Strange Stories

Volume 1

Titles Available from Forty-Two Books

Peaks of Madness: A Collection of Utah Horror, 2nd Ed.

Putrescent Poems: Horror Poetry Vol 1

Satan Speaks! Contemporary Satanic Voices

Monster Brain: Conversations with OCD

Strange Stories Vol 1 (Hardcover)

Forthcoming Titles from Forty-Two Books

2020

They Walk Among Us: A Collection of Utah Horror
by the Utah Horror Writers

Available on Amazon.com or from Forty-Two Books

Strange Stories

Volume 1

December 2019

Edited by Daniel Cureton,
Kylie Williamson,
and Amy Pittman

42
Books
Salt Lake City

A Forty-Two Books, LLC. original publication.
Salt Lake City, UT, USA.
www.fortytwobooks.com
Printed in USA on acid free paper. Broadway, Poor Richard, and Times New Roman fonts.

Cover art by Tithi Luadthong. See "Bibliography," page 611.

ISBN-13, Hardcover: 978-1-7340067-4-2
ISBN-13, Paperback: 978-1-7340067-0-4
Library of Congress Control Number: 2019913426

Editors
Daniel Cureton, MA
www.danielcureton.com
Amy Pittman, MA
Kylie Williamson

Contact
P.O. Box 57474
Murray, UT 84157
USA
info@fortytwobooks.com

First Edition. First Printing.

Dedicated to the Memory of

Mak Adamson

(1995-2019)

Mak was a talented writer and poet. She was published in *Metaphor Undergraduate Literary Journal* where she also served on the staff and curated a collection of poetry, fiction, nonfiction, and art.

Mak was a reader for *Strange Stories*, one of the four who helped on the project's development and helping select finalist for inclusion. She was ever so excited for the publication, and we are sad that she did not live to see it in print, but we are glad that she will live on in its pages!

Letter from the Editors

We are extremely grateful to all the authors who responded to the call for this first volume of fiction. With so many entries (nearly 400), we were overwhelmed! Thank you for your patience, and flexibility. It is highly satisfying to have worked with so many wonderful writers from around the world. We look forward to many more volumes to come!

Daniel Cureton,
Kylie Williamson,
Amy Pittman,
Salt Lake City, UT, USA
July 1, 2019

Introduction from the Publisher

The idea for a new pulp anthology came while perusing the old magazines of the 20th century. Frustrated that the field is almost gone and the ones that are still alive have only released a few issues in recent years, the lack of pulp fiction is being overshadowed by the rush for novel writing, the publishing of literary works, and the disguise of genre fiction as "for the masses."

The legacy of the pulp era cannot be overstated. At a time before radio, pulp and the earlier dime/penny dreadfuls got students and adults reading when there wasn't much else they could afford. While the rich could buy the leather bound hardcovers, the early cheap paperbacks increased literacy and fueled the imaginations for tomorrow, giving hope to the often bleak existence of the lower strata of society (Flanders).

Having had our own stories be rejected too many times with the one liners, "it's not for us," I thought of the idea to make a "for us" type of work. Thus, *Strange Stories* was born. The original *Strange Stories* only had a three year run from 1939-1941 with 13 issues. It was a failed competitor to *Weird Tales* by the uncredited editor Mort Weisinger (Ashley, 901-902).

Careful not to tread on past legacies, *Strange Stories* Vol 1 pays its respect to the previous fore runners with certain formats and images, but moves forward into the 21st with original content, audience, and styles.

Each story is a piece of art, put together in a collection that is a public exhibition. Creative writing, as a fine art, allows us to tame the inner demons and understand the human condition. As in the words of Karl Paulnack, director of the music division at the Boston Conservatory, "Art is part of survival; art is part of the human spirit, an unquenchable expression of who we are. Art is one of the ways in which we say, 'I am alive, and my life has meaning.'" Creative writing thus gives life meaning.

It is my aim as a publisher to produce fine craft and writing that is of high caliber—showing talent—old and new from around the world. In this new, first original Forty-Two Books publication you will enter a world of the weird, the strange, the offensive, freakish, unconventional, surreal, mystifying, standard defying, bizarre, unexplained, moral breaking, and all the types that "didn't fit" someplace else.

Though so many responded to the call, and we couldn't accept them all, we are happy to make a home for those who showed their craft, sincerity, and commitment to the field of writing through evocative and engaging stories.

I am proud, as chief editor, to present to you:

Strange Stories

Volume 1

In Weirds,
Daniel Cureton, MA
Forty-Two Books, LLC.
Salt Lake City, UT
January 23, 2019

Strange Stories

Published Annually

Forty-Two Books, LLC.
Salt Lake City, UT, USA

Read Stories by Authors from Around the World!

THIS ANTHOLOGY CONTAINS NEW STORIES. NO REPRINTS ARE USED

Volume 1 | December 2019

Contents

---A Strange Adventure Awaits!---

Flash Fiction

STRANGE STORIES

Play

Book Chapter

Novelettes

Film Scripts

Contents

Novella

Short Fiction

STRANGE STORIES

Author Biographies

Anthony Rafael Worman has taught English in South Korea, Santiago de Chile, and New York City. He wrote *Valley of Tigers* while living in Yellowstone in the winter. He enjoys travel writing, survival stories, and weird fiction and sometimes tries to combine all three. You can hear him ramble on about current events and (in)formally interview people on his podcast the LAN Party Upload. He currently lives in Montana in the U.S.A. This is the first story he has published and someday will write again.

Aunte Mame is one of two pseudonyms for a local Chicago artist, hailing from the barren Southwest side. A life-long admirer of the arts, she started off as a writer in her elementary years, then went on to visual arts, before pursuing her love for music in highschool. Throughout the heavy adolescent traumas of her teen years, her creativity was her outlet. For each thing she writes, there is a unique version of herself for it.

Ben Gamblin was born and raised in the Pacific Northwest, which gave him his dark imagination, crippling caffeine addiction, and disdain for umbrellas. He studied creative writing and journalism at Western Washington University, and currently lives in Tacoma with his partner and several furry roommates. Ben's work has also appeared in *Ink Stains Anthology* and *The Dark City Mystery Magazine*.

Brenda Bowen Wright has always been a writer, but only recently has begun to put her stories on paper. After a career teaching middle school, nothing much scares her anymore. Brenda has spent her entire life in the State of Utah living and working in many cities, now calling downtown Salt Lake City her home.

C.R. Langille spent many a Saturday afternoon watching monster movies with his mother. It wasn't long before he started crafting nightmares to share with his readers. An avid hunter and amateur survivalist, C.R. Langille incorporates the Utah outdoors in many of his tales. He is an affiliate member of the Horror Writer's Association, a member of the League of Utah Writers, and received his MFA: Writing Popular Fiction from Seton Hill University.

Cathy Bryant has won 27 literary awards, including the Bulwer-Lytton Fiction Prize and the Wergle Flomp Award for Humorous Poetry. Her work has been published all over the world in such publications as *Magma*, *The Andromeda Spaceways Inflight Magazine*, and *Eye to the Telescope*. She co-edited the anthologies *Best of Manchester Poets* vols. 1, 2, and 3, and Cathy's own books are *Contains Strong Language and Scenes of a Sexual Nature*, *Look at All the Women* and *Erratics*. Cathy lives in Cadishead, UK. See Cathy's monthly listings for skint writers at www.compsandcalls.com/wp

Cheryl Zaidan is a full-time marketer, part-time writer, constant dreamer, and jaded horror addict who loves to create characters just so she can do bad things to them. Her short stories have appeared in *Every Day Fiction* as well as in the *Robbed of Sleep* and the *Strangely Funny* anthology series. Currently she resides in Michigan where she has sadly never been haunted. If you would like to see what she's up to, you can find her on Twitter @FeralCherylZ or visit her website www.cherylzwrites.com.

Claude Lalumière (claudepages.info) is the author of five books including *Objects of Worship* (2009) and *Venera Dreams: A Weird Entertainment* (2017) and more than 100 stories, several of which have been adapted for stage, screen, audio, and comics. His work has been translated into seven languages. Originally from Montreal, he's now headquartered in Ottawa, Canada.

Daniel Cureton grew up in South Carolina, moving to Salt Lake City, Utah in 2008 to pursue university studies. He has an MA in English from Weber State University. Daniel is an Avant-Garde writer. He has previously been published in *Peculiar: A Queer Literary Journal*, *The Rocky Mountain Review* academic journal, and *Metamorphosis: A Collection of Poetry & Prose* by the League of Utah Writers. Read more at www.danielcureton.com.

Emily Dye Grounds has been writing since she can remember—drawing scribbles and telling stories before she could read—but this is her very first published short story. Emily earned her BA in English at Oklahoma Panhandle State University and her MA in professional writing from Oklahoma State

University. After graduating, she packed up and left Oklahoma, and moved to Cambridge, Massachusetts, where she started working as a freelance editor and ghostwriter. Emily currently writes and lives in Los Angeles with her husband and their husky.

Evelyn Deshane's creative and nonfiction work has appeared in *Plenitude Magazine*, *Strange Horizons*, *Bitch Magazine*, and other publications. Evelyn received an MA from Trent University and is currently completing a PhD at the University of Waterloo. Find out more: www.evedeshane.wordpress.com.

Geoff Hart has spent over thirty years working primarily as a scientific editor, specializing in authors who must write in English as a second or third language. He's a prolific author of articles on writing and editing, with more than 400 published, but also writes fiction in his spare time. Visit him online at www.geoff-hart.com.

Iona Murphy is an English Literature Master of Research student at The University of St Andrews. Her current research focuses on disordered eating and domesticity in the poetry of Sylvia Plath and Anne Sexton. When she isn't submerged in academic writing, she's creatively writing instead. She has poetry published in Black Bough's *Lux Aeterna* collection, Teen Belle's *Catharsis* anthology, and others. She has creative non-fiction published with *Ayaskala, Ang(st) Zine* and *Mid-Heaven Magazine*.

Jack Lothian is a screenwriter for film and television, and is currently the showrunner on the HBO / Cinemax series *Strike Back*. His short fiction has appeared in a number of publications, including *Weirdbook*, *Hinnom Magazine*, *The Necronomicon Memorial Book*, and the forthcoming *The New Flesh: A Literary Tribute to David Cronenberg*. His graphic novel *Tomorrow*, illustrated by Garry Mac, was nominated for a 2018 British Fantasy Award.

Jack Wells has been writing on and off since grade school. *Monochrome Noir* marks his first physical publication of an original story. When not putting pen to paper, Jack can be found spending time with his sweet but quirky children, hiking, kayaking, and sipping whiskey by his fire pit. Outside of all the fun activities, Jack spends much of his time herding cats as a beleaguered government employee.

Jared Linder lives in Portland with his fiancée and a furry white potato named Finny. Jared studied creative writing at the University of Southern California and the UCLA Extension Writers' Program. He works part-time as an attorney to supplement the oodles of cash being a writer brings in every week. He is working on a novel, which he hopes to start getting rejected by agents within the next year.

Jim Lee is from a small Pennsylvania town better known for producing Olympic swim champ/movie Tarzan Johnny Weissmuller. He graduated from Windber Area High School in 1976 and attended the University of Pittsburgh at Johnstown. He's been a published writer since the 1980s and his various stories, poems and nonfiction articles include such anthologies as *Fantasy for the Throne* and *Frostfire Worlds*, and periodicals such as *Outposts of Beyond* and *Sci Phi Journal*.

Jocelyn E. Marshall is currently based in Buffalo, NY. She is a reader for Palette Poetry and is co-editing a collection on trauma-informed pedagogy. Her work has appeared or is forthcoming in *Assaracus: A Journal of Gay Poetry* (Sibling Rivalry Press), *Tripwire: A Journal of Poetics*, *The Bellingham Review*, and *Twentieth and Twenty-First Century Literature in Context* by ABC-CLIO, LLC.

Joe Baumann's fiction and essays have appeared in *Electric Literature, Barrelhouse*, *Hawai'i Review*, and many others. He is the author of *Ivory Children*, published in 2013 by Red Bird Chapbooks. He holds a PhD in English from the University of Louisiana-Lafayette. Joe has been nominated for three Pushcart Prizes and was nominated for inclusion in Best American Short Stories 2016 and was a 2019 Lambda Literary Fellow in Fiction. He can be reached at www.joebaumann.wordpress.com.

Joe Schwartz's stories happen to people in and from the City of St. Louis, Missouri. In the tradition of writers like Charles Bukowski, Ray Carver and Pete Dexter comes Joe Schwartz whose darkness is as funny as it is chilling.

Schwartz puts a thrill into reading, making it seem as dangerous and decadent as it should be.

Joel Martin is a fantasy writer and freelance editor based in Melbourne, Australia but originally hails from Whanganui, New Zealand. Along with traditional fiction, Joel dabbles in the unusual world of video game writing. He specializes in fantasy, and his love of the genre spans from sword and sorcery to epic fantasy and he is currently working on a weird fiction novel. He is the host of the monthly literary podcast The Morning Bell, and the director of Speculate, a speculative fiction festival.

Johannes Black is a graduate of Cambridge, now studying and working in Trinity College, Dublin. Johannes is passionate enthusiast of literature, primarily modernist and mid-to-late English, Irish and American fiction, including prose and poetry within that remit. Inspiration for her work is also drawn from the cinematic visions of several film directors, including the work of Nicolas Roeg and Krzysztof Kieslowski.

Joyce Frohn has been published over 200 times, including postcards, bumper stickers, and recipes. She graduated from college with a biology degree and became a free-lance writer. She is married with a teen-aged daughter, two cats, a gecko, chickens, and a Patreon account.

Jules Zucker is a writer, music supervisor, and amateur gardener based in Los Angeles, California. Raised outside of Berkeley, she moved south to complete a BA in Narrative Studies at the University of Southern California, where her short fiction piece “Hoppin’ John” won first prize in the 2017 Edward W. Moses Creative Writing Competition. Jules returned to California to work in music licensing and write spooky little stories after a stint in the American Southwest.

Justin Zipprich a freelance writer and blogger based out of Las Vegas, Nevada. He is an admirer of the written word and the amazing worlds that these words create. His true passion being fiction, Justin has written a multitude of short stories, numerous full-length screenplays, and is currently working on a debut novel. His works have appeared in publications such as *Ne-*

crology Shorts, *Foliate Oak Literary Magazine*, *Fiction and Verse*, and *Whisperings Magazine*.

Kev Harrison is a writer and English teacher from the UK, living in Lisbon, Portugal. His short stories have been featured in a number of anthologies, magazines, and podcasts, including *Lost Films* from Perpetual Motion Machine Publishing and *In Darkness, Delight: Creatures of the Night* from Corpus Press. His debut novelette, *Cinders of a Blind Man Who Could See* is available now from Demain Publishing and his debut novella, *The Balance*, is coming in 2019 from Lycan Valley Press. Find him on twitter, @lisboetaingles or on his website, www.kevharrisonfiction.com

Kiki Gonglewski is a storyteller avidly exploring different media. She is a winner of the National Gold Medal for Scholastic Art and Writing, and received 17 gold keys in their Southwest Regional levels. Kiki has also been published in literary magazines *Gypsum Sound*, *Madness Heart*, *Unfading Daydream*, as well as anthologies, *Terra, Tara, Terror!* And *I didn't Break the Lamp: A Historical Account of Imaginary Friends*. She is a large fan of movies, Kurt Vonnegut novels, long naps, and sushi.

Linda Kay Hardie has been a writer since she learned the alphabet at age four. She's had a book published, as well as numerous stories, poems, and essays in magazines and anthologies. Linda often writes poems in the wee hours, when she's watching old sitcoms on TV, trying to recover from insomnia. She has been a disk jockey, newspaper reporter, and library aide. Linda is now an adjunct instructor teaching English composition and core humanities to unwilling students in Reno, Nevada.

M.X. Kelly lives in St. Petersburg, Florida with her partner Val, a coffee pot, and their three cats. Her work has appeared in *Star*Line*, the poetry magazine for the Science Fiction Poetry Association, *Abyss & Apex*, *Scifaikufest*, and other magazines and anthologies across the known 'verse. M.X.'s website can be summoned with the typed incantation of mxkelly.weebly.com

Mark Daponte has published four short stories, three full length screenplays, nine short screenplays (including two animation scripts) and punches up screenplays—because they don't punch back. When he isn't sinking down to the teen level to make his 14 and 16 year old sons laugh, he can be found seeking signs of not-so-intelligent life in his hometown of Brooklyn, NY.

Martin Zeigler writes mystery, science fiction, and horror. His stories have been published in journals such as *Mystery Weekly* and *Over My Dead Body* as well as in various anthologies like *Insidious Assassins* and *A Sharp Stick in the Eye And Other Funny Stories*. Besides writing, Marty enjoys taking long walks, watching movies, and dabbling on the piano. He makes his home in the Pacific Northwest.

Meggie Nelson received her degree in creative writing from George Mason University with a concentration in fiction, but if you ask her family they will inform you she has been writing since before she knew how to read. A fan of wildlife biology, gastropods, tattoo art, and all things fantasy, she is of the opinion that learning more about our world is the best way to harvest inspiration for worlds of one's own. Currently, Meggie lives in Fairfax, Virginia with her boyfriend and four ferrets.

Michael Anthony Lee's fiction has appeared in magazines and anthologies throughout the world. He currently lives in the countryside of Ontario, CA.

Michael McClure teaches writing and literature at Virginia State University and lives with his wife Rebecca and their lemon-colored Walker Hound Cassie in Petersburg, Virginia. He is the co-author of a textbook on world mythology, *Myth and Knowing* (McGraw Hill) and, under the pseudonym Frank McArthur, a post-apocalyptic novel, *2020: A Novel* (Kindle). A core belief in his writing (and his life) is that stories are the cause and the result of all human activity.

Paul J. Lashway is a writer, musician, poet, and artist originally from Buffalo, NY. He has donned many hats throughout his career, including Music Instructor at a Western New York after-school program serving Autistic individuals. Although he primarily enjoys writing stories of the weird and off-kilter, his poetry and paintings have also been previously featured in *Name Magazine*. Paul is currently pursuing a PhD in English while attending SUNY Albany in hopes of one day living beyond the yellow brick road with his lady-friend, their rescue greyhound, and two hairless cats named Sméagol and Gollum.

R. J. Howell is a writer and an artist. A Chicago native, she earned her BA in fiction writing at Columbia College Chicago and her MFA in creative writing: popular fiction from the University of Southern Maine's Stonecoast program. Her short fiction has appeared in anthologies such as Jayhenge Publishing's *Unrealpolitik*, Mt. Misery Press' *Neon Druid*, and *Zombies and Ghosts*. You can find her online at www.rjhowell.com./landlocked.

Ransom Wall is a young writer living in Canada whose work usually contains elements of horror and dark comedy. He has been published in *Weird Mask*, *Twilight Madhouse*, *Gruesome Grotesques*, and now *Strange Stories*. He is hard at work on a novella and more stories.

Rebecca Rowland resides in a landlocked and often icy corner of New England. She accrued graduate degrees in English, Education, and Information Science and works as an editor and librarian but vacations as a dark fiction author. Her first collection of short stories, *The Horrors Hiding in Plain Sight*, debuted in 2018, and her first novel, *Pieces* (co-written with writing partner Michael Aloisi), was released September 2019. Shamelessly judge her painfully pedestrian website www.rowlandbooks.com

Roxy Thomas is an aspiring writer in the horror, paranormal and suspense genres by evening and a psychiatric nurse by day. She lives with her husband, 2 cats, and a dog on 20 acres in Alberta near a national park where the bison roam. Find out more https://storiesbyroxy.com/

Stuart Hardy lives just outside London and runs the Youtube channel, Stubagful, where he posts video essays, comedy sketches, horror cartoons and adaptations of his short fiction. He's been volunteering in community radio projects and posting strange and obtuse content on the internet for over a decade.

S.E. (Stephen Edward) Greco was born and raised in the Philadelphia suburbs. He moved to New York's Hudson Valley where he worked as a physicist and engineer at a major technology company before turning his attention to writing and painting. His fiction has appeared recently in the magazines/e-zines: *The Dark City, Literary Hatchet, CommuterLit,* and in the anthologies: *Society of Misfit Stories, Suspense Unimagined,* and *Going Down Swinging: Pigeonholed.* His work has been nominated by a small press for the Pushcart Prize anthology. Follow him at www.segrecoauthor.com.

Shaun Avery has been published in many magazines and anthologies, normally with stories of a horrific or satiric nature, and often both at once. He has won competitions in the mediums of both prose and comic scripting, and he also had a short movie script shortlisted in a screenwriting contest. A lifelong fan of comics and graphic novels, he is the proud co-creator of a self-published horror comic, more details of which can be found here: www.comicsy.co.uk/dbroughton/store/products/spectre-show/

Ted Snyder hopes that the missing cats in his neighborhood, just outside of Milwaukee, Wisconsin, are the result of the local urban coyote population and not a wolf man living in nearby Pulaski Park. His fiction has appeared in *Leaping Clear* and is forthcoming in *From Seoul to the World*, and his narrative mythopoeic poetry has appeared in *The Mythic Circle*. He also has an article on ancestor simulations in science fiction coming out at NewMyths.com later in 2019. Find out more on his website at www.tedsnyderonline.com.

Thomas Vaughn is an author of dark fiction who resides in the Ozark Mountains. He is a refugee of the debris field of rural Arkansas, an experience that informs much of his writing. When he is not writing fiction, he poses as a college professor whose research focuses on apocalyptic rhetoric and doomsday cults. If you would like to see what he has been up to you can visit him at www.brokentransmitter.com.

Will Riley is a Vancouver-born postgraduate student at Dalhousie University, focusing on the two poles of medieval literature and graphic novels. He is currently finishing his MA thesis. Will has previously had creative articles on current affairs published online and in print, and was a finalist in the Canadian Authors' Association's short fiction contest. Most recently, he has finished work coordinating the 2019 Mosaic multicultural festival in Halifax, Nova Scotia. His cumulative late fees at public and university libraries currently exceed twenty dollars.

Via D'Agostino is originally from the wilds of Massachusetts and now attends the University of New Hampshire for her MFA in fiction. She earned a BA in creative writing and Spanish (with minors in psychology and literature) from Ohio Northern University and graduated summa cum laude in 2019. She has over 20 works published, including fiction, poetry, non-fiction, and photography, in journals such as Sigma Tau Delta's *The Rectangle*, The TownVibe's *The Berkshire Magazine*, and Drake University's *Periphery Literary Journal*. She plans to read and write her way around the entire globe—right after grad school. You can find her on Facebook at @barefootwriterviadagostino.

Wol-vriey is a tall Nigerian living in Nigeria. He writes horror fiction—for adults only, please—and some surrealist stuff. To date, he has published over twenty novels in both genres. His horror novels include: *666*, *Hell Dancer*, *Girls Are Not Smiling*, and the *Brainchew* Series. On the surrealist side of things, he is the author of *Pussy Transmission*, the Bud Malone *Boston* Series, *Vegan Zombie Apocalypse*, *Vegan Vampire Vaginas*, and the disturbing and unsettling *Dr. Orgasm*.

Strange Stories

-ᔕA̲Tᔓ-

Flash Fiction

Penny Fiction

Michael Anthony Lee

The Hangman's Rope

Hangman's rope was justice in bygone days. When it broke, instead of his neck, He changed his wicked ways.

A Fisherman's Tale

When it came out of the water, that moonlit night, he realized he was the one that was caught.

Under the Bed

"The monster under the bed isn't real!—I'll prove it!" she said. She was never seen again.

Death of a Controversial Word Wizard

Jim Lee

Excerpted From: *The Penn's Woods Gazette,*

Windber, Somerset Shire of Penn's Woods,
Samhain Night, the Year of Our Mage-Lord 2116

Jim Leeward-Facing, the imaginative yet often erratic writer who in mid-career attracted wide acclaim and intense scorn in equal measure for his controversial subject matter, died unexpectedly at his home this evening. Although there were no signs of physical assault and the usual preliminary scrying has ruled out any of the more commonplace death spells, hexes and curses, foul play has not been ruled out.

"He was only 158 and in apparently robust health," noted Steve Widdershins, Coroner-Adept for the West-Central Shires of Penn's Woods. "And we must consider the ominous timing: Samhain is of course a holiday traditionally marked by death, taking inventory of one's life and ridding oneself of what is no longer desired. Finally, I would remind everyone that there are very many differing Schools of Sorcery extant, many of which feature Magicks of such obscure and arcane subtlety that only a true Specialist-Adept in that particular School would be able to recognize and identify them. Me, I'm just a humble civil servant—capable, I dare say, but hardly such a Specialist."

Accordingly, a full-scale Coroner's Magick Circle composed of experts from around the world will convene in the vicinity of Leeward-Facing's mysterious demise within a fortnight.

The work that Leeward-Facing is most likely to be remembered for came in the middle period of a prolific, if uneven career. Despite some entertainingly gruesome action sequences and decent characterization, Leeward-Facing's earlier publications gave few hints of the passion much of his later output was destined to engender. More often than not, these initial short stories and books centered on the fictional small Penn's Woods town of Riverton, which he modeled after his lifelong home of Windber, which was reputed to be merely "five miles down the road" from Riverton. The background of one such tale even detailed the misguidedly whimsical juxtaposing of syllables in naming the town after its founder. Berwind the Coal-Mage failed to see the humor in the backhanded "tribute," resulting in the now-infamous Windber Curse (thought to factor in Leeward-Facing's problematical love life, as noted below).

While competently written, such strictly realistic books as *Riverton's Werewolf*, *A Cunning-Woman of the Laurel Highlands* and *The Twin Magick Invasion* met with only middling success—and zero outrage.

"Entirely too conventional," Leeward-Facing would later admit to his equally notorious speculative biographers, Edgar the Divination-Man and Wise-Woman Stella.

However, a novel he published in the Year of Our Mage-Lord 2026 proved anything but conventional. In *The World Without Magick*, Leeward-Facing imagined an alternative universe where the physical laws of nature somehow excluded any sort of conjuring, spellcraft or even the most ordinary of sympathetic magick. In what fellow writers—including ones otherwise quite critical of the book—acknowledged as a monumental act of world-building skill, he speculated how such a bizarre, fascinating and ultimately terrifying reality might function—or at times disastrously fail to do so. It was a place filled with barely comprehensible technologies, all of them resolutely lacking any Magickal basis.

This was far from the first book to attempt portraying this strange concept, but none before had so fully realized the concept of a magick-free lifestyle. And *The World without Magick* was followed by several additional books and many shorter works that fleshed out in great detail such a society's inner workings, strengths, and drawbacks. It was acknowledged even by Leeward-Facing's most vocal literary critics that for the first time an author had overcome the difficulties inherent in defying the famous dictum known in writing circles as Clarke's Law.

Years earlier and late in his own extraordinary career, Arthur C-is-for-Conjure-Man Clarke, the Official Literary Grand-Mage of Sri Lanka (by way of the Celtic Isles), had written an extensive essay on the many problems faced by previous writers who had dared to attempt creation of an even marginally believable non-Magickal world. Having outlined the many pitfalls in achieving verisimilitude in such a work, Clarke concluded famously that: "To be fully convincing any such technology must—must!—seem indistinguishable from magick!"

Leeward-Facing's work flatly rejected this and the public's explosive reaction to it demonstrated the level of his success. To say the novel attracted immediate attention and vigorous comment would be a gross understatement. Many people were utterly charmed and even entranced by the volume's many vivid speculations. Yet many others were outraged. Social conservatives and religious fundamentalist groups were particularly, indeed often extremely, angered. There were protests, boycotts, and even death threats although at the time none of the latter bore fruit. At the time, many observers credited the well-known Threefold Law of Return for deterring Magickal reprisals by the faithful.

The controversy had to the greater degree subsided when a well-known writers' group, the Imaginative Mages of Publishing (IMP) chose to honor Leeward-Facing's overall career by voting him their newest Grand Master of Word Wizardry in the Year of Our Mage-Lord 2101. Predictably, this briefly reignited the controversy.

While criticism is still heard today, the notorious book's several sequels triggered progressively lesser reactions as the idea became more familiar to an ever-wider segment of the reading public. Even some of the most critical have come to view Leeward-Facing's controversial work as a basically harmless, if wildly unusual and almost unnaturally virtuoso example of creative speculation.

"Still," as the Coroner-Adept commented above, "all possibilities must always be thoroughly investigated, particularly in a case involving such a prominent and so far unexplained death."

The last even partially living member of his immediate family, Leeward-Facing never married, despite a number of often well-documented and lengthy relationships, most prominently with "A-Certain-Succubus-Whose-Name-Must-Never-Again-Be-Invoked-By-This-Or-Any-Other-News-Agency-Under-Penalty-Of-The-Most-Severe-Curse" (as per a Spell of Restraining imposed in 2107). Therefore, he is officially survived only by Furball-19, the latest in a long line of Feline Familiars whose antics inspired the hugely popular (if highly conventional) series of talking cat detective books that did so much to soften Leeward-Facing's image and further normalize his literary reputation in the last third of his authorial career.

Dial

Emily Dye Grounds

I used to feel special, the way you pressed against me. But it's just routine. You come in here each day, touch me to your skin, work me into a lather, and then get dressed. Just like that. You dry off, then leave me alone. You run your hands over me till I'm shards, blunter and blunter. And then what? I'm just residue on your body, on your shower wall. Soap scum. Clinging to your tiles, calcified in the grout furrows, I'll watch you do it all over again with a different bar.

Teeth

Jules Zucker

Elias Markowitz has thirteen teeth left. He was never much of a smiler anyway, so it really only bothers him when he speaks. He can no longer enunciate for fear of revealing those jagged rows of teeth like rotting old picket fences, here and there a board missing, here and there an empty space. Instead, he has mastered a lipless mutter so impressive that he seems during conversation like a ventriloquist without a dummy.

The doctors don't know why it's happening. Elias has seen every dentist in the county, thrown his pension each month at professionals and received nothing in return but furrowed brows, shrugs, and the bill. On his 76th birthday, he lost two teeth while he ate his cake alone in the kitchen. Felt them painlessly loosen and orbit a wad of icing and sprinkles as he chewed. Elias spit them out and left the rest of the cake untouched on the table, where it's been now for two and a half weeks.

He remembered the first tooth to go, a back molar that called it quits the day they took his driver's license away. His shaky hands, they'd told him, made him unfit to operate a vehicle. But Elias knew it was all a cruel trick, a bureaucratic kick in the groin that said, "Cars are for *working* people, old man. Where have you got to drive to now anyway?"

By the rainy fall evening his daughter came by with the nursing home brochures, Elias had lost three teeth. He kept them in a little grey box on the nightstand, as if he could pop them back into his mouth in the morning. While his wife pored over pictures of smiling senior citizens playing backgammon and doing water aerobics, Elias researched periodontal disease and dental implants.

He could still remember the following week, when his wife found out he'd spent the nursing home savings on gum surgery. "What about our future?" She'd cried, huddled in her wheelchair in the corner. She'd picked a bright red wheelchair, as if eager to flaunt her slow decay, and he hated her for it. "Glorified hospice care," he'd spat. "Have we no dignity? No self-respect?" The words had barely passed his lips when he felt his front tooth come loose.

Elias dreamt that night that he stood on a stage before a massive crowd. He opened his lips to speak, but instead of words came a torrent of marbles, tumbling out of his mouth like glassy vomit, clattering to the floor. The harder he tried to speak, the faster they spilled until Elias was doubled over with his hands on his knees, spewing marbles by the hundred onto the stage. The crowd laughed and took pictures, and when Elias tried to run, he slipped and slid on the marbles until he fell flat on his back.

Today, Elias lost another tooth. This time, he did not fret; a chilling acceptance washed over him like anesthesia. So this is what he was destined to become, a sad, shriveled man with a cavernous mouth moaning sounds that never quite became words.

The future was as clear as it was bleak. So he grabbed his little grey box off the nightstand and walked eleven miles to the Golden Gate Bridge. As the sun melted behind the jagged San Francisco skyline, Elias stood staring down at the black water. They would find him, he hoped, still clutching the box in his rigid hands, proof that he once was complete, with all parts in their proper place. He climbed onto the railing and peered into the abyss beneath him—so dark, so utterly empty. He opened his toothless mouth and screamed, one black chasm echoing into another. One black chasm, he decided, much larger than the other.

Tonight, the doorbell rang at an assisted-living home. A bright red wheelchair rolled to the foyer. Nineteen teeth sank to the depths of the San Francisco Bay. Tonight, when the front door swung open, there stood Elias Markowitz and he grinned.

Death Takes a Holiday

Linda Kay Hardie

The last thing I remember is turning out the light on my nightstand. I didn't think I would fall asleep, not after all the leftover chocolate and candy corn I couldn't bear to waste, but now I'm in some sort of Cosmic Starbucks. I rap the table in front of me and feel my knuckle strike hard plastic. I smell the acrid scent of coffee brewing. My dreams aren't usually this clearly detailed and concrete—cool.

I'm in a booth with an iced caramel latte in a plastic cup. I sip the sweet and creamy brew, which I like precisely because it doesn't taste much like coffee. Outside the windows all I can see is fog, swirling clouds spinning hypnotically. There's nothing out there but the mist: no parking lot, no people, no world. The view fits my recent mood. I've been feeling a bit melancholy lately, maybe on the verge of a crisis of faith? I take a gulp of my drink, seeking the bitterness of the coffee.

A dark form sits down on the bench across from me, blocking my view of Nowhere. It's Death, complete with empty-socketed skull, hooded black robe, and scythe. Death's venti cup, full of a very dark liquid, emits a sharp smell of coffee and sulfur.

"Mind if I sit with you?"

I wave my hand, "be my guest" gesturing him.

"You're not afraid of me?" Death sips the coffee, which lends to the dream feeling, because how does one sip without lips?

I may be nervous—I wonder how much dying hurts—but I'm not usually afraid. As a Wiccan, I believe death is just a door through which we all pass eventually. Beyond is the next life. I'm actually a little excited at that prospect, but I'd rather wait until I've finished a few things in this life before moving on to the next. I hate being a quitter.

I get the feeling Death is smiling at me, despite the lack of lips. Perhaps it's the twinkle in those dark eye sockets. Relaxing, Death tips that black hood back onto exposed clavicles, fully revealing a harsh skull.

"Since you seem sympathetic, let me bend your ear, so to speak..."

-ര A ര-

"I wasn't always feared and reviled," Death said. "Through the millennia, I have been welcomed, worshiped, and accepted. Now, in your so-called enlightened age, people go to great extremes to avoid me or cheat me. There."

Death points out the window to my left, where the fog has cleared to show a hospital bed. Initially I think it's just a collection of machinery, then I make out the emaciated human form in the center of the tubes and wires.

"Or there." This time I see a woman with a face like a drum, her skin stretched unnaturally tight over her bones to give her a permanent expression of mild surprise. I grimace and gulp more of my sweet coffee.

"Ah, the days of my youth. When Death was a part of Life. We worked together, Life and I. Life worked the spring and summer, the festivals of birth and growth. You humans called them by various names. Your particular ancestors celebrated Imbolc, also called Candlemas, in the middle of winter, during my reign, as a time of hope for Life's rebirth."

As my eyes follow Death's gesture, I see outside the window figures on a dark hillside, dancing around a bonfire, lighting torches from the blaze, more and more torches, until the whole window frame is filled with light. My heart beats in time with their drums, filling me with exhilaration.

Death sighs and sips again. "Now February second is a day when you watch rodents run from their shadows. Ostara, the spring equinox, used to signal the indisputable beginning of Life's time. Then May Day, or Beltane, was when Life became more and more visible in the spring growth. Then came the solstice in the middle of summer, when Life rejoiced.

"I crept in for Lammas in early August. The First Harvest may seem to be about Life, but actually it's about the beginning of Death. Next came Mabon, the fall equinox, when I began to make myself visible to the world, and I openly reveled during Samhain, the original end of the year. This sacred time of death, once a time to respect one's ancestors, is now celebrated as a day of begging for candy. Pah!"

I see a carrot appear in those bony fingers. With a snap, Death breaks the carrot in half. Death sighs, then tosses the carrot. I don't see it land anywhere. It's simply gone.

"Yule—the winter solstice—was also mine, a time of deep sleep, or Death, for the world. But even in Death there is a spark of Life for the next generation, when the new year is born and the circle continues. Your ancestors saw Death as a necessary part of Life, millennia ago, before this current era of fear. No one lives without another one's death. No one.

"I don't know exactly when it all changed. Much of it came with the New Religions, the ones that sprouted and grew in the recent millennia of this Common Era, and preach of a better Life after this one. Yet so many of their people seem especially fearful of me, as though they don't believe their own tales of eternal bliss."

Death peers into the cup of noxious brew, as though hoping to find better news in the dark liquid's surface, then sighs again and gulps down the dregs.

"Thanks for listening. It's been a few centuries since I had the chance to relax like this, to let my hair down, so to speak."

Death flips the hood back up and sticks a hand my way. I reach out and grasp the collection of bones. Death has a surprisingly warm handshake, and I feel a rush of serenity.

"See you April 12, 2048!"

What? I sit up with a jerk, to find blankets tangled around my legs in my own bed. There's a bitter aftertaste in my mouth, and I feel jittery. I turn on the light and the TV, and search for a mindless sitcom. I'll never get back to sleep tonight. But first I light a candle on my altar. I feel the Goddess infuse me.

April 12? At least I won't have to do taxes that year.

The Wolf Man's Wife

Ted Snyder

During a moonlit Saturday night in the fourth year of Maureen's marriage to Bill, what should have been a pleasant dinner at home turned into one of the worst nights in her life. They had just sat down to eat when Bubbles the cat jumped up on the table. Bill shoved his plate aside. She watched it hit the wall and shatter into six almost identical pieces, and as the food splattered against the plaster, she momentarily thought of Jackson Pollock, then shook her head and instead thought of Mr. Clean and his Magic Erasers. A frenzied yowl brought her attention back to Bill, who was in the process of using surprisingly large canines to devour Bubbles.

Maureen screamed, ran, and hid in the bedroom closet. From her hideout, she could hear the sound of wood snapping. Closing her eyes, she could picture her prized Stickley coffee table, a third anniversary gift from her brother, Mark, becoming nothing but splinters of quarter-sawn oak. She cringed as she heard glass shattering. The Tiffany lamps, she thought. Around midnight, after the racket had died down, she opened the closet door slightly. The house was dark. The bedroom had an emergency flashlight on her side of the bed, so she grabbed it and investigated.

It was worse than she feared. There were scratch marks in the plaster, deep and wide. She stepped in a wet spot and realized that he had urinated on the parquet floor. Bad, very bad, she thought, urine stains are so hard to get out.

When she married Bill, she didn't know he was a wolf man. He didn't know either.

Fortunately, Bill recovered. The fur fell out, his nails shrank back to normal, and his canines seemed to retract too. His eyes did seem off, but Maureen wasn't sure if there hadn't always been a crazy look in them. Her mother hadn't liked Bill from day one. Was it the eyes?

Outbreaks of wolf man became a regular full moon occurrence. Maureen started ensuring that Bill was outside before moonrise to protect the remaining furniture and to prevent the parquet floor from getting additional urine stains.

Before his bouts started, there had been a coyote problem in town that the Milwaukee County Fish and Wildlife Control Department had unsuccessfully attempted to eradicate. Bill's lupine compulsions changed that. Coyote traps started to go untouched and people stopped calling to report sightings. However, calls about the disappearance of neighborhood cats and football sized dogs put out to potty at night continued, causing great confusion for the wildlife control agents. As for Maureen, she tried not to think about what this all might mean. She was a vegetarian and had insisted Bill give up meat when they got engaged.

Bill's nights out on the town kept getting longer. The morning after, his nails didn't fully lose their sharpness. His canines seemed a bit too long. He developed a hairy back. And the eyes, well, maybe her mother was right.

On the night of the full moon in September, he came back, climbed into bed, fur matted with blood (Rufus the dachshund from across the street—Maureen had always hated that dog), feces (he had realized three months prior how good it felt to roll in fresh poop), and leaves (maple tree, two blocks away in Pulaski Park, likely now the former home of prideful Simba). In the morning, Maureen woke up to find Bill still in wolf form, his tongue lolling out and his breath just wretched. Gagging, she investigated the house while he slumbered. In the living room, she discovered a new urine stain in front of the sliding glass door and a suspicious nose print on the glass.

They gave it several days. She tried picking up raw meat at the grocer.

He tried holding it all day. Neither worked.

She couldn't live with a wolf man, so she filed for divorce.

She kept the house. He got Bubbles' scratching post.

Maureen's brother, Mark, tried to help as much as he could. He could glue the Stickley furniture back together. He had a knack for getting urine out of flooring, and when that failed, he had a band sander that could grind off the discoloration, allowing him to restain and varnish the wood. Relationships were much harder to mend than a broken coffee table. The stains of the past did not come out of people's hearts and minds easily. Mark ran his hand over the course grain on his sand paper and imagined taking the band sander to Maureen's heart, removing her pain. Then he stopped his hand with a jolt, having realized exactly what he was envisioning. He closed his eyes and tried to think about something else.

Mark also started visiting nearby Pulaski Park. He had a keen eye, and he caught glimpses of poor, wolfy Bill prowling in the woods. Bill saw him too.

Once, after nightfall, Mark drove his pickup to the park. He dropped the tailgate and put out a cut of rib eye steak, rare and bloody, and a can of Coors Lite.

Bill caught the unmistakable scent of steak and cheap beer. He slunk out of the woods to Mark's pickup. While Bill sat on the tailgate eating, Mark talked, telling him about how Maureen was doing. Bill didn't say a word and, after he finished, had started back towards the woods when Mark offered to take them for a drive.

He got into the back of Mark's pickup and they drove to the local middle school, the wind running through Bill's fur and his tongue lolling out.

Bill wanted to jump in the pool, but Mark warned him against it. Coarse fur floating in the pool would look suspicious, Fish and Wildlife Control might be called in to investigate—their agents had already been stalking the area, looking for Simba's killer.

Several showerheads jutted out of a wall leading to the boy's locker room behind a baffle that afforded some degree of privacy. Without saying anything, Mark set out a bar of soap, shampoo, a towel, a razor, and nail clippers.

Mark drove back to Maureen's house. She was still up, binging on the latest BBC historical melodrama to arrive on Netflix, *Ravensgate Manorhouse*.

He didn't tell her about Bill.

An hour later, there was a knock at the door.

Maureen went to the door and opened it. Outside stood Bill—not quite Bill from before, but most of his body was shaven (aside from the top of his head)—his nails looked manageable, and his eyes, well, maybe her mother had been wrong about that look. Around his waist was a towel.

She thought about reconciliation. But, when he looked at her, he didn't smile. He shyly covered his mouth with one hand and asked for a toothbrush. She sighed and let him inside, going to the living room with Mark and Netflix. The heroine of *Ravensgate Manorhouse*, Elvina Becket, had an opportunity to reunite with her dastardly lover, Lord Millifont, and the outcome was impending.

Several minutes later, smelling like fresh mint, Bill came into the living room. There was a moment of silence—then Elvina Becket turned her nose up at Lord Millifont for his rakish behavior. Maureen pointed the remote control at the image of Elvina Becket and pushed the power button. Looking away from the TV, she saw Bill standing just inside the doorway.

Mark told Maureen about finding Bill in Pulaski Park, about taking Bill to the local middle school and its shower—Maureen had a tear in her eye. He also happened to mention a vending machine by the pool and that he had seen enough change at the bottom of the pool to buy a bag of Crunchy Cheetos.

That was more than Bill could handle. His tongue lolled out and he got that look in his eyes that her mother didn't like and bounded out of the house.

Mark went down into the basement for the tool bag so he could repair the front door.

Maureen started the next episode of *Ravensgate Manorhouse.*

She didn't think it was fair how Elvina Becket had treated Lord Millifont. The show's writers, however, did not seem to agree, as the next episode was clearly setting up a story arc for her to fall in love with Wilhelm von van der Gast, a portly Dutch man who wore a signature orange Lacoste polo shirt and was ostensibly in Britain on business.

She threw down the remote control.

Getting in her car, she drove to the local middle school. Bill, smelling of chlorine, sat at the edge of the pool, holding his knees to his chest. His lips had a strange orange coloration, and his hair was more disheveled than before, yet neither seemed off-putting.

She sat down next to him and put her arm around his shoulders.

"We can figure this out, together."

His nose was cold and wet.

The Squeaky Wheel Gets the Blood

Roxy Thomas

The 9 PM reminder on his computer chimed and instinctively Dr. Grainger leaned back in his desk chair rubbing his eyes. No longer immersed in spreadsheets, he heard that infernal squeaking sound from the hallway that had been annoying him all week. The cleaning team had left hours ago, so it wasn't them, but it sounded like someone was pushing a cart. He turned back to his computer and the budget cut memo before him when the squeaking returned, louder, and more grating. Annoyed, he pushed the chair back and strode to the door, looking into the hall—seeing nothing—but sucking in his breath when a freezing cold draft instantly numbed his face. It felt like he was in a biting cold snowstorm without a scarf, something that never happened since he hated the cold. Heading back to his desk, he jotted a note for his secretary to have maintenance check the heating system. This was the third time this week the icy cold had permeated his office for no reason, usually bring with it a pungent rotting scent.

Looking at the clock he decided it was too late to call home, he had missed diner and it was best to avoid the inevitable fight by staying a while longer until she fell asleep. She would complain about the long hours and how the promotion to Chief Medical Officer should mean he could finally be home at night, now that he wasn't stuck in the emergency room. It was hard to explain how important the opening of the new cardiac wing was to his career, and how much work it took. She would never understand about the other programs he had to cut to make this a reality. Flashy new units with the latest equipment, did not come cheap, even when they had a big name sponsor paying for the privilege of his name on the wing.

Luckily, no one would even know about the new mental health clinic proposal for the homeless shelter; he hid that document from the board. In fact, when he lost the actual physical copy of the proposal on the way to the office, he did not even bother to report the privacy breach. Rich business men with heart conditions gained more press and attention than the homeless. But every time he walked by the rag covered guy and his squeaky shopping cart at the exit to the subway, he felt a quick twinge of guilt—it passed quickly whenever he thought of the accolades he would receive.

Sighing, he sat down and immediately slid forward on the leather seat slick with something wet. Jumping up, he looked down and saw black ooze staining the tan of the chair and the tan of his khakis. Checking for some sort of ceiling leak, instead seeing a shimmery smoke winding its way towards the window. As he turned on the desk lamp to get a better view, it seemed to dissipate, leaving no trace. If it weren't for the residue on the chair, he would have sworn he was seeing things.

Not wanting to touch the substance with his bare hands he grabbed a tissue and swept up some of the ooze for closer inspection. It wasn't blood, or oil, but something foreign and vaguely sinister. He recoiled when the scent reminiscent of old beer and leftover soda pop assailed his nostrils. As he stepped back, he saw his reflection in the pane of glass illuminated by the downtown nightscape. Heart pounding, he also saw the image of a man behind him—how could that be?

Turning slowly, trying to avoid the inevitable, he came face to face with the homeless man from the subway. But there was something wrong—very wrong—he was like an irridescent shadow of himself; he looked translucent. The look on his face was both tortured and angry, and the anger seemed to be directed at the doctor, emanating from his eyes and bringing with it a deadly chill.

Before Dr. Grainger could move, his feet were encased in ice, freezing him to the spot. He tried to recoil when the spirit in tattered rags reached out to touch his arm, but could not escape. As the black tipped fingers touched him he felt an intense pain in his temples. Like a slow motioned movie trailer, a sudden vision penetrated his mind:

An ice covered dumpster in a dark alley covered in snow. A shopping cart filled with plastic bags and empty bottles. An elderly man in tattered clothes trying with frost bitten fingers to reach into an empty prescription bottle once filled with nitroglycerin.

The vision stopped when the man removed his hand from the doctor's arm, replaced by unbearable cold permeating his body, sending shooting pain to his limbs and a heavy flutter to his heart. Gulping to get enough air, he tried to move, but the ice was now encasing him to the waist. How could this be happening, it was not logical, or even medically possible. He called out for help but the man touched his temple again and another vision dominated his mind:

A frail man in a dirty coat standing at the doorway marked nursing station. A nurse telling him that the clinic was closing and he would have to get his heart pills at his doctor's office. The man trying to explain he had no doctor and the nurse kindly holding his hand with tears in her eyes, giving him directions to the closest Emergency Room.

This time when the vision stopped the cold was suffocating, his breath now coming in labored sobs. His heart was trying to keep up and even a fancy cardiac wing would not save him now. Looked into the sunken eyes of the homeless man, he sensed sadness, not revenge, which was even more jarring, as if he somehow knew the doctor's fate. He pushed the doctor over so he fell to the ground hitting his head. Ice was covering his arms so he lay helplessly, unable to touch the blood now oozing from the wound.

The homeless man looked down at him briefly before he went over to get his shopping cart, and that dark squeaky sound filled the air. The doctor could see the rusty wheels of the cart immersed in the expanding pool of blood surrounding him. The homeless man took some papers from his cart and groaned as he bent down and placed them beside the doctor. As he left the room, the squeaking was gone, the blood now lubricating the wheels.

-~A~-

The secretary shivered as she entered the executive suite and on her way to the thermostat she found Dr. Grainger clasping a coffee stained and bloody proposal for a health clinic at the homeless shelter.

"Make sure this gets on the agenda for the Board meeting," he croaked before take a final shuddering breath.

Neighbor Bites

Cathy Bryant

Oh God. Not again. He couldn't take it anymore.

Jake put his hands over his ears, but the strains of ten or so drunken people singing "Hey Jude" still reverberated through his skull. Hell, even his *bed* was vibrating. The walls between the flats were membrane-thin, of course, but that made it all the more important for residents to be considerate. It was decidedly inconsiderate to throw a party and sing "Hey Jude" *four times* at 4 A.M., when Jake had to work in the morning—it wasn't even the weekend.

What a crappy day he'd had. At work in the park, while he was weeding a flower bed, a little girl had come up to him. She was as sweet as summer in her peach dress, and when she smiled at him, he smiled back.

Then she bit him, tiny jaws snapping at his bare tricep, and by hell it hurt.

"Yow!" Jake yelled, trying to detach her without hurting her. He looked around for the child's parent/keeper, and saw a shambling figure, dull-eyed and silent.

Parents today, thought Jake, and then felt guilty. Judging by the man's arrhythmic walk (or rather stagger), he had some sort of medical condition.

Jake was forced to pull the girl's hair to get her off his arm, and she came away actually growling, her mouth lip sticked with Jake's blood. She loped back to the man and held his hand, and the peculiar pair lurched off.

Jake was thoroughly upset. He carefully cleaned and dressed the wound, which was of the type that was small but deep and might scar. What had really got to him was the child's ferocity—that feral bloodied face. He felt seedy and faintly aggressive all afternoon.

And so of course his neighbors had to pick that night to act up, didn't they? He wasn't an unreasonable man, and he didn't mind a fair bit of noise at weekends, but these louts would get in at 2 AM and *start* the party then, on any day of the week—and it was day when they finished, usually around 6.

Oh no, *Not* "The Timewarp." "Hey Jude" had been bad enough, but at least they hadn't *danced* to it. With "The Timewarp" came a great thumping that punched into Jake's already aching head.

That was it. He was going to have to say something. He'd knock on their door and complain and they'd have to be quieter. It was that simple, or else he'd eat their brains or something, damn them.

-❧A❧-

It hurt to get out of bed at that time of night. Being over 40 is no joke. Jake pulled a dressing gown on over his pajamas, slid into his slippers and stumbled next door.

The door opened with surprising swiftness when he knocked. An elfin redhead answered it; Jake had no idea whether or not she was a fellow tenant.

"Could you turn the music down, please?" he asked, letting his annoyance show in a brusque tone. "I have to work in the morning, and it's ridiculously loud."

"Ah-yer-sure," said the young woman. "Mo-kill the sound a bit, yeah?"

A lad nodded vaguely and the room was suddenly quieter, with that muffled quality that comes after loudness. Jake's ears ached. Just how high had the volume been?

"Thanks," he said. "I appreciate it."

And so, to bed. He could still hear the music, but maybe he'd be able to drop off now that it was at a reasonable level. Ah, what a day. His breathing began to even, his body to slump into relaxation.

WHAM! THUMP! YELL! "Who Let the Dogs Out"-at a million decibels. Oh no, no! Some thoughtless thug had just ramped the volume all the way up and now the choir from hell was at it again.

Rage filled Jake the way noise fills a small flat. He flung himself out of bed and stormed next door, slipperless and dressing-gownless. He didn't so much knock on the door as whack it to within an inch of its life.

A lad answered this time, a grinning fool who laughed openly at Jake. Something snapped, and Jake launched himself forward like the dogs at the park when their owners let them off the leash.

-∞A∞-

God, it was quiet. Where was he?

Jake raised his head. He was on a sofa, and he felt…good. He felt fine, even energetic. What was that stuff on his face, though? He raised a hand to wipe, and it came away red—red, and smeared with bits of jellied matter like—oh dear God in heaven, what?

Jake looked around then and saw the bodies. A heap of them, torn and twisted and mutilated, the heads cracked like Conker shells from the big horse-chestnut tree in the park. Had he—? What had he—?

No. His mind simply couldn't take it in. This was a dream. Shock was numbing him, and he shambled (like the man in the park, he thought to himself in an idle, casual way) back to his flat. He washed his hands and face, careful not to look in the mirror, removed his stained pajamas and put them in the bin.

There's still time to sleep. I can get a couple of hours in before work, his traumatized mind reasoned, and he lay down. Soon he was snoring peacefully as the sun rose and the birds began their (mercifully gentle) chorusing.

What woke Jake was a strange rhythmic banging that was nonetheless familiar.

Thump-thump-CLAP! Thump-thump-CLAP! Thump-thump-CLAP!

What the hell? Oh, not again! Jake needed more sleep. And weren't they—? Hadn't he—?

Suddenly the source of the noise became clear as the chorus kicked in: it was "We Will Rock You" by Queen, and Jake's neighbors were singing as if paid to do so by masochists.

But it wasn't just anger that sent Jake next door—fear and curiosity were pretty high up the list too. What exactly had happened last night? And what on earth was happening now?

The elfin girl answered the door.

"Hey neighbor!" she said with a rictus grin, seemingly unperturbed by the fact that a large lump of her head and one whole arm were missing. "Why don't you come in?"

"Wh-what?"

"Party time!" yelled Mo from a corner, cranking the music up even higher. "Look how we woke up! No more studying for us, right? It's party, party, par-*tay* all the *way* now, twenty-four seven, three-six-five!"

Jake nodded slowly at the hideously vibrant throng, and backed away without a word, closing the door gently behind himself as he left. Back at his flat he pressed a couple of buttons and waited for his ancient computer to warm up. He really hoped that it hadn't died on him—he very badly needed to go online. How else would he be able to find out how a zombie can commit suicide?

Home

C.R. Langille

She had curled up in the corner of our ramshackle cabin, a tattered wool blanket wrapped around her body like a grey cocoon. It reminded me of when she was a child. Small murmurs and cries slipped through her lips as she slept. Maybe she felt what was wrong with me on a subconscious level, or maybe it was just a bad dream.

I didn't want to leave her all alone. A part of me knew she was old enough to take care of herself. A part of me didn't care. I didn't want to leave.

I almost didn't.

Yet it was that kind of thinking that would lead to her dying horribly and probably by my hand. My fingers brushed the bandage around my arm and the pain was motivation enough to get moving.

We only had one gun between the two of us with a handful of shells. She would need it more than me, so it was a parting gift.

I didn't leave a note, I didn't say goodbye. Going through those motions would only make me weak. She wouldn't agree with what I was doing, but hopefully she would at least understand. We'd seen too many good people turn and she didn't need to add me to that list. I blew her a kiss and left.

The wind outside howled across the barren landscape, burning my chapped skin and making it almost impossible to maneuver without goggles. Unfortunately, my only pair were scratched and blemished to the point that they were almost unserviceable. Better than nothing since the alternative was going blind.

Although this would be my last journey, I had a purpose, and it wasn't to wander aimlessly until I turned to bone and sand like everything else in this godforsaken landscape. I was going home.

My family had owned a small plot of land up Sardine Canyon in the small town of Mantua, overlooking a large pond that thought it was a lake. When I was younger, I couldn't wait to get out of town. Once everything started to wilt and burn, people couldn't get out fast enough.

Red clouds churned in the sky, casting the land below in a rust-tinged shadow accentuated by the occasional blast of lightning. It made it difficult to judge the sun's position. The pain throbbing up my arm was enough to tell me I was a dead man walking. However, that didn't mean I wanted to get torn to pieces caught in the dark.

The wind and dust made it hard to navigate and I had to keep the mountains to my right, using them as a guiding line to the canyon. It wasn't much longer until mountains opened, showing me the way to Mantua. A few more miles up a broken stretch of asphalt and I'd be home.

The hills crept along either side of me as I made my way into the canyon. I was lost in thought staring at dead trees lining the road when pain lanced up my arm. My lungs refused to work and after several agonizing moments, I dropped to my knees and hacked up a wad of black tar that scratched my throat to shreds on the way up. I wiped my face with a ragged scarf, and was about to stand up when something moved in the gravel behind me.

"You left."

It was her.

"You shouldn't have followed me."

It wasn't my voice anymore. It was tinny and jagged, like the voice of one of *them*.

She didn't say anything but helped me to my feet. Her flaxen hair floated around her dirty, tear-streaked face like wispy tendrils. The world turned upside-down and I almost fell over again, but she caught me.

I hugged her, partly to steady myself, and partly to hold her close one last time. She trembled in my arms, her soft sobs muffled against my chest.

"You don't have to do this," she said, her voice trembling and quiet. She knew what would happen—what *was* happening.

Her purity was a stench, like rotten meat. I had an urge to rip it out of her, piece by little piece.

"You have to go, honey. It's getting worse."

"I don't want to."

Tears streamed down her face in tiny tributaries, blazing new trails through the dirt. I had no idea when it would get dark. That's when they would come for her—when I would turn on her.

"Go. Before it's too late."

I gave her a kiss on the forehead, resisting the temptation to sink my teeth into her soft cheek. We shared one last embrace and then I left her for the second time. I didn't look back, but the weight of her eyes was heavy on my back.

I rounded the bend and Mantua came into view: it was as I feared. The small town had burnt to its foundation, the small lake nothing more than a stagnant pool. Up the hill sat my family's land. Like the rest of the town, the house had burned in the purge; however, part of the structure was still intact.

I started up the hill when a gunshot rang out in the distance stopping me in my tracks. Two more followed shortly thereafter, echoing through the hills. Then it went silent.

I tried to imagine she was okay, but nothing was okay in this world, not anymore.

The sun was setting and as the light receded past the mountaintops, the whispering started. I couldn't understand what they were saying, but as I neared my old house, and as it got darker and darker, the whispers became more and more clear.

They were welcoming me home.

Worship

Daniel Cureton

Perun floated in front of the cathedral with the onion domes—so many dotted the landscape in Rus. *All high and mighty, Christ and angels, he can go fuck himself.* It was hard these days having no worshipers, no followings, no festivals. Life in the thereafter for gods wasn't what he expected. *One of these days, I'll be able to squeeze through a mouse hole.*

He slinked into the church, watching all the worshipers praying to icons and Christ. He could see the sustaining currents, feeding the angels and would be savior of the masses. Golden streams poured into the wooden reliefs—into the murals on the walls. The old twinge of desire surfaced; bearable but uncomfortable.

Disgusted, he wandered listlessly towards the forest, which is where the deities lived. Some were sitting, others swaying on the branches—all varying in size.

The ground started to tremble. Perun bolted for the trees. He looked back, seeing Christ—a mammoth titan—stomp into view. Christ inhaled the energy being sent up, exclaiming, "This is some good shit!" with moaning satisfaction.

It was time to go, to slide back into the shadows unspotted. Sitting on the edge of her porch was the local witch. "Baba Yaga, how do you never shrink like the rest of us?" Perun asked.

"*Children!*" she said giving a loud cackle. "I'm the boogie woman, people give me life through bed time stories to children, threating that I'll come and…EAT THEM!"

Some let out a laugh, others slumbered away and yawned with disinterest.

"Ah, well, the benefits of being an ungoddess. Did you hear Christ? I barely made it back to the woods. You remember what happened to Veles when he was sneaking around the 7th Day Adventists last year…"

"He is still flat! Ha!" yelled Ozwiena.

Morana came strolling around to the collective, just in from a trip to India, "You should see the dead gods there, many have turned to little sleeping figurines! I saw Shiva sitting at a temple, snorting worship like crack. Ganesh was baking it into little sweet balls. I got to know Dhumavati and she gets enough traffic at the funeral grounds to eke out an existence on the single and widowed—tough crowds."

Some deities had time to ween off worship, some didn't. Those dissatisfied with the changes in the status spent their days haunting the descendants of their followers who converted...if a domovoi wasn't guarding the house.

Perun sighed. "Well, I don't feel so bad. I got news about new Slavic worshippers." Several gods perked up. "Dogoda, over in Poland, says that they have groups of Slavs and spiritualists who are returning to their roots. They have enough followers there to avoid our fate. Some of the Polish gods are even growing again, very slowly."

"Well, what are we waiting for?" said Morana, hoping off a branch. A few of the larger gods followed suit, leaving those too tired to move.

The group moved deeper into the woods, heading to open spaces where worshipers were likely to gather. They happened upon a few forgotten cathedrals, but gave a wide berth due to sniper angels on the rooftops.

Passing a thicket of aspen, they heard the sounds of chant and the beating of drums. A large group of Pagans with a bon fire, deep in a village, were dancing and singing in Russian. Glinting in the light were pendants of ax and hammer, symbols of the old faith. They adorned traditional garb—vyshyvankas—which filled the gods with longing desire.

The familiar energy was palpable—the rise of the hair on the back of the neck, the quickening pace of the blood—the gods moved to surround the circle. Small streams of blue light went up to the sky. They sucked in the streams, taking in the high. Eyes rolling to the back of their heads, they reclined with satisfaction and relief, filled with distant memories from so long ago.

Perun jumped up, grabbing the currents, stealing them away from the smaller gods who protested; their cries went unnoticed.

With a look of madness, he let out a bellow, "I am CHIEF of the Gods!"

Wind dimmed the fire and the dancers paused to look around the thicket. The gods scattered, retreating to the woods. Perun grew into a titan, eyeballs bursting out of his head, veins pulsing on the skin, foam forming at the mouth.

He fell to the ground, convulsed, and overdosed on worship.

Autopsy Report

Iona Murphy

Who is the deceased?

Name: Jane Doe

Age: 21

Sex: Female

Length: 152cm

Weight: 38kg

Eyes**:** Dull. Glazed over. Remnants of a spark that's been extinguished.

Hair**:** Thinning. Straw like. Limp.

Blood Type**:** O Negative. Anaemic.

Probable Cause of Death**:** …

P*robable Cause of Death.* The question stumped me. What could I say about another Jane Doe; flesh but barely, her wrist fractured from self-induced osteoporosis. Nose to nose, I tried to breathe life into the gaunt child, slapping her cheeks, trying to induce a rosy complexion. But she just stared back, hollow, lifeless. Another victim. How many more Jane Doe reports am I going to fill out with the same cause of death? The unexplainable malnourishment. Slowly I traced my fingers across the ribcage of her decaying corpse. Turning her on her front, tiptoeing my fingers up the ladder of her protruding spine.

That's when I felt it grab me. First my arm, taking measurements. I tried to push it off, but it gripped too tight. I couldn't scream. I couldn't move. I couldn't feel anything. It made its way up to my lips, caressing, trying to force itself into my mouth. Almost paralysed, I tried to keep my lips pressed firmly shut, swearing to never let anything pass into my stomach. It grabbed my nose. Suffocation. Thoughts racing. Heart thumping. Mouth opening. Gasping in desperation, trying to get some oxygen, clinging on to life by a thread. In it crawled, making my body its next vessel. Clawing up through my throat, finding a way to infect my brain. It ran through my body, tearing my vital organs, eating me alive. I couldn't fight back.

I looked at my reflection in the clinical clean surfaces: hollow, gaunt.

Another Jane Doe.

Bad Day at Bull Funk's

M.X. Kelly

Brett whistled as he stocked the shelves with the new shipment of José Cuervo. He noticed that most of the other brands of tequila were also running low, and it wasn't even close to Cinco de Mayo. He made a mental note to look into it and place orders for the depleted stocks later. He couldn't wait to start looking at the new magazine he bought at the porn store down the street on his way to work. He saw no problem with doing that, once the boss man left. Business was generally slow until about 10 o'clock, anyway. That's when all the street winos started wandering in for the medicine to cure their shakes. He always replenished the discount wine and beer sections first thing in the morning for that reason.

The owner emerged from the back of the store, jingling his car keys. He ran his free hand over his crew-cut. He was a retired Air Force Master Sergeant and old habits die hard.

"Okay, Brett. I'm outta here. See you tomorrow. And thanks for covering," he said as he went out the door.

Thanks for covering. If the new clerk they had hired ever showed up again, Brett would kill him. He hadn't been to work for over a week now and he wasn't answering his cell. It was only the little punk's third week, for fuck's sakes. So Brett was stuck working doubles until they found a replacement. He didn't really mind. He would have a fat paycheck.

He finished restocking, walked behind the register and removed his magazine from under the counter. He began to thumb through it, thinking to himself that it was a great morning to be alive. With the shop to himself, alone with his *Busty Babes*.

-❧A☙-

Several blocks away, in the parking lot of Artesia Acres Retirement Center, an elderly man sat behind the wheel of a Chevy Astro van and frowned, looking impatiently at his wristwatch.

"C'mon, gawtdamn it!" he muttered to himself. He sighed and kept an expectant lookout on the front door of the nursing home.

After five minutes, during which time the oldster looked at his watch fifteen more times and rattled off even more obscenities, the entrance of the home opened and out drizzled six hunchbacked, shuffling seniors. Three of them climbed into the van with the geezer, and the other three got into a 1966 red Ford Thunderbird, parked alongside. A white-haired woman slid into the driver's seat and rolled down the window.

"Jimmy, for Christsake, don't let Melvin take a wrong turn."

Melvin stuck his hand out of the window and displayed the universal finger gesture for "shove it sideways" and began backing the van out.

"Guess that's your answer, Bev," said Jimmy from the passenger's side of the van.

"Asshole," Bev torted. She pulled the T-bird out and followed the van.

-❧A☙-

Brett was taking a cigarette break. He was standing outside the store under a neon sign that read "*Bull Funk's Wine & Spirits*." There were three paper signs, one each taped to the windows on each side of the door and one in the window of the door. The one in the store's entrance window was the posting of the hours, for the benefit of tourists unfamiliar with New Mexico's Blue Laws. And they got a lot of tourists given the proximity of a certain infamous town, Roswell, almost within a stone's throw up Route 285. The sign in the left window read "*No Personal Checks*" and the one in the right stated "*Liquor Up Front, Poker in the Rear*."

Brett stared at this sign and snorted at his boss's cheesy sense of humor, blowing out a puff of smoke from between his thin lips. He smiled and turned facing the street, watching the women who worked in the office building around the corner walk along the sidewalk in their tight pencil skirts. He leered and grinned and scratched a raw, red pimple on his nose; one of many placed in random patterns across his face. In his favorite subreddit forum, he blamed his inability to get a date on feminism, but it was really just his gross zits and shitty incel personality.

He threw his cigarette down and was about to squash it under his heel when two vehicles pulled up. A Chevy cargo van and a classic red T-bird. Six elderly people got out. One woman and five men. A seventh man remained behind the wheel of the van, scowling.

Shit! thought Brett. *Six customers? And all of them older than blame.* His eyes roamed over each of their sour pusses. *So much for an easy morning.* He stomped his cigarette out and returned inside the store. He waited behind the counter as the old farts filed in with their canes and walkers. The last one in the door (a gent with a limp and a bushy iron-gray beard) turned and shut the door. He flipped the sign in the window over from "OPEN" to "CLOSED."

Brett watched with mild amusement. "Waddidya do that for?"

The old woman went behind the counter. She pulled a Colt .45 Automatic out of her handbag and jammed it between Brett's eyes.

"Oh, you gotta be shitting me!" Brett cried. "You're fucking robbing us?"

"Yes and no," said the woman.

Brett laughed nervously. Grandma Bev jammed the gun harder into his skull.

"Hey, that hurts!" Brett said.

"It's supposed to," Granny said. She glanced at her accomplices. They were rummaging through the section where the tequila display was. "Hurry up and get it together, fellas! Jimmy, you get the boxes from the back."

"Okay, Bev. We're on it." Jimmy propped his cane against the shelves.

"What? You're stealing *liquor*?" Brett asked, shocked.

"Only what we need," replied Bev.

Brett tried to make a move to subdue the old woman, but she grabbed his arm and twisted it behind his back. He yelped in pain. *Christ, the old bitch was STRONG!* Bev walloped him on the back of the head with the butt of the gun. He swayed, but didn't pass out. He ceased struggling. Bev leaned in close to him.

"There's a smart boy," she whispered. She licked his earlobe. Brett shivered, frightened and grossed out at the same time. He twisted around and looked up at the security camera. Fake, but still...

"We know it doesn't wo-ork," Ironbeard sing-songed from the door.

Brett didn't ask how they knew. He watched silently as the others began loading up the boxes with bottles of tequila.

"Why tequila?"

"Nosy little jerk, 'aint he?" Jimmy said. "And brave. Last punk didn't say or do a fricking thing."

"Didn't help him in the end, though, did it. He was still..." said one of the other men loading boxes. *What did he say? It sounded like exyunitch. What the hell was that?* Brett wondered. *Did the old bitch damage his hearing when she hit him?*

"Now, Rocky. It's okay," said Bev. She still had a hammer-lock on Brett. The business end of the gun was jammed once more against his head. She leaned in to whisper. "We have a craving for fermented agave." She was licking his ear again. "Among other things. It helps keep us young."

"You couldn't just buy it?" he asked, hesitantly. He was starting to get worried. *What really had happened to the other clerk?*

Rocky opened a bottle of Don Modesto and drained it down in three gulps. He tossed the empty bottle aside and wiped his mouth on the dirty sleeve of his flannel shirt.

"Any more questions, zitface?" Rocky asked.

Brett said nothing but stared dumbfounded as Rocky went back to hefting cases of booze and hauling them up to the front of the store, stacking them next to Old Ironbeard. The man hardly seemed affected by the alcohol. In fact, he bounced up the aisle with the bottle-laden boxes like a much younger man.

Eventually, the five men came to stand in front of the register. They all looked at him. Brett trembled. Somehow he found some courage. "You can't kill me. Your fingerprints are everywhere and when they find my body..."

"What body, sweetie?" said Bev. She stuck her tongue, suddenly barbed, into his ear canal and it snaked deep inside.

Brett's eyes widened and rolled into the back of his head.

He screamed once, then gurgled and fell to the floor, lifeless.

A stunning, blond and thirty-something woman with reptilian yellow eyes licked her lips and grinned; her mouth was transformed into a slit filled with sharp white teeth.

"Jimmy, go tell Melvin it's time for lunch."

The Ghost, The Magician and The Jellybeans

Joyce Frohn

The only thing that bothered Boouregard more than being small was the fact the magician that lived in his house, "Mervin the Magnificent," didn't believe in ghosts.

One night Boouregard went to his friend, Clyde, who lived in a haunted theatre across town.

After Clyde pushed aside some cobwebs so they could sit down, Boouregard said, "I want to be scary."

"Have you tried rattling chains?"

"I'll try that," Boouregard said. "Can I borrow some of yours?"

"Sure, I'll even carry them over for you." Clyde set up a nice set of rattling, clanking chains in Boouregard's attic. "Try these, he's sure to be scared."

That night Boouregard tried dragging the chains across the floor but he couldn't lift them. He hunted around the house to try and find something that he could use.

He tried paper chains but they were silent. Floating over Mervin's desk, he thought he found the perfect idea—paperclips. He made a nice long chain of them and dragged them across the attic floor for hours.

The next night when he woke, Boouregard found Mervin's answer to the noise; three mousetraps. He went back to Clyde. "It didn't work. I couldn't lift the chains. Could you come and haunt my house for me?"

Clyde snapped his ghostly fingers. "I know. You're too neat. You look like a handkerchief. I'll get you nice and spooky looking."

He materialized a pair of scissors and shredded Boouregard's bottom edge. "There. Now you'll scare that magician."

Boouregard went home and materialized in front of Mervin. Mervin was practicing his disappearing handkerchief routine. "How did one of my handkerchiefs get so frayed?" He grabbed Boouregard and carried him over to the sewing machine in the corner. "I have to hem it." Boouregard was so shocked that he forgot to dematerialize until Mervin had hemmed half of his nice shredded bottom. "Stupid thing fell apart. I've got to get more handkerchiefs," Mervin muttered as he went back to his handkerchiefs.

Boouregard went back to Clyde. "And the worst thing," Boouregard told Clyde. "Is that I'm smaller than ever. And my left and right sides don't match."

Clyde patted his shoulder. "Cheer up. It's Halloween night. Let's go out and be spooky." Boouregard joined the ghosts from the haunted theater. The pack of them swooped and whistled down alleyways, tapped on tricker-or-treaters' shoulders and swooped around jack-o-lantern's candles. They boo'd in one trick-or-treater's ear so loud that he dropped his bag of candy and ran home.

Boouregard looked at the bag. "I wonder what that tastes like." He picked up a small bag of red jellybeans. "These look yummy."

"Be careful. Human food can be dangerous for us ghosts," Clyde said.

"I'll just eat one," Boouregard said. He popped one in his mouth. "It tastes great. I think I'll take the bag home with me." He tucked the bag of jellybeans into his ghostly body.

On hour later, Clyde said. "Be careful with that candy. You've been munching those pretty fast."

"How can you tell?" Boouregard asked.

"I see some pink spots."

Boouregard waved good-bye and went into his attic room. He looked into the cracked mirror of the old dresser. Sure enough he had faint pink spots. If I ate more jellybeans, would I turn red? That would scare Mervin for sure.

"I'll do it." So Boouregard ate the whole bag of jellybeans.

And the pink dots seemed have spread evenly.

He appeared in front of Mervin, who was practicing his handkerchief routine.

"There's my best pink one but how did the lace come off?" He grabbed Boouregard and a strip of lace and went straight to the sewing machine.

This time Boouregard managed to dematerialize before he got lace sewn on. He went to his attic and sulked. Then a thought came to him, *If one small bag made him pink wouldn't more, a lot more, make him a nice spooky bloody red?*

That night he glided to a closed store and slipped through the wall. He picked up three of the biggest bags of red jelly beans he could find and tried to go back through. He went through, but the candy stayed on the inside. He tried tucking the jellybeans into his body but the candy still couldn't go through the wall—the sun would be rising soon.

Boouregard tore open all three bags and ate the jellybeans as fast as he could. Then he rushed up to his attic as the sun was rising.

He lay down feeling good. But soon his stomach hurt. He began to moan and groan. He rolled from side to side and rocked. He whimpered and cried.

Mervin woke to the wailing. "This house is haunted." He grabbed his things and ran out. "I'm gettin' the hell out!"

The Flesh Game

R.J. Howell

Maureen riffle-shuffled the cards. "All right, boys and girls. Ante up."

Three of the four gamblers seated at the folding table in the bar's storeroom raised their knives and, with a groan, a moan, and a choked scream, contributed their bets to the pool. Maureen's gaze flicked up to focus on the fourth. Her thin lips compressed a fraction thinner.

"Look, Larry, either you ante or you bow out. What's it going to be?"

Larry gnawed on a knuckle, considering. Then he sighed.

"I'm in," he said, and took his knife to his right thumb. Better start winning back some fingers soon, else he would have to move on to toes and Ryan was sure to give him hell for it. Win back his fingers and the ears he'd lost last week, and he'd finally break even.

He added the digit to the sad little pile of meat.

Maureen dealt the next hand, all ten of her fingers spread and fluttering. Driving home the point, he supposed.

Odds always favor the house.

An Angel's Love

Cate Dexter

I met my angel at the 7-11 I work in. It was 2:32 in the morning and I was exhausted.

My angel was a beautiful being, dark skin and gold eyes, hard lines and strong thighs. Gold dust littered their skin, stray feathers caught in their cloud-of-curls hair. They were scoping out the candy aisle and the way the light caught on them, I could almost see their halo.

My angel picked up three of the four cup Reese's packs, a large bag of Skittles, and a double-layered slushy. For the life of me, I'll never be able to figure out why this detail stood out to me, but my angel had more cherry than grape in their slushy. My angel also grabbed a Sprite, which they poured in the slushy once they got outside.

"I'm Azrael," my angel said with a sweet smile as they paid. "I'm new to earth."

"You're gonna get a stomach ache with all that sugar," I blurted out as I rang up the items.

They laughed, reaching a hand out to trail over my face. "Sweet human, I will be fine." They had a smile like the sun, dripping golden rays and scorching me to the bone. "Goodbye, my human."

I stumbled home, hands shaking as I unlocked my door. I found a feather on my bed, white dipped in gold. I tucked it in my pillowcase with shaky hands and fell asleep, dreaming of scorched earth and my angel crying.

"Sweet human."

I jerked, ears warm as I yanked my earbuds out, staring at my angel. This time they had a massive caramel Frappuccino in their hand, a stray feather caught on their gold bracelet. Their body was different this time, light skin and golden hair, tattoos I couldn't understand marking their chiseled form.

"Thanks for the feather," was all I could say.

"Anything for you," they promised, taking a sip of the caramel confection in their hand. Homework forgotten, I stuffed everything into my bag and followed my angel as they left, heading for the cathedral a few streets away.

It felt wrong, standing there when the whole world said that I was going to hell for what I was.

My angel didn't care, motioning for me to follow them as I paused in the doorway.

"Don't be afraid," they laughed, practically glowing in the candlelight. "Nothing here will harm you."

I swallowed hard, stumbled to the altar and knelt, my angel next to me.

"Do you pray?" My angel asked innocently.

"No," I croaked.

"That's alright," they smiled. "I shall pray for you."

Their prayers were liquid gold and sweet as honey, running down my spine and pooling at the small of my back. I felt like they were opening me up and pouring sunlight in, letting its rays chase out any darkness I held within.

By the time they finished I was shaking—raw, all over.

"Angel," I said, as they helped me stand. "Angel I-"

They hushed me with a kiss on my lips, cupping my elbows in their warm hands. I was helpless under their sway, and went down like I had no other duty in the world than to be theirs at that moment. It felt dirty, being in a church at the time. But, I was so utterly entranced, accepting their touch and begging for it as well. The act itself was a blur, and when I came out of the haze, shaking and gasping, my angel was there, looking equally as debauched and ruined. Their wet gasps were like a sob, their open mouth pressed against my shoulder to stifle the noise.

Sex with an angel in a church was perhaps the worst thing I've ever done, but I had no regrets as we lay on a blanket of clothes, intertwined in the most unholy of ways.

I could have sex a thousand more times and it would never compare to that brief hour I spent with my angel.

-ᨓA-

"Hello sweet human."

"Hello Angel," I breathed, stunned that they had picked one of my classmates this time. They sprawled in the seat next to me, a lean graceless-ness in this new form. Their warm gold eyes flicked over every inch of the lecture hall, intrigued by everything.

"Angel," I said. "Angel why?"

"Because," they grinned at me, running long fingers through their hair. "Because."

I could hardly hear what the professor said that entire lecture, the physics of stars and tesseracts forgotten in the warmth of my angel's thigh pressed against mine. The burn of dwarf stars was in the palm of their hand as it rested on my knee, rubbing the heat of a nebula into me from the smooth swipe of their thumb.

-ᨓA-

"Angel." I found them first this time, their new body slumped against a wall, shaking and clammy.

"They took something," they croaked, reaching for me with trembling hands. "They thought it would make them feel better, take away the hurt in their heart and in their head."

"Oh Angel," I said helplessly, cradling them. "Angel why?" I'd never seen an angel cry before; but they did—wet tears that burned when they dripped onto my shirt.

That was the longest my angel stayed with me, and the longest they stayed in any one body, purging it of the drugs they took to mellow out the pain they felt. When they left, they looked different, a little more haunted. I hadn't quite realized it before, but my angel was new, unknowing of the darkness that lay in humanity.

-ര⩚ര-

Their next body was a little older, a little wiser, used before by one of their brothers or sisters.

"It's like an old sweater," they described it, swiping hands up their arms. "Soft with a long life, and warm with love."

I watched them move around the diner their vessel worked in, serving coffee and juice with that sunshine smile. But, the sun was dimmer, had a worn edge from years spent too long on it.

-ര⩚ര-

"Angel," I sobbed, "Angel."

I was lying in the wreck of a car, bleeding from my forehead as a classmate lay dead next to me. They weren't my angel, but they didn't deserve to die because the other person had decided to drive while drunk.

All I wanted at that moment was my angel, for them to rescue me, to hold me in their arms that had cradled galaxies, to kiss me with lips dusted by moons. I wanted them to scream at their father for stealing my classmate too soon, that Joong-Ki didn't deserve to die.

That's not quite what happened.

My angel came, this time as an EMT, pulling me from the wreck with careful hands that had once crushed planets with ease.

"Sweet human," they cooed as I laid on the gurney. "Never fear, I am here."

Joong-Ki was mourned on campus for a few weeks, my teachers let me skip class without fuss. My mother called and talked about coming down to see me. I refused, and instead went to visit Joong-Ki's grave.

"Angel," I blinked at them, strangely unnerved by their presence at his resting place.

"Sweet human," they murmured with a shaky smile that didn't quite reach their eyes. Their new form was smaller, skinnier in a way that was worrying. They kissed my forehead and left, I didn't see them for a few weeks.

"I'm leaving." Their final form was a warrior's form, hard grace and calloused hands.

"I love you." I felt sick to my stomach as I said that, like I was begging them not to leave. In a way I was, praying to a god I never believed in that it would affect their decision.

"I love you," they repeated back to me. "But I'm leaving."

They stayed with me for one last night. I woke up alone, a dreamcatcher made with their feathers hanging above my head when I did.

I never saw them again.

Play

Frank and the Baby

Johannes Black

[Curtain.]

Empty room; set some time in the past, although this is never fixed. Small wooden table in centre of room—an old phone placed on top. A small wooden chair is tucked neatly into this. Other than this the room is cold and bare —with the exception of an old radiator fastened to the left stage wall, a tall closet and two curtained windows. Right front stage lies a large cot, unsettling to the minimal symmetry of the scene. Over the whole structure is cast a white, thin net—Transparent enough to see through, yet, in accordance with the sheets and bedding, diffuses and illusion of cloud-like whiteness. A slight movement is detectable from within: the slow intake and exhalation of breath, or the yearning movements of a child's passing dreams. Industrial noises surround the stage—quiet, however, as if from old machinery. This is sometimes interspersed with the low sound of rain and wind. A stillness, nevertheless, has settled over the scene. This is broken by a low wail from a child. Extends for about ten seconds.

[Child's voice is that of a young woman, projected from either speakers or an actress within the cot.]

CHILD: Ten…nine…eight…seven…six…*(Pause).* Five…four…three… two…one…*(Pause. Quiet Exhalation).* Ahhh…*(Long pause. Whispered).* Frank? *(Pause. Louder).* Frank! *(Pause. Quieter, but gradually rising).* Oh,

CHILD (CONT'D): Frank! My sweet, sweet man…did you do it? *(Pause).* Did they find you? Did they—did they—hurt you? Please, tell me they didn't hurt you. No, oh please, no, I couldn't, I couldn't hear that! To think of the, of the horrible things they might have done—the questions they might have asked! *(More tentatively).* Frank? Are you out there? Somewhere in the rain… somewhere on the road…all and dark in the headlights. *(Asides, melodious and quiet).* But hush, but hush, but silence...in heaven…I close my two eyes; *(Fearful).* the rain, it beats on the door...in heaven, everything is fine. *(Resumed urgency).* Frank! Can you hear me? Come quick Frank, kiss me—yes, right now—kiss me quick. Frank! Frank! Come as fast as you can, tell me you did it, tell me you—

The door slams open, rebounding against the wall. FRANK *is standing, panting like a dog, his face and shirt dripping with blood. Brain matter is visible. It is unclear whether or not it is his. In one hand he holds a large bloody torch. He uses the other hand to smooth back his hair—a habit he repeats throughout—biting his tongue and exhaling in the process. Long pause.*

Frank! Frank—is that you?...

FRANK: Yes.

(Long pause). Attention is drawn to the space between them.

CHILD: I knew it was you. *(Pause).* I could hear the steps of your feet…one, two…three. *(Pause).* Did you do it?

FRANK: Yes.

CHILD: And did anyone find you? *(Pause).* Did anyone see you go in to her? Catherine.

FRANK: No.

CHILD: So it happened. *(Pause)*. Like a dream, a passing dream…

FRANK: Yes, it happened—

CHILD: And you made the call, Frank—for the police? *(Pause)*. They must be there to find her…and then him, wading in his filth, in hers, between the walls… *(Asides. whispered)*. Dancing to the red room, oh—like Sinatra, like a man…

FRANK: Yes.

CHILD: Oh good, oh good! This is wonderful, just so, so…

Her voice trails off. Slight jerk of movement within the cot. FRANK*, wavering, considers instrument in hand, then walks a few steps forward to look into the cot. He parts the netting with his hand to look in.*

Oh my sweet, sweet Frank—what have we done? (*Pause*). Such acts of violence are never forgotten. (*Pause*). Where are we now? It is like some dream.

FRANK: A dream?

CHILD: Yes, a dream. Like the one I had the night I was born—in the hospital.

FRANK *slowly withdraws his hand, letting the net fall back into place, and goes over to sit on the table, focusing the torch's beam on the scene around him. Light dims, whilst* CHILD *recounts, matching her description..*

I remember walking down a long dark corridor, the walls lined with paintings I couldn't see, yet their inscriptions shone out like numbed eyes. A trumpet, or a saxophone, cried out in the farthest distance; a long, far cry, that seemed to open my eyes wide, but cloud the air with a blue mist. And in this moment, of seeing and not seeing, parting the mist with my hands, I could now make out one of the paintings.

FRANK *Puts a cigarette in his mouth. He lights a match, holding it out.*

FRANK: You could now see one of the paintings?

CHILD: Yes, and the nearer I drew the more I realized. *(Pause. Breathing rapidly increases).* That the painting was of me—of me—a newborn child, warm from the womb, lying there helpless and afraid and pale. *(Pause).* It was a disgusting dream.

FRANK *Blows out match, throwing it on floor. Lies back on the table facing upward.*

FRANK: But a dream nevertheless…nothing more…

FRANK *slowly draws in his outstretched body, stands up and walks over, leaving the torch—switched on—on the table.* FRANK *is a lean, broad-shouldered man of around 20, although his age is not reflected in his appearance. A sadness weighs over his every move. This is stifled, however, by an exterior presentation that fluctuates between thoughtfulness and indifference—both to violence and* CHILD. CHILD *rolls up his sleeves and parts the curtain net. A single, long-drawn note of a saxophone is heard. He quickly reaches two hands in and begins the process of lifting her out.*

CHILD: Careful, Frank! Slowly, slowly…that's right, cradle my head…

He lifts her out, slowly. CHILD *is wrapped up in a thin white blanket, which drapes down several feet as* FRANK *lifts. It is larger than would be expected. He holds her close to his chest, nestling the soft load between the inner sides of his black jacket. Then, in rhythm to the industrial noise, rocks her back and forth, whilst pacing, in the line of a waltz, around the room.*

CHILD: Oh Frank—what it is to see you, to see your eyes looking at mine…to see from such a height!

He stops pacing at the left side of the table.

Now, Frank—I must tell you something. I must tell you how I see things happening, that is, now that Catherine is dead. Are you listening?

FRANK: Yes.

CHILD: Before that, peel away the blankets from my face…I want to see everything that will happen.

He does, winding it away as if it were a bandaged limb, letting the sheet and blanket trail down into a small heap on the floor. More and more clothing is peeled away. FRANK *stops and resettles the load in his arms. The shape is now smaller and almost luminous against the dark of his jacket. In exhalation.*

CHILD: Ahhhh…yes, yes, perfect. Everything is just right. Now, then—

CHILD *is interrupted by the sound of the front door being tried. A key is slid into the lock and, likewise, tried to a similar effect. A thump. The door is tried again, to no avail, and then, with a grunt and shove, it violently opens outward to reveal* JORR. *Brief moment of stillness. The phone suddenly commences a loud, penetrating ring, repeating four times.* JORR *stands still, waiting for this to pass. Pause of ten seconds. He turns to lock the door and, whilst removing the key from the lock, the phone commences to ring again—this time without an apparent endpoint: it is felt that the ringing may never cease, rather expand beyond the confines of the small space. Keys are left in door. He walks briskly over to the table and looks carefully at the phone. He places an inspired hand on its top but pauses. It rings twice more. He returns his hand to his side and crosses over to the chair, pulling it out slowly and sitting down. This is done with a minimum amount of effort. He raises his hand a second time. Pause. He quickly picks up the receiver, cancelling the increasingly harsh reverberations. Pause.*

JORR: Hello? *(Pause).* Catherine—is that you?

CHILD: (*Breathless).* Yes, yes, Frank—a dream, a passing dream…But enough of this! *(Pause. Humorless).* Oh Frank. *(Pause).* Come here and pick me up, I wish to tell you something. Stop! *Shouting.* Stop!

The scene pauses. JORR *is frozen in place with the phone to his face.*

CHILD (CONT'D): Do you see Frank? Do you see? This is how it will begin: Jorr will walk back home to his apartment, after having left the factory for the night, come in and then before he does anything…*(Pause).* receive a phone call. It will keep on ringing until he picks it up. But Jorr is deluded, don't you see? He will talk to anyone. *(Pause).* Back!

JORR *reverses his previous action until the moment of first seeing the phone.*

Shouting. Now!

JORR *walks briskly over to the table and looks carefully at the phone. He places an inspired hand on its top but pauses. It rings twice more. He returns his hand to his side and crosses over to the chair, pulling it out slowly and sitting down. He raises his hand a second time. Pause. He quickly picks up the receiver, cancelling the increasingly harsh reverberations. Pause.*

JORR: Hello? *(Pause).* Catherine—is that you?

(Long pause). FRANK *peers forward at this, then picks his torch from off the table. He proceeds to shine it in* JORR's *face.*

Are we not—*(Pause. Slower)*—Catherine…Catherine, if this is you—is in fact you, not some other—then just say something. Say my name—yes!—say my name and then tell me what color the sky was on the day—*(Longer pause).*

His voice fades out, in contemplative thought.

—on the day…*(Long pause).* Catherine? Tell me you still love me. I know you were going to. Just before you commented on the sky; yes, your lips had parted—as they do so often. You looked up at the sky, the, the…blue, red, yellow, cloudless sky…*(Pause).* You might as well have said it, Catherine, you might as well—you were practically screaming *fire*. *(Pause).* It was not even raining and still you insisted on taking a coat. The long, pale white one you held in your hands, just as you held it behind the church door…in the darkness…as we touched and kissed and told each other all those…*(Longer pause).* It was not even raining. *(Pause).* Your lips had parted and the words were there, as they so often were, and yet…and yet—as if against your will—you refused to allow them room in our apartment.

His posture tenses and straightens.

CHILD: *Shouting.* Stop!

The scene freezes in place.

He believes he is talking to Catherine—as I said before, Jorr is deluded…he will hear what he wants to hear, speak to whomever he wants to. Why, why President Reagan could phone him anytime he wants!

She bursts out into laughter. FRANK *remains silent.*

But of course, he will talk and talk and talk away his little lips…until the sun has sunk and gone from the horizon.

FRANK: *After a pause.* Who is on the other end of the line?

CHILD: Why Frank, that would be our mutual friend, Harry, you must have met him, the old man in the wheelchair.

FRANK: Harry…

CHILD: But that is beside the point, the point is that anyone can call him—from Singapore to Sheffield...it does not matter! He is fixated on the woman—even after everything she did to him…*(Pause). Shouting.* Now!

JORR: *(Desperate).* Those unspoken goodbyes—all blue. Christ! Christ—it was all such a fantastic dream! *(Pause).* I've been waiting for you to call again. No sooner than you left had those thoughts—planted far back in some glasshouse, some old room—tore up the floorboards of the apartment and raised up a forest, hundreds of them crowding and breathing around me like animals. *(Pause).* The hours and days loosened themselves from some hold…*(Pause).*

He stands

…and suddenly that was it. Hour upon hour, upon other hours. I sat here

JORR (CONT'D): waiting, like some pilgrim. You only had to say something: tell me you love me. That was it. *(Pause).* Please, just say it! Catherine, are you listening to—

The sound of a sudden vibration—industrial, like the background hum—resonates from the radiator positioned left stage wall. A glow shines out from within its structure. FRANK *slowly turns around to look. The harmony of sound and light causes* JORR *to momentarily yelp and drop the phone on the table.* FRANK *quickly turns.*

JORR *picks the phone back up, wiping the mouthpiece and clutching it with both hands to his ear, yet retaining his stare at the radiator. Slow declination in sound and light until neither can be seen or heard. Long pause.*

JORR: Catherine? *(Pause).* Hello. Catherine, are you still there…here

Looks at radiator.

…here, with me? Are we not just voices on a line—*(Pause).* Just voices on a line—have we not—*(Pause).* Have we not got more to say to each other? Words and sounds...sounds and words. There are words, yes, oh so many things to say. If only we had said more. Goddam it Catherine, just answer me for once! Once! Listen and say something. We had a child together, does that mean anything to you?

(In resolution).

I will not speak to you again—yes, do you hear that?—I will neither call nor speak to you. Goodbye

He quickly hangs up the phone. JORR *leans back in the chair and sighs. An expression of indifference swells over the features of his face. This, however, changes as he glances again at the radiator—the industrial hum low in the background.*

In heaven… in dreams…everything is fine. My Catherine, my Catherine…

He stands and walks over to the radiator, placing a hand on either side and peering into it.

CHILD: It is beautiful, in a way, to see how things will happen. Don't you think? Look at the way he walks, the way he moves from thought to thought—all this, all this leading up to one final choice.

JORR: *(Asides).* Catherine…everything will be fine. It's all just fine.

FRANK: Is this how you think he'll really talk?—

CHILD: And then I think I'll send another call his way—Jorr.

The phone starts to rings again. JORR *appears not to notice. However, the ringing gradually becomes too much.*

JORR: Leave me alone! I will not talk to you again

JORR *stands, clearly agitated by the incessant noise. He paces anxiously, moving between the chair and the main door in steady yet anxious steps.*

What do you want from me? Just leave—leave me alone!

CHILD: And then cut it—

The phone cuts off. Surprised, JORR *darts over and raises the receiver to his ear, draws it away and then returns it to his ear, listening with a ravenous curiosity. Nothing of interest appears to have been heard. With trepidation,* JORR *slowly draws it away from his ear, then, as if in triumph, replaces the phone in its holder.*

And again!

Only for it to burst into an even louder ringing several seconds later. The suddenness of this causes him to fall to the side in shock, immediately sparking a revolt of anger within him. He draws his arms to his head then, crying out in frustration, rushes over to the phone, raises high the receiver and crashes it down onto the switch hook. He repeats this twice more then lets go of the hand receiver, letting it fall off the table and swing back and forth underneath. He collapses onto the chair, out of breath and seized by the exhilaration.

FRANK: *Now laughing.* The man is mad! He's mad, he's completely nuts!

CHILD: *Shouting.* Stop!

JORR *freezes.* FRANK *moves forward a few steps.*

(Pause). Yes Frank, once Catherine left him he had no one else to talk to. Other than himself of course…and me. On the day she had me, in the hours we lay there on the hospital sheets, she told Jorr everything. Everything, every little detail about how much she despised him—wanted nothing more to do with him. I lay there, quiet, and new…and took it all in. Of course I could have said something…I waited later for that…

FRANK: What then?

CHILD: She left the hospital two days later and went to live with another man. Jorr took me home and left me in the cot…he didn't know what to do with me, how could he? Just floated about the room, like some ghost, crying and screaming all these awful things for hours and hours…it was terrible. He didn't feed me for weeks and weeks. He didn't care…neither of them did. If you hadn't of found me, walking in one morning as you did, I—I don't know what would have happened Frank. My sweet, sweet Frank…

FRANK: So, (*Gesturing toward* JORR *at the table)* what happens now?

After a long pause—in which we are reminded of the industrial noises resonating in the distance, as well as the stillness of the current scene—she whispers.

CHILD: Now I talk to him, persuade him to change his mind, not to the point of action, of course, but enough to tilt the bridge. Place me back in the cot, quickly; I must imagine how this will feel.

FRANK *hastens over*

Gently! Gently!

Then returns to his previous position next to the pile of sheets.

(Pause). Now!

JORR *is still sitting in the chair, breathless and shaking slightly. He mumbles a little.*

Tonal difference to voice with FRANK.

CHILD (CONT'D): Oh, Jorr…

JORR *stands up, panicked, and looks from side to side—then at the large cot.* FRANK *is clearly excited by the whole process.*

Catherine…she doesn't love you anymore. No, she doesn't.

A look of terror comes across JORR*'s face. He takes a step back toward the closet, then, stammering, tries to say 'Hello'.*

Cut it out Jorr, you know who I am. *(Pause).* I'm in this very room with you… why, it has been a long while though…yes…

JORR *is still and silent, looking intently at the cot.*

Oh, Jorr…how long has it been? Not more than six—

JORR: Six months, six months—*(Takes a breath).* You said you wouldn't talk to me again, not since the hospital. You told me that.

CHILD: Yes, Jorr, I did. But that was then, and this is now—times change, you know. Haven't we all felt time's winged chariot at our back, stepping on our heels? I was never just going to go away. *Laughs.* —I am your daughter after all! Of your own seed and blood.

JORR *slowly walks over as she talks and carefully looks into the cot, parting the net with his hand.* FRANK *moves toward the cot as well, stopping a few feet short.*

Why you look tired Jorr. So very tired. *(Pause).* You've missed me, haven't you—?

JORR *quickly retracts his hand, looks for a little longer, and then walks back over to the chair. He places his hand on the phone, letting it fall to his side.* FRANK, *meanwhile, still rapt, slouches down to sit against the table. He plays with the torch in his bloody hands*

JORR: *(Long pause)*. What is it that you want?

CHILD: What is it that *I want?*

JORR *holds one hand against his face—an expression of grave worry.* FRANK *spotlights him with his torch for a little while.*

(Long pause). I want you to be happy. I've been watching you, Jorr. Yes. I've been watching you pick up that phone…over and over, time after time. To Catherine, or so I presume?

JORR: Yes. Who else would it be?

CHILD: (*Pause*). Why, lain here over the months, I have heard everything that you've said. Everything: the tap of your teeth, the scratch of you fingernails, your voice railing and breathing in and out those tired three words, over and over. It strikes me, Jorr, that Catherine has had very little to say back to you…

No response. JORR *stands and moves to front center stage, his head slightly bowed. He carries the phone over with him.*

JORR: You're wrong—

Interrupting JORR.

CHILD: What exactly *has* her response *been* to your words? (*Pause*) Jorr, Jorr…you really do miss her, oh—don't worry—I knew you loved her, and I know you still do.

FRANK *has now come over to look at* JORR: *walking around him, peering into his shirt, lifting layers and dropping them. Tone changes. .*

What with her eyes, and her breasts, and her little ways that she never quite shook off over the years you were together. I may have only been a part of your lives recently, alas, six months is no time at all—I am a second to the clock that you are gradually filling with hours…and yet I'm not a fool Jorr, I know things and I hear things.

JORR: *Sinking down to his knees and clutching the phone.* She knows things and she hears things…

CHILD: It is more than clear to me that Catherine was not a good wife to you—oh no, no—she was not a good friend, or a good person if you will. The things she said…the things she did to you…She never cared for you, Jorr, she never laid an eye or hand to care in all the years you had together. Do you not see this? *(Pause).* Are you so blind? *(Pause).* She hasn't been calling you—she was never sat at the other end of the line. *(Pause).* And she didn't love you. *(Pause).* It is out of care for *you* that I say this—

JORR *rises to his feet and charging to the front, the phone still in his hand. In uproar.*

JORR: You're wrong!…and you're a child. You have not lived! And you certainly did not know Catherine—no—you were an accident, the offspring of a cold lonely night, then a fetus, and now you're a six-month child!

CHILD: *Shouting.* No, Jorr!

FRANK, *laughing in background, falls on floor in silent hysterics.*

JORR: You have not known Catherine—not like I have. And she does love me! She does, she always has, and she always will! Who do you think you are?

Brief pause. Then laughter is heard from CHILD, *starting low and quiet but gradually getting louder and louder until the effect on* JORR *is considerably pronounced. Slamming fist on table.*

What is it you find so funny? Tell me!

The laughter fades away as quickly as it came. Pause. FRANK *has now stopped laughing and sits perched on the edge of the table.*

CHILD: Oh Jorr…how very strange and pathetic you are. Although I imagine it is fun…living in a world of your own—nothing is quite fixed, is it? No blue bus to take you home, no hidden explosive to shatter the glasshouse that you call an

CHILD (CONT'D): existence. Wake up Jorr! Open your eyes to what lies in front of you. Catherine, Catherine, Catherine

Each utterance seems to cripple him.

The bitch lied and left you—she left you here…with me…

JORR *starts shaking his head.*

In this room…

JORR: No—

CHILD: To live with another man.

JORR: No!

CHILD: To dance in the red room, with all those—

JORR: No!

CHILD: Yes! *(Pause).* And she never loved you. She hated you. She just ran you down and left you in her taillights…*(Pause).*

JORR *suddenly drops the phone, then falls to the ground, himself bursting into tears. Activity in the cot gradually increases.*

CHILD: Yes! Yes! Cry, cry for me…

JORR: She left me, she did. Catherine. That, that…bitch! And after everything I did for her—

FRANK *is now standing pointing the light down at his quivering body. Embracing this change.*

CHILD: Oh yes! Oh everything you did for her!

JORR:—and this is my return? This is my reward to nail on the wall—her filthy lies and senselessness! Christ!

CHILD: Yes Jorr—her utter, utter senselessness. She left you. She walked out of your own door.

JORR: She walked out—

CHILD: She gazed at another man's ceiling…maybe even several…she laid it all there for him, bit by bit.

JORR:—for him, for him…

CHILD: And now she's leaving you all alone, with me, to spend the rest of your life here—to gather dust, to rot…*(Whispered)*…to die.

No response from JORR.

Such acts of violence cannot be forgotten. She must be taught a lesson—taught discipline…*(Long pause).*

No response again from JORR *who now sits motionless against the table leg.*

Kill her. *(Pause).*

FRANK *points the light at the cot. Moment of absolute stillness.*

JORR, *in terror, looks up at the cot.*

Yes, kill her…tonight!

FRANK: (*Whispered)*. Ohhh, what will he say? What will he say?

JORR: *(Long pause).* T-Tonight?

CHILD: Yes, tonight! With your own two hands…

JORR *stands up, his face one of numbed shock*. FRANK *walks over, putting the torch in one of his open hands. He clasps the fingers over it and then walks over to the cot.* JORR *looks at it intently, then to front, slowly raises his hands as if, almost, reaching out to someone—some invisible presence.*

CHILD: *Shouting.* Stop!

JORR *freezes.*

(Pause). Do you see? Do you see Frank?

FRANK: Yes…I do. *(Hushed).* Everything will be fine…

CHILD: He'll find her body, maybe even touch it…and just in time for the police. *(Pause).* Oh Frank, this is wonderful…it is like some dream; some long, long dream that I now can see. No detail amiss! Everything as it should be. *(Pause. Laughing girlishly).* I want you to dance for me Frank, I want you to dance! Just like before…

Slow music gradually floats over and rises above the industrial clamor. FRANK *raises his head, walks over to* JORR, *taking the lit torch from his hand. He starts dancing to the music—his feet mostly still, but his body swaying in rhythm—using the bloody torch, turned on, as a pretend microphone.* CHILD *laughing as this scene evolves.*

FRANK: *Singing.* "But just before the dawn
I awake and find you gone
I can't help it, I can't help it, if I cry I remember that you said goodbye"

Whilst this is happening, CATHERINE, *a living corpse, walks in and stands by* JORR, *caressing his face slowly.*

"It's too bad it only seems
It only happens in my dreams."

CATHERINE *then leaves.* CHILD *sings alongside.*

CHILD: "Only in dreams
In beautiful dreams…"

Music fades away. FRANK, *still for a moment, goes and puts the torch back in* JORR's *hand. He then restores to the phone to its place on the table, neatly arranged in symmetry to before. He leaves* JORR *and walks over to the cot, parting the net with his hand. Gently, now, and slowly, he lifts* CHILD *out and holds her close to him, rocking her slowly.*

FRANK: Oh Frank, oh…my sweet, sweet man…what have we done? If this is how I see it happening, how I imagine the events to play...nothing can go wrong. *(Pause).* Such acts of violence—Yes. Everything will be fine.

CHILD: But hush, but hush, but silence…in heaven…I close my two eyes…the rain, *(Joyous).* It beats on the door…in heaven, everything is fine. (*In ecstasy*). Oh Frank! *Shouting.* Now!

JORR *lowers his two arms, looks at torch.*

JORR : I'll kill her.

He leaves the room.

FRANK *carrying* CHILD *moves to front center and looks outward. He rocks her slowly, for a little, then tilts back his head into the light.*

Pause. He returns it slowly to the previous position, before looking down into the baby's face. It is an image of serenity—the calm before the storm.

The sound of a door being tried breaks this moment. A key slides into a lock. Sudden alertness

CHILD : *(Abruptly).* It's him. It's him! Quick, Frank, this is how it all begins, hide—hide somewhere before he gets in, he must not see you before!

FRANK *rushes over and lays the baby in the cot. He stumbles to the side, falling into the table and chair—the latter of which falls over in spectacular fashion—to which he hastily rectifies and searches, in vain, for a hiding place.*

In the closet! Now, quick!

FRANK *quickly leaps in, shutting the door behind him. A grunt, then heave, another try of the lock, then suddenly the door opens and* JORR *is standing there: sad and lonely. A brief moment of stillness. The phone suddenly commences a loud, penetrating ring, repeating four times.*

JORR *stands still, waiting for this to pass. Pause. He turns to lock the door and, whilst removing the from the lock, the phone commences to ring again. He walks briskly over to the table—keys are left in door—and looks carefully at the phone. He places an inspired hand on its top but pauses. It rings twice more. He returns his hand to his side and crosses over to the chair, pulling it out slowly and sitting down. He raises his hand a second time. Pause. He quickly picks up the receiver, cancelling the increasingly harsh reverberations. Pause.*

JORR: Hello? *(Pause).* Catherine—is that you?

[Fade Out.]

[Curtain.]

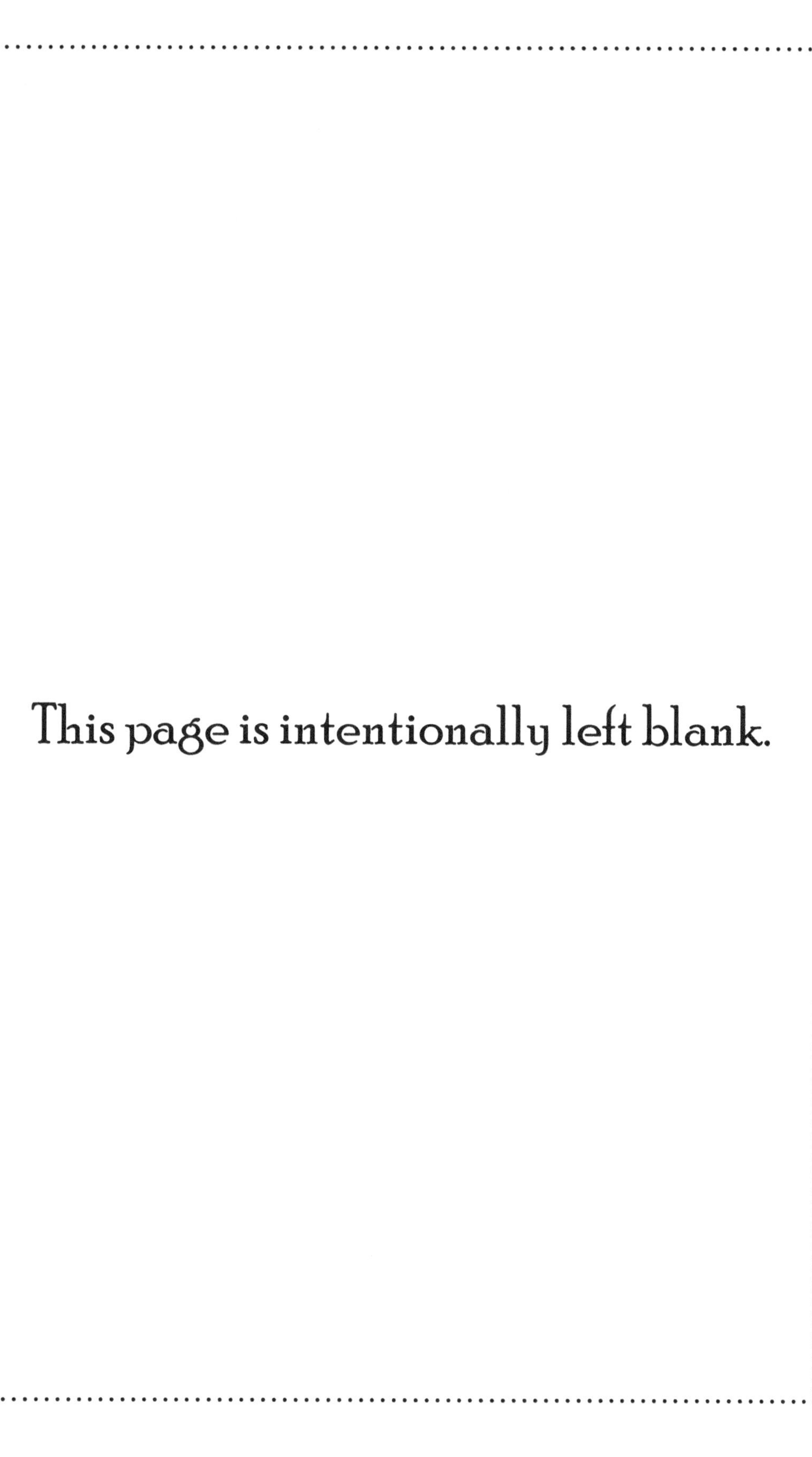
This page is intentionally left blank.

Book Chapter

Monochrome Noir: Chapter 2, "Flash of a Neon Light"

Jack Wells

While the outside of Henry's apartment-office could hardly be classified as classy, even with the custom stencil work on the door, the inside made the exterior seem positively lively. Henry was a simple man of basic needs, and his tastes reflected that, with furniture that was decidedly hand-me-down, and a significant lack of any decorative touches on the walls.

His was a working environment, and he generally didn't make much time or effort for knick-knacks or things that had no use. His desk was large but plain, the office chair had lost its comfort and sheen years ago, and his bookcases were mismatched and of varying heights. Plain carpet blended with plain walls, creating a completely nondescript space, but Henry felt that since most of his work was done in the field, ostentatious living arrangements seemed like a waste.

Which meant that, even more so than usual, Miss Victoria Davies stood out like a sore thumb, like a near-literal explosion of color in his gray space. With her golden-blonde hair, creamy skin, and a startlingly blue dress, she was difficult to look at, seeming almost alien and ethereal. She was also much taller than he would have expected, standing closer to six feet than to five, and with her thin frame and coltish legs she could have passed for a fashion model.

She was standing in front of his liquor cabinet, a tumbler in her hand, running her fingers along the sides of assorted bottles, looking pensive and bored. While nothing else in his office could be considered anything more than shabby or serviceable, his liquor selection was another matter entirely. He felt an instant surge of fresh, hot anger at her audacity. *First, she breaks into my office, then her goons manhandle me like luggage, and now she's invading my booze?* His internal dialogue threatened to explode out of his mouth in some unprofessional and discourteous manner, but she turned to him, her finger resting lightly on a bottle of Blanton's Single Barrel Bourbon, and the green of her eyes stopped his words before they formed.

Henry was so distracted by her and her unexpected presence in his space that he didn't immediately realize that she was speaking to him. His brain struggled to catch up. "…was prepared to leave the way I came in, thinking that surely I had made some gross error in judgement. But I see from your rather spirited spirits collection that you are indeed a man of taste. It feels good to be right."

Her voice was quiet but authoritative, a touch haughty and accustomed to being heeded, and he found himself feeling slightly cowed, then instantly berated himself for it. *Get it together*, he told himself, *no matter her prestige she's still just a person. Just keep it professional*. He was acutely aware of the bodyguard standing mere inches behind him, a poised panther at his back. *Very professional*, he reminded himself.

"Henry Hardcastle at your service, ma'am." He gestured to the liquor cabinet. "Is there something I can make for you?"

She tapped a Hued fingernail against the Blanton's, the sound crisp and clear in the otherwise quiet office.

"Oh, I'm perfectly content with this, if that's okay with you, Mr. Hardcastle." It might have been stated like a question, but she obviously had not been asking.

He eyed the bottle askance, weighing the options. The Blanton's was a recent acquire, and also one the most expensive bourbons he had—each pour was like heedlessly dipping into an investment. While she was rich enough that she could bathe in the stuff, it was a rare commodity for a man with his kind of income. Still, what was he supposed to tell her? No? As tempted as he was, just on general principle, even he wasn't immune to the sway of celebrity. Henry was also a little old-fashioned—when a pretty lady asked for a drink, a gentleman delivered. So, he did the next best thing to saying no. He deflected.

"Are you sure you wouldn't prefer a Cosmopolitan, ma'am? Or maybe a Tom Collins?" He hadn't been trying to inflect condescension in his voice, but a little came through anyway.

The look she gave him could have wilted flowers. He sensed more than heard the bodyguard stiffen, a sudden charge in the air that he was all too familiar with, like imminent violence was about to ensue. Henry suddenly felt very small again, and hated the sensation, though he was powerless to stop it. He was fairly certain that the bodyguard could rip the heart right of his chest if Colorist Davies ordered it.

Her voice was no longer quiet, and when she turned to face him, her vivid colors and her frosty gaze threatened to overwhelm him. "Do I look like some naïve sorority sister visiting her first bar, Mr. Hardcastle?"

He swallowed involuntarily, suddenly realizing the sheer magnitude of her being in his office, and that so far, he had been doing his level best to completely shit all over whatever intention brought her here. He was *not* being professional—he was being a heel—and he knew that he needed to get his act together.

"I apologize, Miss Davies," he said, completely sincere. "It's been a rough night, and I'm a little on edge. I didn't mean to offend. Of course, I'll pour you whatever you'd like."

She gazed at him a moment longer, her emerald eyes boring into his, capturing him like a deer in headlights. But then she blinked and nodded, and the moment passed. The violent current of tension behind him eased slightly as well.

"Thank you, Mr. Hardcastle. That would be wonderful." She handed him the tumbler as he passed, and he grabbed another for himself before taking down the Blanton's and pouring each of them several fingers worth, and then another half finger for good measure. He figured that, with the kind of night it was becoming, he might as well go for broke.

While he was pouring the liquor, she had moved to the guest chair opposite his desk, settling herself in with measured movements, everything poised and practiced.

She looked at the bodyguard, who had not removed his gaze from Henry. "Michael, I think we are good here. You may leave."

The bodyguard, Michael, took a step forward. "But, Miss…"

She raised her hand, stopping him in his tracks as effectively as if he had hit a brick wall. Her unflinching gaze gave no quarter.

"I said you may leave."

Michael stared at her for a moment longer, obviously struggling with leaving her alone in the office, before glancing over at Henry and giving him a very meaningful look. He then cautiously stepped out of the office, closing the door quietly behind him. With the muscle gone, the oppressive cloud of danger dissipated.

Henry handed her the tumbler as he walked back to his desk, then took a seat in his less-than-comfy office chair, appraising her as she took a slow, deliberate sip. Every inch of her had color, from the gold of her hair to the black of her heels, and the sight was both breathtaking and unnerving. He had encountered more than his share of Hueys around the city, sporting a Hued vehicle or piece of jewelry, and had even seen completely-Hued celebrities on TV. But he had never been face-to-face with a fully-Hued person in the flesh before. Given her ability and the celebrity that surrounded it, it was like being in the presence of royalty. Regardless, he pushed himself to see beyond her color and past her fame, to look at her like a PI.

He had to admit, Victoria Davies was as cool and collected as anyone he'd ever seen. Even in an unfamiliar place, sitting across from an unfamiliar man, she was at ease and firmly in control. She sat perfectly still, devoid of nervous fidgeting or subconscious movements that could give clue to her emotions. Surprisingly, she was bereft of rings or bracelets and had no earrings or necklace. Given her wealth and status, he would have expected to see her bedecked with gaudy jewels and some fashion designer's custom runway creation. So the casual, everyday clothes, even Hued, and lack of jewelry had him slightly off-balance. She looked as plain as she could, given the circumstances.

But even in plain clothing, he had to confess that she was beyond stunning. Even the cool detachment that she projected could not diminish her natural beauty. With high cheekbones, a striking nose, and contoured eyes, she had a strangely exotic allure. Like a mermaid out of water, she was strange, and surreal, and supremely seductive. But there was also the air of risk about her, like she was a brewing storm on the horizon, distant but approaching fast. He did not want to be drawn to her—only fools turned towards the storm willingly. But he might as well have been fighting gravity itself. Her otherworldliness, and her mysterious presence in *his* office, was like a siren song. He had an addictive affinity for the mysterious and enigmatic, and Colorist Davies were those things made flesh.

She took his casual appraisal in stride, sipping the Blanton's with no outward enjoyment, no doubt used to being the source of attention and scrutiny. "I suppose that this is the point where I tell you to take a picture because it will last longer."

The quietness had returned to her voice, but it still had the edge of command, of authority. *She probably never needs to raise her voice*, he thought. He couldn't tell if her remark was joking or serious. Her face was a mask, those green eyes expressive and yet, completely guarded. He was unused to conversing with someone so stoic, so again, he deflected.

"What brings you to my office, Miss Davies?"

She didn't respond right away, but instead looked around his office with casual interest, eyes taking in everything while never lingering too long in any one place. Finally she returned her gaze to him.

"This place could use some color, Mr. Hardcastle," she said in that infuriatingly indecipherable tone.

He raised an eyebrow. "I think I'm perfectly happy with how it is, ma'am. I'm a simple man, and it suits me."

"A simple man? Maybe. But word is that you have no small amount of talent with investigations. So, a simple man, but one with a not-so-simple gift." She sighed, though it was so slight that he wasn't quite sure that he truly heard it. "We all have our gifts, don't we?"

He took a slug from the tumbler before responding. "We may all have our gifts, ma'am, but those gifts aren't all created equal."

"Touché, Mr. Hardcastle. I imagine that being a PI and being a Colorist have very different…hardships."

He nodded. "I would assume so, yes. And they each have their own measure of usefulness, as well."

He wasn't trying to antagonize her, but he didn't like how she was taking her time and bandying about, so he couldn't quite keep the sarcasm out of his voice. He hoped she didn't notice.

But she was far too shrewd for that. Her eyes narrowed slightly, a predatory look washing over her features so fast that it might have been just his imagination. There was a long pause before she responded.

"You don't care much for what I do, do you, Mr. Hardcastle?"

"No, ma'am, I do not." He had briefly thought about lying, or deflecting again, but decided he wasn't in the mood to pussyfoot around. As far as he was concerned, if she couldn't handle the answer, then she shouldn't be asking the question.

The slightest arch of a perfectly-shaped golden eyebrow was her only visible reaction. *The lady must be a hell of a card player.*

"And might I ask why not?"

He stared at her for a moment, gauging whether or not she was baiting him. With that damn poker face, he couldn't be sure either way.

"You can ask," he responded, not sure how invested in the conversation he wanted to be. He was getting frustrated, and he wasn't good at hiding it. He set the tumbler onto the desk just in case things got heated.

Still betraying no emotion, she leaned forward.

"Humor me, Mr. Hardcastle. I'm only asking because it would seem that Hueing would actually make your job easier," she said, never once breaking her gaze from his. "The added color would, I assume, make it easier to identify and locate people and things. Is this not correct? And yet, I hear you are set firmly against it, which seems like a rather blatant contradiction."

He gave her the briefest of nods, conceding her point. It was not the first time he had heard that counter argument, and it would not be the last.

"Sure, looking at it that way, you would be right. Assuming all my job entailed was tracking down missing Hued things or people. Which, as you can tell by looking around, isn't really my primary source of income. Hell, not even my secondary source. But…let me tell you how it is on the streets. How things actually play out." He was starting to get a little riled up, and wasn't sure if he should rein his emotions in or let them run their course.

"People hurt other people for all sorts of reasons. Religious differences, racial differences, greed, jealousy, you name it. Crime is as old as humanity itself. And though we make lifestyle progress, and inventions to make our lives easier, we never seem to overcome our base desires. Wouldn't you agree?"

She sat back in the chair, appearing to settle in for a prolonged verbal siege. She folded her hands in her lap, and gave him a slight conciliatory nod—a minor point in his favor. "I suppose I would."

Now it was his turn to sit forward in his chair. Reaching into his inner jacket pocket, he pulled out his zippo lighter, which shone with a dull gleam in the soft office lighting. He set it on the desk between them, and she gave it a cursory glance, before returning her gaze to him.

"Take that lighter for instance. If I'm on the street, in a random crowd, and someone needs a light, I pull that out and light their cigarette for them. No big deal, a quick 'thanks' from the smoker, and nobody else cares. Most people have a lighter like that, or another version of it that achieves the same result. Nobody would even look twice."

He then reached into his middle desk drawer and pulled out his Colt .45, setting on the desk next to the lighter with a weighty thud, barrel pointed slightly to her left. It was dull black on the white desk blotter, standing out like a bull in a pig pen. She hadn't given the lighter more than the briefest of looks, but she scrutinized the weapon with more obvious interest, and if she was nervous having a firearm partially pointed at her, she betrayed no emotion to confirm it. Henry was almost disappointed in her lack of reaction. Again, he found himself reassessing her, realizing there was so much more to Miss Davies than he had initially realized. Still waters ran deep.

"Now, say I'm in that same crowd, only I have a Hued lighter instead. Something silver. Or even better, that liquid gold that is *your* signature. I pull that out to light someone's cigarette, and what do you think happens?" The last part was a query directed at her, and his meaningful gaze told her he was expecting an answer.

Still, she was slow with her response. "Everyone notices." It was a statement, not a question.

"Exactly. Everyone notices. And I mean *everyone*," he agreed. "My mundane item all of a sudden has the keen interest of everyone in the vicinity. It's like I just flashed a million dollars in cash, just held it up for all to see. And all those people take notice. Some people are merely jealous. Hell, some people might not even care too much. But, at least one person in that crowd is now thinking about how he can possibly get that lighter from me. And that person may not have the social restraint that most law-abiding citizens possess. Maybe he's thinking of petty thievery." Henry then pointed at the pistol. "Or maybe he's thinking of a more violent approach. Something bloody and permanent."

His voice had risen slightly, and he noticed that he was now sitting on the very edge of his seat, hands clenched atop the desk. He forced himself to take a breath, and scooted back into the chair, regaining his composure.

"So, now I might be losing my life because of this thing," he said, tapping the lighter to drive his point home. "Or maybe someone just ransacks my place, hoping to find it while I'm not home. Or maybe a group of them jump me when I'm alone, and beat me to a pulp."

She gave a pointed look to the newly-forming bruise on his cheek, corners of her mouth turning up ever so slightly.

He touched the shiner without thinking. The skin was more tender than he'd expected.

"Unrelated," he muttered. "But my point is that, if everything was Hued, it wouldn't matter, and we wouldn't be talking about a lighter. Because if everything was special, then nothing would be special. But there's so few of you Colorists out there, and you are so selective about what you Hue—and for whom—

that there will never be enough supply to meet the demand. In my opinion, all you've done is give people yet another thing to be covetous about. Another thing for people to be hurt or killed over."

Again he found his hands clenched, and stood up and paced behind his desk, trying to regain control of his emotions. Everyone had their hot-point topic, and Hueing was his, rather than the usual religious or political debates. But, losing his cool in front of a distinguished guest, and a Colorist at that, wasn't going to help in any way, so he focused on his breathing to help calm himself.

"Mr. Hardcastle, I appreciate your candor. I apologize if I've upset you." Her voice had changed slightly, a softness edging in where there had been none before, showing a warmth that had been previously absent.

He waved her apology off, returning to his seat across from her. Fishing out a cigarette with feigned laziness, he picked up the lighter from the desk and lit up, the familiar habit bringing an immediate sense of calm.

"But, all that hurting and killing…isn't that good job security for you?"

He looked up sharply, fury threatening to rise again, Colorist be damned, only to see that she was openly smiling, her face no longer the mask of cold indifference that she had worn until that point.

She put her hands forward in a placating manner. "I'm kidding, Mr. Hardcastle. Only kidding."

Leaning back, she crossed one leg over the other, suddenly seeming a very different person. The icy veneer and control were gone. In their place was a person like any other, Hue notwithstanding, and he struggled to adapt to the change.

"I'm actually relieved to hear you say that, Mr. Hardcastle," she began.

"Henry," he said, surprising himself, as he had no intention of easing the formality between them.

A slight smile graced her lips. "Henry. Like I said, I'm glad to hear you say that. While I may not see things quite the way you do, certain events have transpired which have given me a new perspective, so I don't necessarily disagree with anything that you've said. In fact, I think we might have more in common than you might realize."

He looked her up and down pointedly, a dubious expression on his face.

"Look past the exterior, Mr. Hard…Henry, and you might be surprised."

He took a drag on the cigarette, buying himself some time. She had initially behaved and spoken exactly how he had assumed she would—haughty, entitled, and detached in the way that only the filthy rich could achieve. But he was seeing a different side of her, and he had to concede to himself that he needed to look past his own prejudices and preconceived notions, otherwise he was likely to miss something. He couldn't get so wrapped up in his own narrative that he overlooked something simple.

"So, is there anything else driving your disdain for my contributions to the world?" she asked, a hint of playfulness in her voice, though the question was sincere enough.

He thought about it for a moment, trying to formulate an answer he hoped would sound valid.

He made sure to keep his tone light, attempting to keep the casualness of the conversation alive. "I guess, if I had to put a finger on it, I would say that it has no real purpose. I mean, what does it actually do? Hueing doesn't make anything better. It only has value because of how rare it is, and how new it is. It only has value because we choose to think it has value. Like diamonds or pearls. They provide no actual benefit to the world. I just find Hueing to be entirely superfluous."

"You don't like diamonds or pearls, then?" she asked, feigning shock.

"Do you see me wearing any?" he countered, his sarcasm back in full effect.

Her genuine laughter, sounding far too raucous for someone so important, caught him by surprise. But he found that he enjoyed hearing it. It was pure and transparent, like a window, allowing him a glimpse into her real personality.

"Very well, Henry. You prefer things with actual purpose. With a real value to the world. I get it." She gave him a long look. "Like that cigarette you're smoking."

He nodded. "Right. Very valuable. Smoking calms me down. This cigarette is helping me think, and keeping me relaxed."

She gave a slight, victorious smile. "As you say. But, cigarettes themselves are not relaxants. They contain no ingredients or additives that induce relaxation or calmness. They only have that trait, that value, because you've assigned it to them, even if you've done it subconsciously; your perception of them relaxing you gives them value to you. But in truth, like diamonds and pearls, cigarettes provide no actual benefit to the world. Some would say they actually create issues instead of fixing them, like causing difficulty breathing, or contributing to more garbage on the streets, or being responsible for countless accidental fires. When you really think about it, any benefit they provide is entirely manufactured by the person smoking them. Face it, Henry, like diamonds and pearls and even Hueing, cigarettes are superfluous."

He stared at her for a long moment, cigarette halfway to his lips, his hand unmoving. Then he leaned forward and stubbed it out in the ashtray.

"Nobody likes a smartass," he mumbled, not entirely happy with how she had turned his point back at him so easily. The conversation was starting to feel like a tennis match, volleys back and forth, and he was losing—badly.

She gave a short, sharp laugh. "On the contrary, Henry, almost everyone loves a smartass. It's the dumbasses that we cannot abide."

The levity only lasted for a moment longer, however, before her expression grew serious again. Some of the control returned, as if she was putting the public armor back on, though her posture remained casual.

She sighed before continuing. "Anyway, we could spend all night debating the merits of my ability, but as much as I'm enjoying this conversation, I have neither the time nor the inclination to do so. There are things I agree with you on, and things that I do not, but there's only so much time in a day. So, let's get down to brass tacks. As I'm sure you've guessed, I am here on business. I have a situation that I believe requires your specific talents."

He held a hand up, stopping her before she could explain. He had been waiting for her to get to the point, but the more he thought about it, the more certain he became that she was wasting her time.

"Miss Davies, while I am more than flattered that someone of your… standing…decided to come to me with a job, there are numerous high-profile investigative firms that would more likely suit your needs. People with experience dealing with situations at your level, with the kinds of resources that make police departments jealous while, as you can see, I am just one man. I doubt I'm what you're looking for."

She fixed him with a hard stare, her green eyes piercing and otherworldly, and he found himself withering. Her voice came out hard and flat, not quite hostile, but very near to it. "I like you Henry, and I've enjoyed our little tête-à-tête, but do not for one moment presume to tell me what I am, or am not, looking for."

"Yes ma'am," he managed. He dropped his hand and took an involuntary gulp of air. While he wouldn't call Victoria Davies traditionally intimidating, she still had a way of making him stumble, catching him off-guard far more than he was accustomed. He couldn't tell if he liked it or not.

"Good," she said, the icy visage disappearing as quickly as it had manifested. "Yes, there are high-profile firms and celebrity investigators and all manner of expensive options that I could look into. And if I wanted my business known to all, those are the avenues I would pursue."

She never once blinked as she continued.

"But I don't want high profile. I don't want visibility. I want discreet. I want unknown. I want someone that nobody else would suspect. And I want someone who isn't going to be so goddamn distracted by me that they can't get results. I have neither the time nor the patience for sycophants, Henry. I need someone both skilled at finding things and completely immune to the allure of Hueing. And that someone, I have decided, is you."

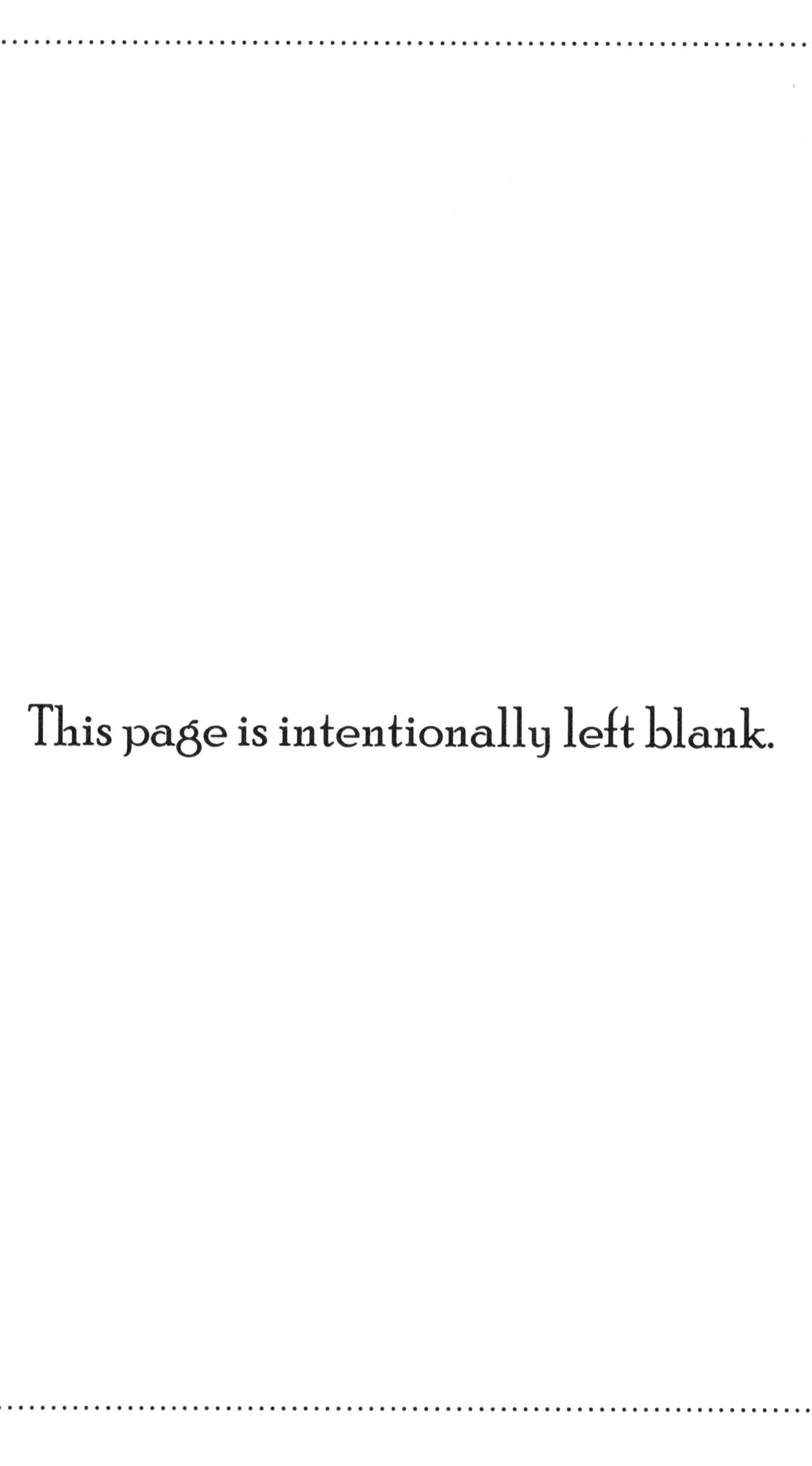
This page is intentionally left blank.

Novelettes

The Good Doctor Mankel

Martin Zeigler

Dr. Mankel heard the screaming, and it was good.

It meant that his new patient was conscious and kicking.

Why his patients always screamed during recovery was a mystery. He kept telling himself that someday, when he found the time, he would dig through the medical literature for a reason. For now, though, with only his experience to guide him, he had to assume that the shriek of a patient, like the robust cry of a newborn, was a healthy sign and a good indicator that the patient had pulled through the intricate and demanding procedure.

And the scream he heard as he vigorously scrubbed his hands at the sink was nothing if not robust. It penetrated the solid steel door of the patient's cell, traversed the maze of underground corridors, passed through the granite wall of Dr. Mankel's office, and ultimately reached the good doctor's ears, still retaining the brunt of its high volume and pitch, of its anguish and panic.

Of its pure, undeniable goodness.

When the world returned to Jeremy Lakehurst, he failed to realize at first that the world had left him at all. In his mind he was still standing outside his apartment building, his key poised for the lock of the lobby door.

But what he now saw was a door at the far end of a small room, no longer an all-glass door but one of solid steel, save for a thin rectangular eye slit.

A moment ago he'd been standing out on the walkway, pleasantly aware of the evening breeze and the rustling leaves behind him, and now here he was inside a room.

Inside a room and no longer standing. But lying on...what, a hospital gurney? Covered up to his neck with a yellowed sheet and a threadbare blanket?

In his mind, he remembered the rustling of leaves, remembered gripping the key and going for the door with the "Verdant Arms" etched in its glass. Remembered the urge to race through the lobby and bound up the stairs to his apartment.

Yet here he was, no longer feeling the breeze at his back or the key in his fingers or the urge to do much of anything. Instead, he lay on his back in a soiled gown, groggy, dull, slightly in pain.

The key. He could have sworn it was in his hand not more than a second ago. Maybe it was still in his hand and he couldn't feel it because of this odd sluggishness that had overcome him.

He lifted his hand up off the gurney. As he did so he glimpsed a flicker of movement. To his left? To his right? It looked as if it could have been both, but it didn't matter. What did he care about flickering when he could see that a key was no longer in his grasp?

Had he been dreaming?

He must have been dreaming.

Otherwise he'd have the key.

Otherwise he'd be standing outside an apartment house called the Verdant Arms.

Otherwise he'd be feeling the breeze at his back and hearing the rustling behind him.

Maybe he had been scheduled for some kind of surgery and was now coming out of it. Yes, that explained the gurney, the drugged feeling, the dull pain. He was here recovering from an operation.

And while he was under, he'd dreamed everything—the apartment, the key, the rustling.

Except for one thing.

An operation for what?

He recalled nothing about a diagnosis, making an appointment, fretting about it.

But he did recall a conversation.

What conversation?

Why the conversation that was coming back to him, that was breaking through the cloudiness and becoming vivid again. The conversation that had made him want to jump for joy and take those stairs up to his apartment two at a time.

That conversation.

The one with—Julie, that was her name. He'd met her earlier that evening—the evening he was now beginning to suspect was not a dream after all. He'd been sitting alone at a restaurant—The Riviera out on Spring Street, yes, that was it; awaiting his meal, taking notice of the woman at the next table sitting by herself.

He now remembered everything. The details of her face in profile. Her voice, when placing her order. The butterflies in his stomach as he worked up the nerve to say something to her that wouldn't sound uproariously stupid. The question he finally did ask and most of all her reply.

"No, not at all," she had said. "I wouldn't mind company at all. Won't you join me?"

And then, of course, the resulting conversation. He remembered it all. Its give and take. Its natural and preposterous digressions. Its initial awkwardness and ensuing grace.

No, that was no dream. Neither was returning to the Verdant Arms later that evening, after promising to see Julie again. Nor was gripping his key and wanting to leap up those stairs. Nor was—

Jeremy remembered something else.

The rustling he had heard behind him as he approached the lobby door was not due to leaves or trees or bushes.

But to rapidly advancing footsteps. He recalled the fabric pressed against his face. The pungent, vaguely fuzzy odor before sinking into oblivion.

And now here he was. Coming out of surgery. Surgery he had no say in.

"God damn it!"

The first words he had spoken since his world came back to him, and they sounded strange to his ears.

In a fit of rage, Jeremy slammed his fist on the bed. Again he noticed the flicker of movement to either side. This time he turned to look. First to his right, then quickly to his left to confirm what he had seen.

Both walls, covered floor to ceiling with mirrors, revealed the same nightmare. And he let loose a scream—a frightened, horrific, deafening scream—in the hopes it would wake him.

-ൟA൞-

Dr. Mankel peeked through the eye slit and spotted the empty gurney. Concern coursing through his veins, he slid his key into the lock and threw open the massive steel door, letting it clang and echo against the corridor's stone wall.

From the wider view of the open doorway, he scanned the entire room. His new patient, Jerome Lakehurst, was nowhere in sight.

Jerome. Jerome. Was that the correct name?

Dr. Mankel flipped open the file folder he'd been carrying and skimmed the driver's license clipped to the inside. No, not Jerome. *Jeremy*. Jeremy Lakehurst, twenty-six years old, residing—or, rather, once residing—at 1447 Verdant Arms Place.

"Jeremy?" he called out, pleased he had taken the time to verify the name before causing any undue hurt or embarrassment. "Oh, Jeremy."

It wasn't as if the young man could have gone anywhere. The room had been under lock and key ever since he was admitted. Still, whenever the good doctor found his recovering patients up and about, it distressed him, flooded him with an anxiety a father might feel upon discovering that his child had wandered jacketless into the biting cold.

He was about to call out again, when a movement at the far corner of the room caught his eye. That had to be Jeremy, he surmised. Experience had taught him over the years that these tiny, cramped cells offered little in the way of hiding places.

Sure enough, as he stepped forward and peeked around the gurney, his patient came into view. He was on his knees, his face up to the mirror, sobbing.

Perfectly normal in Dr. Mankel's experience. In fact, these tears of joy and gratitude were such a natural part of the recovery process, he hardly noticed them anymore.

He set his folder aside, kneeled down alongside Jeremy, and gently placed his hand on the young patient's back.

"I understand," he said.

And he did understand. He understood perfectly the desire to get up and look at oneself close up and delight in the monumental improvements. After all, that's what the floor to ceiling mirrors were for.

But first and foremost he needed to impress on his new patients the absolute need for bed rest. Later, they would have an entire lifetime in which to revel in their newfound perfections.

Jeremy jumped at the touch of the cold, damp hand and quickly drew away as if a thick, fleshy insect had landed on his back. He glanced at the face in the mirror—the other face, the normal face—and then over at the man kneeling beside him.

Who was he? And why was he smiling? And why was he saying he understood?

Jeremy hadn't seen the man enter the room—or heard him, for that matter. He had been staring all this time into the mirror at his own face and pawing, by turns, at the things on his forehead and at the holes near his upper jaw. Tugging at the two flaps jutting out of the front of his head and then running his fingers along the holes at the side of his head. Pulling, again, at the two flaps, wishing they would snap off, but again feeling the intense pain at the effort, as if the flaps had always been there. And then once again cupping his hands around the holes, trying to picture himself with ears, with ears that were no longer part of him.

And all along he'd kept whimpering, pleading, crying out for help in the desperate hope someone would rush into the room and see him cowering in the corner and wash away these unspeakable abominations and remove these flaps and restore his ears and return everything back to the way it was.

And now—from out of nowhere, it seemed—here was this man beside him who was smiling and telling him he understood.

Was he here to rescue him?

Jeremy looked him over, this man in the white coat, with the white bushy hair and the white eyebrows and almost pure white skin devoid of any blemish or wrinkle or iota of wisdom, and he slowly arrived at his own understanding—that this man would not be his deliverer any time soon.

"You—you did this to me, didn't you?"

Dr. Mankel shrugged, and hoped he wasn't blushing. Because, frankly, the way his recovering patients always seemed to ask this question embarrassed him terribly. He wished they would come right out and say what they mean—"Doctor, thank you so much for doing this to me," or words to that effect. Then he could respond with a slight nod and a simple, "You're welcome."

But this way—being asked, as it were, to step forward and proclaim, "Yes, it was I, Dr. Friedrich Mankel, who restored your humanity"—placed the doctor in the uncomfortable position of having to toot his own horn.

And yet he did feel it proper to introduce himself, and so he held out his hand in as modest a way as he could. "Hello, Jeremy. I'm Dr. Mankel. Friedrich Mankel."

Only to get his hand swatted at.

"Okay, *Mankel*, I'll ask you again: was it you who did this to me or wasn't it?"

The good doctor realized that Jeremy, in his own way, was trying to lavish praise on him, but he would have none of it. He hadn't chosen this profession to bask in his own glory. All the mirrors on all the walls in all the private cells in this facility were meant for his patients, not for him. And so, as he had done so often in the past, he tried as best as he was able to steer attention from himself and direct it to the person who truly mattered.

"Jeremy," he said, "it isn't about me. Don't you see? All these marvelous changes have been lying dormant within you all this time. All I did was give them life."

"What are you talking about? What *marvelous* changes?"

"Why, your ears, of course. I see you've been ogling them."

"Ogling? Is that what you call it? Is this the marvelous change you're talking about, you sick son of a bitch? Cutting off my ears?"

"I understand," Dr. Mankel said. After all, he *did* understand. He recognized that the hostility Jeremy was expressing was directly at odds with the joy he was really feeling. It was the kind of contradictory reaction the doctor had observed in many, if not all, of his other patients. And he hoped someday to present a paper on it.

"What do you mean—you understand? That I want to wring your neck?"

"I understand, Jeremy—from listening to you, observing you—that you are no longer self-conscious about your ears, the way you were just a few hours ago."

"Not so self—are you kidding me? How can I not be? God damn it, look at me! You've cut them off! You've cut my ears completely off! Nothing sounds right anymore! And I look like a goddamn freak."

The patient's wailing, his anger, his nonstop fussing over his surgery—all classic signs of expressing elation through rage.

"I understand, Jeremy," Dr. Mankel said. (And he did understand.) "Now compare this to how you were at the restaurant last night."

"Restaurant?"

"Trying to drum up a conversation with that young woman."

"Julie? How do you know about—"

"I noticed right off how afraid you were to talk to her. And I knew why. And I think you knew the reason too."

"You were there?"

"Of course I was," Dr. Mankel said. "It's part of my mission, to seek out the broken so that I might make them whole again. In your case, I just happened to walk into that particular eatery when I spotted you. I suppose my eyes have been trained to recognize the symptoms. I could see, right away, how utterly insecure you were about your ears."

"My ears? Why the hell would I have been thinking about my ears?"

"Oh, I think we both know the answer to that, don't we, Jeremy? Surely you must have realized at some point, if only subconsciously, how huge your ears were in comparison with your face. And I believe this self-awareness on your part was the one thing preventing you from conversing with that young lady."

"What are you talking about? I did—*converse*—with her. And before that, I was trying to work up the courage, that's all, just like anyone would. Had nothing to do with my ears, for God's sake! Besides, my ears aren't any bigger than anybody else's. Or they *weren't*. I mean, they..."

Dr. Mankel cherished these moments when his patients fell silent and began to work things out for themselves. Some took longer than others, and he allowed them all the time they needed, but already he could see the light dawning in Jeremy's eyes.

"You see? You see?" Dr. Mankel whispered excitedly. "Now that your ears have been removed, they are no longer bigger than anyone else's—or smaller for that matter. They transcend comparison."

"What'd you do with them, you sadistic bastard? You get them right now, do you hear? You get them and you sew them back on or stitch them or whatever it is you have to do, god damn you, but you put them back the way they were. So I can hear like I used to. So I can look like a normal human being again. Or I swear I'll break every goddamn bone in your body."

One thing Dr. Mankel could not understand was why his patients always seemed to feel that their newfound blessings could go only so far—as if their good fortune was a limited quantity. Couldn't Jeremy see, for example, that just because he attained absolute perfection without his ears didn't mean there wasn't a proper place for them?

As if pointing a child to an as yet undiscovered Christmas present under the tree, Dr. Mankel extended an eager finger at Jeremy's reflection in the mirror. "Open your eyes, my friend, to all your possibilities!"

Still on his knees, Jeremy turned again to the mirror and ran his hands yet one more time over the flaps extending from his forehead. Like a blind man gleaning shape through touch, he felt his way, with thumb and index finger, along the meandering furrows of flesh and cartilage, and confirmed what he had been denying up to now—that these were his ears. Transplanted and useless, no longer connected to any hearing mechanism at all, they had become something ludicrous and hideous, like deranged, vestigial flippers on some animal doomed to extinction.

He didn't cry. He didn't sob as before. Instead he simply rammed the base of his palm into the nape of the doctor's neck, driving Mankel's skull full force into the mirror. He then grabbed a fistful of white hair, yanked back, and did this again. And then again and again, like some relentless machine, until, exhausted, he let the head drop where it would against the shattered glass.

He then burst into laughter.

Blind, shrieking, hysterical laughter.

The kind of laughter that made him wish he were dead.

Dr. Mankel understood, as he shook off what appeared to be the last of the blows, that his patients tended toward a certain celebratory exuberance. But he wouldn't have it any other way. His patients' joys, however expressed, were his joys, and he tried to encourage such free-wheeling displays of enthusiasm whenever possible.

He peered closely into a pristine section of glass at his own eyes. He couldn't recall from his brief medical training whether it was dilated pupils or constricted pupils he should be looking for, but it didn't matter. The size of his pupils appeared normal, which indicated, to his relief, that he had suffered no concussion as a result of Jeremy's overexcitement.

Although, as he mentioned to his young patient, "I do believe I'll have quite the headache for the next few hours."

Jeremy was kneeling at the broken mirror, his head in his hands, his protruding ears poking through his fingers.

"Now, now, don't you worry about me," Dr. Mankel said, laying a comforting palm on Jeremy's shoulder. "I'll be all right. Nothing a couple of aspirin won't take care of."

Feeling that shoulder muscle tighten, he added, "Hey, you know something, Jeremy? You have quite the arm on you."

He had said that to lighten things up, to ease the sting of whatever guilt Jeremy might be feeling over accidentally clunking the doctor's head into the mirror. But as he reflected on this further, he wondered if young Jeremy might have overexerted himself. If so, then now, more than ever, was the time to insist on bed rest.

Dr. Mankel slowly stood up, assisting Jeremy to his feet as he did so. "Uuup we go," he said.

Carefully, his hands tucked under Jeremy's arms, the good doctor helped him onto the gurney, then covered him with the sheet, followed by the warm, comforting blanket.

"You're doing fantastic," Dr. Mankel said.

And as if there weren't enough good news for the young man to absorb in one day, the doctor leaned in and whispered into Jeremy's ear—which is to say an ear hole and not one of the actual ears on his forehead—"Wait till you see the surprise I have in store for you."

Dr. Mankel then left the room, leaving Jeremy alone to happily contemplate the thousand and one possibilities inherent in the wonderful word *surprise.*

-∞A∞-

What Jeremy first saw when Mankel threw open the door to the adjoining cell was her face in profile, almost as he remembered it from the restaurant, except this time ravaged and worn by tears.

He wasn't surprised it was Julie. Devastated, yes, but not surprised. He'd deduced it the instant Mankel entered his room just now and whipped away his blanket like a magician performing the tablecloth trick and shouted out, "Let's go, lazy bones! It's time to share in a friend's celebration!"

Julie didn't turn in his direction, not even in response to the metallic creaking of the door. She just sat on the edge of her gurney and kept staring straight ahead at her room's mirrored wall, defeated, as if having exhausted everything in her meager arsenal—her morbid screams of anguish, her desperate cries for help.

Long before Mankel had burst into his cell, Jeremy had awoken to those screams, surprised they weren't his own. Surprised he could even make out a word or two, given his degraded hearing and the thickness of the walls. Words like "leg" and "back" and "blood."

And for that reason, he resisted looking away from her face. By avoiding the truth perhaps he could render it false. But despite his efforts, his gaze fell to her gown, and then to the blood-soaked bandage where her right leg had been shorn at the knee.

His cut-and-pasted ears suddenly seemed trifling by comparison. What could be worse than losing a leg?

He then saw the leg and got his answer.

A deluge of pity and rage hit Jeremy at once. He wanted so much to rush forward and hold Julie in his arms, wanted so much to swing around and clip the throat of the monster standing behind him, but was so torn between the two actions, he couldn't budge.

He took a deep breath. With a steady calmness that surprised him, he whispered back to Mankel, "Can you please leave us alone?"

"I understand," Mankel whispered in reply. "The time has come for you two to get *further acquainted.*"

Jeremy heard the massive door bang shut behind him. He now approached Julie slowly, so as not to startle her. He quietly said her name, and she turned. Her eyes grew wide, accompanied by an almost delightful smile that quickly became an openmouthed look of horror. "Jeremy! What are you doing here? I...oh, no. What have they done to you?"

"To *me*? Jesus, Julie. My God."

Somehow, by some cold, harrowing technique known only to Mankel, her amputated leg had been surgically attached to her in such a way that it jutted straight out of her back. It was an image Jeremy knew he would never forget—the thigh stitched crudely to her upper back, the foot pointed downward, its skin purple and already reeking of decay.

Certainly Julie was aware of this. She had screamed of it the night before. And yet all she did now was reach out with both hands and caress the sides of Jeremy's earless face.

Jeremy took those hands and held them in his own, gently stroking them with his thumbs. "Did Mankel say anything to you?" he said.

"Mankel?"

"That thing calling himself a doctor."

"Oh, yes," she said bitterly. "He told me how he watched me enter the restaurant—the one you and I were at—and saw me limping. He told me he fixed things so my leg wouldn't trouble me anymore. He told me it would accompany me until medical science figures out how to repair it. He told me a lot of things, and I don't understand any of it, Jeremy. I had a blister on my foot. That's all it was, a simple blister that was bothering me. That's all. That's all. That's all."

"I don't understand any of it, either," Jeremy said.

"I know where we're at. At least I understand that much," Julie said. "We're in Hell. I just don't know why."

Jeremy knew that anything he said wouldn't come close to being an answer.

There was a faint clearing of a throat, and he looked toward the door.

In the darkness of the slit, two eyes gleamed.

-ꟹA❧-

The chime of an amiable bell resounded throughout the maze of corridors.

Dinnertime!

For Dr. Mankel the most enjoyable time of the day, and he imagined the same held true for his patients. It was the one time of day when they could eat, and certainly that played a factor, but more important, it offered them an opportunity to bond with others just like them, to share their thoughts and experiences, and to simply have a good time.

Having pushed the button to activate the electronic dinner bell, he now threw a lever, and immediately he heard the familiar ca-chunk of three-hundred cell door bolts sliding open in concert.

He stared raptly at the bank of closed-circuit monitors in his office as his patients slowly emerged from the comforting cocoons of their cells and made their way, some more easily than others, to the cafeteria.

He wished he could remember all their names as they appeared in the monitors—the blind patient who once could see but now, with her eyeballs attached to her elbows, would never again suffer through eye exams. The deaf patient who once could hear but now, with eardrums removed and stitched to his nipples, was blessedly exempt from asking for clarification. The mute fellow who once could speak but would never again stumble over words, what with his mouth having been patched over with his amputated nose, the nostrils affording a convenient vessel for one straw or two.

He watched them all in their happy procession—the countless patients of his with limbs and organs removed, reattached, and adapted in every permutation imaginable in order to improve their lot in life. He watched as they stumbled, fell, crawled on all zeroes, all the while celebrating with cries and moans the blessings they had been given.

And look! Who's that inching their way into the crowd but his new arrivals, Jeremy and Julie, and—oops, Julie faltered there a bit, but reliable old Jeremy caught her before she took a nasty tumble. In time they would learn to adapt, but there was no need to rush things. They seemed happy together, so why not let love determine the proper course?

-A-

Jeremy picked at the lettuce leaves. Julie, sitting next to him, didn't even bother and just swept them aside.

Last time Jeremy had eaten was at The Riviera, and who knew how long ago that had been? Julie, he guessed, was in the same boat. Which was why, when that bell had rung and her cell door had snapped open and someone limping by had rasped that this would be their only meal of the day, the two of them had inserted themselves into the procession.

But somewhere along the way, as they passed all those wretched, tormented souls struggling to make their own way, they had lost their will to eat.

And yet they kept inching forward, as everyone was doing, Jeremy managing somehow to support Julie despite her missing leg, despite the same leg wobbling malevolently from her back. And by and by they found themselves in a vast, cavernous hall that apparently served as a cafeteria. Except without the serving lines. Without the stacks of trays, plates, and silverware. Without the workers in white aprons and caps. Without the beverages on ice or the meat sizzling on the grill.

Just row upon row of decrepit picnic tables that looked as if they'd been hauled away from rundown rest stops and neglected city parks.

And yet the tables were filling up. Not fast—nothing here moved fast, Jeremy was beginning to notice—but for those with the ability to sit, a dry-rotted bench on the point of collapse and permanently encrusted with bird droppings might have seemed like heaven when compared to the alternative—the soiled drop cloths scattered about on the cold granite floor.

Jeremy had chosen one of the better tables and helped Julie position herself on the bench, but wondered if it made any difference. The offerings before them looked equally as grim as those on the drop cloths and on the other tables. Just lettuce leaves, nothing more. Some fresh and green, most yellow and wilted, all of them in evenly dispersed clumps, like fallen leaves raked in a yard.

"Grab a leaf and eat it."

Jeremy, startled as if shaken out of a daydream, looked up at the man across the table.

"Go ahead," the man said. "It's okay to eat with your hands." He pointed to the faucet at the end of their table. A patient, his gown soaking wet, was greedily cupping his hands under the running water and slurping it. "Or drink with them, if you're thirsty."

Another patient, legless and armless, lay on her back under another spigot, and with the aid of someone at the faucet, let the water rush down her throat in gulps.

"Course," the man across the table added, "this all depends on your having hands."

He then held out one of his own. "Name's Holman. Billy Holman"

Jeremy shook hands and introduced himself, then lay his hand gently on Julie's shoulder and introduced her.

Holman nodded. "Pleased to meet you."

Jeremy could tell she was in pain from the way she leaned into the edge of the table in an effort to counter the weight of the leg growing out of her back. If she had kept quiet, he would have understood. In fact, he didn't feel like talking all that much himself. So he was pleasantly surprised—relieved, even—

when she spoke up.

"Hi, Billy," she said, smiling through the obvious pain. "You don't seem the worse for wear."

"Let's put it this way," he said. "My name—Holman—whole *man* no longer applies."

"Jesus," Jeremy said, catching on instantly.

Julie shrugged. "I don't under..." And then, with a glint of realization, "Oh, God, I'm so sorry."

"No reason for you to be sorry, young lady."

"Mankel did that to you?" Jeremy said, his blood rising— mostly on Billy Holman's behalf, but some of it, he admitted, at the thought of Mankel's doing the same thing to him.

Billy nodded and sat silently for a moment. "What I'm about to tell you probably falls under the category of too much information, but what the hell. This whole goddamn place is too much information."

He rested his elbows on the table, looked at Julie, looked at Jeremy. "Three years ago," he said. "I was sitting in the station, waiting for my train. I'm on my cell talking to a girl I'd met on a chat line. She's whispering to me things she plans to do to me once I get to her place, know what I mean? She's going into detail. She's telling me there'll be no fighting it. I'm sitting there listening to her, knowing no one else around can hear, and I'm picturing what she's telling me real good, and I'm wishing for that train to pull into the station right this second."

Billy glanced around to see if anyone else at the table was listening in. "I remember getting—how do you put it—a sort of physical reaction to the scenario I was forming in my head. And I'm hoping no one else is noticing. I look around the waiting room and all I see are a mother and her kid playing some game. A guy reading. Another guy, sort of pale-looking with white hair, staring off into space. Still, I figure I better get some fresh air, think about something else, otherwise I won't be able to stand the two-hour train ride. So I push open the door to the station and step out into the cold night air. Stamp my feet for a while and I'll be good. Next thing I know, I'm in a mirrored room. The guy with white hair is patting me on the back, telling me he's cured me of the nightmare of rigidity and, if I want to take a look, he'll leave me alone."

Jeremy thought about Julie's leg and about his own ears and about the other perverted subtractions and additions he'd seen. About how it never seemed enough for Mankel to remove something. He had to go that extra sick mile. He suspected the same held true for Billy, but didn't want to go there.

Holman seemed on the verge of going there but then waved it off. "Welcome to Saint Friedrich The Perpetually Sadistic," he said.

Julie placed a hand over Billy's and said nothing.

"God damn him!" Jeremy slammed his fist on the table, sending a feeble shock wave through the slat of wood he'd struck. Others at the table looked up, but only briefly, then resumed picking at the small mounds of lettuce they had claimed for themselves. "We have to kill him. All there is to it."

"Never work," Holman said.

"What do you mean? There's an army here. We can overpower him in a matter of minutes. Put a quick end to his miserable life. Then we can get out of here."

"An army?" Billy said. "Look around. We're slaughtered before we even start. Besides—some of us tried it."

"Killing him?"

"Escaping."

Julie looked up. "Really? You tried getting out of here?"

Billy offered a single nod of his head. "Oh, yeah. It's not that hard. See that hatch over there in the corner? Crawl through it, climb a ladder, push open another hatch, and you're at the surface."

"Did you say *surface*?" Jeremy said. "We're underground?"

"Yes, sir. Turns out this place is a child of the sixties, a fallout shelter built back during the duck-and-cover days. Topside, you can still see one of those rusty old yellow Civil Defense signs with the three triangles."

"But the cells, the locking mechanisms—what's that all about?"

Billy shrugged. "Government probably figured there'd be mass panic during a nuclear attack and we'd need a way to protect us from ourselves. You know the government, always looking out for us."

Julie said, "But you're still here. You weren't able to...uh...get away?"

"Kind of looks like that, doesn't it?"

Julie shrugged. "I guess. But why—"

"I'll tell you what else is up there, Ms. Julie, besides that tin sign. Forest. Woods, woods, woods. Three-hundred-sixty degrees of deep and black and forever. Those of us topside all looked at each other and shook our heads. There was no way in Hell. But, hey, we tried."

Jeremy said, "Look, Billy. We just need to try again. Recruit others, get more people involved. We can do this."

"Oh, can we?" Holman slapped his hand down and addressed the length of the table. "Hey, all of you. Show of hands. Those of you who have hands. How many want to attempt an escape?"

As before, the others acknowledged they had heard the question, then resumed eating.

"Come on," Jeremy said, addressing the same bunch. "We're talking a chance to get out of here. To lead normal lives."

Other than a shake of a head from one or two, which could have meant anything, no response.

"I'm telling you," Holman said, "no one here wants to leave."

"Bullshit! Look at these people! Look at—"

Holman pointed, not to any of the picnic tables this time, but to one drop cloth after another, each littered not so much with human beings as with living, writhing body parts. "No, Jeremy, you look. You look good and hard. You want to know why we gave up on escape? You think it's because of all the damn trees? No. It was knowing there's a world beyond those trees.

"You think anyone here wants to get back to that world and be seen in public? Be gawked at by normal people? People with eyes to see with and ears to hear with and legs to walk on and mouths to eat with? Looking at us like we were freaks. It's not even 'like we were freaks.' We are freaks. I'm sitting across from Mr. Bat Ears and Ms. Ship's Boom. And you're sitting across from Mister Miss It. You think I want to be around people, around women, who'd just as soon have a life with a pile of dog shit as with me?"

"But there are real doctors out in that world, Billy," Julie said. "Decent doctors. If they can separate conjoined twins, they can certainly fix Jeremy's ears or remove this leg from my back or—"

She hesitated, and Billy filled the silence. "Uh-huh. Go on. And what's that about your leg? What, they'll just clamp it into place with a few spring clips and you'll be on your way to the Summer Olympics?"

"I'm no doctor, Billy. But they can do amazing things."

"She's right," Jeremy said. "Escaping is our only hope. You can't tell me you want to stay here and let Mankel continue doing what he's doing, capturing innocent people from the outside, locking them up, mutilating them for whatever demented reason."

"What can we do to him?" Billy said. "He knows where the lettuce is hidden."

Jeremy felt the loathing rise up in his throat like bile. He came close to assailing the lot of them for their acquiescence and cowardice. But he held his tongue. After all, he *had* taken a good, hard look, just as Billy had said. Their situation was so indescribable, so impossibly obscene, he couldn't begin to imagine living in their skin, even given the rigged, perverse deck he'd been dealt.

"Well," he said, "if no one will go with me, I suppose I'll go by myself."

Jeremy had quietly decided this would be the best way. Once he made it to safety, he could alert the authorities and effect a rescue, whether these poor bastards wanted it or not.

"I'm going with you," Julie said.

Jeremy turned to her. There was simply no way she could do it. He would be forced to carry her and support her all the way, however far it was. She would prove a burden and little else, and that's all there was to it.

He squeezed her arm. "I'd like that," he said.

Billy Holman seemed to mull something over, then leaned forward and whispered, "Hey, look. If the two of you go ahead with this, it would have to be at the beginning of dinner. Dinner's the only time we're out of our cells, and Mankel's usually in his office when it starts. When chow's close to being over, it's a different story. He'll come down the hall and stand at the entrance like a third grade teacher on lunchroom duty, watching all his little charges parade back to their cozy little classrooms."

Billy took a quick look back at the entrance. So far, no sign of Mankel.

"But here's what I can do," Billy continued. "Whenever you two feel you're ready, give me the word. I can talk a few people who still have their feet and a couple of others who still have their hands into helping out. We'll keep him occupied. Tell him he's the next best thing to Hippocrates. Try to give you enough time to make some headway through those woods before he sees who's missing. How's that sound?"

"I appreciate that," Jeremy said.

"Maybe you do. Maybe not. Because how long it will take for you to find a highway or the nearest town is anyone's guess. And we can stall him for only so long."

"That's all we can ask. Isn't that right, Julie?"

Julie nodded, reached out and squeezed Billy's hand. "Thank you."

Holman smiled back. "Just say when."

Jeremy looked into Julie's eyes and saw the same answer he had arrived at.

"When?" Jeremy asked. "We're thinking right now, this minute."

-A-

Give them time to be by themselves. That's how Dr. Mankel looked at it.

Those vibrant, hearty souls, with the fire of youthfulness in their blood, certainly didn't want some old, white-haired fuddy-duddy hanging around all the time, lingering over their shoulders like some fussy chaperone.

Which is why the good doctor preferred to wait a good forty-five minutes before leaving his office and joining his patients for dinner.

Now, approaching the cafeteria, he came across a handful of those same patients blocking the entranceway in a tight semicircle.

"To what do I owe the pleasure?" he asked.

The man he remembered as Holman seemed to act as their spokesman. "It is we who owe you, Doctor. We feel it's about time we express our undying gratitude for the life-restoring changes you've made in us."

"Why—"

"No, you listen. We know there must be times when all your hard work seems thankless and unrewarding. But please don't ever think we haven't been paying close attention to your persistence and selfless dedication. Why, even a seemingly minor task as preparing our daily meal doesn't escape our notice. One cannot help but marvel at the ceaseless effort you must expend, each and every morning, to present the mounds of deliciously wilted lettuce leaves in such a tasteful and decorative fashion, both on our tables and on our drop cloths."

"That's very kind of you, Mr. Holman, but...." Dr. Mankel couldn't go on. He felt himself close to tears.

"Oh, kindness. What a weak, flimsy thing human kindness is when compared to the acts you perform, doctor."

Dr. Mankel searched his adorers in vain for the two patients he really wished to hear from, and believing they were still in the cafeteria, he proceeded to sidestep the group through an opening on their left.

Immediately, the group shifted en masse to fill the gap.

"Now, now, kind doctor," Billy Holman said, waggling a scolding finger at the physician. "We're not through with you yet. We know how you shun praise, but there's no escaping it this time. I, for one, pledge my undying devotion to you from the bottom of my heart. And the rest of us, at this time, wish to do the same, even those of us without hands to place over our hearts. Unfortunately, those without hearts couldn't make it."

All this overflowing of admiration was becoming unbearable for the doctor. But a spark of romance was about to be kindled between Jeremy and Julie—he felt it deep within him—and all he asked was to be there at their first kiss. That alone, that quiet touching of their lips, would be thanks enough for his dedication.

This time he moved to the entourage's right, but as he did so, a woman at the edge jumped in sideways to block his path.

"Now where do you think you're going?" she said, holding her hand out like a crossing guard. "Don't you realize how my life has changed for the better since you removed my left kidney, removed my gall bladder and spleen, removed my stomach, then grafted them all onto my liver so it wouldn't function as well, forcing me to follow a stricter diet and lose weight? Never mind that we're all losing weight anyway, it's the thought that counts."

"Enough!" Dr. Mankel cried. The happiness he felt was almost excruciating. If they kept this up he would surely double over with joy. "Please, please, return to your rooms at once. Please reflect on your perfections and what they mean to you, not to me. I am but a mere man of medicine, doing his duty. Nothing more."

And with that, he gently but firmly pushed through the center of the small crowd, persuading them, in an almost parental way, to step aside.

-∞A∞-

Julie couldn't go on.

The attached leg kept pulling down on her like a massive weight, as if at any moment it would rip the flesh and muscle off her back. Her arms and hands and face were so scratched, scraped, and bloody, she doubted anything would be left of her by morning.

But she remained quiet. It was just pain, after all, something she would have to live with for the rest of her life, whether the two of them stopped or not. And she wasn't about to jeopardize their only chance of escape by making noise about it.

So she continued to ride piggyback on Jeremy's ever-sagging shoulders, gripping the front of his sweat-soaked gown with one hand while stoically hacking away with the other at the ever resistant branches and foliage.

And poor Jeremy—it was all he could do to keep her steady and keep pushing forward in the dark and keep waging his own battle against the dense, packed forest that showed no sign of surrendering to open space.

"How you—how you holding up, Julie?" Jeremy said, his panted words a struggle.

"I'm okay," she said. "Are you—"

Something gave way.

At first it seemed as if Jeremy's legs had finally buckled under the weight. Then it was as if he'd stepped into a knee-high ditch. And then he was gone, completely gone, as if he'd dropped out of existence.

For the briefest second there was an almost liberating sensation of weightlessness, of soaring through the darkness of space. Then came the crash and the crisp, precise snap of her good leg.

She didn't want to scream.

But she screamed.

And kept falling, now tumbling over herself, striking hardpan, exposed roots, unforgiving rock, her arms hitting things and flailing about and hitting things again, her good leg shattering more and more with each blow, her attached leg tearing away from her back like a tree uprooting from the earth.

And still she kept falling, picking up speed, no longer screaming but consumed by a silent panic. A dread fear that this was eternal damnation—not an end but an endless descent.

And when she finally did come to a stop—on a patch of thick, damp moss—the relief was so palpable she almost burst into laughter. Until she realized she could not move at all, that everything, everything about her, was broken. That she was little more than a damaged heap.

"Julie? Julie?"

She could move her eyes. Yes, she could do that much. And even here in the dead of night at the bottom of a bottomless ravine, she somehow discerned Jeremy as he slowly worked himself to his feet.

And, yes, she could speak. "Jeremy. Are you hurt?"

He worked his neck, pulled his arms back, tested himself. "Shaken up a bit," he said. "Bruised, probably. But I can get around. I think."

"That's good."

"But Julie...oh, my God, Julie."

He knelt before her and ran the back of his hand over her swollen cheek. "Let me take a look—"

"Please don't," she urged, unable to signal him to stop. "Just shaken up. Like you."

"You sure?"

She nodded ever so gingerly, but even that slight motion sent jolts of pain down her spine.

"We probably need to get going. Can you stand—sort of?"

"Uh, not yet. Look, Jeremy, I think it'd be better if you went on without me. I'll only slow you down." She smiled the best she could. "Should have thought of this sooner, huh?"

"We'll rest a bit, then."

"No, Jeremy." She wanted to place an encouraging hand on his dirt and blood-streaked face. "It's best if you go on alone."

"Look. Maybe we should turn back."

"No, not that!" she implored. "I can't go back!"

"I can't leave you here."

"I'll survive. If I get hungry, well...anything around here's bound to be better than that daily dinner."

"Come on, Julie. I've carried you this far. I'm not going to give up now." He patted his own shoulder, several times in succession, and Julie could see he was trying to put on a good face. "Climb aboard, and we'll be on our way," he said. "We can do this."

"You can do this," she said. "For all of us."

Jeremy looked at her. The slightest glint reflected off his eyes, as if light from a solitary star had somehow found its way through the forest's suffocating canopy. He wrapped his arms around her and held her gently, but even the pain from that tender caress was too much for her to bear.

"Please don't let go," she said.

She closed her eyes in anticipation and felt the press of his lips on hers. And for a long moment she wished that this was how it would all end—with the terrible pain and with his kiss.

But then came the letting go, which she knew would come. She took as deep a breath as she could before opening her eyes.

"You won't forget me, will you?" she asked.

"You'll be my first stop on the way back."

That wasn't what she meant, but this was no time for details. "I better be," she said.

Jeremy planted a kiss on her forehead and gave her a smile. He touched her neck. Touched her face. Then turned and began the long climb back up the steep ravine, quickly becoming another dark entity in the forest.

Julie watched and listened for a time, then closed her eyes and quietly awaited the solace of her own private darkness.

-ᕱᕲ-

At first he figured it was a mirage brought on by exhaustion, that what he saw through the trees was nothing more than wishful thinking.

Half the night, it seemed, had passed since he left Julie behind. For all that time he'd been waging an endless war against the pitch dark, against the roots, vines, bracken, fallen trees, and low-hanging limbs, not knowing where the next step would take him. Knowing only that Julie was dying and that he had to press on.

No, Julie was nowhere near dying!

That's what he kept telling himself, out loud, as he fought his way forward. And yet he could still feel the gaping hole in her back from hugging her, the warm blood oozing from the wound. He could still picture her arms twisted at sickening angles and her once good leg reduced to a misshapen tube. In his mind he still felt the blood-soaked moss all around her.

So he knew what precious little time she had left. And given the hours lost so far against this implacable, godforsaken forest, he knew also that he could very well have exceeded that time.

Still, he kept swearing he was mistaken. That in the heat of battle, even his certainties were suspect. That just beyond the next set of trees there would be light. The shining light of civilization and salvation.

But when the lights suddenly did appear, he doubted them.

They moved slowly, steadily from right to left, flickering through the thicket. A white light followed closely by a red.

He stood still, bracing himself against a tree trunk, the first time he stopped moving since clambering out of the ravine. Dead tired, on the point of collapse, his lungs afire; he told himself, no. This was nothing more than the forest's form of an imagined oasis in the middle of the desert. The lights were something he desired, and therefore they were there. Nothing lay ahead in the blackness but more blackness.

He shut his eyes tight in an effort to lock out all illusion. He kept them shut and waited, and in doing so, he heard the faint rumble of a motor. Opening his eyes, he still saw the pair of lights sliding leftward, blinking through the trees, and now accompanied by an engine's rumble.

They were real!

The head and tail lights of a car!

He was near a highway!

Now was not the time to rest. Jeremy pushed off from the tree and broke into a run, swinging furiously at everything in his path. He could make out shapes now, the edge of the forest silhouetted against the lighter darkness of the night sky. And so he pushed ahead all the faster, all the while hearing the sound of the car fading away to his left.

"No! Wait!"

But the going became worse. A blockade of briars and sticker bushes stretched out before him like a barbed wire fence, as if the forest, at the last moment, had deliberately thrown this obstacle in his path to prevent his escape.

"Wait!" he screamed again.

He plowed ahead through the barricade, slashing violently at the nettles, not giving a good goddamn how they sliced him up. These injuries were nothing compared to Julie's. Julie, who was still alive, still alive, still alive.

And then he was clear. Clear of the stickers, clear of the blackness, clear of the malicious forest, and out into the blessed starlit open.

He spotted the car. It was speeding away faster than he'd thought. He raced across the open field, shouting at it to stop, but by the time he reached the shoulder of the road, its red taillights had receded into mere pinpoints.

"No," Jeremy cried.

Doubled over, his hands on his knees, he told himself he needed to keep going. And so he stood erect again, or as best as he could manage, and continued along the road in the same direction the car had taken.

It was a highway, he told himself. There would be other cars. And now and then he glanced behind him for signs of approaching headlights.

Up ahead, suddenly, those distant pinpoints turned bright red. The car had braked to a stop. Meaning an intersection, possibly road signs.

The brightness let up and a ray of white came into view, moving to the right. The car was making a turn. That's the way he would go, Jeremy decided.

He also decided he could no longer afford to walk along the road hoping for a car to pass. Reaching into his ever dwindling reserves, he began a slow jog, hoping for the strength to move faster.

The taillights had disappeared now, and the ray of white light had become two distinct lights, side by side. The car wasn't turning right. It had made a U-turn and was coming back.

Maybe the driver had heard him yelling or had somehow spotted him in his rearview.

Spurred on by this imminent hope, Jeremy found the boost of energy he needed and broke into a sprint toward the ever advancing headlights, waving his hands frantically, shouting, "Over here! Over here!"

The lights grew larger, brighter.

"Over here!" he shouted again from the road's edge. He heard the crunch of tires on loose gravel. "Please, I'm over here! I need help!"

And then he realized. This was no highway. There was no dividing line, no white line marking the road's edge. No pavement. It was a private road. A private, gravel road connected to the forest.

Through the bright white of the headlights Jeremy could barely make out the driver, but there was no mistaking the white lab coat and the white hair.

And there was no doubting that this was Mankel's private road. The road he used to set off on his demented missions and return with his human, soon to be anything but, cargo. The road he used to conduct his searches, his back and forth patrols, in the event of escape.

Heart pounding from an insurmountable fear, Jeremy did an immediate about-face and took off running. But what hope did he have on gravel of fleeing an oncoming car?

At least he had a chance on the grassy field. And an even better chance in the woods beyond—yes, *those* woods—that fearful void he had spent all but his last ounce of energy escaping.

He veered away from the shoulder, glancing back. And in veering away and glancing back, his foot snagged in something, and an instant later he was face down on the gravel, his foot twisted in a pothole.

He turned his eyes toward the car, now stopped a few yards away, its engine idling, its headlights still blaring. He heard a door creak open and the sound of shoes on the loose rock. He squinted into the brightness at the figure moving toward him.

-❧A❧-

Dr. Mankel rinsed his hands at the sink in his office, relieved he had found the two lovers before they made the mistake of returning to a world that would only have viewed their perfections with envy and contempt.

Julie, sad to say, had succumbed to the vagaries of nature. Why a perfectly healthy young woman would bleed to death in a peaceful forest was something he would investigate—when he had the time.

Jeremy, fortunately, had seemed none the worse for wear. Except, of course, for his limping back to the car and his squinting against the headlights. But those were problems easily remedied.

In fact, that was probably him screaming now.

Mason Jar

Joseph Schwartz

Jeremiah lay flat under his truck. Daniel stood above him offering occasional support, handing his neighbor a tool here and there, looking down through the engine compartment occasionally able to see a grease stained finger or a single searching eye.

"You want something to drink?" Daniel asked.

"Sure," Jeremiah said.

"What ya want? Tea or water?"

"Yeah, sure, just go already. Crackers and cheese! I can't hear myself think."

"I'll get us some tea."

"Yeah, okay…whatever."

Jeremiah cursed as the metallic sound of his wrench hit the garage's speckled cement floor. Daniel went inside before things could get worse. The immediate relief of the AC was glorious.

He stood in the kitchen taking a few deep breaths, sucking in the cold. Daniel wiped the sweat from his face and hair, smearing his hands down his jeans in two dark streaks.

"Gross."

"Delly," Daniel said. "I didn't see you there, pretty baby."

"Better not let Daddy hear you talking like that," Delilah said. It was a rush for them both to know Jeremiah was steps away. The danger was half the fun. "I'm his sweet little virgin and will be until my wedding day."

Daniel said, "What Daddy don't know won't hurt him."

"It ain't Daddy I'm concerned about," Delilah said. "You, on the other hand, should be scared to death."

Delilah sat at the kitchen table wearing a faded green baby doll shirt advertising the Baptist Church both their families attended. With her foot pulled up to her thigh on the kitchen chair, her dark blue satin shorts with white piping slid back to her hips. Delilah was painting her toenails with a bright cherry red allowing Daniel to see her daisy yellow underwear.

"Where's your momma?" Daniel asked.

Delilah laughed, setting her thumb to her mouth, tipping her wrist back. "The Baptist woman's expo."

"Oh, yeah," Daniel said, smiling not really liking the joke. Mary's drinking was no secret, but faking ignorance was next to Godliness.

Matter-of-factly, Delilah said, "Let's get out of here tonight."

When it came to Delilah, Daniel was helpless.

He remembered one plain and ordinary Wednesday afternoon when Delilah skipped school and Daniel called in sick to work so she could go see a horror movie.

The theater had been empty. Delilah, dressed in her skinny jeans, Metallica t-shirt and flip-flops sat sidesaddle on Daniel's lap grinding her bony butt against his swollen jeans, leaving him ready to cry with frustration.

That night Daniel took two Oxycodone and made numb love to his wife, using her body to ejaculate his memories of Delilah.

"Be careful your Daddy don't catch you."

"Crap! Whatever," Delilah said. Before Daniel could stop her, she smeared nail polish on the crotch of his jeans. A small but noticeable stripe of red.

"Gosh dang it! Why do you have to be such a damn brat all the time?"

"Careful Elder Dan, you almost took the Lord's name in vain."

Delilah quickly kissed Daniel on the lips. He greedily watched Delilah jog from the kitchen shamelessly raising her shorts show Daniel her partially bare bottom.

It was difficult for Daniel to will away his erection, but when he went back out to the garage, back into Jeremiah's shrine of grease and sweat, presto, he was as soft as pudding.

The iced tea was sweet. Daniel licked his lips several times enjoying the taste as it mixed with the memory of Delilah's most recent kiss.

"Where the hell did ya go for that tea, China?" Jeremiah asked, sliding out from under his truck.

When God was making assholes, Daniel thought, he must've given Jeremiah a double scoop.

"You get that bolt out?" Daniel asked.

"It broke. Fragging head snapped clean off. Going to have to send it down to the shop. Might as well light the damn money on fire just to watch it burn."

"Lucky you still got Mary's car."

"Lucky," Jeremiah said with a hiss. "That's me alright."

-∽A∽-

Daniel's anxiety, when it came to a date with Delilah, was a soft pressure he found nearly unbearable. To clear his mind, he would pretend to work in the garage.

Hidden by the raised hood of the car, Daniel unceremoniously masturbated into an old tube sock he kept in a toolbox.

He did not enjoy this as much as he found it necessary. Daniel knew tonight would be unendurable if he didn't relieve himself before going out.

He flattened the sock and put it back in the toolbox. Light headed, Daniel fastened his pants and shut the toolbox, covering up his secret although he had nothing to worry about anyhow. Karen could give a shit. Her puritanical ability to just lay there and take it was how she kept Daniel in his place. How, he wondered, did he ever end up marrying such a bitch?

Then there was Delilah.

She was everything Karen had forgotten to be. When Daniel was with Delilah, he was just a cool guy with a pretty girl that liked to get in trouble only to see if he would save her. Daniel knew he was her fool, but some things were irresistible.

It did occur to Daniel someday Delilah would be no different than Karen. Her hips would spread and these silly games would become stupid and annoying traits.

Karen was loyal, faithful, a good mother and wife who mostly gave in to whatever Daniel wanted.

In a few years, Delilah would grow up and move the hell away forever.

Until then, Daniel was helpless.

-~A~-

A few hours felt like an eternity to Daniel as he and Karen moved through their typical schedule of a Wednesday night.

Once married, Karen had been able to get knocked up easier than a college freshman. She refused to get her tubes tied and still made Daniel use rubbers. When Daniel bitched and begged not to put one on, Karen reminded him it was a simple matter of him getting fixed. Whenever Karen said shit like that, Daniel wanted to remind her he wasn't the one who was broken.

After a bath for each boy, a couple of juice boxes and a kiss on the forehead, it was just Daniel, Karen, the TV, and Karen's box of wine. Karen criticized their neighbor Mary's drinking because she did it publicly. Daniel was glad to get Karen shit faced at home any chance he could get—at least when she was passed out she didn't complain.

Daniel checked one last time on the kids before he threw a blanket over Karen. He turned the volume up on the TV—Karen slept better with the noise.

-~A~-

Delilah was invisible in the night except for the orange tip of her cigarette. Her eyes and cheeks glowed. She was beautiful.

"C'mon," she whispered. "Let's go."

"Don't pee your pants," Daniel said.

He could see her smile in the dark before tossing her cigarette away. She opened the driver side door to the Honda. They'd done this before, but he was still proud of how good she was at it.

Delilah put the key in the ignition turning it halfway, making the dash burn with warning lights before releasing the shifter from Park to Neutral. She steered while Daniel pushed. Sweat broke across Daniel's brow. A crisp, sour smell of his BO crept up through his cologne and deodorant. Once down the driveway and past the stop sign, Delilah stopped the car.

Daniel walked to the driver's window. Delilah was waiting for him, hands at ten and two. "Ma'am, do you know why I pulled you over?"

"Oh, gosh, Officer, was I speeding?"

"Afraid so. I'll need to see your license."

"My husband will be so upset with me. He warned me not to get in trouble. Isn't there anything I can do to change your mind?"

When Delilah looked up at Daniel with her amazing brown eyes, so wet and full of sincerity it caused him to forget they were just pretending.

"Dang it, Dan. You're doing it again."

Delilah scooted over the transmission hump dragging her Keds over his dash. Goddamn it if he couldn't just blister her ass for that. Crazy as it sounded, Daniel wasn't mad at her anymore.

"Aw, don't be like that," he said, putting his hand on her knee.

Delilah put her hand over his, giving her best fuck-you smile. She brutally dug her nails into his hand. Daniel refused to react, leaving his hand motionless. Despite the throbbing crescents imprinted into his hand, he was oddly happy as he started the car.

-❧A❧-

Cars were parked in the driveway, on the lawn, and in the street. Daniel was cautious. If he needed to get out of here, he didn't want some asshole blocking him in.

Delilah leapt from the car—no kiss, no goodbye, no fuck you. Delilah's rejection of him made his eyes water with hate and shame. If Daniel stopped doing this, then what? Back to Internet porn and darkweb chat rooms? It paled in comparison to Delilah no matter how fucking awful she really was.

Daniel moved among children, searching for Delilah as he wandered about this absentee family's split-level ranch. There were many beautiful girls here but there was only one Delilah.

In a blue and white cooler, beer cans floated amid silver cans of generic cola. Daniel reached in and took a soda. He did his best to ignore their whispers.

"Who's the narc?"

Jesus, Daniel prayed, *give me strength.* This was only a test. Therefore, Daniel rationalized, Delilah was a test too.

He stood in the living room looking at a wall filled with framed photographs. Who were these people and why were they so goddamn happy? Lost in thought, Daniel spilled his soda when Delilah grabbed his arm, her eyes wild and filled with fear.

"What's wrong?"

"Let's go," Delilah demanded. "Now!"

"Geez, Louise. Okay, okay."

Daniel stumbled after Delilah as she practically dragged him with her down the front steps. Shouts were already beginning to follow from behind them like police sirens.

"Where's that bitch, Delilah?" a girl yelled. "I want my phone back, bitch!"

It didn't matter to Daniel what she had done. Delilah was perfect no matter what, and if that meant running like hell to preserve that belief, he had no problem with it.

Eventually, somehow, they would be together. It was at times like this that Daniel hoped Delilah might fall in love with him.

With delight, they jumped over and slid across the hoods of parked cars. Breathless, Daniel unlocked the Honda using the key fob remote. He smashed into the car as a pair of man-sized hands shoved him from behind. Like the childhood dream of robbing a bank and shooting it out with the cops, the chase excited him in a way he hadn't felt in a long time. His ribs hurt like hell, but this wasn't a bank. It wasn't anything. He could do whatever he wanted. Seriously, who the fuck was going to stop him?

He swung a right hook in the general direction of his would-be tackler. A tall, lanky boy winced when his fist rammed into the kid's ear. The boy fell to the ground, clutching his head. Daniel watched hoping someone else wanted to fight, but the crowd that had eagerly followed the kid lost its nerve.

Jumping into the Honda, he pulled around a blue Ford, cringing as the bottom of his car grated against the pavement, refusing to stop. He sensed luck was on his side. If the cops came, his alibi was already at home sleeping. Karen would swear to his being home all night. Where else would he have been? People only get caught lying when they know they are lying. The trick was getting everyone to believe your lie.

Delilah giggled, the brightness from the cell phone making her look like a ghost in the darkness. Daniel felt confident no one had memorized his license plate. Besides, who would be willing to shit a perfectly good night drinking beer down the drain by calling the cops? Nobody, that's who.

Delilah was deleting pictures from the phone. A boy, sometimes shirtless in a mirror and sometimes in a pack with friends, seemed to be the problem. Whenever he appeared alongside a cute brown-haired girl with braces, the picture got deleted.

"You could've told me what was going on back there," Daniel said.

"Whatever," Delilah said.

"I could get into big trouble ya know."

"Nobody is gonna tell. Besides, I'll give slut face Leslie her phone back at school. I told her that. She's lucky I only took her phone and didn't hit her in the head with a hammer."

"What the hell, Delly. You'd do that?"

"Ain't you the pot calling the kettle black?"

"I'm not going around stealing people's phones and handing out hammer lobotomies, young lady."

"Remind me the next time Karen comes over to play cards how much you care about my friends."

Bitch. Gripping the steering wheel, it was times like these he vowed never to do something like this for her again.

Delilah didn't say a word when Daniel parked. She disappeared almost immediately into the darkness. This was it, he promised himself. If it meant selling the house and moving to another state, he had to stop this shit with her.

Daniel's cell phone vibrated in his hand. He refused to read the text out of spite, still riding the high of self-righteousness from his recent decision. He planned to call a real estate agent in the morning. Karen could bitch, and she would, but it wouldn't matter. In the end, Daniel would get what he wanted. As long as the bills were paid, the kids were fed, and Karen didn't have to take it up the ass, a new house with ten acres and a couple of four-by-fours to go mudding with the kids seemed like no big deal.

Karen was still asleep on the couch, with the TV on and relentlessly selling foot insoles guaranteed to change your life.

He quickly looked in on each of the boys, pleased to see them asleep. The master bedroom was quiet as he undressed. Setting his phone on his nightstand, he tossed his dirty clothes in the basket.

Lying in his briefs, the bed all to himself, Daniel picked up his phone. In the preview, there was a smiley face from an unknown number.

He touched his pointer finger against the glass. Delilah had sent him a picture, a selfie of her red nail-polished fingertips spreading apart her labia..

-∞A∞-

It had been a week since Delilah's text. Daniel knew he should erase it but he couldn't. He was pathetic when it came to her. The two times he'd been able to convince Karen to have sex with him since sneaking out were routine. Daniel thought of Delilah, the image of her from his cell phone foremost in his mind as he came. Although Karen came too, her pleasure paled in comparison to Delilah's disdain for him.

It was one of those Saturdays. The sublime hum of the engine practically hypnotized him as he mowed the grass.

Aimlessly riding, thinking of nothing at all, he almost drove straight into Delilah. He had not seen her until she was in front of him. Daniel slammed the brake, shoving his stomach hard against the steering wheel. It hurt, but as usual when Delilah appeared, nothing else mattered. He reached down and turned off the engine, fingers tingling with pins and needles. He opened and closed his hands, grimacing as the blood came rushing back in.

"Cripes, I hope I die before I get as old as you," Delilah said.

"You're never going to get old. I promise," Daniel said.

"God, how I want to get out of here."

"Maybe we can get over to the twenty-four hour bowling alley Friday night."

"Not like that. I mean for real…forever."

"You're serious?"

"Would you do it, Dan, take me somewhere? I just can't stand it here with *them* anymore."

"I don't know, Delly. I mean, that's a lot to ask."

"Yeah," Delilah said. "I should've known. All you want is some pussy, right?"

"Jeepers, Delilah, keep your voice down!" Daniel looked around the yard. They were alone.

"Maybe you should go inside and ask Karen to watch you jerk off. I bet if I asked, she'd make up some sun tea and we could both watch you—"

The sound of Daniel's palm rang out like a gunshot against Delilah's cheek.

"Now you listen to me," Daniel growled, taking hold of Delilah's elbow. "You can't ever say anything to Karen, do you understand me? Ever!"

Daniel's anger drained away the moment he saw the look on Delilah's face. She cried soundlessly, not daring to breathe a word. He let go of her arm. The bright red dots where his fingertips had landed glowed against her skin like cigarette burns.

"Delly, I…I've just got to think about it."

Daniel put his foot on the tractor's brake pedal and released the transmission. The mower turned over and Daniel returned to where he'd left off. Like waking up from a dream, he couldn't quite remember the details except to say he was asleep.

The pride he felt for asserting himself with Delilah felt good. He refused to look over his shoulder and give her the satisfaction of contrition, even if only implied.

For once, Daniel was in control.

When he finally made the wide turn at the end of the yard, guiding the riding mower along the path, Delilah was gone. She'd disappeared, likely back to her room to sulk. He realized she may never talk to him again, or could someday wind up becoming a mother to his children. Either way, he was deeply satisfied with what he had done.

-∞A∞-

Daniel thought about Delilah's offer for the next three days.

Could he do this?

Leave Karen and the kids and just start over?

It seemed harsh, if not unfair. In one more year, Delilah would be eighteen, an adult in the eyes of the State—it was only a matter of time.

He could do it.

Leave.

The only question was how.

Thankfully, the Internet is a hell of a thing. Ask a question and a flood of information will spill out. In less than an hour, he knew what he would do. The first step was to get cash and plenty of it.

Daniel's mom had brought him to First National Bank as a kid. No wonder he chose to bank here. Some choices in life were easy. There were four teller windows. The bank had undergone a renovation, restoring a majority of its original charm. At ten in the morning, a skylight once covered with sheet rock and fluorescent lights flooded the bank's lobby with sunshine forcing everyone to stop for a moment as if to admire it.

After less time than it took to microwave a bag of popcorn, the light relented and it was business as usual again. Daniel found he possessed an unusual clarity this morning. He felt different, inspired, what folks might call "born again."

"Next, please," the teller called.

He preferred the short and fat teller Trish, but she was busy right now with an old lady who didn't understand how she'd overdrawn her account by eleven dollars and fourteen cents. Tall, and black as tinted glass, Lenova took

Daniel's check and deposit slip with a smile.

"Oh, my," Lenova said feigning awe. "That's a whole lot of money."

"Yeah," Daniel said. He'd been working on a lie since he came up with this idea, but hadn't found one he liked. Instead, he blurted out the first thing that came into his head. "Big vacation. Taking the whole darn family, even the in-laws." It was a relief to hear it out loud. It was a good lie. He liked it.

"You're a very generous man."

"You can't take it with you, right?"

"Exactly," Lenova said typing on her computer. "Okay, all done."

"That was painless," Daniel said.

"Nothing to it," Lenova said.

"So…it's here now, in the bank?"

"You can write checks against it early as tomorrow morning."

"No, I mean the money."

"You mean cash?"

"Right."

"Three days."

"But it's my money."

"Those are the rules, honey. Nothing I can do about that."

"What if I need it now? If it was an emergency?"

"I can get you the bank manager, but I've done everything I can."

"It's a stupid rule," Daniel said. "Very stupid."

"That's what everybody says. Anyhow, don't be sad, honey. Have a nice vacation."

Daniel left the bank unhappy for the first time in years. There was a palpable lump of anger and frustration in his chest. That damn woman at the Credit Union had said all he had to do was take a draw against his 401k and put it in the bank. "Consider it a loan to yourself when you need it most," she had said. All this jumping through hoops was for nothing without the money.

He had wanted to leave tonight, to take Delilah half asleep in her pajamas and leave. Daniel supposed three days wasn't that long to wait for anything, especially with ten thousand dollars. He decided he'd at least tell Delilah about his plan. Before he left the bank parking lot, he looked at the picture on his phone again and texted her.

Daniel was happy again.

-∞A∞-

Two days later, the money was ready. He had a meeting with the vice-president of customer service at First National scheduled for five minutes after the bank opened.

He would have to sign a form and give the goddamn bloodsuckers his thumbprint before they would let him have the money. The VP had told him this over the phone as if he was a child. Why did he need so much cash? It seemed ridiculous. Daniel told him to mind his own business and just do his dang job. Christ almighty, Daniel thought to himself, people are such nosy pricks.

It didn't matter. Nothing mattered except Delilah.

She finally texted him back, "u still mad?" Daniel almost cried —this was as close to an apology as he would get.

Daniel texted back, "I love U," with a heart emoji.

"ur sweet," she sent.

His hands shook, "Do u still want to leave 4 real?"

The seconds were practically eternal as Daniel waited, wondering if he could still do this. What about jail? Could he do the time? Would Delilah wait for him? But then his phone vibrated and he no longer needed to think about it.

"OMG!! YES."

The money felt light. There wasn't a dollar missing. Ten grand, all in hundreds, and all brand new bills. Daniel had brought a backpack with him. The last time he'd used it was for a gym membership that expired four years ago. He had snuck out of the house dreaming how heavy it would be—the fortune fit inside the pocket of his windbreaker.

Daniel parked in his driveway. Delilah was waiting for him, smoking a cigarette and pushing herself lazily back and forth on the porch swing. *Thank God, Karen is at work.* His heart pounded with excitement.

Daniel smiled as he turned off his car. He walked up the stairs and sat down next to her. Although faded, bleached pink by the sun, the wide red cushion Karen had bought years ago for the porch swing was still comfortable.

Daniel could not remember the last time he had sat on the porch swing. He was nervous. Delilah took hold of Daniel's hand, slipping her soft palm in against his. His heart raced—the thought he might be having an honest-to-God heart attack occurred to him. After a few deep breaths, he regretfully realized he was still alive.

"You have the money?" Delilah asked.

He reached in his pocket and took out one of the banded packs of money. Delilah held the money up to her nose and smelled it. Daniel hoped he didn't look as disappointed as Delilah did happy.

"I'm ready if you are," Daniel said. He felt dizzy, like he might puke. This girl and the shit they were about to do, there would be no turning back.

Despite all that he could lose, he had never been more ready for anything in his life. The rules applied if you liked them, if they favored you. They could play by the so-called rules everybody else blindly followed, or they could make their own rules and never look back.

Despite her bad breath, Daniel wanted to kiss Delilah. It was likely she had not brushed her teeth today. Her fingernail polish was chipped and chewed at and there was a tan sludge of earwax visible just above her tarnished silver stud earring. A zit coming in on her chin that would be a whopper. Daniel couldn't help but laugh.

"What's so funny?"

"Nothing," Daniel said, taking back the money. God how he wanted to tell Delilah how much he truly loved her. "I'm just happy. That's all."

-A-

Midnight.

Before Karen had come home, he'd packed his clothes into the backpack he'd taken with him earlier to the bank. He put most of the money inside it, too, camouflaging it in between t-shirts and his tried-and-true Levi's.

He left behind his razor, shaving cream and toothbrush, but took his deodorant. When Karen got up, she probably wouldn't notice something like that. Daniel needed time. He had to get as far from here as possible before anyone figured it out; his wife, Delilah's parents, most of all the police.

His boys were asleep in their beds, Peter in the top bunk because he was oldest, and Paul on the bottom. Daniel lovingly combed the hair over each of their brows. This was the hard part.

These boys would have a hell of a time with things. Growing up with a son of a bitch for a dad was one thing, it was a whole other thing to have no father at all. Daniel didn't expect Karen to forgive him, much less understand. He didn't know why he was doing this except he wanted to start over.

Twice Delilah's age, he knew things she didn't have a clue about. Dumb shit like doing laundry or making good coffee and smart things like how all men are gullible assholes when it came to sex and how there wasn't some magical god living in the sky. Life wasn't complicated if you didn't make it that way to begin with.

Daniel closed the front door to his house and walked to his car. Delilah was already there, waiting for him, holding her pink backpack.

For a change, Delilah pushed while Daniel sat in the driver's seat, guiding the Honda silently out to the road. It seemed ridiculous now, as they would never be coming back, but the act seemed almost sacred.

When Daniel gently applied the brakes, Delilah scurried to the passenger seat, kneeling with the door still open to kiss Daniel. Her lips were filled with fear and happiness and immortality.

Delilah yelped with delight as Daniel slammed the gas to the floor. Daniel forced himself to memorize her, the way her hair blew back, the taste of her tongue still fresh in his mouth. His memory to cherish forever.

Daniel had always wanted to see the Pacific Ocean and seriously doubted Delilah had ever seen anything bigger than a lake. They could do it together for the first time. It would be uniquely theirs alone.

They stopped at an all-night convenience store built into a truck stop. Truckers were there in droves, up at 3 AM. working, eating, and getting gas by the hundreds of gallons. Maybe someday that was what he'd do—heard it was good money. He imagined taking Delilah on the road and driving across America. They could see the world one mile at a time.

Aside from nineteen dollars in gas, and a large coffee, Daniel bought Delilah two bags of chips, a candy bar, a multi-colored bag of salt water taffy big enough for Halloween, a slice of pizza, a country sausage corn dog, a bag of beef jerky and a fountain drink a toy poodle could drown inside. The clerk scoffed at the hundred-dollar bill. She pulled the cap off a yellow marker and put the top between her thin lips as she swiped the pen with across the money. When nothing happened, she conceded by opening the register.

Daniel had not thought about how he would ever convert the money he had over to smaller notes. Fast food places usually had signs that said "NO BILLS OVER $50 ACCEPTED." Restaurants and bars were definitely out, but there was one place that wouldn't blink at cashing a hundred dollar bill: grocery stores. They could give a fuck if you paid them with bags of change or gold bullion.

Daniel loved the idea. First, it would keep them on the road, moving. Second, the odds of someone connecting the dots of the mystery one-hundred-dollar-bill shopper were about as likely as finding the corpse of Jimmy Hoffa sitting on a park bench.

Daniel drove while Delilah gorged herself. Occasionally she took a large drink of soda and let out a belch only slightly more pleasant than someone shitting in public. She pushed the buttons on the radio until she found a song she liked, turning up the stereo full blast. It hurt Daniel's ears, but he played along as if he enjoyed shitty dance music. Delilah sang and bounced in her seat, spilling her soda, oblivious to the fact she was running away from home. When the song ended, he killed the radio.

"You're a really good dancer," he said. "Maybe you could get a job dancing or something when we settle down?"

"Whatever," Delilah said kicking off her shoes. She tilted her seat back so that she was sitting at a forty-five degree angle. It delighted her that it bothered the hell out of Daniel when she put her bare feet on the windshield, walking her naked toes up the glass, leaving smudgy toe marks in her wake. "I'm not gonna end up some skank swinging around a pole."

"I didn't mean it like that," Daniel said.

"You'd like that, wouldn't you? Me naked and dancing around."

"If it was only for me, yeah."

"You're such a perv!"

Daniel didn't want to talk anymore. He turned the radio back on but kept the volume down. He was beginning to feel tired. The truck stop coffee was bitter, even with all the sugar he'd added. He wished that he'd gotten something else, a soda like Delilah's, but they put so much shit in those things it was probably healthier to drink Pine-Sol.

A light in the passenger seat caught Daniel's attention. The horn of the eighteen-wheeler passing by was deafening as he swerved over the centerline.

"What the fuck is that?"

"That's a dollar in the swear jar, mister."

"Goddamn it, Delilah. I'm talking to you."

"Oh. My. God. You have got to chill out. I'm just texting Susannah. Besides, Jeremy is totally cheating on her, and she is like 'no he's not' and I'm like, yeah bitch, he is."

"You've got to get rid of it. Now. Or I will."

"How stupid do you think I am? That piece of junk momma and daddy got me last year is on a charger in the kitchen. This is Tina's old one. She gets a new phone every dang year. All ya gotta do is buy a new sim card with minutes. Cheese and crackers, you act like the FBI is looking for us. Nobody cares."

"I…I just don't want to get caught, that's all."

"Don't bitch out on me now, Dan."

"You're right, I guess."

-A-

Daniel picked the Princess Motel. It was a good head start, two hundred miles from where they began. Besides, Delilah liked the name.

He paid for the room with cash. The clerk didn't blink when he took the money, handing Daniel back his change along with the key.

The room was drab, with beige carpeting and cream-colored walls that blended together like camouflage. There was an old TV mounted to the dresser, its corners worn down to the bare metal. The king size bed sagged in the middle. Pillows with mismatched cases were stacked at the head of the bed against a headboard, so plain it could have been bare wood.

The sound from the bathroom was all too familiar. Daniel could hear Delilah gagging. She had locked the bathroom door behind her with the sink water running. If there were two things Daniel knew for certain that women felt embarrassed about, puking was one of them. The other was taking a shit. To this day, Karen still did her best to go either when Daniel wasn't home or before he got up for work.

Daniel knocked gently on the door. "You alright in there?"

A muffled, "okay, I'm okay," came back so faint Daniel had to press his ear flush to the door to hear it.

"C'mon, Delly. Open the door…please."

Delilah unlocked the door. Cautiously, Daniel pushed the door open. Poor Delilah looked like she'd eaten a bug. She was on the floor with her elbow cocked on the rim of the commode, waiting to vomit again. Daniel leaned over Delilah and pulled her hair back until she was finished.

Delilah's heaves turned into whimpers. Daniel knelt and put her face against his chest, basking in the moment as she allowed him to coddle her, notwithstanding the reek of vomit in the unmoving air.

"Are you okay?" Daniel said.

"Yeah. Something I ate. Feels like it's out."

"Ya wanna go lie down?"

"Okay. Sure," Delilah said.

Daniel helped Delilah to her feet. He subconsciously had led her to what Daniel would have considered Karen's side of the bed.

Delilah raised her arms as Daniel pulled her faded cheer squad sweatshirt over her head. Her hair stood out with static electricity, jutting in fine lines like a spider's web. Underneath her sweatshirt, she wore a black t-shirt with a picture of a wild-eyed cat hurtling through space. Delilah kept her arms raised, waiting until Daniel pulled the t-shirt over her head. He had never seen her like this before, vulnerable, and truly innocent.

Delilah unbuttoned her jeans and pushed off her low-top Chuck Taylor's. She stepped out of the pile naked except for her white panties and a navy blue sports bra. Delilah pulled back the cover and sheet and slid into the bed, taking care to pull her long hair over her shoulder before resting her head against the pillow. She put herself into bed like a child, tucking the cover under her chin with the balls of her fists.

Daniel could hear himself, breathing heavily. He felt drunk with excitement. No fantasy he'd ever had for her could compare with this reality.

"Your turn," Delilah said coyly.

Delilah watched as Daniel undressed himself. He folded his clothes and put them on the dresser next to the TV. First his shirt then his pants. He tucked his socks back into his shoes and ritualistically set them next to the door just as he had a million times at home.

Daniel slid into the bed next to Delilah wearing only his white cotton briefs.

Delilah lay unmoving, staring expressionless at the ceiling while Daniel's hand searched under the covers for Delilah's thigh. He placed his palm against her hip and followed the outline of her panties until his palm was resting on her stomach's soft flesh.

He kissed Delilah softly on the cheek and then her chin while he moved his hand over her bony rib cage until he was cupping her sports bra covered breast. Delilah, aside from breathing and blinking her eyes, simply didn't move.

"Are you okay?" Daniel asked.

"I don't know," Delilah said. "I guess."

For all her bravado and nastiness, all her unfulfilled promises and demands and his blind servitude to please her, Delilah had only been using Daniel. Now that he had called her bluff, she was shit out of luck.

Then Delilah let out a long sigh that infuriated Daniel—she was bored.

Daniel pulled his underwear off and lifted Delilah's stiff body with his left arm, rolling her over onto him, clutching her greedily against his erection.

Delilah was alive again, struggling to free herself. Her resistance pure rapture to Daniel. Black spots danced in explosions behind his clenched eyes as he came. Weak and unable to hold her any longer, Daniel let go and Delilah leapt off him, red faced and disgusted by his semen on her abdomen.

He watched as she dug through her clothes and pulled out the phone, her thumbs tapping swiftly at the screen. Daniel felt bad. Maybe he could apologize. Jewelry always did the trick with Karen. A few hundred dollars for a diamond ring from Walmart seemed like a reasonable place to start.

Without taking a second look at Daniel, Delilah walked across the room and unlocked the door.

"Where the fuck have you been?" Delilah demanded.

You goddamned fool, Daniel moaned silently to himself.

"Whatever. You were supposed to get the money and split. Wait, what's wrong? Did he——"

Delilah was crying now, her words like underwater burbles. Daniel started preparing a plan as soon as he saw the boy. He knew he needed to get out of this room. It was when the other boys crowded the door, big sons of bucks blocking the light of day as they stood behind their buddy when Daniel realized he was most certainly fucked.

Daniel pulled back the covers and stood up naked as the day he was born. The boys looked at him disgusted as Delilah played the victim for her cast of rescuers, burying her face in her hands at the shame of it all.

Daniel made a break for the bathroom. The door wouldn't keep these gorillas at bay for long, but the thumb lock might give him the edge he needed. When they took off to chase him, he would have the advantage. One at a time, and even stark naked, he could knock the shit out of few of them. Together though, he'd be lucky to block their best punches.

The door gave before Daniel could get the small window open. A big blond headed boy hit him with a right cross to the temple. Dazed, Daniel stood there dumbly as another punch devastated his left eye.

Consciousness came in spurts after that.

One-minute blackness, the next excruciating pain as a tooth broke in half, tearing across his tongue. The snap of his elbow being broken like the crack of a bat. A thundering rampage of shoes against his back, his head, his stomach.

The worst of it, though, was Delilah's shouting, "Get him! Kill that son of a bitch!"

-∞A∞-

The hospital room seemed incredibly white each time Daniel woke up. Intensity, the doctor had said, was a side effect of the trauma. It would pass. However, he would never quite be himself again.

It could be worse, Daniel thought. Nobody had said anything about those boys or Delilah. So far, so good, Daniel comforted himself.

He was wondering if he should call Karen, when the door opened.

Pastor Chris and Sister Roselyn came to his bedside with smiles wide as heaven. Sister Roselyn had a bouquet of purple hydrangeas cut from her own flowerbed. Pastor Chris had a "Get Well Soon" card big as a family portrait under his arm signed by the entire congregation.

Sister Roselyn arranged the flowers in a bowl next to Daniel's bed. She consoled him by patting him on the arm saying, "There, there, dear. The worst is over now."

"Mother, would you excuse us," Pastor Chris said touching his wife's arm. "The men need to talk."

Sister Roselyn patted Daniel's arm one more time, then left the room as quietly as smoke through an open window.

Pastor Chris squeezed next to the bed, leaning over until he was close, Daniel thought the pastor might try to climb in with him.

"You rotten son of a bitch," Pastor Chris said. "You're lucky we don't hang you."

Daniel tried to move despite the pain. The bruises, contusions, fractures and breaks were like a prison. Whatever was on the Pastor's mind, Daniel would have to endure.

"If I was Brother Jeremiah, I'd be digging your grave right now. The Lord says, vengeance is mine, I shall repay, but how do you think that sort of thing gets done, Daniel? By men of God, that's how!"

Shock and anger began to twist in Daniel's chest like stripes on a barber's pole. What had Delilah said to save herself?

Daniel could forgive her. He had loved her and always would. Of course, she had one hell of a spanking coming for her part in this shit. The idea of blistering her lying ass briefly caused Daniel a small amount of joy.

His head ached from having to listen to Pastor Chris. If Daniel had fallen off a three-story building and immediately been run over by a train he couldn't have hurt any worse. Those goddamn jocks sure knew how to hurt a guy.

"You are dead to the church. Your name and your family's name have been removed from our rolls. If you show up to a service, deacons will remove you. If you persist, we will involve the authorities. You will be arrested. We will press charges. If it comes down to it, we will put an armed guard at the door.

"Brother Jeremiah's family, however, will be there every Sunday as we worship the Lord, while you have condemned your family to Hell.

"I hope I never see you again, Daniel. If you were on fire, I wouldn't piss on you to put the flames out.

"And if you ever put your hands on any other member of my flock again, I will not hesitate to shoot you between the eyes."

Relieved, Pastor Chris smiled. It was that same 'gosh-I-love-life' smile he wore for parishioners every day. The hypocrite. Pastor Chris was no different from those boys who had beaten him.

Daniel watched Pastor Chris leave. Although the good pastor had not raised his voice, Daniel's ears were ringing. He wished he could scream, to smash those damn flowers, smash their beauty against the wall.

He would not cry, though, this he had promised himself. No matter what, do not cry. That was his dad's solid advice, which was always tempered by his mom's, "For chrissakes, be a man, Danny."

But when Karen walked into the room, Daniel couldn't help himself. In spite of what he had done, Karen had not forsaken him.

-A-

After six months of physical therapy, Daniel could walk crookedly with a cane. His new dental implants felt funny against his tongue. Surgeons had to use cadaver bone to reconstruct his jaw. The pins in his arm were unnoticeable except on an x-ray. In those black and gray pictures, his arm looked like a pincushion.

The doctor said Daniel was lucky his spleen hadn't ruptured, and it was touch-and-go there for a while on his left kidney. Daniel's knee, though, was ruined. The collateral damage of having a broken femur in the same leg, as his doctor said, "A guy couldn't have gotten more unlucky."

The story that Karen told him in the hospital was simple and conniving. Seeing as no one was fingerprinting him, he found it easy to go along with it.

Daniel had been the victim of a vicious carjacking. He had been going to see a piece of property in person, a place where Daniel hoped to build a vacation home. He'd been discovered behind the Donut King across the street from the Princess Motel in Joplin. A twofold miracle, the first his life being saved considering the nature of the beating he had taken, and second, the officer who had come across Daniel was none other than Pastor Chris and Sister Roselyn's son-in-law, Officer Jethro Morris.

Daniel, in spite of the pain, believed he had been lucky, twice as much as any man could ever hope.

There was a long way to go physically. It would take years to regain Karen's trust again, but she sincerely loved him. Now that he thought about it, he loved her, too. She had been kind to Daniel since coming home from the hospital—fed him, helped him bathe, gave him his meds as prescribed, and never again brought up what had happened.

Daniel tried to apologize. No matter how sincere or heartfelt, Karen seemed unfazed by his repentance.

"Karen, I'm sorry. It just got out of hand. It was like I was possessed or something."

"Well, it's over now and you're home. Let's just try and concentrate on that."

Remarkably, Daniel held no feelings of ill will toward Delilah. The sacrifice he'd had made with blood, body parts and pain seemed to cleanse the slate. Despite Delilah's ignorance and greed, she had inadvertently given him the second chance he wanted.

Tonight's party was the ultimate test. Jeremiah and Mary were having a dinner get together. Mary was openly celebrating her sobriety these days. The idea that they could remain friends and put this ugliness behind them was surreal to Daniel. The short walk across the lawn to the neighbor's house was difficult for him, but Karen was with him every step of the way.

By the time Daniel and Karen sat down at Jeremiah and Mary's kitchen table, the sharp needle-like pain was a more manageable fleabite discomfort Daniel could rub away.

"Ready when you are," Mary said sitting down at the kitchen table. She took hold of Daniel's hand and gave it a squeeze. Her smile made him comfortable, and aside from Delilah not being here, the evening was perfect.

Jeremiah brought a pile of meat to the table on a white serving platter as big as an eighteen-wheeler's hubcap. Daniel's mouth watered looking at the succulent buffet of meat. There was enough to feed an army.

"Geesh, guys, is the freezer broke?" Daniel quipped.

Mary answered. "Oh, you know how it is. Tom and Jenny were supposed to come over, but their son Mack has the flu. They're both fine, but the flu this year is a real b-i-t-c-h."

Jeremiah looked concerned over his tumbler of brown liquor at Mary. She had become something of a free spirit since coming home from rehab.

"Oh, poo, don't look at me like that. I spelled it out so that don't count."

Mary and Karen laughed, ignoring Jeremiah.

Leaning close enough to Daniel he could have kissed him on the cheek, Jeremiah tilted his glass back and forth, tempting his neighbor. "Want a snort?" he asked.

"I'm not really sure I should, the meds and all," Daniel said looking to Karen for permission.

"Oh, go ahead. A little nip won't kill ya," Karen said. "Besides, you deserve it."

Daniel smiled at his wife. She was a hell of woman and he certainly didn't deserve her kindness. He didn't deserve any of this.

Daniel felt like such an asshole. The Scotch Jeremiah preferred went down silky and hot, turning on a furnace in Daniel's stomach.

"Delicious," Daniel said trying to hand back the drink.

"Go ahead," Jeremiah. "There's plenty more where that came from."

Daniel looked again to his wife. She smiled and Daniel drank. Life was good.

It occurred to Daniel he hadn't had much to eat today. His head was swirling a bit.

Daniel held the glass in front of him, examining it. All that remained was a razor thin line's worth of the booze. Sure, he was a bit out of shape when it came to getting a buzz, but he couldn't believe how woozy he was beginning to feel. The pill he'd taken before coming over had an express warning on the label not to mix it with alcohol, but this was ridiculous.

"Jesus," Daniel slurred as the world slowly began to spin.

Daniel wanted to talk except what came out was incoherent. It was taking all his strength not to collapse. His wife and friendly neighbors had transformed from carefree dinner guests into steely-eyed gunslingers.

Oh, Christ, Daniel thought. Not again.

"Time to get to work," Jeremiah announced.

-A-

Everything was black, but Daniel was awake. He knew he was because he could hear Karen and Jeremiah's voices.

"I think he's waking up," Karen said.

"'Bout time," Jeremiah said.

"You sure about this?"

"Sure about what?"

"This place… it's not exactly sanitary."

"Karen, you and I both know this is for the best. And you know the deal."

"You're right, you're definitely right about that."

Daniel found it painful to open his eyes. His body seemed paralyzed.

The world was blurry, everything seemed covered in a blanket of fog. Daniel found the weight of his own head tremendous. He could see his arm and hand tied down. Unable to muster the strength it would take to turn his head, he presumed the other to be the same way.

The wide chair he'd been strapped to was like the pews at church, functional but uncomfortable. He could feel the grain of the seat, the coarse wood digging hard against the back of his thighs. The most sobering thought, though, was that from the waist down he was naked.

"Daniel," Karen said. She was close enough that he could smell her perfume.

Daniel willed the fog to lift. They were staring at him. Karen looked worried. Jeremiah, though, was a rock—absolute and without emotion. He was wearing a full-length black leather smock that bisected at him at the shins. Daniel recognized it. The apron was what Jeremiah had worn last year when he had gutted a nine-point buck in their shared backyard.

"What's…going on?" Daniel was relieved to hear his own voice again. "Karen, my leg is hurting. I need my pill."

"Daniel, please," Karen said. "Shut up."

"You put something in that drink."

"No shit, Sherlock," Jeremiah said. "Boy, you ain't as stupid as you look."

"Karen, untie me. Let's go home."

Karen turned away. Daniel could see a rim of tears by the fluorescent light of the garage. She was scared.

Daniel watched as she shook her head, willing the fear away as she walked to the door that led from the garage to the kitchen, leaving Daniel alone with Jeremiah.

"Jeremiah, I'm sorry, I really am," Daniel said. "But you have got to believe me when I say nothing happened."

"Satan, get thee behind me."

"You can stop this now. I get it, you hate me. I'll move. Whatever you want."

"There's nothing you can say, Dan, that can change what you've done."

Daniel stared at Jeremiah. He couldn't think of anything to say. Quietly, he began to whisper to himself the twenty-third Psalm, hoping for a miracle.

"You're praying is just talking out loud, won't work. In fact, it's disgusting to me. You should've stopped when you had the chance, come to the Church and confessed. They could've helped. But now…here we are."

Karen came back through the door carrying a white towel. She was wearing purple rubber gloves, the kind hospitals used. Jeremiah pulled an identical pair from his back pocket and put them on, snapping the latex with sharp, small cracks.

Karen unwrapped the towel on a metal rolling cart. The clatter of surgical steel against the sheet metal was an all too familiar sound to Daniel.

Jeremiah smiled as he handled the instruments, showing them cruelly one at a time to Daniel. He recognized the scalpel instantly. There were two different sized tongs and a box of surgical rubber bands, whatever the hell those were, and some assorted clamps for holding slippery veins in place.

Karen had a syringe. She was drawing a white, milky substance through a rubber cork of a brown bottle smaller than a shot glass. Daniel realized they were about to anesthetize him.

"Oh for Pete sake," Jeremiah said. "He's pissing."

"Don't worry about it. Urine is sterile. Perfectly natural according to the book," Karen said.

The floor crinkled and crunched under Karen's shoes as she brought the needle toward Daniel. Karen pushed the plunger down as the needle punctured Daniel's arm. The drug was Propofol, a fast-acting anesthetic emergency rooms preferred. Of course, you had to be a doctor to have it. The thing about hospitals was that they were busy places and sometimes nurses who regularly worked sixteen-hour days were careless. Daniel understood Karen and Jeremiah had been thinking about doing this for a long time.

"Karen," Daniel groggily whispered. "I'm sorry."

"Please, Daniel, please, please, please just shut up already."

An anesthesiologist would have told Daniel to relax and count backwards from one hundred.

Ninety-nine, ninety-eight, ninety-seven…

-❧A❧-

Daniel watched them through binoculars. He wasn't welcome. It hurt but at least it was clear. A NO TRESPASSING sign had been posted on the west side of the old great oak facing Daniel's house. It provided, as Daniel learned via a letter from an attorney for his neighbors, legal notice. If he violated the sign, the matter would be pursued in court.

A decision had been made among Karen and their neighbors while Daniel was being reconstructed with screws and mortar and parts from cadavers.

Per the attorney, Daniel could be arrested, but the premeditation shown by Delilah, not to escape her captor but to rob him, was just as enforceable. It would all be a matter of public record. The media trolls who hung out in courthouses would love it. It would be scandalous.

Daniel would be branded as a pedophile, go to prison, be unemployable and become a cancer to Karen and the kids. Delilah would likely stand trial as an adult. She'd easily be found guilty and serve a soft two years in a women's minimum correctional, where she could get her high school equivalency diploma and possibly take a few college courses. However, she'd be a felon forever.

The boys Delilah had hired to whip Daniel's ass would also be going down for three to five. They'd become hardened criminals. Their dreams would be filled in like potholes.

All this in the name of justice.

-A-

Jeremiah and Mary were getting fat, growing soft with relief. Their little girl had grown up and gone on to do what was expected of her. She wasn't married but she was engaged to a young man and it looked like she would finally get a new ring along with a new last name.

Daniel sighed and put the binoculars down. Karen had left for the weekend. Daniel suspected she had a boyfriend now, likely one of the real estate agents she'd met working in the title insurance office. Daniel didn't mind so much, as he preferred the peace and quiet when Karen was gone. While his wife was shitting some poor asshole's bonus check down the tubes on a roulette table, and gleefully allowing him to revenge-fuck her later for the loss, Daniel mostly worked in his garage.

Mason Jar

Daniel had subdivided a corner of the garage into a studio. It was his little world where nothing bothered him. A shrink had told him he needed to find something that didn't matter except to him.

Out of frustration, he'd gone to the garage. There was an orange five-gallon bucket with leftover rebar rods from a concrete pad he'd helped Jeremiah pour. The first time Daniel pulled a piece of the eighteen-inch long rod out of the bucket and looked at it, really looked at it, he felt inspired. Something was there. He put it in the vice, and using a piece of pipe he had inherited from Jeremiah as a cheater for prying off frozen lug nuts, Daniel began to shape the metal.

It took all his strength, bending and pulling, but eventually he had something. A month later, Daniel made a sculpture, a plump iron ball of intertwined rebar rods.

Curious if what he had done was bullshit, he dared to enter it in the library's local art show. He won second place, losing to a blurry watercolor by an octogenarian of her beloved Cocker Spaniel. The library gave his name and number to a lady who'd fallen in love with the piece, simply titled "Ball #1." She called, they met, and for the first time in Daniel's life, he had made money doing something he enjoyed.

The workbench, the lights, the pipe bending tools were Daniel's refuge, his private island escape from his suburban nightmare.

His boys were growing up. They hardly needed Daniel for anything more than money, shelter, and food. As for Karen, he knew they were staying together for the kids. Her parents had divorced when she was thirteen and it had been hell on her. Besides, they made better roommates than they ever did spouses anyway. Whereas before, they took each other for granted, they now politely kept their distance from each other—Daniel out of guilt and Karen out of shame and anger.

In a way, Daniel was happy. Things had worked out for the best. They certainly could've been much worse.

Daniel turned on the grinder with its large, thick red wheel. The sound of the machinery filled the air with an industrial hum. He put on his faded yellow leather work gloves. The angle iron he was working with screamed, sending a shower of sparks into the air like a fountain on the Fourth of July.

On a shelf high above Daniel's head, one he couldn't reach except when he stood on a stepladder, there were models he'd built from strips of sheet metal, trimmed and shaped with tin snips of found objects like the paperclip used to by the DMV clerk when he got his handicap plates.

There, among the shapes twisted together, against the wall and almost invisible, was a small Mason jar commonly referred to by folks as a jelly jar.

The gold top, like all metal in this garage, had begun to oxidize with rust.

Inside the jar, pickled and preserved for eternity, were Daniel's testicles. A reminder he rarely thought to look at nowadays.

It simply was best not to think about how things might have been.

The Valley of Tigers

Anthony Worman

NIGHT

I

One night, in my mid-twenties, when I was living in Seoul as an English teacher, I decided to ride my bike home after several hours of drinking. It was already late, but one could never tell with the bright lights of the city washing away the veil of night.

The city of Seoul never slept. Private karaoke rooms were open all night, so were countless 24-hour bathhouses, fried chicken joints and dim, underground pubs. The nightlife would thrive all night, without hesitation, even after the first rays of sun peeked from over the mountain-lined horizon.

Around midnight I could tell it was going to be one of those nights: our group would be out all night and we'd drunkenly disperse only after the first trains started running in the morning. I probably could make it another hour or so, but my body craved the comfort of being in a soft bed, even if it would take me two hours to ride home by bike.

I suggested to the group that we split the cost of a taxi, but nobody else had any desire to go. With considerable difficulty, I was able to break away from the pressure of feeling obligated to have just one more drink. And so, it began, my 40-kilometer bike ride out of the city. I had taken this route countless times during daylight, but never so late, never after sunset. I'd ridden into the city earlier that day with plans to head back before sunset, had I not run into a group of old friends picnicking along the river. I was riding westward along the riverside around noon when I heard some people shouting my name, “Hey! Toine! Over here!” I slowed my bike and glanced around. Sure enough, there were four of my hiking pals snacking and drinking along the river.

It was then that my day took a turn for the unexpected. I joined them for some rice balls and marinated beef and raw vegetables, locking my bike up at a rack nearby. From there we joked around by the river and tossed a frisbee by some landscaped gardens. It was a perfect late summer day and yellow daisies, pink hibiscus and lavender were in full bloom. Before we knew it, dusk had approached, and we proceeded to make our way into the nearby college district to have some barbecue ribs for dinner.

Ribs and shots of soju propelled a profuse but circular conversation about global trade and earnest travel recommendations. The restaurant was very noisy: the din of people shouting over and at each other, a hyperactive waitstaff frantically serving everybody, dishes clanking on tables and glasses clanging as people cheersed and shouted, vociferously enjoying the good times. I don’t remember a thing we talked about after the debate, but it must not have been very important, because I only remember feeling the lifeblood circulating all of us, our faces flushed, our thoughts exaggerated and the calm of my riverside bike ride just a distant memory from a sunny afternoon long ago.

It wasn’t until we left the restaurant and finished two more rounds, at two other nearby bars, that I finally decided to depart. I was strongly persuaded to stay, to have one more round, to enjoy myself, but I could feel the fatigue setting in and strongly desired to sleep in my bed. I resolved to say my goodbyes and return to the bike rack by the river.

The air was cool, a crisp late summer break from the mild humidity of the day. I took a deep breath and stared at the moon. It was a giant ivory orb glowing as bright as the sun, an unusually illuminating tone that might have been inviting to werewolves. It helped to imagine my journey as something even more adventurous, and with such a long ride ahead I welcomed these inventions as a sort of insurance for the monotony of the dark ride ahead.

Satiated, tipsy and feeling not quite as inebriated as I probably was, I put the bike chain in my day pack, mounted the bike and turned back east, against the current of the Han River. The Han River bike trail was completely free from car traffic. It was a paved path weaving through parks, underpasses, bridge ramps, gardens, and recreation areas the whole way down—a visionary accomplishment of city planning. I would be riding on a paved path wide enough for eight to ten bikers to travel together side by side, had they tried to do so. After the first fifteen kilometers, I would turn north from the city, riding paved trails that would fade into small stretches of road and then turn into a network of farm paths weaving among rice paddies and greenhouse tents. The town I taught English in was an isolated little hamlet in the midst of transforming into a towering city of high-rises, about twenty-five kilometers north of the eastern city limit.

II

The city lights whirred past me as I picked up speed, the chill of the wind felt refreshing on my flushed skin. The dark ripples of the river reflected lights like a disco floor. The city was above me, casting shadows as I passed under the occasional bridge. The trees and shrubs along the path had become dark shadows of themselves. They protected the bike trail from the cement wall that rose up to the city. Only the roar of traffic from high above, which had settled into a hum, broke the illusion of tranquility. Across the river, tall buildings clustered into groups gave authority to the night, like beacons for lost ships. I was the only bike rider on the trail. The river banks were sparsely populated with couples seeking refuge from the city, cuddling up in private enclaves along the embankments of the river at night.

The night was a comforting blanket. It enveloped me and protected me as much as it hid everyone and everything else. I felt safe in this cloak, riding at my own pace, steadily accelerating as I gained confidence in the stillness of my surroundings. The couples dwindled as I rode further from the city, as did the frequency of light-shadows across the river. The bright yellows, reds and greens of the lights became less frequent and there was an increase in colorlessness. Under the moon, everything became blue, and in the shade, color was lost completely. Even trees and water turned black, becoming defined only by their shapes as outlines against the blue-black night.

The overpasses grew quiet, too. I felt calm. The din of the restaurant seemed far away and long ago, yet the excitement still vibrated through the looseness of my nerves. Time had already passed at a rate inconsistent with the earlier hours. The time-factors of riding a bike and traversing a novel landscape at night were multiplied by the variables of doing so in a country that was not my own. Time-rates seemed to change whenever I landed at an airport to another country.

When I first put my feet on the foreign ground of the Korean peninsula, something characteristic of that land began to take hold. It was not linked to the architecture, or the sounds, or even the smells. It's a feeling derived from the detection of a wholly new and nuanced set of norms channeled by every interacting person bound to the ground by the parameters of gravity and place.

Granted that people have souls, those souls are echo chambers for the social boundaries of the surrounding society and culture. If people don't have souls, they might also lack a social and cultural frequency. A culture without souls would feel like an empty field. It would be dead, inert, approaching extinction, coalesced into stone.

The soul of Korea at night took on a different air, calmer and more decompressed than the tiger-soul that pulsed during the day. If Seoul is the city that never sleeps, then its soul at night is calm and chaotic, opposed to the frenzied approach to order during the day. This soul emerges as drunks pass out, desires are met, and the exhausted slip from the conscious into the unconscious.

As I rode my bike, the calm took control, rice paddies soaked, and a chilly stillness promised that anything could happen.

III

I turned on to a tributary of the Han and made my way upstream. In the stillness of night I rode, not a soul in sight nor a sound to be heard. Even the flow of the river was quiet. As I steadied into a rhythm I sort of lost myself, pedaling in a meditative trance that negated all conscious thought. The hypnotic night induced this peculiar sort of zen. The path was flat and straight. I proceeded without distraction.

The nocturnal promise of my bed tantalized me. It was still so far away. The alcohol drew out my metabolism and the pedaling wore away at my quads. I grew increasingly numb and increasingly alert in the dark. My focus sapped my motivation, and my desire to sleep became more immediate. The initial shot of adrenaline that had fueled the early ride had worn off. I was now stranded in the middle of a monotonous journey. A slight incline crept under me as I wobbled and powered forward. Upwards I went, steadily, frustratingly, coveting the soft mattress that seemed only to exist in my imagination when suddenly a red-white ball of fur leapt on to the path. It materialized hardly a meter in front of me. A long, bushy tail, nearly as long as its body, appeared then quickly scurried off. Was it a fox?

I halted the second I saw it, putting both my feet on the ground, and now it was gone. Had I imagined the whole thing? I questioned my perception at this point. In search of an answer, I convinced myself that there was no way I would have fabricated such a thing. This animal had no significance to me, not here. The fox might have had mythic meaning in this land, but to me its mythos was as obscure as a bear-woman or a zelkova tree.

IV

Enervated by the subtle thrill, I kept going deeper into the darkness. It grew darker as I rode northward, away from the city lights. The city continued to emit a distant glow behind me, a glow that became more concealed by the mountains as I rode further from it. Yet it never completely went out, softly polluting the night from its concealed source behind the mountain horizon.

Night was darker out here. Had it not been for the moonlight, I might not have been able to see anything at all. Stars perforated a small slice of the sky, but clouds concealed them in one direction while the distant light pollution behind me concealed them in the other. Almost everything seemed a contour of a shadow, a shape colored black or deep-blue. My night vision was still sharp, and I could not imagine the unfilmable darkness that would soon engulf me, a darkness so complete that it could only be felt or trespassed through a veil that does not let anyone out.

A small town was visible in the distance, some five meters ahead. A light from somewhere in it glowed. The glow was faint and flickering, more orange than yellow. Individual windows were sharply outlined in contrast to the night, which seemed not only darker than the urban glow of Seoul but darker than anything I could remember in these parts. I could not remember this town but was happy to see it disrupting the darkness encroaching my path. A town meant that larger buildings were likely nearby, and that the suburbs of my remote neighborhood wouldn't be too far off. Still, I did not remember this town. I didn't dwell on it long enough to question why the glow from those high-rises was absent. Had I taken a different route? If I had, it couldn't have led me too far away, or so I rationalized, because there was only one main artery of bike trail along this one tributary—only one—that ultimately led to my bustling satellite suburb in the northeast valleys of mountainous, greater Seoul.

The mountains enclosed me on all sides. If I had somehow taken the wrong path, I had no idea where I would be or what tributary I was along, or how it could have existed given the mountainous geography I was familiar with leading up this way. Regardless, I kept riding. I was hopeful that this new route would eventually connect with the circuit of roads I knew, the ones that would lead me back to my soft bed. There was no way I was going to backtrack all the way to the source of my error, only to continue navigating my way after adding an unknown amount of distance on to my tired journey. It was late, now, probably past two or three. I could not check the time because my phone had died.

I stopped and looked at the black screen on my phone, somehow hoping I could turn it back on. I pressed and held the button for several seconds. Nothing. I glanced at my reflection on its black surface. Reflected in the dimming moonlight, everything seemed darker than it should. I had no "control" memory to test its variability against, no measure of darkness over time or relative to space. I couldn't tell if this was a testament to my poor night vision or the weight of the darkness.

Hesitantly, I started pedaling again. The bike felt more deadweight now than the bike I had come to know. Tired and hungry, I wanted to discard it even knowing I could not get anywhere without it. The town was getting closer. It was quaint and let itself be seen only by lamplight. The town did not have any high-rises. It could only be a small farming town. I was surprised it had been out here in the solitude of the mountains this whole time. Surely no one ever came out this way. I couldn't imagine this enclave lasting much longer. The big city lights drew out younger generations in greater numbers every year.

I had been through small farming villages before, in isolated valleys buffered by endless arrays of rice paddies. They were living history. Something great would be lost if they disappeared completely. Their untold serenity characterized the land as if they were living art, centuries-old landscape paintings informing the present about something simple and pure.

V

What made the town spectacular was its simplicity. The single-level traditional-style houses were points on a plane of rice paddies connected by segments of dirt roads. At this time of night the air was still. Fields of crops quietly emitted a stillness of sustenance. It was like any one of those other small Korean towns, quaint, food-producing, humble. This locality was oblivious to the onslaught of globalization sweeping the rest of the globe. Maybe its people didn't even believe in a globe. In the dark, the town was so still that I felt like an intruder coming near it. As I approached I felt a knot in my gut. I was nervous. Why should I be nervous? This was just a quiet, Korean village.

I could not grasp the danger awaiting in the night. I could not fathom the history that lived in an enclave, as full of life as the mountains and trees secluding it. I passed a colony of rabbits on the side of the bike trail. They were white and grey. There were about a dozen of them eating the grass that grew where the edge of the asphalt met the soil. As I approached them they grew scared and hopped away. Somehow this emboldened me, and I felt a rush of courage as I approached the town.

Closer to the town, I noticed two men in uniform standing on each side of the road. Each one had a flat-topped hat on with a red band around its base. I slowed my pedaling, removed my feet from the wheels, then suddenly stomped them down to come to a quick and complete stop. I could not see the whites of their eyes, couldn't tell if they had seen me, although with such a straight line of sight they must have known that somebody was coming. What kind of town was this, an army holdout? I took these guards as evidence that I was somewhere I should not be.

VI

I couldn't turn around to ride away from the soldiers. My curiosity was taking hold of me. For a moment, I looked back down the dark path I came up on. The trees rustled in the darkness and the emptiness promised nothing. My physical and mental state had been eroding, and I was hesitant to ride either way, the guards' foreboding presence weighing on me in a peculiar way. I allowed myself to come to another standstill, immobilized as if part of me knew something another part didn't. My body was so worn out I even thought about sleeping along the path right there. I grasped for the best solution and finally, in my desperate yearning to find the shortest and easiest way to get to my bed I decided to ride up to the guards and ask them what I could do. Maybe they'd let me ride through.

I put my feet back on the pedals and pedaled slowly, not much faster than a walk. As I rolled closer, the soldiers did not move. They stared at me intensely. I looked the taller one in the eye. I saw duty, but no compassion. I asked him, in my elementary Korean, "How do I get to Jinbeoli from here?" He continued to stare at me, stern and imperceptive. He said something. I did not understand anything. It was not Korean. He had a different sound palette. He spoke mutedly and stoically, but something was off. The other man nodded. What was going on? Something was wrong. I felt a hand grab my arm from behind. It pulled me back with force. These men were speaking not Korean, but Japanese. Closer than before, I could make out the details. They were not wearing national uniforms, they were wearing dark-colored tunics.

I was aggressively pulled off my bike from behind the two soldiers. The bike clattered to the ground. Who wanted to hurt me? I lost track of my thoughts. I was on high alert, but also had no idea what was happening. Another rush came over me and I was ready to do anything necessary, without sense or context. I had absolutely no time to rationalize. I regretted not turning back to the city. The arm that had grabbed me from behind pushed me away with substantial force. I was pushed for several meters and stumbled over rocks and down the embankment to the tributary that I had been following this whole time. It was steep. I rolled for several meters on cold rocks, giving no resistance, too confused to figure anything out or decide on any action.

Ultimately, I came to rest in a cool trickle of shallow water over smooth stones. I laid still for a moment under the stars, wondering where the moon went. A black, curled tree branch watched over me like a wicked arm, as if I had fallen into some sort of nightmare.

What had happened? I looked up, both fatigued and fully alert, physically bracing myself for a counter attack. Then, I suddenly ducked—but there was nothing to avoid—just a phantom of my imagination. Really, I had no idea what to expect and tried to embrace for anything. I was panicked and afraid. Calming myself, I listened. The roll of Japanese consonants and vowels sounded familiar, if not a little more ancient, more slurred, deeper, and more formalized than the Japanese I was used to hearing. There seemed to be a negotiation going on up above. I could only imagine what they were talking about. Was I an anomaly, a white-skinned man in shorts, riding a bike, who spoke bad Korean with a Western accent? Or had I simply violated a rule by speaking Korean and not Japanese? Was I not supposed to be outside the town at night? I surmised that I could have broken any number of laws, and probably more than one.

The voices raised to a shout, and then I heard a loud noise, alien to me on this peninsula: a gunshot. It was so loud and ruptured the night like an earthquake. I fell on the rocks below me. My fight or flight response suddenly took hold, flight being the definitive mode of action. I got up and started running as softly and quickly as I could down the river, back towards where I came from. Endorphins kicked in and gave me another stress-high. In the darkness and under the partial cover of the river bank, I had some advantage of getting away from this horror without any more trouble.

Suddenly, another loud boom. A spatter of mud smacked the back of my calf. There was no mistaking that they were aiming at me. I did not look back. I ran. I stumbled, crawled, and regained my balance when another shot echoed even louder through the night. I nearly fell over again from the sound. I felt no splash or debris this time. I could not delay any longer. As I fumbled and ran, I remembered a short story about a man escaping a group of armed men by jumping into a river and swimming to safety under the protective cover of the water, which softened the bullets by reducing their speed. From deep under the water, he could see the bullets slow to harmless droplets and rain down in slow motion.

Decisions driven by panic are instantaneous. All I thought was that I did not want a bullet in the back of my skull. I dashed frantically into the water, shoes and all, and continued to go under as deep as I could. I was fully swimming now, as bullets hit the water around me, making odd "gulp" sounds a fraction of a second after each loud, explosive burst of gunpowder. The explosions were muffled now and sounded as if they were underwater and not me. I stroked my arms outward and back, outward and back as I swam in the dark water. I couldn't see anything and didn't bother trying to open my eyes and hoped that I was headed in the right direction. The downstream current was my only guide to safety. The water felt colder now, and for a moment I worried about how I would recover later—when a muffled "boom" and an immediate "gulp" landed louder and closer than before, and I thought I felt a warm stinging sensation land on my lower back. I refocused, feeling the direction of the river and guiding myself along with it as fast as I could.

Breathing had become a voluntary act, and I held the air in with more willpower than I had ever used before. I felt pressure push against my diaphragm from the inside-out. My head felt light and all I could think about was nothingness as I saw flashes of red. I felt myself losing control of the organs of my body.

I stayed underwater and swam for as long as I could. I had no idea how far I had gone. I finally resurfaced for air after the gunshots had gone silent. I could not know whether the soldiers had abandoned their pursuit, and I could not see anything in this darkness except for shadows of curled tree branches. The arms reached for me from all directions, and I wondered when one would wrap a cold, dark hand around me and pull me into another nightmare. I noticed a thick cluster of curled trees on the opposite shore of the river further downstream. There were wide, shadowy trunks. I jumped out of the river and into the haven of wooded protection. Pausing, I steadily regained my breath, not without a good amount of fear and paranoia. Soaking wet, I briskly walked through the thicket as far and deep as I could.

I heard no more gunshots as I jogged, but still I jogged to be safe. Branches grabbed me, tugged at my arms and scratched my legs and face. I fought them with explosive strength while others snapped and cracked against me. My shoes made a loud squish every step I took. My clothes were cold and wet, yet my body heated up. I breathed furiously until I could not breathe anymore. When I could no longer breathe, I could no longer move. At this point, I leaned against a gingko tree. It was an old tree. The familiarity of this tree grounded me.

I felt a weight in my pocket, heavier than what I remembered being there. I reached in and my hand stuck to the wet fabric. I pulled out my phone. It was still a hand-sized rectangle but now it was a slab of rock. No face, nothing to differentiate its front from its back. It looked like an oversized paperweight. There was no reflection upon it, not even in the moonlight that shone through the tree.

I felt something move inside my shirt, as well. I jumped back and swatted myself, suddenly startled at the muscular kicking and scraping and fur against my abdomen. I hopped back and flapped my arms. When I pulled up my shirt, a tiny, wet rabbit hopped out and fell to the ground. It did not hop away, but rather looked at me, as if lost, hoping that I could feed it or help it find its way. I looked it in the eye. The rabbit stared back, still. Seeming to understand, it hopped toward me. As I extended a finger it extended its snout toward me. I felt more relaxed, and then more tired, and realized that I had to get dry and warm and find somewhere to sleep. I had given up all hope of sleeping in my warm bed tonight.

VII

In an attempt to stay warm, I shed my clothes and wrung them out before going any further. I set the rock slab in my pocket atop a ball of roots protruding from a nearby tree. The rabbit sat on the ground and studied me as if it were creating an hypothesis on human behavior. My shorts and shirt were both made of cotton, and their cheapness was now getting revenge on me. I slapped my shoes against the same sturdy gingko tree to excise as much water from them as I could, making a loud *thwap* with each slap. Without my phone being a phone anymore, I had no idea what time it was. My biological clock told me it must be well past midnight. I considered the rabbit who was studying me and wondered if it could have some use or meaning to me. After quiet rumination, I didn't think so, at least until I got so hungry.

After reluctantly putting my damp clothes back on over my goose-bumped skin, I decided to move on. I was worried about my safety, so I proceeded away from the tributary and back towards the city. Maybe I could find a public bathhouse and rest there for a while. Most were open twenty-four hours. If I could spend the night there, I would refresh myself and catch a commuter train back home in the morning. My best odds would be finding a bathhouse closer to the city. I continued barefoot, my shoes still soaked despite my thwaps.

Beneath my feet the dirt and branches crunched and pricked my soft skin. It felt quite good. The soil was soft and cool, but not cold. I considered the round moon overhead. It was bright, like a quarter-shaped bioluminescent organism in the sky. On the moon there was an outline of a rabbit, pounding rice into cakes. The stars in the sky resembled familiar arrangements. Astronauts landed on the moon in 1968. How underappreciated it has become, how mundane. Was it possible for a man to walk on the moon, and would anyone ever do it again? The sky presented a sort of sacred anchor for me, my knowledge of it limited by everything anyone had ever taught me about it. I proceeded through these dark woods, tired, chilly, and increasingly hungry.

Barefoot and hopeful, I walked the earthen ground over roots and sticks, the rabbit inexplicably hopping two strides behind me. Finding the city again did not seem like a certainty. Its urban glow from the other side of the mountains had disappeared. I justified this as a trick of the moonlight. I worried that it did not exist anymore or hadn't been built. This unreal hypothesis weighed on me with an irrational complexity. I resisted it by weighing the meaning of things I could perceive with my senses. I had kept my slab of rock in my pocket as an anchor to what I knew, used the moon as my spiritual leader, and took comfort in the nature of the earth and trees surrounding me. The rabbit behind me didn't bother me but didn't comfort me either. Without any idea of what to make of it, I led it with confidence into the forest. This rabbit, with its deliberation and careful study, reminded me more of a raven than any rabbit I had ever met, yet it was a rabbit. A sort of love washed over me. I respected the rabbit.

-A-

Beneath the canopy of trees, darkness sheltered its silent dwellers from moonlight. There came a cackling and a murmuring from off in the distance. The rabbit stopped before I did, and his ears stood up. The sounds were deep baritone voices, reverberating in rhythms that sounded like thoughts. There was a continuity to them that was unmistakably human. Their voices were also guttural, slurred and accented, as if from some distant time before the modern Korean accent. I copied Rabbit's listening stance by trying to discern the characteristics of the murmuring tongues—were they safe or threatening? Rabbit and I noticed a faint flickering coming from the same direction as these sounds. A muted red-orange that resembled the color of flames reflected on tree trunks in the distance. We were careful not to make a sound. I noticed several *imnidas* and *haseyos*, distinct sound patterns of the Korean tongue.

The sound of a semi-familiar language brought relief and comfort. They should not want to kill me, or at least I hoped. I looked at Rabbit and Rabbit looked at me. I guess we hoped we would give each other permission to proceed. We were both lost and tired and sought refuge and hoped someone could lead us. In Rabbit's eyes I read something of a "let's go," and I wondered if he interpreted the same thing from me.

VIII

As we approached the small group of Koreans by the fire in the woods, they looked at us with fear and doubt. They peered at us through the flames with red and orange flickering faces. I was equally fearful and doubtful. Rabbit, being the only non-human creature among us, was the only one brave enough to make a move. It hopped naturally to the bare feet of one of the three men behind the flames and sniffed his toes. They were all dressed in rags covered in dirt. Their faces were rugged, callous and blotchy. They held their stare at me while rabbit examined their smells.

And then they started to speak amongst each other in a dialect of Korean I could not understand. Rabbit watched. One man glanced back and forth between me and his companions. He turned to his fireside friends and began to talk. He seemed to have made his point, which stirred up some fury in the man to his side. The other man raised his voice and pointed his arms frantically to make his point, seeming almost unable to control himself. The middle man nodded in agreement of both sides, then interrupted with his own statement, gesturing at the rabbit, who watched them intently. I wondered whether the rabbit understood, whether it sensed danger or something else.

I studied the men, and they studied me. Finally, one of them said something. It was accented thickly in a rural drawl, an accent that did not belong in the pulsating, densely-packed towns of twenty-first century Korea. It was a voice that had fermented a long time ago, saturated with life. Listening to him was like eating a full-bodied, organic cabbage. I did not understand a word. I ran the code through my head, desperate to decipher something, anything. No. No luck, I thought about my response. I hesitated, then spoke, with as much an apologetic inflection as I could, with the appropriate polite ending: *Please, sir, I do not understand.*

From there, the man who had the floor unleashed a rapid string of words more slurred than anything that came before. He continued to go on as my thoughts wandered. These men, if they were as much an embodiment of history as they sounded, might have had no exposure to any other language besides their own. They had no idea of "another language," how it could exist, or how it could work. My hopes of being comprehended might take months, or years.

My role, I imagined now, was to be as compassionate and passive as possible. I did not in any way want these men to confuse me for an aggressor. My survival *depended* on it. I acted like a guest in their home. I should offer them a gift, I thought. I had a pair of wet shoes and a rock slab in my pocket, both of which I wouldn't mind doing away with. My shoes, though wet, were performance-brand hiking shoes. My rock slab, while not a phone, was a well chiseled piece of rock that might be of use in some unforeseeable context.

At the end of the man's spiel, he turned silent and receptive. I could offer no words. The other two men fidgeted impatiently. I had still been holding my shoes, so I set them down. I did not impose myself and communicated my willingness to accept them. *Shoes*, I said, in Korean. *Gift*, I followed, also in Korean. These words were basic words, old words and simple words. I wagered that if my words hung in the air long enough they would transcend the moment and the minds of the men, into unknown space.

My offering of wet shoes rested on the soft ground. Rabbit approached them. Everyone watched the shoes and the animal carefully. The eyes of the men followed the rabbit, paying attention to every detail. The rabbit stopped at the shoes, sniffed them and thoroughly examined them. The rabbit looked at the three men, as if it were transmitting a message to them. No one knew what to do. The men shifted their bodies awkwardly. They became silent.

IX

The three Korean men are named Sung, Jo, and Hyuk. They are by the fire in the woods, discussing the mysterious outsider who has presented himself before them.

"Do you think he is dangerous?"

"No, he is not dangerous. He is not aggressive."

"He might be a spy. What do you think, he could be tricking us, right?"

"No, I don't think so. He is alone and unarmed. He is offering us a gift."

Sung, the man on the left, denied the gift. No, he said. Instead, he asked, "Where are you from?" The outsider seemed to understand this, but hesitated. Sung asked again. The outsider simply said he was a foreigner. This did not help. Was he dumb? How could he not know where he was from? "Are you Japanese?" Sung asked. The outsider said, no, he was not Japanese. He would not say where he was from.

Hyuk, the man on the right, shouted impatiently: "Who are you!? Where are you from!? Why do you come here!?" Taken aback, the outsider balked. "Beautiful-country" he finally said. Ha! What is that!? The United States of America, translated into Korean, is derived from two Chinese characters: beauty 美 and country 国. These men, probably local farmers who had no worldly experience, had never heard of such a place. Therefore, there was no translation for such a word.

"Beautiful country! Ha! What is that? Is that where gods come from?"

"He must be insane. But he is scared."

"Yeah, right. I don't trust anyone who doesn't speak."

"He brings gifts. And look, he is accompanied by the rabbit. That is a sign."

"It's just a rabbit, not a sign. We should eat it, if anything."

The rabbit was the medium mediating the two isolated worlds. It hopped over to the skeptic who wanted to eat it and nuzzled his bare foot. Then, after a pause of wonder and consideration, returned to the outsider and rubbed its snout against his still exposed foot. No one was wearing any shoes. The rabbit, if anything, was not food, but a third party to the two human tribes. It was outside of reason, an irrational mediator. If it was not a sign, it was at least a peaceful presence, an accepting third, free of judgment, incapable of wrath, not a symbol of peace or war but a stand-in circumventing disorder and disintegration.

X

The young stranger in a strange land was welcomed into the tribe of three men gathered by the fire in the woods. They did not have much food to eat, and they were all considerably tired. It was late in the night. The fire was dying and as the embers glowed, images faded. One man would stay awake to keep watch as the others slept. Toine, granted the opportunity of sleep under their protection, suddenly realized how tired he was. He might fall asleep sitting right where he was, hardly able to bear all the aching muscles in his body, with all his other systems having been exerted beyond their means. He was *burnt out*. What a night, he thought to himself. It took all his remaining energy to lift himself up and lie down on the soft dirt surrounding the embers. The embers felt warm and inviting. He could relax. He listened to and tried to decode the exchanges in Korean. He guessed that they were deciding who would take the next watch, and he imagined the exact words they might be using by recalling the memories of a Korea he knew from before. He imagined one man not understanding the other, asking to clarify what he meant, then disagreeing with his terms, negotiating, and restating the newly modified conditions. He felt something soft cuddle by his feet and imagined that it could be the rabbit. It must be the rabbit. The rabbit was rubbing his foot, and it lulled him into a deep sleep.

As Toine's mind abandoned conscious thoughts to a deeper, unconscious control he solemnly imagined rabbits and men fighting each other, as if at war. The war was brutal. A man picked a rabbit up off the ground that had been aggressively gnawing at his toes. The man's toes were covered in blood. The man ripped the limbs off the rabbit, and then other rabbits hurried to flank the man, using their sharp teeth as weapons to bite him wherever they could. Where his skin was not exposed, they would tear at his clothes, spitting pieces of fabric out before ripping off strips of flesh.

They did not eat the flesh, though. Rabbits began climbing on top of other rabbits to get at the thighs and the waist of their prey. There were thousands of rabbits climbing over other rabbits to take him down, only it was no longer a man, because its head was not a human head, but began to take on the form of a tiger. The tiger's face showed no human expression of fear or mercy, but simply a predatory expression that lacked inhibition and moral discretion.

The anthropomorphic tiger began flinging rabbits off its human body, tossing them out of its mouth as it swung its head and released them from its fangs swiftly. Rabbits continued to climb and bite, and the tiger-man continued to tear them away with his fangs. Thousands of strips of flesh covered in orange fur hung and bled, sore and exposed. The tiger-man suddenly leapt on to all fours, his body no longer resembling that of a man, but that of a full-blown tiger, and began taking rabbits in its mouth two to three at a time, aggressively whipping them this way and that, its powerful neck muscles inflating to the size of pipes. He thrusts rabbits several meters up and over, some of them hitting the ground with loud thuds. The tiger's neck muscles pulsed as it ripped through the sea of rabbits, their white fur slowly turning to red under splashes of blood from all the damaged bodies falling around them. The army of rabbits extend to the horizon, and the lone tiger's odds seemed slim, but he continued to fight for its life with fang and claw.

The rabbits did not look like rabbits anymore. Their natural state started to take on a wretchedness. Their eyes appeared envious, their paws fingerlike, their snouts less perceptive. They leapt with an awkward gait, less elegant than their natural hopping. Their hind legs grew longer, less coordinated. Some stumbled as they tried to lunge in their attack, falling face-first into the ground. The tiger now could move about more freely, less encumbered by the relentless onslaught of rabbits. The tiger bit and clawed, clearing a path wide enough that it could leap from the ground. It leapt into a tree so that it could get of view of the rabbit army it would have to kill. It saw rabbits all the way to the horizon, to no end, their white furs bouncing and fumbling with a fervor that this tiger could never match. The tiger knew it would need friends to help him fight. From deep within the tiger's throat, a sound like a growl unfurled.

What started as a slow purr amplified into a full growl, which steadily grew in volume until the whole field of rabbits came to a halt, their ears not perked up but bent downward as if to protect themselves from the offensive noise. The roar was full and uninhibited, bordering on infinite. It blocked out all noise. It silenced everything. Tigers from the furthest corners of the peninsula could hear it and knew what it meant. It was a call to arms. Suddenly, every tiger in the land rushed towards this one valley full of rabbits. They leapt over mountains and towns and rivers.

They approached the rabbit army from all sides, flanking their perimeter and ripping the creatures apart limb from limb. The tiger in the tree was wounded, and hid. He watched a bleeding redness permeate the perimeters of the field. The concentration of rabbits lessened as trampled grass and dirt emerged. This dirt was drenched in blood, too, which colored it a brownish, purplish red. The concentric circle of earth widened as less rabbits held their ground.

Suddenly, the tiger felt enormous guilt, the weight of loss you would feel only by admitting murderous guilt. Its fur retracted as a smooth, porous skin spread over him. The tiger began to remember who it once was. It felt a conscience unlike it had ever felt before. It felt both helpless and responsible. It was responsible for the death of the rabbit. No one would ever know that any such thing as a rabbit had ever lived, and the tiger would live on as its species inherited the earth, responsible for the eradication of rabbit without penalty. Whoever needed rabbits, anyway? They were only ever just a delightful snack, tasty detritus from an abundant world of food. No, it did not matter. Rabbits could disappear forever, and no one would know the difference. The world might even be better off without them.

The guilt nagged at him, no matter how hard he tried to ignore it. The pain ebbed and returned. This had happened. Consciousness could not explain it away. It was an extinction and a genocide.

No, this tiger thought, I must do something. The tiger leapt down from the tree and, on all fours, straightened his legs to elongate his body to maximize the intake of air before letting out another echoing growl. In fear of it not being heard, the tiger released every last volume of air from its lungs. No sound. Nothing came out but a human-sounding plea of hopelessness and frustration. It was pathetic.

The whole species of tiger now allied with bear, bird, and all other carrion-eaters to eliminate the malformed rabbit-species from the land. They picked at rabbit carcasses, cached them in hidden trees, feasted on them for days, and left them there to rot. The tiger tried again to make a sound, but nothing came out. It tried one last time in anguish and desperation, then sighed, and resigned to its exasperated state. At least it was safe to stay in the tree. The rabbits ran to their death as unforgiving predators stopped them at the perimeter. Unless they found somewhere to hide, they would all die. The tiger slumped in defeat, its victory having come at such a high and unimaginable cost. It was a psychic cost only known to him and the rabbits. It was a chimeric man-tiger now. It was fundamentally a different kind of creature. It was guilty, remorseful, sad, defeated. It fell to the ground without making a noise. It was alone and no one would ever notice it again because it was not a tiger or a man, but an anomaly. It held his abdomen and curled into the fetal position. It felt nauseous. The only thing it could do now to stave off the pain was to fall asleep.

XI

Toine suddenly woke up on the cold dirt by the burnt embers to painful bright rays of sunlight. All the men were gone. It must have been dawn, the sun being low in the sky, still clear and powerful. He had never dreamt so vividly before. He stood up instantly, looking around on high alert. He hated the feeling he had awoken to, that vivid dream stirring him so disturbingly. He wanted to run away from it as far as he could, but it was just a dream. He thought that maybe he would forget it, but also knew that he could not afford to forget it, and that the power of this nightmare would stay with him no matter how hard he tried to hide from it. He hated this feeling.

He looked for the rabbit that had been sleeping where his feet had been, but even the rabbit was gone. He was in the same spot of forest he remembered from last night, though it looked substantially different in the daylight than it had at night, and now it was deserted of human and animal life. Only the trees remained. Toine studied them carefully to see if they had changed, but he could not tell.

He was wearing the same clothes, his shoes off to the other side, where the fire had been, were still there. The men must have left them. Perhaps they were too big to fit them. He was bewildered. He only had one task: to get home, to get somewhere safe. He was a vagrant in the middle of the woods. Alone again, he had to decide which direction to make his way. Broad daylight flooded the forest. He could either try to walk back to his apartment, try to find his bike and ride back, or go back into Seoul and catch a train.

He decided against navigating his way back to his apartment on foot. He briefly considered retracing his way towards where he was forced to abandon his bike but rejected that idea out of uncertainty. The best option for him at this point—the best and quickest way for him to get home—was to go back in the general direction of the city and catch the train back at the first station he came to. Finding the city should be easy enough. He knew the shape of the mountains that marked the direction where it had been and would walk towards them until things began to become familiar again. He slipped his shoes back on and began to walk.

NATURE

XII

The morning was quiet. The walk was rather serene, new dawn gave off false promises of a beautiful day hike through the woods. I remembered all the trail-heads I had ever began, their quiet promise of escape calmed me with a nostalgic quiétude. I was thirsty and hungry, and I felt odd. The lingering horrors of the dream still tugged me out of the present. Realistically, I was not prepared for a day of hiking even on flat land. I hoped that getting to the outer limits of Seoul would not take too long. I had not eaten or drunk anything since getting on my bike in Seoul. I also felt the rough aftermath of the soju on my whole body. I hoped that there would be a store or a natural spring somewhere along the way.

I checked both my pockets and the ground for my phone. I thought I remembered putting it on the ground somewhere nearby, and checked there, but all I saw was just a pile of loose rocks that looked like a collapsed cairn. I could not find it anywhere. I surrendered, giving in to the idea that it must have fallen out of my pocket in the river at some point, or while running, and that the rock I remembered pulling out of my pocket later in the night must have been some bizarre coincidence, not much more bizarre than the rabbit-medium or my frightening dream.

I began not to trust my memories. With the thought of the rabbit again, last night's dream panged at me like a dagger in my torso. Where had reality ended and the dream begun? Had I really met three Korean men at a fire in the woods who sounded like living history? That had seemed quite real, as did the imperial soldiers. As much as I tried to enjoy the beautiful day, I couldn't shake an invisible darkness from the glimmering gold and green. Time was out of joint, and I had a nagging feeling that would not go away, a feeling like the reality surrounding me was trying to sneeze but couldn't. What could I do? I didn't have much of a choice but to walk towards the city. As I walked, I scoured my periphery for anomalies. My attention was on high alert, homing in on every possible danger. Every weird-looking tree, and every rustle in the bushes made my heart skip a beat.

A squirrel darted through the grass and I flinched, preparing to defend myself. I must have looked strange walking through these woods, but who was there to observe me? Everything was so green and so calm and so golden, and in between my stretches of high alert I began slightly to enjoy the serenity of the day. My pace settled into a rhythm, and the forest normalized. I became quite seduced by nature.

I only had the clothes on my back and my damp shoes at this point. I needed a shower. Last night's inexplicable events began to settle in my mind. I eased my way through shrubs and trees of which I did not know the names. There was no muffled sound of car engines, no voices, no barking dogs, nearly no sound at all. This was a little peculiar. I kept confirming the mountain outlines in my mind with the ones on the horizon to reassure myself that I was going the right direction.

My body ached as I walked. The trees seemed older. Had there been this many trees before? It didn't seem coherent with what I remembered. I was beginning to feel plagued with a paranoia, feeling that I was not somewhere I should be. I had been on several hikes around here before and the trees today seemed larger, more ancient. Wide trunks flanked both sides of me. This seemed off, especially here, so far removed from the mountains. I was used to seeing more small farm plots and vegetable gardens crammed into every small plot of open land. As people packed into a small country, the Koreans I knew made as much use of flat land as possible. This was necessary in a country with such a dense a population.

Mountains remained sacred, though. Every mountain I had been on was still thoroughly wooded. Mountains were also havens for many Buddhist temples. But given any flat, square plot of land, the ground-dwelling denizens would be farming it, building high-rises upon it, landscaping it for gardens, clearing it for roads or houses—almost anything that could fit there would be built or cultivated there. No space went unused, not as long as the land was usable.

But wherever I was, that principle did not hold true. I was walking through a flat, very old growth forest. There were no bodies of water to guide me. I had left the tributary in pursuit of the mountain outline that now was concealed by the canopy of trees overhead. I could name the gingko trees and guessed at what might be zelkova trees, but they were all just trees, which were as universal and as general as dirt or the sky or the sun itself. From where had this old growth came? How had it survived all the raids of imperial Japan, all the shellings of the Korean War, and all the economic ambitions of the postwar boom? These woods beat all the odds, I surmised, and I was lucky to be walking through them alone, unimpeded by crowds of hikers that surely would have flooded these places had they known about them.

In broad daylight, I now felt more deeply entrenched in history than I had before. This was deeper than any of the stranger, more metaphysical anomalies from last night. There was no metaphysical doubt about this now, it only kept getting more vivid and more real. The sun blasted through the trees with intensity and warmth in powerful rays of gold. That light colored the trees a hearty brown and their leaves vibrant green.

I was overwhelmed with a desire to take off my shoes again, not just to relieve my feet of their dampness but to liberate my feet from their cosmetic protection. I grounded myself in the softened earth, letting the nutrient-rich humus take in my soles and softly carve out space between my toes as I walked, sinking into every step with natural joy that soaked up through my feet and into my legs, groin, abdomen, and arms; the whole forest channeled into my heart as if I were part of a root system soaking in water and conducting messages through networks of fungi. I was no longer alien, but part of the ecosystem. I allowed myself to adapt, and the forest-home adopted me as it adopted squirrels, bird nests, caterpillars, and butterflies.

I carried my shoes in my hands. I had worn them down in the last twelve hours almost as much as they had been worn in the last twelve months. This, I observed, seemed like an accelerated amount of wear, but then as I looked at the shoes again they had indeed reached their limit. They hardly looked like my shoes anymore. If I hadn't been so superficially concerned with the purity of this forest, I would have discarded them right there. Right then, I realized how superficial my ecological morality had been. At the rate they were going, these shoes would decompose in a week. In the moment of this law-redefining moral assessment, I decided to leave my dilapidated shoes by the base of a tree. Perhaps some animal would make good use of them, I thought, or a colony of insects might make them their biome. Somehow, I knew they would not be shoes much longer—that this greater ecosystem, or microcosm of past ecosystem, would make *them* a part of *it*, that the shoes would turn to dirt that would cultivate new growth in their vestiges of factory production from a capitalist past.

XIII

The woods did not continue forever. Their canopy thinned again and gave way to new clouds and a blue sky. Cumulus puffs filled out spaces of pure sky, moving over the land thoughtlessly. I walked into the openness, feeling vulnerable and exposed. I glanced around with hope that I would see a rabbit friend nearby. There were none. I stumbled upon a road. The macadam road I remember was now only a dirt path. The smell of morning dew and growth permeated the air, vaguely familiar but off by a degree.

Nothing looked recognizably familiar, but I convinced myself that it was. The dirt road was not paved. In a ghostly way it resembled a road I once knew. Two effluent bodies of water joined several meters from where I stood. I had a geographical intuition that these two waters fed into the Han. I had certainty that the Han led into the city. These aspects of geography were comforting, even if my identification of them was only guesswork. I could not reason why they appeared so changed, but I rationalizing whys had become quite taxing. I could not afford to invest myself so much in whys when the instrumental knowledge of getting me from point A to point B had become so much more dangerous. Geographical features were something to go on, signs that sent messages for me to follow. Most roads and waterways led to some sort of civilized life, but of what sort I wasn't so sure.

XIV

I walked for a couple of hours along flat land by the bank of the river. Birds chirped, and the steady current of water rumbled. Two cranes floated on a spot in the middle of the river. Faint, in the distance, I heard a gentle hum. It could have been the rumbling of an enormous generator, or the steady but muffled noise of city traffic. The hum only approximated either sound, as if something had changed slightly in the technology. The hum oscillated like a sine wave. The noise was faint, and I continued to pay close attention to it—I couldn't ignore it. It set off a spark of curiosity. I stopped and held still for a moment. I hadn't realized how much noise my footsteps had been making, and how quiet everything else had been. Silently, I stood there, my ears perked like a rabbit sensing a predator. A slow, steady hum reverberated and unraveled discordantly from beyond the horizon, where the city should be.

I tried to try to gain some elevation. An elevation gain would provide me with a wide enough view of the city. I was somewhat lost, thirsty and shoeless. I reminded myself that I really had no idea where I was but was still grounded to the Earth. I took precaution. I could trespass enemy lines at any moment. I was, in military terms, AWOL: absent without intent to desert.

My strategy was to climb to a high position and assess the terrain. It took an hour for me to reach the beginning of the hill. I found some pine nuts growing on a tree and gathered them for later. Then, I attacked the branches and shelled the seeds with a ravenous appetite.

XV

The noise grew louder the further up the mountain I climbed. It rose from a hum to a growl. The motors purred up and down, loud and soft, making waves of sound that rushed over the mountain and downwind where I climbed over roots and glacially carved rocks. Trees grew out of crevices and I grabbed onto bulbous roots that protruded outward like loops of tied shoelaces. With my bare feet I was able to grip the vertical surfaces of stone with confidence. I ran upward at an accelerating pace towards the loudening sound upon an increasing slope, grabbing cracks and propelling ever-forward.

Thermal winds carried a peculiar smell over and down the mountain. It smelled like nothing I had ever smelled before. It smelled like thousands of raw steaks. It was the smell of offal, of mass carnage. It was a primal smell that must have attracted hungry animals to carcasses for hundreds of millennia. The purr-hum now sounded like thousands of individually oscillating growls. Some volumes grew loud while others calmed down. They rose and fell, their unique fluctuations blending into a sea of cumulative noise.

I worked hard to climb the rest of the mountain as quickly as I could. Once I got to the viewpoint, the vista before me was unspeakable. At first, it was unclear. Then, as everything came into focus, I had to turn away. I couldn't accept what my senses sensed. There was not a sea of buildings, roads and modern infrastructure. No houses, no fences, not even plots of land. There was nothing where a part of the city should have been. There was a vast, undeveloped valley with a river flowing through it, but nothing normal was there. There were thousands of orange and white and black giant striped cats. This was all that populated the valley: giant cats. They were tigers. They were far away from where I stood at the top of the mountain, and I would not hesitate to call them beautiful, even miraculous creatures. Yet their sheer number was disturbing and unnatural. What were they doing down there?

In broad daylight, their fierce oranges and blacks were visible. Everything was so clear, unbelievably clear compared to the smog-plagued city I once knew. I could see for distances I had never been able to see before. I could make out distinct tigers down below, though from where I stood they were the size of tiny rodents. Most tigers were on the river plain, but some were beneath the cover of trees in the riparian buffers and woodlands as well. Without the roads and buildings, everything was colored differently. Besides orange and black, the valley was a blend of rolling greens and blues, an otherwise serene habitat now invaded by an ambush of tigers.

XVI

I suddenly realized I could not go any further. I could only hear the ambient chorus of growls from down below. Why did it smell so bad? I peered below again—was there fresh meat down there? The tigers were feasting on a field of carcasses. The smell was a mix of putrid air, with the fresh smell of offal, the smell of a cold butcher's kitchen. A few tigers were ripping into their food, tearing pieces of sinew apart with their mouths, shaking their heads and whipping aside strands of red.

I tested the limits of my vision from the top of the mountain, peering down into the valley. All I could see, up to the vanishing point, were tigers. I had no doubt there were several thousand of them. How this could be was beyond me. At the same time, the air of the day was warm and comforting, and resistant to doubt. The sun bathed me at my viewpoint as I looked down in awe and shock. Mesmerized, I sat down on a rock to watch the valley. In a lapse of short-term memory, I reached in my pocket for a camera. All I found were pine nuts. I grabbed a few raw pine nuts and ate them.

A thermal breeze blew up from below and wafted a butchered meat smell in my face. For a moment, it felt as much a perfect day as any. I sat on the warm rock, burying my toes in the dirt, and remained calm despite the foreboding sense of permanent time displacement that my predicament now wrought with its own peculiar hammer and anvil.

The predicament I was in did not hit me suddenly or harshly. It permeated my state of mind slowly. I tried to think back to the fox, when things started to unravel. All I thought was that I wasn't quite sure where I was, or how I'd gotten here. With that, something became clear, but it did not hit me wholly or all at once. I peeled back layers, from scene to scene, until now, with thousands of hungry tigers before me: a new conscious dawn rose like sepals falling off an emerging flower.

Here I realized that I could not go forward—I could not find a train, a taxi, or a ride of any sort. I doubted that I could get anywhere at all. I was in a sunken place. There was nothing for me down in the valley of tigers. I was prey in a land of predators.

Watching the tigers, I noticed they were eating from carcasses of dead animals. They ripped the flesh off the carcasses as if it were plastic wrap. Blood spattered on their faces and all around them. In unison they growled, and sometimes at each other, as if to say, back off. They licked and chewed and purred as they ate in small groups, side by side, satiating their appetites.

I considered going back again, but go back to where? I had lost my place. The best I could do was try to find my bike, or even try to find the transient Korean men, but at the risk of ending up shot or imprisoned or treated as food. I couldn't assume safe haven anywhere. I had to get out, but there was no guaranteed way of doing so in any direction. Again, I thought of reaching for my phone. Instead, I grabbed a rock next to where I sat and threw it out over the ledge, towards the valley. I watched it fall.

I thought about the rabbit. I glanced around for other creatures in my vicinity, but it was just me and the dirt, with the trees and the rock I sat on. I accepted the possibility that I may have reached a dead end. I didn't know what to believe in anymore. Reality had ripped open and nothing seemed consistent. The horror of being untethered to anything real sunk in. Sometimes, in the world I knew, I'd wake up at 3AM and feel this same existential malaise.

Doubts covered me like sediments over a speck at the bottom of a drain. There was no way in my power to recover anything I had lost. Courage seemed like an alien concept. How could I have courage without an idea of what to do? I weighed this in anguish. Anguish took control and persuaded me to give up. Against this surrender a part of me that fought even while my mind and my body had been taxed out of their last resources shouted back: keep going! You can't stop now, you can't die here.

So, I decided to set up camp. I would run to stay in place, until a better answer might come.

I made a lean-to, gathered some nuts, started a fire, boiled some water, and regained my strength. I did all this at the top of the mountain over the span of several days. I anticipated rabbits to visit my camp, but none came. I tried to live the best life I could up here, isolated from the world. It was a pretty good spot with a pretty good view. No one bothered me here, and I lived off the land. Night came after day. The stars came out. I prayed, and hoped, and meditated, and gave thanks to the mysteries beyond the night sky, which felt right. The moon up there stared back down at me with the silhouetted face of a rabbit. I could not help but see it now. The shiny white pearl in the sky waxed and waned over the course of the year and I grew a beard and my skin turned leathery. I must have been the last man, because I had talked to no one in that time. I was not sad or happy, but merely there, hoping, waiting, falling asleep every night to the growling chorus of a thousand tigers, and waking up every morning at daybreak to the same sounds. Nothing much changed here besides the seasons. Sometimes I fed squirrels, and those were my happiest moments. I marked each day with a stone. I aligned them in linear rows in the dirt. This may have been the only thing that kept me sane. It stabilized my reality with the rotation of the Earth. I may have been without material wealth, impoverished of humankind, but for that year I was more in harmony with nature than I had ever been before.

XVII

A year passed before I talked to another person again. One day, while I was foraging for berries, a bearded man emerged from behind a tree. He said hello as if I had been just a friendly face passing him on the street. I was startled and nearly tossed the stone in my hand at him. Fortunately, I restrained myself, remembering what man was like and sensing a warmth from his smiling face. He was rugged and old but walked firmly and youthfully.

"What are you doing out here, young man?" he asked. I wondered how much I looked like a young man, and how old he was. His face was chiseled with wrinkles. He had a long beard that resembled Confucius. He spoke to me only in Korean.

Even though I'd gotten used to living out here, I still didn't know where I was, or why I was here. I asked him: *"Who are you?"*

"This is my home."

I asked him a better question: *"But what is happening on the other side of that hill? Why are there so many tigers?"* I said all this in the best Korean I could put together.

"Oh, the tigers...You saw them? They have been invading the valley unlike never before. They are eating everything, and soon they will have no food left. The valley is in great danger."

Sure, I thought, this was obvious as well. I decided to go for a more direct question, one that would get to the bottom of where my fate hung: *"What year is it?"*

"What year? Ha!"

Great. He was just a mote of obviousness. Yet he was human, and we could understand each other, at least to some degree. *"Why are you here,"* I asked.

"This is my home. I could be here just as much as I could be anywhere else. I just happened to see something unusual in my path today, and that is you. It must be a lucky day for both of us, for I could have been a hungry tiger, or you could have been, and then either one of us would have met our end right then. Fortunately, we're not tigers."

I thought about that for a few seconds and had to agree that I guess I was indeed lucky—lucky to still be out here.

When I realized this, everything suddenly became new to me. I was lifted out of my fog of inertia. I was stuck on a mountain over an overripe population of tigers, but with this man, there was now hope, and I would ask another question and he would answer me just as enigmatically, and I was left with the impression that I might never see him again. There was love, and there was hope, and there was, just for a moment, a shared culture—a verification that everything that had happened to me was not just an insane series of hallucinations. We lived side by side, and I did, in fact, see him time and time again. He was always just as enigmatic, joyful and friendly. Sometimes we'd exchange food. We began sitting down together on the rocks that overlooked the valley of carnage and having deep conversations about what it all meant. We did so over the rumbling din of growls.

Life went on like this for months, and then years went by before I finally decided to leave. The day I left I did not see the man, and I did not tell him I would be leaving. I woke up one morning and there was no noise from below. I did not see even a hint of orange. The mountain was still and quiet. Trees forbid themselves to move. The wind was still. I knew it was long past time for me to go. Reluctantly, as I had felt glued to the terrain I had come to know, I abandoned camp. I walked further into the forest than I had ever gone before. I passed new groves of trees with a sense of longing. I started crying over some feeling I could not identify. I approached a new dawn, sad and hopeful, with tears mediating how I felt, conducting energy from one intangible source to another.

The Love Hunters

Shaun Avery

An Anti-Climax

The escort, all six-foot, sculpted barefoot wonder of her, has been sucking and pulling on his flaccid penis for what feels like hours without much success.

He looks down at her bobbing head, the frustration in her beginning to become apparent behind her professional front, and he surprises both himself and her by saying, "stop."

She does so.

Then sits up on the bed and looks at him.

"It's not happening tonight," he tells her. "You might as well go."

She stares at him, shocked.

This is something that has clearly never happened to her before, and she's having trouble dealing with it.

As if confirming his thoughts, she says, "you can't do this to me!"

"Oh, sweetheart," he says. He reaches into the bedside cabinet and pulls out a huge bundle of cash and drops it on the even huger bed. "I'm afraid I can."

Criminal Connections

Die, Bitch!

Henry smiled at the two words he had just written on the screen, finger hovering over the "enter" button on his laptop, poised to send the message out onto somebody's online profile.

"Come on, man," his best friend Eric called from downstairs. "We're gonna be late!"

Probably correct. But he was enjoying being naughty. They'd already skipped school, and would soon be going…somewhere else. He now just wanted a few seconds to revel in this hateful message he had typed out to a stranger.

He hit down on the button with a smile, feeling pretty pleased with himself.

"Last chance!" Eric shouted. "Don't make me call your parents!"

Don't make me call yours, he thought. But of course, he dared not say that. Instead he replied, "all right, all right. I'm coming!"

Then he headed down to the front garden, where Eric was parked. There was plenty space there—his parents had been forced to sell their vehicles recently, and though Henry had passed his test a few months ago he had yet to save enough money to buy one of his own. Meanwhile, Eric and his whole family still drove. Just one more way his friend was superior to him. One of the many.

"Better late than never," Eric said, tapping his watch.

"Yeah, yeah," said Henry, clambering into the passenger seat. "Let's go, huh?"

So, they did.

-A-

"Good morning, good morning!" shouted the auctioneer an hour later, greeting the small crowd. "Let's see what we have here!"

Henry looked around the crowd, feeling like an impostor. He knew they both had fake ID, and from what he had heard, the guy that had produced it was pretty good, but still he felt edgy; certain that someone would look at them and just *know* they were too young to be here.

Perhaps sensing this, Eric nudged him.

"Relax," he said. "Chill."

Henry tried to do what his friend said, tried to adopt a more relaxed, casual stance.

But then the auctioneer's eyes fell on him.

Henry froze.

Understanding what “blood runs cold”—a phrase he had read in many books—actually meant.

But then the auctioneer’s face split into a grin.

“First time here, bud?” he asked.

Henry nodded, relieved.

“Well,” said the auctioneer. “Are you in for a treat.”

A New Plan of Attack

One hasty and slightly awkward retrieval of massive-heeled boots later and she’s heading out of the front door towards a taxi whose driver he always keeps on call.

He watches her go from his bedroom window.

It’s a shame, what just happened.

She’d been pretty. But then, they always were. He had the type of money that meant he could hire the best, the most beautiful.

So, if the retreating escort had been so gorgeous—and she was, no doubt about that—then why had she been unable to arouse him?

Plus, he had to be honest, tonight had just been the culmination of a problem he had been aware of for a while. This had been the first time he had been *completely* unable to perform, true enough—but with the last of the escorts he had been with, maybe the previous six or so, it had undeniably been a struggle. Several time he had suffered from premature ejaculation, and had to give them a couple of extra hundred as a bonus from sheer embarrassment.

He sighs.

Perhaps something new is needed.

“Arthur!” he calls, voice huge and echoing in the vast emptiness of the house.

The butler appears within seconds, poking his head around the bedroom door. “Sir?”

“I’m afraid that did not go terribly well, Arthur,” he says.

“Sorry to hear that, sir.” Arthur looks at him. “Anything I can do to help?”

He thinks about it, heads back over to the bed and lies down with his head against the backboard and ponders the question.

"Yes," he says. "I think there is."

He's excited now, loving it when a new idea comes from nowhere and grips him, making him see the way that things could work.

"Call the agency," he says. "Tonight. Straight-away." He smiles. "But *you* pick the woman for me, Arthur. Don't even tell me her name until she gets here."

"As sir wishes," Arthur says, and retreats.

Alone in the bedroom, he lies back down to nap.

To wait.

Henry's Big Find

It was one of those storage locker auctions they had gone to—much better than school, right? Or so Henry thought at least—and it was the only one in town that was not the subject of its own TV show. Which was partly why Henry and Eric had chosen to come here—less chance of being picked up by the camera. It was all just for a laugh, but they had brought a little cash too, and were more than willing to spend it.

On what, though?

They had no idea.

Until they came to the sixth locker.

Which at first appeared empty.

"Huh," said Eric. "Nothing to see here." He placed a hand on Henry's shoulder, tried to pull him away. "Let's check the next one."

But Henry resisted.

Seeing something propped up in the corner of the locker, surrounded by shadows.

Actually…

Some*one*.

Henry took a step forward.

"Hey, hey, hey!" cried the auctioneer, standing behind them. "I know you're new here, but I *told* you the rules—no going inside unless you've bought it!"

"Then I'll buy it," Henry said, not looking at the older man, eyes still on the item in the locker. "How much?"

"For that?" the auctioneer said, coming over to stand beside them and take a look at the content of the locker. "Three hundred?"

"Deal," said Henry, and reached for his wallet.

"Hey, wait up," the auctioneer protested. "This is an auction. I have to open up the bidding to everyone else." He looked around at the crowd of prospective bidders. "Anybody?"

There wasn't.

And that was how a happy Henry bought his very own sex doll.

Greetings from a Stranger

The new woman walks through the front door, and he can see instantly that Arthur has done a good job in picking her.

"Hi," she says. "I'm Melody."

Arthur's in his room, doing whatever he does in there. So, it's just the two of them: her just inside the entrance, and him, standing in the main room—looking at her. Liking what he sees.

The long dark hair. The long sleek legs. And the huge heels that give the latter such prominence.

He looks at them, smiling.

"Shoes," he says.

And points to the items in question.

She stares back at him, a bemused look upon her face.

"Your shoes," he says. "You'll have to take them off before you can come all the way in."

"Whatever you say," and slowly starts to take them off.

He watches her.

He knows what she is doing.

She knows what she is doing.

She's making a show of unleashing her feet, trying to turn him on with it. And he's amazed to realise, trouser pants jutting out to prove the point, that it's working.

She stands there smiling when she's done, the huge-heeled shoes held in her hand.

"Good," he says, nodding, pleased. But he's not done yet, adding, "give them to me."

She walks over, never taking her eyes off his, and she places the shoes in his waiting hand.

"There you go," she says. "Sir."

His arousal is growing by the second, his failure with the last escort already fading from his mind, becoming the stuff of dark fantasies.

He brings the shoes up to his face.

Sniffs them. Smells where her feet have been. The combined aroma of flesh and fabric almost intoxicating to him.

Then he licks them.

Takes that scent onto his tongue and man does it feel *good.*

"Why, that's a sexy big tongue you've got there, mister," she tells him. "Want to use it somewhere else?"

That's all the invitation he needs, and he grabs her and kisses her.

And they only make it as far as the stairs before their clothes are gone and the ravishing begins.

Home

"God," said Eric, looking at the doll, now propped up in the corner of Henry's bedroom. It was a solid rubber affair, not a blow-up kit, but he still didn't much like the look of it. "I can't believe you bought that thing." He folded his arms in front of his body, wanting as much of a barrier between him and the prosthetic woman as possible. "I mean, are you really going to *use* it?"

Eric had been saying much the same thing for the duration of the car ride back to Henry's house. And now, seeing his friend's face, Henry realised that he really didn't like the look that he saw there. It made him think he would perhaps even send Eric a few online death threats later. Under a pseudonym, of course. He liked using words like that. They made him feel like a real writer, like his threats were absolutely the best in the business.

"Might do," he eventually said. "And get that look off your face," he added. "I mean, it's all right for you—you *already* have someone to sleep with."

Eric grinned.

And Henry remembered:

They sat together on the sports field—Eric had just been playing football, but he was taking a rest now. Henry, naturally, had been waiting for him the whole time—waiting for him to get tired messing about with the other guys and come back to him. Which he always did. And this time Henry could tell that he had something to say, something on his mind.

"What is it?" Henry asked.

Eric looked at him, grinning that grin of his, the one that girls always loved. "What's what?"

"You know. Something's happened, hasn't it?"

"What makes you say that?"

"I can tell from your face. What is it?"

Eric looked at him. "It's me and Alison."

Alison being—what? His ninth girlfriend since they'd been in high school? Something like that.

"What is it?" Henry asked. "Have you guys split up or something?"

"No," Eric said. "Actually, it's the opposite."

And Henry knew.

Nine girlfriends, yes—but Eric had never gone the full way with them. They'd wanted him to, or so he said. But he'd relented. Had always claimed, at least to Henry, that he wanted the first time to be, in his own words, "the right *time."*

And now, it seemed, that time had come.

"No way," Henry said.

"Yep," said Eric, nodding.

And Henry looked back to the kids playing football.

Thinking, *fuck, there must be some hope for* me, *yet!*

But as of today, that hope had come to nothing.

"Yeah, well," Eric said, bringing him back to the present. He pointed to the groin area of the doll, which seemed to be well used, frayed, bits hanging away. "I'd use something if you did."

"Come on," Henry said, walking over to the doll. He wiggled its mouth, the lips the only part of the face that moved. "Admit it. She's hot."

"She's rubber."

Henry nodded, conceding that point if nothing else.

"And what are you going to do with it when your parents get home?"

"That's what I have a closet for," Henry replied, pointing to the location in question.

Eric shook his head. "Lot of effort to go to for a doll, man."

"I know," Henry said. He looked to his purchase, feeling oddly proud of her. "But I'm sure that she'll be worth it."

Spite Fight

He hates leaving the house, and tries to do so as little as possible. But sometimes, like today, it's necessary.

Still, at least he knows Melody will be waiting for him when he gets home.

Not that he's under any illusions about that, of course. He knows it's just a cash thing. That's how he got her to stay, in fact—offered her more money than anyone else could give her.

The person he's going to meet, Rod, would kill to be in that financial position.

But instead the guy is sat in a grotty café in a tatty black cardigan, staring down into a murky cup of coffee as if it contains the answers to all of life's problems.

He comes up behind the man.

"Hello, Rod," he says.

Rod looks back at him.

"Hello, Connor," he says. "You haven't changed a bit."

"So they tell me," Connor replies, taking a seat across from his half-brother, sitting far enough away from the café table that he can cross his legs. "How you been doing, Rod?"

"Shitty."

He guesses there's not going to be much small talk done here.

"I lost my job again," Rod replies. He smiles, revealing poor dental hygiene. "You know what that means."

Yes, he does indeed know what that means.

Connor sighs.

This is why he always dreads his special phone ringing, the number that only his half-siblings have. This is why he'd kept it from Melody, when she'd asked who had called earlier. But it's his cross to bear. And you can't say he hasn't earned it.

He pulls out his wallet.

Rod's eyes, as always, bulging when they see the thickness of the wad in there.

"Has, uh…" Rod licks his lips, tries again. "Has anyone else been in touch this month?"

"Not yet." Connor removes half the wedge, hands it over, glad they're in a secluded corner of the café so no one can see what's going on. "But I'm sure they will."

"Yeah, well." Now that Rod's got his money the belligerence is out in full force, all pretence at friendliness and solidarity now departed. "We haven't all got *your* luck, man."

"If that's what you want to call it," Connor says.

Then stands and leaves, Rod's jealous eyes burning into his back all the way.

-ↂAↂ-

Heading home, he asks himself why he still does it.

He had not been exaggerating back there in the place. Today it was Rod…next week it could be any one of a dozen other people. All bound to him by blood. All expecting a handout. And none of them knowing the truth about what he'd really done.

Once again, he curses fate, feeling, and family.

But most of all he curses his mother.

And almost has a dark, dark moment when he gets home and walks into the bedroom with his head down and hears the purred words "hi, lover" and thinks for a second that it's her.

But, looking up, he sees it can't be.

The woman lying atop the bed waiting for him is *nice*.

"Lover," he says, taking off his shoes, unbuttoning his trousers. "I should pay you extra for a greeting like that."

Melody giggles.

He wants to talk to her, wants to tell her all about his day, his meeting with Rod. But that's not what he's paying her for. Not yet, at least. So instead he sheds his clothes and joins her on the bed.

And as he kisses her, enters her, it seems for a second that all is finally right with his world.

Homework

Henry's parents, Noreen and Brad, employed a pretty hands-off style of discipline with their son, thinking that they had brought him up well enough as a child to give him a certain amount of freedom and flexibility now that he was a teenager. So, when he announced at seven that evening, that he was heading up to his bedroom to go on his laptop for a bit, they thought nothing of it assuming that he would spend the next few hours chatting to his friends online.

Well, that was what Noreen thought.

His dad instead said, with a chuckle, "bet he's looking for girls."

"Bradley!" Noreen said. She only ever used his full name when she was admonishing him. "Our boy's far too young for *that* sort of thing!"

But although they disagreed on that one thing, they both assumed that their son was engaged in innocent, legal online pastimes.

They had no idea.

Bitch…asshole…loser-creep….

Henry looked through his little book of insults, tried to decide which ones he'd been underusing lately. When you wrote as many death threats as he did, you had to work to keep yourself fresh.

Today's target? Some pop singer who'd been pictured pigging out at some all-you-can-eat place. No shame there, of course—Henry had been to similar places himself. But then, he wasn't female. And he wasn't famous.

FAT WHORE, he wrote on the singer's message board. Then, as a final flourish, added WATCH YOU DON'T SWALLOW YOUR WHOLE FUCKING HAND, TOO!

He leant back in his chair, satisfied.

Then his eyes swung to the closet.

He'd put the doll away in there just after Eric had left and a mere half hour before his parents got home from work. He'd had a little fool around with her breasts, but he had gone no further with her yet. Hadn't even *kissed* her, though looking at those pliable lips he'd been tempted. Question was, dare he make a move on her when his parents were both in the house? Sure, he had a lock on this side of the door so they wouldn't be able to walk in on him, catch him in the act…but would he really be able to face them at the breakfast table in the morning if they *heard* him going at it, the bedsprings squeaking and the doll squelching?

He didn't know.

But thinking about the doll had made him eager, excited.

He went to take a look at her, stuffed back in the corner of his closet.

She was his.

Bought and paid for.

Who needed an Alison when you had that?

The thought reminded him of Eric's earlier comments about the doll, and he headed back to the laptop, ready to bring a little fear to his friend's online profile. Using—naturally—that most beloved of all words to him: a pseudonym.

He started typing.

Then a *thump* suddenly rang out behind him.

Henry jumped.

Then stood, shaking his head.

"Honey?" his mother called from the bottom of the stairs. "Everything all right up there?"

"Fine, mom," he replied, eyes still rooted to the source of the sound. "Just dropped a book, that's all."

"Must have been a big book."

His mother chuckled as she spoke. They never laughed, his parents, he had found that they…always *chuckled.* It drove Henry mad. He'd sometimes laugh too loud just to show them how it should be done.

"That's right," he shouted back to her. "A big one. Sorry, mom."

He waited for the sound of her heading back into the living room—probably still *chuckling*, he bet—then Henry walked over to the fallen object.

Lying there, on the floor like that…

The doll looked more tempting than ever.

But he wasn't sure how it could have fallen so far out into the room. Not propped up in the corner like it had been.

But who cared?

She was *his*.

He put her back where she had come from, closing the closet door behind him, before sitting down at the laptop to send a few abusive messages to his best friend.

The Question

He senses Melody is getting a little quiet around him, looking at him like she's about to say something but then never actually coming out with it. This worries him, but not too much—if she's about to spoil this good thing they've got going between them by asking something stupid, well, he knows that she is easily replaced.

They're sitting in bed when it finally comes.

She has the blanket around her lower half but the upper is totally, gloriously, naked, long hair cascading down over bare and slender shoulders. He was both surprised and delighted to discover that she possesses naturally curly hair, and she's not bothered to straighten it for a while. A sign of her growing comfort with him? Or just a trick designed to make him think that way so she can get more money from him? And why does he even care?

He's looking her over, thinking all of this, when the question finally comes.

"Babe," she says. Babe is what he is to her now, and she a few different terms of endearment to him. "Babe," she then says again, "what is it you actually *do*?" She motions around the expanse of the mansion. "I mean, what *pays* for all of this?"

A-ha, he is thinking. *Not what…but* whom.

What he actually says though, is "well, Melody, what do *you* think I do?"

"I don't know," she tells him. She reaches down for the bottle of champagne he always keeps near to the bed, presenting her bare behind to him, and even now, in the midst of this conversation that he'd rather not be having, the sight makes him lick his lips, make him want to take her there and then. "I tried searching for you online." She comes back up, holding the bottle in one hand and two glasses in the other, cradling them at the stem. "Nothing."

And he looks at her.

Wondering, *could I tell her?*

Could he break bonds not just sacred but legal and tell Melody about Rod? About the other half-brothers and sisters? Even about…*her*?

He wants to.

Oh, how he wants to.

It's a burden that he and Arthur have shared alone for all too long.

But then his eyes meet hers, and even though he knows she's just here for the money, he still can't do it to her. Can't lay all of that bad history on her.

So he just smiles and tells her, "I'm in business."

She doesn't seem terribly satisfied with that response. But there's still enough of a master-and-servant relationship between them for her not to push it.

Instead, she pours their drinks then snuggles up to him and says, "maybe you can tell me about it one day."

"Yes," he says, stroking her curly hair. "I hope I can."

Awakenings

"Henry…"

He tried to shake the word away, tried to stay in his awesome dream of watching women change into their bikinis on the beach.

"Oh Henry…"

He snuggled in closer to the doll, brushing it with his erection. He'd managed to resist for a whole half hour after his mother had tucked him in, but then his need had grown too much, and he'd got up and checked the door was locked and then headed to the closet and got her out. He still wasn't going to risk having sex with her, not when his parents were in the house. But that didn't mean he couldn't use it for company.

"Henry!"

The bikini babes vanished in a puff of smoke.

And he came awake.

To see that the doll was staring at him.

But it wasn't like earlier. Although her eyes had always been open, no eyelids there to close them, now it was different. There was something *behind* them. And it was looking right at him.

"B-babe?" he said.

And like something in a nightmare, the doll's mouth slid slowly open.

"No," the doll said. "The name's Roberta."

The next thing Henry knew he was lying on his bedroom floor, the doll standing over him.

"What…what happened?" he wondered.

"You fainted," said the doll. "You wimp."

"Hey." Henry pulled himself to his feet. "You can't talk to me like that. I own you!"

"Think so?" the doll said, looking at him again.

And suddenly there was a pounding inside Henry's skull, like something was hammering to get out.

He fell to his knees, mouth opening wide.

"Uh-uh," the doll said. "Don't scream. Because if your parents come in here…I'll have to hurt *them*, too."

Henry clamped his mouth shut.

"Good boy," the doll told him, and finally looked away.

The pain stopped, and Henry flopped onto his back.

The doll, meanwhile, headed over to the computer.

But not by walking, Henry saw.

It sort of…*hovered.*

Henry couldn't believe that this was happening. Had he slept with the doll without realising and picked up some sort of disease that made you hallucinate? Had Eric's warning been right? God, he hoped not. That might almost make him feel guilty about all the stuff he'd put on the guy's profile.

And speaking of which…

The doll flipped open the laptop's cover, exposing the screen that still shone there.

"You really should exit this stuff before you hit the sack, Henry," it told him.

Then read out loud:

"Watch your back, heathen…die screaming from God's holy judgement, bitch…" It looked back at him. "This stuff is *good*, kid."

"I don't…" He swallowed, licked dry lips. "I don't know anything about that."

"Yes you do," the doll said. "I could smell it on you, what you like to get up to up here. That's why I chose you, made you buy me."

"No," he said. "That was my choice."

"Was it?" came the reply, and though her facial features did not, could not move, he thought he sensed a smile in there somewhere. "Think back, kid."

He did so.

And sure enough, it was difficult to describe the urge that had come over him, that had made him pay three hundred for a clearly used sex doll. He'd thought, at the time, that it was just lust, mixed with an envy of Eric for popping his cherry before him. But now—could what the doll was saying be true?

"Don't even bother wondering," the doll told him. "It is."

"Fine," Henry said, going for a brave tone but sounding mostly petulant. "So now you're here, what do you want with me?"

"Why, Henry," it said, and suddenly the doll was right there beside him, stroking his hair. "You're going to help me *get* somebody."

Dear Dad

Melody stands by the front door and looks at him, hands on her hips, designer handbag slung over one shoulder.

"Is this because of what I asked you the other night?" she says.

"No," he replies, waving the question off. "God, no." He nods back towards the kitchen, where Arthur is putting breakfast together. "Just got a little business, is all."

"Then you're not just getting rid of me?"

He still can't tell how much of this is acting, whether she really cares or she's just trying to hold onto a pretty good money-stream. Nor is he sure of where and when he started giving a shit about her motives, when he began to see her as a real person and not just a fuck-machine. That's never happened before, not with anyone. The closest thing he's ever had to a companion before this is Arthur, and they are more partners-in-crime than partners-in-friendship.

"No," he eventually tells her, and he's not sure how he feels when he realises that he's not lying. "I'll call you when it's done."

"Call *me*?" she presses. "Not the Agency?"

"No, sweetheart," he replies. "I'll call you."

She seems to believe him, and with one last longing look she steps out of the door.

He breathes a sigh of relief, then heads into the kitchen.

"Business, sir?" Arthur asks, sliding his lunch across the table to him.

"Yep," he says. "The best kind." He reaches into the fridge, pulls out a six-pack of beer. "Drinking business."

-∿A∿-

And business is good that day, the beer gradually promoting him to the level of "tipsy" before forming a merger with the twin interests of wine and champagne to put him firmly in the category of "blotto."

By nine p.m. he's drank every drop of alcohol they have in the house.

But what the hell.

He can always afford to buy more.

He's lying on the floor in his private study when he thinks this, and the thought makes his eyes flicker slowly up to the picture that dominates one wall.

He wishes he'd taken it down, burnt it long ago. But he could never quite bring himself to do so, and now still here it remains. As penance, perhaps.

"Dad," he murmurs. "Dear Dad. You always were the big one, weren't you? Always the one she wanted most, the one she worked for."

He uses the edge of a table to pull himself up, regains his footing in a world suddenly spinning.

"Dear Dad," he says again. He sneers up at the picture. "Mr. Fucking Money-Bags." He grabs an empty bottle. "The guy I've never even met."

And he hurls the bottle at the picture, satisfied at the crash that occurs when the two of them meet.

Then just before he spirals down into a blackout he peers out of the window.

But, what he sees there must be a hallucination, another after-effect of the drink.

For why would some spotty teenage kid be out there looking in at him?

On Patrol

He'd been out there all day.

For a place as big as this, it sure was low on the surveillance: no CCTV, no armed guards, nothing.

In one way, Henry was glad of this—it made his job a whole lot easier. But in another, it kind of disappointed him—it exposed his fantasies as unrealistic and bizarre, and no teenager wanted to be made aware of *that*.

Then again, some of the stuff that had been happening to him lately had been *beyond* fantasy.

Take last night, for instance…

The doll sat looking at the computer, reading his work. This was the night after she had first presented herself to him—yeah, he thought of the doll as a *her* now, having heard her speak—and how he had managed to get through a whole day at school after that whole thing was beyond him. Every time Eric's hand fell on his shoulder—which happened often, his friend liking to give him a scare—he just about jumped from his skin, certain that it was her, that she had come to harm him in some way. But it never was, and when he got home she was in the closet where she'd gone after their little chat.

But Roberta came out when he returned, and went straight to the computer, where she soon looked to him and said, "this shit's all new to me, kid. When I was killed, there was none of this "social media" stuff. I mean, what the fuck does that even mean?"

He hadn't got past the first part of her sentence. "When you were… what?"

"Killed." She swivelled her doll's head back to the screen. "Didn't you know, kid? I'm dead. A ghost."

Yep, he never could have fantasised *that* one.

But he could well believe it, seeing how hopelessly clueless she was about the Internet.

"So you just sit here and send threats to people?" she said.

Henry looked to the wall, nervous that his parents might hear her voice from next door.

"Don't worry, kid," she said. "You're the only one who can hear me. For now."

Oddly, that didn't do much to reassure him.

"How do you find these people you threaten?" she asked him.

He had given up trying to deny his illicit activities—why bother, when she seemed to know everything about him, had apparently read him the first moment she'd seen him?

"Just search for them online, I guess," he said, shrugging.

She nodded, looked back to the screen, read some more of his work: "maim, mutilate, dismember." She looked back at Henry. "You must really hate this guy."

"Actually," Henry said, looking at a picture of Eric, "he's my best friend." And he looked really buff in the picture in question, showing off his six-pack at the beach. The bastard.

"Right," said the doll, suddenly more interest in her voice than he had ever heard there before. "So, how does that work? If I just type in a name, will I find everything out about them?"

"Well," he said, "not quite. But almost."

"Good," she said.

Then she told him to type in a name.

One he'd never heard of.

But he looked.

Nothing.

"Ah well," she said. "Never mind. Bet I still know where he lives, anyway."

And now Henry was here, at the address she'd given him.

Not much had happened so far, and he wasn't really sure what he'd come for, just that the doll had told him to "go and watch," and after that explosion in his head the other night, he hadn't been in any mood to defy her. Though he'd been tempted to abandon his post and follow the dark-haired, long-legged beauty when she stepped out of the big house earlier.

He hadn't.

Pussy that he was.

Still, around nine that evening he was thinking of calling it a day.

It had probably been more interesting than school, this little patrol, but that wasn't really saying much. As to where he'd been tonight, he would tell his parents he'd been out with Eric, if they asked. Which they probably wouldn't.

He took one last look through a window.

The guy whose name he'd searched last night—Connor McWilliams—looked pretty merrily drunk.

Henry headed off to report that back to the guy's mother.

Memories

The next morning (well, it's actually afternoon by the time he comes around, but what the hell) brings with it the hair of the dog, more drink.

But not alone this time.

"Arthur," he says, knocking on the butler's door. He's always up to something in here when he's not working; but Connor never asks him what it is, gives the guy his privacy. Arthur's earned all that from him—and more.

"Yes, sir?" comes the reply.

"Put on your best clothes. We're going out."

"Out?" Arthur queries, opening up the door. "Where, sir?"

"The pub."

Arthur looks at him. "You want to go to the pub?"

Well, no—he *doesn't* really want to go to the pub. But he wants a drink, and he drank everything they had in the house last night, so yes, it's the pub it must be.

"Come on," he says. He pats down his hair, smells his breath, which now thanks to toothpaste and mouthwash is only 85% proof. "Let's go."

"As sir wishes," Arthur says, and puts down the polish.

And pretty soon they're at their local pub.

Both of them new to the place, and getting funny looks from the regulars, a couple of whom look like they *live* there.

"Don't worry about that, Arthur," he says. "They'll sharp change their tune when I buy drinks for everyone."

He's right.

They do.

It's amazing how many best friends he has a mere hour later.

By that point they're in the corner of the bar, eyes on a pool match being played being two young and hip-looking guys in their mid-twenties.

That's when he says:

"I nearly told Melody."

Arthur puts down his glass of beer, wipes foam away from his lips. "About you-know-what?"

"About you-know-*who*."

"Well," Arthur replies. "She's a lovely girl."

"Did you know," he asks, "when you picked her? That I'd like her so much, I mean."

"I wish I could claim that, sir." Arthur smiles. "My magic's not that good."

Connor thinks he meant that as a joke. But the comment seems to make it physical, the memory that always lies between them, the one that bonds them. You could almost reach out and touch it. Touch *her*.

"Do you think I should?" he says.

"I doubt she would believe it, sir."

Connor nods, seeing the truth of this.

"Why stay, Arthur?" he then asks. "You don't have to, you know. You could leave anytime you want. I'd give you all the money you needed, if you ever wanted to."

Arthur says nothing for a while, just watched the boys and their pool game. "I was the second thing she bought," he finally says. "When you were just a baby, when the paternity tests came back. First the house. Then me." He smiles, looking to his master. "But she never knew what would happen. That I would feel so protective over you."

Connor didn't know what to say to that.

"I was already too old for a kid of my own, back then." Arthur laughs. "Too old to find a wife to *have* one with. That was why, when I saw you…"

He places down the glass, empty now.

"I just wish it hadn't taken so long," he concludes.

"Better late than never," says the younger man, and orders up another round.

But even as they descend into alcoholic oblivion, Connor can't help but feel a little bit uneasy.

Can't help but feel the presence of his mother is somehow still watching them.

And judging.

The Things You Do for Love

"So," Eric said. "I didn't see you at school yesterday."

Henry grinned. "That's because I wasn't here."

They were sitting at the edge of the football field again. Eric had been waiting for him, not bothering to play with the sports kids like he usually did when Henry wasn't around, and something about that made him nervous.

"You mean you knocked off without me?" Eric said.

"Yeah, but don't worry," Henry replied. "I didn't get up to much."

Eric leered at him. "I bet I know *exactly* what you got up to…"

"Wrong," Henry told him.

That had actually happened last night, when he got back home.

He'd expected his parents to be in bed by that time, and he was not disappointed. He had headed straight up to his room, and though the laptop lay switched on, he hadn't really felt much like sending death threats. Instead, he'd opened up the closet door.

And found the doll waiting for him.

"Tell me," she said.

He looked back, making sure the bedroom door was locked.

"I saw him," he then said, turning back to her. "Some old guy, too. And a woman, but she left just after I got there."

"An old man?" said the doll. "Describe him."

Henry did so.

"Arthur," she said.

Then took a step forward, hovering in that way of hers.

"You did good, kid," it told him. "You want your reward?"

He did.

And oh God was it worth the wait.

"Come on," Eric said now, nudging him. "You must have done the do by now."

"A gentleman never tells."

"Hey," said Eric. "I told you all about Alison, didn't I?"

He had indeed. On many separate occasions. With some decorum first time around, but with increasingly graphic detail every time since. Including where they usually like to go to get up to shenanigans.

"Hey, that reminds me," Eric went on. "If you're not busy tonight—you fancy double dating with me? Alison's got this real cute cousin."

Once upon a time these words would have brought joy to Henry's ears. But not now. Not when he had Roberta waiting for him at home.

"No thank you," he said.

Eric shook his head. "Your loss, man."

That was when a football sailed by them, slamming into the wall behind Eric's head.

"Hey, you fuckers!" he shouted. "Watch it!"

"Geez, Eric," Henry said, shocked by this outburst. "Relax."

"Sorry, sorry," Eric replied. "Just a little edgy, that's all. Some shit's been harassing me online."

"Oh really?" said Henry. "That's too bad."

-ೋΛೋ-

They went at it again that night.

And they were sneaky.

They used the floor, no squeaking bedsprings to give them away.

When it was done, his semen trickling out of her soft plastic vagina, Roberta said, "I've got another name for you to search."

"Sure," he said, and padded naked to the laptop.

She gave him the name.

And surprisingly, he had *heard* of this one.

The guy even had his own website.

"God, is *that* what he looks like now?" Roberta nodded towards the cover photo. "He's let himself go!"

Something about the familiarity with which she spoke intrigued Henry. "You know that guy?"

"Once," she said. She seemed to be considering something. "Now I think I'd like to get to know him again."

"How?" Henry felt a chill, realised he was still naked and went on put on some clothes. "I saw his house on *Padz* one time—it's at the other end of the city."

"Well," she replied. "That's where *you* come in." She looked at him. "You can *drive*, can't you?"

"Well, yeah," he said. "But I don't have a car."

"No. But I bet you know someone that does."

And he did indeed.

His best friend—and favourite online victim—Eric.

-A-

"Oh Eric…oh God don't stop…oh Eric you're the best…"

Alison groaned, pushed him away. "Will you knock that shit off?" she said. "It's weird when you keep saying your own name."

"Saw it in a porno movie one time, babe," he told her. "Sorry. Thought it might turn you on."

"Well," she said, "it didn't."

"Oh yeah?" he said. "Does this?"

His mouth descended, his hands finding her once more.

They were in the backseat of his car, where so many of their sexual encounters had taken place, although not, thankfully, the first one. No, that had happened at a party…and if Henry hadn't been such a wimp and come to that same party, Eric would bet that *he* would have got lucky too—even if only with someone that was drunk.

He sighed inside, thinking of his friend.

He still couldn't believe that Henry had turned down his offer of a double date.

He sometimes wondered if they should still be friends. Alison certainly couldn't stand him…Eric had had to *beg* her to set up that date. And now that

Henry had rejected it, there was probably no hope of them *ever* getting close.

Man, Eric thought.

When did being young get so complicated?

He tried to banish these thoughts, tried to lose himself with Alison.

But then he realised she was pulling away.

She was on top of him now, and looking out the window.

"I think someone's out there," she said.

Eric froze.

Remembering the online harassment, remembering all the death threats.

Then his fear turned to anger.

"Wait here," he said, and did up his trousers and stepped out into the night.

And he did indeed see a figure at the other end of this deserted park.

Eric couldn't believe that they'd been rumbled, that someone else had found them out here. The park was creepy at night, which was why no one ever came here. He'd even recommended it to Henry, for use in the unlikely event that he had someone to bring along.

"Who's there?" Eric called. "Who the hell are you, pal?"

His hands formed fists as he remembered the violence of some of those threats.

But it was no stalker that stepped out of the shadows.

It was just Henry.

"Taking me up on that offer, are you, buddy?" Eric said. He looked at his watch. "Well, it's a little late, but—"

He didn't see the knife until it was in his stomach.

"Need your car," he heard Henry say as he fell to the floor. But it was no voice Eric had ever heard from his friend. It was dull, monotone, robotic. Like something else was controlling him.

Then all he could hear was screaming and slicing as Henry reached the car. And Alison.

And finally, nothing.

"But what if they come out of their room and see me?"

"*Your* parents?" Roberta replied. "I doubt it."

"But I don't want to take the chance." Henry crossed his arms, trying to make a stand with her, and was surprised to find they felt sore, achy—whatever he had just done outside, it must have been pretty strenuous. "I don't want you hurting them."

"Fine," she said. "Push me out the window, pick me up outside."

"But won't that hurt?"

"Not as much as you will," she warned, "if you don't get a move on."

Henry took the hint.

Despite the pain in his arms, he did as she'd instructed, then ran outside to where she had landed and bundled her into the backseat.

"God," she said. "I can still smell the death. I like it."

"Cool," he said, getting the car going. "The knife's still somewhere back there, too."

"Good," she said. "You'll need it."

Hesitation

Ten numbers.

He's typed in ten numbers.

But he's too scared to tap the eleventh.

Why can't he call her?

Why can't he just call Melody and tell her everything?

It's not just about the sex, either—in fact, after what happened with the escort that came before her he suspects that he is incapable of going back to emotionless sex, anyway. No, he's at a crossroads. One that seems to demand he strive for something more with his life.

He looked out across the main room—Arthur was messing around with the security pad on the front door. The butler's always on at him about increasing the security around here—maybe putting in some CCTV. But surrounding yourself with cameras, that seems more *her* style than his. And there's no one in the world he wants to be compared to less than his mother.

As if prompted by the thought, his phone rings.

But not the one in his hands.

No, the other one.

The special one.

He picks it up, unsurprised to see Rod's name there.

"What's up, Rod?" he asks. "You spent that money already?"

But Rod is laughing crazily over his words.

And he hears more of them in the background.

Voices he recognises, mocking, and laughing.

The rest of his half-brothers and sisters.

"Turn on the news," Rod says through guffaws. "Channel 87."

"What for?"

"Just do it."

A shiver running through him, he does so.

And he sees immediately why they're laughing.

On the Road

"God, that was such a rush!" Henry looked at Roberta in the rear-view mirror, the ache in his arms long, now feeling nothing but joy and energy. "We got time to pull over for a quick one?"

"Better not," she replied. "The police might be looking for this car by now. But soon. Very soon."

"All right, all right." He stroked the gun in his pocket, the gun he had taken from a dead guy's hand. "But tell me, why'd you want to kill that guy?"

Actually, she *had* killed him. Done her head thing like she'd done with him, only took it through to the end this time.

"He should have killed himself long ago," she replied. "How dare he go on living without me?"

Oh-kay, Henry thought. *Better leave that one there.*

Instead he asked, "where we headed next?"

"I think you know."

"The drunk guy in the big house? Cool."

And they sped through the night towards Connor McWilliams.

Bad News

It's still playing on the news, the story getting bigger now. He's called Arthur in to watch it with him, the old guy shaking there as his eyes take in what's happened.

"At roughly 8 a.m. this morning," the newsreader gravely stated, "a car ploughed through the front door of the mansion of hip-hop legend and actor Big Bo Bob. Two bodyguards were stationed at the door, and it was these brave souls that the car struck first, killing both men instantly."

Big Bo, he thinks. *Though I'd call him another name, if I ever got to meet him. Dad.*

"The driver then exited the now ruined vehicle and removed a pistol from the holster of one of the bodyguards," the newsreader went on. "This he used to spray the house of Big Bo Bob with bullets, killing his wife and two teenage sons instantly."

That would be his *legitimate* sons, of course. The one whose money didn't come to them via a secret, highly guarded back account.

"The only survivor was a maid who remained hidden in a wardrobe the entire time." And here the newsreader's face took on a strange look, as if they could not quite believe what they were about to report. "And it is here that the story takes on the strangest twist of all, as this courageous woman now tells."

The screen cut to the woman in question, talking to a reporter at the scene.

"They found a car in the garage," she said. "One of Mr. Bob's. They took that. But the guy doing all the shooting didn't just get straight in it. He took something out of the *other* car, the one he'd crashed the place with. It was one of those sex doll things. And the guy was talking to it, kissing it."

"And is that," the reporter asked, "when the man shot your employer, Big Bo Bob?"

"I'm not sure he *did* shoot him," the maid said. "They were just standing there in front of him, the guy, and the doll. And Mr. Bob's head, it just sort of…exploded."

"Thank you," said the reporter. "Back to you in the studio."

And in the house, he clicks off the TV.

Arthur looks to him, eyes going wide. "Did you hear that?"

"Yeah," he says. "She's alive. And that means she's coming here."

"She's already here," came a voice he'd wished never to hear again.

They pair turns to see the boy who is a stranger and a prosthetic woman they know all too well. "Really should have changed the security code for the door," she said.

Conor looks to Arthur, confused, but the older man wasn't looking at him. Conor's eyes turn towards the boy. "I know you," he says. "You were outside the other night, watching me."

"That's right," the boy answers. "Name's Henry—and I've been making pretty good friends with your mother."

"You're not the only one," he says. "She tell you what she used to be?"

"That's not something he needs to know," his mother says. "And since I'm the one who's in charge here, I think you'd better just shut the fuck up."

"Why?" he replies, feeling courage come from somewhere, some place Conor never had back when she was alive. "What you going to do to me?"

"Oh, I've learnt a few new tricks," she says. "Let me demonstrate." The old man starts to scream, clutches at the top of his head. She gives him one last sorrowful look before his head explodes. The force of the blast knocks Connor from his feet. But not for long, and soon he's on his knees beside his friend, cradling Arthur's body.

"Is that how you killed my dad?" Conor screamed, looking up and over at the doll.

"And a few others," she tells him. "The guy who found me in the skip where your little friend dumped me, and all the guys that came after him. Took me a while to find somebody that was of some use to me." She nods back towards Henry, hanging slightly behind her, gun in his hand. "But Henry here was worth the wait."

"You're disgusting," he says.

And he remembers:

He was fourteen.

"I wanted a girl," she said. "That would have been easier. But so long as I'm stuck with you, I'm going to teach you what I'm all about." She pointed towards the item in the room, the big thing that's covered up with a blanket. "Go on. Take a look."

Conor looks at Henry. "You don't know what you're doing, kid."

"Yes he does," she replies. "Which is more than you ever did, remember?"

He does.

It was like some surreal moment from a movie—what the hell was a sex doll doing propped up in the corner?

"She's a monster," he continues. "She had about a dozen kids, all with different guys." He stands up from the body. "A dozen *famous* guys."

"I'm going to train you how to seduce a woman, kid," she said. "Using our friend here," she added, pointing at the doll. "But don't waste it. You're only going to go with famous chicks. Like I do, with men."

He went on "She got pregnant every time, but she wasn't very good in court. Most times she only got the dads to make a one-off payment. She ditched the kids, then passed them onto foster parents. Claimed she "couldn't cope." And just a few months later she'd be pregnant with another one."

Conor turns to face his mother fully, a scowl coming across his face. "Guess what, mother? I've made contact with them. All of them. Had to—to try and make up for what *you* did to them."

"But Mother, I don't want to!"

"My dad was the big one, though," he says. "The only one who's still successful," he added, thinking of the destitute states of Rod and all the others. He motions around the house. "He paid for all of this—*still* paying it, in fact, though I guess not for very much longer. He did it all in secret, so his wife would never find out—the only rule was, we were to have no contact with him. Ever."

"Get the fuck on there!" she cried, and slung him atop the doll.

He fell to the floor, crying.

"Pussy," she said, walking away.

Then he felt a hand on his shoulder.

Looked up, expecting her.

But seeing Arthur instead.

"Know how she fooled him?" he asks Henry.

The boy had a glazed expression on his face, like this is all a dream to him.

"Magic." Conor spits the word out with disdain.

"I'm not going to let her do this to you anymore," Arthur said.

He rubbed snot away from his nose. "What you going to do?"

"Have her sign this document making me your legal guardian," he said. "Then...you don't want to know."

But he had an idea.

He'd seen the magic books she left around. When he heard a scream coming from her bedroom the next morning...He rolled over, went back to sleep, smiled. When he came down, both the doll and his mother were gone. A new era of happiness began, with Arthur bringing him up.

"Yeah," she sneers. "Magic."

"Magic?" says Henry, reminding them both he was still there. Conor points towards Arthur's body. "What did he do to you?"

"He made my physical form disappear," she says, "fused my soul with the doll, then dumped me in a skip. But he wasn't good enough to kill me."

"Not then," comes a voice. "But I never stopped practising."

Arthur rises from the ground. Nothing there above the shoulders, and yet somehow he still hears the man's voice.

"Go," Arthur said, leaping towards Henry. She tries to stop him, but Arthur is on her, knocking the doll form to the ground.

Henry, watching them, doesn't lift the gun until Arthur is on him. By then, it was too late; Arthur's hands are on Henry's wrist, wrestling, trying to wrest the gun away from him.

"Bastard!" she cries at Arthur. "He was mine! How dare you take him from me?"

The gun goes off, bullet sinking into the ground.

Henry screams, seemingly forgetting that it was *he* that fired the shot.

"No," Arthur's voice somehow all around them, floating through the air. "Not your property—a person, even if you never saw that."

The doll growls and roars. Conor rages forward with a sudden anger, lashing out with a punch that knocked Henry off his feet.

Mother looks impressed.

"That's my boy," she says. That's when Arthur's a hand smashes through her body from behind, punching its way out of her rubber stomach.

Something black and burnt-looking in his hands, squirming in his fingers.

"Your soul, Roberta," he says. "Your evil, poisonous soul. I wasn't able to do this last time we met. But now I've grown."

The black thing screams as he crushes it.

"No!" Henry cries, and swings the gun. But Connor is ready. He kicks out, hits Henry full in the face, and sends the boy flying across the room.

Arthur slides his arm out of the doll, crumpling to the ground, lifeless. "Had a feeling," he says. "Ever since our little chat at the bar the other day. That's why I changed the door code back. Couldn't shake the idea she was coming."

His voice growing quieter now, fading.

"How many more times can you save me, Arthur?" he asks, fighting back tears.

"Afraid that was the last, sir." It's barely a whisper now. "You'll have to find someone else now. So ask yourself this: are you going to tell her?"

Arthur's body falls to the ground, his spirit extinguished.

"Goodbye, my friend."

Conor walks over to Henry, who seems unsure of what to do. The boy is just another victim of his mother's evil, just like him, but he picks up the gun, regardless.

Henry eventually comes to his sense. "Hey," the kid says. "You can let me go. It was all her. Honest. She was...controlling me."

"You think?" he says.

His eyes noticing the boy's hand sliding round the floor behind himself.

"Can I trust you, son?" he asks.

"Course you can," comes the reply, and he wants to believe it—almost *does* believe it—until suddenly the child moves, snarling, lunging with a bloody knife.

But not quickly enough.

The gunshot is loud, almost deafening.

A sound he never wants to hear again.

Now that it is done...he sits down and weeps for what he lost so long ago.

What Comes After

"Hello?"

She calls through the letterbox.

"Connor, Arthur called me last night, he said I should come over and see you today."

The door slides slowly open before her. "Connor?" Melody walks through.

"Babe," she says. "The door was open. Are you all right?" She stops. Seeing the carnage before her: two dead, headless bodies. A sex doll with a hole punched right through its centre. And the guy she'd come to like sitting among it, crying.

Part of her wants to run.

But then—

-A-

He sees her.

Coming towards him, looking scared. So scared. But not running away. And suddenly, that means so much to him.

So, he holds out his hand and he says her name. And when she sits down beside him he finally tells her.

Everything.

This page is intentionally left blank.

Film Scripts

Culdesac

Aunte Mame

EXT. SUBURBAN NEIGHBORHOOD—NIGHT

Standing on the sidewalk is a young girl, dressed as a baby doll. She bends down to fix her stockings.

CLOSE IN

On her face when she straightens back up. We see—framed by her flouncy pigtails—an altogether pretty face, abruptly ruined by a swollen lip, fresh gash on her cheek, and menacing black eye, glistening with a thin layer of glitter eyeshadow.

After looking both ways, she leaves the safety of the sidewalk, and begins walking down the street. It is eerily quiet. No one but her seems to be out there, existing.

Then a car suddenly appears, creeping up slowly behind her. She pays it no mind; keeps her eyes out ahead of her.

BEEP! BEEP! (O.S.)

Now she turns, facing blinding headlights. From behind them, it seems, a voice calls out:

MAX

Hey! You lookin' to get hit?

DOTTY

You lookin' to run me over?

MAX

With that attitude, I might as well.

The young girl—DOTTY—draws closer, and sits on the front hood. A face, speaking volumes. "I wanna see you try."

Surprisingly, this results in a laugh than any sort of protest from the voice behind the headlights—MAX.

MAX

(Laughing)

Alright, alright. You got me. Ain't nobody doin' nothin' to anybody, okay? I was just looking for you, okay? Heard you walked these parts.

DOTTY sneers. MAX continues.

MAX

What's your name?

SCENE 2.

DOTTY

Heard that I walked these parts, but didn't hear my name? Kill the headlights.

MAX

Or what?

DOTTY

Or nothing, that's what. Consider your search ongoing!

Counting 5 seconds or so. Then the headlights go off. The dim night aura returns.

Leaning out from the Driver's seat window is MAX, a seemingly grungy teenage boy, about Dotty's age. Now seen through the windshield is another boy, appearing younger; smaller. His name is TONY.

Through thick, black-framed glasses, he locks eyes with DOTTY, who all but smiles at him. It leaves just as quickly as it came, once she moves her gaze back to MAX.

DOTTY

I like to know who I'm messin' with, is all.

MAX

And now you do. So...

DOTTY

Dotty. But I go by Dot.

MAX

Swell. You know Marco, Dotty? That's where you're headin', right? To see Marco? To Marco's?

DOTTY

Yup.

MAX

Ain't even gonna lie. Well... Marco don't like you roamin' in the dark. Says you need a ride.

DOTTY

I don't need anything. Especially a ride. But I want one. I'd like one.

MAX

Yeah? So what you gonna do?

SCENE 3.

DOTTY

Tell your friend to give up the front seat.

MAX

I ain't gotta tell him. He can hear you.

(Turns to Tony)

Right, Tony?

Without a word, TONY climbs over to the back seat, his sneakered feet being the last thing we see before disappearing into its darkness. All the while, DOTTY is already settling into the passenger seat.

She slams the door beside her, and Max takes that as his cue to start driving again.

He reawakens the engine, and they drive off.

CUT TO

INT. CAR—NIGHT

MAX in the driver's seat. DOTTY on his right in the passenger. And TONY nowhere to be seen in the back.

DOTTY reaches in between her legs, and pulls out a compact mirror. She opens it, and examines herself. Pressing the swollen purple flesh of her eye; pinching the skin of her lips and cheek, making them an even more vibrant red than before. Even shedding a trickle of blood.

MAX sneaks glances as she does this.

MAX

Pretty crowded down there for her, I'm sure.

DOTTY

Her name is Henry.

MAX

(Incredulously)

Ha! Henry?!

(Laughs)

Motherfucking Henry!

SCENE 4.

DOTTY

(Pats her own cheek)

Not like it belongs to this doll here. And no Susy, Ethel or Maggie's comin' outta her. I can tell you that now. Not if you and me have any say in it.

MAX

Me?

DOTTY

You and every other.

MAX

Jesus Christ.

DOTTY

Him, too. Shit, legends in that 'How to be a Holy Violator' manual tell of him and the Magdalene whore. Only he wanted a king, right? Just like his ol' man? A king for himself. And her? She wanted a king in her. To hell with whatever came out.

MAX

"Man wants man, you'll give a man. As long you get a man..." Is that what I'm hearin'?

DOTTY

Is that what you're likin'?

MAX shakes his head, smiling; taking his eyes off the road to crane his head back to where TONY is. Finally do we see him, deep within the shadows. The glint of the occasional street light reflecting off his glasses.

When MAX turns back to Dotty, she says:

DOTTY

And Marco didn't warn you about me?

MAX

He told me what I needed to know.

DOTTY

And what's that?

SCENE 5.

DREAM SQUENCE

A plastic bag flashes right before DOTTY's line of sight, and encloses about her whole head, tightening around her neck.

Holding it there from behind the passenger's seat, is TONY.

Baring his teeth, he tightens it.

DOTTY claws at the bag, thrashing back at TONY - Laughing.

Her hand catches his glasses, and she knocks them off, TONY roaring as they dangle from his face, then fall silently to the ground.

MAX, still casually at the wheel, calls back to TONY:

MAX

Hey now. Watch the hands. Told you to leave those fucking glasses, anyway.

TONY only glares at him, and keeps at it with the bag.

DOTTY's laughing falters to a breathless cackle. Then to short gasping breaths.

Her legs kicking. Feet clomping.

Hands lowering to tear at the console, seat, and windows.

Through the bag, the mold of her teeth gnaws, failing to break through.

Inhale...

And then silence. Joined by stillness.

Completely limp, DOTTY lulls forward when the bag is

taken off her head.

MAX brings the car to a halt.

She hits the dashboard with a painful 'THUD'.

END DREAM SEQUENCE

CUT TO:

EXT. SUBURBAN NEIGHBORHOOD; STREET-NIGHT

DOTTY still sits on the hood of the car.

MAX, still leaning out from the window.

TONY at his side in the passenger seat.

SCENE 6.

MAX

Ain't even gonna lie. Well... Marco don't like you roamin' in the dark. Says you need a ride.

DOTTY

I don't need anything.

(Beat)

I'm swell. I'll be that way when I get there.

MAX

Will you, now?

DOTTY

I *will* now. And I *will* then, too. Thanks, though.

And with one final pat to the hood, DOTTY leaps off from it, and walks off, still in the street.

MAX watches her for a minute, then gets back into the car.

He slams the door beside him.

TONY doesn't so much look at him, as he does cock his head in his direction. Peaking his ear to listen, more or less.

Listening for him to break the silence.

MAX

...Now.

TONY springs into action, reaching into the backseat for a white plastic bag, before throwing his door open.

Halfway out, MAX calls out to him:

MAX (CONT'D)

And take off those fucking glasses!

TONY rips them off, tosses them back into the car, and slams the door behind him. We hear him sprint off.

MAX, looking on from the driver's seat.

CUT TO BLACK.

BESTIAS de CARGA

AUNTE MAME

TITLE CARD:

BESTIAS DE CARGA

THEN CUT TO BLACK.

Three LOUD KNOCKS on a DOOR.

BENIGNA (O.S.)

What is it?

CUT TO:

INT. ROOM - NIGHT

AMANDLA - meekly dressed in black - opens the door ever so gently, and is greeted with the sight of a small young *bruja*, standing high up on a wooden table.

Clad in all white, she performs a *limpia*, holding a fat cigar in her hand. From her mouth, spilling thick clouds of smoke.

She blows them onto the face of SENOR CHAVEZ,

who stands shirtless with his arms outstretched, glaring at her.

She - BENIGNA - glares back.

AMANDLA

(Hesitant)

Someone here to see you, Benigna.

BENIGNA

Is that so? Well tell them that I'm busy.

AMANDLA

I can't do that.

BENIGNA

Oh?

Slowly and dramatically, does the door open wider, revealing three, menacingly dark figures, looming behind AMANDLA.

The one in the center is the first to move, entering the room as if he owns it.

He...is DON MATEO - The *Narco*. And like death facing a soul who has evaded him for too long, he barrels past SENOR CHAVEZ, towards BENIGNA, and doesn't stop until he is mere inches away from her face.

From the door, AMANDLA looks on, terrified. The other two figures stand firm.

BENIGNA, all the while, simply takes a drag from her cigar, and blows a great puff of smoke in DON MATEO's face.

Calm as ever, she speaks:

BENIGNA

(To Amandla)

Let me guess. Yemaya let them in.

On cue, YEMAYA - a vibrant little girl - comes bouncing into the room, past AMANDLA and the two figures. And bumping right into DON MATEO's leg, she reaches into his pocket, pulling out a piece of candy. Without taking his eyes off BENIGNA, DON MATEO pets the little girl's head.

YEMAYA giggles, cramming the newfound treat in her mouth, wrapper and all.

BENIGNA (CONT'D)

Alright, then.

(To Yemaya; gesturing towards CHAVEZ)

Would you mind taking this one outside with you, mijita?

YEMAYA nods, then turns to SENOR CHAVEZ, grabbing hold of his hand. He pulls it away.

SENOR CHAVEZ

Now wait a minute -

BENIGNA

I'll get back to you as soon as I can, Senor Chavez. I promise you. But for now, just follow my niece.

YEMAYA - nodding again at the sound of her name.

YEMAYA

(sing-songy)

This way! This way!

She grabs hold of his hand once more, and with a slew of protests in his wake, he is dragged off, AMANDLA and the two figures making way for them as they leave.

Beat.

BENIGNA and DON MATEO - facing off still.

The silence barely settling back in.

With the slyest of smirks, BENIGNA is the first to break it:

BENIGNA

Buenos Noches, Don Mateo.

DON MATEO

What the fuck did you give me?

BENIGNA briefly turns her gaze to AMANDLA, and very gently begins her descent from the table.

BENIGNA

See the other two gentlemen
out as well, Amandla. I'll
speak with their boss alone.

DON MATEO - briefly turning to the figures.

DON MATEO

Go.

The two gape at him.

DON MATEO (CONT'D)

Vete, Cabrones! Ahora!

They all jump to the task, AMANDLA herding the two figures off before closing the door loudly behind them.

DON MATEO turns back to BENIGNA, her smirk lesser,

but not entirely gone.

DON MATEO (CONT'D)

(Sarcastically)

Are we safe now?

BENIGNA

We are.

DON MATEO

Good. Now you can answer my question.

From his other pocket, he produces a shiny gold necklace and slams it onto the wooden table.

DON MATEO (CONT'D)

What. the fuck. Did you give me?!

BENIGNA looks down at the necklace.

For the first time, she seems...surprised.

BENIGNA

You took it off.

DON MATEO

Obviously.

BENIGNA

Since when did you ever do that of your own volition?

DON MATEO

Since I found out you put your bullshit on it! My Grandmother's necklace? Really?!

BENIGNA

(Shrugs)

Had to hold some sort of significance. Otherwise, it wouldn't have worked.

(Beat)

And if you're here, that means it did.

DON MATEO glares viciously.

BENIGNA (CONT'D)

...Did it?

DON MATEO

(Rage)

Made me look like a fucking idiot, is what it did! Standing in front of a man who had the balls to think he could tell me how to run my business! And rather than make an example of him, I do what? WHAT?! NOTHING! Just sit there, huffing and puffing! WAITING! Only for literally NOTHING to happen! Is that what you wanted? Is that what you were after?

BENIGNA feigns surprise, "clutching her pearls."

BENIGNA

What-What I wanted?

(Laughs)

What could I possibly want from you that's actually yours to give? The drugs you steal?

The women you sell? The threats that were once wasted on you, oh so long ago?

(More Laughter)

What are they for, other than to remind others as to who you are? As if I don't already know who that really is.

All traces of laughter gone, BENIGNA persists:

BENIGNA

You don't remind me - of anything, 'Don Mateo.' I remind you. I am the giver here.

(Beat)

And what I am giving you is the solution to what will no doubt be the MOTHER of all your problems...In the very near future.

DON MATEO

Snaking it around my neck isn't exactly giving it to me, now is it?

BENIGNA

Would you've rather I strangled you with it?

(Beat)

I'm not your dead mother, and you are far from a child. You're so-called embarrassment today was how you were going to figure it out, one way or another. Maybe even a few times after that, since you like to cross-examine every fucking thing, just like your precious white powder.

BENIGNA picks up the necklace, dangling it before DON MATEO's seething gaze. Not as if to hypnotize, but to tease.

BENIGNA (CONT'D)

Only this - you can't put through a sifter.

DON MATEO

You're not putting that thing back on me.

BENIGNA

You say that as if you have a choice.

And right before another word could be said from either one of them, in bursts SENOR CHAVEZ, absolutely raving:

SENOR CHAVEZ

Alright, now I've had it with this shit! I was here first, wasn't I?! Why does he get to buy my time, huh -?!

BENIGNA

Senor, if you could please just go back with my niece -

SENOR CHAVEZ

To Hell with that bitch! I'm not paying for her company -!

BENIGNA

LISTEN! YOU JUST NEED TO -

Stop.

She stops...because a low, heavy growl cuts her words short.

And BENIGNA'S eyes - once set on the man before her - now stop dead on an unseen horror, standing - still growling, and heavily breathing - directly behind SENOR CHAVEZ.

And before he could get so much as a glance, a clawed hand grabs for his gaping mouth, and pulls him back.

He disappears beyond view.

A symphony of bone crackle.

Gurgled shrieks, a demonic roar, and then an assault of blood, hitting BENIGNA like paint splatter.

She watches - listens - in completely silent fear.

That is until she hears the distinct creak of a door; slowly, ever so slightly opening -

BENIGNA (CONT'D)

No, no, no, NO -!

BENIGNA lunges for the door, hopping over what looks like a lifeless body lying over another, until we see it's claws move.

His claws move.

The sound of YEMAYA's shrill little voice, singing "Dulce! Mas dulce!" from behind the door, beckons DON MATEO's head up, revealing his MONSTROUS FACE.

BENIGNA meets it like before - fierce, and completely unphased of its danger, as she tries with all her might to hold the door closed.

BENIGNA (CONT'D)

She wants one of those stupid candies of yours!

CUT TO:

INT. ROOM - LATER

DON MATEO now sits at the wooden table, still completely covered in all his gore.

BENIGNA - sitting right across from him - holds that damned necklace from before in her hands.

Carefully, she places it over his head.

We CLOSE IN on its pendant, glistening atop his bloody shirt.

And when we CUT BACK to the two of them once more, even he is astounded.

DON MATEO is back to normal.

His eyes, his teeth, his hands...All human.

His natural colored eyes look about at the mess that he's made. BENIGNA, watching him do so.

When they hit SENOR CHAVEZ - or rather, what is left of him - he asks:

DON MATEO

What the hell was he even here for, anyway? A spell?

BENIGNA nods.

DON MATEO (CONT'D)

For what?

BENIGNA

As fate would have it...Good fortune.

(Beat).

DON MATEO throws his head back, and LAUGHS.

CUT TO BLACK.

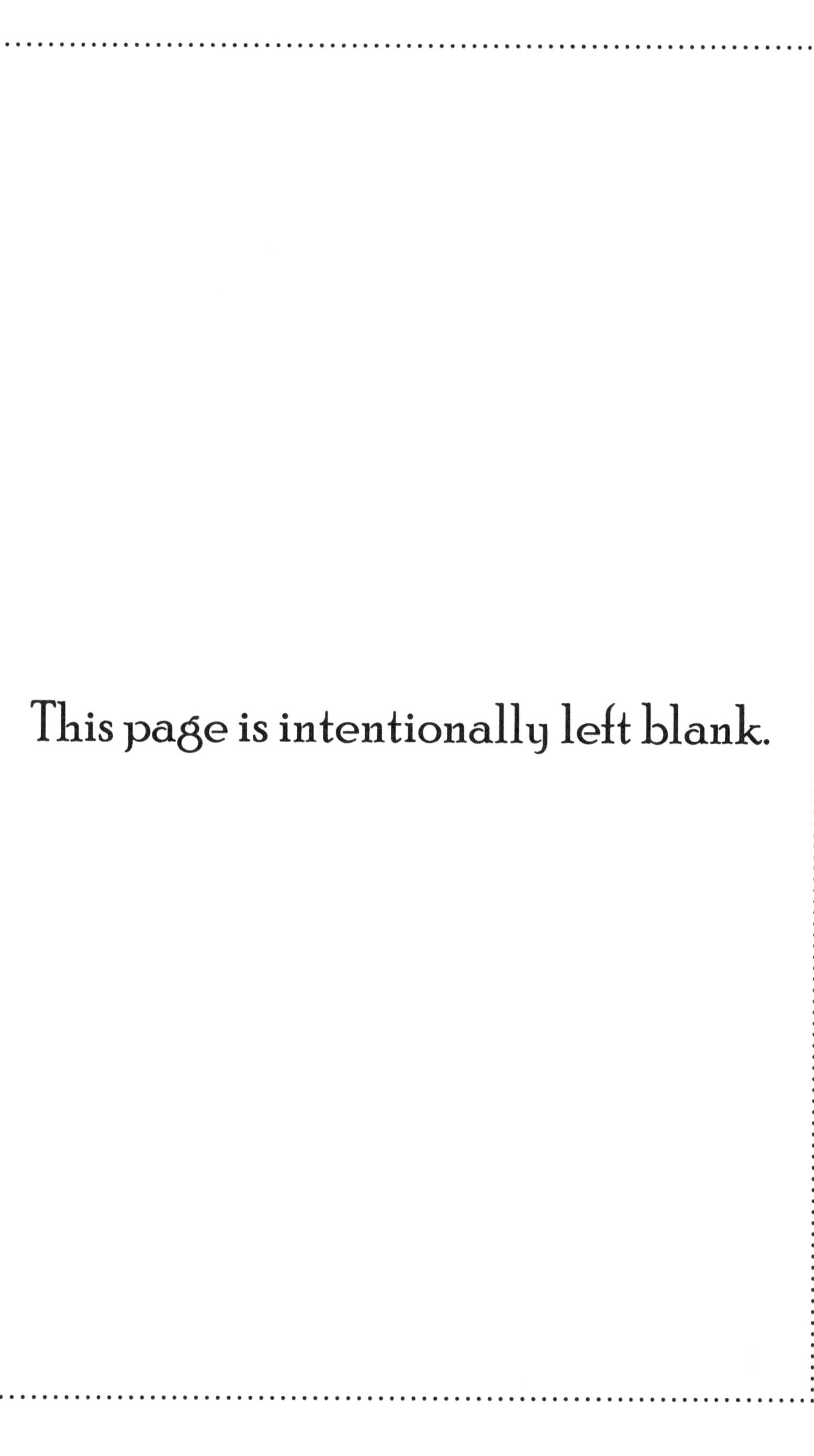
This page is intentionally left blank.

Novella

Painted

Via D'Agostino

Author's Dedication:

To Drs. Pullen and Moore, who helped breathe life into this story, and Dr. Kraynok, who saw me when no one else even thought to look.

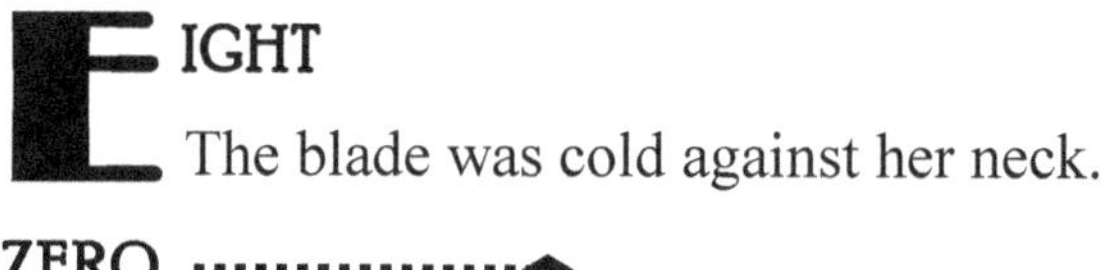

EIGHT

The blade was cold against her neck.

ZERO

In the beginning, there was a girl. She was young, bright, and full of potential, but in the end, she was nothing.

FIVE

The blade was cold against her wrist, the handle hot in her hand. The edge was wickedly sharp—she had made sure of that. One quick slice—push down, pull across—and it would all be over. It was that easy. Down and across, down and across, down and—no. Better to slide the blade up the inside of her arm, peel the skin open like a fish—free the life-giving blood from her veins.

Cut, cut, cutting, and cold. The words echoed across each other inside her head, lyrical and alluring. Sera knew that many people preferred the catchall "self-harm," but she liked the word *cut*. Something about the syllables, the way the letters looked jagged next to each other, appealed to her. Thinking about it was almost as good as actually cutting herself, and imagining the blood was its own kind of release.

It would spill, hot and dark, and red; it would spread, thick and viscous. It would pool, painting the tiled floor in a memory that would never wash out. Exactly a year ago, it had been a beautiful day that ended tragically, and that ending had been her fault. Today—after she had suffered for so long, knowing nothing could ever right the wrong—today would be remembered as her final act of penance.

April was about new beginnings, but sitting on the lip of the battered old bathtub, safe behind a locked door—at too steep an angle to see her own haggard reflection in the mirror—Sera knew there were no new beginnings for her. She knew there had been a time when she had been happy, but she couldn't even remember what it felt like to be whole. When Remi had left this world, left *her*, he had taken a piece of her heart, and nothing could replace it.

Sera trailed the tip of the knife up her arm, but not quite hard enough to do any real damage. A tingling sensation spiraled out from where it touched, coursing through her body. This was her choice. This was a power she had control over—her, and no one else. No psychiatrists telling her to take this and that pill. No people who claimed her as a friend but did not know the first thing about her. No one promising her it was not her fault. It had been out of her control—but that didn't mean it was not her fault.

The blade left a fiery path in its wake: a thin, crimson line set over top of the blue-green channel trapped beneath her flesh. Sera lowered the blade back to her skin, setting the tip into the curve of her wrist, shaping her body to fit the blade. She let it linger, slowly winding her arm around the edge, tracing her fingers across the smooth metal. Sera was alone, had always been alone, but the slide of the blade over her skin felt almost like a caress, a kiss from a lover.

A cold, biting kiss, and an end for all I've done, she thought.

This would be her release, her repentance, and her final plea for forgiveness.

Sera remembered all the times she cut herself before. Once, it had been an art form, back when she had needed a way to express her pain—her skin a canvas, her blood the paint when brushes and acrylics wouldn't do. Back when it had been a plea for help written across her shoulder or her thigh.

Back when Remi had been alive.

This time…this time there wouldn't be a next time. This time, she meant to kill. This time, as she again placed the tip of the blade against her skin, as she pressed down, this time it would all be over. Sera dug the edge of the blade into her wrist. She did not wince; she barely registered the pain beneath the rushing relief.

She felt the blood begin to flow.

ZERO

In the beginning, she knew only that she was hurtling towards the end.

In the middle, there was confusion. They told her it would abate, that it would ebb away so slowly that she would not even notice it, but that, one day—*one day*—she would wake up and everything would be clear, and then her life would go on.

One day never came—or, maybe it did, but it didn't come in the middle. Life did not intervene in the form of months or years or decades. Life was reduced to the space of a few breaths, heartbeats crushed so tightly together it seemed they were trying to make up for all the time they would miss.

In the end, there was a girl.

In the end, there was clarity.

In the end, nothing else mattered.

In the end, she could only remember the beginning.

ONE

The thing that people didn't understand was that there wasn't one specific moment when everything fell apart. It wasn't like turning on a faucet: one minute, nothing, and the next, water everywhere. There wasn't one particular event that everything could be traced back to, no simple, easy answers. No neatly wrapped package, no pretty little bow. Only the truth—the truth was that Sera did not know when the darkness had begun to creep in on her.

It was like the way she'd begun to self-harm. It hadn't been cutting—nothing so intentional. At first, she hadn't even known what she was doing. Scratching bug bites until they bled; picking at scabs to intentionally reopen accidental injuries. Chewing the insides of her cheeks, gnawing her lips, biting her fingernails so short they stung and bled. Kicking at curbs until her toes throbbed. Sera hadn't understood what it all meant then, but like a picture made clear only after all the pieces were assembled, she understood what she was doing now, even if she did not know when everything had started to be less accidental, and more purposeful.

But. If Sera had to pick a place to start her story, she supposed that the crash—the catalyst that shattered her world, rather than taking it apart painstakingly, piece by piece—would work as well as any other.

It had been a beautiful spring day; the kind that made every freshman yearn for summer, just so they could get out of high school English. Mr. Darby started in on another lecture about how the sparrow was symbolic of a boy and the ocean was secretly a woman. *What the actual hell? Not another story about men and the ocean and some chick's poem about her head in the oven door—* the bell rang.

She was on her feet in an instant. She was always desperate to escape the school and consistently beat her brother to the car. Since he was the one with the license, he was also the one with the keys, which meant standing around awkwardly while she waited—but anything was better than spending another minute in the school.

"Finish reading Hemingway," Mr. Darby was calling over the noise of the students packing up. "Next week we're starting something even better."

Oh, joy. Now what?

"We're continuing our studies in American literature with another classic: *The Great Gatsby*. I know you're going to love it—"

Sera shoved her earbuds into her ears and cranked the volume. She bobbed her head to the opening chords, tapping her fingers against her leg to keep time as the guitars and drums melded together, overlaid by words she knew like the beat of her own heart.

"I heard you crying loud…"

What a joke, Sera thought.

She tightened her fingers on the straps of her backpack, resisting the urge to rub at her shoulder where the thin, red lines stung. Last night had not been a good night. In her dreams she had been running—running from her parents' concerned faces, from her brother's outstretched hand. All she wanted in the world was to stop, turn back, and fling herself into their arms, but her feet were tangled in something. She fell, sprawling across the hard ground, and something began to drag her away; she twisted and thrashed to no avail.

When she looked back, her parents hadn't even been chasing after her. They were surrounded by all her siblings…too distracted to notice that one was missing. Only the sibling she was closest with, her brother and best friend, Remi, had looked up.

"Where's Sera?" he asked.

No one had heard him. She was no stranger to nightmares like these. She was dragged, kicking and screaming against the invisible force, beneath the surface of a lake so black that there was no reflection. When she awoke, she'd reached immediately for the knife.

There had been a time when she would have reached for Remi's hand, but she did not want to be a burden, and so she bore her pain alone.

Sera had not always felt like this. She knew that there were organizations meant to help, that she could tell her parents or either of her older siblings and they would drop everything to see her safely locked away. She knew, too, that she would become just another number, a face in a crowd of people with scars—and what was her pain compared to theirs? She could not bear the way her parents would look at her, the disappointment she would cause them, the pain in their eyes.

Sera knew that her parents would blame themselves for anything wrong with her, that they would spend hours tracing her life back, trying to figure out where they went wrong, instead of letting her be at fault. She could not imagine how it would wound Remi to know that even his friendship, his love, had not been enough to save her from herself.

She could not compare to those around her. Her parents were kind. Her siblings loved her. There was food on her table, shoes on her feet, and laughter in her life. The paint supplies in her closet were all different shades, each more vibrant than the last, from her favorite companies: Liquitex, Sennelier, Winsor & Newton.

Surrounded by a family that loved her, she was utterly alone.

She stole glances of the others in the hall—did they feel the same way? Did others carry a broken razor blade, hidden in their backpack? Did her classmates lock themselves in bathroom stalls when it was all too much, using paper towels to cover the damage done, rubber bands or old hair ties holding them in place?

Sera knew that she couldn't be alone, but even as she gazed into face after face, she saw no trace of her own suffering in their eyes. They did not understand, and they did not notice. Sera could have opened her mouth and screamed, but she knew that no sound would come out, or that no one would hear her—and really, what was the difference? So she marked herself to relieve the pain, and covered the scars with the fabric of her shirt. Hid behind her too-thin brown hair, afraid that if anyone looked into her eyes, they would see. Afraid of what would happen if no one bothered to look. Afraid, like a hunted rabbit.

She pushed her way out into the hall, shoving past the other kids, doing her best not to be shoved in return. The walls didn't make for a good crash-landing, even with a backpack as padding. Sera knew when to hold her ground, and when to leap out of the way to avoid being knocked to the floor.

Sera was just reaching her favorite part of the song, *When I Come Around.* She was at the last turn before she reached her locker when someone snagged the cord and tugged the earbud from her ear. With a tickling sort of sensation that made her cringe away, the left earbud popped free. Sera looked up to see a lanky, bright-eyed boy grinning down at her, the earbud dangling from his fingers.

"You may find out that your self-doubt means nothing was ever there," he said, in perfect time with Billie Joe.

Sera snatched the earbud back. "Remi."

He mimicked her exasperation. "Sera."

"How did you know what I was listening to?"

"You always listen to the same shit."

"It is *not* shit."

"It's like four years old at this point. You need some new jams."

Remi casually ran a hand through his dark, curly hair and flashed a flippant grin that was more for the blonde across the hallway than it was for Sera. He was so like the never-ending, ever-changing list of heroes and heroines he loved to describe to her. When Remi was reading, the suave attitude he adopted at school would melt away and his eyes would shine bright with some fresh adventure gleaned from the book clutched in his hand. As he recounted the tale to her, he would gaze off at a horizon she could never see, full of dreams she would never dream. Sera told herself that he was only teasing about the music. He was, after all, the one who had introduced her to Green Day.

"You were whispering the words. Thought I'd chime in."

His eyes were brilliant, distinctive, the color of blue jay feathers—the kind of eyes that made girls swoon and found themselves written into love songs with blonde girls like the one Remi was smiling at. His grin was not genuine; it was meant to impress. The one she had always counted upon to see her—to see past it all to her core, to see her as she truly was—looked right through her.

Sera knew that one day, Remi would find a girl he loved and who loved him in return. She was his sister, that is all, and someday—someday soon—there would be a girlfriend, and then a wife, and then children, who would supersede her. She would fall from most important to second, third, fourth... someday, he might not even remember her at all.

Sera knew this. She had always known this, but recently, it had been weighing on her mind more and more. Remi was changing, and she was not the same to him as she once had been. Sometimes her nightmares showed her the uncaring family with too many kids who only half-noticed when she was gone. Sometimes, it showed her Remi in ten, twenty, thirty years, his baby sister no longer his best friend. And sometimes, it showed her not the future, but the present. In it, she was always alone.

The memories seemed to rush in on her, as if the school hallway was constricting around her, crushing the breath from her body. Remi's still casual smile was like a knife twisting into her gut. The happiness at the prospect of seeing him, of complaining about her day to the only person she could count upon to care, drained out of her faster than water in a bottomless bucket. Kirstin, the blushing, giggling blonde still lurking in the background, did not help. She was Remi's latest heartthrob, and that meant Sera had to endure Remi's doe eyes every time her name came up. Sera knew that it was unfair of her, but she hated Kirstin anyways.

She thought another moment in that hallway might cause her to rip her eyes from her head, or worse, murder Kirstin on the spot. Sera turned stiffly, a toy soldier wound too tightly, and walked away.

"Hey, wait," he yelled.

Remi's voice was behind her, and then he was in front of her, blocking her path. Sera knew that her own eyes, plain, dull, and brown, paled in comparison to her brother's, but Remi seemed to see something in them. The blue sought out the brown, but she found she could not hold his gaze.

Sera wadded the earbuds up, forced them into her pocket, and kept on going. Today had not been a good day. She had been banking on Remi's face making it better, his easy smile brightening her abysmal mood, his banter curling the corners of her mouth up instead of down. She wanted things the way they had been, back when the girls could giggle all they liked and he never noticed. Back when he was too caught up in his books, in their games of make-believe, in being both her best friend and older brother to bother with things like girlfriends and reputations

I will always be your little sister, Sera thought. *But soon, that is all I will be.*

She could feel him slipping away, from best friend to brother to stranger. Now, rather than laughing with Remi, she found that she just wanted to go home, curl up alone in her bed, and forget that any of this had ever happened, where *this* meant *her entire life.*

Sera threw herself onto the floor so she was on a level with her bottom locker. She started spinning the dial on the combination lock, keying in Remi's birthday: zero-six-two-four. The lock popped open. She shrugged off her pack, ripped open the zipper, and began stuffing the books she would need for the weekend into it.

"Hey, take it easy there, Ser," Remi said. "You're like low-key killing that thing. What'd it ever do to you?"

Sera gave the zipper a jerk. It caught, stuck, held fast. "Would you—you stupid—God damn it." But it refused to budge no matter how she wrestled with it.

"Crushing it." He sounded mildly amused until she shoved the bag away from herself in frustration. "Hey, hey. It's cool. Look." He pulled the pack back towards them, wriggled free the fabric that had jammed it, and slid the zipper up with ease. "See?"

"Yeah, okay, great. Thanks."

Sera swung the bag from the floor onto her shoulder, where it thumped heavily against her back.

"Another rough day?" Remi asked.

Do you care, or are you playing the role of cool big brother because it's a part you know well—one that all the giggling blondes of the world love?

"Yeah. You could say that."

"What happened?"

"What the hell didn't?"

"A tree didn't fall out of the sky and take root in your soul."

"Fuck off."

"Oooh. Pulling out the big guns, are we?"

Sera didn't answer, just turned and started trudging her way back through the school. The throngs of students were thinning out as Sera reached the edge of the mob, but there was still a fair amount of jostling required to get through. Behind her, she could hear Remington's voice rising over the general hubbub, chasing after her.

Like a wild mother fucking polar bear tearing down a tundra, she thought.

"One. Twenty-one guns, " he sang.

Sera quickened her pace.

"Lay down your arms. Give up the fight."

Heads were starting to turn. Sera broke into a jog. She could hear Remi's shoes hitting the floor behind her, keeping time. Keeping up. The jog became a run.

"Alright, calm down. I'm sorry," he said.

She felt something catch at her backpack, attempting to pull her up short. She twisted, wrenching herself free of Remington's grasp. The run became a sprint. Sera hitched up her pack, hooking her fingers onto the bottoms of the straps and holding it against her spine so that it wouldn't bounce.

"Sera!"

She kept going.

"Ser, wait up!"

She swung around a corner, her feet skidding, almost toppling over. She ricocheted off a wall, slammed into the front doors, and felt them give way beneath the impact.

"Sera!"

She burst out into the daylight, still going at full tilt. She heard Remi hit the doors before they closed all the way, heard them fly into the brick wall with a crash. She didn't know why she was still running. She didn't understand why her feet were beating a tattoo into the pavement: *get away, get away, get away.* Whenever she had felt like this before, her legs had carried her *to* Remi, not *away* from him. What was the matter with her?

"Sera!"

She tried to stop, but like in her dream, she could not seem to control her own feet. If she did stop, if she did look back, would Remi still be chasing after her? Or would he only glance her way with a semi-curious look that said more than words ever could?

She streaked across the road, knowing full well that, in all likelihood, there would be cars. She should stop. She should not go careening into the school parking lot, weaving between buses and moving vehicles. The traffic wasn't too heavy yet—her sprinting had gotten her outside before almost anyone else—but all it took was one careless driver.

The streets in Cleveland were always clogged with traffic, and Sera never forgot to look both ways before crossing. But some days she made the conscious decision not to look. Sometimes, she took a chance. Some days, she hoped that she would get hit. Today was one of those days.

To her left, she saw a flash of hideous, puce green, the color of bile. She heard the blaring of a horn, Remi screaming her name. She ran, but not away. Directly in the path, she waited for the impact. She felt the hand of Death slam into her shoulder, felt the world tilt beneath her feet. This was it. This was the end. This was the first time she had truly been about to die. Her own name was echoing in her ears, Remington's shout ringing through the air.

Sera felt herself begin to fall, and she was not afraid.

EIGHT ················◆

The blade was cold on her neck, the touch of Death imminent upon her shoulder. Her own life was so far out of her control.

ONE ················◆

The asphalt was cold against her cheek.

Sera breathed, and the world smelled of blood. Reeked of human commodities. Underneath the stench of the pavement, Sera could just make out the scent of spring, so faint it was almost lost to the world.

She opened her eyes.

The first thing she saw was a patch of snow that had not yet deliquesced in the early April sunshine. It was melting in the middle, and the edges had already turned to millions of tiny, shattered crystals, a network of starbursts radiating cold. Trickles of water curved around it, caressing its edges and then running away, stealing little bits and pieces of the whole.

Her entire body was tingling from the impact with the unforgiving ground. Her breaths where short, the wind knocked from her chest. The skin on her hands had been sheared away, her jeans and her knees both torn open. She struggled to draw ragged gasps into her lungs, her backpack pressing on her, smothering her. Her thoughts were as disjoined as her movements, each moment its own snapshot, each motion unconnected to the whole. She dragged in another, shuddering lungful of air. Let it escape. Pressed her bloodied hands to the rough tarmac. Levered herself up. Pulled one leg underneath her body, her knee scraping over the ground, the melted snow soaking into the denim.

She got her second leg under her and peeled her hands up. She could feel tiny pieces of asphalt sticking to the raw flesh, could see the smudgy red prints her blood had left. Her heart thumped in her chest, echoing hollowly. It was as though she had been wrapped in cotton, muffling the world. Sera slipped out of the backpack, the straps falling away and freeing her from its weight. It tumbled away, but she ignored it as she staggered to her feet.

This was not right. She had been the one running. She had been the one to sprint through a parking lot. She had been the one in the path of the speeding car. It had been fast, had been on the verge of a blur, but she knew she had seen Rhett Crisinski's hideous, puke-green, wanna-be Mustang flying towards her. He always drove too fast, always had something to prove. He had been coming for her, the car Death's chariot and he the charioteer. He had hit someone. She had heard the awful sounds a body makes when it breaks beyond repair. She had felt the touch of Death, had hit the ground, and she had surrendered her life.

So why had her eyes opened? Why was she standing here, back on her feet? Why was Remi's shout still lingering, her name the last word to leave his lips?

Rhett's car was stopped only a few yards from where she had fallen. Its hood and fender were badly dented. It looked as though some giant had reached down and molded the car into a new shape, bending and twisting the metal into this new configuration. The windshield was cracked—not shattered, but cracked, a cobwebbing of hairline fractures, a spider web of scars that would never heal. The roof curved up, then bowed in, a sharp puncture that was never meant to be there—or, at the very least, was meant to fit the shape of her body.

"No," Sera whispered.

This couldn't be happening. This couldn't be true. Her eyes were lying to her. Her brain was deceiving her. This couldn't be real because…because—

"Remi."

The word was barely audible. It was the only sound she could make. His name—just that, and nothing more.

"Remi."

It was a murmur, a plea, and a sob all at once. And yet, her tears did not fall. She knew that they should, *goddamn it*, they ought to course down her cheeks like the first spring rain after a long, harsh winter, but she was too frozen, too dry, too numb and empty.

Her feet did not move. She knew that they should. That they ought to carry her to his side, that she ought to clutch his hand, hug his body close to hers. There might yet be life trapped beneath his skin. His vibrant eyes might still cling to their vivacity.

And yet, she could not. She could not bear it if his eyes were empty.

She knew that they would be.

"Remi…"

Sera knew that it should have been her. The hand that had sent her toppling to the side, out of the path of the car, had not been the touch of Death coming to pull her away from life, she realized. It had been Remi's hand, desperate to save her, shoving her out of Death's way—and his life had been forfeit.

Remi, no. Remi, I'm sorry. Remi, come back. Please don't leave me. I can't do this alone.

"Remi…"

Her voice trailed away. There was more, so much more, that she should have said. He had been chasing her, coming after her, trying to help her. And she had led him to his death. All that remained of him was only a few steps away, but her feet would not move. She could see the crumpled side of the car, and the smear of blackish red. She could see the shape of a body, broken on the ground, facing away from her. His hair was matted with blood and his clothes were streaked in grime, torn as though he had been running through brambles. Even when she blinked, the image remained, imprinted on the insides of her eyelids.

This was her fault. *Her fucking fault.* She knew others would tell her it wasn't, that it was an accident, or that it was the driver's fault—*Rhett, you bastard*—for going too fast in the parking lot, for not looking where he was headed. She knew that they would tell her. She knew that she would agree.

She knew that she would be lying.

EIGHT

Her hands slick with sweat. Did she even want to live?

FIVE ……………◆

Sera sprawled on the bed. Her wrist was throbbing, and small, red blotches were already starting to appear on the white. Terrasen, her only sister, must have taken the red hand towel—*again*—and Sera had learned the hard way not to wrap wounds in toilet paper. It wasn't easy to explain why there were fluffy white bits stuck in congealed blood on her flesh, even with Middie, the slightly psychotic attack cat, hissing in her lap.

The echoes of Terra's overly-bright voice still filled the room. She had waltzed in, bold as brass, and pounded on the bathroom door, demanding that Sera come play some game called *Sleeping Queens.* Sera had once been as bright and as full of vivacity as her little sister. Now, it was all she could do to drag herself from her bed every morning.

"Oh, I'll put your fucking queens to sleep," Sera grumbled at the door.

"What?" Terra demanded, her voice un-muffled and undeterred.

Sera sighed. "Nothing. I don't want to play."

"You never want to play anymore."

"Go away."

"Please will you play?"

"That's a negatory, Ghost Rider."

"Sera, please?"

"Go away."

"Make me."

"Fuck off, Terrasen."

"Mommy's told you not to say that word."

"So go tattle on me."

Sera knew she wouldn't. Terra had in the past, and the fallout had not been pretty. Sera and their mother had had a lovely little conversation that resulted in several dozen of the worst curse words either of them knew being screamed at each other, a broken flower vase ("That was from my wedding! What the hell is *wrong* with you, Seraphim?"), and one of the first scars to be on her wrist instead of her shoulder or leg.

"Seeeraaaa."

Terra rattled the doorknob. If that door opened and Terra caught sight of the knife in Sera's hand and the blood smeared across her arm and the bathtub, they'd drag her to the psych ward for sure. But the lock held.

"Terrasen." Sera lifted the blade from her arm. She hadn't had the chance to slice deep enough to do any real damage, but if Terra hadn't interrupted, she might even now be bleeding her life out on the floor.

"Seraphim," Terra mimicked her older sister's tone.

"Fuck. Off."

"Fine." Sera heard Terra's little foot—she was very small for her age—hit the door. It rattled in its frame, but nothing else happened. "Fine," Terra repeated. "Stay in there, you stupid jerk."

"Hallelujah," Sera muttered as Terra stormed away.

She sat in silence for a while, staring into nothing. The throbbing of her arm brought her back, the pain tethering her to life. She found that she did not have the energy to again press the blade against her skin, so instead, she dumped it into the sink.

Then she set about cleaning up the bathroom, the long sleeves she always wore rolled to expose her hands, a towel wrapped around her still-bleeding mark. When she finished, she barely managed to drag herself into her bed before collapsing. The bedroom she and Terra shared was painted in the bright shades of childhood: rainbow shadows cast by multi-hued lights dotted the walls and ceiling. Terra had begged so hard for the differently colored bulbs, and even Sera had to admit they were kind of cool, with their polychromatic shadows and shattered dreams of ephemeral hope.

The lights weren't shining now.

They weren't glowing, or burning, or flickering.

Were they even on?

Sera couldn't tell, and leaning over the side of her bed to check was far too much effort. Even climbing into her top bunk had been a struggle and the mere thought of climbing down again, for any reason, exhausted her.

Sera tightened the towel on her arm. Pain shot through her, lancing from her fingertips to her elbow as the edges of severed skin grated against each other, reminding her how they had once been whole, screaming in agony from the separation they now endured.

She had once been whole, too.

She had once cared. She had once wanted to see the sun rise, to wake up every morning and go to school, to paint and display her artwork. She'd run through the streets and roamed the woods with Remi, playing pirates, time travelers, wanders lost in the desert. She had been the princess in the tower and he had rescued her every time.

No one was coming to rescue her now. Every day was the same as the last, as though she had been locked away in a game of make-believe. An endless loop of *wake, school, fake a smile, pretend to eat, sleep, sleep, sleep pray you don't dream tonight* with no conceivable change. No way out but to end it all.

Remi had once told her of an old, long-dead poet who counted coffee spoons instead of days. Although Sera did not understand poetry the way Remi had, this small phrase now made sense to her. The sun still rose, but her days were not illuminated by it. Time was measured in coffee spoons, in pills she did not swallow, in layers of dust settling over the paintings that had once adorned the walls. That day of blackest spring three years ago had not been the end of all things. It had not even been the beginning—only the push that sent her spiraling into an endless, ever-gaping hole.

She couldn't remember, exactly, when the hole had begun to gape, or what had happened to cause the first tear. Perhaps it had been gradual, too subtle a shift to pin down to any one specific moment, like when Terrasen had taken over the room. Slowly, little by little, Terrasen had begun taking over the room, tacking up pictures of kittens in hammocks where Sera's artwork had once hung. The light bulbs became rainbow colored; the curtains still bore half-finished pink flowers from Terra's embroidery phase; Terra's bookshelves were filled with books Remi would have read, books on everything from dragons and modernized mythology to Sherlock Holmes and volumes of poetry Sera could never understand.

Sera hated those shelves.

She hated everything that reminded her of him.

Maybe that was why she'd thrown all her brushes and paints into a box and shoved it on the top shelf in her closet. She had promised herself she would never open it again, and she meant it. But somehow, it had ended up only hidden, not thrown through the window or at the bottom of a dumpster. She had scrubbed the flecks of paint from her hands, but she still expected to see the smudges of color when she looked down.

Sera sighed, swore idly to herself, and shifted. The movement jarred her forearm and the skin that had been so neatly parted by the knife blade burned. It hurt like hell, but anything was better than focusing on the void inside her chest.

Sera let her head loll to the side, skimming her eyes over the once-white towel. If her parents or siblings saw this, it would be back to the hospital. She didn't want to deal with that. Trips to the hospital required effort.

She forced herself to sit up. "Shit. Fuck. Goddammit," she muttered as the skin peeled apart and tore. The red blotches on the towel darkened. Sera pulled her arm into her lap and slowly unwound the fabric. The skin was angry and red, the edges of the thin cut she had made forming a crimson river that carved its way up the path laid out by her veins.

The knife she used wasn't particularly large, but she kept it sharp. When Remi had joined the Boy Scouts, Sera had not been allowed to follow him. To console her, their parents had bought her a knife just like the one Remi was learning to whittle with: a silvery, open-framed Gerber.

The blade was maybe three or four inches long, but it cut into her flesh the same as any other knife would. On her worst days, though, the knife reminded her too much of Remi. Those were the days she cracked the blades out of unused razor heads. She experimented with both implements the way she once would have tested paintbrushes. Razors left thinner lines, drew more blood. The pain they left was slower to bloom but sharper once it came. The knife was more satisfying in her hand, but tore the skin raggedly, leaving messier edges to knit back together.

Occasionally, she still resorted to kicking walls, pressing her hand in door jams, or holding her fingers to a hot stovetop just long enough for the skin to start to smolder. Never enough to leave a blatant mark she couldn't hide. Never enough to break the bones. Just enough to relieve the pressure building inside.

"You're never going to heal on your own, are you?" Sera asked her arm.

Its only answer was another twinge of pain.

"Right. Well, in that case…"

Sera reached behind herself and fumbled for the box she kept tucked against the edge of her bed rails. It was an old, wooden thing with a simple flip latch on the front. It had been a gift from her grandmother, and, when the back had begun to crack, Remi had repaired it with duct tape and wood glue.

She opened the lid and lifted out her sewing supplies. Needle, thread, and safety scissors her mother had given her years ago. A small bottle of rubbing alcohol and an eyedropper. A stained red hand towel folded at the bottom.

"Well, fuck me."

Terra hadn't stolen it after all.

Working almost completely one-handedly, Sera unraveled a length of tan thread, cut it free, and threaded the needle. She tied the ends together, leaving the needle to hang on a loop. She'd learned the hard way that single strands weren't the strongest. Doubling up was faster and easier.

Using the eyedropper, she doused the needle and thread in the rubbing alcohol, keeping the towel positioned underneath the whole affair so that her sheets would stay clean. She settled her arm, palm up, between her bare feet, deliberated for a moment, and decided to start at the end closest to her elbow.

The smell of the rubbing alcohol permeated the room and the wet thread trailed unpleasantly over her leg. Blood was still leaking from the cut, running sideways across her arm and smearing on her feet and the towel.

"Red on white like a virgin's wedding night," she recited. "Red on red, no bloodstains on the bed."

It was something she and Remi had come up with, back when their dad had been trying to teach them how to jump a car battery. *Never red to black,* he had cautioned. *Red to red, and black to the frame.* Unable to remember it any other way, she and Remi had crafted the little rhyme they were careful never to recite within earshot of either parent. Remi had changed black to white, insisting it was more poetic, but neither of them had ever forgotten again.

She closed her left hand into a fist. Pain lanced up her arm and she had to pause to dab at the warm, scarlet rivulets coursing over her skin. She blotted up the worst of it, set the tip of the needle against her skin, and pushed.

Sewing her own arm closed was…interesting, to put it mildly, but Sera had gotten quite good at it over the years. If she didn't want to take a trip to the hospital, then she had to be. Besides, it wasn't like a doctor would do much differently. She had watched them do almost the same thing she was doing now, but with individual blue strips instead of thread.

She had watched, and she had learned. That night hadn't been the first time she'd gone to bed with a knife, but it was the very first time she took that knife to her wrist. It was the second time she almost ended her own life. She had slipped out of bed, blade in hand, feet quiet on the ladder, and kissed Terra's head goodnight before locking herself in the bathroom.

Except *goodnight* had actually meant *goodbye*, where *goodbye* was attached to *forever.*

TWO ················◆

It started as a wonderfully normal day. Sera was feeling good for once, probably because she'd slept through the night for the first time in months. It was a beautiful summer's afternoon, and school had let out a few weeks ago, so everyone was caught up in reveling in their new freedom, not yet bored out of their minds. It was a perfect kind of a day.

Sera had not known these kinds of days still existed.

Her father, Carter, had long since left for the airport where he worked in the communications tower. She usually heard him get up and clatter as quietly as he could around the house, pulling out of the driveway just as the sun kissed the horizon.

Today she had slept through it all.

"Good morning."

There were six Malik children in total, each one with a mouthful of a name and nickname to boot. Malakai, named for his grandfathers Mallean and Kai, was in grad school, and Sarah, their mother, was always good-naturedly heckling him to *hurry up and marry that boyfriend of yours* before she got old and gray. *Well*, she'd always add with a laugh. *Older and grayer.*

Five years after Malakai had been born, Remi had joined the family. Carter and Sarah could never agree if he was named for the firearm or the type-writer, but there was no question that Sera's name was a distortion of her mother's. She wasn't quite two years younger than Remi, but they couldn't have been closer if they were twins.

It took seven years, two miscarriages, and numerous doctors' appointments Sera could remember being dragged around to, before her mother had become pregnant again. Terrasen, named for the earth, had been born. While Remi was the one Sera loved the most, Terra was the one that she most wanted to be—young and fresh and always so full of life. She did everything with more passion than ten people combined and whirled through life like a skater gliding over the ice.

When Terra was two, the twins were born. Unlike the others, their parents had not planned out names for the twins. They were born with brilliant, matching blue eyes, even more stunning than Remi's. Years later, their irises, all four precisely the same color, were still vibrant and dark, a shade of blue nature had not conceived of before. *Cobalt*, Sarah had said. *And Indigo*. Thus, Co and Indi became the youngest members of the Malik family. Sera had always wondered what their names would have been if their eyes had been brown, like hers. Mud and Dirt? Tree Bark and Dog Shit?

Sarah slipped into a seat at the kitchen table, brushing back a graying lock of hair. She wore an old sweatshirt, the cuffs dangling off, and looked mostly asleep. As the first daughter after three sons, she had been named "Seraphim" after her mother. Sera and Sarah looked nothing alike, and by rights Terrasen should have been given the name "Sera," since she was the spitting image of their mom. But instead, Sera had the angelic variation of an already Biblical name. It was a connotation she had quit trying to live up to long ago.

Sarah's blonde hair curled gently around her shoulders and her blue eyes were clearly visible. They were rimmed with red and shadowed with bruises from lack of sleep. Sera combed her own, much darker, much messier hair out of her eyes. Stifled a yawn. Tugged the sleeves of her t-shirt farther down her arms, making sure the thin red lines cut into her shoulders were well hidden.

"Good morning."

Cobalt was bouncing in the seat next to hers. Sera put her hand on his head and tried to hold him still, but it was like stopping a rocket that had already been launched. She was in peril of losing her arm, but Co certainly wasn't going to stop.

"How do you have this much energy every morning, Co?" Sera asked him.

Co waved a Cheerio at her in answer.

"Sera. Hey, Sera. Seraphim," Terra interrupted, waving one batter-covered hand in an effort to catch her big sister's attention. Terra was at the kitchen counter, standing on tiptoe to reach a bright red mixing bowl. "Wanna help?"

"What are you making?"

"Pancakes."

The twins screeched in perfect two-part harmony. Sarah rubbed her eyes. "Children," she said, but the admonishment was only half-hearted. "You're hurting my ears."

"Mama Mama," Indigo said. "Mamamamamamama." Cobalt joined in, and then Terra. Sera considered fleeing back to her room, but part of her was enjoying the commotion.

"I wanna waffle," Co said.

"Waffles?" said another voice Sera knew well. "I thought we were making pancakes!"

Sera turned and saw Mal coming down the hall. He must have been in the bathroom the whole time. He ruffled Sera's hair and gave her a hug. He smelled of city and aftershave.

"What are you doing here?" Sera asked.

Mal's eyes darted away from hers. *He's about to lie to me,* Sera thought. Then he smiled, his face relaxing. "Can't I want to see my siblings once in a while? Beside, I like—what is it now? Waffles."

"Pancakes," Terra insisted.

"Waffle," Indigo shrieked.

"Why are we making…waffles?" Sera asked.

"Pancakes," Terrasen corrected.

"Waffles," Co argued.

Sera waved a dismissive hand. "Whichever."

"Besides, *we* aren't doing anything," Terra said. "*I'm* the one doing all the work over here."

"You're sitting on the floor. That's hardly a fu—a struggle."

"Seraphim."

"What?"

"Be nice to your siblings."

"Yeah, be nice to us," Malakai said, faking hurt.

"We're the only siblings you're ever going to get," Terrasen put in, spoon in the air, one hand on her little girl hip. She had more sass than any seven-year-old had a right to.

"Only got us," Co said, giving another bounce in his chair.

Sera refrained from pointing out that she was hardly suffering from a lack of siblings. Terrasen, on the other hand, had no problem with ragging on her brother for being one of so many. "She should be nice to me, at the very least," she said. "Since I'm her only sister. It isn't like there's ever a shortage of brothers. *I* am special. *You—*" she jabbed the spoon at the three boys for emphasis, "—are all replaceable."

Sera felt her heart turn over. *Remi.* It was as though the whole world had frozen, and Sera knew, as sure as her good mood was slipping away, that there was something she had forgotten. Something to do with Remi.

"Terrasen," Sarah said sharply.

The room unfroze, and Sera blinked back into focus. It didn't just seem like the room had been turned to stone, it actually had been. Terra and Mal were both still, Sera was motionless in her chair, and their mother was as stiff as a board, her face ashen. Whatever her mother was feeling, she did not share it with Sera. She did not even glance her way.

"How could you say something like that—" and Sera heard her mother's voice change. There had been an ache to it, a pain buried so deeply that Sera didn't notice it until it was gone. "On such a beautiful day?" she finished, the lighthearted tone forced but convincing.

Sera looked more closely at her siblings and mother. They all caught her stare, one by one, and turned back to whatever it was they had been doing, but Sera wasn't fooled. They were keeping something from her, and she was certain it had something to do with her uneasy feeling of forgetfulness.

"What's up with you guys?"

"Nothing, sweetie," her mother answered, taking the bowl from Terra and measuring out the first dollop of batter. It sizzled on the skillet.

For just a moment, silence hung over them all like an executioner's blade. The house was full of children and quiet, something Sera thought she had heard never in her life. She had the wild impulse to throw something, to hear something shatter against the floor, just to create noise.

"Would you like some waffles?" Malakai asked, breaking the tension.

"Pancakes."

"What if I want waffles, little sis?"

"Too bad; we are having *pancakes*."

Sera wasn't buying the happy-go-lucky attitudes they all had for sale, but she didn't feel like arguing. Not when she could still feel the ghost of her good mood echoing in her chest. Not when the sun was shining, Terra was smiling, and the smell of fresh pancakes filled the air.

She couldn't remember the last time she'd bothered with breakfast.

"Sure."

Soon, Sera, Mal, Terra, Co, Indi, and their mom were gathered around the table, a heaping pile of steaming pancakes set before them. Malakai, despite being the oldest, was making an even bigger mess than the twins. He was smashing a banana into a mushy puddle while the rest of them passed the plate of pancakes around the table. Middie, the family cat, deemed this unacceptable. She must have decided that Mal was disrespecting bananas everywhere, and she expressed her feelings by trying to steal his plate. Sarah had to shoo her off the table with a roll of paper towels amid gales of laughter from the children. The ghost of Sera's good mood had been saved from its second death.

"Sera, will you please—Middie! For heaven's sake, *get off the table!*—

pass the syrup?"

Sera waited until her mother's hands were unoccupied by cat before sending the syrup her way. The barest hint of a smile touched Sera's lips as she bit into the pancakes. They were warm and fresh and so, so good.

"Any plans for the day?" she asked the table at large.

"Yes. Mal and I have some errands to take care of. And I need to go grocery shopping soon. Anyone else want to come?"

Sera expected a chorus of *no*. Grocery shopping wasn't an event. It was an ordeal. Instead, the table fell silent, as though their mother had mentioned the morgue and not Giant Eagle. Sera stared around at her siblings. None of them would meet her eyes. None of them would even glance up from their half-empty plates.

"None of you have to come," Sarah said gently. "It won't make a difference."

Indigo was the first to shake his head, and the other two followed suit.

"Sorry, Mom," Terrasen whispered.

"Sera?" Sera's head jerked around to her mom, her eyes slipping from one small, anxious face to the next before meeting her mother's blue eyes. "Is it alright if I leave you in charge?"

It was a question, but it wasn't. After seeing her siblings' reactions to grocery shopping, telling her mother that they had to go with her wasn't really an option. She couldn't help but notice that there was never any hint of an expectation that Sera would go with their mother—not so much as an cursory invitation.

"I guess so."

"Are you sure? I can call—"

"No, it's fine…wait." Sera had no watch of her own, but Malakai was wearing the same one he'd had for the last six years. She made a grab for Mal's wrist, missed, fended off his retaliatory swing, and succeed in her second attempt. She checked the time. "Don't you usually have some sort of fu—" she caught herself just in time "—um, funky three o'clock thing on Sundays?"

Mal jerked his arm back, nearly smearing his elbow through her syrup. Sarah sifted uncomfortably in her seat, pinned under her daughter's cold gaze. "You must have lost track of the days of the week. It isn't Sunday."

"Then why aren't you at work?" She turned to Mal. "And you should be in class."

"It's administration day," he explained, all calm and collected. He didn't even bat an eye.

"Uh huh." Sera wasn't convinced, but she turned back to her mother.

"The law firm was closed today."

"Uh huh. Sure."

The law firm was *never* closed on weekdays. Sera figured its doors would stay open even if there were six feet of snow, a power outage, and rampaging tigers that had escaped from the Cleveland zoo and were terrorizing the streets, all in the same night.

"Because I had to go grocery shopping."

Sera could feel the blackness edging back in. She pictured it as some indistinct black blur, crunching her good mood between its fanged teeth. The image would once have sent her running for her paintbrushes, but now she longed for something with an edge. There were only butter knives on the table, too dull to properly cut away her insides, and the stove was too cool to burn this feeling out of her.

You can't do anything like that in front of them anyways, Sera reminded herself. *They can't know.* She balled her hands into fists, digging her fingernails into her palms. It wasn't nearly as calming as an Exacto knife would have been, but it was better than nothing. She wasn't even supposed to have those blades, but she'd once had a stack of them for working with the more viscous paints. The night after Remi's funeral her parents had taken them, but they had not found all of the replacement blades. It had been the same night they'd changed the combination of the gun safe. A week later, they'd moved the safe entirely, but Sera thought it might still be in the house somewhere. One of the shotguns was old, a relic from her mother's bloodline. An heirloom Sarah wouldn't sell—and there was no one she trusted enough who would be willing to hold the gun for her—even if she didn't trust Sera with a weapon in the house.

Sera felt her nails beginning to raise welts. It centered her, balanced her ever so slightly. Sera scrutinized her mother. Sarah turned away, busying herself over Indigo's sticky face. Any reason not to look at Sera. She was off-kilter, too.

"Don't lie to me. Why—"

"Because, Seraphim," her mother said, turning back. The cat leapt onto the table again, scattering pancakes and knocking over the syrup bottle and sending any chance Sera had of getting an answer flying out the window.

"Middie!" their mother bellowed as the psycho cat began clawing at the tablecloth and yowling. *"Get off the table!"*

Middie yowled some more.

Sarah sighed and set about disentangling Middie from the tablecloth. Middie, for her part, did not want to be disentangled from the tablecloth and put up a terrific fight to stay right where she was, trapping herself further. After a minute of hissing, coaxing, and clawing from both parties, Sarah managed to bundle Middie out of the room. Then, before Sera could pose the question to her again, she began directing them in cleaning up.

Sera found an excuse to slink away as soon as she could and crept up the stairs to her room. She could still hear the others clattering around, but their noise seemed more subdued than usual. They were all probably still terrified of being forced to go grocery shopping.

"Goodbye, everyone. I love you all," Sarah's voice echoed up to Sera.

"See ya, kiddoes," Mal chimed in.

"We'll be back in a few hours," Sarah called up the stairs. Sera didn't bother to answer. Her voice would have been lost beneath her siblings' even if she had tried.

Sera stared at the rectangle of sunlight spilling across her bedroom floor. Downstairs, the door slammed shut. The noises children make when left un-monitored rose up to Sera, but she couldn't bring herself to care. The idea that she was forgetting something kept resurfacing no matter how many times she pushed it from her mind. It was something important, something that had to do with what her siblings and mother were refusing to tell her. She began pacing.

"What the fuck is it?" Sera demanded of the empty air.

The space was feeling more confined by the step. She wanted out—out of her head, out of this room, out of the house—but someone had to take care of the fleet of little siblings. She should have told her mother to stay, or to take them with her.

A twinge of pain shot through her ankle as she took another step, reminding her that only a few weeks ago, her left leg from the knee-down had been encased in a plaster cast. She quickly chased the thought away before she could remember that frigid April night and *why* she'd needed a cast in the first place.

Suddenly exhausted, she wilted to the floor and sprawled across the carpet. The white ceiling glared down at her, the curtains fluttering on a breath of air. Terra had left the window open again, and the June breeze was pleasant on her skin.

Sera didn't want to be heckled by fresh, springtime winds, filled with a hope that she knew she'd never feel again. She curled up on her side. Maybe she should just go back to sleep. The world always looked better when seen through a veil of dreams, a haze of non-reality. Anything was better than wondering what she had forgotten and simultaneously trying to suppress the idea, because she knew that, whatever it was, she wouldn't like it.

Maybe she should listen to some music. Maybe that would help.

She rolled onto her back again.

Maybe she should paint. She hadn't touched a brush in weeks. The counselor said it would help, and her parents had bought her a rainbow of colors so vibrant it hurt to look at them. She'd uncapped the red but the color looked exactly like blood—*Remi, Remi, Remi*—and she'd almost vomited. Sera quickly screwed the lid back on, all the while pretending to be pleased. She hadn't touched art supplies since, but the nightmares of his crumbled body, blood spattering his face and her hands and the asphalt, had tormented her for weeks.

"C'mon, Sera," she said aloud. "Do something with your life."

But Sera didn't feel like it.

She didn't feel like doing anything—and that included lying there. She didn't have the energy to paint, to cut, to breathe. She didn't want to be there. She didn't want to be anywhere. She didn't want to exist.

"You're a waste of space."

She rolled onto her other side.

It wasn't any better.

The world still looks like shit. Maybe the world will always look like shit. Maybe that's all there ever was, and all there will ever be.

And then Sera heard the scream.

ONE

The lock clicked. Sera leaned back against the door. The wood was cool on her exposed skin. The backs of her legs, her forearms, the palms of her hands—even through her t-shirt and shorts she could feel her heat being leeched away, but it didn't matter.

Soon, nothing would.

Sera let the air trapped in her lungs escape and sagged back, her body sliding down the wood, crumpling on the floor. She knocked into the door, felt it quiver in its frame, and then she hit the ground with a muffled thud.

Her knee collided with a stack of over-full shelves and three things tumbled down. She ducked, covering her head with her arms as a sealed package of dried apricots bounced off her elbow and a cylindrical tube of lemon-scented Clorox wipes rolled away from her feet. The third thing was soft and heavy, draping over her like a wadded-up blanket someone hadn't quite managed to unroll.

Sera lifted her head, tugging the object off of herself and holding it up. Even in the dim light she knew immediately what it was: Remi's favorite hoodie.

The cuffs were frayed from years of use. The sleeves were stretched out because Remi always pulled the hems down to cover his hands, snuggling into the soft fabric. She remembered his elbow, pale and angular, poking out after he'd ripped a hole in it while jumping the playground's fence. Malakai had noticed it to and had waved his sewing kit at them.

"No thanks," Remi always said. "It gives it character."

Every rip, tear, and stain was just where she knew it would be—right down to the splotch on the shoulder where infant Terra had thrown up baby formula all over him. The smell had come out, but the discoloration remained.

It had been a year since she'd seen Remi wearing it. Their mother had yelled at Remi that it looked terrible, was worn to rags, and needed to be thrown away. She'd threatened to swipe it and just pitch it while Remi was asleep. Distraught, Remi had asked Sera to stash it in her room.

"Mom will think to look there," she'd said.

"Then where can I put it?"

Sera had pondered. "What about the bantry?"

It was what they called the defunct bathroom squashed into a corner of the second floor. It had once been a fully functioning third bathroom, but it had been broken even before the Maliks had moved in. Their dad had been promising to fix it for years, but as time spooled out and the family expanded, their mom had ended up converting it to a storage room. There were stacks of dried goods, shelves of cleaning supplies, and a shower full of items Sera couldn't identify but that her mother insisted had a purpose. Part pantry, part bathroom, the bantry had become Sera and Remington's secret hideout. The window above the toilet, which opened out onto the roof of the first floor, was the gateway to their refuge.

Sera pressed the hoodie to her face. It still smelled like him. There was the tang of cleaning supplies and a slight mustiness to it, but when she closed her eyes and inhaled, it was almost like he was there again. She could detect the new shampoo he'd started using because he wanted girls to lean in, not run away. Underneath that was the same laundry detergent the whole family used, but flavored with the scent of dirt and woods from all the time spent roaming among the trees, wood smoke from family campfires, and the lingering hint of old books.

If poetry has a smell, Sera thought. *This is it.*

She couldn't do this.

She had to do this.

Sera slipped the hoodie over her head. It had once been far too big, but now fit almost perfectly. The stretched-out sleeves left the cuffs dangling just past her wrists, the hem resting against the tops of her thighs, just barely shorter than her shorts. It was cold from sitting so long, but she hardly seemed to notice.

She crossed the cramped room to the broken toilet. It was crooked and a bit cracked, but that didn't matter. What Sera cared about was the small window behind it; she had to straddle the toilet to reach it. It had been years since she and Remi had last snuck out onto the roof, but back when Mal was still living at home, they'd made midnight excursions all the time.

That had been before the blackness had begun to creep on Sera. Everyone had written it off as teenage angst—and it had probably started that way—but Sera didn't think this was something you aged out of. Not anymore. Not since the accident.

Her world had been full of siblings throwing food at each other, a mother too busy chasing them all to notice the scissors until Mal had cut off all of the cat's fur, a father who came home from work to fix the house and the cars, but always somehow had time for his children. They were each loved and individualized, even as their ranks grew.

It was this, more than anything, that Sera could not understand. Her parents loved her. Her siblings adored her. She'd never been popular, but she had never truly been alone, either. And yet she somehow felt as if she were the only person in the world. Her mother and father would take the time to listen to her and do their best to make her feel validated. And yet it was as though she were standing in the middle of a crowded room, screaming her head off, and not a soul even glanced her way. Her whole life, she had been encouraged to follow her dreams, no matter how far-fetched, to be her own person, to find what she loved and be passionate in everything. And yet, when she looked in the mirror, all she saw was a blank slate, devoid of personality.

She had been meant for a world painted in color, but the brightness had slowly begun to leech away. On the day of the accident, it was like a reverse *Wizard of Oz*—she fell asleep in a world of color, and woke up in stark black and white. Now, alone and barefoot on the cold, tile floor, the blackness was all there was.

She worked her fingers around the edge of the frame, digging her nails into the wood. Bits and pieces of old paint flaked off, fluttering to the floor like butterflies made from crumbling ash, like paper birds with their wings ablaze.

Her fingernails cracked. She felt the wet warmth of blood, but she refused to relinquish her grip on the window. "Would. You. Fucking. Open," she muttered.

At last, Sera managed to pry the glass pane up just enough to wedge her hand beneath it. The window had always stuck, but Remi had never seemed to have so much trouble with it. Maybe she was just doing it wrong, messing things up, as she did with everything.

Unbidden, an image of tomorrow crept into her mind. Her, in that awful starched black dress her mother had laid out. Remi, still and cold in a coffin, the smile gone from his face and the life from his eyes. Their parents clutching each other amid the array of siblings. Malakai sobbing quietly onto his husband's shoulder, whose own face was blank and unreachable. Terrasen, eyes bright with tears, cheeks soaked in sorrow. Cobalt and Indigo, worst of all, clinging to each other, inseparable the way that Sera and Remi had been. All bathed in black, as dark as a raven's wing, as inky as the pages of Remi's books.

And she knew she couldn't do it. She couldn't go. She couldn't stand there, surrounded by people who were supposed to bring her comfort but who could never understand. People who would offer condolences, say that they were sorry.

They were sorry? What did they have to be sorry for?

It was her fault. All of this was *her* fault.

She had been the one to run through the school halls. She had been the one to slam through the double doors—doors she now refused to go through, even if it meant walking an extra five minutes to class. She had been the one sprint into the parking lot. She had been the one seeking death, and she had been the one to fail.

Sera jammed her hand upwards as hard as she could. Pain lanced through her arm as the bones in her wrist jarred together in ways they had never been meant to. Good. She deserved to suffer, to feel her body break and bend in ways never intended. She slammed her hands into the frame again, then bit her lip against a cry. Was this how Remi had felt in those last few moments? Was this the pain that should have been hers?

Again, harder. Her elbow skid off the window sill and smashed off the lid of the toilet. Sera froze. The clang echoed around the room, bringing the threat of discovery.

But the house stayed silent.

Sera breathed.

The night air was cool on her face.

She forced the window up the last little bit, opening the gap as wide as possible. The wood creaked in protest, as it always had, but without Remi's smile to fill the silence it seemed so much louder, as though the intervening years were somehow amplifying the sound.

Sera sighed, long and slow. It had been three years—*could that be right?* Yes. At least three—since she and Remi had crammed themselves through the window. The opening had been bigger then.

She clambered onto the toilet seat, fingers gripping the windowsill so hard it hurt. She put her head through the window, eyes straining to see in the half-light provided by the street lamps on the other side of the house. Her shoulders scraped against the frame and she worried Remi's hoodie might tear, but then she was through. Her feet slipped and slid over the top of the toilet, boosting her up. She got one knee underneath her, then pulled her foot through so she was straddling the frame. The ledge bit into her hands and bare legs.

How had she and Remi once done this so easily?

She perched there, precariously balanced, almost teetering, before getting her second leg through and half-jumping, half-falling to the roof. It was a graceless affair, and loud enough that she worried someone might hear, but everyone, half-dead with grief and already exhausted by tomorrow, slept on.

The world slept on, and silence fell again.

There had been a few days of warmth and sunshine, but even the weather seemed to be mourning Remi's loss. All things bright and welcoming had been encased in frost, suspended mid-life. Sera knew how it felt.

The night was cold and dark, the single star that was visible harsh and stark against the blackness. Sera hugged herself, curled in the hoodie that had once been Remi's. The inky air bit at her legs and the roof was so cold it burned against her feet, more like mid-December than mid-April.

She hardly felt it at all.

Sera followed the slope of the house as it curved up, walking the path that she and Remi had trodden so many dozens—maybe hundreds—of times. The over-crowded bantry had been their hideout, the unwilling window above the broken toilet their gateway, but it had always been the highest point on the roof that had been their refuge.

It wasn't a long walk but the roof was pitched and Sera's extremities were numb, so it seemed to take forever. Sera waded through the fog of her own thoughts, struggling to swim to the opposite shore, but none ever seemed to appear. All she could see was herself in that awful black dress and Remi dead before her.

Your fault, her thoughts mocked. *It's all your fault.*

Yourfaultyourfaultyourfault.

And Sera knew that the voice was right.

She made it to the spot, two stories up, where she and Remi had once sat, stargazing on clear nights, huddling together under a tie blanket their mother had made Sera when the weather had begun to turn. On summer nights, they used to perch, side-by-side, feet dangling over the edge, heels kicking in the air, legs swinging back and forth. They used to be together.

She was so tired of being alone.

She had felt the space between her and Remi growing, increasing as their interest diverged. Remi was all sunshine and smiles, his eyes following girls who would one day take Sera's place as the most important person in his life. She knew she was wrong to think that a sister could compare to someone Remi had chosen to love, but this had only made it worse. She couldn't tell Remi, her one confidant, and so she had begun to retreat. She would grow up sour and more bitter than poison. He would fall in love and have a house full of children. He would be a great husband and father, and he would always be her brother. He would always be her best friend, but someday she would not be his.

There had been more awkward silences, and they didn't fall together as easily as they once had. Sera knew the problem lay with her, but she did not know how to fix it. She had felt abandoned, even as she acknowledged how absurd it was to feel that way. She had thought she had known what suffering and loneliness were. She had thought things could not get worse.

She had been wrong.

Was this rock bottom? This time, were things really the worst they could be? Everyone said it would get better. Everyone said that time would heal all wounds, things would be brighter, look better, in the morning. But how could they know that? How could anyone know that?

She had been wrong before; she would not be wrong again.

Remi would have pulled her down by his side, wrapped his arm around her, and they would have laughed their troubles away. At 12 and 13, life had been so uncomplicated. Sera wished she could go back, turn the clock to those happy years, and warn herself of what was to come. Tell herself not to walk the path that gaped before her. Find another way.

But had there ever been one? Or did all roads lead here?

It didn't matter. Nothing mattered, because Sera couldn't go back. She couldn't fix what had gone wrong, couldn't change the past. She did not want to face the future. And so she did not sit. Did not swing her feet over empty space, carefree and happy the way only children can be.

Instead, she walked to the edge. Looked down at the darkened ground below her. It would still be frozen. It would not yield. Her body would bend and break, her bones would shatter. It would be over. For the first time, Sera knew what her actions would result in, but she continued despite that. No, not despite—because of.

She was at the highest point of the house, perched above the attic, almost three stories up. She prayed to a god she did not believe in that it would be enough, and then she prayed to Remi's ghost, the only thing in the world that she knew for sure was real.

If he had been there, she would not be balanced on the edge. He would be sitting beside her and they would be pouring over some old poetry book or counting the stars—but ensconced in his hoodie, surrounded by his smell, with her own body heat radiating back to her, she could almost believe he was there. She could hear his voice in the wind, calling out her name the way he had as she'd tumbled to the pavement that day in the parking lot.

With her eyes tight shut, she could see him there before her, reaching out to her. If she opened her eyes, she thought she might see him for real. "Sera," he whispered, and there was more, but the meaning was drowned in the darkness, in wind, in her own misery.

"Remi," Sera whispered into the wordless night. "Remi, I'm so, so sorry."

And then she jumped.

TWO

She jerked upright, suddenly wide-awake, but the house was deadly silent. Had she fallen asleep there on the floor of her room and dreamt it? Nightmares bordering on night terrors weren't uncommon these days, so she supposed that was possible, but the scream had sounded very real.

"What the fuck?" she breathed, afraid to disturb the silence, but afraid to leave it unbroken as well.

There came another scream, but the voice sounded different this time. Was it someone else? It was still a child's voice, and in a house full of siblings—all of whom were under the age of ten—it could have been anyone. Still, if Sera had had to guess, her bet would be that this was Terrasen.

The scream came again, this time as her name. "Seraphim!"

Sera was on her feet in a heartbeat, smashing into the door, spilling into the hall, almost tripping and tumbling down the stairs, crashing to the floor. Her ankle and shin throbbed where the shattered bones had only recently mended, but she sprinted across the room all the same.

She slammed into the wall, ricocheted off, and skid to a stop in the middle of the kitchen floor. Terrasen was still shrieking, kneeling on the ground, huddled over something. Sera couldn't see what it was.

"Wh-what…what happened?" Sera gasped, clutching at her side as her body remembered that running meant an elevated heart rate and heavier breathing. She hadn't moved anywhere with any urgency since that day in the school parking lot, and her body was not readjusting well.

Her ankle and shin burned.

The doctors were going to kill her. *Fuck them.*

She should probably sit down. *Fuck that, too.*

Terrasen, Cobalt, and Indigo were all there, in the kitchen, but it was Terra who Sera's eyes were drawn to. It was she who had screamed Sera's name. Terra's eyes were wide with terror, her mouth slightly open, her chest heaving.

"What happened?" Sera demanded again.

Terra stared at her, chest heaving. If it had been cold in the kitchen, if the spilled water spreading over the counter and dripping onto the floor had been ice instead of liquid, if there had been frost on the windowpanes, the clouds of breath billowing from Terra's mouth would have filled the kitchen with their haze.

But billowing white breaths were not words. They did not offer an explanation.

"What. Fucking. Happened."

Sera didn't know if it was her tone or the swear word that did it, but this time, her voice jarred her little sister. "W-we were putting away the dishes. Like Mom asked."

"I can see that," Sera said, scanning the room.

The skillet was precariously balanced in a puddle of water, mixing spoons were everywhere, the dishwasher was open and half full of dirty plates, and the red bowl Terra had made the batter in was upended on the floor. The dishtowels that usually hung on the oven door were scattered around the room, some on the floor, some tossed on the counter. Terra was crouched down, her body blocking most of the twins, who were on the ground behind her.

"And the knife from last night was still out."

"What knife?" Sera flipped furiously back through her memories. What had they had for dinner the day before? Some kind of seafood…salmon fillet. Her stomach dropped. "The fillet knife?"

Terra nodded.

"I told him not to," she whispered. "That he wasn't old enough to handle that knife. Mom said…she said you were supposed to put it away."

Sera's eyes roved over her sister, looking for injury, but Terra looked fine. And then she knew. She knew without having to be told, without having to see. She could picture it in her mind's eye. One of the twins had picked up the knife. Terra had told them no, they weren't to handle it, that it was too dangerous. The other twin, concerned for his brother's safety, had gone to take it. At least one of them had probably been climbing on the counter, as both boys loved to do, and had jumped. Or had fallen. The water had spilled, the dishes had clattered, and the knife…

It was Remi all over again. Remi, crumpled and broken on the ground. Remi, who had died because of her.

Sera pushed down the pain. She opened the door to the vault in her head and shoved the agony inside. She could take it back out and examine it later, but for now, she could not afford it. She could not let another brother suffer because of her carelessness.

"Where?"

Terra understood. She held out her left arm and touched her right index finger to a place just above the inside of her wrist.

"How bad?"

Terra dragged her finger up her arm—one inch, two? Sera wasn't sure. It didn't matter. A knife that sharp would go through soft flesh like butter, and there would be blood. If the blade had cut into something important…Sera didn't even want to think about it.

"Which twin?"

Terra staggered to her feet and lurched to the side, so she was no longer blocking Co and Indi. Sera moved towards the boys as though in a dream, every step forwards seeming to push them farther away.

They were hunkered down on the floor together, the fillet knife lying near their bodies. Indigo had his hands pressed over Cobalt's arm, but it wasn't working. Red rivulets ran between his fingers, streaking down Co's arm, dripping off his skin to pool on the floor.

The twins were only five years old, but it did not surprise Sera that Indigo knew to apply pressure. She remembered their father, Carter, walking her and Remi through the basics of first aid when they were too young to fully understand what he was saying.

"If it's bleeding, you push on it, okay?" he had said. "And then you get Mommy or me, or one of your brothers."

"Carter, they're too young for such talk," Sarah had told him.

"You never know when you'll need to know something like this."

"Oh, honestly. You'd think we live in a war zone."

"In a household with all these kids? You bet we do. Malakai, Remington, and Seraphim will have to be able to help if something happens to Terrasen or one of the twins."

Sarah had placed a hand on her swollen stomach. "Sera's not even eleven yet."

Carter had just gestured at each of the kids in turn, then at the mess they had made of the living room. "War. Zone."

Sarah laughed and had let it go, but Sera had never forgotten. Neither, it seemed, had Indigo, who had, no doubt, received his own lesson in first aid. No, the thing that surprised Sera was how calm both boys were. Terrasen seemed to have forgotten how to speak, which was her favorite pastime, but the twins were calm and collected. Indigo pressed on Cobalt's arm. Cobalt stared at his brother indifferently, as though it were a rubber glove sewn to his shirt that was bleeding, not him.

Sera knelt by the twins, her hands moving to replace Indigo's, but he would not relinquish his grip. His hands and wrists were slick with blood and Sera could feel the warmth of it staining the knees of her jeans.

"Indigo, you have to let go. I need to see."

Indigo shook his head.

"Indigo. Look at me."

Four matching, dark blue eyes sought out her brown ones as both Co and Indi looked to her. Their startling shade was the reason for the twins' colorful names and the one of the ways Sera could tell them apart; Indigo's were just a hint closer to purple than Cobalt's.

"Mom, Mal, and Dad are all out. I'm all you've got. I can help him, but you have to let go. I need to see where he's hurt."

Indi's lips trembled. "A-accident."

"I know."

"S-s-sorry."

"I know. I need you to let go, okay?"

Indigo's mouth worked, but no words came out. His hands slipped away. Sera took Cobalt's arm and inspected it. It was smeared crimson, and there seemed to be a long slice—at least three inches—parting his flesh. There was too much blood to tell just how deep it was. Sera's hands were wet and coated in scarlet in seconds.

"Terra, get me a towel."

"But—"

"Terrasen. *Now*."

Sera didn't take her eyes from her little brother, but she felt Terra moving, could hear her scurrying around the wrecked kitchen. Sera reached her left hand out behind her, the right one still pressed tightly over Co's bleeding arm. Fabric was pushed into her fingers. She clawed at the towel as Terra relinquished it, put it against the place where the blood was the darkest, and pressed down.

Co's eyes widened and he gasped in pain but did not cry out.

"I'm sorry. I'm so sorry," Sera murmured. "I'm sorry, Co. I have to stop the bleeding. Then we can get you to the hospital. It'll be alright, okay? It'll be okay. I promise."

The towel was soaked through already. Terrasen had started sobbing silently, her hands pressed against her cheeks, her fingernails digging into her face, but when Sera looked up at her, she held out a second towel without being asked. Sera took it and pressed it over the first.

Indigo remained on the opposite side of Cobalt, clutching his uninjured hand tightly. Neither boy said a word, but silent tears were tracking their way down Co's face, running sideways towards his ears.

She needed to get him to the hospital. *The hospital.* The very idea sent a rush of panic rising up inside of her, threatening to choke her. She hadn't been back there since the time she had jumped, right after Remi—

Calm down, Sera ordered herself.

She drew a deep breath, calling up the blank façade. The erasure of emotion was a trick she had been practicing for years. Though Remi's death had, at first, seemed to shatter her mask, in the end, it had strengthened it. The morning of the funeral, when they had found her crumpled and broken on the ground, within inches of escaping life's chains, she had learned how to construct a wall strong enough that nothing got through. Now, calling up the blank impersonality was as easy as putting on a hat.

She assessed the situation, plotted a course of action, and began to follow through. Her priority was Cobalt. Anything else was just getting in the way. Sera looked at the twins' hands, their fingers locked together. Sera remembered Remington holding onto her the same way on her roughest day, promising her there would be a better tomorrow. That he would always be there for her.

You were wrong, Remi. You were so, incredibly wrong.

She forced down the pain.

"Indigo, I have to take him to the hospital. You have to let go of his hand."

Indigo did not respond. His grip did not loosen at all.

"Let go."

He shook his head, once, barely more than a jerk.

"Indigo."

"No."

"Let go of his fucking hand, Indigo."

"No."

"Godammit, I don't have the time to deal with this shit."

Some part of Sera's mind reminded her that she shouldn't be swearing in front of her little siblings. The rest of her didn't give a damn.

Sera released pressure on Co's arm, leaving a red handprint on the white towel. Immediately, it began to fill out, spreading as the blood began to flow again. She gripped Indigo's wrist and pried his fingers free. He thrashed wildly, kicking and biting, lashing out at every part of her he could in his desperate attempt to reach Cobalt, but Sera was far stronger. She wrenched him right off his feet and carried him bodily into the hall.

"Terrasen," she commanded as she struggled. "Hold him."

Pulling Indigo off Co hadn't been too hard, but pulling him off of herself proved to be a much more difficult task. She grabbled with him for a moment before succeeding in wrestling him to the ground. He kicked and screamed, writhing as Terra moved to take Sera's place.

"Just until I get out of the house," Sera panted, and then she was gone, sprinting back to the kitchen, scooping Cobalt up and carrying him outside. In her head, the moment when she had wrenched the twins apart was playing on repeat. How desperately Indigo had fought. How the color of Co's eyes had gone from vivid to washed out, a pale imitation of its true beauty. How his uninjured arm had flopped hopelessly back to the floor. How Indi had to be overpowered and forced away from the one dearest to him.

How a barrier too strong to cross had ripped her and Remi apart, too.

"Pull yourself together," Sera ordered herself aloud. The sound of her own voice breaking through the roaring silence in her head grounded her somehow. "Co needs you. You can pity yourself later."

She took the pain that was threatening to crack through her wall and shoved it into a vault in the back of her head. That vault had started life as a box, but there had been too much sorrow and blackness for a single, wooden case to hold. Before the latch had burst, she had transferred the contents to the vault.

For now, she banished this new, unexpected pain, trapped it inside where it would not get in her way. Where it could do her no harm. She knew it would leak back out later—it always did—but for now, she was safe in her placidity.

Sera bundled Cobalt into his booster seat in their Mom's car, then raced back for the keys. Indigo's screams echoed in her ears as she pulled the door shut behind her.

Sera only had her permit. Every minute she spent behind the wheel she was breaking the law, but she didn't care. The drive to the hospital seemed endless. She knew it shouldn't take this long to get across her suburb and into downtown Cleveland, but the distance dragged by. Even the clock in the dash was running slow.

Sera screeched to a stop in the hospital parking lot. She jumped out of the car so fast that her arm tangled in the seat belt, whipping her around and sending her crashing to the asphalt. She was up again in a moment, slamming the door shut while simultaneously shoving the keys into her pocket. She wrenched open the back door. Cobalt spilled out into her arms.

The two of them, both streaked in blood, Co still in a daze, made quite the scene as they stumbled through the sliding glass doors. Nurses swarmed around them, asking questions, trying to pry Co free from her arms. The next few minutes were a blur, a haze of white and red, blood transfusions and disinfectant, a jumble of words Sera could not understand. Sera refused to let go of her little brother, and, eventually, the doctor and nurses gave in.

"What are you going to do to him?" she demanded of the doctor.

"I just have to stitch the wound closed. It'll only take a few minutes, and then it will be able to heal much more easily and quickly than it would otherwise," she explained to Sera.

Sera watched, wide-eyed, as the doctor sewed Cobalt's arm back together, the clean gap made by the knife closed again by her hands. Sera remembered watching as her mother had taught Malakai the same magic, only with a needle and thread. She had taught him how to mend a tear in the hem of his favorite shirt—dark blue, with the number of their father's favorite football player on the back. Malakai couldn't stand sports, but he loved the shirt, which had once belonged to their dad. This seemed to be almost the same, but with skin instead of fabric.

The doctor talked as she worked. "These are called sutures. They come pre-made with the needle attached. We use different gauges, or thicknesses, for different areas of the body. The more delicate the tissue, the higher the gauge and the thinner the suture."

Even encased in purple surgical gloves, her movements were deft, her stitches even and clean.

"I'm using what's called 5-0 nylon. It'll hold the edges of skin together so that they can heal properly. Then we'll remove the stitches and he'll be as good as new."

The blue sutures were stark against the red blood and Co's pale skin, but once the scarlet had been wiped away, even Sera had to admit that it looked much better.

"See," the doctor said. "That wasn't so bad." She smiled at Co, who gave her a befuddled smile in return, and then Sera, who looked at her stony-faced. The doctor's expression turned forced and she ducked out of the room and into the hall.

"Your parents will be here soon," the nurse said, patting Sera on the shoulder. She didn't remember giving them her phone number, but they had asked so many questions so quickly. "Why don't you go to the bathroom and wash up a bit, just so they don't freak out as much, okay? You look like a horror movie victim."

He smiled the sort of smile that said he wanted to be her friend. Sera knew it was a lie—she was just a frightened kid to him, and so he tried to lend her support. She'd rather he treated her like an adult because then it was easier to remain impassive.

He kept on smiling. Sera looked away, down at her blood-soaked shirt, still damp and clinging to her, the red crust streaking her arms, the flakes peeling off her hands. He handed her a clean shirt—scrubs—and pointed down the hall.

"Third door on your right."

Sera nodded and took the clothes. She kissed Co on the top of the head. "I'll be right back, okay? I promise."

Co nodded. He was still a bit dazed and woozy-looking, and there was nothing but trust in his big, round eyes. She squeezed his hand on the side that wasn't damaged before leaving. She locked herself in the bathroom and stripped off her shirt, splashed water over her face and down her front.

"Fucking shit, that's cold."

She fiddled with the knobs and tried again. Pink-ish red water streamed into the sink, faster than it could drain. Sera swirled her fingers through it, like finger paint. She smiled as she remembered herself and Remi, maybe four years old, scribbling outside the lines while their mother read a book and pretended to be paying attention to them. Mal had joined them and introduced his two younger siblings to the magic of washable markers—and then to the wonders of drawing on each other. It had taken a full twenty minutes of splashing and shrieking to rub all the ink off, the colors blending into a muddy brown in the kitchen sink.

Sera scrubbed—at herself, at her shirt, at the memories trying to creep out of the vault in her head. The image of Co and Indi as they were ripped apart kept flashing before her eyes. The sound of Indigo's screams echoed in her head, mixing with the sound of Remi's laughter and the sink running in the background.

She turned the water back to cold and doused herself again. She let it run until her hands were numb. She patted herself down with paper towels until she was as dry as she was going to get. Her fingers were stiff with cold and she fumbled with the hem of the shirt before successfully pulling it over her head, but maybe if she were physically numb, then she would be emotionally numb, too.

By the time she made it back to Co's room, he was much more awake and talkative. Both of their parents were there. They looked up from Cobalt when she pushed open the door. Both of them had red faces, eyes swollen as though they had been crying, and dirt on the knees of their jeans.

Jeans? Sera thought. Her mother, sure. There wasn't anything fancy about grocery shopping. The mud was a little strange, but her father? He was supposed to be at the airport. He wore a shirt and tie to work every single day. If he was dressed like this, then he hadn't gone to the coms tower. And if they were together, then she hadn't gone to Giant Eagle.

And, Sera realized for the first time, she hadn't taken her car. Sera had just driven it to the hospital.

"Hey, Sera," Co said, waving.

There was a medical bracelet around his wrist with all the information she'd given the nurses and receptionist. She walked to his bedside and took his hand. His fingers were warm against hers.

"How are you?" she asked.

"Good. I got sewn up like when you drew me into a monster last Halloween."

"You mean Frankenstein?" Sera had had a devil of time getting him to sit still long enough to get the face paint to come out right, but in the end, Co had looked like a slightly smudgy version of Frankenstein's monster. No one could tell in the dark, anyways, and he'd been proud of his big sister's artwork.

He showed her the stitches now, just as proud, even though she had been right there when he'd received them.

"You were very brave."

The words sounded flat even to Sera. Indigo's screams were roaring in her ears. She linked her fingers through his and let their conjoined hands rest on the bed. The bracelet was turned so that Sera could read Cobalt's name. His date of birth. And today's date:

June 24, 2015.

Sera nearly feel over from shock. This explained everything. Sera's parents hadn't gone to work because they had been at the cemetery. Carter must have left that morning for something, and then come back to pick Sarah up. Malakai had taken the day off to mourn—and everyone had been worried that she would realize. That she would do something rash. And so they had all kept quiet, and she had forgotten.

She could smell candles burning, hear the laughter that had pervaded their house for so long, that was still there behind the wall that divided her from the rest of the world. It had always been a day spent outside, a day with friends and family and the old, stained picnic blanket spread out in the grass.

Indigo's cries, echoing from inside the vault in her head, drowned out everything else, real and remembered. The pain washed over her again. She could feel the threads holding her heart together ripping apart. She gripped the side of Co's bed, forcing herself to hold it together, to tamp the emotions down. Tonight, she would let herself feel. Tonight, the blade of her knife would carve through her arm. Her grandmother's old sewing kit would be enough to put the pieces back together, and she would pretend for parents and all her siblings.

But tonight, she would languish in her loss and revel in the physical pain that was the only thing she could still control. She deserved to suffer. She deserved to bleed. She had forgotten, and that could not be forgiven.

Today was Remi's 17th birthday.

SIX

That simple plastic rectangle was more than a red ID card with her picture on it. No matter how ridiculous she looked in her photo, no matter how horrendous her signature, this meant freedom—and Sera intended to fully use it.

Somehow, driving calmed her. Sometimes she just needed to feel like she was heading somewhere. Even when she was driving in circles, it gave the illusion that she was going somewhere, even if she was only fooling herself. She could think clearly, or clear her head and not think at all. She could crank the music and sing along, forgetting the burning trails her knife had left, or disappointment she knew would be in her parents' eyes if she dared look. Most often it was the guilt writhed inside her, gnawing on her innards like a rodent living in her chest and gut. When she was drowning in herself, driving was a reprieve, a breath of fresh air. Sometimes she could even conjure an image of Remi as he would be now, just a little older than her, his smile brighter than ever, his eyes sparkling with unhatched plans.

She was behind the wheel now, alone and running from the possibilities of a future she could never have.

Sera had always been a fan of loud music—in her headphones, through speakers—wherever. Whenever she turned a drive into a means of escape, a life raft bobbing towards her, the volume of the radio was never loud enough. She could never jam out hard enough to chase her demons away, but the louder the music, the better they were held at bay. What she listened to depended on the day. Sometimes it was Rise Against, sometimes Linkin Park, My Chemical Romance, The Foo Fighters, maybe even a little Three Doors Down. Today, like so many days, it was Green Day.

The volume was cranked up all the way as she drove, too fast, down the rain-slick streets.

Am I bleeding? Am I bleeding from the storm?

Sera didn't know how, after all this time, she could possibly have any blood left to spill. Not when she had spent every minute of every day since the accident bleeding out. Not when every little thing set her off, sent her spiraling out of control.

She had thought she would learn to stop it, or, at the very least, to cope. To staunch the wound before the blood could really begin to flow.

She had been wrong.

My head's above the rain and roses.

Only barely. Only just. She could feel herself sinking fast.

Still breathing on my own.

But for how much longer?

Sera jammed on the brakes, slewed around a corner, and slammed to a stop in a parking space she had picked at random. Mostly in it. There weren't enough people around to care that she was crooked, anyways.

She stumbled out into the sleeting rain, slamming her door and yanking her hood up over her hair at the same time. She sprinted for the back door of Common Grounds, one hand clenched around the keys in her pocket, the other holding her hood in place. The car beeped behind her as she slid across the wet asphalt and collided with the cement wall of the building.

Inside, it was dry and warm. The place was nearly deserted, but even though it was close to three in the morning, there were a few people still hanging around the 24-hour coffee shop. The homeless man, who was a permanent feature of the place, was crashed out in his usual corner, last month's newspaper stuck to his cheek and two coffee cups on the table in front of him. One was on its side and a small puddle of dark brown liquid had pooled beneath it.

Spike was behind the bar and he smiled when he saw her. "Seraphim—it's good to see you. It's been a while."

Sera yanked her hood down, her rain jacket dripping water everywhere. Before she had a chance to reply to Spike's greeting, he was handing her a steaming hot cup.

"Crazed Englishman?" she asked, taking it and inhaling the vapor.

"With a touch of extra toffee."

"Spike, you are the absolute best."

"So what brings you here at this late hour?"

Three A.M. was far from the latest that Sera had been in Common Grounds, but somehow, Spike knew that she needed to talk. He looked the part of a too-skinny, too-tall hipster, with his tattoos barely visible beneath his shirt sleeves and his ever-present slouched beanie. The toothpick poking out from between his teeth made him mumble a bit when he talked, but despite all of this, he was the best listener Sera knew.

She collapsed onto one of the barstools and took a long drink from her cup. It burned her tongue and throat as she swallowed, but Sera found that she didn't care. Spike watched her, knowing that she would talk when she was ready, and not a moment before. That was one of her favorite things about him: he never pushed you. He let you get where you were going in your own time. Maybe it came from working at a 24-hour coffee shop, where someone was always coming, someone was always going, and the majority of the customers were sitting around doing nothing. Common Grounds never closed its doors, and no one was ever in any kind of a rush to leave.

That was probably why Sera like it so much: it was one of the few places left to her that offered any kind of peace. The other customers were never in a hurry to get somewhere, and so she never felt that they expected anything out of her. For someone with nothing to give, this was the closest to belonging she could get.

Sera set her coffee cup down on the counter and wrapped both hands around it, drawing warmth from the liquid. She let her head fall forwards and rested her cheek on the top of the cup. The plastic lid bit into her skin and she could feel the heat radiating up towards her. She let all the air whoosh out of her lungs in one long, slow breath.

Without looking up, she said, "Do you ever feel like…have you ever…" she stopped. The words did not want to come. Spike didn't say anything, just let her regroup and find a place to start.

Spike knew that Remi had died in a tragic accident in a school parking lot. It seemed that everyone knew. He knew that she struggled with this, that she and Remi had been closer than peanut butter and jelly. He'd seen her hobbling around on crutches and he watched her tugging on the sleeves of her shirt, always making sure her arms were covered.

He never asked her for the details of what had happened that day, or how it affected her still. It wasn't because he didn't care, and it wasn't because he was too unobservant to notice. It was because he knew that she would tell him, in her own time, if ever she decided to.

Sera was so thankful for that. All anyone ever wanted to know was what she was feeling, how she was coping, why she had not moved on with her life. Sera never wanted to tell them. To this day, she didn't think there was a single time when she had decided, of her own free will, to talk to someone about that day in the parking lot.

"Spike?"

"Mm?" He looked up from wiping down the counter and held her gaze. His eyes were honey brown and full of concern, but he did not ask any of the questions everyone always did. He did not ask anything at all.

"Do you ever…" she trailed off, unsure how to start. "Has something ever happened to you, something terrible and irreversible? Something truly… devastating?"

He nodded once. "Sure."

"Was it something you knew would haunt you for the rest of your life, but no matter what, you could not change it? Something you would give anything to fix, but you just can't?"

Another nod. "Suppose so."

"What if it was your fault?"

A long pause. "What do you mean?"

"If this awful, horrible, unfixable thing were your fault. If everyone told you it wasn't, that it was just an accident and that tragedy is a part of life, but you knew. Deep down, you knew. It was your fault and nothing you do can ever change that. Nothing you do can ever make it better. No sacrifice, no amount of suffering, seems to be penance enough. There is no justice, no retribution, and all I keep thinking is—"

She broke off suddenly. Stared down at her coffee cup and tried to blink away the blurriness on the outlines of her vision.

A warm hand touched her forearm. It wasn't an aggressive or possessive move, or even protective. It wasn't sympathy or pity or sheer curiosity. It was… friendship. Camaraderie. A gesture to remind her that she was not alone in this vast, cold world.

But she was alone. Without Remi, she had no one. She had had other friends, of course, but after the accident, she had neglected them. They had given up calling, asking her to join them, and eventually, they had stopped including her in their friendship. She couldn't blame them—she wouldn't want to be friends with her, either—but it left her to face the world entirely on her own.

She felt the tears, deep in her throat, ready to rise up and strangle her. She forced them back down, but a small choking noise escaped. Before Spike could say or do anything else, she pulled away, half falling from her chair, her feet hitting the ground unevenly. She staggered upright, already moving across the room. She did not turn around, but she could feel Spike's amber eyes on her.

With one hand she braced herself against a wall that was painted to look like red brick. It was splattered in neon blue and green streaks, as if a firing squad had been armed with paintball guns for the execution. The other hand pressed against her chest, as though she could hold the sob inside by clutching at her shirt. She pushed past a circular table with its conglomeration of chairs, ignoring the blinking lights of the retro arcade games. One solitary man played Attack from Mars pinball. Mrs. Pacman, controlled solely by the computer, died.

In a place that was open 24/7 and modeled like an 80's movie, time stood still. For a moment, Sera was sure that Remi was here with her, as he had been so many times before. He was just beyond her reach, just out of her sight, out by the car, behind one of the pinball machines, in the bathroom for just a moment.

Sera wheeled, her feet taking her to the last place her mind had hit upon. In the back corner were the bathrooms—two bright blue doors set against the neon green wall. The men's had been broken for years now, but inside the women's the walls were covered in posters and graffiti. Inside the women's, there was a Skyrim print tacked up next to an advertisement for a game called *No Man's Sky.* Behind the two posters was a poem, written in Remi's careful hand. Written by the two of them, locked in together, giggling like children. Now, that was all that remained of him in this place. Memories scrawled on walls and echoing in her own head, louder than reality.

She was going to be sick.

She staggered past the bathrooms and, at long last, Sera reached the extreme back corner of the room. Her clutching hands found what they were seeking. She threw the door open wide just as lighting streaked across the sky. Overhead, thunder rumbled, hitting her straight in the chest. She thought she heard someone say her name, but the voice was lost to the howling wind.

The night beckoned. Without so much as a backwards glance, Sera plunged into the pouring rain.

EIGHT ……………◆

The blade was cold against her neck, her hands slick with sweat. She could feel the edge slice into the first layer of skin, and she did not have control.

THREE ……………◆

"How would you say that affects you? I mean, how does it make you feel?"

Sera glared at the psychiatrist. Rebecca Something. She was short, fat, and, in Sera's professional opinion, as ugly as a pig in a wig. Rebecca Something clicked her pen expectantly, the papers on her clipboard rustling. She'd been scribbling furiously the whole time they'd been talking, which Sera found mildly impressive. She had no idea what the woman had been jotting down, since Sera herself had hardly said a word. Rebecca Something was a clearly a master of both saying and writing copious amounts at the same time.

"Sera—can I call you Sera?"

"No."

Rebecca Something frowned. "I'm trying to establish a connection with you, but trust is a two-way street. I can't help you if you won't let me. You have to talk to me in order for this to work."

"Mm." She didn't bother to point out that she'd heard that cliché a thousand times before.

Sera picked at the frayed edge of an overwrought pillow. It was a hideous hodge-podge of pink and yellow squares of gossamer fabric stitched together rather haphazardly and fringed in golden sequins. It and its twin took up half of the small, gray couch, looking just as uncomfortable and stiff as Sera felt. She occupied the other half of the couch and kept fidgeting around, trying to find the best way to sit. The couch was at an angle to Rebecca Something's velvety, wing backed chair, so in order to face the woman, Sera had to position herself diagonally on the too-small sofa, elbow propped on the back, her feet sticking out in front of her like a broken doll's.

Possibly this was an intentional arrangement and it was supposed to make the patients recline and feel more comfortable.

Sera did not feel *more comfortable*.

"I'm only trying to help, Seraphim."

She did not feel comfortable at all.

"You were telling me about the night before your brother's funeral," Rebecca Something continued.

Sera refrained from pointing out that she hadn't said a word and Rebecca had been reading the outline of the sordid tale off the clipboard. The story had been pieced together by her parents and the doctors after they'd found her the next morning with a broken leg. She'd been frozen half to death but was still alive. They had known she'd been trying for a little further than halfway and instead of landing in the afterlife, she had found herself here, trying and failing to play nice with a counselor.

Her mother had even apologized.

"I'm so sorry, Sera. We should have taken you to counseling immediately after the..." her voice cracked, and she'd needed to pause for a moment to compose herself. Sera had stared at her listlessly, counting the thrum of her pulse as it pushed against the constraints of her cast.

"I mean, we were just so busy...it'd barely been a week...I can't believe I didn't see something like this coming. I've just been so lost in my own grief... but it will be okay, Sera, I promise. We'll get you the help you need. I love you, baby girl. It'll be okay."

She'd hugged Sera. Sera hadn't had the energy required to hug her back and had sat, as useless and unmoving as a broken doll, in her mother's embrace. Tears that should have been hers dripped off her mother's nose and onto her shirt, leaving dark splotches on the material. Sera had wondered for the millionth time why she couldn't cry.

"How did you feel about the funeral?" the shrink asked Sera.

Sera felt like chucking one of the absurd pillows across the room, flipping the table, and storming out, but she knew she couldn't. For one, it would only land her right back here again—or worse, in a psych ward. For another, she couldn't storm anywhere. Not with her leg encased in white plaster up to her knee.

The doctors had told her she was lucky. Both her knees were relatively undamaged and only the one ankle had been broken. They'd had to carefully persuade her shinbone to go back where it belonged and secure it there with a metal pin, but really, she was in remarkably good shape after such a long, cold night and such a long, dark fall.

That was what everyone called it. A *fall*. As though she had slipped. As though it had been an accident. As though she ought to be grateful that it was her leg and not her neck that had snapped.

"I feel like shit would be a lot better if I'd fucking swan dived off the roof rather than just jumping."

Sera knew she shouldn't have said it and regretted the words the moment they left her lips.

Rebecca Something leaned forwards in her chair. "Now, I'm not going to force you into anything, and it's important that you be the one to make the decisions, because it's your life and you need to be in control. I would never push drugs on you, okay? With that being said, I think you could benefit from some antidepressants. How would you feel about taking amitriptyline?"

"Which is?"

"Elavil."

The name made Sera picture an elven village, but the meaning was clear.

"You want to medicate me."

"I want to help you, Seraphim."

"By drugging me."

"Don't think of it like that. Think of it as…a little pick-me-up. Like a cup of coffee in the morning."

"And if I don't want it?"

"It's ultimately your choice, Seraphim, but it will help you feel better."

I don't want to fucking feel better. I want to be dead. Sera almost said it, but stopped herself at the last minute. "I feel fine."

"Your doctors and parents and I all agree that it would help, but you have to be the one to decide."

Except it wasn't a decision. It was never a choice. Not really. No matter how prettily the doctors and her parents painted the picture or insisted she was free to decline, she knew the truth. They would give her the pills in nice, cylindrical tubes with her name printed on the side. They would tell her how many to take and when. They would stand by her side, hold the glass of water, until they were sure she had swallowed. Then, and only then, would they leave.

Then, and only then, would she kneel over the toilet and force herself to throw up the contents of her stomach, purging her body of their poisons. Every time the idea of making herself sick appealed less, but every time, the urge to expel the pills was stronger. She would sit on the bathroom floor, shaking, in cold sweats, until there was nothing left inside of her but the guilt that nothing could ever eradicate. She did not want their help. She wanted to be left alone. She wanted the pain that she so deserved, and she wanted to suffer from it. She wanted Remi back.

She wanted to die.

FOUR

Sera was a specter. A mere shade of a girl, ghosting down the halls and through her house. Life was not about living; it was about going through the motions. Get up, get dressed, brush her teeth and her hair. She had to at least look like she was alive, or her parents would stop her, try to talk to her. She was forever pretending—no, lying. Because it was easier if no one knew, if no one suspected.

If they all just left her alone.

"Hello?"

Sera froze, mid-way through shutting the back door. She held her breath, waiting for discovery. The house was silent. She eased the door closed as quietly as she could and slunk around the corner to the stairs. She hadn't snuck out of class early to deal with her parents. The house was supposed to be empty: her mother at the law firm, her father at the airport, Terrasen and the twins at the elementary school. It was supposed to be just her in an empty house until the bus rolled by, leaving her siblings at the curb.

"Hello? Is someone there?"

Sera's foot hovered over the next step, wondering if she could get away with pretending not to have heard her father. Deciding that she could, she continued to advance up the stairs. They creaked beneath her weight, betraying her presence.

"Sera?"

Silently cursing her bad luck, Sera schooled her features into a pleasantly surprised expression. At least, it was what she hoped looked pleasantly surprised. She had been promising herself that she would practice in a mirror, to make sure the lie she presented to the world was believable. If they believed her, there were less questions. The less questions, the less effort required to keep up her lie.

She turned, forcing a bright smile onto her face. Her father was standing at the foot of the staircase, a dishtowel in one hand, a white ceramic mug in the other. Sera could just make out the image of the NASA logo with the words *I need my space*. It was a souvenir from the trip they'd taken to Houston, Texas, back when Sera had been small—maybe four years old. Malakai and Remi had been there, but neither Terra nor the twins had been born yet. The three of them, all less than 12 years old at the time, had run all over the building, and their parents had spent half of the day chasing them down.

"Sera? Are you alright?"

Sera blinked. The world refocused and she was back in her house, hand on the railing, foot on the stairs, twisted to look down at her father. She dragged her gaze up from the mug to her father's face, trying and failing to push away memories of Remi in an over-sized, space-themed shirt, of Malakai accidentally-on-purpose chipping the edge of a mug on its display shelf so that they would have to buy it, of her parents yelling at him and taking away his allowance until they'd withheld enough to pay for it, of Remi using the mug every single morning to pretend that his milk was really coffee.

"Hello?" Her father waved the dishtowel. "Earth to Sera?"

Sera crash-landed back on the stairs. "Oh, um. Hi, Dad. Dad, hello. Um, what are you doing here?"

"I have the day off, remember? I traded shifts with Demaenkin last week when his wife had the baby." He flipped the towel back over his hand and resumed drying the inside of the mug. Sera could see the place that Mal had chipped it.

"Oh, yeah. I'd forgotten about that."

"I thought I'd get some housework done while I have the time."

Sera nodded. Silence fell. Before he could toss her own question back in her face—a question she hadn't thought she would need a pre-planned answer for—she went for the distraction tactic.

"How's Demaenkin's baby."

The words fell from her lips, flat and uninterested. Her father looked up again, peering at her face. Sera realized her eyes were on the mug again, that her expression was dangerously close to revealing some small amount of the pain she felt. She searched for her smile and managed to conjure up something closer to a grimace. She opted for what she hoped was a bland, neutral look instead, painting on an expression the way some girls painted on make-up.

"Are you okay?"

"Hm? Me? I'm fine."

"Seraphim…"

"I'm fine, Dad. Fit as a fiddle."

"What are you doing home so soon?"

"School let out early."

"Why?"

"Pep rally."

"Now? Isn't it the wrong season for that?"

Fuck. Is it? Sera honestly didn't know.

"C'mon, Dad. Pep rallies are always in season and never in style."

Sera managed a smile. Her father laughed. "Isn't that the truth. What are you going to do with all the free time?"

"Um…"

"There's always homework."

"I don't have any," she said truthfully before she realized that it would have been the perfect excuse.

"Maybe you can help out around the house? I don't want you sitting in your room all alone, and I could use an extra set of hands. I'm going to try to fix the hinge that keeps sticking in the—"

"Oh, I just remembered. Ms. Tattersail assigned us a paper yesterday that I forgot about. I should probably work on that."

Her father peered at her. "Are you sure you're okay?"

Sera nodded. "I'll be up here if you need me." It seemed like the sort of thing a normal person would say. Before her father could question her further, Sera turned and, barely restraining herself from flat-out sprinting, hurried up the stairs.

She burst into her room, barely managing to shut the door behind herself before she sprawled across the floor, her book bag sliding from her shoulders with a thump. She lay on her stomach, her cheek pressed to the cool ground, staring at the cracks that ran between every strip of wood, following each line until it disappeared beneath the rug.

When she had visually traced out every crevice in the boards that she could see, she lifted her head just enough to look to the other side. Her chin slid over the floor, the skin bunching on one side, taut on the opposite. Then her head tipped and flopped back down, crushing the other cheek to the floor. Her head didn't turn this way as comfortably, but moving back was too much work. Besides, there were new lines in the floor on this side.

It only took a minute for Sera to realize that, though the lines were different, all the patterns were the same. Even the grains of the wood, which had, at first glance, all seemed to swirl uniquely, blurred into the same, homogenous mess.

Sera gave up and let her eyes wander. In paintings, people's eyes were always drawn towards the lightest part of the canvas. Artists used this to their advantage, choosing the colors and posing their subjects in carefully coordinated ways to direct the viewer's eyes in a certain direction.

Lying on the floor, Sera did the reverse. She found the darkest corners of the room, the deepest shadows, the recesses most devoid of light. She avoided the window with its gossamer white drapes fluttering around it—*like the wings of fairies*, Terra had said as she'd arranged them. She tucked her chin, sheltering her eyes from the bright winter sun as much as she could without really moving at all. Her gaze landed on the closet door, and on the strip of utter blackness beneath it.

Inside that closet, all the way up on the top shelf, pushed back into the furthest corner, there was a box. Sera hadn't looked at it since the day she had put it there, hadn't wanted to think about it. She had sworn she would never open it again.

She stood, almost as though she were in a trance, and walked to the closet. The knob was cold against the palm of her hand as she turned it. The door creaked as she pulled it open. The top shelf was, as ever, far above her head.

Sera left the closet gaping open and walked across the room to the old, wooden rocking chair. Her mother had rocked her and every one of her siblings to sleep in that chair when they were infants, from Malakai, when the baby shower gift had been brand new, right down to Cobalt and Indigo, just over a decade and a half later. The rocking chair had taken up permanent residence in Terra and Sera's room because there wasn't space for it anywhere else, and it usually sat alone and forgotten in a corner.

Possibly Sera sympathized with it far too much.

"It's just a shitty old rocking chair," she muttered to herself and she dragged it across the floor and over to the closet. It swayed beneath her as she stepped onto the seat, rocking as rocking chairs are wont to do.

There, just where she had known it would be, was the box. It was brown and cardboard and so very unsuspecting, but Sera knew the horrors it contained. She knew exactly what she was getting herself into as she pulled it towards herself and lifted it down, as she blew away the dust and teetered on the chair, as she settled herself back on the floor, kneeling before the box, and cut into the masking tape holding it closed.

It had been over a year now since she had last seen the contents of the box. She did not understand why she was going through it now, what was compelling her to free this piece of her past. She only knew that she had to.

Sera took a deep breath, closed her eyes, and opened it.

THREE

The paintings were staring at her.

She knew every brush stroke, every dab of paint, every little nuance and mistake. She had poured her heart and soul into every one of these pieces, and then she had hung them around her room, a smorgasbord of portraits, still lifes, nature scenes, and creatures from her own imagination. She always paid careful attention to eyes as she sketched and then painted them, drawing out the precise color, shape, and texture of the iris, trying to capture the subject's thoughts and feelings in their glassy reflection.

And now they were staring at her as she had once stared at them.

"Sera?" The door creaked open and Sera's mother stuck her head inside.

"Ever heard of knocking?" Sera said, but she was too tired to muster the energy to really be pissed.

"Sorry." Her mother was smiling. "It's good to see you painting again."

"Mm."

Sera hadn't actually painted anything yet. She was just standing at her easel, pallet in one hand, brush in the other. The blank canvas was staring at her, too.

"The kids and I heading to Trellis soon, but I just started a load of wash. Will you please finish it for me?"

"Mm."

"And then I have to go back to Walmart. Again."

"Weren't you just there yesterday?"

"Yes, but they botched my prescription. Yours and Dad's came through alright, though. Just mine. It isn't like I've been getting the same thing for how long now?"

"Mm." Sera's interest in the conversation had already waned. She went back to staring at her easel. She still didn't have a clue what she was going to paint.

"We'll be home sometime after seven, so dinner will be late tonight."

"Mm."

"You know where the kitchen is if you get hungry."

"Mm."

"Laundry, please, Sera. Don't forget."

"I won't."

"See you later."

"Have fun at garden club."

"It isn't garden club."

"Then why's it called trellis?"

"You know, you might find you like it if you came. It's all music and art."

"Mm."

Sera had no desire to spend her Sunday afternoon in a church with her mother's friends and their children. Maybe she would paint a shadowy sinner whose skin bubbled off the moment they set foot on holy ground. She could paint it all in black and white, with just the subject's blood in vivid red. It would make a nice color contrast.

Her mother sighed. "Goodbye, Sera. I love you."

"Mm."

Her mother's head withdrew and the door clicked shut. Beyond it, Sera could hear Indi, Co, and Terra rushing around the house, gathering all the random detritus they would need for their not-a-garden club.

She stood there, obsessively tracing the edge of her hand with the tip of her brush, listening to the chaos. Feet pounded up and down the stairs. The plastic dishes they always brought for the potluck clattered together. Books thumped against the floor as someone dropped them.

"Terra, did you shut the kitchen window?"

"No."

"Why not?"

"Because it's such a beautiful day out."

"Terra, I told you to shut that window."

"Why?"

"Do you like having a cat?"

"There's a screen."

"Middie has claws."

"Middie wouldn't do that."

"Middie likes exploring, you know that."

"Middie isn't stupid," Terra insisted, just as stubborn as Sera once was. The memory of herself at that age almost brought a smile to Sera's lips, but then the feeling was gone. She would never be like Terra, and she hoped that Terra was never like her. Not the way that she was now.

"Go shut the window."

"But Mommy—"

"Terrasen."

The argument ceased and Sera heard the window creak shut a minute later. She listened to her brothers' banter as they all piled out the door. She heard the car start, the doors opening and closing, someone sprinting back inside for a forgotten item.

"Did you remember to lock it?"

"Sera is still here."

"Everyone got everything?"

The front door shut again, but their voices still drifted up to her through the bedroom window Terra had left thrown wide open. As her mother pulled out onto the street, she watched Terra roll her window down.

"Put that back up right this instant, Terrasen."

The one on the other side of the car rolled down as well.

"Indigo!"

Then they were too far away for Sera to hear anymore. Silence fell, unbroken, settling over the house like night over the world, and even the wind forgot to whisper. Sera stared blankly at her canvas, and her blank canvas stared back.

FOUR

The house was silent.

The world was holding its breath.

The earth seemed to have stopped spinning.

Sera knew this was a bad idea. Knew that this could only lead down a road she should not travel. Knew that, by reopening this box, she was reopening the vault in her head. Her demons would escape, and they would not be forced back into confinement easily. She knew she should stop, fold up the flaps, and put the horrors back in their corner of the closet.

She knew she wasn't going to.

THREE

Sera did not know how long she stood before her easel in the empty house, waiting to paint something. The gruesome image of the churchgoer had fled, leaving her with an empty head. The seconds stretched into minutes, maybe even hours. Days could have passed and she would never have realized. All she could do was stand and stare, drowning in the off-white of the blank canvas and the swirl of unmixed paints: inky black; bruised blue; sea foam green; dusty, regolith gray; twilit, dusky violet; soft, baby pink; a single streak of sunshine yellow; a puddle of vivid scarlet.

Her eyes wandered around her room, seeking inspiration among the things that she had already painted. She had dabbled in a wide array of different styles over the years, from sharp, angular abstracts to sfumato still-lifes. Most were acrylics, but there were a few watercolors showing the lake, sailboats, and lighthouses. There was even finger painting of a cat, based loosely on Middie, perched in a tree that looked very much like the one across the street.

She set her brush down and dipped her fingers into the paint. The red smeared across her skin like freshly spilled blood, but too cool, too viscous. The yellow blurred it into sunset orange, tinged by the color of her flesh beneath. Sera turned to the canvas and pressed her whole hand against it, dragging her fingers down, leaving three long, orange-red-yellow streaks behind.

The violet engulfed the side of her hand, leaving a curl the shape of her pinky finger when she peeled her fist off the white. The heel of her hand smeared in the blue, changing both canvas and flesh to midnight, then it was dusted over in gray. Her thumb dotted in green, leaving blots that would take hours to dry.

She stepped back to survey her work and felt her heart drop to her toes. On the wall directly behind her was the first painting she could remember ever making, ever hanging in her room. It, too, was a finger painting, crafted of all the colors of the rainbow, swirled and blended in ways nature never intended, so many hues that in places they were nothing more than muddy brown.

She had been four, and the outline of her small hand was still visible, smudged on one side where Terra, who had been a kicking, writhing heap of a child, had put her foot in the paint. But not all of the fingerprints were hers, because she hadn't been painting alone. Sitting on the floor next to her, both of them stripped down to their underwear, had been Remi.

The pain exploded through her so forcefully that, for a moment, she went blind to everything else. When the world swam back into focus, she was on the floor on her knees, paint spilled everywhere, the canvas she had been working on knocked to the ground. A deep, diagonal slash carved it almost into two separate pieces. The knife was in her hand. She did not know how it had gotten there. She found that she did not care.

The sound of ripping canvas echoed in her ears. It was a sound she needed to hear again. She was up in a moment, her colorful hands reaching for the nearest painting. She tore it from the wall, her fingers smearing new shades on top of the old, curling around the handle of her knife. She drew her arm back, then plunged it into the very heart of the painting.

She half expected the starry night sky to bleed blue and black blood, tinged with the yellow-white of the stars. When it didn't, she realized that, more than expecting it, she *wanted* it to bleed. She raised the knife again, let it fall, dragged it down, slicing through loving hours of time spent guiding brushes.

The ribbons of the canvas lay scattered around her, but dried paint did not flow like blood. She wanted—no, *needed*—to bleed. The feel some small part of the agony she had caused Remi to suffer in those last few moments.

He had been chasing after her.

It was her fault.

It would forever be her fault. She did not deserve to stand there and paint, to create something new, or even to look at the beauty of life captured in paint, when he was gone and she was to blame.

She reached for another canvas.

FOUR ....◆

The contents of the box were just as jumbled as she knew they would be. After all, she had been the one to forbid anyone to touch the remains of her art. She had thrown the ribbons of her heart into confinement—four sides, a top and a bottom. She had sealed them inside, intending to leave them untouched forever. She had shoved them to the back of her closet, just as she had pushed her thoughts to the back of her mind, refusing to so much as acknowledge their presence for five seasons.

But she had not thrown them out. Even in pieces, she could not bear to let go, and the memories crept out of her head when she least expected it. She dreamt of Remi's death, swept away by her own guilt.

She could remember the day of his death as though it had just happened, and her own pain was the only instrument in each and every one of her paintings. Even those made long ago were tinged with it. It was anguishing to recall how she and Remi had smeared colors across a canvas and across themselves and each other. How their mom had smiled, how Terra had gotten a single foot in on it, how they had laughed and splashed in the bathtub later.

How proud they had been of their creation. How she had smiled every time she had studied their childhood art. How they had planned to get matching tattoos on her eighteenth birthday. How, until that day in the school's parking lot, they had never spent more than two weeks apart.

All of those memories, turned to dust, to ashes, to dreams. To nightmares to torment her both day and night, to keep her awake and haunt her in her sleep.

Sera reached into the box, pushing aside the tattered strips of canvas. Flakes of paint cracked off and fluttered down around her, dusting her hands in a rainbow of colors. A splinter of a wooden frame dug into her flesh, but she didn't pull away. Physical pain meant nothing to her anymore.

There, at the very bottom, she found what she had been seeking. Her fingers searched out the corners, feeling their way along the edge, ensuring that the whole thing was still there, still in one piece, before she tugged it free.

Everything shifted, slipping and sliding to the sides of the box as she began to wriggle her prize free. It caught—stuck—held fast. Refused to relinquish its place beneath the heap of rubbish that had once been art.

Then, a last tug, the square-framed canvas surfaced. She lifted it out of the box and cradled it in her arms. With all the care of an archeologist discovering a shard of ancient pottery half-buried in the earth, she blew the dust and bits of debris off the canvas, revealing the painting beneath.

It could hardly be called a painting at all. It was a swirly, smeared mass of colors, with low spots so thin the canvas was visible and high spots where the paint formed ridges that had taken hours to dry. The chaotic design was imprinted with the outlines of small fingers and hands. It looked like the work of a child—two children to be precise. Three if Terra's foot-smudge counted.

The pain rocked through Sera, so intense it was like a physical blow. She fell back, clutching the painting to her chest, curling in on herself until she was the smallest ball she could be. The edges of the wooden frame dug into her chest, stomach, and legs as she began to rock back and forth, head tucked down, shielding herself from the world, the pain, the crushing guilt.

She could not breathe. She could not think. She could not go on like this, forever trapped by the agony of what she had done.

Sera did not know how long she sat there for, trapped in her own mind, imprisoned by her own failures. She did not know how long the war waged within her, but when it ended, she lifted her tearstained face, filled with new resolve.

One hand clutching the painting to her core, Sera stood. She rummaged in a drawer until she produced a pen. Using a scrap of shredded canvas, Sera scribbled a note. Her final goodbye. It was the first time she had written a suicide note, and she had no idea what to say.

She tried out several different headings in her mind: *Dear Mom, Dear Family, To Ye Who Finds This.* None of them fit. In the end, she forewent a greeting and skipped straight to the message.

It was my fault, and I'm sorry. Please don't feel guilty for what I've done. None of you were to blame. It was all me. It was always me.

Remi, I'm so, so sorry.

Sera didn't bother to sign it. She set the finger painting on her dresser and placed the note on top of it. She rubbed her wrists, the skin rough from the scars cut into them. Scars she had cut into them. She pulled on her winter coat, tugging down the sleeves to almost completely obscure her hands.

Her feet clattered on the stairs and she hurried down them. Her father looked up from where he crouched on the floor, hunkered down over a door that had been removed from its frame, an array of tools spread across the floor and sticking out of various pockets.

"Decided to come help?"

Sera had completely forgotten he was even there. "Um…no. I'm going…to Common Grounds."

"Thought you had an essay to write?"

"I'm going to write it there."

"Oh."

He returned his attention to the hinges. Sera thought she was in the clear. She was turning the doorknob, car keys in hand, boots hastily laced up her shins, when he paused again.

"Wait up a sec, angel." It was a nickname left over from childhood. She wished her father wouldn't.

Sera closed her eyes. "Dammit," she muttered under her breath.

"What did you say?" His tone was pleasant enough, but Sera knew she was on dangerous ground.

"I said, "What's that?" I didn't hear you."

He surveyed her faux innocence. "Where's your laptop?"

"Huh?"

"You're writing an essay aren't you?"

"Oh. Um. I've got a notebook. In the car. And a pen. You know I think better on paper."

He didn't look convinced. "And your wallet?"

"In my jacket pocket."

This, at least, was true. She flapped one side of her coat at him, inviting him to come check. He didn't. She edged closer to the door.

"Good luck with the hinge," she hinted.

"Good luck with your essay. I love you, Sera. You know that, right? You are my beautiful baby girl and you can tell me anything."

The anguish welled up in her again. She just managed to bite it back before her face betrayed her.

"I know," she choked out.

Then she opened the door and was gone.

THREE

The accumulation of several years' worth of labor had once adorned the walls, each painting lovingly, painstakingly crafted, each stroke considered before it was made, mistakes altered into something that seemed to belong, the swirls and blots more familiar to Sera than the memory of Remi's face. No longer.

When she opened her eyes, fully conscious of herself and her surroundings, she did nothing but survey the damage listlessly. There was no point in trying to fix what she had done. She was the flotsam and jetsam, thrashed and churned by the sea, spewed up upon shore, broken and tattered, useless to anyone.

She did not have the strength to stand.

She did not have the will to live.

She had a knife in her hand, one that was perfectly capable of ending her life, spilling her blood, taking away the pain she suffered. It was an agony she deserved—if there was a hell, she knew that she would burn in it—but it was unbearable.

She did not have the gumption to plunge the knife into her heart or her wrist. She did not lack the resolve, but that was a high-energy death. She wanted something easier. Less dramatic. To slip beneath the jagged waves of a storm-tossed sea, sinking slowly out of sight, never to be heard from again. Not to leap from a rooftop screaming a battle cry and painting the streets in her own blood.

Somewhere deep in the house, a buzz resounded.

Her mother's words echoed back to her. *Do the laundry. Please, Seraphim, don't forget…I have to get my prescription refilled—they botched it—but yours came in alright.*

In the bathroom in the medicine cabinet, there was a bottle full of pills.

In the bathroom in the medicine cabinet, there was an easy way out.

In the bathroom in the medicine cabinet, there was, at last, a blissful end.

Sera summoned all her remaining strength and, gathering her legs beneath her, she willed herself to stand.

FOUR ···············◆

The rumble of the engine was comforting. Her Subaru Outback was as cold as the January afternoon, but inside, she was safe from the wind. Inside, she could drive as far as she wanted and never come back. Maybe she would look up from the road and find herself in California, or on a plane to England. Maybe she would find some answers, a release for her pain.

Maybe she would find her way to the doors of death.

The white paint looked gray and shabby next to the gleaming, freshly fallen snow that glittered in the sun like scattered pixie dust. The interior of the car was cold and bleak and black, but it did not demand an explanation. It did not ask for a destination. When she put her foot on the gas pedal and applied pressure, it did not ask questions.

It simply went, and she simply drove.

THREE ···············◆

The door to the bathroom creaked as she pushed it in.

FOUR ···············◆

The door to the car was not shut all the way. The light flashed. Without lifting her eyes from the road, Sera reopened and then slammed it closed. The sound reverberated through her bones, straight to her core.

THREE ···············◆

The counter was cool beneath her hands.

FOUR ···············◆

The wheel was perforated against her fingers. She knew there would be indents in her skin when she let go, but she did not care. Her hands were sweating. Her palms were slick with it. The wheel was going to be coated. But she did not care.

She did not care.

THREE ••••••••••••••••◆

The mirror showed her a glimpse of herself—haggard, disheveled, as destroyed as the detritus left in the wake of a hurricane—as she swung it open. Her sunken eyes glanced away from the hollow cheeks, the matted hair.

She did not care to look.

She did not care to see.

She did not feel anything.

FOUR ••••••••••••••••◆

The air was bitterly cold, the wind biting as it flung small flurries against her skin, stinging pieces of fractured ice.

THREE ••••••••••••••••◆

The pills rattled in their bottle.

FOUR ••••••••••••••••◆

The automatic sliding glass door rattled in its frame as the wind threw itself against the panes.

THREE ••••••••••••••••◆

The cap was on the counter.

FOUR ••••••••••••••••◆

Past the ticket machine, up the stairs, across the bridge over the tracks. She had not intended to come to the Puritas Station. She did not know where she was going to take the Rapid to. She did not know anything anymore.

THREE ••••••••••••••••◆

The pills were in her hand.

FOUR ••••••••••••••••◆

There were only a few people waiting at the station, forming a small knot as they subconsciously allowed the wind to herd them. None of them paid her any heed. She did not glance at them. They did not glance at her.

She stood a little apart from the cluster, hands deep in her pockets. Where was she going to go? Far down the tracks, as far along the bend as she could see, she could just make out the shape of the train. It was hurtling along towards them. It would be there soon.

She would board it. She would ride it to the end of the line. She would get off. And where would she go?

It was halfway around the curve, racing along the line.

She walked to the side of the platform closest to the train. She closed her eyes. She edged forwards ever so slightly. Both feet had already been in the center of the yellow warning strip of paint. She eased her way closer to the drop off.

The train was flying down the straightaway, fast enough to kill.

She was balanced on the ledge, the tips of her toes about to be dangling over. Her pulse was thrumming in her ears, louder even than the train, and yet, she still thought, for the briefest moment, that she heard her brother call her name. Thought she felt him there beside her, standing just a half a step away, waiting for a train that would take them both away.

She drew a breath. Looked up and to the left, still alone on the edge, counting the heartbeats remaining to her. She could fall forwards, directly into the path of the train, and it would be over.

It would all be over.

THREE ················◆

The pills were in her mouth, a glass of water clutched between her fingers, pressed against her lips. She looked over the rim of it into the reflection that stared back from the mirror, haunted and alone, straight back into her eyes. The barest hint of a loving caress touched her wrist, as though her brother had laid his fingers against her skin, and then it was gone.

FOUR ················◆

A little girl, the only child waiting for the Rapid, broke away from her mother. She had shiny black hair tied in low pigtails that draped over her shoulders. She wore a pink and blue striped hat with a bobble on top, purple flowered rain boots, and a long, crimson jacket. She was a collision of color, a neon nightmare, a brilliantly shining star in the dreary station.

THREE ················◆

She swallowed.

FOUR ················◆

The girl would be a good subject for a painting, but she would never sit still long enough to be effectively captured. She had an aura, an energy about her that could never be transmitted onto canvas or paper, or even into a film. It was a vitality, a sparkling quality that was visible only if you looked closely, paid attention to the flitting edges, intangible but more real than a hand upon your shoulder.

She was alive.

She alone, in this cloudy-gray, abysmal realm, was really and truly alive.

Her dark eyes shone with life as her fingers caught at Sera's sleeve, tugging her away from the edge, gentle but insistent. Irresistible. Sera staggered back as the train hurtled to a stop, inches in front of her nose, ripping the air from her lungs with its speed.

That was her death, and here she stood, still alive. Her heart seemed to restart in her chest, and her lungs expanded. Suddenly, she was gasping for air. It was as though feeling had suddenly been restored to her numb limbs.

"Careful," the little girl cried. "My mom always warns me not to stand on the yellow, or you might get bit. Didn't yours ever teach you not to get to close to the trains? She says they bite."

"Seika," the little girl's mother cried as she rushed towards them, her arms stretching out to her daughter. "Seika, what are you doing?" She caught the girl up, hugging her close, then held her at arms' length and stared her in the eye. "You scared me—how many times have I told you that you have to be careful around the trains?"

"I know, Mommy. But I didn't get bitted." She held out her arms for inspection. "See?"

Sera watched, trying to force her limbs to unfreeze, as the woman hugged the girl again. Her skin was pale from fright and blotchy from relief, her frizzy blonde hair wild from the wind. "Thank goodness. You can't go running off, okay? Stay by my side, always."

"I'm sorry, Mommy, but I was worried she was going to get bit."

The little girl gestured to Sera, whose feet came unstuck at last. She teetered, unsteady, as she began to walk away. Her life had almost ended. She had almost thrown herself onto the tracks. This girl, this innocent, bright-eyed little girl, had saved her life, and she didn't even know what she'd done. She hadn't just looked—she had seen Sera. She had known what was going to happen and had cared enough to change it.

The woman's voice followed her back up the red metal stairs, but Sera wasn't listening. She thought of her father, tinkering with hinges and waiting for her to come home. She thought of her mother, who always found time to spend with each child, no matter how large the gaggle of siblings. She thought of her brothers and sisters, a whole fleet of them, living their lives, making something of themselves, planning for the future, romping the city with the care-free innocence of childhood.

She thought of the little girl who had saved her life, and how much her mother must love her.

Sera climbed back into her car and she drove for home.

THREE

Sera knelt on the floor, the tiles digging into her knees, head in the toilet, as she forced her body to purge itself of the pills. Coughing, gasping, desperate to be sure they were all gone, she clutched at the rim of the toilet bowl.

She was no stranger to forcing herself to throw up medication—she had been doing it with the antidepressants for as long as they had been shoved down her throat. But this was different. This had been a choice—a choice to die, and then the decision to live.

Someone she loved had given his life for hers. She would not end hers, would not waste the gift he had given her. There was a purpose to this, a reason for her continued existence. She could not tap out until she had found and fulfilled.

Sera knew she would have to go back into her bedroom, would have to clean up the wreckage she had left behind. She would bury it in a box, shove it into the back of her closet, and forget it had ever been there. She would fold the laundry. If anyone asked, she would pretend she had spilled the pills down the sink or something—by some mistake, she had been forced to pitch the whole lot. She would not let anyone know. She would get back up, and she would face the world again. She would regain control, but for now she just wanted to lie there, face pressed against the cool porcelain, breathing in and out.

SIX

The night wind seemed to careen wildly and out of control, throwing itself against the house, ripping through the trees, and battering itself into Sera. The rain came down in sheets, soaking her clean through. It was only October, but already, it felt as though it ought to be snowing. The rain ran in icy rivulets down her face, sneaking its way under her shirt and down her back. Her dark brown hair was plastered to her skin, almost black from the water.

Her car was just up the hill, up the set of steps she had almost fallen down in her rush to reach the shoreline. She could go back up there, climb into the dry space, and turn the heater on full blast. She could drive back to Common Grounds, apologize for running out on Spike like that. There were a lot of things she could do, but somehow, she could not seem to pull herself away from the edge of the lake.

It crashed against the sand, breaking over the rocks that made up a sort of pier. She and Remi had long ago dubbed it Adventure Pier, and to this day, Sera did not know its actual name. To her, it had always been and would always be Adventure Pier.

An image of her mother flashed through her mind, calling her and Remi back when they'd walked too far out on the rocks Sera stood on now. Their mother had been standing on the beach, her hair billowing around her face as the wind whipped off Lake Erie.

"The rocks are slippery when they're wet," she'd warned. "And those waves are big enough that you could easily get drenched."

Sera and Remi had stopped in their rock hopping, turned to look back at their mother. She had beckoned them towards her. "It's dangerous; come back here."

They had looked at each other, and then at Malakai, who had been leading their little adventure. Mal had grinned at his little siblings, then waved back to Sarah.

"Coming, Mom."

There was no one there to call Sera back now. She could walk as far as she wanted, heading towards Canada, until she fell in the lake and drowned. No one would say a word. They would find her body, bloated and swollen with water, after the storm had passed. Her family would move on. They had gotten over the loss of a child before.

Sera found herself perched on the edge of the last rock that made up the pier. The lake stretched before her, endless and foreboding. She could do it. She could jump. She was a strong swimmer, but she knew that once she pitched herself into the lake, there would be no coming back out.

And yet, Sera only stood, watching the waves break around her, showering her in spray and threatening to sweep her feet out from beneath her. Another wave crashed over her, but she was already as wet as she could be and did not mind the cold—only the rattle of her own teeth. She stuffed her tongue between them to quiet the sound. She felt as though she was standing on the edge of the world, and nothing could harm her anymore. She flung her head back, letting the rain course down her face. Its chilled caress snaked its way down her front, beneath the collar of her shirt.

She thought back to all the times she had walked the line between life and death: leaping from the roof the night before Remi's funeral; slicing into her own wrists; the pills; the Rapid—and yet, never once had she gone through with it. She had stitched what she had torn, done her best to put the pieces back together. She was still alive. She was still breathing.

She did not know what she wanted, not anymore. Things could never go back to the way they were. She knew that. She had always known. Without that elusive dream, there was nothing left for her to desire.

Standing there at the edge of the world, in the pouring rain with the waves breaking over her, she only knew two things. The first was that she was not there to end her life. And the second was that this, at least, was something she could control.

EIGHT

The blade was cold against her neck, her hands slick with sweat. *Breathe in, breathe out.* She could feel the edge slice into the first layer of skin. *Breathe in, breathe out.* It was her life on the line again, but this time, she did not have control.

This time, she knew that she wanted to live.

SIX

The lock slid into place with some difficulty, but once it was engaged, Sera breathed again. She had been worried that Spike would try to stop her when she came in. She knew he had seen her—the only other people in Common Grounds at this hour were a young, tattooed couple so full of piercing holes that between the two of them they could sink a ship. She had made a beeline from the back door to the bathroom, but she was soaked through from standing on the pier and wasn't exactly inconspicuous.

Sera went to the sink and began doing her best to wring out her sopping clothes, sending the water down the drain rather than letting it drip off of her and puddle on the floor. It didn't make that much of a difference, but she felt bad about leaving a mess that Spike would have to clean up.

As she twisted the fabric of her shirt, something someone had scribbled on the wall caught her eye: *THE WORLD IS BEAUTIFUL.* Someone else had added *SO ARE YOU* and, beneath that, *SEEN YOUR NUDES.* Above it all was a caricature rose, its stem too thin to ever support the blossom.

When she was a wrung-out as she was going to get, Sera dried her hands on a paper towel and peered at herself in the mirror. Around the scratches that spelled out words Sera couldn't read, she could see herself, still sodden, looking like a half-drowned cat. Next to the mirror, a soap dispenser hung on the wall. A sticker with cursive letters looked back at her, agreeing with her reflection: *yikes.*

Sera turned away and looked around the bathroom instead. Every inch of it was covered in posters or graffiti, some of it pictures, some words, and some just scribbles. There were entire conversations written along the walls, pen covering everything but the sink and toilet.

The back of the door had the same, repeating pattern drawn all the way down it—letters that did not spell out words. In the corner by the toilet, scrawled in huge, black lines, someone had written, *MADSAN, I AM A CREATURE OF WORTH.* There was no signature, but next to it someone had drawn a hand holding a lit cigarette, and others had commented, some including arrows to show how the conversation had been written. *Bitch, you thought. Fuck you whore. Suuuuure you are.* At the very bottom, almost inked on the floor, were the words *what a beautiful little butterfly you are. Fly angel, fly.*

Sera leaned a little closer. Had that one always been there? She didn't think so. The writing looked vaguely familiar, but she couldn't quite place it. Still, the words whispered through her head, as though someone had set them on repeat. She found them oddly comforting.

She stepped back from the wall and let her eyes scan over the posters. There, just where she knew they would be, were the two that covered Remi's writing. Sera slid her fingers into the seam between two posters. The one on the left was a sea foam green with a blue swoosh at the top and a pink swatch at the bottom. There were planes in one corner and a solitary man in the center below the words *No Man's Sky.* The poster on the right showed a desolate mountain scene, painted in blacks and grays, the jagged peaks of the mountains framing someone's illegible signature. White words written over the black at the very bottom proclaimed it as a Skyrim poster.

Careful not to rip either, Sera peeled the two pictures away from the wall. Beneath them were the words Remi had penned there years ago, still untouched in the curling frame Sera had drawn around them.

This living hand, now warm and capable
Of earnest grasping, would, if it were cold
And in the icy silence of the tomb,
So haunt thy days and chill thy dreaming nights
That thou wouldst wish thine own heart dry of blood
So in my veins red life might stream again,
And thou be conscience-calmed—see here it is—
I hold it towards you.

Sera did not understand what it meant, not really, not the way Remi had, but seeing him write it and listening to him read it had warmed her to the core. Even now, she felt a gentle flush sweep through her, radiating out from her right wrist, where the bangle Remi had given her dangled. To her surprise, there was none of the pain she expected to feel. The calm that had washed over her on the edge of Lake Erie remained, and there was no desire to get back in her car and drive to Suicide Bridge. It was nicknamed that because so many kids had leapt over the side—and more than one had escaped from the nearby mental hospital to do so. Sera had thought of ending her life there nearly every time she'd crossed over it. It would be so easy, and it would be almost a quiet death, because it would not be original. But somehow, seeing the words of a poet Remi had loved, rather than stabbing through her like hot knives, calmed her.

It was clear that she was not the only one who felt this way. The posters had not been put up until at least a year after Remi had written the poem, but it had been left untouched in a space of white. Even the frame Sera had drawn around it remained unmarred by the hands of others. The rest of the walls were covered in layers of writing, but this one, small patch had been left untouched. Pure. Unscarred by any hand but Remi's and her own.

Sera fingered the hems of her left sleeve, then pushed the fabric up her arm, revealing the rough ridges cut into her skin by her own knife. The scars were jagged and ugly, but in that moment, Sera didn't hate them as she usually did. She didn't feel the immediate urge to cover them again. Instead, she traced her fingers along them, feeling the puckering. They had been gaping and bloody once, but they had healed. Her arm would be forever changed, but it was not damaged beyond repair. The scars were jagged and ugly, yes, but they were wholly hers.

"Red on white like a virgin's wedding night," she whispered.

Remi was not there to answer her the way he had before, but she heard the echo of his words just the same.

"Red on red, no bloodstains on the bed."

Sera thought for a moment, then pushed her right sleeve up to mirror her left one. She did not realize that her hands were shaking until the moment she went to open the bathroom door and the knob rattled in her grip. She clenched it to steady herself. If she opened the door and walked out into the main part of the café, she would be exposing the truth. She had not worn anything that showed more than the palms of her hands since the day that should have been

Remi's 17th birthday. Not since the night when she first sliced into her wrists as retribution for forgetting the date. She had cut and then sewn, stitching herself back together, and had hidden the damage beneath long sleeves. If her parents had noticed, they hadn't done anything.

No one ever did anything.

That was the way of the world, wasn't it? If you wanted to see a change, you had to change it yourself. If you wanted something to get better, you had to make it better. You couldn't just sit idly by and blame your problems on someone or something else. This was her life, and she was the only one who could live it.

For the first time in a long time, she wanted to survive. No—she wanted to live. She was tired of hiding. She was done letting the world walk all over her. She was ready to find her purpose, to make good on the gift Remi had given her. To have a life worth living, and to *live* it.

And so, sleeves rolled high up her arms, the scars that twined their way up the insides of her forearms proudly on display, she pushed open the door.

EIGHT ···············◆

This time, she knew—a shadow of a doubt eclipsing hope—that there would not be a next time.

SIX ···············◆

A steaming cup of Crazed Englishman sat on the counter, waiting for Sera the moment she stepped from the bathroom. Her name was written on the side in the same handwriting she had found nearly on the floor.

What a beautiful little butterfly you are. Fly angel, fly.

Spike pushed the drink towards her and smiled around the toothpick jammed between his lips. "This one is on the house."

Sera slid onto one of the bar stools and wrapped her hands around the cup. "I'm sorry."

"For?"

"Running out on you like that. I—I just…I'm sorry."

Spike shook his head. "Don't be. There's few things a walk in the rain can't fix."

Sera glanced up. He was smiling, and she had known—she had just known—that everything would be alright.

SEVEN ···············◆

She did not know, exactly, why Malakai was there. She felt as though she had once known, at some point in the long-forgotten past, but she did not know now.

She supposed that it did not really matter.

She had been on the steps, listening to Mal rant while Carter and Sarah tried to soothe him. She had not been lurking in the shadows, but she had taken her time coming down the stairs, Mal's voice echoing up to her.

"What am I supposed to do? If they're going to fire me, they're going to fire me."

"Getting laid off and fired are not the same thing."

Sarah's voice was calm, reassuring. Mal was unaffected.

"And what difference does it make? I still lose my job. Where am I supposed to get another one? Noah and I barely make rent as it is. Oh, and Noah! He's been so…so *difficult* lately. Screaming at me over the smallest of things… He slept on the couch last night, did you know that? Refused to share a bed with me. I was honestly surprised to see that the ring was still on his finger this morning. Although maybe if he stopped wearing it, we could pawn it. Then maybe we could pay to get the car fixed…"

"What's wrong with the car?" Carter asked. "I can get my tools—"

"I don't want your charity."

"It's not charity. You're my son and—"

"Just forget it."

Malakai burst through the door and collided with Sera, who had just reached the bottom of the stairs. She staggered back a step and almost fell over, but Mal caught her by the wrist and hauled her back to her feet. She flinched away from his grip as his fingers pressed into the ragged flesh of her arm.

With the pain came the memory of the smell of coffee, rich and thick, and the faint traces of smoke and worn wood. A counter touched by too many hands and a smile in the place Sera had least expected it. Her talk with Spike in

Common Grounds over a stack of empty coffee cups had not righted all the wrongs in her world, but it had helped.

She had not cut herself since then, had not felt the need to. She had found herself, knife in hand, just for something to do, but she had forced herself to replace it with a brush or pen. She'd taken to tracing the veins in her arms, but ink was not the same as blades.

Her forearm was still healing. It would never again be smooth, never again be whole, but someday it would be better. *Baby steps,* she told herself.

Still, the pain must have registered on her face. Malakai noticed. Rather than release her arm, he turned it over and jerked up her sleeve. It was appropriate weather for a long-sleeved shirt, but once Mal had yanked the fabric up to her elbow, the scars were conspicuous. It looked worse than it was: scores of half-healed red lines scattered over old cuts, some faint white lines, some thick enough to be tiger stripes. Black ink swirled between the marks, accentuating the red and white, the bits of old scabs still peeling off.

"God, Sera. You are such a mess."

Sera did not know what she had been expecting her brother to say, but it certainly had not been that. *No,* she told herself. *You just heard him wrong. Mal wouldn't say that. He loves you. He's your brother.*

"What?" she asked, but there was a roaring in her ears. The screeching of tires, metal crunching, screams that should have burst from her mouth and rung out across the parking lot. Those screams were still trapped in her head, still echoing against the inside of her skull. Suddenly, it didn't matter what Mal said—only what she heard.

"You're such a mess. You sit around all day, wallowing in your own self-righteous self-pity. Ever since Remi died, you've been blaming yourself, hurting yourself, acting like life can never get better. When are you going to grow up and move on?"

He did not see how far she had come—where *he* meant *the world.* They did not see how their words had the ability to wound her, how she was only just managing to hang on.

She tried to fight it. "Mal, I—"

"Don't try to explain yourself to me. I already know what you're going to say, and I don't want to hear it. Maybe you are right. Maybe it is your fault. If you hadn't been so consumed by your own self-hate, if you hadn't gone sprinting out in front of a moving car… Remi saved you—he died so you could live—and you sit around doing nothing but pitying yourself and making yourself bleed."

The wounds that had been healing, so excruciatingly slowly, took only those few seconds to tear open again, worse than before. Every breath was a struggle. Every heartbeat seemed like her last. Her hands itched to hold a knife, but this went beyond cutting. This time the hatred did not come from within herself, and so she could not let it out of her skin. This time it came from the outside, and it would crush her in on herself. She could not fight it—not when he was right.

"You think it's my fault Remi died?" Sera whispered.

Malakai looked stunned. He dropped her arm as though he had been burned, but then reached for her immediately. She backed up out of his reach. The screams were fading, leaving a horrible silence. She saw her brother's mouth moving, her parents' eyes wide with shock. On the other side of the window behind them all, the wind was making the trees dance. Sera's gaze caught on a leaf of the tree that stretched over their home. As she watched, it broke off and flew away from the rest, caught in the wind, slowly spiraling to the ground. It was like a message from above.

Sera looked again at the people who claimed to be her family, but all she saw was a hallway filled with strangers. Their hands reached for her, but they all missed. Malakai's mouth was still moving. Sera thought she could make out a few words, but her ears will still empty. She thought to read his lips.

"No—I didn't mean that. That's not true. Not what I meant, I—Sera!"

It did not matter.

She wrenched open the door.

"Seraphim, I'm sorry."

It did not matter; it was too late.

She was already gone.

SIX ....◆

For the first time, Sera felt she could breathe.

SEVEN ....◆

The shotgun was heavy in her hands. Her thoughts were heavy in her mind. Malakai's words pounded through her head. They were harsh, and cruel, and unforgivable. He was right; everything he had said was true. And she was done with living in the ruins of her sins. She could not go on like this.

She had thought she had made her peace, that night in Common Grounds, as the rain had washed away the footprints she had left on the shores of Lake Erie. She had thought that she was strong enough to face the world. The words written on the walls had given her that strength—both the ones spun by a long-dead poet and traced there by her brother, and the ones that Spike had given her.

What a beautiful little butterfly you are. Fly angel, fly.

She had thought she found her wings again, but while the words of one brother had lifted her, the words of another had slammed her back down to earth, the fragile wings that had borne her up so easily broken. A fledgling fallen, another hope lost. Another dream shattered.

She should have known.

Sera had believed that things would get better before. She had thought that she had been spiraling ever downwards, but that things could improve. That there was a way to reverse her path and climb back up, someday. She had been dead wrong.

Her foolishness had cost Remi's life.

She had dared to believe it again, to make her peace with his death. To begin to accept that it had been an accident. She couldn't have known. Yes, she had been stupid, but maybe, just maybe, it wasn't her fault.

This time, for her foolishness, her own life would be forfeit.

Sera's feet had taken her immediately from the house, but she had been forced to return by nightfall. Her mother had tried to reason with her. Her father had promised it wasn't true. Malakai had apologized.

"Sera, I am so sorry. I shouldn't have said that. I didn't mean it—it isn't true. You can't believe it's true. It wasn't your fault."

She had looked at him, her brown eyes devoid of all emotion. He had prattled on.

"It's just that Noah and I have been fighting and they're laying people off at work…I know my marital stress and work shouldn't affect you, and it's no excuse. What I said was inexcusable, and I'm so sorry, Ser."

She had flinched. Only Remi had ever called her that. Mal had noticed.

"Sera. That day in the parking lot—it wasn't your fault. It wasn't. There was nothing you or anyone could have done. It was an accident."

She had regained control of the emotions roiling inside of her and kept them off her face. She was a statue. She imagined herself as one of those stone angels placed over graves in cemeteries: cold and unreachable and inextricably bound to death.

All her recently conquered nightmares flooded in on her again, but on the surface, she stayed as calm as a sea before a storm. She was stone on the outside and molten lava within. Mal hugged her. She stood there and let him before going up to her room to formulate a plan.

She had thought, at least she had her family, but even that was a lie. She'd believed that they truly thought that it was not her fault, and that they did not blame her for Remi's death. Even if she did not believe it herself, it had been comforting to know that they did not hold her responsible. It had kept her anchored. It had kept her alive.

But after what Malakai had screamed at her, no matter what any of them said, she knew the truth. Even now, two years, eleven months, and a thirty days after Remi's death, they blamed her for it. They had harbored their hatred all the while, and it had only been a matter of time before one of them slipped up. What good little actors and actresses they all were. But it didn't matter. Sera had seen beyond their veil, past the guise. She knew the truth.

They did not want her, and if they did not want her, then what reason did she have to stay? The letter was on her pillow, several feet above Terrasen's head. They would find it sooner or later, but it would be too late. She was setting them all free.

She was setting herself free.

It had not been hard to steal it. The 20-gauge shotgun was one of the few weapons left from her father's purge back when she had leapt off the roof, surviving only because of the sentimental value it had—"It was my father's," Sarah had said, touching the stock lovingly. "It's one of the last things I have from him."

They had locked it. Hidden the safe. But Sera hadn't been fooled, and the safe had been waiting for her in the closet. It only took her a few tries to guess the combination—it had been the day her parents had gotten married, but was now the day her grandfather had been born. She did not hesitate to take it into her hands. Her parents had made sure there was no ammo in the house—as uncommunicative as they could be, they were not entirely stupid—but it had not been hard to procure some, and so she had two slugs tucked into her back pocket, her favorite jacket zipped up tight against the cool April air.

Tomorrow was the anniversary of Remi's death. The day was fast approaching as the sun sank towards the horizon; soon it would stain the sky in its blood. And soon she would spill her own blood. It would finally be over.

That night in Common Grounds, she had breathed for the first time since Remi's death, but Malakai's words had again stolen her breath. She had been smothered, strangled, until she had decided. And now, the evening air fresh around her, she finally felt free.

When Sera was in approximately the middle of the woods—only about a quarter of a mile from her house, but as far from civilization as she could get—she settled herself with her back to a tree. She did not want the shot to go astray. She did not want to hurt anyone else. This pain was hers alone to bear, and soon it would no longer matter.

Nothing would matter anymore, but she had enough blood on her hands, and some stains never washed out

EIGHT ···············◆

Her blood would stain the streets. Hers, and hers alone. Her blood would stain the streets, leaving stains that would never wash out.

SEVEN ···············◆

The shotgun was loaded, laid across her lap, ready to be fired. The tree was rough against her back, the ground hard beneath her. She had been here for hours. Sera checked her watch. It was past midnight. It was exactly three years from the anniversary of Remi's death.

She had contemplated enough. She had no reason to live. She had no friends. Her family blamed her for Remi's death, and why shouldn't they? It had been her fault all along. Hers, and hers alone.

Suspended in the sky, half of a silver-white disc shone. It seemed brighter than a half moon ought to have been, as though her anguish multiplied its illumination. She could see just fine—she even cast a faint shadow on the forest floor. The barrel of the shotgun was cold as she turned it.

She had fired it before, of course—popping cans off of a fence, hunting small game with her father. With her brothers. With Remi. But she had never aimed a firearm at another human, and she had never had one aimed at her own face. She had thought it would be easier to stare down into the bottomless black depths of the barrel.

Her confidence had gone, but her resolution remained. She would not subject the others to her presence. She wished she had taken her life sooner and saved them all the trouble. She wished her leap from the roof the night before Remi's funeral had been fatal.

Sera had removed her socks and her shoes, ready to pull the trigger with her toe, but that seemed so undignified. She did not want to die like that. Her hand was calm, so deadly calm, as she reached for a tree branch that had fallen not too far from where she sat. It was the exact right length to reach the trigger of the shotgun, like it had been put there exactly for that purpose. Sera did not believe in a god, but sometimes small miracles were enough to make her wonder.

She leaned forwards, pressing the end of the barrel into her forehead. She supported it with her left hand, the stick gripped in her right. There was even a little notch in the end of the branch, creating a cradle to press the trigger into. It was perfect.

Sera closed her eyes and breathed in, one last time, and waited.

There was no sense of a presence, as she had felt before. No hint of his hand on hers, his breath on the back of her neck, his voice whispering her name.

Nothing. The woods were heavy with the scent of the coming summer and the reek of loneliness.

She drew another breath. What her family would think of the letter she had left them? Would her mother criticize her penmanship, as she had her whole life? Would they even be able to make out what her looping, slanted cursive scrawl said?

Mom, Dad, Malakai, Terrasen, and Cobalt and Indigo,

I am so sorry for what I have put you all through. I never meant to hurt all of you so much, but it is my fault. It was always my fault. I know you blame me for Remi's death—and you're right. It was my fault. That was my fault and so is this.

I am sorry. I am so sorry. None of this is your fault and none of you are to blame yourselves. I am sorry I took Remi's life. I am sorry I am going to take mine, but I cannot live like this any longer. I can't be such a burden.

I have tried. I have hoped. For a time, I even believed. But there was never any hope. Not for me. I know you all know that it is my fault Remi died, and I can't subject you to living with me any longer. And so, I will take my own life. I am sorry and I love you all.

You will find my body in the center of the woods. Don't let the little ones come; I took the shotgun.

I love you all,

Sera

And then, at the bottom of the page, she had written one of Remi's favorite quotes. He had been planning to get it tattooed on his arm when he turned 18. He had never had the chance. Instead, it was Sharpied on the inside of her left arm, the letters rough and hard to read because of her scars. And it was written across the edge of the page, the black ink stark against the pure, snowy white.

To die, to sleep. To sleep perchance to dream.

"Red on white like a virgin's wedding night," she recited. "Red on red, no bloodstains on the bed. I'm coming to join you Remi. I'm coming to join you, and I've left them a letter so they won't waste their lives looking for us."

Sera thought again of the note, unaddressed, folded in half only once, lying on her pillow. But was it? Suddenly, she wasn't sure. She could not remember putting it there. She could recall writing it, folding it, tucking it into her pocket. She had laced up her boots, retrieved the shotgun and the two slugs.

Carefully, Sera pulled the stick away from the trigger and lay it on the ground beside her. She lifted her head from the barrel and patted her chest pocket with her right hand. The little slip of paper was still inside, waiting to be left where they would find it.

She couldn't die without leaving a note. She could not be that cruel.

Sera lowered the shotgun to the ground. She had to stand up, gather her shoes, the shotgun, the remnants of her life. She had to walk back through the woods to her room. She had to…had to…Sera collapsed in on herself, curling into a ball, hugging her knees to her chest. And for the first time in a long time, Sera began to cry.

EIGHT ················◆

In the end, there was a girl who understood.

ZERO ················◆

In the beginning, there was a girl who knew nothing.

EIGHT ················◆

In the woods, there was clarity.

In the streets, nothing else mattered.

In the blood, she could only remember the beginning, and oh, how she had painted.

SEVEN ················◆

The door to the safe clicked as Sera shut the gun inside. The ammunition was still in the woods, buried beneath dirt and leaves. She did not know what else to do with it, and so she left it to mark the place where she had almost lost her life.

The place where she had almost taken her life.

The place where she had chosen, instead, to live.

She sat there in the woods, each tear like revelation. She was crying. At long last, she was crying. But she did not cry for Remi, for the life he might have had, and she did not cry for herself. She cried for the family she would have left behind, the broken look on her mother's face, the hollow cold that would fill Terra's eyes. One day, Cobalt and Indigo would be grown, and they would have remembered her only by the scar that marked them as two separate beings instead of one whole. There would be the brother, already half-forgotten, who had died to save the sister who in turn took her own life. Her father, who had argued in favor of giving the gun away, would scream at her mother. Sera did not know if their marriage could survive the death of another child. And Malakai. Malakai, who had been so hurtful, who had said such hateful things. She had to believe he didn't mean it, and that even if he did, she somehow still cared about him. Cared about them all. Her tears were the proof of it.

As she walked back through the woods, her boots dangling by their laces from her fingers, the gun heavy in her other hand, she thought of the future. Face still wet with fresh tears, she allowed herself to see beyond the blackness. To believe that there had to be some sort of point to her life. She had a purpose, and she would find it, fulfill it, fight for every inch of happiness she could find.

Remi had prevented her from throwing that purpose away, long ago in a parking lot that seemed far away, and she had hated herself every day for his choice. But it had been his choice. His, and no one else's. She had not asked him to save her life. He had chosen to. Maybe he had found, in that split-second moment, that his purpose was to save her. Maybe she was destined for something greater.

Maybe there was no such thing as fate, no destiny.

Maybe it didn't matter.

Sera did not think she would ever be alleviated of her guilt and her grief. Some part of her would forever feel responsible for that day. But that did not mean she had to hate herself. Remi had loved her enough to give her his life. The tears were proof that she could still love, that she could still feel any emotion at all. And if she felt something other than emptiness when she thought of

Terra sleeping alone in their room, of Indigo and Cobalt barely remembering her as more than a smudge in their childhoods, then maybe she could feel something other than pain and bleakness. Maybe one day, she could love herself enough to begin to forgive herself for all the things she had done.

Sera did not know how long she had sat in the woods, how long the walk back had taken her. She only knew that she had locked the rifle away and snuck up to her room to wash the dirt and tears from her face and hands. When she had come back downstairs, her father was at the kitchen table, coffee cup in hand.

"Good morning, angel," he said. "You're up early."

The sight of him almost brought her to tears again. To think that only hours ago she had thought she would never see him again. She had not even said goodbye.

Sera wanted to say good morning back, but she found that her voice did not work. Before the tears that clogged her throat could find their way out, she bent and wrapped her arms around her father.

Startled, he set down his coffee mug. Sera did not know how long it had been since she had hugged him. He stood to hug her properly, pulling her tight to his chest, his arms winding around her. He did not speak. He did not ask. He did not seem to feel the need to understand.

Or maybe he understood far more than Sera had ever realized.

EIGHT

Sera was drunk on life.

SEVEN

"Is everything alright?"

Sera pulled back from her father at the sound of the voice. "Mom!"

She flung herself into her mother's arms. Like Carter, she did not ask. She simply held onto her daughter.

The suicide note, still pressed against Sera's heart, felt like a secret that wanted to be spilled.

"I'm so sorry, Mom."

"Oh, honey, you have nothing to be sorry for."

Every heartbeat was a gift, every breath a chance to see the world as it was: an endless wheel of colors, not a sketch of black and white. Her life could be the most detailed painting in the world, if only she tried.

"I know. I understand that now."

EIGHT ················◆

She was high on the feeling of being alive.

SEVEN ················◆

"What's for breakfast?"

"Terrasen!"

Sera attacked her younger sister, engulfing her in a hug that almost knocked them both over. Terra screeched and flailed. Sera laughed and held her at arm's length, smiling at the shocked expression on the small face.

"Are you alright?"

"Never better. Do you want to make waffles?"

"What?"

"And then maybe we can play *Sleeping Queens*?"

"Who are you and what have you done with my sister?"

Sera laughed again. Carter and Sarah were smiling. Terra wrapped her arms around Sera's middle and squeezed as hard as she could.

"I missed you," Terra said.

"I missed you too, little sis."

"I just have one question."

"What's that?"

"Can we have pancakes instead?"

ZERO ················◆

She had been born to paint, and they all expected her to paint great things.

EIGHT ················◆

On the day of Remi's 19th birthday, Sera's car took her east, up and down streets, winding her way through the points of the compass until she turned off Euclid Street and into the Hough neighborhood.

The refuge of her car began to feel like a cage. Sera wanted to taste the night air on her face, the cool breeze on her skin. She wanted to hear the sounds of the city: people wandering the streets, their footsteps slapping on damp pavement, their voices echoing off the buildings, the cars honking, motors rumbling. She wanted to smell the harsh, pungent odor, the reek of unwashed bodies that pervaded the air of cities jam-packed with people.

Sera did not remember leaving her car, but the sidewalk was beneath her feet, her legs carrying her to a destination she did not know. The world was both dark and light at once, all of the lines blurring together, as though she had fallen into an abstract painting.

She felt as though it had been a million years since she had been really, truly aware of the people surrounding her. Now, she could feel every breath, hear every heartbeat. She was just one among many, another walker on another night in another city. She breathed the industrial stench that she called home.

And then she heard the gunshot.

ZERO ....◆

They never expected her greatest work to be painted in her own blood

EIGHT ....◆

Sera was running before the echo had faded from her ears. Her boots, left only half laced, slipped on her feet. One came entirely loose and her foot pulled free. She left it behind her, lying on its side on the pavement.

She skid as she slowed at the corner, grabbing onto a sign post and swinging herself ninety degrees onto the next street. Then she was off again, leaving the second shoe by the still-quivering post that read *Linwood Avenue.* Her heart was in her throat, her feet protesting the rough ground. Halfway down the block, she paused to listen.

"What the fuck you think you're doin', little girl?"

It was a man's voice, harsh and unforgiving. Sera drew closer, passing a car that had been abandoned with both the driver's side doors dangling open.

Sera was more cautious now than she had been on her wild run through the streets. Her heart was pounding like a stallion's hooves against the earth, her breath whooshing in and out of her lungs like bellows stoking a fire. It had been so long since she had felt so alive.

It was freeing. Intoxicating. Exhilarating.

"No, please. Take whatever you want."

A woman this time, the plea evident in her voice.

"You think you gonna git to tell me what Imma do? If I wanna take what I want, Imma take it. The fuck you think I need your permission for?"

"I'm sorry. Please…"

"Shut your damn face, lady."

Sera did not think. She did not plan. She did not wait to see where life would take her.

She acted.

Several hundred feet down from the corner of Linwood Avenue there were three figures. The first was facing towards Sera. She could see his sallow face and sunken eyes even before he noticed her. His clothing was torn and stained, as though he had been living on the streets for a while, and his limbs were too thin, his body battered. In his right hand was a gun.

Cowering before him, backed up against the side of a building and in profile to Sera was a woman. She was clutching a little girl to her chest, tears running down her face. The girl couldn't have been more than three years old, with wispy blonde hair pulled into pigtails that puffed out from the sides of her head. She was dressed in hot pink footie pajamas with a purple unicorn stitched on the front. Her face was buried in her mother's shoulder.

Sera knew that it wasn't uncommon for robberies to go down like this. The man had likely jumped in front of the woman's car. For whatever reason, she must have been driving down the lane. Rather than run him over, she had stopped. He had pulled a gun, ordered her and her daughter from the car and backed them into the wall.

"I ain't gonna tell you again," the man threatened.

"Please…" the mother begged. Her eyes darted around desperately, searching for an escape. Seeking help. Her gaze found on Sera's. Her eyes widened as she begged, silently, her lips forming words that she did not speak. Sera did not have to hear. She knew.

She stepped into the alley.

"Hey!"

The man spun and Sera found herself staring down the barrel of a gun for the second time in her life.

She did not have it in her to be afraid.

"Leave her alone!"

"Who the fuck are you?"

"Who the fuck are *you*? What are you doing, robbing this poor woman in the dead of night?"

"She bin drivin' on my turf. Makes her fair game."

"Oh yeah?"

"Yeah."

"Says who?"

"What the fuck you mean, 'says who?' I don't need no permission. Who the fuck you think you are, girl?"

"My name is Seraphim."

"The fuck kind of name is that?"

"The name of a girl who is no longer afraid."

He looked at her like she had gone mad. The woman, too, was staring. She had pushed her daughter behind her and Sera could see the soft curve of her belly, just beginning to bulge.

"You are going to let these innocents go. They probably don't have anything of any value on them anyways."

"You think you can tell me a damn thing? Fuck off."

Sera was about to step closer, to get in his face, *the gun be damned*, when she felt hands close on her upper arms. She twisted, tried to pull away, but the grip was too strong. Before she could really start to put up a fight, something sharp cut into her neck.

She knew all too well what the blade of a knife felt like, but this was the first time the hand that held it had not been her own.

"That'll teach ya," the man with the gun said. "Fuckin' bitch, rattlin' off her mouth. Never thought to look for a whatchamacallit."

"Accomplice?" Sera suggested, her tone perfectly civil despite the wickedly sharp edge that grazed her skin with every breath.

The first man pointed his gun at her in acknowledgement. "That's the one." He swung his aim back to the mother and daughter, still cowering together. The little girl had begun to cry, softly but audibly, the sound smothered by the mother's shirt.

The blade was cold against her neck.

"Now. You got a purse or somethin'?"

The blade was cold on her neck, the touch of Death imminent upon her shoulder. This was so far out of her control.

"N-no. I l-left my house in a r-rush. Emergency call from work—I only had time to buckle in my daughter—"

"Shut the fuck up. This ain't story time." He pivoted. "And you?"

Her palms slick with sweat, her fingers scrabbling at the backs of the hands that held her, trying to pry the knife away from her throat. The rush of life was still singing in her veins. Never before had she been so grateful to be alive.

"Nothing."

For the first time, the man seemed to notice her disarrayed state. "How the fuck you get here?" He glanced at her bare feet, her tousled hair. Her suicide note, which she had taken to carrying with her as a reminder of all that life had yet to give, was still safe in her pocket, right over her heart.

"I ran."

"You ran?"

Sera swallowed. The blade was cold against her neck, her hands slick with sweat. She could feel the edge slice into the first layer of skin, but she forced herself to remain calm. She shoved the panic into the vault in her head, the practiced stillness of those who are dead inside stealing over her. *Breathe in, breathe out.* It was her life on the line again, but this time, she did not have control.

"Yes. I heard a gunshot, and I ran."

This time, she knew that she wanted to live.

"The fuck you run towards the sound of a goddamn gunshot for?"

This time, she knew—beyond a shadow of a doubt—that there would not be a next time.

"Because I understand now. Whether or not Remi's death was my fault, I have to make amends. A life for a life—maybe I can even save three."

The woman's hand fell to her stomach and Sera knew she had been right.

Trusting whatever instincts had lead her here, Sera acted. She did not know how to fight her way out of this, or how to save the mother and her children. She only knew that she had to. Remi had saved her so that she could live. Could be here, for this moment. Could save this family.

Sera went limp in her captor's hold. Even though her fingers were curled around the tip of the blade and the man's wrist, she felt the skin of her neck break. She heard the man swear as her weight dragged him down. Her legs puddled beneath her. She was choking on her own knuckles as she forced her fingers between the blade and her neck. Blood welled from her hand and streaked down the knife.

"Help me," her captor yelled to the man with the gun. "Fuckin' shoot her!"

She heard the second gunshot that night.

Sera's body rocked backwards. She thought, for a moment, that she had been shot. She waited for the pain, but none came. Her captor's body slumped to the ground, the knife clattering away. Sera fell, gasping, to her hands and knees. Blood pumped from her left hand and oozed from the red line cut into her throat.

Sera forced her feet back underneath herself and pushed herself upright. The man who had held her lay in an ever-growing pool of his own blood. His companion had aimed for her, and missed.

The knife was still on the ground. It skittered away as Sera dove for it, but her fingers closed over the handle. It fit into her hand as though it had been made for her. She had been meant for this—she had found her purpose in life: to save the lives of these innocents, here, alone in the streets of the city she called home.

Her blood would mark those streets, leaving stains that would never wash out.

Her purpose in life was to die, yes, but not to end her own suffering. Her purpose in life was to die so that another might live, as Remi had died to save her. His gift would not be wasted any longer. So long she had tormented herself, wallowing in the past, convinced her life had no purpose, no direction, that Remi's sacrifice would been in vain. It would be meaningless no longer—she would not let it.

The knife glinted wickedly in the streetlights' glow. The woman screamed as the man again took aim with the gun. Sera did not have faith in a god, but as the blade left her hand, she prayed. She had never thrown knives more than a few times, but it flew, straight and true, borne upon her brother's love. Upon hope and suffering and pain, and the prayers of an angel who, for so long, had not been able to believe. Upon the will, not to live, but to save another.

The knife flipped, end over end, and embedded itself up to the hilt in the stomach of the man with the gun. He staggered back, ducked his head to look, growled. With a howl like a dying wolf, he ripped the knife from his body. Blood poured down. He followed it, falling in a heap on the spattered pavement. The man lifted the gun but he did not point it at Sera. The mother and daughter stood, screaming in terror, several feet to Sera's left, and Sera acted before the man could. She dove. He shot. Blood stained the streets, but it was not Sera's alone.

She had been born to paint, and they all expected her to paint great things. They never expected her greatest work to be painted in her own blood.

ZERO ……………◆

Sera lay like the Vitruvian Man as her heart pumped its last. She stared up towards stars that she could only just see. Dimly, she was aware of someone screaming, but the problems of the world seemed very far away. She did not have her I.D. on her, but the note was still in her pocket. It would be soaked through with blood, but if they could read it, they could identify her body.

A single word formed on Sera's lips. "Remi." It was a breath, a hiss of air, too quiet to constitute sound. But he heard her, and he came. He knelt by her side, as she should have knelt by his. He was whole and pure, and just as she remembered.

His dark brown hair fell over his forehead as he leaned over her, curling the way it always had. His eyes were bluer than a summer twilight and dancing as he smiled the smile she had loved so much. The smile she had missed every day since his last. Behind him, the sky was growing lighter with the approaching dawn.

"Remi…" Sera tried again.

"Shh, sis. It's okay. I'm here now."

"Remi," she insisted. "Remi, I'm sorry."

He pressed his finger to her lips. "Ser, You have nothing to be sorry for. You gave your life for another, just as I gave my life for you. You didn't take it. You didn't ask for it. It was a gift, freely given as an act of love."

Sera found that she could not speak. She found that she did not need to—there were no words Remi needed to hear. He understood her, all of her, even her silences. He had come for her, as he always did, to shelter her from the world. He had brought her the dawn to end the black night through which she had wandered for so long. He was here, and everything would be alright. Remi gathered her limp body into his arms and lifted her from the ground.

EIGHT

In the beginning, there had been a sister who was lost and a brother who was found. In their reunion, in their deaths, there was the hope of life. Remington carried Sera away into the blossoming light of brilliant new day, gilded in gold, leaving the cool obsidian night far behind.

In the beginning, they had each other.

In the dawn, they were together.

In the end, there was nothing left but a street painted in the blood of the angel.

Author's Note:

Painted was inspired by the stories another student told me about his past during our freshman year of college. Like Sera, he lives in Cleveland, OH, and many of the places that Sera visits are taken from his life. Common Grounds is real, right down to the graffiti, the broken bathroom, and Spike. So are the Rapid train station, the pier Sera goes to in the rainstorm, and Suicide Bridge. The woods also exist, and the scene with the rifle and the tree branch are all true to his life. I even gave Sera the same car as him, and the same drink order—a Crazed Englishman. Sera's music tastes, Remi's birthday, and Middie the cat are borrowed from a different classmate, one who also engaged in self-harm and suicidal ideation. While Malakai, Cobalt, and Indigo are all completely fictional, Terrasen, and Remington are very loosely based on my own brother and sister. The street where Sera dies exists, and the words *Fly, angel, fly* are written on the wall at Common Grounds to this day.

Short Fiction

The Disagreeable Dinner

Mark Daponte

Will Fasso walked into his kitchen to see his wife, Susan, wearing a bathrobe, a long face and bags under her blue eyes. He opened the curtains to let sunlight in and noticed that their local TV weatherman was finally right.

"Look! It really *did* snow three feet last night!" Will exclaimed. "Hurray! Now we won't have to go and visit your parents!"

"You know the roads will be cleared by the afternoon."

"Unfortunately, I do know. We'll dig the car out after breakfast."

"I'm way too tired to dig," Susan replied.

"Oh no. Was it because I was talking in my sleep—again?" Will asked.

"I wish you were talking. At 3AM, you were singing in your sleep!"

Will walked to the refrigerator and removed a half gallon of orange juice.

"Did I at least sing on key?"

"Nope. You 'sang' 'Oye Como Va.'"

"That's weird," Will said as she yawned and he twisted opened the orange juice. "We've known each other for twenty years and I never talked or even hummed while I slept. Now, that makes that—God, how many nights in a row have I woke you up?"

"You started yapping in your sleep two nights ago, hon," she said.

"Now I'm singing at 3AM!? Maybe it was something I ate."

"Hmmm. Could be. You know, it all started after we went out for Mexican food."

"It did. I—"

Will shivered as if he was just shoved into a closet sized freezer.

"Th-th-at's weird. I'm f-f-f-reezing. Maybe it really was something in that f-f-f-f-f-f-ood."

Susan stood and looked closer at his now pale face.

"What's wrong?"

"I-I feel weird...bloated...gassy...Excuse me. This isn't going to sound or smell pretty."

Will stood and lifted up his right leg to release gas. His bathrobe moved like a flag getting hit by a violent gust of wind. Suddenly, he and Susan heard a male's voice sing:

"Oye como va, toledo. Bien como va."

Susan laughed and said, "You can throw your voice so it comes out of your ass? Talk about a marketable talent."

"But that voice wasn't mine! Who-who-said that?"

"I'm right behind you, muchacho," the voice answered.

Susan ran behind Will and hopelessly looked for the voice's owner. She lifted up his bathrobe only to see his backside.

"Show yourself!" she demanded.

"Put your right hand high in the air, señorita."

Susan obeyed.

"It's in the air. Now what?"

"Slowly lower that muy bonita hand, señorita."

As Susan's hand lowered, the voice said:

"You're getting warm...warmer...warmest to me!"

Susan's hand rested and covered Will's butt. A muffled voice then cackled:

"Get your hand off me! Help! Policia! I'm getting muy pawed!"

Susan's palm covered her opened mouth as she gasped.

"Honey! Your butt just vibrated when that guy talked! Unless…were you using huh, my vibrator in the privacy of our home and you had an, uh, a sexual misadventure?"

"Of course not!! Just w-w-ho are you in me?" a frightened Will asked.

"A ghost on crack. Perdone. I should say a ghost in your crack."

"What are you doing inside my husband?" Susan asked.

"My name ess Juan Jimenez. In my mortal life, I cooked for Consuelo."

"Is that the same Consuelo who owns 'Consuelo's Restaurante?'" Will asked.

"Where we had that Mexican food two days ago!" Susan added.

"Sí. Two years ago, I was Consuelo's secret lover. Well, I was secret until Consuelo's husband caught us canoodling and 'cocaine-ing' in his kitchen. Consuelo's gringo husband suffocated my pretty face in a pot of refried beans at 12AM—midnight. On the anniversary of my murder, my soul rises from the bottom of a pot of refried beans and settles in—a gringo!"

"You mean—me?" Will said, his voice cracking.

"Sí. You ate me one night, now you have me this morning."

"Great. I've got a spirit in my sphincter?"

"Sure do! Just don't ask to move in with me. There's not much space in here…only room for one. And you got this one!"

"Scoot! Vamos already!" Susan ordered, smacking Will hard on his backside.

"Ow! What are you doing?" Will asked.

"I'm just trying to get Juan to find another ass to haunt."

"Tough tamales. I'm staying in your man's can."

"Me amigo, Juan. Isn't this between you and Consuelo?" Will asked.

"Si. So?"

Susan picked up her cellphone and speed dialed "Consuelo's Restaurant."

"Then maybe Consuelo can talk you out of him. Hello? Who am I speaking to?"

"This is Consuelo. May I help you?"

"Yes. My husband has a man in his ass!"

"If that's what he likes, that's what he likes," Consuelo replied.

"No! I mean—oh, you talk to him."

Susan placed the phone flat against Will's butt; only to hear Consuelo say, "May I help you? Hello? Hello? What the hell is this?!"

"Hable, Juan. Por favor? Double por favor?" Will pleaded; only to get back silence.

"Sorry but I'm not in the mood to talk to an asshole—like you!" Consuelo said before she hung up.

Susan left the kitchen and turned on their bathtub's water.

"Now you listen to me, Stevie," Juan slurred. "The cocaine I took—I feel it's wearing off. So this is what I want you to do. Go and swallow ten pounds of cocaine. That oughta last me a year until I rise up on my next anniversary."

"Where am I going to find 10 pounds of coke?" Chill. I'll give you a number to call. My dad would love your business."

"But—if I eat all that blow, it'll kill me."

"Sí and so? That's a small price to pay for me getting real high! No? Ha ha ho!"

Susan entered the kitchen and motioned for Will to follow her into the bathroom. Will saw the tub of water, nodded and removed his clothes.

"Hey Will. Is this butt cable-ready? Maybe I'll get 'Cine-Ass.'"

Will sat in the filled tub.

"Drown you loco psycho!" Susan exclaimed.

Suddenly, the bath water turned black, wildly bubbled and Juan's voice gurgled:

"Nice try but this ghost is staying! Rent free!"

"That's what *you* think!" Will said. He ran to his bedroom and removed the old wooden crucifix that his mother had given him for him confirmation from the wall. The crucifix was at least two feet long.

"Don't put it in! That won't fit, honey!" Susan said.

"I have no choice!" Will said. He bent over, held the crucifix high in the air and barked:

"May the power of Christ compels you to—leave already!"

"Look, ass hombre. If you're trying to shove a cross up you, that just won't work, man! Besides, if a cross on a colon isn't a mortal sin…what is?" Juan laughed.

Will threw the crucifix on the floor, ran back to the bathroom, rummaged through the medicine cabinet, and removed a dusty bottle of "Ex-Lax."

"Let the ass-orcism begin!" he announced.

As Will guzzled the bottle, Juan cried out. "No! Not that! Stop! Alto! Por favor!"

"Hasta la vista, keister squatter!" Susan said.

"I'm melting away....melting...melting...adios...What a world, what a… Oye como…Ahhhhhhhhhhhhh—dios!"

"We killed my ass clown! We did it!" Susan exclaimed. They danced and hugged their way back to the kitchen table.

"Whew. Talk about food haunting you!" Will added. "If this doesn't call for a celebration, nothing does!"

"Hmmmm…How should we celebrate?" she cooed then kissed him.

"We celebrate a killing by killing brain cells! I hereby proclaim this a Mimosa morning!"

"Sorry. It's too early in the morning for me to drink fine French champagne."

"It's never too early for me."

He went to their liquor cabinet, removed a bottle of champagne, popped it open and tilted it into a pint beer mug. After Will added a splash of orange juice to the bubbly, he raised his mug high in the air.

"To a guy's death—and this guy's 'rebirth!'"

After chugging his Mimosa, Susan reminded him, "And to digging out our car and visiting your in-laws. Remember?"

"I, huh, 'almost' forgot. Okay. After Mimosa-ing, we'll go and get this latest family obligation over."

After Will polished off the bottle, he and Susan walked outside and found their SUV buried in a snow drift. Will leaned on his snow shovel and gawked at a six foot white oval mound with four black tires peeking out from its bottom.

"Staring at snow isn't going to melt it," she laughed.

"Ya think?"

As he jammed the shovel by the front of this car, he shivered.

"Whew—it got extra-cold all of a sudden."

Susan looked closer at his now pale face.

"What's wrong?"

"I-I feel weird...and I—I—really, *really* have to pee."

"Can't you hold it in and do it in our apartment?"

"No! I wish I could but I-I—can't!" he screamed as he unzipped his pants and waddled to the sidewalk. "I have to do it…now!"

As a steady stream of urine poured out and fell on the snow-filled sidewalk, he heard a deep voice with a French accent hiss.

"Bonjour! My nom is Jacques Gabin; a painter in mortal life but now I'm inside you in death."

"He…that guy's voice…just made my dick vibrate!" Will gasped.

"Wait. Are you—in Will's member?" Susan asked.

"Oui. I'm a member of his member. And today must be the anniversary of my drowning in that vat of French champagne."

"Don't tell us," Susan pleaded.

"Yes. He drank me, now he drinks in my words whenever he pees."

"No! Someone is throwing a French voice at us!" Susan said.

"Yeah. Whoever it is…show yourself!" Will demanded.

"Oui, pee monsieur."

Suddenly, Will's penis behaved as if it was on auto-pilot; moving and squirting yellow lines in the snow to draw a smiling wavy-haired man, a cigarette in a corner of his mouth underneath a mustache and a beret on his head. As pedestrians approached, stared at the still-urinating Will, then stepped over his "painting."

"Hurry! Buy my painting before it melts!" the voice said. "Pablo Picasso had his 'Blue Period;' now Will Fasso has his 'Yellow Period'…*period.*'"

Will's sobs were interrupted by a police car's siren and a burly policeman who didn't appreciate that Will was relieving himself on a sidewalk in broad daylight—and screaming that he couldn't stop. The cop could only shake his head and chuckle.

"Just finish up, buddy. Are you going to conceal that water gun—or do you want an indecent exposure ticket?"

"I can't stop! I—I really can't!"

"Why not?"

"Ask that French guy!" Susan said, pointing at the yellow-lined portrait on the sidewalk.

The cop closely examined the face and gasped.

"I—I'm pretty sure I know this guy," the cop replied. "Yeah, it's definitely him."

"Who is 'him?'" asked Will.

"This creep named Juan Jimenez. I was the first cop on that crime scene."

"Was he suffocated in a pot of refried beans two years ago?" asked Susan.

"That he was. And I wonder if—"

The cop bent down, placed his head near Will's penis and asked it, "Juan? Are you now 'making believing' you're French?"

"Si! I'm es muy French-o!" Juan cackled. "But believe this. Senor Will ate me one night, he still have me this morning—and *every* morning!"

Hunting Time

Joel Martin

I tightened the noose and the thick cords pressed against the witch's pale, cold neck. The horse that she sat on whinnied, as if sensing that murder would soon take place upon his back.

I patted him gently.

The wind rustled the grass in front of me and billowed out my unbuttoned coat. The smell of the pines all around us drifted pleasantly in the air. I walked a few paces from the witch and grasped the reins of my own horse. I looked up at the witch's face.

She might have been considered fair, in better days. Her hair had been cut back, perhaps so one might mistake her for a boy. Her gaze locked with mine and, I thought for a moment that her eyes, so hard and blue, had been replaced with more innocent eyes. All these hunts had begun to blur into one. I ran my fingers over my stubbled face before pulling my gloves from my saddle and slipping them over my cold fingers.

I swung myself astride and with a click of my tongue my horse, ambled over to the witch. I reached forward, my gloved fingers brushing her frigid skin, and pulled the gag from her mouth.

"Have you anything to say before the sentence is carried out?" I said.

Her mouth twitched in undisguised rage. "Only that I curse you, Vane.

You will not wake from this hunt. I swear it."

I stuffed the gag back into her mouth and pulled up the reins of the horse under her, the leather taunt in my hands. She slid off, struggling off the saddle. As the noose tightened savagely, her feet kicked out in protest and the veins in her neck bulged under the pressure.

I had hunted this witch for more than a month. The Church of the Red Lily had sent their dogs and their men who were little better than the hounds, and yet she had evaded them all—but not me. Two weeks in the saddle, marking the witch's path from the steep mountain passes into this, forested valley. She slept little and travelled light, but all creatures leave tracks. Signs of life.

I watched her struggle for those last minutes of her life. This was the work. I needed to know she was dead when I pulled her down from that tree. I had seen many hangings, and a few too many accidents for my liking, especially out here in the middle of nowhere where it was hard to ensure smooth proceedings in the variable conditions. A broken branch, a weak thread in the rope. Usually, this type of affair would take place in a town square where the platform was released from under the victim and the pressure suddenly exerted on the neck was enough to snap it, if not cleanly but quickly.

I did not have the convenience of such a setup here. It would take more than ten minutes for her to die as the air leaked from her body. That throbbing feeling at the base of the skull, near the ears, pulsing like some tortured heartbeat growing louder to the clanging of drums. It was a terrible way to die. I touched my own neck in reaction, the dark bandana hiding old scars.

By law, witches were condemned to die by the rope or the pyre. And fire was no option here. I would need to gather wood, and should the clouds prove more than an idle threat, rain would put an end to any such death. The rope was the simplest option, and here in the forest, every fell looking tree was the perfect height.

Something broke through the sounds of wet leaves drifting past and the creak of heavy oak and the gagging of a dying woman. It was a howl. Not quite wolf like. There was something in the timbre of the voice that made me reach for my musket. I swung it easily into my hands and I watched behind the witch, where the noise had originated.

If she heard it past all the dying she didn't show it. As she struggled her gaze never wavered. She looked into my eyes and deeper still. I considered the musket in my hands. One lead ball straight to the heart would have been quicker and cleaner. More humane? Maybe, although death was death. But I had orders. And I wanted to get paid. It was hard to get fair coin for a witch killed with a bullet. Had to kill it the way any good church man would.

As the colour bled from her already pallid face, her struggling slowed.

And there was something holy about the noose here. I had heard stories of groves where scores of victims were hung for heathen gods in days past. It wouldn't be too long before hangings in the name of our new church surpassed them. And I'd be there, with a fat coin pouch in hand.

The body had stopped shaking. She was dead. She still twitched, but it was those shivers that passed through a body like that from a headless chicken. I waited a few more minutes more, eyes still wary on the trees around me. I slung the musket back into its leather sheath under the saddle. I urged my horse closer to the witch, drew my sabre and cut the thick rope with a few strikes.

I dismounted and lashed the lifeless corpse over the saddle of my second horse. The ride before me would be short. Leave the woods and then a straight trot to town.

But the day was not going to make it easy on me. As I cinched the saddle tightly, the clouds that had been threatening finally released their watery burden.

Then I heard it again. The howl was at once both animal and human. A fear made evident through broken vocal chords that once held some semblance of coherent speech.

I squinted. Two figures, shadowed in the distance by the forest's dull light were locked in a struggle. My first thought went to my musket, but it would be no good in this weather. I didn't rush forward. As I moved forwardly, slowly, the figures became clearer. A vaguely human shaped being was tangled with something more like a beast.

I drew my sword, but my mount swung his head around, his eyes wide and terrified. I tried to regain some control, but he reared up sharply and I lost hold of the reins of the other horse.

A sickening, crunching sound came from the fight. The beast pulled a bloodied maw from the other's neck. Then it's maddened, bloodshot gaze locked with mine. Snarling, it raised its claws high. Viscera dripped from its tips.

It howled again and bounded towards me, first on its back legs and then on all fours. My horse bucked again, toppling me. I hit the ground and my breath was knocked out of me for long moment.

As my vision swam, I grabbed my sword from the mud and scrambled to my feet. The creature moved like a blur. Its claws scythed across my horse's throat and the terrified creature fell to the mud, kicking and flailing as life left it. The second horse, with the witch's body still attached, bolted.

I tried to make out what was standing opposite me. The pale body was human in form, and its face, though covered in blood, looked hauntingly familiar. Like something from a half-dreamed nightmare. Water dripped down my face, clouding my vision, and I could not make out any more of its features in my dizzy state. It wavered as it looked at me. Then it turned about and ran for the woods, following the path of the escaped horse.

Hands on knees, I took in a few deep breaths. Then I cautiously approached the other beast, which lay silent on the ground. Its face was a bloody pulp, from savage bites and the rending of sharp claws. Its hands were elongated and ended in deadly claws. Its body was thin and ribs jutted out from pale, sickly-looking skin. I had never seen a creature of its like before.

I kicked the dead thing and slumped down next to it. I had no horse, no witch, and no money waiting for me in town. And the thought of heading into town empty...

I would be damned to lose my bounty to these things. That witch was mine.

Although just dead, the body stank of disease and rot, the stench overpowering the pine musk of the wood around me.

The rain had ceased, leaving only the sound of water trickling from the treetops. I followed the tracks of the runaway horse, which was easy to do, as the terrified beast had crashed through branches and the forest floor was well disturbed.

Through the trees ahead I saw a large form lying on the forest floor. I drew my sword and crouched low as I made my way through the trees, careful not to disturb branch or twig. Coming across my other horse, its neck was slashed open, just as my own mount had been. Blood soaked the muddy forest floor.

I sheathed my sword and wiped sweat from my forehead. The ropes that had bound the witch were slashed and her body taken. Why?

The creature had to be human, for no animal would think of doing such a thing. Maybe some forsaken man, too long alone and naked in these cursed woods. A cannibal, possibly. Yet why didn't he simply eat it on the spot? He must have kept it intact, for there was no blood trail leading away.

It was cold, deliriously so. The thought had hit me suddenly, cutting through my previous clarity. I shook my head. The weather, the madness of this entire day, had seeped into my mind. I had to concentrate.

Something moved in my peripheral vision. The beast had not left, but was watching me.

I calmed my breathing and waited, sword slightly raised. I readied myself and waited, my hand inching close to my sword.

As it lunged, I turned and swung my sword. The pale creature swayed out of the way, then dashed back in. It grabbed hold of my sword arm and bit into it.

I yelled and slammed my knee against its lithe body, but it clung on doggedly. I planted a fist in its face and it released me, bleeding profusely under its swollen, yellowed eyes.

Fire pulsed through my body and my armed throbbed.

The beast stood back, and its elongated tongue slid over the blood that coated its lips.

It snarled and turned on its heel.

Without hesitation I took off after it. It had my prize, I was sure of it.

The beast was only a few paces ahead of me. The trees closed in about us, the heavy branches around me suddenly sinister, claustrophobic even, as we hurtled through the forest.

Just as I neared the creature, my booted feet clanged against something different. I chanced a glance. Cobblestones, thick with ivy and moss. The ground shifted and the very foundations of the structure rumbled beneath me. Ahead of me, the earth gave way and the pale naked creature plunged into the depths.

As the ground fell from under my feet, I leapt forward, looking for a handhold. My fingertips scraped against old stone but they slipped free and I fell. My back hit a sloped rock wall and I slid down. Earth packed in what must have been numerous floors. I twisted around and tried to grab hold of anything. My skin burned as it chaffed against the stones.

Finally, my fingers wedged inside a crack and I hung with my feet dangling off the abyss. My sword fell into the darkness, which snuffed the light from its glittery steel in an instant.

I looked up. Just above, a stone floor loomed just above me. My arm burned strongly again with the pain from the bite. Gritting my teeth against the pain, I swung my body up and found another hold. With bleeding fingers, I pulled myself up the collapsed section of the floor until I reached the lip, hoisted myself onto it and collapsed against the cool stone.

I looked up at the two or three floors that rose above. It was hard to be sure how many. Grey shafts of cloudy light streamed down from the forest above.

I sucked in deep breaths. There was no way to get back up. I sat up and tried to peer into the darkness that surrounded me. It was a room of some kind or perhaps a hallway; it was too dark to tell.

I unwound the bandana that hung over my neck and bound it over a branch that had plunged with me during the fall.

Some flint and steel later and light flared from my makeshift torch in a burst of embers.

The walls were smooth, and water trickled down the surfaces, from the forest floor above. This place, these walls, they belonged to some structure more impressive than a forgotten cave or tomb. Perhaps it was part of a fortress or something much larger.

The creature I pursued, he would be trapped here as well. I was sure of it.

Now that the adrenaline had passed had subsided, a deep hunger swelled within me.

There had to be creatures here, perhaps insects or rodents that could satiate my hunger. Crude, but at this stage I had to eat something. The intensity of the desire overwhelming any thought of escape, at least for the moment. I scraped and scrounged for anything, for what must have been minutes, but each moment felt agonizingly long, and for all my energies I could only snatch up a single rat.

The thing was sickly and thin, the only one unable to escape my pursuit. It could have been a king's feast for all I cared. I fashioned a simple fire and placed the dead thing upon it. I didn't even wait for it to cook through completely. I ate it all, fur and bone even, spitting what I couldn't swallow.

As its juices ran down my chin, the flesh and blood warmed me to my core, comforting me.

I wiped the gore from my mouth with my sleeve and sat back against the stone wall. I felt wrong. I was hungry, bloated and ill all at the same time. This place had to be the reason I needed more food.

I shuffled down the silent halls, my torch illuminating the way ahead.

After some time, I stopped and listened. Occasionally, there was an odd scratching sound, the squeak of a rat, perhaps, fearing for its life after finding what little was left of its brother. But largely, there was nothing. It felt like the place hung in a void. It was the silence of a place long dead and I was trespassing on its slumber.

The walls were old and I feared a collapse at any moment, but they didn't rumble or groan as old buildings were usually wont to. Alcoves ran along the old passages, and statues filled some of them. Most were missing heads and limbs, but some still stood mostly complete. Tall revenants guarding this otherworldly place.

Light appeared through an open doorway. I clutched my torch, my only weapon, with both hands.

A voice called from within the lit room. “Come in, Vane, don’t be a stranger.” A cackle burst from his lips and echoed down to me.

The room was bathed in flickering light and I spotted the man sitting in front of a small fireplace. His back to me, he wore an old coat, red and faded. A church hunter by the colors. Smoke drifted up through a crack in the structure. A few lights shafts splayed out from it. His back was to me.

I moved closer. “Who are you?”

“Oh, just an old hunter.”

He turned and held out a red, bloated rat on a stick, glistening with blood. Grey hair fell over his left eye, a bandage around his jaw. His teeth were a stark ivory, his lips split in a wide smile. “Hungry?”

Hunger overcoming my trepidation, I snatched it and crunched into the plump morsel. He laughed again and, turning back to the fire, stoked it with a makeshift poker.

“How do you know my name?” I said rat and blood dripping over my lips.

His lips curled up. I couldn’t decide if it was a snarl or a sneer. “You’re a regular guest. One would think I would run out of rats by now.”

“What are you talking about? I’ve never seen you before.”

“You have. You just can’t remember me. You never can.”

I said nothing and looked about the room. There was a small cot and table, a collection of boxes here, some sealed, others ripped open, and a candle burning low.

“You live here?”

“I’ve had enough time to get used to the old one’s place.”

“Old one?”

“Well you’re here, so I assume you’ve met her. There are enough tunnels here to make a man mad.” His cackling laugh started again and was replaced soon by a hacking cough. His body shook with illness. “Ah, I welcome the company nonetheless. Though I fear you’ll be moving on soon.”

“I have a beast to hunt. My prey has taken something of great worth to me.”

He looked at me and that sneer reappeared on his face. “Your hands.

Started early this time."

I was confused for a moment then I pulled my hands to the light. They were pale and the nails were black. Veins, thick and corded, snaked up my arms.

"What…what is this? A spell? What have you done?"

He laughed again. "Do you think that bite was nothing more than a wound? You think the beast you track carries no greater weapon? Poison runs in your veins, a poison that will overtake you soon."

"This cannot be. I must find a healer, an apothecary, they can reverse this, surely."

He pointed to the other door. "Then you better hurry, Vane, for that poison will spread quicker than you think."

The revelation leant me speed and I hurried from the room and the strange old man. The light of the room fell away as I journeyed deeper within the halls.

Finally, my torch illuminated something wet on the ground. I knelt beside it. Not rain, it glistened red, with that beautiful coppery scent, filled with salt and hot like the sun. I inhaled sharply trying to find the next droplet. I ran, the scent giving me direction. I knew I was close.

Soon it was bright enough for me now, though there was still no natural light. The darkness had done its work on me and my eyes had grown used to the place, the light of the torch harsh to my eyes. I dropped it and stopped as I heard a scraping sound, and the sound of bare feet pounding along the stone. I felt the vibrations through the ground.

Finally, I spotted a shape running through the corridor towards a blinding ray of daylight that speared into the underground cavern.

I had been down there for hours; I was sure of it. It should have been moonlight, but it was not. The grey gold light of day was unmistakable. This made no sense. I gritted my teeth as I saw the creature bounding up a long flight of cracked and broken steps.

The ascent was long and I found myself falling on my hands and feet to climb up the honeycombed surface. The rays of light finally struck my body and its warmth was suddenly unbearable upon my skin. My clothes weighed me down. I shed my heavy jacket when I finally made it to the forest floor.

I felt neither the touch of the rain upon my skin nor the chill of the air brushing past my hair. There was no exultation as I stepped into the surface world. All I felt was bloody vengeance upon this horrid creature that had robbed me of my prize. I growled and rushed after the beast.

The trees lashed against my undershirt, ripping at it and hindering my progress. I shed the shirt like dead snakeskin—naked against the elements—pale and ill-looking. I was nearly upon the fleeing creature. I saw its back and clawed hands.

I leapt upon the creature, dug my hands into its sides, and raked it with my nails. It thrashed and turned. I snarled and slammed a fist into its face. It struggled from under me and cut past a line of trees. I bounded after it. I realized that the creature had led me back, back through the forest to where our chase had begun. The rain was coming down heavy.

He lunged at me, taking me by surprise, and pulled me down. His jaws snapped at my neck, my clawed hands digging into his face, trying to hold him off.

I withdrew one hand and slammed it into his side, my sharp nails puncturing the thin skin of his ribs. He howled and fell back. I grabbed his neck and pulled him up. I heard hooves in the distance.

The blood was draining from his face. I saw his eyes, past the beastly ferocity that lay in them. Past the pallid skin of his neck and old rope burns that might have been lost to anyone but me.

His lips turned up in a horrible lipless smile.

I couldn't think. My jaws closed over his neck and I ripped out a chuck of flesh. I spat the flesh away, though some of it lingered within my mouth. Shaking, I stood there over the dying creature. The rage bubbling over, my claws tore at his dead face, removing his nose, lips and eyes. Everything that resembled me.

I looked up and I saw two horses, a man standing close to the one which had the witch's body over it. The man drew his sword and his horse reared in fright.

I began to laugh and weep, my laugh sounding coarse, like the barking of a dog while hot tears poured down my face.

I howled.

Beloved Evanescence

Kiki Gonglewski

"Oh well. It wasn't built to last," she whispered with a shrug, "and neither were we."

"The world you mean?" He cast her a brief sideways glance before focusing on the receding reality. "I suppose you're right." They were alone, this corner of existence had long since been abandoned.

"Why are you here again?" She inquired, her face tilted, vision made blurry by the edges of one thing melting languidly into another in the light. She could no longer stand to look him in the eyes. His irises were a fascinating blend of colors, she recalled, yet not for the life of her could she remember the exact colors.

"I guess I'm here for the view."

She nodded, finding this answer satisfactory. She didn't mind his presence anymore. And if she wanted to, she could forget about him entirely, reduce him to a fuzzy smudge in the corner of her field of view or to a small section of her mind until he just disappeared.

"You won't get any better than this," she agreed. "What better way to see the world than to stand on the very edge of it?"

And that they were. This was the place of timelessness and time, infinity and evanescence after all, of everything contained within a great nothingness, and the death of the world. And they were standing on the precipice, a small island of existence eternally deep and high. Beneath their feet was the last frontier before the great leap in the dark. And the world was ending before their very eyes.

A piece of reality cracked and chipped, before breaking off eventually from the world to leave a vacuous cavity behind, drifting silently past them, followed by another, and another, and would continue to disintegrate until nothing was left at all.

"It's…it's beautiful," he said at last, letting the slowly ephemeral view envelop him. "In it's own way."

"Yes, it is." She agreed, "You know, it's no surprise. Humans have always found something impossibly alluring about destruction. Like moths to a flame."

"I don't understand it. I should feel sad. I know I should, but it's almost beyond that. It's a terrible, terrible thing, evanescence…I don't see why we'd find everything slowly decaying towards its end to be at all alluring and beautiful."

"But don't you see? That's exactly what makes it so beloved. It is inevitable that the human race will die out, the universe will one day end, and nothing will remain. No one will remember Shakespeare, or Picasso, or General Relativity. Although the transience of all things has bothered me, bothered everyone, it also provides incredibly valuable perspective. Without the shadow of impermanence, there would be no contrast, weight or value to everything we hold dear. How could we love something without a flickering thought to the eventual thieves of time and death? We value precious things simply because we know that, like the world, like love, they won't last forever. And maybe that's why we love it too, because it allows us to love in the first place. And for that, I suppose I'm thankful, even if it's the thing that takes it away."

They were silent for a moment. The contours of their faces flickered momentarily and they were provided with some brief insight in those moments. There was indeed something so elegant about it all, and they could feel each other's acknowledgement of its magnificence, even as they knew that as they were drawn into their crumbling surroundings, they also found themselves evermore lost until there would be no going back. There was a feeling of forever here, but like all things, they both knew now more than ever, that it was simply a human illusion.

"You know, it's funny…it doesn't always look like it's dying," he said to her, "It looks like it's waking up."

"You don't really believe that do you?" she whispered quietly. "This is the end." Neither was sad nor afraid—for they were both too far gone to feel.

"This is the end," he repeated dully, "the end of everything. The end of us, the world…" There wasn't much else to say. Their voices were made redundant by their surroundings. Their love was made extraneous by their circumstances. Their fates were made irrelevant by all the yesterday's conspiring against them. And everything around them was tumbling down. It was only a matter of time before they followed.

"I…I love you," he faltered. His voice had gone suddenly hoarse, as if some tightening force was crushing him from the inside out. He was in very real danger of imploding any minute.

She shook her head sadly. He thought he saw a tiny little piece of her hair break away like the rest of the world and wondered if they too were truly disintegrating. "No…no, you don't."

"Please. Don't say that," he insisted. "I love you. I love you, I love you so damn much, I love you, I love you!"

"And I love you too," She said, tilting his face towards her. She thought she saw a little piece of him break away at her touch, and wondered if it was their time yet, if they were ending too. But her words rang empty and heavily, like the sound of someone striking a lead pipe. Both of them knew by the sound alone that it had superficial or no meaning at all.

"You see it now, don't you?" she continued, "they're just words. The meaning has been sucked out of them so that they're left dry. They shatter with a touch."

"I love you," he repeated hopelessly, but he knew deep inside that she was right. The words had formed in his mind, but there was a small delay travelling to his heart. He knew with seeping dread that it would eventually catch up to him. "I love you."

"No," she told him gently, perhaps for her own benefit as much as his, "you don't." His eyes were two small mirrors that conveyed the breaking down of the world. She looked at him and watched them shatter in the reflection.

"You loved me. Loved. And I loved you."

"There's so much we were supposed to do together, so much I wanted to say. So much I never got to tell you. You have no idea how much that hurts,"

"Well, actually…I think," she said slowly, "I think I do."

There was silence again, as both pondered miserably what was lost. They used to finish each other's sentences. They worked as one-hive mind, and even their hearts beat in time at one point. No more. It wasn't one moment in which everything fell apart. In fact, they couldn't for the life of them remember how it started. But it was by far easier to recognize when something was over.

"I loved you," she continued sadly, and she couldn't tell if she was crying or not because the ending world warped and blurred around her, as if it were being viewed from heavily-curved lenses, "but there's no going back. We'll never go back…the world is ending."

"I know."

"Good. At least we can finally learn to breathe again now. Maybe, after we get that under control, we can even talk about it."

"Can I at least stay, then?" he asked finally, "with you…one last time? For the view?"

"Okay. Is that what you've come for? For the view? Or to see the world fall apart with me?"

"In part," he answered, "and to say goodbye."

"Goodbye," she said to him gently. It seemed for a second that life had crept back into her again through her pores, before she breathed it all out again in a long sigh.

"Goodbye."

Neither moved. Neither spoke. But the world kept on falling…falling apart. And even the slowing of time could not break the spell cast over them.

Distantly, she spoke to him, of one ghost voice and two melding minds, "But…but if you could find a reason to stay…just for a little while…you could. And just for a while, we could…we could watch the world end until there's nothing left of us to watch or feel at all."

At this moment, everything became irrelevant—even their past—and time could have stopped for all they noticed or cared. This was their universe, now: the two of them, and an ending world.

No past, no present, and no future awaited them outside the moments out of time they shared with each other and their surroundings. Their shadows had already broken away from them like much of the world. As it fell apart, they could feel themselves becoming ghosts, as if this one transition, state change, and metamorphosis was intrinsically linked to the other. In many senses the pair already was.

Piece by piece, one impossibly small fragment at a time, everything was flaking, thinning, cracking, drifting away from itself. It shattered like a mirror that sent its spider web cracks to reach the extremities of existence. It crumbled like a million colored stars falling from the sky to leave a checker-board of reality behind. It was a delicate, fragile process that drew like towards like, which sought some meaning from the other and only partially found it.

They couldn't for the life of them decide which one they most felt they were: the small, hopelessly lost fragments of reality that painfully broke away from the world and floated away, or the empty voids that each orphan piece left behind.

"Now where were we?" she asked him. She looked out from two hollow eye sockets, a vacant head, and wondered what happened to her voice. She once had a beautiful voice. Empty, all empty. She breathed in through an empty chest, and realized she was full of holes. She knew she was always a delicate thing. But now, with an exterior of only a thin layer of translucent skin, she knew the next time she tripped and fell, she would shatter and break.

He didn't respond at first, but looked up and pretended to be observing the fleeting world. The ossification had already begun within him. There was a great aching pain in the cavity of his chest that blocked out everything else. Soon, it would spread and everything else would be a stranger to him, the festering thing inside him turning him to dust. A process he knew he would have to learn to live with, or give up and deteriorate into dust forever. He did not yet know which fate awaited him.

"I'm sorry," he said, turning to her. She was no longer beautiful in the hoary light that surrounded them. He wouldn't have minded even if he had noticed. "I'm sorry, I guess I just forgot."

"That's okay," she responded, "I don't mind."

He reached out slowly and took her hand. She didn't shrink away. Perhaps she didn't notice, she wouldn't have minded if she had. But it was different. Once they could sense an overwhelming current of love pulsing from one soul to the other, like a closed electric circuit that went around and around forever. Now, somewhere along the line the circuit had been broken, and their hearts had long since run away from each other to leave large caverns behind while they hid in the deep where they'd never again be found. But it made sense to them both. They didn't resist or resent it anymore. For nothing could ever be the same. Yet it served as an infinitely small, faint reminder that once upon a time, they had indeed been very much in love. But those days were behind them now. Ahead lay the abyss.

He suddenly had the desire to squeeze her hand with all his might, to feel something, or maybe if only to remember. But he knew it would only cause her more pain. Besides, there was really no point; he could barely tell that it was there anymore.

The ground beneath their feet was nearly gone, and they could have floated off if they wanted to. But neither did, both stayed anchored to the earth, for they knew they didn't deserve such things.

"Where were we?" she repeated softly, and the sound of it continued to exist long after her lips had closed once again. "Where were we, where were we?" If she said it enough times, perhaps, she could find an answer. Her mind wandered slowly back to her.

"Right," she said distantly, "the world is ending."

"That it is," he said to her, "that it is." And their silhouettes thinned as his voice echoed softly within the vast, empty expanse of everything.

Last Slice at Luca's

Ben Gamblin

Pascal fidgeted with his latex gloves whenever a customer displayed rude or unsavory behavior in one of his restaurants. A few light tugs were usually enough to temper his nerves before the inevitable confrontation. This, however, was an altogether different matter. He yanked the elastic bands until they hung loose and misshapen around his wrists, and he could feel pools of sweat forming in the gaps between the gloves' fingertips and his own.

The customer was *smoking.* Smoking a damned cigar, right there at Table 14. Never in the three years since Café Fromage opened its doors, nor in the seven since he'd entered the restaurant management business, had Pascal witnessed such a flagrant violation of dining etiquette—never mind the statewide ban on indoor smoking in public places. The café was small, a mere sixteen tables from end to end, and the stench would overpower the entire dining room in no time. Quick, decisive action was needed.

"I brought him a menu and he just...lit up right there at the table," explained Stephanie, the server who first alerted Pascal of the disturbance. She was one of his most reliable employees, a stalwart pillar of the weeknight dinner shifts. Now she cowered behind him at the front desk, peering over his shoulder every few seconds to steal a glance at the brazen rule-breaker. The other on-duty server, Joel, remained by the kitchen doors. The sourdough chowder bowls on his tray were no longer steaming.

"How long has he been here?" Pascal asked Stephanie.

"Ten minutes, if that."

"I see."

"But what are—?"

"Leave him to me. You take care of the other tables. Make sure everyone has enough bread."

Pascal yanked each wristband for good measure and scuttled across the dining room, offering a polite smile to the other customers as he held a watchful eye on the lone, cigar-smoking male at Table 14. Seventy, Pascal estimated, maybe seventy-five years old. As he approached, he realized the old man was seated in a decrepit wheelchair with rust patches along the rims and raggedy-edge foam padding. Closer still and Pascal noticed his sallow, oatmeal-grey complexion and rheumatic eyes pitted with cloudy cataracts. He sported at least a week's worth of salty stubble, and wore a red-and-white Hawaiian print shirt, loose-fitting trousers and shoes that were...well, like the kind of shoes every old man seemed to own. Brown, dull and comfortable-looking, with the heels worn down from years of being slipped on and off.

The old man gave Pascal a squinting smile and set the cigar on the table. The lit end dangled precariously over the edge, sprinkling ash onto the carpet, while the other end, gummy and saliva-coated, left a brown smudge on the white linen tablecloth. The sight of the cigar, combined with the odor, made Pascal's stomach twist.

"Sir," he said shakily. "You...need to put that out immediately."

"Problem with the smoke?"

His voice was low and froggy. Pascal nodded curtly. Rather than complying, the old man picked up the cigar and carried on.

"Don't worry," he croaked, "I'll be done in a minute."

Dementia, Pascal deduced. That was the only explanation for such unapologetic deviance from someone who was certainly old enough to know better. It *was* half past five. Weren't senile folks prone to these sorts of episodes when the sun went down?

Any other time of day, Pascal would have evicted this noxious miscreant without a moment's hesitation. However, like most evenings, the dining room was full to capacity. How would that look to the other patrons if he kicked out an elderly man in a wheelchair, cigar or no cigar? And at dinnertime, no less. Café Fromage had a pristine reputation—and an enviable Yelp! rating—to uphold.

"Sir," Pascal repeated, this time enunciating the S, "you cannot smoke inside any commercial establishment in Washington state. The law has been in place for more than a decade. Either extinguish your cigar at once or you'll have to leave."

The old man narrowed his eyes at him.

"I gotta ask," he finally said, "what's with the gloves?"

The random question caught Pascal off-guard.

"Well, the...health code requires it," he replied.

This was a slight lie. Pascal preferred to wear his gloves when working the restaurant floor—or the 'germ farm,' as he privately referred to it—but he was not legally obligated to do so unless he was preparing food or cleaning.

"Health code, my ass," the old man grunted. "I've been to tons of places where the waiters don't wear gloves."

"I am the *owner* of this establishment."

"So what do you need gloves for? You don't even handle the food."

"I assure you, I handle food all the time," Pascal lied again. "Now, the cigar...I must insist."

The old man smiled again. "In a minute, bub. I paid good money for this."

Pascal felt his composure slipping away. In addition to Café Fromage, he owned two other restaurants—Hollandaise, a popular brunch spot in Fremont, and Pierre's Bistro near the market—along with the Vigne Exquise Wine Bar in Pioneer Square. A man of his stature in the Seattle restaurant community could not afford to lose his temper in front of paying customers, no matter the circumstances. But indignation swelled inside of him as he peeked at the nearby tables and saw his other patrons reacting to the spectacle. Arched eyebrows, stiff shoulders, flaring nostrils, lips forming phrases like *Dear God* and *Oh, that's disgusting*.

The old man took a long puff and released a thick plume that sailed across the dining room like a phantom ship. This was the final straw for Pascal. He reached down, snatched the cigar away and dropped it into the old man's water glass. The embers snuffed out with a sickening hiss. He wiped his gloves together, smirking with self-satisfaction. A couple of the customers even clapped.

The old man glared at the cigar as it sank to the bottom of his water glass. Mumbling to himself, he reached into the chest pocket of his shirt and produced a second one. Pascal's smirk vanished as the old man bit off the end, spat it onto the carpet and lit the tip with a gold-plated Zippo lighter.

"Listen, pal," the old man said, lowering his voice. "I hoped it wouldn't come to this...but fact is, I'm gonna enjoy my cigar. Then I'll be on my way."

"I beg your pardon?"

"Look."

"You think you can just waltz in—?"

"*Look.*"

Pascal noticed the old man was, in fact, pointing to an object in his lap. Upon closer examination, he saw it was a thin, yellow tank of compressed oxygen. The old man held his Zippo next to the tank's release valve.

"All I have to do is open her up," he said quietly. "Nice place you got here. It'd be a shame, you know?"

Pascal swallowed hard, and a bead of sweat trickled down the hook of his nose. Surely this man wasn't...oh, but he was, and most assuredly judging by the wicked twinkle in his eye.

The customers seated closest to them began their mass exodus. Some stomped toward the front desk, where Stephanie fielded their indignant questions, while others beelined for the door without bothering to lodge a complaint, much less pay their bill. However, no one seemed to fully grasp the standoff unfolding at Table 14. This felt like a small miracle to Pascal. A stampede was the last thing he needed.

"All right," he said quietly. "What do you want?"

"I got some bad news from my doctor recently. He told me to spend the next few weeks doing things I love. See my kids, travel to places I always wanted to visit, even buy a sports car if I want. Not like I'll be making monthly payments where I'm headed."

"But why are you *here*?"

"I'm getting to that," the old man snapped. "So, doc says this and my first thought is, I'm gonna grab one last slice at Luca's Pizzeria. Best deep-dish pie in the Northwest, not that that's saying much. So, now I'm here and Luca's is gone. What gives?"

Pascal wrinkled his nose at the thought of Luca's Pizzeria. The place was filthy when he'd signed the deed three years earlier. Mold spots in the kitchen, water stains on the dining room ceiling, ancient knob-and-tube wiring that was a five-alarm fire waiting to happen. And that pizza oven, coated in decades-old grime that even a steel brush couldn't scrub off. If Pascal hadn't completely gutted the building, it may very well have been condemned. The idea of anyone forging an emotional connection with that rotten grease trap was inconceivable to him.

"Luca's closed down," he said softly, trying to cushion the blow. "Three years ago."

"No shit? Gianni finally decided to retire, huh?"

Pascal tugged at his gloves. "That's right."

"What a shame. He owned Luca's for what, thirty years?"

"Thirty-two, I believe."

"Bastard could've told me. We served in Nam together, 4th Infantry Division. I was one of his groomsmen, even helped christen his son." The old man sighed. "You ever eat at Luca's?"

"No, I can't s—"

"Oh, it was something. Gianni was second cousins with Lenny Montana—you know, the guy who played Luca Brasi in *The Godfather.* So, he named the restaurant after him and decorated the whole place with pictures from the movie. Weird, right? Not like he was related to Brando or Pacino, or even Jimmy Caan. But I guess when you make a pie like Gianni, you can fix up the place however you want."

Pascal nodded faintly, feeling lightheaded from the smoke. Over his shoulder he could hear coughing, groaning, more scuffing chair legs, the door swinging open and slamming shut. It would take weeks—perhaps even months—for Café Fromage to recover from this incident. Assuming that the place wasn't a mound of rubble by evening's end.

It occurred to Pascal that the old man might be bluffing. The tank could be empty for all he knew. And supposing it *was* full, could an open flame actually make an oxygen tank explode? Or was that just something that happened in movies? Regardless of his suspicions, Pascal knew calling the old man's bluff would risk everything—quite literally, life and limb. He had no choice but to appease this man in the same way he had appeased so many rude and unsavory customers over the years: with poise, civility and endless patience.

"Perhaps...you'd like something to eat while you enjoy your cigar," he said, gesturing toward the unopened menu on the table. "This month's charcuterie plate has been quite popular, and some say we have the best veal in the city."

The old man ignored the menu and scratched his chin. "Fromage...that means cheese, right?"

"Correct."

"Seeing how I came here for Luca's...you got any pizza?"

"Not exactly. We have the Monterrey flatbread, but it's closer to a bruschetta."

"I was *really* hoping for some pizza today." He rattled the oxygen tank and chuckled. "Think you could make that happen?"

"Let me see what I can do," Pascal whimpered. "Anything to, uh, drink?"

"Water will do just fine, garçon. Oh, and don't even *think* about calling the cops. If I see one cruiser pull up..."

Pascal nodded dutifully and scurried away before the old man could finish, weaving through the tables and chairs like a mouse searching for the exit of a maze. A few of the customers who were still seated raised their hands and snapped their fingers to get his attention, but he brushed past all of them without so much as an errant glance. Stephanie met him at the front desk. Her cheeks were flushed, and sweaty strands of hair clung to the edges of her face. Joel held the door open for the departing customers as they snatched their hats and coats from the foyer rack and hustled outside.

"Pascal," Stephanie whined, "what does he want?"

"Oh, he's just a little...you know." He twirled a finger around his ear.

"Everyone else is leaving!"

"I am *aware*, Stephanie."

A middle-aged man, red-faced and trembling, stormed over from the coat rack and thrust a shaky finger in Pascal's face. The man's wife attempted to placate him with a few taps on the shoulder, but he brushed her aside.

"I have emphysema for Christ's sake," the man snarled. "What kind of outfit are you running here?"

"My deepest apologies, sir. We are dealing with an—"

"This'll be the last time I ever set foot in this shithole."

Pascal watched, helpless and deflated, as the man stomped out the door without another word and his wife scampered after him. *Shit*hole? Surely he didn't...oh, but he did. Pascal felt a tug on his shirtsleeve and turned to find Stephanie at his side.

"What are you going to do?" she asked.

Pascal's eyes met hers. Up to that point he'd been so preoccupied by the potential damage to the café itself—both physical and financial—that he'd neglected to consider the employees under his care.

"Come with me." He gently took her arm. "You too, Joel."

He guided them through the swinging doors that led into the kitchen. Karl, the head chef, threw up his hands when they entered. The line cooks, Ramon and Aaron, stood behind him looking equally perturbed.

"The hell's going on out there?" Karl demanded. "We haven't had a new order in more than ten minutes."

Pascal tore off the tattered remains of his latex gloves and tossed them in the wastebasket, then fetched a fresh pair from the cardboard box on the counter.

"Karl, do we still have some of that gruyère we got last week?"

"A little. What for?"

"A...pizza."

"*Pizza*? With this thing?" Karl pointed to the oven. "It'll take a half an hour for the dough to proof in there, maybe longer. I told you before, I don't like going off-menu."

Pascal frequently butted heads with his head chef. Karl viewed himself as a culinary virtuoso, an essential ingredient to the café's success. He and the line cooks seemed to regard Pascal as a mere check-signer, a stuffed-shirt businessman without a modicum of gastronomic talent despite the many years he'd spent working in kitchens before becoming a restaurateur. Pascal usually let Karl win these arguments—the owner always had better things to do than engage in petty squabbles with the hired staff—but this time he felt compelled to stand his ground. Waving him aside, Pascal cleared his throat and addressed the entire kitchen.

"My apologies for the...situation tonight," he said solemnly, "Right now, I need all of you to pack up and head home. You'll be paid for the full shift, I assure you."

Stephanie's eyes narrowed. "Tips too?"

"Of course."

"Who's gonna cook the damn food?" Karl asked.

"I'll take over."

Both line cooks snickered and a derisive smile crawled across Karl's face. "You think *you* can replace the three of us? When was the last time you even set—?"

"I'll be fine. Leave everything as is. I'll see all of you tomorrow, same time as usual."

Despite some added grumbling, Pascal ushered everyone toward the back door in a timely and effective manner. Karl was the last one to exit. "I didn't go to culinary school for this bullshit," he sneered, slamming the door behind him.

Pascal wasted no time once he was alone in the kitchen. After cranking the oven dial to 500°, he raced to the mixing bowl and threw in yeast, sugar, olive oil and a few dashes of truffle salt, followed by a cup of flour and some warm water. The dough was shaggy when he dumped it onto the counter a minute later, so he pounded and kneaded vigorously, adding more flour with each flip. When it felt sufficiently chalky, he put the dough back into the mixing bowl, covered the rim with a towel and set the bowl on top of the warming oven. This would help it settle faster—a trick he'd picked up years ago working for a family-owned pizzeria. "Need half an hour to proof," he grumbled. "Culinary school...idiot."

Next, he shredded the gruyère and gathered the other toppings on the countertop. Tomato sauce, sliced prosciutto, spinach, onions and minced garlic. Once everything was ready he returned the dough to the counter, rolling and stretching it into a flat circle that measured roughly eight inches in diameter. Any larger and the pizza would take too long to bake—and really, how much could a sick old man actually eat? He applied a thick layer of tomato sauce to the dough and tossed on several fistfuls of grated cheese, followed by the meat and veggies, and slipped the pie into the oven just as the preheat timer chimed. Only then did he stop to wipe away the sweat on his forehead.

The next few minutes ticked by slowly as Pascal watched the dough rise through the oven window. His eyes kept drifting toward the back door. He could leave too, slip out unnoticed like the others, and be blocks away if or when this deranged old coot decided to annihilate himself. He wouldn't be able catch up with Pascal in that rustbucket wheelchair, either. But as quickly as this thought occurred to him, a feeling of deep shame took hold. He couldn't simply abandon the café. If captains were expected to go down with their ships, what made restaurant owners any different?

The timer dinged and he removed the pizza from the oven. The crust was pocked with air bubbles and the cheese was singed in a few spots—far from a showstopper—but Pascal hadn't made pizza from scratch in years and, under the circumstances, he thought it looked appetizing enough. He transferred the pie onto a ceramic serving plate. With no proper pizza cutter on hand, he snatched the chef's knife from the magnetic rack above the oven.

He emerged from the kitchen with the platter in one hand and a full water pitcher in the other. Bluish smoke hung in the air like evening fog. Predictably, the dining room was empty save for the sole occupant of Table 14.

"About time," the old man growled as Pascal approached. "Thought you took off on me."

"Of course not."

Pascal set the plate onto the table, along with the pitcher, and used the chef's knife to halve and quarter the pizza. Then he stepped back and swept his hand through the air like an artist unveiling his latest work. The old man did not look impressed. As he squinted suspiciously at the plate, Pascal filled one of the empty water glasses.

"What *is* this?" The old man poked at the crust with his finger.

"Ah, so...for our toppings we have Fribourg gruyère, Prosciutto Toscano, some—"

"Doesn't look like a Luca's pie, that's for sure."

"Deep-dish pizza takes much more time to prepare. I didn't want to keep you waiting...sir."

The old man set down his cigar on the edge of the table and picked up a slice. Despite his evident apprehension, he bit into the bottom tip and a smile formed as he chewed.

"Not *bad*," he said. "Little heavy on the garlic, but...I gotta say, I'm impressed. Didn't think you had it in you."

"I'm glad you're enjoying it."

As he nibbled at the slice, the old man gestured to the back wall of the dining room. "Gianni used to have a big-screen up there," he said between mouthfuls. "We watched the Mariners beat the Yankees in '95 on that TV. Watched 'em lose to the Indians in the ALCS too. Tell me, how does a team with Griffey, Randy, Edgar *and* Buhner not make it to the World Series?"

"Tell me about it," Pascal muttered, not having the faintest idea who any of these people were.

"Yep, lots of good memories at Luca's. I came here at least once or twice a week, and every time Gianni knocked a few bucks off my bill. He always did for the other vets. Then I got the cancer back in '09 and doc told me I couldn't eat pizza anymore. I still popped by every so often to see Gianni and the other guys, but Luca's wasn't the same. After a while, I stopped coming altogether. Now, shit...I don't visit for a few years and the place disappears on me. That's getting old, I guess. Soon it'll all be gone."

The old man took one more bite and chased it with a long glug of water, loudly belching at the end.

"Goddamn heartburn. I need a break." The tip of the cigar had gone dark, so he relit it and resumed smoking. "Shame about Gianni, though."

"What do you mean?"

"Oh, you didn't hear? Last winter. Heart attack."

"He's...dead?"

"Yep. Only got to enjoy his retirement for three years. Not that he enjoyed it much."

"I'm very sorry, I..." Pascal trailed off as the old man's words sank in. His chest tightened and his knees softened to jelly. "Wait, you...you knew Luca's was closed?"

The old man winked.

"Then why did you come here?"

"I spent a lot of time with Gianni near the end. Broke my heart, seeing how he sold his restaurant for less than half what it was worth and then died piss broke because of it. Couldn't even afford the pacemaker that would've saved him. Tell me that's not criminal for a guy who served his country."

Pascal slumped into the chair directly across from the old man.

"I can explain," Pascal said.

"Explain what?" The old man nipped vigorously at the cigar, his eyes fixed on Pascal through the smoke. "How property taxes shot up in the city and Gianni couldn't afford to keep the lights on anymore? How some asshole swooped in when times were really tough and made a lousy offer he knew Gianni couldn't refuse?"

"That is *not*...you have to understand, this is a very competitive industry and—"

"Oh, I understand. I read up on you, Pascal. You own three restaurants in the city, and a bar too. Paid below-market value for all four properties. You know this is public record, right? Took me less than ten minutes to find it."

Pascal knew he couldn't wait any longer to act—there'd be no appeasing this customer, after all. He could sprint for the kitchen. If he was quick enough, he might escape the blast. He also contemplated snatching away the lighter and the lit cigar, rendering the oxygen tank harmless. Surely his hands were faster than the old man's. But at that moment he found himself too petrified to blink, let alone attempt a daring act of sabotage.

"Let me ask you a question," the old man said. "Where do you think you'll go?"

"Go?"

"I open this valve, light the flame and we go kablooey. Which direction are you headed, north or south?"

"Well, I don't...um..."

Pascal fiddled with his gloves on the tabletop, searching for the right words but coming up empty. The old man reached over and tauntingly tapped his cigar over the pizza plate. Bits of ash fluttered down, melting into grey freckles over the warm gruyère.

"Maybe you haven't given it much thought," he said. "Never needed to, right? You're young, got all that money in the bank and those yuppie customers licking your boots. But I'll bet my entire estate you're thinking about it now. Wondering if it's too late to make peace for all the hard-working people you screwed over in this city. Am I getting warm?"

Pascal gulped and gave a flimsy shrug.

"It's funny," the old man said. "How you think about things near the end. You don't have to tell me."

He tapped the cigar again, scattering more ash onto the pizza. Pascal watched his hand come to rest on the table with the cigar between his index and middle fingers. The knife lay on the other side of the plate. Suddenly, Pascal saw an opportunity, but it needed to go exactly to plan. Otherwise, well—kablooey.

"Gianni sounds like he was a fine man," he murmured.

"Damn right he was. Prick like you could've learned something from him."

"Undoubtedly. You...you said he had a TV somewhere?"

"Yeah." The old man craned his neck toward the back wall. "Just over—"

As his eyes drifted away from the table, Pascal snatched the knife by the handle and plunged the blade into the meaty center of the old man's right palm. A guttural wail echoed across the dining room as blood gushed from the wound and the cigar slipped from his fingers. The old man frantically attempted to extricate the knife with his free hand, but the blade had penetrated the wood beneath the tablecloth and wouldn't budge. Both of them reached for the lighter at the same time. The old man lunged forward but Pascal slapped it off the table and it soared across the dining room, striking one of the chairs at Table 9.

The old man went for the cigar next, which had fallen on the carpet and rolled between the wheelchair casters, but with one hand pinned to the table the other couldn't quite reach the floor. Pascal staggered around the table. In a final act of defiance, he stamped out the cigar with the sole of his shoe and doused the crumbled remains with water from the pitcher. Foul-smelling smoke plumes spiraled toward the ceiling.

The old man groaned in defeat. The linen around the wounded hand was saturated in blood, and his complexion had faded to a milky white. As he attempted to hoist himself back into the chair, his backside slipped off of the seat cushion and the wheels rolled back. Soon he was dangling limply from the table, the knife pinning his hand as gravity pulled the rest of him toward the floor.

"Oh Christ, pull it out!" he howled.

Pascal looked on in horror as the blade sliced through the flesh like a table saw. As the last strand of tissue was severed, the old man collapsed to the floor. He held up his right hand in a daze and Pascal recoiled when he saw the injury. A jagged, V-shaped cut extended from the center of his palm to the webbing between his middle and ring fingers. Both halves flapped in different directions as blood oozed down the old man's forearm.

Pascal didn't know whether to catch his breath or throw up. Either way, he needed a seat. He collapsed into the nearest chair, hiccoughing as sour bile bubbled deep within his gut.

"Son of a bitch," the old man sputtered from the floor, gazing at the wound with wild blue eyes. "Didn't think you had *that* in you."

"Me...me neither."

"Guess this means you won, huh?"

Pascal nodded slowly as it sank in. He *had* won. He was alive and Café Fromage was still intact. When the public found out about what had happened, how he'd singlehandedly foiled this maniacal plot, he'd be lauded as a local hero and his offended customers would surely forgive the 'cigar incident.' It might not even hurt the Yelp! reviews—on the contrary, they'd probably skyrocket. He was so overwhelmed with relief and gratitude that he began to cry. Mad, hysterical giggles escaped his lips as the tears mixed with the sweat beads, cascading warm and oily down both of his cheeks.

The old man mumbled something under his breath.

"Sorry?" Pascal asked, barely acknowledging him.

"I said, that's why you gotta come prepared."

He slipped his unscathed hand into the pocket of his trousers and removed something round and palm-sized. Pascal rubbed the tears away to get a better look. Then his bladder seized. It was a hand grenade. Round, green and textured in a grid pattern, just like in the movies. The old man brought the pin to his mouth and smiled.

"Thanks for the slice, asshole," he gasped, tearing it out with his teeth.

The grenade slipped from the old man's fingers and rolled in a wobbly half-circle across the carpet. Pascal stared down at the object, tugging furiously at the ends of his gloves as it came to rest at the tip of his shoe. Then he closed his eyes and took a deep breath. Sour cigar ash flooded his nostrils, chased with hints of garlic and sweet gruyère.

Trials

Jack Lothian

It had smiled at Sarah.

"Bullshit," said Johansson. He grabbed a Styrofoam cup, placing it under the nozzle of the coffee machine. They were in the canteen, middle of the night. Empty Formica tables, harsh strip lights over-head, the ever-present scent of disinfectant.

Sarah sat down at the nearest table, tore open her juice box. "I swear. Just for a moment."

"Sure it did," said Johansson, as he sniffed his coffee cautiously. "What are we talking here—a big old grin, showing off those lovely yellow teeth? Did it wink as well?"

They had their own work sections. The fortified door, with the keypad lock. The secure area. The control panel. The firearm underneath, always loaded, always ready. Then there was the reinforced glass, with all the scratches and gouges in it.

And beyond that, were the subjects.

"I'm not saying it acknowledged me or anything like that. We're not talking individual cognition." Sarah hesitated, trying to find the right phase, and failing. "It smiled. That's all."

Johansson took a sip of coffee, leaned back in his chair. The canteen was empty. Everyone was either at work or sleeping—shift life. Sometimes you could go weeks without seeing someone you knew unless you made a real effort to catch up. The long hard hours meant that effort was in short supply. "You gotta introduce me to this guy," he said. "Sounds like a real charmer."

"Screw you. It was just…seeing him standing there like that…for a second there it was like, y'know…"

She didn't have to say it. They both knew what she meant. Normal life. The old days. All that came before.

Her subject was male. Mid-thirties, average weight, decent head of hair. He didn't have a wedding ring when they'd brought him in, but he didn't have any clothes or identifiers at all, so maybe that didn't mean anything. When she started, she'd tried to imagine how their lives had been. Families. Friends. Jobs. She'd wonder if her own life had ever crossed over with them. Maybe they'd been on the same subway once or passed each other in the street.

Now she saw them for what they'd become, not what they once were. The slack jaw, the jittery motion, the jaundiced eyes that only sparked into life when they sensed some form of prey.

She had the current one for nearly two weeks, close to a record. Her last subject collapsed after two hundred and fifty volts had shot through its body and it couldn't get back up. The clean-up crew came in and took it away, and she'd had a day off before they assigned her a new subject. She'd spent that day sleeping and hoping she wouldn't have any dreams.

It could be worse. She could be outside.

"Sorry, back up there. I'm just gonna quote what you said— 'him standing there,'" said Johansson, a smug look pooling across his face. "*Him*. Your words. Not mine."

"Him. It. You know what I meant."

"Oh god. Please tell me you've not gone native."

"Slip of the tongue."

"This is not your family—" started Johansson.

"Okay, yeah, very funny."

He continued, mimicking the tone of the warning broadcasts. "This is not your co-worker; this is not your friend. This is not a person—"

Something welled up inside her and broke as fast it came, and it caused her to reach out and slap the Styrofoam cup from his hand, sending coffee all down his front.

"Jesus—what's your problem—?"

"I told you to stop it."

He grabbed some tissues, started wiping. "No, you told me I was very funny."

She tried to hang onto her indignation. Johansson knew what she'd been through. Then again, they'd all been through something though.

One day it had started, without warning; an aggressive neural condition, that targeted around seventy-five percent of the population, inducing a terrible form of primal behavior. It was like someone had flicked a switch and changed the world forever.

Their job was to try and understand what had caused this, and if there was any way to reverse it, to return the afflicted to the previous state of being. It was brutal work. They used live subjects, and they'd gone through a lot of them.

The prevailing opinion was that the condition was both irreversible and all -encompassing. It wiped away any trace of the original person, with no detectable brain activity beyond instinct and response. Like Johansson often said, they were worse than animals because at least you can teach a dog to beg for a bone. She felt bad for being so sharp with him. She usually found him pretty amusing.

"I'll get you another coffee," she said, trying to sound conciliatory.

"Don't worry about it. Tasted like crap anyway."

That was Johansson. He'd always throw you a rope, make sure you were okay. She nodded, pretended to look over at the clock.

"I better get back to it then."

She headed for the door, the one marked red that lead to the corridors, the people with the armor and guns, the thick doors and the workspaces beyond. To where the test subjects were waiting, always waiting.

"Hey," said Johansson. "You fancy hooking up later?" He held up his empty cup at if it was a deal breaker.

She thought of the way the subject had turned towards her as she left for her break. How it had held her look for a moment.

"Raincheck."

Johansson nodded. "Alright. You know where I am if you need me."

-ↂAↂ-

She dreaded the walk back. It wasn't heading past the different doors, the knowledge of what was going in there, the way words like *vivisection* were never far from her thoughts. She was used to that by now. It was going back to her section. Back to him. *To it.*

She hadn't been entirely honest with Johansson.

It hadn't smiled towards her.

She wished it had. She wished it was just a motor reflex. Old muscle memory.

She had entered the room, and it had turned around. Usually, when they focused on you, there was a predictable, visceral response. Fury and rage. Sometimes there was nothing, like something in the cortex had misfired and failed to trigger. Not this time though.

It saw her. It tilted its head. It took an unsure step forward.

Sarah had given it a sarcastic wave. "Hey there."

It had smiled. And it had tried to raise its hand in response.

-ↂAↂ-

Sarah entered, moved to the console, keeping her head down. The subject stood in the middle of the secure room. The door closed behind her, with the whirr and clicks of unbreakable locks. Sarah could feel it watching her. She tried to block it out, tried to busy herself with the work.

She checked the schedule. Mild voltage followed by sound files fifty through to sixty. These were a range of noises—some from nature, some from the city, some artificial—bombarded at the subject at high volume while she noted any variances in responses. It was a slow and thankless task. The subjects needed at least ten or fifteen minutes to settle back into a state of inertness before the next file could be played.

Sarah went to increase the voltage as per instructions. Electric shocks aimed at stimulating the prefrontal cortex. She inputted the new levels, and she went to push the switch that would send the charge down the wires that were attached to the subject. She caught something out the corner of her eye.

It was shaking its head. She hesitated.

Anthropomorphization—ascribing human attributes and emotions to creatures that had no capacity for it. This had been one of the most significant issues that authorities had to overcome. The brain couldn't help sketching in emotions and feelings where there were none. These things looked like us, moved like us, once upon a time they had been us. But like the warning messages had said: they are not your family, they are not your friends. Not anymore.

She was tired. She was losing her grip. She took a breath and went to press the switch again.

It took a half-step forward. Looking straight at her. And once again it shook its head.

If she had to write down a word for what emotional state she was currently ascribing to test subject #508M35, that word would have been ***pleading***.

-ෙA ෙ-

"You need help."

She nodded at Johansson who was standing over his control panel. "Yeah. No shit. That's why I came for you."

"No, I mean—"

"— that I'm crazy, yes, I know what you mean. Just come and take a look for me."

Johansson's subject was currently lying on the ground, with what was either drool or phlegm seeping out the corner of its mouth. His remit was more chemical than stimulation and she wondered what had been pumped into those veins to bring it down like that. Sarah half thought of asking if she could try some herself.

"You know the protocol. Anything out of the ordinary goes upstairs."

She stepped in close to him. "That's for a twitch. For a clench of the jaw when we don't expect it. Tiny details. This is…this is different. You know that."

She could see Johansson was torn. For all their bitching and moaning, this was one of the better jobs. He'd need a good reason to risk it.

"I'm not allowed in your section."

"Please. Two minutes. That's all."

He hesitated, and she knew he'd say yes. But she asked him again anyway, to make it easier on them both.

-∞A∞-

Her subject was staring at them as they entered. Johansson walked to the control panel.

"It's watching you," she said.

"I'm a good looking guy," said Johansson. He ran his hand over the console, moved to the switch. "So, when is it going to tell me to stop? Before?" He suddenly flicked the switch, and its body jerked spasmodically as the volts charged through it. Johansson took his hand off the switch. "Or after?"

The subject staggered backward. Johansson regarded it wearily before turning back to her. "Can I get back to work now?"

Sarah didn't say anything. She was looking beyond him to the secure room. He turned, followed her gaze. It had its hands out, palms facing towards them. It was a symbol that could be recognized the world over, no matter what language you spoke.

It was saying "stop"

Johansson was quiet for a moment. "It's a—it's some interneural reaction. We're reading things into what isn't there—"

She edged past him, to the console, and brought her hand to the switch. She let it rest there for a half-second so that the subject could clearly see what her intention was.

It shook its head.

"Son of a bitch," muttered Johansson. "Do it again."

Sarah took her hand away from the switch. The subject visibly relaxed. She brought her hand back, and it shook its head, raised its hands again. *Stop.*

Sarah puts her hands by her side. She took a very deliberate step back from the console. And then one to the side, so there was some space. Then she forced a smile at it.

It stared through the glass at her for a beat. And then it smiled back.

"You still think I'm crazy?" she said, almost a whisper.

Johansson didn't say anything. She caught his expression and felt herself go cold. She knew what he was thinking; she didn't need him to say it.

Johansson had had a family once. A wife. A seven-year-old daughter. He'd told her his story one night, his voice soft and level, unable to meet her eyes, staring down at his hands as he related every detail, his words only cracking and breaking as he reached the terrible end.

She had her own story. She wouldn't ever let herself think about it, about what she'd been forced to do to survive.

They are not your friend. They are not your family.

She remembers staggering down some stairs, the blood in her hair, on her arms, her dress. Screaming and howling into the void. Everyone had a story. And the remorse, the guilt, the horror that ate away at you; that was what it meant to be human. That was what separated us from them.

Yet here was this creature in front of them. Looking at her and Johansson with an uncertain smile. With what could even pass for hope in its eyes. Just like a human would.

If there was some vestige of a person left within that thing…what did it mean, with all they'd done? All the test subjects, thrown and burned in landfills. And before that. Family. Friends. Loved ones.

It was almost too much bear. And it was still smiling. That awful, human, smile.

Sarah turned away. "Do it," she said, quiet. "Just do it."

Johansson nodded. He reached for the switch and increased the voltage, all the way up to maximum levels. A warning light flashed on the console, but Johansson ignored it.

The subject started to shake its head. For a moment she thought it even tried to speak. But then the volts flew down through the cables and the moment was gone. It didn't smile or shake its head. It didn't move again.

Johansson moved past her, and she let him go. She heard the door close behind her. The churn of locks snapping into place.

She thought of her sister, of life before all this. The real world. She walked over, touched her fingers to the glass. She looked at the subject, collapsed on the floor, wires still attached. She stood there for a very long time. Then she pressed the intercom. She asked for a clean-up squad. She took out the file from under the console and flipped to the back, and filled in the required forms. She placed a request for a new subject, one that she knew would be delivered by the morning, so that she could get back to work, so that the trials could go on.

His Master's Voice

Geoff Hart

Bob only talked to me when we'd been drinking, but it wasn't something one bragged about. After all, how many talking dogs do you know? My faithful canine companion, it turned out, was something of a philosopher, and as with most philosophers, his ideas flowed most freely when he'd lubricated them with alcohol. It was a late-March night, and we were sitting exhausted by the fire after a ski loppet at the Stokely Creek ski area, and I was consoling myself for the aches and pains of middle age with Irish coffees that were mostly Irish.

"Pour me another one, chief." I reached for the Dalmore—Bob was quite definite in his tastes—and sloshed two fingers worth into his bowl.

"Did I ever tell you the story about why dogs no longer rule the world?" he asked, licking his lips. Bob had reached that exalted state in which the most secret of confidences could be safely divulged among drinking buddies. I nodded approval, interested to hear how he was going to explain this one.

"It's quite simple," he continued, after dipping his muzzle. "Our historians tell us that some ten thousand years ago, one of our colony ships landed on this planet, and found it to our liking. It was two or three generations into the settlement process before we discovered we'd made a mistake; apparently, some crucial mineral was missing from the soil, and our bodies had stopped developing normally." He paused to lick a paw, a mournful expression on his homely face. "The result was simple, yet potentially fatal to us as an intelligent race: we lost our opposable thumbs. By the time this became apparent, it was too late to do anything about it."

"Wait," I interrupted, "You're telling me that dogs came from another star to colonize Earth?"

"Indeed, that's what I'm telling you. And no, not the one you're thinking, though we were flattered you named one of the brightest stars in your sky after us. In any event, we were fortunate that our minds were largely unaffected by the mineral deficiency; indeed, there was a side effect that turned out to be quite beneficial. Our mental powers grew beyond their strongest former limits, and we became even better able to control our environment—in all ways except direct physical manipulation, which is why we bred you humans to help us in these matters. It was fortunate indeed that you showed both remarkable physical dexterity and such adaptable and controllable minds.

"Now hold on a second, Bob. Interstellar travel is one thing, but telepathy and mind control are dogs of another color. Surely you don't expect me to believe you can control human minds?"

"Of course not. Now be a good fellow and let me have a sip of your coffee."

"Don't be ridiculous, Bob, you can't drink from my glass. Why the germs alone," I continued, wiping the dog slobber from the rim of the glass.

"As I was saying, you humans made ideal companions, and it helped that you were compatible souls for the most part. We've been breeding you for millennia now, and suspect that within another few centuries you should be sufficiently advanced to help us do the necessary genetic engineering to give us back our hands. Then we can dispense with this master/slave relationship and begin treating you as near-equals." Tears glistened in his eyes at the thought of this magnanimous gesture, and he lapped delicately at his Dalmore.

I looked at my glass and back at my dog, then shrugged off the doubt that had begun forming at the back of my mind. "Bob, that's an interesting story all right, but it's full of more holes than you had fleas last summer. I could name a dozen flaws with your theory."

"A challenge! Proceed and I shall endeavor to correct your misapprehensions."

I began mustering my argument. "All right, take medical research for example. If you dogs are really our masters, then why do humans use you for— pardon the mixed metaphor— medical guinea pigs?"

"Child's play, my dear. Have you not noticed that all medical advances are tried first on animals, then transferred to human applications years or even decades later? It's simple enlightened self-interest. We get the benefits of medical research first, often decades before your people, then magnanimously pass it on to you once we have selflessly proven it to be safe. In the meantime, many dog lives are saved that would have been lost had we tested our medicine on you first. Besides, there's the ethical question," (he repressed a shudder), "of experimenting on sentient beings like yourselves."

I shot from the hip. "Dog shows!"

"Access Hollywood? The Oscars? MTV?" He grinned, and took another sip. "Intelligence does not imply good taste. Anyways, those who live in glass houses..."

I paused, then came up with a sounder objection. "What about dogs that are mistreated, beaten, abandoned or starved? How could a master explain that...maybe a slave revolt?"

Bob chuckled, and lapped again at the Dalmore. "Just as not all humans are as bright as you are, my friend, not all dogs are as bright as me." He coughed modestly. "Some have surprisingly weak minds, and it's our practice to let them make their own way in the world. *Think of it as evolution in action*, to borrow one of your species' better phrases. And it's not like your people lack their Kardashians and Trumps, is it?"

"Wolves?" I was flailing, and we both knew it.

"There are those who choose to turn their backs on the benefits of civilization, who return to the way of tooth and claw. We've had our share of Thoreaus, Abbeys, and Leopolds over the centuries. *Going native*, we call it, and not all return from that heart of darkness."

"All right then," I replied after a bit more thought and a lot more coffee, this time with less Irish in it. "How about dogs who give their lives to save humans? Not a very 'masterly' thing to do, is it?"

Bob sighed his disappointment. "Really? You'd best lay off the booze; your wits are weakening. Surely you're not implying that my race is without honor? That we feel no emotional bonds for our lifelong friends and servants? Yes, I have no doubt that's *precisely* what you were thinking. Well, let me assure you, we're as bound by honor, by responsibility to our pets, as yourselves. Perhaps more so. Do you not, yourself, have tales of heroes who gave their lives to save dogs, horses... even…"—he shuddered—"cats?"

He took another snort of the Dalmore. "Try again."

I'd grown desperate by this time, for his arguments made a certain amount of sense, though the whisky might have had something to do with it. "What about cats, then? Why permit your mortal enemies to live with men and even displace dogs in some cases?" I was clutching at straws, but by his reaction, I'd scored a point.

"That's indeed a good point," he mused, "and one that our most eminent philosophers, among whom I number myself, continue to debate. The opinion I favor is that the feline kind are tolerated to remind us that for every good in the world, there must be some offsetting evil—for every light, some offsetting darkness. I confess, my people are a superstitious lot at times, and none has ever come up with a sufficiently compelling justification for exterminating the creatures. Perhaps someday, when reason triumphs over sentiment." Bob yawned extravagantly, showing off pearly white teeth, products of the finest soup bones money could buy.

"Dog food," I blurted before he could go on. "Why do you eat that horrid stuff when you could have filet mignon?"

Bob grinned his lopsided grin, albeit a bit sleepily. "*Horrid*? Well, perhaps not a gourmet delight for the most part, but eminently preferable to a diet rich in salt and saturated fats." He cocked an eyebrow at me. "*À chacun son goût*, as my French brothers say. And then there's Kraft Dinner and Ramen." He shuddered. "When was the last time you read about a dog with diabetes or coronary artery disease? Did it not strike you that there's a disproportionate expenditure on nutritional research for dogs? No coincidence, that. We're still hoping to find that missing mineral that prevents us from growing useful hands.

Your researchers draw closer with each new generation of kibble, but I confess there's a real possibility the necessary elements simply don't exist on Earth in sufficient quantities. Incidentally, did you ever ask yourself why the first sentient terrestrial being in space was a dog? We may very well have to look for the missing minerals in the great beyond, of course. Once we'd proven that you could design rockets, albeit not up to our safety standards, we deemed it wiser to set you to puttering about your solar system on our behalf."

At that point, my wife entered the room, a superior look on her face. "You still plying that dog with whisky? Honestly, you spoil him." She knelt by his side and began scratching his tummy with long, practiced strokes, and he wriggled on his back in a passable imitation of ecstasy. Bob's voice continued to sound in my mind, but my wife, who was a teetotaler, heard nothing.

"Ah! We bred you well, we did. Those nails are perfect for scratching tummies and other unreachable spots. We're an ascetic race for the most part, but we have our guilty pleasures. Yes, I do suppose that we do spoil you shamelessly, the things we let you get away with."

Bob wagged his tail and *woofed* once, quietly, then licked my wife's hand.

Humanarians

Brenda Wright

Good morning my little babies," said petite Ms. Apple as she shivered an undetectable tremble in the morning's dewy light, which triggered many of her babies to drop to the ground. Most of her children still clung hungrily to her breasts, suckling on her sugary sap.

Ms. Fuji Apple bowed and said good morning to her best friend, the solid and strong Ms. Red Maple living next to her. Red's children had finished breast-feeding on their mother's rich maple sap a few months ago. These babies wore elegant clothes resembling helicopters. When Red shivered, children released from her nipples with their clothes spread out wing-like and proceeded to gently float along with the breeze. Eventually the little Maples would land on their somewhat inhospitable daycare center on the surface of the ground.

Both of these plant mothers knew it was pointless to talk to their departing newborns, as they were fast asleep. But it didn't stop the mothers from singing aching good-byes to those babies as they detached leaving raw wounds on their mother's breasts.

"I love you sweethearts," Fuji Apple crooned into the warm caressing breeze. If you looked closely at all Mother's, sweet tears were running down many trunks in memory of the long growing season they all had spent nursing these sweet infants.

However, both mothers agreed, despite the sadness of early fall, it is much easier to breathe this time of year. All leftover sperm had long ago dropped to the ground or been consumed by small winged creatures. All that male sperm thickly wafting in the air in the spring is choking and stinky. Clouds of air-born sperm clogs everyone's stomata during the frantic, lusty spring breeding season and last spring was no exception.

All female genitals have nicely healed over by this time of year. The resulting pregnancies all eventually mature to the point that the sleeping seeds are encouraged to leave home.

"I can't believe how many pregnancies I had this year," said Fuji to Red.

Red shivered in the delicious, vivid memories of last spring's breeding season. Her experience, she concluded, had been an over-the-top series of orgasms like never before. She had enjoyed last spring intensely and was even yet still basking in the after-glow.

Red fondly recalled the little fuzzy insects, smothered in sperm, rhythmically dancing all over her female genitals. This dancing produced in her such wicked stimulations. Each successful penetration of sperm propelled her to release intoxicating orgasmic scents which lured even more sperm-coated insects to her exposed and highly decorated vulva.

"I know what you mean." Red said, "I was so heavy with infants this year my arms were absolutely sagging."

"Did you notice one of my arms broke the other night from the weight of all my many children?" said Fuji. "That arm is now hanging in a shattered mess after the horrible pain of splintering. But the worst pain is seeing dozens of my under-developed babies struggling to drink my sap which no longer flows to them. Soon those infants will die and simply rot in place," cried Fuji Apple. "No animal will want to eat that rotted fruit and take those babies to different locations. And I carefully took so much time and energy to pack deep, luscious clothing around them."

"Let me have a look," said Red Maple as she slowly turned her head to fully view Fuji. "Oh, my bark, that is so sad. I am so sorry for your loss Fuji," said the truly horrified Red. "May your sap flow and heal you quickly, both from your wound and lost children."

Red always found it more favorable to have the wind blow her lightweight sleeping children to new locations. The heaviness of all that fruit surrounding her offspring and hanging on her beautifully formed branches was just too grotesque of a thought. Her strategy was to use the wind rather than fruit-munching animals to transport her babies to faraway places. Most trees, like her and Fuji, wanted offspring to grow up as far from parents as possible so there is never a challenge between parents and siblings over nutrition sources.

Fuji Apple would argue she had the better strategy, with her use of delicious wrapped babies. Her children were sturdy enough to withstand the digestion process of fruit-eating animals. The animals walk long distances before excreting her kids. Along with a splat of luscious feces, her babies would grow pre-nourished into their own successful lives far from her.

All infants from seed-bearing plants stay in a state of suspended animation until the conditions are perfect for them to awaken. Baby plants eagerly sprout into adolescence and grow as quickly as they can. When these new individuals hit maturity, and if the growing season is sufficiently wet and warm, they too will be warmly welcomed into the springtime breeding orgy.

Unfortunately, the fact is that few infants will actually awaken and find conditions in which they can successfully grow. Both Fuji and Red stood still and were lost in wondering how many precious children would flourish and grow into successful citizens. It was such a big gamble each year—only the hardiest survive. But for now, both mothers are grateful their offspring are nestled deeply in sleeping pods awaiting the primal call of nature to awaken and grow.

Red secretly hoped all her children would live to populate an entire mountainside. Fuji longed for a huge secluded grove filled with her descendants. Actually they knew that all plants wanted to fulfill the covenant to multiply and replenish the earth.

-∞A∞-

"Are you going to the humanarian club this afternoon?" Red broke the silence asking Fuji.

"Why yes, of course I am," said Fuji. "I even had time to copy off my best dish for the entire group. Are you bringing a recipe?

"Actually, I am presenting the new enchilada recipe I tried last week," said Red.

They both agreed this was so exciting and socially responsible of them to join the movement.

Later that day, as the sun was at the highest point in the sky, an amazingly large group of plants gathered in the western meadow. The Aspen family had to squeeze tightly together to make room for the Wild Onion and Sagebrush families. All who came found a perfect spot to their liking.

The leader this week, Ms. Roma Tomato, let everyone dig their roots in while she finished hanging up the club's banner carrying their motto high into Mr. Living Oak's tallest branches. Seeing it, Ms. Tomato decided the cost of the banner was well worth it as now everyone could read for themselves and become rededicated to the group's goal.

"Ahem!" said Roma to the group along with a sudden burst of scent from her leaves to get everyone's attention. "Ok, let's all settle and quit rustling so we can get started."

She waited until the air was calm and comfortably moistened by everyone's transpiration.

"You know we have a goal in this club to try and reduce our intake of plants," began Roma. "And I quote; 'We are trying to erase all vegetables, fruits, herbs and spices from our diets. We believe this is one of the most effective choices an individual can make to reduce the suffering of all plants, to help the planet, and to improve personal health'."

There was a giant rustling shiver and chemical release from many of the plants as they agreed in the group's resolution for change.

"Who has the first recipe to share with the group today?" asked Roma.

"Oh, I do," said Red Maple. "I have altered my mother's favorite enchilada recipe to be perfectly humanarian."

"Alright Red Maple, please try and communicate as loudly as you can. You all have a copy in front of you printed on the finest white Scandinavian skin. These fine sheets of humanarian writing skins have been graciously donated by the Norway Spruce family. Feel free to jot down notes as we go along," said Roma Tomato.

"Okay," began Red, standing tall and tossing her branches back proudly, "you will need: One-half cup of German fat. Add to the fat, over medium heat, two young Aborigine testicles, peeled and minced, and one-half of ovary, preferably older Caucasian, chopped finely, and then add three cups of cubed rump meat from your preferred ethnicity. Sear it all nicely brown.

For the tortillas, mix twelve un-born baby bones, crushed and powdered, with a cube of cold Asian fat. Slowly add two tablespoons of unfertilized Egyptian eggs. Mix gently then fold in the bone dust, fat and egg mixture and roll into balls to be flattened into your tortillas. Brown the tortillas tenderly."

Red continued after all finished writing, "We received the human milk cheese recipe last week, so use that. Add as much of your preferred human cheese as matches your taste. I really liked the native Eskimo milk cheese.

For the Enchilada sauce, add three cups of blood. I prefer Native American, but I know that is hard to find in most stores. Add in some crisply fried Mongolian toe scrapings and sprinkle with salt."

"Yes, Mr. Rhubarb, salt is humanarian!" shouted the little Asparagus. Everyone giggled at the young sprout's out-burst. Old Mr. Rhubarb turned a bit red at this quip.

Red calmly waited until everyone quieted down, "Put the enchiladas together and pour the sauce over the top. Heat in your chloroplast ovens for thirty minutes or until done."

The group was buzzing as everyone had comments for their neighbor about this recipe.

"Do you think I could substitute scrapings from skin cancer victims or maybe charred livers of cirrhosis victims if I can't find any Mongolian toes?" asked Ms. Avocado.

"Hass Avocado wants to know if she can substitute skin cancer scrapings instead of fried Mongolian toes? Does anyone have an opinion?" yelled Roma above all the noise and rustling.

Mr. Almond, one of many openly bisexual hermaphrodites in attendance, stated for the group that he much prefers the blanched lips of a young Hispanics over anything else. There were a lot of different feelings expressed over that opinion.

"What do hermaphrodites know about cooking?" spewed Ms. Sweet Cherry suffering from a postpartum funk. "I like the taste of female Spanish belly buttons or bloated belly-skin of Eastern Indian dancers. I think you can more easily substitute those," Ms. Cherry added with a smug but depressed whisper to her partners.

"Thank you all and thanks to you, Mr. Almond for your tasty additions. Now, if we can settle a bit longer, we have a special treat from Sir Bristlecone Pine. Bristlecone, the floor is yours," said Roma.

"Howdy," said the extremely old Sir Pine. It took a moment for him to untwist and raise a bit higher above the crowd so all could see and hear him. "I have altered my family's famous and until now, secret dessert recipe for you all. My family has been eating what we used to call, 'Fig Balls' for nearly four thousand years. But before I give you my humanarian version of the recipe, I'd first like to apologize to you all. I never considered that my delight in eating nuts and seeds for all those years was hurting so many of you in such a deeply personal way. It grieves me intensely to learn those were your infants. Ms. Spring Wheat, Mr. Black Walnut and Black Sesame, also Ms. Oat, Ms. Pinto Bean and especially to you Ms. Spanish Peanut—I ate your infants, by the cupful. I am heartsick about it. Maybe even more disrespectfully, I simply discarded to the trash all the infants of Ms. Fuji Apple, Ms. Butternut Squash and Hass Avocado, after devouring their fruit."

"And to the rest of you," continued Sir Pine, "you who suffered bodily wounds as I tore off and munched on your arms or unearthed your legs to boil and eat, I apologize. I even scraped some of your skin raw for nothing more than a simple splash of zest to enhance flavor. I consumed and tortured you and your loved ones for my own pleasure, I beg your deep forgiveness as I pledge to join all in adopting a humanarian lifestyle."

With that heart-felt plea for forgiveness, Sir Pine broke down and wept. Big drops of sticky sap ran down his branches and trunk trapping many exotic insect that had wandered too close to his flowing tears.

Everyone cheered and whipped their leaves and stalks in the energizing sunshine as a show of support for the ancient, wise Sir Bristlecone.

When he got a grip on himself, he settled the crowd and continued, “so, as penance, my altered secret recipe goes as follows,” said the ancient Pine, “take twenty-five deboned Indonesian babies and soak them in one-fourth cup of hot water. Mash the babies after they have soaked long enough to be fully moistened. Add in two tablespoons crushed and flaked French eyelids, which are soaked in the Italian saliva wine we learned about last week. Add one tablespoon crushed, dried bitter Caucasian penises, and one teaspoon of extract of sour Russian males. Roll the mixture into small balls and then roll each ball into a dusting of pounded and shredded Polynesian intestines for an amazing coating. You may want to dust each ball with dried mother’s milk glands for additional sweetness. Enjoy.”

And with that came a round of applause as the grand old Sir Bristlecone Pine relaxed and twisted back down to his tired weather-worn posture, sinking deeply back into earth’s rocking chair.

“Well what a fine meeting, what a fine meeting indeed,” said Roma as she and Mr. Boxwood standing next to her waved their stinky leaves in sync with the entire gratified crowd.

Pointing to the banner and slogan high up in Living Oak, Roma said, “Let’s all repeat our slogan and then we’ll adjourn until next week.”

And with that, all eyes turned to the banner and all shouted in unison, “Plants are not ours to experiment on, eat, wear, use for entertainment, or abuse in any other way. I pledge hence-forth to be a humanarian.”

With that, all left in no particular hurry, to assume their plots and to carry on their everyday lives as Earth’s living creatures who honor all types of plant life—no matter how big or small. Someone was heard to yell as the crowd dispersed, “I only eat things with faces!”

Red Maple helped Fuji Apple by supporting her heavily pregnant branches as they sauntered with entwined limbs back home exclaiming how wonderful so many have now pledged to protect all the living, breathing green families and neighbors with whom they share this wonderful blue speck of floating dust we call Earth.

G.H.O.S.T.S

Cheryl Zaidan

"Welcome to The Ghastly Hauntings of Spectral Transients Society."

These words were spoken by a tall, gaunt man in a top hat and black cloak. His thin lips twisted into a smile and his black eyes shifted back and forth as he surveyed the room. Most of the participants were seated in a circle, except for a few which were hovering around close by.

"We have a new member today," he gestured towards a young man with bright red hair and an earnest face who stood behind him. "Everyone say hello to Bob."

"Hello Bob." A chorus of voices greeted him although some of them simply moaned.

The man looked uncomfortable but nodded slightly in return. "Hello," he mumbled back. "It's nice to, uh, be here."

One of the members, a teenage boy, laughed. Another, a lady in period dress, just sat there looking as if she was about to cry. A little girl of about 5, came up to Bob. She was holding a red ball in her hands.

"Hi Bob. Wanna play?" The child's smile was sweet but there was something off about it. Her grin widened, exposing what looked to be an adult set of teeth inside of her small mouth. Bob smiled back uneasily and was about to reach for the ball, but he caught the eye of the teen boy who was on the other side of the room. The boy shook his head and mouthed the word "no."

"Maybe some other time, kiddo." Bob tried to pat her head but failed as his hand fell through.

"No one *ever* wants to play with me." The little girl wriggled her nose in mock disgust and skipped over to where the boy sat. She stuck out her tongue at him and he responded in turn.

"Cindy, we are nice to new people," the thin man scolded her. "Perhaps we should properly introduce ourselves. That was Cindy, she looks young but she's not really. I would say she's been around for about 150 years old or so. You've met me, I'm Edgar." He bowed slightly. "Who wants to go next? Victoria? How about you?"

The sad woman looked up at Bob with haunted gray eyes. She had stopped trying to stifle her sorrow and was instead weeping openly, occasionally pausing to dab her eyes with a lacy handkerchief she held to her bosom.

"On the night, my lover killed me…" she began. The teen boy rolled his eyes and groaned audibly.

"Not THIS again," he said. "We've heard the story."

"But *he* hasn't!" The woman's voice rose defensively, "*and* Edgar said I could speak!" She looked over at Bob, who attempted to make a sympathetic face back at her.

"Let her talk, it makes her feel better," Edgar admonished the boy who sighed somewhat dramatically and sat down.

"I was awaiting him on the balcony," the woman continued. She was no longer crying, but still had an unhappy, faraway look in her eyes. "We were to be wed the very next day. He was my everything. I had even forsaken my family to be with him. They didn't like him, you see. But I was headstrong and thought them wrong. If only I had listened." She paused again to suppress a sob.

"Blah blah blah," the boy interrupted, but the angular man shushed him one more. "Go on," Edgar urged, ignoring the boy's exaggerated eye rolls in his direction.

"He came to me that night—eyes wild. I thought it was perhaps because of the storm which had suddenly taken hold, or perhaps the passion we felt for one another. The wind felt like it was whipping us as I stood so close to the edge of that cliff. It was as if God himself was angry and about to strike down wrath upon our sins. I tried to wrap him in my embrace but his touch was cold, his eyes were frightening and then he..." The woman started weeping again uncontrollably. This was followed by an awkward silence as everyone in the room tried to stay respectfully quiet. Bob was staring at his shoes, uncertain of what to expect next.

"He had planned it all along. You see, I was not his only. There was another and she was with child. His child." She buried her face in the handkerchief once more.

"What did you do after you died?" The little girl asked innocently. The ball dropped from her hands and rolled toward the boy, who made no attempt to touch it.

"I made sure neither of them found peace," the woman continued. "Oh, I haunted them terribly. My face would appear when he was looking out a window. I would call his name softly in the same voice I used to use when I thought he was my faithful lover. Eventually he was driven to madness and killed both he and his wife."

Bob shivered. The boy looked a little upset. "I didn't know THAT part," he mumbled.

"What happened to the child?" Edgar inquired.

"The baby, a boy, survived. It was naught but an infant when the brute took their lives. The boy was raised by the woman's aunt and led a long, fruitful life. I dared not do anything to harm a child!" Her voice was defensive although no one seemed to be openly accusing her of anything. However, a few members looked on with disapproving eyes.

"Served the bastard right." The boy kicked the ball back to the little girl, who picked it up and sat down cross-legged on the floor. "Glad the kid was okay."

"Thank you very much Victoria." Edgar waved one long thin arm in her direction as he spoke. "Ricky, since you seem so keen to talk during this session, tell us what you've been up to."

The boy looked up. "Nothing much. I'm not going to tell my damn story again."

"Nobody's asking you to," The tall man responded, not unkindly. "Just tell us what you've been doing."

"Haunting. Stealing keys and stuff."

"Where?"

"Oh, just this house—total goody two-shoes family in the middle of a normal street. Been freaking the heck out of the Mom. One time I sort of let myself appear to her in the basement. She dropped the laundry basket and ran screaming up the stairs, then she tripped over the dog and did a full face plant." The boy snorted. "It was really funny."

"That sounds dreadful!" exclaimed Victoria who had ceased her sobbing, at least for the moment.

"More dreadful than murder-suicide?" A thin pinched-faced woman who was seated off to the side spoke for the first time, arching one eyebrow accusingly as she did so. Victoria fell silent and looked at her feet.

"Now, now," Edgar walked quietly into the middle of the circle. "There's no judgment here. Also, there are no limits as to *how* you haunt or *why*. Just tell us what you're doing. Let's do a round robin, okay?"

Some of the ghosts nodded, a few just stared, and the pinched lady let out an audible sigh.

"Okay Ursula," Edgar continued as he nodded towards the thin woman. "What have you been doing?"

"Misplacing books and scaring the college students in the basement library late at night." She crossed her arms. A satisfied smile framed her wan features.

A few other ghosts spoke. There was the bespectacled man in a bowtie with a clipped British accent who appeared to only one person, so his flatmates wouldn't believe him. An elderly gentleman in a prim waistcoat and cravat noted how he refused to leave the house he had been born in, raised in, gotten married in, and died in and how several mediums were rude to suggest he do so. A priest with a cheery attitude and bifocal glasses gave sermons to a church in the middle of the night after most of the people had departed. Bob listened intently to them all, but there was one burning question in his mind.

"Hey," he whispered to Ricky who had floated over to where he stood.

"What's up with the little girl?"

"Don't mess with her if you know what's good for you," Ricky spoke a little too loudly. Edgar cleared his throat and glared over at him.

Bob waited a few minutes then leaned forward casually towards Ricky. A striking blonde woman was talking about her death by poison as though she was discussing taking a coat to the cleaners.

"She's not a normal ghost," Ricky spoke softly this time.

"What is she?"

"A demon."

"Are you kidding?" Bob's face showed a great deal of worry.

"Nope." Ricky removed his cap, scratched at his tousled hair and threw it back on his head. "Just talk to her and see." The blonde woman was still speaking but her story seemed endless, so Bob beckoned towards the little girl who came to him immediately with the ball in hand, smiling widely.

"Can I see the ball?" He asked quietly.

The girl licked her lips. Two thin tongues darted out, each had a notch in it like a snake and her eyes began to glow a deep crimson. Edgar grabbed both her shoulders roughly, pushing her back quickly before Bob had time to react.

"Ricky was this your doing?" Edgar raised his eyebrows quizzically at the boy who looked away, trying not to snicker. Cindy held her ball tightly in her hands, her small mouth frowning in disappointment as she sulked away to a corner of the room, wafting through several members as she made her way back. No one made any attempt to stop her.

"Hey, he wanted to see what she was," Ricky was practically choking back the laughter as he saw Bob's face which was even paler than it had been before.

"Well just for that young man, you'll be the one to take Bob out on his first haunting. I trust you can come up with something not so…traumatizing I suppose." Edgar glared at Ricky who hadn't stopped grinning.

"Yeah I guess. Hey Bob," he turned towards the red-headed man. "Who do you wanna haunt first?"

Bob sighed. "Well I guess haunting my ex-girlfriend might be kind of fun." He shrugged nonchalantly.

"Good. C'mon let's go." He patted the man's shoulder lightly. "Um, do you know what time she takes her shower?"

Bob frowned slightly. "No, why?"

"I have an idea." The two departed from the room, the rest of the members watched them as they left.

"Well, that's over with now." Edgar clasped his hand briskly. "Cindy my dear girl, tell us what happened during your last exorcism."

Cindy grinned and waggled her double tongues and threw the ball at him.

A Drink of Water

Wol-vriey

It was mid-evening, the sun half-eaten by the horizon. Above that realm of sunset orange, the sky was a cold metallic gray, the color of a knife's blade.

Heading vaguely east, Jude staggered across the dusty Utah prairie. With slow, calculated paces, he inched his painful way along. About him the sparse prairie grass danced in a desolate breeze.

Jude was very thirsty. But somehow, there were no cacti anywhere in sight.

In addition to being thirsty, Jude was badly wounded. He had three bullet holes in him. The one bothering him the most was the one just under his navel and a bit to the left. *That shot definitely hit something vital,* he figured. *It feels like I've got a brave's spear stuck inside me*. He reconsidered, the wound couldn't be as bad as he'd thought. He'd made it this far, hadn't he?

But the darn thing burnt like someone was twisting a poker in his gut. A sudden stab of agony made him glance down at his belly; he almost expected to see his intestines hanging out, but no, it was the same as before: a sticky red patch all over the front of his shirt with the red seeping down to his crotch and pants.

His other two wounds—one in his left shoulder, the second just beneath his right ribs—were more an of inconvenience than anything else.

But the one in his *belly? Ouch.* And, oh, the darn, godforsaken thirst. Where the hell had all the cacti run off to?

A Drink of Water

He was *so* thirsty. He'd do anything for a cool beer now. Okay, even a warm beer would be fine. Water would be good too.

Jude was certain he was lost. By his fuddled reckoning he should have hit a creek or stream ages ago; this part of south-eastern Utah was rife with tributaries of the Colorado River. But no, there were none, like all the rivers and creeks had vanished, or were purposely avoiding him. Damn, he'd not even seen a mirage. Now you *knew* you were in deep shit when you couldn't even find an illusion to tantalize you.

He stumbled and lost his balance. For a moment the dusty earth approached and receded as his eyes lost focus, then he got his legs under him again.

He stood bent over, gripping his sides, wincing as he felt a thin dribble of blood spill from his punctured belly. That was the real danger, he knew—dying of blood loss. He needed a doctor, and fast. Which meant he needed a town. But getting to a town quickly would require a horse, and he'd lost his.

No, he'd not lost it. Butch Higgins had taken it. The son-of-a-bitch.

A flock of shadows made Jude pause. Shielding his eyes against the sun—he'd lost his hat four miles ago—he gazed up at the expectant buzzards. No way to scare them off; Butch Higgins had taken his guns too.

So instead, Jude gave the scavengers the finger. "Screw you lot. I ain't 'bout dying out here. Go find someone else to eat!"

The birds kept circling him though. Taking their insistence on hanging around as confirmation of how much on his last legs he seemed, Jude resumed his dogged trudge across the sunburnt land.

While placing foot ahead of foot, he thought grimly back on how he'd gotten shot.

-A-

Butch Higgins was big and ugly. He was also strong as an ox which, in addition to the fact that they were cousins, was why Jude had called him in on the job.

Butch had first sniggered. "A sack of injun gold laying about in the Abajo Mountains? You sure 'bout this, Jude?"

"Lower your goddam voice!" Jude glanced uneasily around the Red Devil Saloon. None of the other drinkers seemed to have heard Butch's outburst. “Yeah, it’s there, alright. All we need to do is ride in, the two of us, dig it up, and get out.”

Butch looked suspicious. “Why just we two?”

“‘Cos we need to stay hidden, that’s why. The larger the party, the more likely it’ll be spotted. There’s a Navajo village nearby. They’re friendly, but… it’s *their* missing ancestral gold we’ll be digging up, see? They ain’t gonna take kindly to us palefaces carrying it off.”

Butch sipped his beer and looked thoughtful. “They don’t know it’s buried up there?”

“No they don’t. Look, Butch, the gold’s there. Now which is it, you want in on this or do I find someone else?”

The ugly grin that split his cousin’s ugly face was answer enough.

Riding down south from Moab, it took them two days to reach the Abajo Mountains. That night they climbed up to the cave and dug up the gold. It was as easy as Jude had hoped it would be.

“Damn Navajos’ll never know we stopped by,” Butch said, his eyes gleaming a greedy green in their torches’ flicker as the heavy coins streamed through his fingers. There was also some gold jewelry in the money sack: rings, necklaces, and earrings.

Jude had been pleased. They’d descended back the way they’d come, while the moon spotlighted the Navajo village below.

Their luck held. Riding all night, by the time the sun cleared the eastern mountaintops, they’d put a good distance between them and any possible pursuit.

Jude could finally relax. Then he turned in his saddle and saw Butch pointing his six-shooter at him.

“I’se think it’s time we both went our separate ways,” Butch drawled. “Me, I’m taking all this Injun gold and heading east for Memphis.” He laughed. “While’se you, Jude, is taking a real short trip down to Hell.”

Jude went for his gun. Butch shot him thrice, grinning as Jude toppled out of the saddle. He dismounted and shot his own horse, a black mare, while Jude writhed in pain on the ground. Butch Higgins took Jude’s white stallion—he’d been eyeing it ever since they’d set out—and rode off across the plains on it.

A Drink of Water

Butch had made a point of not killing Jude. Not because he was against murder, but because he wanted the buzzards and coyotes to finish the job for him.

-ᘛAᘚ-

The buzzards circled lower over Jude. Jude though, was less concerned about them now; up ahead he could see a long line of trees which meant there was water nearby, likely a stream of some sort.

That hope reinvigorated him. His steps picked up strength, till the circling carrion birds realized he wasn't about dying just yet. Still, not to be outdone, the buzzards flew ahead of Jude and perched in the tree branches, just in case he did croak.

Jude trudged on. Soon, he could hear gurgling water. Which river was this? He had no idea. In any event, it would do to slake his thirst.

Jude walked in between the trees. Through their levels of overlapping leaves he saw the river now, a fat silver line that reflected the falling evening sun.

One of the adamant buzzards dropped a turd close by his head.

With water so close now, Jude's injuries were temporarily relegated to insignificance. Sure, he might bleed to death, but he'd drink his fill first.

Just about to part the last branches and step down to the riverbank, Jude saw his horse. The white stallion was twenty yards to his right, tethered just inside the line of trees.

Jude was instantly alert. His priorities inverted: the pain of his wounds returned, his great thirst was shoved to the rear of his mind. He looked left and right, wondering where the hell Butch was.

The white horse sensed Jude; it looked around and neighed in his direction. Jude winced; Butch must have ridden the stallion extra hard, spurring it violently. Its right side was ripped open, its metal ribs showing through tatters of bloody skin. Maybe Butch had had to dodge some Indians after abandoning Jude; that would also explain Jude catching up with him here.

Then he saw Butch. Butch wasn't alone, however. He was lying on his back on a flat dusty rock up on the riverbank, his head in a naked woman's lap. The woman's flaming red hair hung down to her waist. The sack of recovered gold lay beside them, half covered by Butch's discarded hat.

While making his silent way through the trees towards the pair, Jude pondered the woman's presence at the riverside. He first thought that maybe Butch had ridden ahead into a nearby town and picked up a whore…but why bring a prostitute out here, when there were soft beds in every bordello, or…had he met her by the river? And anyway, where were her clothes?

Jude put that aside. He'd just realized that with Butch's face completely shielded from view by the woman's paint-pale back, there was no chance of his cousin noticing him approach. He'd get to his horse—he was certain Butch had left his guns with it—shoot the damn backstabber in the back, take the gold and ride off. He'd give the woman a lift back to her town too. If she *was* for sale, he'd maybe buy her comforts for himself. Once he'd been patched up, that was.

Once close enough to the couple to see better, and by now his thirst was back redoubled, Jude got a proper look at the woman by the river.

She had no legs. She was fish from the waist down. Her scaly green tail flopped off the rock into the river.

A mermaid? What the hell?

The mermaid was stroking Butch's head and saying something that Jude missed. Butch sat up then, a dreamy look on his face, and rummaged in the sack, after a while coming up with a gold necklace—the fish-woman already had several gold rings on her fingers. Grinning, he arranged the necklace around her neck, letting its oval pendant dangle between the bare cones of her breasts.

"So what'cha think, hon? D'ya like it? I got several more." He settled his head back down on her scaly lap again. Jude, meanwhile, was wondering why Butch sounded like he was drunk with no evidence of alcohol about.

"Oh, it's real purdy, darlin'" the mermaid drawled. Then, next thing, she grabbed up a massive rock and smashed it down on Butch's head.

Jude winced. The impact had sounded like someone shattering a coconut.

Blood began squirting out of Butch's head in all directions, splattering both the rock and the mermaid, while Butch released an oddly prolonged groan of pain, like he wanted to scream but didn't remember how to.

His thrashing legs kicked the sack of gold off the bank and into the river.

The mermaid calmly raised the rock and struck Butch again. Butch twitched a bit more, then fell silent.

The mermaid adjusted her position on the rock slightly—this let Jude see her better: she was pretty, but had blood-red eyes. Like someone stripping an orange, she began peeling the chunks of cracked skull off Butch's head and dropping them beside her on the rock.

Once she'd cleared off a wide enough patch of skull, she dug a hand into Butch's head and scooped out a handful of his reddened brains.

She raised the brains to her nose, smelt them, then ate them. She chewed and swallowed. She grinned broadly, then scooped another handful of brains out of Butch's head and ate those too and grinned even broader.

Jude found it hard to classify her expression while she fed as evil—there was something disarming about it: an almost childlike innocence.

"Aw, yes, mama was right—human brains is jes so darn tasty," she said, licking her lips. The fading day glinted off her tail scales.

Watching the mermaid eat, Jude decided he wasn't about drinking water here. As a last resort to quench his thirst, he searched the horse's saddlebags for a canteen. There was none, which first struck him as odd. Then he understood what had happened. Clearly, Butch had only stopped here for a drink of water… and had met the mermaid.

He winced. With Butch booting their gold into the river, the entire expedition had been for nothing. No way was Jude entering the river with the mermaid nearby. The only remaining parts of their haul on land were the blood-stained necklace now dangling around the feeding mermaid's neck and the rings on her fingers. True, those might fetch some good money, but all shot up like he was, Jude didn't feel up to disputing the fish-woman's claim to the jewelry.

He was alive, though, and more important, he'd gotten his horse back. He looked the animal over, wondering what kind of trouble Butch had gotten into to use the horse so hard: in addition to its exposed metal ribs, it was leaking oil.

He shrugged, it would still go; the damage wasn't anything a blacksmith couldn't easily fix.

Wincing with pain, Jude swung himself up into the horse's saddle and rode off through the trees. He decided to simply trace this river till he reached either the Colorado River or the nearest town, whichever came first.

He sensed the mermaid peering inquisitively in his direction and looked back once, just in time to see her turn her gaze away from the trees and dip her hand into Butch's shattered head again. She raised another handful of brains to her mouth.

Jude laughed coldly. "So long, cousin. Looks like *you're* the one making the short trip down to Hell. Me? It sure don't look like I'll be dyin' today."

Out of the fringe of trees, he spurred the white stallion, making it go faster. The sooner he saw a doctor the better.

And besides, Jude didn't want the damn buzzards following him again. They made for depressing traveling companions. At the moment, the birds seemed happy enough waiting for the mermaid's leftovers.

Metal Grrrls

Jocelyn E. Marshall

New, Fantastically Fierce Frontwoman!

The large, bold text caught me and lead to an article detailing GWAR's newly-appointed lead-vocalist. It was as if the Metal Gods lowered the four words down from their mountaintop to me and other lady metalheads. Wrapping around our bodies and soothing the senses of longing, we hurled back approving growls. These howls carved smiles into the normally stoic, obsidian rock faces, and the Metal Gods harmonized and formed the long-awaited Scumdog. It appeared as if the Gods answered our Metal-Grrrl prayers. It appeared as if they had provided the magnificent, "Fantastically Fierce" Vulvatron as a signal for us to come seek refuge in her expansive bust line. It did not appear to be an announcement that would later be revised, and even later a position completely withdrawn.

With that announcement, we glanced at the new Scumdog, an overdue gift from the Gods, and felt a tingling in our own personal vulvatrons. A sunbeam lit up center stage, illuminated Vulvatron's two gigantic, space-cyborg tits, and highlighted a volcanic eruption of blood from each nipple. Typically, such an eruption would warrant medical attention; but then, those oozing areolas streamed hope, screamed "look at what's possible!" to other busted-creatures of the Universe, and seemed to be equal to Scumdogs Beefcake or Balsac. That beautiful birth, all captured in one headshot-headline pairing, and those bleeding nipples were droplets leaking into "frontwomanhood."

A couple of days after the news broke, "frontwoman" disappeared from the headlines and was revised to "female vocalist," "co-vocalist," and "unlikely new vocalist" with the hiring of singer Blóthar. That single sunbeam illuminating the prosthetic Areolas for Equality faded away—dimming those bloody streams of hope. Vulvatron retracted into the background, and us Metal Grrrls followed her away from center stage.

The revised headlines continue to sting when we watched the new Scumdog's introduction in a Spokane, WA performance. After fighting and defeating Techno Destructo—pulling cords from his tank-filled cyborg backpack, humping his left shoulder as he crouched down in pain, and finally snatching the microphone from his resistant fist, Vulvatron triumphantly walked to front-center stage and greeted her Bohabs. With legs straight and feet together, pushing out her exposed butt cheeks into symmetrical, meaty rounds, and back long and stiff, she commanded attention. Gazing out onto her congregation through a veil of black face paint and spreading out arms to welcome all, she preached, "Look on me and this band. I am your salvation and your doom. I am Vulvatron." At that moment, the Metal Gods seemed to be offering a gigantically-breasted Savior for the followers that mostly resemble her. Strong and in front, Vulvatron appeared to be leading a march toward progress. She headbanged, rhythmically rotating her hips, joined the guitarist in air strumming a power ballad, and then vocals began. Male vocals began.

As his round, hairy figure promised, Blóthar boomed the opening lines:

Tor
Tormentor
Born into the fog of war

With each pause, the antlers sprouting from his mask briefly shook as lungs quickly refilled. Assuming center-stage, Blóthar was framed by the two guitarists, and his wide, alien form blocked the drummer while the battle with Techno Destructo played out in the background. Then, like a dim light in a large, dark room, a faint high-pitched *It left a scar* squealed out of the invisible Vulvatron and into the domineering base line. Resuming his position, Blóthar illuminated further,

He watched his family turn to sludge

He was appalled

Again, lightly elaborating, the next lines

They often are were meekly added. The lyrical volley continued, and each pass of the ball resembled another "correct" headline:

"Co-vocalist!"

"30% lyricist?"

"Co-front man!"

"25%-visible body?"

But maybe we have read too much into the Metal Gods' gift. Maybe there are other frontwomen to look up to that have been missed. Distracted by a longhaired, rhinestone-studded figure, we all turned to another stage.

Lead singers of Pretty Reckless, In This Moment, and Epica stand tall in unison, forming a row of dolls on the well-lit shelf. With breasts protruding almost as far as Vulvatron's do from her Scumdog garb, one Sexy Rocker coyly assumes center stage. Batting her unnaturally long eyelashes, tracing her latex-wrapped curves with long, acrylic nails, the Joan Jett siren cries out:

It's a fucked up world

What do you get from it?

She tilts her head to the side for a moment, streaming a trail of blond extensions across her chest, hair falling forward over her face and microphone.

She answers, *Sex and love and guns, light a cigarette.*

We howl with approval, and suddenly the musical airwaves filter into mere white noise. Captivated by Sexy's pouty lips curling around each syllable, our gazes are met with lustful, half-open eyelids. In unison, all of us look to our left, right, and behind to see whose gaze Sexy is actually addressing: the left reveals a teenage boy, worshipping Sexy's decision to straddle the amplifier in front of his face. The right discloses an adult male devotee re-imagining Sexy's performance in a more personal setting. The metal member behind showcases a Sexy Mini-Her, with a satin corset offering up her chest to the Metal Gods, or perhaps to Sexy, or perhaps to both. The music fades back in.

With a high-pitched, yet rough, whiney howl, the Sexy Rocker doll croons:

Is it sick to make

You beg the way I do...

Is it sick to say

I want you biting down on me

Amidst the male howls, we look down at our own T-shirt covered breasts, our latex-lacking pants, and our flat skate shoes.

"Do we belong here?"

"Will the Metal Gods cast us aside soon?"

Then, with one exhalation the Metal Gods produce a new singer. An '80s metal voice rings throughout the venue, and Jada Koren's strong form rises from the Gods' cloud of debris.

"I love your pain and how it makes me feel inside."

"I love your pain and how it opens you so wide."

"And I love the way you bleed all over me, all over me."

"I crave your pain and how it soaks me in."

"I crave your pain cause I'm its only friend."

Us metal heads sing along, with legs and arms mimicking Jada's intense, committed posture. We lock eyes and passionately harmonize:

And I love the way you feed my hungers, my hunger, my greed

And I love the way you bleed all over me, all over me

As the song ends, smoke clears further, and Will Smith is revealed at the stage's right side. His gold suit and throne of Benjamin's dominate the congregation's attention. Looking at the celebrity shadow, looking at the quick rise in playing as Ozzfest's newest band, the crowd becomes skeptical:

This song is predictable, and Jada is essentially yelling these lyrics.

Wicked Wisdom's tunes are basically average and sometimes overly formulaic, but all are tolerable.

Four words: average, musicianship, boring, power-chords.

They aren't terrible, but their music doesn't warrant repeated listens.

-A-

Disrupting our doubt, a low growl emerges—shaking the rock faces and floor of the venue. Pieces of the Metal Gods slide down into a black, jagged pile. With another tremor sending the obsidian rubble flying, Otep Shamaya arises from the rocky birth canal, microphone in hand, and steps onto the Pittsburgh stage. With her bandmates creating a slow, deep rhythm, she reminds us of their new record and teases with, "Would you guys like to hear a song that's just fuckin' chock-full of inappropriate content?"

Our own vulvatrons begin pulsating, and we respond with a collective howl.

-ᔕA∂-

Otep raises her fist in the air, and all of us mirror her actions as a tide of uplifting confidence swells inside our bodies. Recalling the *YouTube* removal of the video for "violence and suggestive same-sex content," we smile cheekily at one another—the song's controversy being linked to "out lesbian" headlines and Otep's *After Ellen* interview.

"What brought you into metal?"

"Aggression, that's it."

The interviewer must've paused, as one does when asking a question that is meant to allude to a different one, and Otep must've read into that pause, too, as she added.

-ᔕA∂-

"It didn't cross my mind that I'm a lesbian and there were no other lesbians around me—"

"—That are out," the interviewer corrected.

"Why should I hide anything? So far I've only had a few people who seem to have a problem with me being here. Mostly because I'm a woman, and I guess I'm the antithesis of what they embrace as what a woman is. Like, you know, tits and ass. The sexuality of what I do is not even a part of it. If there is anything in there that people can see as erotic, it's not anything overt. Everyone needs an enemy, and all too often it's us."

The Metal Grrrls and I flashback to Sexy Rocker, and then look at Otep's tattooed, muscular arms emerging from her black, cut-off T-shirt. We take note of her concealed chest in comparison to Vulvatron's gigantic, bloody tits, and observe her baggy jeans in contrast to Sexy's tight leather pants. For us, the phrase "Mostly because I'm a woman" echoes around the venue, and

Vuvlatron's Areolas for Equality seem to shrink in size. The droplets of blood that once oozed freely dry up into crusty red caps over her nipples.

-A-

Looking back at the stage, we sing along to Apex Predator and revel in the song "Chocked Full of Inappropriate Content." As it finishes, we're reminded Otep is leaving the band and her music career altogether. She claims, "I feel I've done all that I can as a musician at the moment. I may return to music one day, but for now I'm proud of what I've done and am ready to move on."

-A-

We wait for the lights to dim, look up to the Metal Gods, and pray for more. Sensing our unhappiness, the Metal Gods inhale deeply. Holding their breath, they sway to the left, sway to the right, and exhale with a strong roar. Their faces vibrate, sending shockwaves throughout the, amd debris floats down to the stage. Exerting one more roar, the Metal Gods cause the debris to swirl upward and mold into a female form. She starts to head bang, gets into a lunge position, and lets out a deep growl.

"Is that a dude?" the congregation questions. Band members walk in from behind her, loudly playing their instruments in congruence, and we all chime in to the lyrics:

So rise my spirit rise!
Revel in this dead man's body
Grip his soul, sip the blood . . .
I will be god

Looking on with adoration, we match Angela Gossow's headbanging, and our sprits are lifted. One song turns into five, one hour seems like thirteen years, and eventually Angela appears weary. She stands at center stage and provides a confession similar to Otep's,

"I have to turn a page. I have to enter a different phase in my life."

Bewildered, all metal members look around and wonder, "Who will take her place?"

We secretly send out a prayer to the Metal Gods and ask, "If not her, or Otep, or Vulvatron, who will be our Savior?"

-ᴥAᴥ-

Angela raises the microphone and waves it over the crowd from side-to-side as if it were a forked stick guiding her to water. The crowd looks on to her strong shoulder to her elbow to her clenching hand to the end of the microphone resting in front of a blue-haired woman. She looks up to Angela, and they both begin to growl. The stage shakes as they hold the note, and Angela beckons Alissa White-Gluz to step forward. Once on stage, Angela places the microphone in Alissa's hands and disappears into the masses. Tightly holding the microphone, Alissa begins:

It's times like these
When lines are drawn
Which side of the fence
Are you standing on?

Unimpressed and skeptical, a Metal Boi approaches guitarist Michael Amott and whispers "Have you thought about bringing a guy in to sing?"

He laughs and responds, "Or a transsexual? We're an equal opportunity kind of band. But, really, Angela has chosen Alissa, who is a great singer."

We applaud and hurl howls of approval as Alissa continues growling.

-ᴥAᴥ-

Inspired by the lyrics, or her power stance, or a combination of both, all of us begin circling into a mosh pit. Springing around on the balls of our feet with arms whipping by our sides, we move to the song's rhythm. Gazing up at Alissa, we listen:

They try to change you
Crush and break you
Try to tell you what to do
They'd like to have control of you…
Remember who you are
This is fucking war!

We yell back, "This is fucking war!" and male fans appear alarmed. The high-pitched voices shake walls, and the Metal Gods laugh as vagina-lacking followers appear bewildered. Eventually, Alissa and Arch Enemy finish their set and fade into the background. Eyeing the empty stage, looking up at the Metal Gods, we repeat, *They'd like to have control of you…Remember who you are.*

-∞A∞-

We wonder who we are. We look back to the doll shelf, back to the celebrity wife, to the lesbian, back to the growler, and then back to ourselves.

"Which are we?"

"Which can we be?"

-∞A∞-

With ears still ringing and hearts heavy, we find Jamey Jasta, lead singer of Hatebreed, speaking in a *Metalship* interview. Towards the end of the discussion, the interviewer asks,

"What do you think about metal being a male dominated industry?"

Without any hesitation, Jamey asserts "That's a misconception! The last two tours we outsold guy shirts with girl shirts!"

The two brief sentences, additional stab wounds for the Metal Grrrls listening, let us wonder, *So that's what we are? Numbers of shirts sold?*

Jamey continues, "In the late '90s, it was so male dominated, but from 2002 to 2003 onward there have been a lot of women. We've even toured with bands with female members over the last few years, from Otep to Arch Enemy."

Unsatisfied, we sarcastically question the TV, "So, because these limited anomalies exist, male domination doesn't?"

He responds by generalizing, "Metal is just a welcoming thing, and women gravitate toward metal and harder music now because it's not just boys' fun anymore. People are more open-minded now, and it's not as threatening as it once was."

His final words are cherries on top of the sweet knife carving into our chests: "I actually think Dave Matthews concerts are more threatening. A security guard once told me he had more women assaulted at a Dave concert than at our Mayhem Fest, so there you go."

Together, we spit back headlines: "Dave, the front *man*." "Dave, the *lead* vocalist."

-~A~-

As others doze off, I re-watch the Spokane, WA performance. Perched on the edge of my couch, leaning into the computer screen, giggling with anticipation, I look out to Vulvatron taking center stage again, commanding full attention with her iron-straight posture and arms outstretched. Voice low and steady, she calmly booms,

I am your salvation, and your doom. I am Vulvatron.

The lights cut.

A glowing ooze of jumbled letters streams down her shaded frame, sliding over ears, in-between breasts, over hips, repeatedly spelling out in waves,

"Merely female, just a co-, so unlikely."

Within minutes, the glow fades, letters stop moving, and a defeated woman greets me from the screen.

Recluse

Justin Zipprich

I started collecting enemies when I was just six years old. It was at this age that the first of a long chain of awful and disappointing events would occur, shaping me into the disturbed soul that I am today. Though I call them secrets, the disappointments are well known to the individuals who perpetrated them, although to these people, what they have done to me is probably nothing but business as usual for them. I call these events secrets because, although I have been hurt time after time, I have never let these actions affect my outward demeanor. Instead, all the bad experiences lay dormant inside of me, year after year, stewing within until today. I have finally had enough. Today I will get my revenge on all those who have done me wrong.

Here I find myself ready to take matters into my own hands. The setting is an old, dirty, rent by the hour hotel room. The walls yellowed from stale smoke, the carpets filthy and the drapes tattered. Obviously not intended for wealthy clients, the room consists of only a worn leather chair, an old decrepit dresser and a stained mattress covered with an off-white bedspread, probably newest thing in the room. Unfortunately, you can't simply dress up a turd. Fortunately, I am not in this room to sleep, I should be out within an hour. I am here to do a job and then fade into the background, a place I have become very comfortable with.

So here I sit, next to a small window, the only one in the room. The gun that I hold is aimed at the entrance of the barbershop across the street. My weapon of choice, an AR-15 semi-automatic rifle, bought from a local gun shop under completely legal means. After all, who was to suspect a quiet man like myself would ever have a hidden agenda since I have kept my anger against those who had treated me unfairly to myself. I was patient through the waiting period, confident that the background check would not register any red flags, and was finally awarded the possession that would right all the wrongs. I like this rifle for I have spent many hours admiring it. The black smooth aluminum alloy, the very clear and precise optical sight, and the perfectly distributed weight as I hold it in up against my shoulder; it all feels so right. I hold the gun in the ready position, the bulk of its weight resting on the window's sill, the sight trained, the crosshairs eagerly awaiting their first victim. Soon the front door will open, my target will appear and with one pull of the trigger their life will end. Until then my target lives a perfectly happy existence, without a thought in their mind that this will be the last day of their turn in this miserable experience called life.

The plan is simple, get justice for my many years of abuse by taking the lives of all who have hurt, ignored and treated me like trash and then disregarded their actions like I was just that, garbage thrown out a car window or tossed on the street without a second thought. I had never thought of myself to be a violent person, never hurting a soul but instead always insisting on treating every person I meet with a level of respect that was never returned. I would be kidding myself if I said that murdering my first victim would be an easy task. I am nervous as hell, constantly going over the ramifications of this terrible act over and over in my head. If I do indeed go through with this, it is an inevitable fact that I will eventually be caught, tried, found guilty and possibly given the death penalty. Obviously the thought of being locked in jail for the rest of my life is a frightening image, many terrible things will happen to a person like me in prison, possibilities that I don't even want to imagine. However, getting caught does hold a couple of advantages.

In the opportunity of a trial, I would finally get a chance to tell the world why I had taken so many seemingly innocent lives. It would be then that my wrong doers who were lucky enough to survive will finally acknowledge me, remembering the terrible things they put me through and then realizing that they were no better than the murderer they see before them but instead much worse. The guilt would eat at them until they eventually took their own lives, doing my handy work for me. Those who would not survive the massacre will surely have families who would mourn their losses until they realized the terrible people that their friends and family members had been. The whole country would finally realize that I was a real person, a person who dealt with a lifetime of pain perpetrated by others. After forty years, the world would finally realize that I existed.

The other reason that prison does not seem too terrible is that my entire life I have already lived inside of my own private prison. A prison that contained only one cell that held only one occupant, myself. My entire life has been lived in the shadows. To the rest of the world I am but a ghost, so transparent that when walking down the street, passersby's will glance in my direction, seeing through me as if I do not exist.

It's not like I've really tried to keep a high profile, until this recent endeavor, I have worked as an accountant in a small insurance firm. To most it's a mundane profession, working in a windowless corner office where I was rarely visited or even acknowledged. I work my eight hours and then leave the office, usually with my head down, fully knowing that no one ever say goodbye. When I get home I sit in front of the television, rarely paying attention to the program playing on the screen, a cold microwave dinner on a tray table before me. I live alone with no roommates, no spouse, not even a pet, just me, myself, and my thoughts.

It was about a month ago, late at night, when I deviated from my usual routine and focused on what was playing on the screen. It was a show about the history of serial killers from Jeffrey Dahmer to the car trunk snipers in Washington State. I found myself glued to the television. The program was an overview of their crimes, as well as how they were eventually caught. While watching, I couldn't help but feel a kinship with these monsters. They had realized that the human race was but a stain on this planet. They understood that most people were mindless slugs, going through life without a care in the world, and intent on living their own lives while disregarding all others around them. The scum came in all shapes and sizes. From CEO's who would lay off half their company just to make an extra million bucks to state senators who would strip the rights of one group just to appease another more ignorant group, this behavior even funneled down to the everyday working man who was out only for himself, his actions more important than that of everyone else. The majority of people, the rest of the world, deserved nothing as long as they got what they needed.

Dahmer, the Unabomber, all of them, they knew the truth. They understood that most people needed to be wiped off of the earth. Room needed to be made for the freethinkers, those who could see the truth of this world for what it really was. The ignorant would never understand what I know, that most people deserved to be slaughtered.

That was all the evidence I needed. I bought my gun, made my list and chose a date to exterminate the first of many who have done me wrong, finally dying for their sins. The person inside the barbershop is number one. The individual most deserving of my wrath, for they have put me in harm's way more than anyone else. I planned my first victim very carefully. I watched them, learned their schedule and tied up all the loose ends. Just a few minutes ago, I watched my victim though my scope as they went into the shop. I know it could be at least an hour until they open that door, fall into my sight and are taken out. That's okay, I can wait, I've become very good at waiting. As I sit here, staring through the sight, my finger massaging the trigger, I can't help but think about the list that I have composed and all the individuals who had made the cut.

The first secret disappointment of my life was also my first memory. I was a boy of six looking out the front window of my childhood home as I watched my dad shove his suitcase into the trunk of the family car. He was leaving my mother, claiming that he couldn't stand life with her anymore. He had found another woman who truly understood him, and he was going far away to live with her. He promised to send money but vowed to never return. I could never understand it, probably never will. I thought then and still think that my mother is a great woman. She was beautiful even back then, blond curly hair, blue eyes and a wonderful smile that never seemed to leave her face, at least until that day. She embraced me as we watched my dad drive away into the sunset, trying with little success to hide her tears.

After that day, life became much more difficult. Had I known that my father leaving would be just the first of many disappointments that would come my way; I would have run into the middle of traffic. But alas, there was no way I could know. My mother tried her best to support us both, working for little money at a local factory, coming home exhausted while still trying to maintain that smile. We had very little and after a while we had to move out of our home and into what can only be considered as a shack in the violent, shady part of town. With most of my mother's paycheck going toward rent, we had very little to eat. Our clothes were moth-ridden and our lives generally miserable. My father's departure had left us almost penniless and barely able to survive and he has truly earned his place as the second name on my list.

Of course, being the poor kid in school made me the prime target for bullying. My main rival was a tall chubby kid by the name of Marcus Fisher who made it his mission in life to ruin mine. I was a skinny kid with no hope of defending myself and that was fine when the tormenting focused mostly on name-calling. Inevitably, the bullies soon grew tired of insults and moved on to physical abuse, pushing and shoving me in the halls of school at every chance they got. This trend continued until high school where one evening, while I was walking home, Marcus decided to kick it up a notch. I was walking through the middle of town when he and his friends pulled up in his red mustang. Until this point, my main defensive move was to ignore the torture and try to walk away. Unfortunately, even an animal like Marcus caught on. The car doors flew open as the group ran to me and began verbally assaulting me. I tried to get around them, but they had me cornered, stepping in front of me in every direction. The rest of the episode is a blur. I can only remember snippets. I can recall them surrounding me then being knocked to the ground, followed by flashes of sneakers and fists pummeling me, as I lay there defenseless on the cold sidewalk.

The next thing that I can clearly remember is waking up in a hospital bed, a nurse revealing my grocery list of injuries: five broken ribs, two black eyes, a fractured arm, my nose crushed to a pulp and the remainder of my body covered with bruises. My mother tried desperately to find out the name of the guilty party, but I maintained ignorance and Marcus was never found out. He would go unpunished for twenty-five years, until now. Marcus Fisher is number three on the list.

Not willing to let my financial situation keep me down, I was able to secure a student loan and enroll in accounting classes at the local community college. I had always considered myself a smart kid, which helped me to excel in this higher realm of learning. I was able to grasp basic accounting skills quickly, moving quickly through the material with little distraction. That is until I saw her sitting at the front of the class. She was the most beautiful woman I'd ever seen. Her name was Heather and she was gorgeous, complete with a perfect completion, silky brown hair, a great body and intoxicating eyes. I tried every day to build up the courage to speak to her. The routine was always the same. When class ended, I would follow her as she headed towards the parking lot, racking my brain to think of something to say. Inevitably failing, I would watch her as she reached the parking lot, started her car and drove away, leaving me alone behind the tinted doors, failing yet again.

It was the last day of the semester when I finally built up enough courage to speak to her. When class ended I called her name. She stopped and turned to me, that striking smile leaving me breathless as I searched for the right words. I struggled, finally clearing my throat and stating my intentions. I asked her if she would like to hang out some time. She said that she would like that, and that it would be fun. She told me to call her that night to discuss our plans. Then she gave me her phone number, a milestone for me and we said our goodbyes. I could barely contain my excitement as I drove home as quickly as I could and waited by the phone, wanting to call right there and then but deciding to give it some time.

An hour later I made the call that would change my life. When she answered, she seemed to be in an overly cheerful mood, often laughing out loud when nothing funny was said. I thought nothing of it as she said that she would meet me at a local Italian eatery to which I happily agreed. I arrived at the restaurant an hour early and parked my car. There I waited as I thought about all the great things we would talk about, the compliments I would shower upon her and our possible future together. At five minutes till, I went into the restaurant, got our table and waited for my beautiful date to arrive. I even ordered some wine to make the mood right. There I waited and waited then waited some more. Half an hour later I will still optimistic, sure that she had been held up for one reason or another, that there was a perfectly valid excuse for her tardiness. That half hour turned into an hour, and when the waiter told me that I had to order something or leave, I fully realized that Heather would not be joining me.

Still, assuming that there was a perfectly valid reason for her absence, I decided to give her a call to make sure that she was all right. The voice that picked up the other line was not that of Heather but that of a man. When I asked if Heather was available, he rudely informed me that she did not want to speak to me, and that I had been stood up on purpose. He stated that he was her boyfriend and that they thought it would be funny if I showed up at the restaurant and was left alone. I didn't want to hear anymore and I almost hung up when I heard chatter in the background and then Heather's voice. She tried to say that she was sorry, and that she thought I was a nice guy but I didn't want to hear another word. I was furious as I slammed the phone down on the receiver. I have never forgiven that act of childish behavior, and now Heather is just a memory, and a name on my list.

Although I hold a lifetime grudge against all of those who have treated my badly, I had a feeling that people matured as they grew up. Kids would be kids. They would fight and call each other names like all kids did. It wouldn't keep them off the list but I could understand to a certain extent why children did what they did. I would find out that young adults in college still had a lot of maturing to do as well, especially when it came to working on team projects. There were always those one or two individuals who couldn't pull their share of the work, either because they were drugged up or just generally lazy. I just learned to deal with it, overcompensating for the group in order to get the work done, while being confident that when college ended and we were all shoved into the real world that only the professionals would survive.

I had been wrong again, over time I realized that people never change.

Instead they remained the ignorant scum they were as children. In the real world adults still spoke behind each other's backs, pulled dirty tricks to get ahead and were as lazy and thoughtless as they were the day they were born.

Soon after graduation, I acquired a job at an insurance company, the aforementioned accounting position with my windowless corner office. I had a nameplate next to the door but it meant nothing. It seemed that no one even knew I was there. It was okay, the hours were good and I was paid enough which was a good thing since my mother was still down on her luck when it came to her finances. I always sent her half of my paycheck.

I had been working my butt off for several years under a strict and unfair boss, always doing what he asked regardless of how redundant the assignment. I never received any real acknowledgement for my efforts, but I had been used to going through life without much recognition. Still, I knew that my work was important and when it was announced that a senior accountant position was available, I thought that I was guaranteed the job. There was only one other guy in the office that would give me any competition, a sniveling assistant to the manager by the name of Miles. He was as cocky as they got and I suppose I could understand why. He started with the company out of high school with a position in the mailroom, quickly climbing his way up the corporate ladder, resulting in his position as the primary assistant to my boss. It didn't take a rocket scientist to realize that his rise to success wasn't due to his work ethic or dedication to the job, Miles was a suck up from day one. And that wasn't just my opinion, everyone could see the way he would always bring in breakfast for the boss while complementing his clothes, and constantly congratulating the boss on every business decision he made, regardless of how the decision effected the department.

I tried not to think too much into it. Let him suck up, flattery would only get him so far. I was the one who was at work on time every day, getting the work done and proving my value to the company. What I soon found out was that while he was working, Miles had been taking accounting classes at night at an online college. When the senior position was announced, it was common knowledge that Miles was gunning for it. I knew I had to make my move, and one afternoon I finally built up the courage to request a meeting with my boss. When I stepped into his office I closed the door behind me and took a seat. The boss waved a lazy hand at me, his way of instructing me to speak. I spent fifteen minutes explaining to him all the reasons why I should get the senior accountant position. I bullet pointed my past projects, explained my great work ethic and how effective I would be in the new position. As I spoke, the boss nodded a few times, never glancing in my direction, his eyes seemingly glued to his computer screen with little interest in anything I was saying. When I had finished my speech, we sat for many seconds in complete silence as if he forgot I was even in the room. He finally responded with a simple “okay, thanks. I’ll keep it in mind.” I dismissed myself.

A few days went by while I waited for the decision but hadn’t heard any news. Then at the end of the week, I was sitting at my desk working hard as usual, when I noticed an unread email appear in my inbox. It was addressed to all the employees in the building and it congratulated Miles on his promotion to senior accountant. I could not believe it, after all my years of service and dedication this is how they reward me? The boss didn’t even have the decency to let me know in person beforehand. I had considered quitting that moment, of course not before letting everyone in the company know exactly how I felt about them. However I thought better of it. Besides, I needed the money and I now know that they will get what is coming to them as they have each reserved a spot on the list.

This is what I deal with every day of my life, constant disappointment from anyone and everyone that I come in contact with. I’m sure many of these offenders have long forgotten their offenses. I am sure that Heather has long forgotten what she did to me in college and if ever reminded, she would think of it as just an innocent prank. Marcus Fisher, my middle school bully, is probably living a nice life with a steady job and a happy family. The memory of his brutality pushed back to the farthest reaches of his mind, behind twenty-five years of new memories. I’m also sure that even more recent discretions, such as those imposed by my boss are nothing more than necessary actions, no more hurtful then the act of swatting at a fly.

These people are just a fraction of the many individuals who have treated me unfairly since the day I was born. The list could go on for miles. There was Christy, the girl in high school who laughed at me when I asked her to the senior prom. The kids in gym class who always chose me last when it came time to pick teams. My eighth grade English teacher who decided to give me a failing grade although I tried my best. The banker who refused to give my mother the loan she desperately needed although she was well qualified for it. There's the mail carrier who refuses to honor my requests for my packages to be left at my door and instead leaves them at the apartment entrance for all to see, and my landlord who never fixed my heater after my several requests, resulting in me catching the flu. The list goes on and on, at first figuratively and now literally and they will all get what's coming to them. I know I've got a lot of work ahead of me, and it may take years to cross every name off the list, but as long as I take them one by one, I will complete the task.

So here I am, sitting in this filthy hotel room, my rifle cocked and loaded and my sight set on the front door of the barbershop. Actually, now that I think of it, they don't call them barbershops when they assist female clientele. Beauty shop, that's the proper name. In moments a woman will exit the building, an individual so vile that I can think of no other single person to place at number one on my list of offenders.

When my mother opens that door, her life will suddenly come to a sad and unexpected end. She is the first person on my list, the primary offender, and the monster that birthed me into this terrible world. If it weren't for her, I would have never been through the incredible pain that I have endured throughout my life. She is the reason I have grown up with all of these secret pains within me, and for that she must pay. It may seem like unjust punishment but it is necessary, justice must be served. Regardless of what she has done for me, this is the way it must end. So many terrible memories could have been avoided for both her and me if she wouldn't have fallen for that bastard of a father who planted my seed in her belly.

There is no turning back now and I am ready to do what must be done. Any second now my life with take on an all-new direction. I am no longer afraid, I am ready to accept my fate and do what must be done. I am perfectly at ease with the rifle in position, the target in the crosshairs, my finger massaging the trigger.

The Right Thing

Michael McClure

Sarah was gone when I woke up, but that was not surprising. I often slept late, and she liked to catch the morning light. I'd see her later. She'd come find me drinking Pabst Blue Ribbon longnecks at the Cavalier Inn. We liked to go there at least partly because of a waitress named Ida who only had one eye. Painted on her patch was a big, wide-open blue eye, much bigger than a normal eye, and sometimes, late at night, Ida'd slip us a free longneck. Maybe I wouldn't see Sarah for a couple days. Nothing serious. I wouldn't worry about her; she'd only get mad if I did, anyway. She'd show up when she felt like it.

That was Sarah. The day we met was like that. Jeremy and I were drinking pitchers, and we were well into the second, and there she was sitting across from me. I remembered seeing her our Buddhism class in the big auditorium in Cabell Hall, but I had never spoken to her. Now, here she was, diligently working to catch up with us, her dark eyes bright against her white white skin. She pretended to believe my poetic pretensions. That would work with me anytime.

She was a student in the local art school. She made rubbings from gravestones and hung them around my apartment. William Henry Rittenour, b. 1861, d. 1887, lived over my bed. She liked to take photos in the graveyard, too, especially in the early morning. In the kitchen over the little round wobbly thing that served as cutting board and dining room table, she hung a black and white print of a large dogwood tree practically burning in the dawn light and surrounded by white markers in crooked rows. And she painted an oil in the reddest blood red of Kahoutek devouring the earth. That was the comet that was a buzz of anticipation those days.

We didn't go on normal dates. Mostly she'd come over and surprise me.

"Come on, we're going to a party!"

We'd end up at a farm out in Albemarle County—I rarely knew where we were—drinking grape Kool-Aid, not something to lightly in those days, or smoking hash. Sometimes she'd just show up late and spend the night. And then she'd leave first thing in the morning, often without even waking me. I used to kid her that she was working on the land speed record for getting out of bed and out the door.

One day I bought a blue and white flannel shirt at Montgomery Ward's. We were going hiking up in the woods on the Blue Ridge later, and it seemed like the perfect shirt for a fall day, for playing in the crunchy leaves. When we got it home, I found a tag with red letters in all capitals: DO NOT WEAR UNTIL WASHED. Sarah loved that warning. She immediately insisted I put the shirt on unwashed.

"Don't you dare wash that, Stephen. Maybe the pattern will be indelibly printed all over your chest and back like a full-body tattoo," she laughed. I still think of her sitting on my bed laughing whenever I put that old faded shirt on. It's the oldest piece of clothing I own; really it's worn out, so thin I expect it to fall to pieces every time I wear it on a lazy fall weekend. Somehow I never get rid of it.

-A-

When the time for Kahoutek finally arrived, we drove up to the Skyline Drive. We didn't want the city haze of light and wood smoke intruding in the fiery advent. November 14 was supposed to be the comet's brightest moment.

We couldn't even find the damn thing.

But the drive wasn't wasted. Sarah gave me directions. We turned off the main road onto a gravel drive, the turn almost hidden by overgrown bushes on either side. The road wound up the mountain and finally opened at a rounded peak.

In the middle of a wide trimmed lawn stood a massive marble palace: a white, three-story building that looked to me like it belonged in a rich neighborhood outside of Rome rather than in the mountains of Virginia miles from anywhere.

We parked on the white gravel driveway and got out.

"Sarah, *where* are we?"

Sarah smiled in the rising moonlight.

"It's OK, Stephen," she said, taking my hand and pulling me toward the darkened mansion, feet crunching on the white gravel. We walked around the house, and I was speechless again. There was a garden framed by giant evergreen hedge, no twig out of place, and marble statues, Pan with his pipes and wood nymphs and a 12-foot Jesus, with his heart throbbing outside his chest, and fountains, the musical water falling like the sound of the moonlight growing whiter and whiter.

At the back of the garden, on the very peak of the mountain, stood a moss-covered tower built of large, rough stone, dark, almost black in the moonlight, rising high above even the mansion.

Sarah opened a small wooden door in the side of the tower. I hurried after her up the steep stairs, wondering where the hell we were and why and how and every other question. Intrigued, too, as usual. At the top another wooden door opened to a small round platform with a low stone rampart. In the center of the circle stood a round block of shiny black marble, which Sarah climbed up on at once.

"C'mon," she whispered.

I stepped up beside her, both of us still breathing heavily from the climb up the tower. We held each other lightly against a falling feeling, slight cool breeze blowing against us along the ridge from the south. We were the highest point on earth in every direction. The moon and the stars seemed to welcome us among them.

"I love this place." Sarah spoke in an even voice.

Far down to east I could see the sprawling lights of Charlottesville. City lights can seem beautiful, seen from afar, magic, alluring, but in this case the city was an intrusion—an ugly sore on the sea of black that should have been.

The lights that fit were the single points of far scattered farms, solitary and tiny against the dark world.

Then, just as suddenly, Sarah jumped down from the altar-like stone, and we headed down the stairs. Her battered Volvo clattered into action, and we smoked a joint on the way down to the city without talking, my mind rolling over the images of the night. I turned to say something, and there were tears running down her cheeks, silently. She didn't wipe them away. She didn't answer when I asked her what was wrong. She shook her head when I put my hand on her arm.

-ᏜAᏜ-

Another day I was asleep when she burst into my room. "It's noon, asshole! Get up." By this time I knew better than to ask questions. She'd never answer questions. "Answers are mostly lies," she'd say.

She usually drove whenever she was taking me somewhere new. It was easier than giving directions. And I liked being a passenger; I liked watching the scenery unfold instead of having to concentrate on the road. Don't get to do that much anymore. God, I'd give a lot to know where Sarah is now, to be with her again.

We drove through a clump of trees just outside the city limit. Tucked away in a little hidden valley. Looked like some kind of industrial site. We were waved through a tall wire fence by a security guard, past a small blue sign: U. S. Government Property. Authorized Personnel Only. I looked over at Sarah, her lips pressed tightly together, not exactly a frown. I wondered how we could just drive past the guard without even stopping. She didn't turn to me. There was no smoke, no obvious activity. Just a tall gray building, very tall by Virginia standards, maybe five or six stories high, and a couple cars parked by a red metal door with a security camera mounted above it. No windows, I noticed.

Sarah parked her Volvo, and, as we walked toward the door, she handed me a small plastic badge with a safety pin on the back. "Put this on."

A man opened the door as we approached. He was dressed in a white lab coat.

"Glad to see you, Sarah. How's Chuck these days?"

"Oh, he's *real* fine," she said. She smiled, but I could hear the check in her voice.

"Think we'll see him around here anytime soon?" the man asked.

"I wouldn't hold my breath," Sarah said.

"Yeah, well," the guy smiled too. "Tell him I said hi. Hey, Sarah, remember to give me those badges before you leave. Have to check your levels."

"Sure." Sarah took my hand as we walked toward another red door. Elevator. Standing inside, not feeling any motion at all, still holding hands, we listened to the quiet hum of unseen machinery. She turned suddenly toward me and stared to say something, but just as suddenly stopped, awkward, seeming almost confused.

"What is it?" I said. But then the door slid open facing a black sign with large yellow letters: Radiation Badges Must Be Worn at ALL Times in Reactor Building.

We stepped out, crossed the narrow hallway, and entered a huge room mostly filled by a large pool of dark water. We moved up to the cement wall surrounding the pool; it reminded me of the shark tank at Marine World, Africa, USA. I almost expected to see huge gray shapes turning in the deep water. But there was nothing. Just clear dark water utterly still, the only sound an undertone of the air-conditioning system. All around the perimeter of the room the walls were covered: controls, dials, digital displays, pipes, valve wheels, and different colored lights, some blinking on and off, others glowing steadily.

After looking around, I turned to Sarah, who was leaning out slightly over the retaining wall staring intently down into the depths.

"This is cool, right?" she said, but without smiling.

"Um...,yeah, but what...?"

"Oh, shit, Stephen. Shit! Goddamn it! What do you want, Coney Island?"

For a split second I thought of saying something about Marine World.

"There's not always some ride, y' know." She was actually angry. "Somebody's big funny joke. Look at all this stupid machinery. They pretend and pretend, all so super important, but what the fuck is it really for? They've got this pool hidden way here, like a temple to some secret cult. It is, y'know. This is about death, about killing."

Sarah stopped and watched my face for a reaction.

"Chuck poured himself into this pool. This water is really the melted-down soul of my father."

-ᘓAᘐ-

I was really surprised when Sarah asked me if I wanted to go to her parents' during our Christmas breaks. The surprise was her *asking* instead of telling, but, of course, I was thrilled.

"I know you'll like it there," she said. "I know you'll like my Dad. But it's not Christmas. Just so you know, it's the Solstice."

"OK, the Solstice," I said.

"You know, not a fat man who panders to our greed. We all join to fight back the darkness on the longest night. Otherwise, the world could come to an end."

"Oh, right," I said.

She laughed at that.

Her folks' place was about a two-hour drive north and west from Charlottesville through undulating hills, mostly grazing farmland framed by old wooden fence lines or older low rock walls built from the stones pulled from the fields they lined. When we got there, we entered the house, a two-story white colonial, through a large cluttered kitchen. Chuck was sitting at the big rustic wooden table in the center of the room, a mug of coffee before him. He didn't look up when Sarah bent to kiss his cheek.

"Want to arm wrestle?"

I looked around to see if there were someone else in the room.

"Well?"

"OK, sure," I said. I looked at Sarah.

"Is Mom here?" she asked her Dad.

"No, she's off to Luray for some craft fair or something for a few days. I think she said she'd be back on Tuesday."

After glancing around at the dark room—even the side with the twin windows over the sink was dark, the walls and cupboards all made of a wood almost black and the thick slate counters almost invisible under the weight of kitchen tools and books and pots and machine parts—I put down my backpack.

There was a drumming coming from somewhere deeper in the house, a rhythmic drum sequence repeated and repeated and repeated.

"That's my brother Peter," Sarah said. "I'm gonna go find him. You boys fight it out."

Chuck lit a corncob pipe, drew in quietly, and held it out to me stem first.

"Grown right here, Stephen." He smiled a truly inviting smile at my surprise. "Didn't Sarah tell you I'm a farmer?" He laughed at that.

I didn't know what to say.

"Good preparation for arm wrestling." This tall man bent over the table and used his forearm to sweep one end clear of an accumulation of plates and silverware an unopened mail and a huge roll of silver duct tape. About the tape, Chuck said, "Magic stuff, duct tape, couldn't live without it. Well, sit right down, We'll finish this bowl and see what you're made of."

I didn't stand a chance. Chuck knew that, but he waited a few face-saving seconds before crushing my arm against the boards. He didn't hold it against me. We smoked some more, and then he took me outside for a tour. First, he introduced me to Nietzsche, Sarah's dog, one of the ugliest dogs (if any dog can be said to be ugly) I ever saw but kind of cute, too, in a scary way. He had a fierce-looking face, a little like a bulldog's but bigger. He had short tawny hair except for the hard ridge of longer black hair along his spine.

"Razor-back Dog. From Rhodesia. Rhodesian Ridge-back. Supposedly bred to hunt lions." Chuck glanced at me.

I nodded.

"I guess it's not Rhodesia any longer," he said. "No. Zimbabwe now. Much better, not to have your country named after a British robber baron. Not so great to hunt lions for sport, either."

He led me over to the barn and waited until I entered the warm dark room before he pulled the sliding door shut with a crash. We stood together in the dark for few seconds—the air was humid and thick with a strong, cloying plant odor—then Chuck switched on the lights. Mammoth pot plants hung upside down from the rafters, hundreds of them, dried to shiny olive and brown, the tops hanging low, heavy with thick oily buds.

"Holy shit, Chuck." I couldn't believe my eyes.

He laughed loudly, the full joyous laugh of a man pleased with his own joke and not embarrassed to show it. "Well, Stephen, government pensions aren't too hot, you know, especially when you bail out too soon for the nickel hunters."

I spent the rest of the day with Chuck. Sarah and her brother Peter and a teenage boy named Eddie whom Sarah's Mom had simply brought home from a the West Virginia State fair six months earlier stayed out of sight, the virtually never-ending drumming the only testimony to their presence in the house. In the afternoon, with the air getting icy—the gray sky felt more and more like impending snow—Chuck and I drove out on his land in an open jeep and cut down a crooked pine.

"For the Solstice," Chuck said. "Don't you dare call it a Christmas tree."

"Sarah told me," I said.

"I always pick a bent one," Chuck said. "Seems like the right thing."

We set the Solstice tree up in the living room, more cluttered than the kitchen, full of old, overstuffed chairs, two couches, several odd shaped brass floor lamps, and crammed bookshelves along nearly every wall. An African shaman's mask hung in one corner and large brightly colored painting of the streets leading to the Eiffel Tower in another. We had to shove a coffee table, a rocking chair, and an overstuffed chair out of the way, adding to the jumbled feel of the room, to make space for the tree.

But we got it up, between smoke breaks, and decorated. Most of the Solstice decorations apparently look remarkably similar to Christmas ornaments, though a few of them set a decidedly different tone, a miniature shrunken head and a number of small animal bones gathered from the farm's fields, for example. It was beautiful. Ornaments piled on to the point where we had to hang the remainders from other ornaments since the tree was so crowded.

Sarah finally reappeared, and she laughed until she literally cried at the sight of her Dad and me staggering about throwing tinsel on the sagging branches and nearly as much on the surrounding furniture. Chuck kept trying to sing country songs, but he could never remember more than the first line or two, and, besides, they clashed with the ceaseless drumming still vibrating through the house.

"How long *can* they keep that up?" I asked Sarah.

"Oh, don't worry, they'll keep going all night."

"All night?"

"Yeah, scaring the demons away. Y'know, saving the world. It's the Solstice."

"Oh, yeah, right. Glad they're on the job."

She smiled at me then.

-ᴥ-

After a late dinner Chuck left us alone. We sat in the living room, talking about Chuck and the farm and how her Mom sometimes brought runaway teens home with her from her various journeys and what it was like growing up there for Sarah. I talked about my parents' divorce, about wandering all over New York city from a young age, being captive on a city bus one time when it was hi-jacked and everyone on board was robbed at gunpoint, and watching when my Mom and I came home from seeing *What's Up, Pussycat* and there was a passed-out man in the entrance to our apartment building, so my mom went next door to the fancy address with a 24-hour doorman and in his thick coat heavy with gold braid he came over and dragged the man into the gutter. The man did-n't even wake up.

I wondered if he was alive. My Mom tipped the doorman twenty bucks for his help, then we went inside.

You know, typical childhood memories that somehow make us who we are, all the while washed over by the quiet and then louder rising and falling waves of drumming that had come to seem like the heartbeat of a giant animal, like the house itself was a living being.

Sarah got up and rummaged through the bookshelves for a while. I liked leaning back and watching her pull out a book, consider it for a moment or several moments, and then slide it back into its place while we continued to talk about other things. Research her Dad had been involved in developing "clean" nuclear bombs. About her high school boyfriend who committed suicide. About my boarding school years and the skills to survive its hidden but rather brutal in

-group culture. Some of the time we were both silent and just listened to the drums' steady aural flow. Finally, she pulled a large volume against her chest and came back to the couch and sat down next to me, our legs pressed against one another. That was a good feeling.

She looked at me, kind of a questioning look, then she kissed me, gently, and opened the book to a long series of photographs of kangaroos, close-ups in which you can count the whiskers around a big one's mouth, running shots, families, a little head poking out of a pouch. Sarah turned the pages slowly at a sequence, apparently the culmination of the whole book, showing a large kangaroo leaping over a wide gorge high above a river far below.

Sarah let her hand rest on the page. She looked at the animal, safely across the gap, with satisfaction, even tenderness. I tried to think of something to say, to change the subject. The Sarah turned her gaze up to me, questioning with her eyes.

"Great shots," I said.

"Great shots?"

"Yeah, really great. Beautiful animals."

"Do you see?" she let her hand slide down the page on which the big kangaroo is in mid-air suspended above empty space.

"Yeah, it's far out. What an incredible jump."

"Is that all you see, just the surface?"

"Yeah. What the hell? What do you see?"

She didn't say anything. I stood up, the book fell to the floor, and I walked over to a bookshelf and pretended to look at titles for a few seconds while feeling my own pulse beating seemingly in time with the drums which were suddenly loud again. The lights blinking on the tree were in synch with the drums, too, and they reflected in the glass over the Eiffel Tower so it seemed even the streets of Paris long ago were in the fight against eternal darkness.

"Let's go to bed, Sarah," I said.

"OK," she said.

Sarah slipped the book back onto the tight shelf and clicked off the floor lamp at the end of the couch. Only the Solstice lights on the crooked tree showed our way out.

The Prayer Collective

S. E. Greco

I'm Governor Sule. Very honored to meet you, Ambassador. Welcome to Callisto, the most beautiful of Jupiter's moons."

The governor was a small man in a long silver robe which disguised his squat, pear-shaped frame. He had a pudgy face and his hair was pulled up in a tight spherical bun, a style which had gone out of popularity on Earth a decade ago. He gave an overly ceremonious bow to the Ambassador and then extended a soft hand.

Ambassador Lorne towered over his host as they shook hands. He wondered if perhaps the Governor was hopeful that the bun hairstyle might be poised for a comeback. Lorne was younger by at least ten years, shaved bald, and by contrast, he struck a lean and athletic figure in a neatly tailored dark suit. He looked around the cavernous reception room, which held only a few pieces of furniture and several hanging works of luminous kinetic art. One wall had an array of large circular portholes through which could be seen the stark, frozen surface of Callisto. Lorne wondered why there were no other people in the room.

"Yes, the landscape is quite beautiful," Ambassador Lorne said. "But where are the rest of the humans? I didn't see anyone else, human or Callistan, when I was walking over here from the shuttle bay. And there were no other spacecraft in the bay either."

"There's only me," answered the Governor.

"Just you?" remarked Lorne with surprise. "There's a contingent of eight million aliens working for us on this planet, and you're the only human here supervising them?"

"Not aliens really, as they are native to this world. And yes, I am the only human needed. The station here is completely automated. As for the Callistans, other than having supplies delivered regularly for them, they care for themselves. There is a group of several Callistan supervisors with whom I interact, and Callistan managers below them. They run the entire operation efficiently."

The governor directed Lorne over to the table and chairs. They sat down and the Governor poured tea.

"Is there any human tourism here?" asked Lorne

"Not yet, except for a few extreme adventurers. Callisto presents some unique environmental challenges, and so routine tourism is some years off. But the native Callistans do quite well here in their subsurface shelters."

"This is my first visit to Callisto, and I must admit I know very little about the Prayer Collective. Frankly, it's shrouded in…well, secrecy. As you know, I was asked to come here by the Jovian Central Government, to help negotiate with the Callistans on behalf of the Terran Church of the One True Deity. I'm a rather strange choice for the job since I'm not…er, I've never met a Callistan before."

Lorne had almost slipped and told the Governor that he was not devout. Not a good idea since the Terran Church was extremely powerful and influential, and they had spies everywhere.

Lorne continued. "Perhaps the government picked me simply because I'm based on Europa and I could get here quickly by shuttle. My superiors said that you have an urgent problem with the Callistans and that there might be some benefit to having face to face negotiations. So first of all, let me ask… what are the Callistans like, Governor?"

"They are small in stature, the males about four feet tall on average. The females are slightly taller, but neither gender is suitable for any type of manual labor or military service. They walk upright on two legs, and they have six arms, each one ending in a hand with six digits."

"Yes, I've seen pictures of them. What I meant was, what are they like…mentally? Psychologically?"

"They are very meek and docile creatures, and therefore they were very easily subjugated. And they are not very bright, I must say. One might even call them simpletons. As far as we can tell, they've made no technological progress in thousands of years, and in fact, they spurn technology other than what is specifically needed to run the shelters. Their techno-phobia is one of our challenges in working with them. For one thing, it makes communication very slow because all orders must be passed on by spoken word."

"And as I understand it, the Terran Church has all eight million of them reciting the same prayers simultaneously?"

"That is correct."

Lorne thought, *Six hands on each Callistan, so three pairs of hands pressed together in prayer. I'll bet the Terran Church is ecstatic over that!*

Lorne was an agnostic in secret, but he tried to keep up the appearance of being a true believer. It would be unwise for someone in his position to do otherwise. He was trained as a scientist, and although that did not preclude being religious, he made decisions and formed opinions based only on hard data.

Lorne took another sip of the tepid liquid in the small ceramic cup, out of politeness. To him, it tasted terrible. There must be a million different beverages in the solar system that people called *tea.* No telling what kind of vile weed had been used in brewing this one, or what planet it had come from.

"How long has the Collective been at its prayer mission?" Lorne asked.

"About five Earth years, ever since the Terran Church declared robotic and computerized prayer to be sacrilege."

"I see. And who decides what they pray *for*?"

"The Terran Church decides of course, and the objective of the praying varies. Right now they are praying for the success of our troops in the Lysithean wars. A particular prayer is continued until the Terran Church deems that the desired effect has been achieved."

"And has the prayer made a difference so far in the Lysithean wars?" Lorne already knew the answer to his question. The war had been raging for twenty-two Earth years, with no end in sight, the advantage swinging back and forth between the two opposing sides. He was therefore surprised when a quick affirmative answer came back from the Governor.

"Yes, the prayer has certainly been beneficial," said the Governor in a confident tone. "Although the Jovian Central government has suffered significant losses in the war recently, it would have been much worse without the prayer. You must understand that this is a huge undertaking, praying for success in wars involving over a hundred million souls, so expectations must be tempered."

Lorne nodded politely and said, "Oh, yes indeed. Tempered. And before this war prayer, what were they praying for?"

"A plentiful grain harvest on Mars."

"I see. But I've read that recent storms destroyed a significant portion of this season's crop."

"But without the prayer, the storms would surely have been much worse, as per the long-range weather predictions."

So that's it, thought Lorne. *Every prayer is declared to be successful because they can always say the outcome would have been much worse without it. Sounds like institutionalized ignorance.*

"And have they ever tried praying for some slightly less ambitious goal? Something much more narrow in scope, where success or failure is more of a black or white situation?"

The governor smiled politely and said, "The Terran Church elders seem to avoid narrowly focused prayers. I'm sure they have their reasons."

Lorne nodded again and thought, *Yes, I'm sure they do. They want to avoid the publicity of a prayer effort being a complete bomb...*

The Governor seemed to pick up a trace of skepticism on Lorne's face because he added: "There was *one* case of a narrowly focussed prayer...but it was...unsanctioned." The Governor opened his mouth as if to speak further on the topic, but then abruptly closed it. Lorne did not press him further. He decided to alter his line of questioning.

"Do they pray out loud in the Terran language, Governor? And if so, then I assume they speak it well?"

"They *do* pray in Terran. However, only the supervisors speak and understand it. The prayers are written in Terran by the Church, and then transformed into a purely phonetic form of the Callistan language, which allows the Callistans to make the sounds of the Terran language. But except for the supervisors, they don't understand the meaning of the sounds they are making. They simply speak the sequence of sounds they are given, over and over. We monitor their compliance with microphones to ensure quality control, making sure they are saying the prayer continuously and pronouncing it correctly. Their vocal cords are very robust, not prone to injury or damage from the fourteen Earth hours of continuous speech. That's one of the reasons they are well suited for this work."

"Yes, I was told about the fourteen-hour shifts. And that their complaint has to do with overwork, is that correct?"

"Yes. It's fourteen hours of prayer, then ten hours off, every day. They would like their workday reduced to thirteen hours. They have made no other requests at all."

"And if their request is not met, are they threatening to stop operations completely?"

"Well, they don't make overt threats. They are a very docile people as I said before. It's difficult to explain, but they seem to take great satisfaction in pleasing us, which is why they don't need human supervision. But this satisfaction apparently has its limits. However, the answer to your question is yes. We believe that if we don't comply with their request, they will cease all praying."

"It seems a reasonable request, doesn't it Governor? I know of no other place in the solar system that has a population, alien or human, working fourteen-hour shifts with no days off."

The governor's eyes widened with alarm, and he replied, "But if the request is met, then the Church will not meet their prayer quotas."

"Quotas?" asked Lorne with a puzzled look.

"Oh, yes. The Terran Church has strict quotas which must be met!" said the Governor, as if stating the obvious.

Lorne thought, *This is amazing and actually somewhat frightening. The place seems to be run like any other factory. Production quotas for prayers! The Terran Church is basically running a prayer sweatshop here, using alien labor. And I'm sure they have some cockamamie formula for computing how many prayer man-hours are needed to achieve a certain miracle.*

"Let me ask a very naive question, Governor. If the Prayer Collective is always successful in their mission, why don't they just pray that the Terran Church elders change their minds and accept the thirteen-hour workday?"

"Because they consider interference with the free will of living beings to be…objectionable."

"I see."

Lorne paused as he heard the whirring of tiny wheels. A small cylindrical robotic servant placed a tray of sweets on the table between the two men, and then abruptly left.

"And exactly how are the Callistans compensated for their work?" asked Lorne.

The Governor appeared surprised by the question. "With room and board, of course," he answered.

"But they built their underground shelters themselves, eons ago."

"But we supply and robotically maintain them now."

"They *could* produce their own supplies. They used to grow their own food and manufacture necessary crude materials in the shelters."

"They cannot do that anymore. The Callistans who were involved in the food growing and manufacturing operations are needed…to pray instead."

Lorne shrugged and said, "Well, I have to be honest with you, Governor. The whole situation here borders on enslavement. The Callistans are working very long hours only for subsistence, with no time off, and no means of leaving their assignment. Even if they take satisfaction in pleasing humans, it's simply not right."

The Governor looked flustered and said, "But, Ambassador, the *enslavement* as you call it must be weighed against the good that is achieved through eight million beings praying in unison. There has never before been such a monumental effort in the history of the solar system!"

Lorne was silent. The Governor could read the skepticism in his eyes.

The Governor continued, "You are unsure about the prayer mission, Ambassador, I can tell. Perhaps this will convince you. I said before that there was one case of an unsanctioned prayer that was narrow in scope. It occurred approximately one Earth year ago when an Ambassador such as yourself came here as a negotiator. In fact, that was the first time that the Callistans made the request for the reduced work shift. The Ambassador would not grant the request, and so in their ignorance, the Callistan supervisors composed and had the Collective recite a prayer for the death of the Ambassador because they assumed that another would follow him who might grant the request."

Lorne's eyes widened and he gave the Governor an incredulous stare. "His death? Are you serious?"

"Yes, Ambassador."

A slight smirk emerged on Lorne's face, as he asked, "And what was the outcome, Governor?"

"He died, of course. The situation was complicated. The Callistans did not know that killing the Ambassador was wrong. They do not have the same type of moral compass as humans. They believe that killing for a higher cause results in some type of rebirth of the being in some different place in this universe. It was explained to them that it was wrong in our culture to kill the Ambassador for any reason and that his death displeased us. They accepted that. So they dropped their request for a while. Now it has resurfaced. But I'm certain that the incident will not be repeated. I can assure you that you are in no danger."

Ambassador Lorne raised an eyebrow. "Interesting. And what was the medical cause of death?" he asked sternly.

"Cardiac arrest."

Lorne nodded knowingly. "And did he know they were praying for his death?"

"Yes. But we found out too late to stop all the praying in time because eight million Callistans had to be given orders by word of mouth."

"And I'll bet this Ambassador was quite devout, a true believer. Am

I correct?"

"Why, yes."

Lorne was unable to keep up the pretense of being a religious zealot like the Governor, whom he considered essentially brainwashed by the Terran Church. He leaned closer to the Governor and said sternly, "He didn't die from the prayer, Governor. He died from simple fright. And I don't require your assurances about them not repeating such a prayer, because I can assure you that I am *not* frightened."

Lorne stood up and said, "So, I think we're done here, now that I fully understand the situation. The problem is that I don't have the authority to reduce the work shift. I was told specifically by the Terran Church not to agree to that. Believe me, if I did have the power, I would reduce the shift by appreciably more than one hour. I *do* have the authority to agree to certain other things to make their work environment more pleasant…a greater variety in their food, or perhaps…"

"But as I've already said, they want nothing else," the Governor interrupted in a flustered tone. "That is why we are in a very difficult situation."

"Then I maintain that we are finished here, for now. I plan to appeal to the Terran Church elders. Perhaps I can make them see reason regarding the work shift. Goodbye, Governor."

The two men shook hands. The Governor looked dissatisfied with the outcome of the conversation, but he watched silently as Lorne began his brisk walk to the shuttle bay.

Lorne was soon back in the pilot seat of his craft. He engaged the autopilot and set the destination controls for the number six airbase on Europa.

As the shuttle rose above Callisto and escaped its gravitational pull, sunlight reflected off the thick Jovian atmosphere and flooded the cabin. Lorne turned his head to take in the view of Jupiter's giant red spot through the starboard porthole. He always loved that majestic sight. It was his favorite in the entire solar system.

The comm system beeped and Lorne accepted the incoming transmission. The voice of Governor Sule filled the cabin. And he sounded quite distressed.

"Ambassador Lorne, you must return to Callisto immediately. I just spoke to the Callistan supervisor and I learned that shortly after you arrived, they had the Collective cease the scheduled Terran Church prayer and they began the recitation of an unsanctioned prayer, the nature of which…Well, let me reiterate that I am certain they have no wish at all to harm you because they initially considered having the Collective pray to simply disable your craft so that you would essentially be stranded here for some time to negotiate. They knew you were coming to see me, but they had no idea how brief your stay would be. By the time I walked over after you had left and spoke to the supervisors…"

Lorne interrupted: "Did I hear you say 'Disable my craft by…praying?' Why, of all the crazy…"

"But as I've already said, they are technologically inept and did not know how to go about it. They were afraid that anything they could accomplish in terms of disablement might be easily repaired. So they decided to simply… well, how shall I phrase it…to *pray* your spacecraft *out of existence*. After I explained the situation, they moved to stop all eight million praying Callistans as quickly as possible, but word of mouth communication is slow. Therefore, you must come back immediately to…"

The Governor's voice faded and was replaced by the crackle of static.

There must be something wrong with the comm system, thought Lorne, as he glanced downward just in time to see the floor of his craft vanish beneath his feet and the beautifully speckled orb of Callisto appear below him.

The Thickening

Rebecca Rowland

They called it The Thickening.

Originally, the media tried on a number of monikers, attempting to incorporate the disease's unfortunate first benefactor. Trevor Davison, a hip-hop artist who rose to fame purely through self-produced YouTube videos and guerilla-style social media bombing, was only twenty-four when the first symptoms appeared. Trevor displayed episodes of confusion, started missing appointments, even had to halt recording sessions because he couldn't remember the words to his own song. His entourage chalked it up to drugs, maybe a bit of day-drinking; his girlfriend attributed it to stress: he must have over-extended himself. But his mother Joanna recognized that it had to be something organic.

The doctors rendered a hesitant diagnosis of early-onset Alzheimer's disease, but they were perplexed. Trevor was showing other signs typical of Alzheimer's patients. For one, his symptoms had come on all of a sudden and in full force: one day he was focused, energetic, and articulate; the next, he was confused, lethargic, and garbling even the simplest of sentences. In addition, Trevor would have cursory moments of clarity; he'd speak lucidly to others for hours on end, but within the conversation, he'd spontaneously drift off, sometimes breaking his locution in mid-word. An hour or so later, he'd become intelligible again, but the coherence never lasted more than a day. And unlike in Alzheimer's, there seemed to be no rhyme or reason to when his communication breakdown would begin; there was no so-called "sundowning" as the afternoon stretched into evening.

Trevor, and those who were diagnosed after him, simply slowed; their communication abilities congealed like viscous liquids, thickened. The affected became toys who'd been played with too long or smartphones that were too out of date to accept the most recent software upgrade: they glitched, they did not respond to commands, and soon, they would stop working altogether.

Joanna's documentation of her son's progression transpired accidentally. As his first fan turned tour manager and public relations director, she had always carefully chronicled his every creation from his first notions of prose to the final, sample-woven track. Soon, she armed herself with five separate cell phones with the most advanced photo and video capabilities and quickly became an expert in rapid image editing, and when his YouTube follower number reached one million, she hired three assistants to film, edit, and post twenty hours of each day in shifts.

"Jesus, Ma—" Trevor held his hand backwards over his face like he was shielding himself from the glare of a searchlight. "I'm eating breakfast, fah Christ's sakes." With his free arm, he shoveled a heaping spoonful of sugary cereal into his mouth, the sloppy overflow of milk dripping down his chin and onto his tank top.

Joanna held the camera steady. "T, your fans are watching. They want to know everything about you. Don't leave them hangin'!" she encouraged.

And with this, her son put down his arm, quickly wiped the milk from his face and chest, and smiled brightly into the lens. He closed his eyes and began to sing a cappella, resting his palm on his stomach to feel his own breath.

Social media junkies bathed in Trevor's Instagram, Facebook, Twitter, and Snapchat updates, and when his Periscope recordings expanded to a minimum of eight hours per day, he sometimes attracted an audience of fifty thousand, often nudging out the White House in popularity during times of peace.

And then, during one of Trevor's live recording sessions, his mind began to skip, an ancient LP record traced by a dull needle. And Joanna continued to film.

The Thickening

-∽A∽-

Miriam Cavanaugh had worked her whole career at the Centers for Disease Control and Prevention. Originally from Springfield, Massachusetts, she had earned a full scholarship to Penn State, and though she completed her doctoral work back in the Commonwealth at MIT, she found herself pulled southward again when the government agency wooed her, desiring her expertise in the domestic transference of communicable diseases. It had taken some resolve to adjust to Atlanta's sweltering summers, but by the time she had settled into permanent housing and delivered a son, her body had acclimated.

It was on a Monday that she sat at her desk in the lab and reviewed the most recent spinal tap samples from patients exhibiting symptoms of the mysterious brain disorder that had been slowly devouring the nation. A number of the newest cases appeared much milder than the older, and thus more well-known, ones (the President himself had contracted the affliction, although it didn't prevent him from powering through the fog to send regular, often disjointed and nonsensical tweets to his devout followers), and Miriam could not determine why. The easiest, and most desirable, explanation was that the disease was simply disappearing as quickly as it arrived.

At first, Trevor's Dementia—The Thickening, as Miriam nicknamed it—seemed too much like a B-movie title to her. It had appeared to afflict celebrities, movie stars, and recording artists almost exclusively, but upon further inspection, it seemed to correlate with how large of a digital footprint the affected individual possessed. The more Google hits a patient gleaned within a simple web search, the more severe and quickly his or her dissension was into unintelligible rambling.

"Sounds like we need a social scientist here, not a microbiologist," her lab mate Bridget joked when the research group met to analyze the lack of a disease transference trail. Her colleagues laughed, and Bridget turned to face Miriam. "Speaking of which, how is David?" she asked. Miriam thought she saw a bit of a wink in her eye above the woman's wide smile.

Miriam grinned slyly back at her but said nothing. Her son was a graduate student in anthropology, and he had returned home the previous week to spend some time with friends and with her before the next semester began. David was darkly handsome with high cheekbones, and people, even those in solidly cemented relationships like Bridget, salivated over him, but Miriam was fiercely protective of her only child. He was still young: the last thing he needed was to be hunted, a big net thrown over his broad, athletic body, and dragged kicking and screaming into the chains of commitment.

Anthony, another member of the group, was saying something, but Miriam had been too lost in her own thoughts to have been listening. "I'm sorry—what was that?" she stammered, embarrassed at her distraction.

Anthony buttoned and unbuttoned the cuff on his left sleeve. "We were saying that nowhere in our initial findings does it suggest that screen viewing time has any effect on the disease: neither its infection nor its progression." He rubbed his palms together. "The symptoms seem to be limited to those who are the subjects of online activity—photographs, videos, and the like—those being watched, not the watchers themselves."

"No direct contact transmission," added Bridget. "It's not passed through physical contact nor through bodily fluids. No indirect contact either: animals and insects appear to be unaffected, and there's nothing connecting it to water, food source, or air contaminants either, at least at this point."

Miriam tapped her jaw with her finger. "We're still looking at the spinal fluid transmutation. The viscosity is markedly different in patients showing symptoms—"

"But it's still unclear if the thickening happens all at once or is progressive," Bridget added quickly. "If the fluid shows signs of exposure to the virus or mutation or…"

"We don't even know if it IS a virus," Miriam pointed out. "We haven't isolated one. Not in the bloodstream, not in spinal fluid, nowhere as of yet." She paused. "And god, I hate that term, *thickening*. It makes the body sound like a bouillabaisse."

Anthony began typing frantically on his iPad and the notes appeared on the projected board behind him. "So, it's all suspect-but-not-prove as of now. We know there's a change in spinal fluid consistency. We know patients exhibit changes in thought processes, speech patterns, and states of consciousness."

"And there's some sort of connection to social media presence..." Bridget added.

"Suspect, can't prove. Connection, maybe. Causation? Unclear."

Miriam raised her voice. "So, why is it dissipating?"

The three were silent for a minute. Miriam continued. "Why, after such a flourishing of new cases for months, are we seeing a dramatic dip in infections? Why is the disease waning in some while it continues to spike in others?"

Again, the room fell to a hush. "Schadenfreude phenomenon?" Anthony said and emitted a low chuckle.

"Come again?"

"If it's true that the disease strikes patients based on their social media presence, maybe people are too busy watching the celebrities die to post their own updates, photographs, and videos," he said somberly. "There's nothing more entertaining than watching someone self-destruct."

-A-

Joanna knew better than to put to down the camera. In the early 1990s, she'd joined friends on a coastal pilgrimage to the Pacific Northwest. The Seattle music scene was raging, and her friend Marlene played a mean bass and dated a decent-looking drummer named George, and by some serendipitous accident, they'd befriended a guitarist they called FlapJack who owned the kind of windowless van Joanna thought only belonged to predatory pedophiles and government surveillance groups.

On their journey up the coast, they'd stopped in Los Angeles and the four piled into a roach-friendly hotel for a few hours of shuteye. Joanna, who'd slept most of the day curled up around a beaten-up amp that rubbed raw the skin along her upper arm, was not tired, so she curiously ventured out alone in West Hollywood, hoping to ferret out a cheap drink or a free show. As she neared a well-known bar that hosted the talent from the L.A. rock scene on the Sunset Strip, she spied a circle of onlookers, their mouths wide as two paramedics rushed to the aid of a collapsed patron on the sidewalk nearby. It wasn't until she had reached the crowd that she recognized the victim; the last time she had seen his face, it had been twenty feet wide and she'd dumped half her bag of popcorn onto a new pair of shorts, staining them with slippery, butter-flavored oil.

As the medical team hoisted the actor's lifeless body onto a stretcher, Joanna scanned the crowd. A man stood statue-like, holding a camera at his waist, its lens pointed at the ground. He hadn't taken one shot. Later, when Joanna stumbled upon an article about the fatal drug overdose, she spied a short blurb from the photographer. He stated that he hadn't taken any pictures out of respect for the performer's family.

"What an idiot," Joanna said, and she tossed the magazine in the trash.

-A-

Miriam pushed her work shoes off without bothering to untie the laces, stripped down to her underwear, and stepped into a pair of running pants. She grabbed a t-shirt that had been draped over the back of a nearby chair and sniffed it. It was a few days past clean, but she didn't plan on seeing anyone that night, so she pulled it over her head and padded into the great room. There was still some Scotch in the crystal decanter her co-workers had bought her for a housewarming present many years back. She'd never gotten the gist of pouring liquor into special containers for display purposes, but she admitted, utilizing the vessel made her feel a bit more sophisticated when she drank alone.

She flopped onto her worn sofa and tucked her feet under her thighs. After flipping mindlessly through a series of sports commentary, home shopping, and crime reenactment shows, she finally settled on a softly-lit cooking program. The host, a grandfatherly-looking man with a beard too long to be sanitary for food preparation, stirred something methodically in a large chrome pot on a burner.

"There's nothing more delicious and satisfying on a cold fall evening than a dinner flavored with savory meat stock," he said, staring flatly into the camera. "While you may reduce a large pot of homemade stock reduced down to a *demiglace*, or, even further, to a *glace de viande*, it is of the upmost importance that you do not simmer for an extended amount of time, or the aromatic texture will evaporate along with much of the liquid content.

Similarly, thickening into a sauce will intensify flavor and create a more appealing texture. However, if you reduce your succulent stock too long, its flavor will flatten, and attempting to revive the sauce by adding water will be fruitless. The damage is already done."

The man paused and drew his wooden spoon up from the pot and brought the tip to his mouth. As he slowly parted his lips to taste the concoction, David's voice materialized behind Miriam, startling her. "Sounds delightful," he said, pouring a bottle of water into a glass. He rubbed the inside of his ear and squinted at the television. "Since when do you watch cooking shows?"

"Since when do I cook?" quipped Miriam.

David walked to the front of the sofa and sat down hard next to his mother. He always did that: practically falling into chairs with such force, one would think his body was made of solid lead. Miriam turned to look at her son. "Do you have an Instagram account? Or a Facebook?"

He smiled conspiratorially and sipped his drink before responding. "Why? Are you planning on following me?"

She ignored his playfulness. "What about a Periscope account? Do you make YouTube videos?"

David smiled. "No, I don't have any of those things. No Twitter either, which is sometimes a disadvantage because a lot of people only communicate through their social media accounts these days. I miss a party invite or a big announcement because I am out of the loop."

"So, then, why don't you have them? The accounts?"

David thought for a moment. "Honestly, first it was because you scared the bejesus out of me about what potential college admission counselors and then desirable employers might find out." He laughed. "Not that I'm living some sort of wild, secret life or anything. But I don't know… I guess I'm comfortable just living life as I see it. Maybe I'm behind the times. There have been plenty of cultures who shunned movies and photography."

"In this day and age? I find that hard to believe anyone could avoid cameras these days," said Miriam.

"Yes, well, there have always been slightly ominous connotations associated with recording a person's likeness. The Amish dissuade photography for religious reasons. If a person consents to being photographed, he or she is allowing a graven image to be created, and that is a sinful action. When interest in photography began to build in the mid 1800s, superstitions sprang up, such as in a picture of three people, the person in the middle would be the first to die."

David paused to finish the rest of the water in his glass. "And, of course, there are the Kayapo of the Amazon. In their native language, the phrase *akaron kaba* translates to both 'take a photograph' and 'steal one's soul.'" He paused again, staring at his mother without expression. "I don't think that was accidental, do you?"

-A-

Joanna pawed the screen of her Smartphone awkwardly with her index finger, the long, polished nail scraping the edge with every swipe, making a squeaking sound. On the muted television above the microwave, a 24-hour news station featured an interview with a representative from the CDC as a ticker scrolled excitedly along the bottom of the screen: *Apple releases newest iPhone model... NASDAQ in third day of steady decline...sudden deaths of Singer sisters reinvigorates lipstick line*, the last notation referencing a pair of tabloid celebrities who had become famous simply by starring in their family's vacuous reality series and launching their own line of lip plumpers and butt padding. Joanna owned three tubes of the former; she didn't need the latter.

When the camera's eye gazed upon the scientist from the CDC, a caption below her image read *Government agency discourages people from participating in social media*. Joanna rolled her eyes and with some effort, managed to hit the MUTE button on the remote control and the sound roared to life.

"Are you telling the American public to stay off of Facebook?" asked the interviewer incredulously.

"We're saying, stop filming yourself and posting the images online, at least until we have a better idea of what is happening here. For your own health and safety," answered Miriam. "You can visit as many social media sites as you wish."

The interviewer crossed his arms over his chest. "But without someone to watch, what's the point of going online?"

Joanna hit the POWER button on the remote and the screen image sucked itself into a tiny glittering spark and turned black. Still clutching her phone, she walked down the hall and into the guest room. The lighting was dim, and although it was the middle of the day, all of the window shades were pulled. She flicked the switch on the wall just inside the doorway and paused as her eyes adjusted.

In the bed, nearly motionless, lay her son. His eyes twitched and followed her as Joanna walked to the side of the mattress where his body was completely prostrated. She rested her phone on the nightstand, grabbed Trevor's shoulders, and awkwardly pulled him upward so that he was half-sitting, half leaning on the stack of pillows propped against the headboard.

"How's my superstar today?" she asked him. Without waiting for a response, she grabbed her phone and opened the camera, then connected to the live feed. As she pointed the lens at her son, a distorted response emanated from his mouth.

"Maaaanna…Duck holes kick. Solo," Trevor said. "Red fill twenty… Ma, no," he continued, a few wisps of clarity breaking free. "No…more," he pleaded. "Hiccup fowlers cola pop…pop…no…" His voice drifted off and he turned his head away from the phone five feet from his face.

"T, your fans want to know how you're doing." Joanna's disembodied voice wafted from behind the electronic eye. "They are anxious for you to recover and go back on tour, my love. Tell them how much they mean to you," his mother commanded.

"Me…" Trevor's voice was only a whisper. "Mee. Meee…" he repeated, still looking in the other direction. Joanna could see a trickle of drool sliding down the side of his mouth, and she reached out and officiously wiped it away, hoping the fans hadn't noticed. Her touch seemed to set into motion a shiver that began in her son's mouth and wound its way down his neck and intensified as it reached his spine. Trevor began to buck and seize, his body flailing back and forth; his head struck the wooden headboard repeatedly, the sound of a baseball struck by a bat over and over, a home-run hit on instant replay.

Joanna did not move. She watched as her son thrashed about for a full minute then was perfectly still. As the life leaked from him, his eyes glazed and emptied their memories, and his mouth slacked into a rubber mask, one religiously bleached tooth peering out from behind parted lips.

Joanna was still holding the camera. She hadn't tilted it even an inch.

She swiped her finger sideways and looked at Trevor's video feed. She watched, mesmerized, as his follower numbers doubled, then tripled. The wide expanse of universe had witnessed her only child's violent escape from it. Countless viewers would replay the clip in their feeds, his immolation to immortality.

Joanna sat down on the bed softly next to Trevor, taking great care not to jostle his soft body, and settled into a comfortable position. Then, she turned the camera to focus on her own face. She cleared her throat, smiled prettily into the gaping black hole of the lens, and welcomed her captive audience.

Brass Belt Luna

Will Riley

The lights are throbbing and Brass Belt Luna is rubbing herself all over a patron, but the relationship between them is of course non-existent. Even eye-contact between stripper and patron is rare. Invariably, any communication lies between the man and the other men next to him. The bold ones, laughing with abandon, to get cheers from his gang of friends. Or the shy ones, giving awkward hesitant smiles at the gang of friends who dragged him here. They're not interested much in the woman in lingerie sitting on them, so much as interested in reassuring the men next to them that they're having a good time.

Candee tells Brass Belt Luna that it's like each man is trying to convince the other that they aren't gay, and now Brass Belt Luna can't see it any other way: see how this one's smiling too hard, this one is laughing louder than is natural, this one is cracking bad jokes that he's rehearsed in the mirror…When the speakers call for the sultry Lara Lucia, and Brass Belt Luna gets on the stage, her act has more improvisation in it than the act of the people she dances for.

Luna is gay herself, which in this profession is actually a plus. She's gay, and for those who're alright with that, she also takes off her clothes for a living. And for those who are okay with both of those things individually, the fact she's a mix of those two alienates them. Just, the period of initial revulsion is slightly longer than if you're straight. Once you get over it, though, once you recognize that all you're doing is putting one piece of flesh against another piece of flesh, a bit of fabric between them, you don't get guilty for not feeling anything while you're doing it. You have very obvious reasons not to.

More new girls than you'd be comfortable expecting come in for all the usual reasons, needing to get through college, having nowhere else to turn, and yet *still* treat the job like it's method acting or something, and get all morose once they don't "feel" dancing anymore. For Luna, although acting's definitely a part of her job, "feeling" the role she plays never comes into the equation. You just do what the role you're playing tells you to. She supposes, though, it must be nice for someone to have expectations like that.

So, now that a club for Luna's particular demo's just opened up, and she's low on cash again, she's giving a job there try. But the reactions are exactly the same; this girl's looking at her friends, this one's looking at her girlfriend, this European tourist's looking at her *wife.* Axel tells Brass Belt Luna it's like each woman is trying to convince the other that they aren't straight. One difference between lap-dancing for men and for women, which only a sexologist or a master pervert could give a reason to, is that women want you facing them more often than men do. This makes the fact that the patron's eyes are elsewhere all the more difficult for her to ignore.

The sound system is introducing the bodacious Lana Loveless, which is Brass Belt Luna's cue to get on stage and start her set. She feels like an idiot for thinking things would be any different. Luna's setlist is unconventional: Devo, in particular, turns many heads. But lots of the lyrics are about sex, and the beat is jaunty and electric so no problem, even if the lyrics are still about sex from the male perspective. She's dancing right now to "Don't You Know,"

I got a rocket in my pocket
but I don't know what to do
Like a plug without a socket
I'm just waitin' round for you.

Brass Belt Luna—now a kid again—is also hearing Devo play on the radio, an English-language pop station from inside a beat-down pickup's stereo, parked crooked on the family lawn with the doors open. Devo's more current at this time, but not much more. Brass Belt Luna's at the birthday party of some nephew she doesn't know, staying around the table of food, rather than speaking to anybody there, who she also doesn't know. Her mother's telling her "Stop eating so many chips, Luisa, you need to take better care of your body." Brass Belt Luna, giving her body what it wants, thinks *salt, starch, and most importantly, taste*. Why would a body want something that was bad for it? That thought is interrupted when the crowd masses around the gate to the backyard, as Uncle Oscar comes in with a spherical present under his arm. Uncle Oscar, who donates the most at mass. Uncle Oscar, who's wearing a cheap suit, but unlike everyone else, actually wears a suit. Uncle Oscar, who *almost* got to suplex a mummy with El Santo (and/or Samson, the Silver Maskman) on the silver screen. Uncle Oscar, the White Panther Mask.

He hands the present to the nephew Brass Belt Luna doesn't know and musses the kid's hair up, tucking his cross back into his collar as he walks in. He pats a few of his brothers and cousins on the shoulder, and even signs an autograph for one of the men just married into the family. Of course, he politely refrains from a photograph. He doesn't bring his mask along when he's not working. Been working less and less, now.

He walks over to Brass Belt Luna. "You're getting bigger, Luisa. Might get bigger than me!" He says it as a joke, but it's not actually that unlikely. He's small: you need to be light and compact to take bumps like he does, do flips like he does. "*Bien attendidas, Mascara Pantera,*" Luna replies. Uncle Oscar smiles. He still likes being White Panther Mask, even when he isn't wearing a mask at all. He likes it so much, in fact, that when he dies 12 years later due to a sudden stroke, his mask is placed over a mannequin head on top of his casket. The face of the body in Uncle Oscar's casket is contorted—looking completely different from the man Luna sees at the nephew's birthday party. The man in the box is as much a stranger to her as Uncle Oscar is to fans when he isn't wearing his mask. She can feel the stares of her relatives going right through her as she looks at this stranger in a coffin adorned with cheesy white roses. There's not exactly much to endear her with anyone at this mid-scale funeral.

Back at the nephew's party though, Uncle Oscar, who is not a corpse just yet, tells Brass Belt Luna he's heard from her mother she's doing really well in ballet. "It's fun, I guess," Luna lies. "Our teacher's kind of mean. She makes us stretch our legs out in the air every day until they hurt. Then she shouts at us if any of us put our feet down."

Uncle Oscar chuckles. "Have you heard the phrase, 'pain is weakness leaving the body'?" She has, from her ballet teacher, and she doesn't like it. She was hoping to hear a different opinion and frowns a little. She tries to hide it, but Uncle Oscar sees. "Of course," he says, "I don't have the exact experience with weakness or pain to fully know what I'm talking about." He lifts his right pant leg and shows a giant gash right on his knee. "I got this before I ever put on the panther mask. Courtesy of *Diablo d'Oro.* It was most painful thing you could ever imagine. When this happened to me, all of the weakness I had inside of my body just drained out of this knee all in one go. The pain shoved it out. Then I bounced back as the White Panther Mask a year later. Yet, for all the strength I gained, I'd have gladly taken that weakness back, endured the pain of stretching my leg out in the air for a hundred lifetimes, just so I wouldn't have to have lived out the pain of getting this." He points back to the knee. "Your body can be your friend if you take care of it, Luisa, but it can turn into a weapon against you if you're not careful."

Now that she's grown, Brass Belt Luna knows that her body has indeed turned into a weapon, but she doesn't know to whom or what it's pointed. She stretches her lethal arms up in the air and the crowd whoops and hollers as her back arches. She's a whirling dervish with none of the delicacy of religion, the crowd too loud for anyone but her to hear her feet shuffle with each twist. Her legs don't feel any pain as they stretch and flex in the air at angles they shouldn't be in. Her body is fluid and angular at the same time, a curled spring in a wind-up car, ready to explode into motion without warning.

Then, Nastasha Romana's chunky wrestler's cleat smacks into Brass Belt Luna's forehead, which it is *not* supposed to do, flinging her backwards onto the ropes. Her mask slips over her eyes; the ring is starting to spin out of control, and so is her mind: *Brass Belt Luna (alternative aliases: Lara Lucia, Lana Loveless, Trixxxi) is an adult performer primarily known for exotic dance routines to the music of the American Midwestern synth-punk band Devo.* Goddammit, if the match was real that kick would feel like nothing on account of adrenaline, but she's completely off guard; she doesn't even remember the point when her head bounced against the floor: *Devo is known for its ironic style, irreverence of social norms and, especially on their most popular album,* Freedom of Choice*, its curious and fully explicit sexual themes.*

Nastasha Romana's felt her leg connect, but she can't stop the show. She's bouncing off the ropes opposite Brass Belt Luna, who's stumbling up and closing her eyes, waiting for another hit: *There was a mild controversy after the release of the music video for* Girl U Want, *the first song on* Freedom of Choice. *The video featured cuts to audience members holding signs depicting a directional arrow entering an oval, an electrical socket*...an impact from Nastasha's forearm, and Brass Belt Luna is back on the ground. It shouldn't hurt as much as it does, but it's renewing the pain of the fresh kick.

She's forgetting 7th grade algebra for a minute now, *In the video for* That's Good, *sex is similarly depicted, with a spinning crinkle cut French fry entering a donut, then a cut to smiling woman*...She doesn't even remember getting pinned. There's sparse applause for Nastasha, but most people use the women's match as a bathroom break. Especially an untelevised freelancer match. *Then the same French fry enters the same donut and snaps in half, cutting to the woman frowning.* That kick was real, and it's not a good wrestling match if it looks too real. Maybe, at the very least, Nastasha Romana's performance is bad enough that Brass Belt Luna's will look good.

It is bad enough. Kenny the Killer's nameplate on his desk says "Ken R. Burns, CWP senior talent relations" Kenny the Killer dips a cookie into his tea as he stares serenely, as though transported, into a dainty Japanese woodblock print framed on his wall. He leans back and smiles as he talks to Brass Belt Luna. He says some things about "legacy," about "being a proud addition," about "throwback appeal," but she's not really following much, still woozy from the boot to her face. What she does pick up is that she'll have to start as Heel, and she can't really do anything panther themed yet, not when Wildcat Wendy's already so lucrative, selling so many t-shirts. Instead, she'll get some big white lace-up boots that are designed like a classic luchador's—except they go far above the knee like a pair of stockings—a mask that's open from the nose down and lets her hair out, and, most importantly, a belt with a brass buckle big enough for cameras to see. Brass Belt Luna smiles. Before she's even won her first match, she's getting a belt.

Kelly Saxon, Max Saxon's wife, has *The Big Book of Lesbian Pirate Stories* in her locker. She reads the bumbling sleazy prose aloud sometimes, just for yuks, and to make everyone else in the room squirm with discomfort. She smells like Altoids, and some spice Brass Belt Luna can't place when she gets closer up. Cumin, maybe. Yes, probably cumin.The marriage with Max Saxon is as fraught as you might expect: she's a face and Max Saxon is a heel. Kelly is attempting to get a divorce, but is being obstructed by Evangelist Erica, who believes divorce is against God's law. This culminates in a ladder match on pay-per-view with the divorce papers suspended above the ring, each trying to reach them, one wanting them signed, the other trying to rip them in half. Kelly Saxon (nee Kelly Stardust) loves and embraces trash in all its forms, self-aware or no, with particular ironic glee. She emits a hissing laugh through her teeth every time she reads the synopsis of her upcoming plotlines. The ladder match was actually her idea, and the marriage was half hers, half the writer's. She even suggested to perhaps get some paperwork written, make it official in some regard—just for yuks.

As the announcer calls out her name and hometown, Brass Belt Luna steps into the crowd's eye, her music playing. She's surrounded by boos—boos are the same as cheers when you're a heel—and they're not booing hard enough for her liking. She's jobbed to Wildcat Wendy, because everyone jobs to Wildcat Wendy, but she's also jobbed to Lisa Lisa, Beth Snow, fucking Yukari Kawashima, who doesn't know that when you get a flying head-butt to the gut you should probably sell it.

Even though the script qualifies it as a belt match, she's jobbing to the girl with whom she listens to Devo. *The eyes are always somewhere else*. Kelly Saxon will beat her in two minutes, then Phoenix Jones will dash in and ambush the both of them, leaving them bloodied and Luna out cold. Then the real title match will begin.

Despite whatever closeness she has with Kelly, the only reason she manages to score this match is because she's one of the few girls willing to blade. She feels at the razor blade underneath her wristband, making sure it's easy to get at. Blading's getting more and more frowned upon, but it's *always* been undesired in women's matches. But that's how much pull Kelly has, she can get blading in there, and make their bodies look gross and brutal instead of sexy if she wants, just for yuks.

Everyone but Luna is somebody doing something: Kelly Saxon is defending the intercontinental women's champ belt; Evangelist Erica is starting a 6-woman tourney to solve the elusive mystery of "who German Suplexed my pastor through a folding table?" Even Mariella Dio, who has a minor shoulder injury, gets to show up in a wheelchair and neck brace and yell at people to keep a feud going; Brass Belt Luna is Brass Belt Luna, nothing more.

She's talked with the writers, talked with all the face girls she can get a hold of, tried to pitch some kind of feud. They all just smile politely and say, "we'll see," but she knows that, no, we will not see. Maybe it *is* because she's gay; that the other wrestlers are scared she's feeling something that the others aren't when she's tangled up with them. Or, it could be because of her past employment, the fact that similarities between those two jobs are too uncomfortable for them to face. In these moments of suspicion, she forgets about Kelly Saxon; she's forgets the Iron Sheik—married, three children—and the now-infamous footage of his massive erection, visible through his shorts right after throwing Hogan to the floor or the awful, terrible porn that lots of "early retirees" go into. The job's association with sex has been explored up and down; everyone's consolidated it in their own way by now. The fact she's cashing in on the legacy of her uncle—the stranger in the box—working at a premiere association and making twice as much money as he did at this age for half the matches, doesn't cross her mind.

Nor does the fact that she stares right through people like they're nothing but a body, and that she only ever calls people by their stage-name—even when she's off stage—which is just creepy and would give any prospective fighter second thoughts…except for Uncle Oscar not White Panther Mask, but Uncle Oscar.

She isn't even aware of the fact that she's still new, and that it shows. For all her body is feeling, like the spring in a toy car or a whirling dervish, it really, really shows. And when you look new, and you're in the ring just because someone you're related to was there before you, people know you're a danger. So, when Kenny the Killer is dipping his arrowroot cookie in his chai, gazing at his woodblock print to avoid looking at the fresh pink boot-mark on Brass Belt Luna's face, and gives his "proud addition" a canned filibuster written by someone higher up in the food chain who only wants her there on merit of legacy and throwback appeal, he's not thinking about her so-so farm match with Nastasha Romana at all. He's thinking about Simon Samson's nephew whose newbie hatchet-job of a Frankensteiner is why he's sitting behind a desk instead of standing in the ring.

Brass Belt Luna should have a lot going for her, he thinks. She's a legacy character, with connections to White Panther Mask. *Helps that she's got a nice body, before pro training. Good face too; lots of second generation wrestlers are disconcerting mixes of the ugly sonsofbitches that sired them and the supermodels that gave birth to them. White Panther Mask isn't her actual father, so that problem doesn't exist! But, Ah! She has to wear a mask, or else you can't connect her to the man the company's trying to emulate. Quite the waste, quite the loss. Can't even stick anything cat themed on her. She could be someone with good image, lots of panache. But anyone who isn't a kid, who knows that fights are rehearsed, will see an absence of technique, absence of precision. She's Ultimate Warrior, and even in wrestling, the Ultimate Warriors of the world can only ever get so far and cause so much damage.*

Kenny the Killer's figured out just what to do with her. He passes her the brass belt, her new identity. A brass belt: an insult to tradition, to the necessary hierarchy; wearing a mark of accomplishment before you've accomplished anything. Now, she'll never be written to win a real belt. If she won, you'd need to throw out her gimmick, give her a different name, rebrand all the merchandise; no-one wants that. Brass Belt Luna, newly christened, doesn't understand what Kenny the Killer's just done. She's smiling as she walks out the room, and Kenny the Killer leans back again. In all likelihood, she'll follow in her uncle's footsteps for just a year or two. She'll try to be true to his memory, for just a year or two. Then it'll be out of her system, and before her next contract renewal she'll decide to get on with her life.

What Kenny the Killer never expected, of course, is that in the end Uncle Oscar's legacy doesn't have much to do with her becoming a wrestler—resignation does. This is what Brass Belt Luna is thinking about when she's tangled up with Kelly Saxon in a commercial break rest-hold after a whole lot of bouncing off the ropes, getting ready to take the blade out, smelling the cumin and Altoids. She thinks about the nephew's birthday party, and how even after Uncle Oscar shows her his knee, she continues to express her displeasure with ballet to him; how all the stories about princes saving princesses that the teacher has them do are stupid. She doesn't tell him this, but puberty's already hitting her like a sack of bricks. She doesn't express that she's already wondering if maybe she wants to save a princess herself, or be saved by a princess instead of a prince.

But still she keeps insisting. And suddenly, Uncle Oscar's expression shifts, like yet another mask has been taken off his face. His eyes open up from their usual smiling squint and become wide, sunken, hollow.

He whispers harshly. "All right Luisa. You want the truth? Here's the truth. Luisa, do you see the man I just shook hands with a minute ago? He has a tattoo below his eyelid that says 'Marisa, '84.' You must understand what that means by now, Luisa, Marisa's dead. And this is a birthday party for your *nephew*? He's a nice kid, but you're too young to be an aunt already, and your sister is *far* too young to be a mother. Where is your father right now? Did you really think your mother, who almost never leaves the house, was the one paying for these ballet lessons? This is squalor, Luisa; you need to escape. You aren't going to find an education here, not in anything worth learning; your body is your only way out. You'll take the ballet lessons, you'll take what you learn there, and you'll go into wrestling. You won't be a millionaire, but your name won't get tattooed under some bastard's eyelid."

Brass Belt Luna's eyes twist around and sees the backyard around her take on a whole new layer of grime that was once invisible. She can see it, but she can't accept it yet. "But I'm just a kid," she whispers back, "you can't plan my life for me like this!"

"The fact that you're a kid and you're living here is why I *have* to decide your life for you, Luisa! I've given you a role to play that's better than anything around you! Now play it!" Uncle Oscar's whisper is becoming more strained, laced with panic. Then all at once he sees a car with tinted windows come down the driveway and men in sunglasses coming out, coming in through the backyard, asking where the fuck is Oscar Moreno, and he makes a mad dash, trying to climb the chainlink fence, getting his cheap suit caught, failing to get away as a man in sunglasses grabs him and throws him down, other pairs of sunglasses swarming around him until the biggest of them puts his foot to Uncle Oscar's face in a singular crushing impact.

The whole party divides away from the circle of kicks, punches and baseball bats as the shivering thing in the center of the circle loses its identity as White Panther Mask, as even Uncle Oscar, yet another mask falling off as it becomes something even weaker. The men slowly drift away from the breathing mass of bone and muscle. It doesn't even cry or do anything but breathe heavily and twitch. All the pain in its body has already left it a long time ago. Brass Belt Luna won't understand the nature of this beating until she watches a similar one, inflicted years later in a back alley, to her strip club's manager—The first strip club, that is—the straight one that she works at before going into wrestling. The second one, the lesbian strip club, comes she after she stabs a razor blade deep into Kelly Saxon's knee.

Brass Belt Luna knows the role she has to play. She takes the razor blade and puts the edge between her fingers. Maybe Kelly will imagine this as weakness leaving her too. Maybe she'll believe in herself enough, like Uncle Oscar did, to think she'll come back from this even stronger; or maybe she won't. The blade comes out of Kelly's knee as fast as it went in. She screams, and who knows how many masks are falling away from her as she tries to buck wildly from Luna's grip, not escaping, everything leaving her in this moment until she becomes just a body, shaking, mixing sobs with screams—broken. Brass Belt Luna keeps holding her down, smelling the cumin one last time, keeping her steady and allowing only just enough blood to get on the ring's floor, without it looking too real. It's not a good match if it looks *too* real. The announcers have to pretend that this was all according to plan. They declare Brass Belt Luna the women's intercontinental champion. No one's even figured out what's happened yet, not even Phoenix Jones—she's just standing off stage with her face in her hands.

The crowd hasn't figured out what it's just seen either, but it bursts into thunderous boos regardless, and Brass Belt Luna lets it wash over her. Boos are the same as cheers, if you're a heel. She's the champion now. *My belt will be gold now, not brass. The real contracts will come, the cash—and for a moment*, she thinks she'll be free to use her body the way *she* wants, and not somebody else, and then—

Her music plays and the cameras pop as the lights throb; Brass Belt Luna is rubbing herself all over a patron, but the relationship between them is of course non-existent. Even eye-contact between stripper and patron is rare.

Backwards: The Abandoned Time Travel App

Stuart Hardy

It took Jon a while to convince his supervisor to show him the warehouse. She'd mentioned it offhandedly on his first day and he'd been pestering her about it for his first couple of weeks at Havenware. She'd finally caved and agreed to take him up to the ninth floor one evening when it was just the two of them working late.

"Just don't mention this to anyone else, yeah?" said Sian.

She was an approachable, but cautious boss, and she was always very wary of the occasional visits by the CEO; Jon was far too interested to just let this go. A warehouse full of projects that the company had just abandoned! How *could* she just sit in her office on the fifth floor knowing that there was a pile of half-finished, discarded, and failed ideas just a few floors up?

She told him that it wasn't that interesting. It was mostly just shelves upon shelves of faceless metal and plastic boxes that didn't do anything all that inspiring: games consoles, new types of TVs, personal helper robots, sentient appliances; the sort of thing that you'd expect of any modern technology firm.

That still hadn't made him shut up.

She scanned her security pass, pushed the door open and led him through. The lights automatically flicked on one by one down the long and cluttered room that seemed like it stretched on and on forever. The walls were lined with shelving units and the floor was strewn with storage boxes and wires and bits of unidentifiable plastic and metal.

"Whoa! And all this stuff's just been left abandoned up here?"

"Yep," she said. "Some of it's alright, but it's mostly crap."

She started forward and skimmed over the mountains of faceless junk.

"Ooh, this one was quite cool," she said.

Sian picked up a nearby box full of what looked at first glance like Christmas lights, but they didn't have the long cord stringing them together.

"These were supposed to be neural dampeners," said Sian, taking out one of the little coloured diodes. "They store and recognise common human thought patterns. Y'know 'I've been dumped, oh no,' stuff like that, and they're meant to switch off your ability to think about it." She furrowed her brow at the little light bulb-shaped object. "This one's purple, so I *think* it's a job interview."

"Huh, cool."

"Yeah, you'd think so, but there was just one problem." She put the box down on a nearby shelf and rummaged around in-among the bulbs and brought out a rubber skull cap with tiny sockets covering it. "You had to plug the dampeners into this. They'd only work while you were wearing it; take it off, and you're back to normal again. Sure it'd be good for relaxing at home, stop you thinking about a horrible thing that happened that day, but is anyone really gonna wander around wearing one of these stupid things *all of the time*?"

"Hmm, true," said Jon, taking it from her and running his hands through the tiny sockets. "But couldn't you just...um, I dunno...make a dampener that cancels out feeling embarrassed at being seen in it?"

"Yeah we thought so too, but the investors started asking about everyone who either doesn't have or want one. What do they do? They'd have to look at the ugly freak in the electric skull cap covered in Christmas lights *all* of the time."

"But surely that's just a minor inconvenience?"

"Yes but aesthetics *matter* to the investors, Jon. They take one look at this and just think no one'll actually *wear* that, and that's it: project's dead."

"But, but...but they can't just...*just* because of its appearance? Really? "

"Why did you wear a suit to your interview, Jon? Appearances matter."

"Hmm, true," said Jon.

He turned away from Sian and started skimming through more and more shelves of dusty junk.

"So is this where all of our unmarketable or unworkable bits of tech are gonna end up?" he asked.

"Yep," she said. "Sadly, I think that machine that controls the weather that Sam's team are working on is gonna end up getting chucked up here too."

She went back to skimming along the shelves again.

"Ooh, lemme show you that one time the company tried to invent time travel!" She approached a nearby footstool and went searching on a top shelf.

"What? Really!?"

"Yeah! Time travel! Hang on a sec—"

After a moment's foraging, she brought down a large shiny silver box with a small keypad on the outside and a little blinking Wi-fi light. A logo was embossed on the front.

"Backwards," he read.

"Yep," said Sian, setting it down on top of a nearby box.

"It started out as an old fashioned time machine like in the movies," she went back up the stepladder again as she explained. "Basically; you set the parameters, generate a portal, and you can go anywhere, anywhen, y'know, basic stuff. We then split it into two machines when we realised we could charge double the price for 'Backwards' *and* 'Forwards.' We'd finished these prototypes before the investors dropped out."

She set a nearly identical box with a blinking Wi-Fi light that was embossed with the word 'Forwards' next to the first box.

"Bloody hell...you guys...you *invented* time travel! Why the *hell* would the investors drop out?"

"I was on the marketing team for it at the time and they dropped out about halfway through development and they dropped out because we kept running tests and ended up having to place more and more restrictions on it. The whole thing's a mess all told."

She sighed and leant a hand next to the devices and used the other one for gesturing.

"Okay," she began, "let's say an unlocked 'Backwards' machine is put on the market, and people start buying them. You can go all over history, do whatever you want, see the pyramids being built, watch a first performance of a Shakespeare play, go to the crucifixion, all that stuff. Thing is though: what if someone wants to change something?"

"Ah-alright, I see where you're going with this…"

"Exactly, right: killing Hitler. That's the first thing you think of when you think of time travel, isn't it? Well guess what? *There's only one Hitler.* What's gonna happen on day one when this thing hits the market? Suddenly hundreds of people show up in Nuremberg in 1933 armed to the teeth, all of them expecting that they're gonna get to be the one who gets to kill Hitler. They paid a lot of money for this time machine, that was their dream, *but* it's *also everyone else's dream.* So we've got two choices: we either gate off Nuremberg in 1933, *or* we hire some representatives and send them out there and make all of the homicidal time travellers form an orderly queue, arm everyone with a pair of nail scissors or a stapler or something, and everyone gets to have their turn at stabbing Hitler with a small sharp object until he slowly bleeds to death over the course of...oh, I dunno, several years, maybe."

"I, well I...oh..."

"Oh?"

"Well, I thought you were talking about cause and effect, not business logistics."

"Well yeah, there is *that* too," she sighed, "but we had to at least *try* and think of how it would work, even if it's essentially unfeasible. I suggested this idea that we could curate 30's Nuremberg into some sort of Hitler theme park for time travellers, but when you start taking it seriously: you realise you have to reshape the dream of time travel and the more we reshaped it, the less inspiring it started to sound."

She pulled out her phone at that point and tapped a few things into it.

"Eventually it became an app on your phone. You download 'Backwards' for a small fee, the servers transmit the temporal energy to your phone, and you can do a limited number of things with it, all of it localised of course. Here, we shot this promotional video for the investors when we thought it was actually gonna go ahead."

"Ooh, let's see."

The video loaded and they both watched a small selection of scenarios play out. They were all accompanied by a cheesy voiceover.

"Too hungover to go to work after a night out? Tune in to 'Backwards' and give yourself two night's worth of sleep in one!

"Late for a train? Never again with 'Backwards!

"If you start cooking your dinner and then change your mind about what you want, 'Backwards' can uncook your dinner and you can have it another day!"

The video then went into a brief explanation of how the app worked. Basically you'd open your phone camera, highlight a real world object, person or animal, and you'd create a temporal field that would allow you to reverse a limited amount of time that had passed for that object, person or animal.

"They chose to stop funding it in the end because it started to sound a bit dull," said Sian. "It was only compatible with the most expensive phones too and it'd drain your battery after one use. I never understood the physics behind it. The guy (can't remember his name) he tried explaining it to us in the presentation but none of us got it. Long story short: entire universes had to be created just because somebody wanted to undo a bit of burnt toast."

Jon was looking quizzically at the server boxes. Sian took that to be an invitation to explain further.

"Okay, just think here: Guy burns toast. Guy has no breakfast. Guy stops off to grab a sandwich on the way in. Guy is late for work. Guy doesn't get all his work done on time, stays late, is tired, his work is inadequate, he gets fired.

"Alternatively: Guy *unburns his* toast. Guy *is* on time for work, everything's fine. Another universe right next to it though: Guy is imprecise with 'Backwards,' only *slightly* burns the toast. Guy eats the toast and it doesn't taste nice. Guy goes to work, is annoyed for a bit, does a bad bit of work, gets fired.

"Or: guy does *good* bit of work. Guy gets *promoted.* Guy can't handle the pressure. Guy has a breakdown. Guy gets fired. The app'll typically generate these massive flow charts for any tiny little action and chew through your hard drive space in a matter of seconds and then crash. You've got to have a really expensive phone too; most devices can't handle it."

"Huh," said Jon. "I see your point, but a lot of the outcomes are the same, couldn't you just compress them?"

"Jon: these things were *HUGE!* Sometimes you'd get from burnt toast to a nuclear holocaust, spilt milk to first contact with alien life in a flow chart that's about fifty-million events long. Remember, a guy's out of a job and they find his replacement, the replacement's life is changed completely and so on and so forth. Compression would help, sure, but it wouldn't change much."

"Oh, I see," said Jon. "Was it ever good for anything?"

"Well it did give us the idea for this one here," she said, and she stepped back up on the footstool and brought down a third box. This one had the word 'Sideways' embossed on the front.

"We stripped out the functions that allow the user to affect the world around them and just left the flow charts in. It lets you see into alternate universes."

"Whoa! Cool!"

"Yeah, I thought so too, but the presentation was a total mess and the investors didn't buy it," she sighed again and rubbed her temples.

"Y'see 'Backwards' had kinda killed our ambitions *and* our imaginations. We tried too hard to start thinking *inside* the box. We were struggling to think of what you could reasonably achieve with an app that just lets you *see* what's happening in an alternate universe, but not affect anything, so we ended up marketing it at the socially neurotic. Say if you're at a party and you happen to say or do something embarrassing and spend the rest of the evening stressing about it, 'Sideways' allows you to look into the alternate universe where you *didn't* say/do said embarrassing thing in the first place, and set your mind at ease knowing that pretty much nothing would be all that different, so no harm done."

"Bloody...wow, I would buy the hell out of that!"

"Yes and so would I, but these investor types aren't like you, Jon. The socially neurotic don't really exist in their universe. To the investors the average consumer looks and thinks exactly like them and has the exact same wants and needs as them, and since they're usually secure and confident middle class white men in their forties, fifties and sixties being able to see consumer desires beyond their own limited worldview is kind of difficult for them."

"But-but, surely *everyone* wonders how life would've turned out if they'd taken a different path?"

"Why would they? These investors have had perfect lives. They're rich, they're successful, they're surrounded by 'yes' men at all times, and if 'Sideways' can't actually *affect* anything..."

She sighed and her eyes wandered back to the box. She was wistful for the lost potential.

"I dunno, maybe we should've just sold it as an entertainment product. Watch events play out in an alternate universe where Kennedy never got assassinated, or the dinosaurs were never wiped out, or the...sky is made of hamburgers or something, I dunno."

She stopped and that faraway look in her eyes slowly vanished as she realised she'd just had an idea.

"Wait, maybe that's it!" she snapped. "That's it! It's an entertainment product! Yeah, yeah, just watch some crazy alternate timeline where, wait...wait a second, wait..."

She put a hand to her forehead and rubbed her temples.

"Wait a second, why do I feel like I've done this before?"

Her eyes slowly wandered to the blinking Wi-fi light on the 'Backwards' machine.

The device had been on the entire time.

She realised, sniggered and smirked at Jon, whose face had changed from the false and exaggerated display of whimsy and wonder and was now the grimace of someone who'd been found out.

"Ah. I see," said Sian. "So, lemme get this straight: you convince me to use my pass to bring you up here, distracting me while you turn the 'Backwards' server on. We leave and you link your phone to the server and download the control app. You then use 'Backwards' to get me back downstairs and back to my desk before all this happened.

"You start convincing me to let you back upstairs again. We get back up here, and you get me to explain how all three of them work, the flaws, etc, and you get me to help you think your way around some of the problems."

Jon didn't say anything.

You 'Backwards' me back downstairs again, satisfied with an idea you coaxed out of me, while you steal the prototype Sideways, Forwards, and Backwards servers and you hand them to someone off-site." She finished and chuckled. "Huh, clever.

"Which one d'you work for just out of interest? Digiplex? Multiware? I have trouble keeping track of our rivals."

He still kept quiet.

"So, you steal the three boxes. You take them back to your company with my notes and ideas, see if anyone can figure out how to get 'Backwards' and 'Forwards' working. There's just one big problem though, Jon," she said bluntly, "there *is* no universe where 'Backwards' worked. You think we didn't try?"

"I..."

"Oh yeah, we tried. We hooked 'Sideways' up to a huge server after the project fell through, scoured all of its variables and we could *never* find a universe where this project got off the ground. Why d'you think you could 'Backwards' me downstairs without your phone crashing? The flow chart that it'll have created in this specific case will have very limited outcomes. Time travel *doesn't work*, Jon, it never will. Cause and effect, the technical side, the marketing, take your pick; something *always* gets in the way. Humans just aren't capable of inventing it."

She smirked at the box. "As for 'Sideways', if you did get someone to buy that, it'd be an interesting little novelty for a while, but it wouldn't be sustainable. It'd be like VR or 3D movies or Holotalk or whatever, except it'd be even more ludicrously expensive—a luxury item for spoilt rich kids. You honestly believed that I didn't think of that ages ago? I had that idea way before we abandoned that stupid thing."

Jon still said nothing.

"Well, maybe your investors are more optimistic than ours. Of course that only would've been relevant if I hadn't used 'Forwards' earlier today, watched this entire thing play out already and narrowed and determined the outcome."

Jon's face fell as Sian grinned.

"Yeah, I had my suspicions about you from the start," she said. "There's one outcome here and I know what it is."

He could hear the distant sound of police sirens closing in outside. Jon grabbed his phone and frantically opened the prototype 'Backwards' control app. Sian had flicked the switch on the back of the box before he had the chance to use it. The app froze.

"You-you—" he started to respond, but she then held up her phone and highlighted Jon on her screen.

"How old are you again, Jon?" she asked. "How many years d'you think you'll get for this? Life, maybe? It's unlikely, but I reckon it's possible."

"No-I-Sian, please!"

Sian slid the bar on her unlocked Forwards app to sixty-five years.

"Ready Jon?" she smiled. "Aaaand, Forwards!"

The Hole in Eye's House

Jared Linder

There is a hole in my wall and it gets bigger when I look at it.

Maybe it gets bigger even if I do not look at it. I do want to look to check.

My house is a room. I stand in the middle of it and look around to make sure everything in my house is where it should be. Bed pushes against the wall. Sink hangs across the room from Bed, halfway between the floor and the ceiling. Toilet gurgles near Sink. Mirror sits next to Dresser by the front door. I always look at Mirror last before I leave, to make sure everything on me is where it should be.

Mirror is as tall as me and does a good job of covering the hole. When the hole started, I put the newspaper over it, but it ate the paper. Then I put Mirror in front of the hole, and that has worked much better. Everything on me is where it should be, but I stay in front of Mirror.

The alarm on the watch around my wrist goes off. They gave me the watch a long time ago when I was small and They first told me I was going to be an Eye. It goes off to tell me it is time to go to Their house.

I do not want to go to Their house and write in my notebook and make my official report. Tomorrow, I will have to take my report to the Office of Governance and give it to Them. I do not think They read it. But it is good to do my job, even if my job is not good. Good and not good and other contradictions.

The newspaper waits for me outside. I should have gotten it already and read it all the way through, but I am certain it will be filled with news. There is already too much news, and They always make more.

There is time to say goodbye to Bed, Sink, Mirror, Dresser, and Toilet. I like them because they are not Them. My furniture cannot see, so it cannot see things differently than me. "I am leaving now. Do not make the hole angry when I am gone." I know my furniture cannot make the hole angry, but it feels good to pretend, even when I know I am pretending. Sink lets a single drop of water fall from its long, white nose into its circle mouth. "Do not worry," I tell Sink, "I will be back soon to get ready for The Game."

Refereeing The Game used to be the part of being an Eye that I liked the most because They cannot lie to me when I am refereeing The Game. But it has become hard to tell if Their truths are better than Their lies. Thinking about this makes my head fill with static. This is why I do not like thinking about The Game until I need to. I even skip the section in the newspaper that talks about it.

I pick up my official notebook and try to fill my head with Them and what I will say to Them when I get to Their house. I am glad They are not allowed to talk to me about The Game. Since I did not read the newspaper like I was supposed to, I am not sure what I will say to Them. I would read it on the way, but I cannot read and walk at the same time.

They leave the newspaper just outside my front door. It is morning so there is also a brown, paper bag with an egg sandwich in it. I do not have to open it to know. The paper bag They leave me in the morning always has an egg sandwich in it. I used to like egg sandwiches, but I have gotten tired of eating them.

They act like They do not notice me on the way to Their house. I know They are acting because some of Them whisper things like, "There goes the Eye," when I pass by. Maybe They are scared of me. They are not allowed to take pictures of me or use me in Their videos so there is no reason for Them to look at me, whether or not They are scared. I eat my breakfast and try not to look at Them. Some of the egg sandwich goes in my mouth and some of it goes on the sidewalk.

I move out of the way of a tall One with a large hat that looks like it is made from things I have pulled out of Sink's mouth. They race by me and stare at Their Rectangle and Their eyes go up and down. They are watching videos on Pangaea or looking at pictures on Pangaea or thinking about what They will post today on Pangaea.

Even the big, loud signs that They stick in the ground or on top of buildings are about Pangaea and how some of Them have lots of Presence and some of Them need more. Here is one on top of The Italian Restaurant that has a video on it about how Alonso S. Juarez can get Them more Presence by teaching Them how to make more interesting posts.

It is all so large in my head. It comes in through my ears and eyes and I cannot shut it out. How to watch the most videos in a day and ways to find the best Pangaea profiles to follow and how to take the most beautiful pictures. And all of it to allow Them to make the most Presence so that They can pay to make more Pangaea posts and then use whatever is left over to buy food and clothes and new Rectangles at The Store.

I walk by a faded sign near Their house. The letters are almost all gone, but the arrow at the end of them still points out toward the mountains, far away from The Capital City, where They put The Machine. They do not fix the sign because They do not want to think about what it is pointing at. They do not take it down because They want to pretend They might use The Machine again someday.

I am the Eye for the Capital City of the West Coast League of States and it is my job to make Them feel like They do not have to think about The Machine. I know They use me instead of The Machine because They can lie to me about Their Presence and I will not know They are lying. Knowing and not knowing and other contradictions.

-∽A∽-

Their house is thirteen blocks away from mine. It is much larger than my house and has smooth white walls on the outside. I knock on the door and They open it.

"The Eye's here!" They yell this down the hall behind Them before greeting me. "How's it going, Eye? You're looking mighty chipper for so early on a Saturday."

I do not know why They ask a question when They answer it too. The small patch of hair under Their lower lip has a piece of egg in it, and it hovers in front of my face because They hunch down to make me feel less short. I am not that short.

I say, "I am going well, thank you. How are You going?"

They smile and the egg falls off. I follow Them through a hallway and into Their kitchen, where the rest of Them sit around a long, metal table with glass on top. Two of Them have Their Rectangles out and are scrolling through Pangaea. I can tell because Their eyes go up and down.

"Good morning, Eye," They say.

"What's up, Eye."

"Hi, Eye."

One of them should have been a question, but was not. They have never met me before, but They pretend we are friends because They know I write reports about Their Presence and They do not know no one reads them.

I tell Them, "Good morning."

The One who let me in gives me a plate with egg on it and sits down at the table, and says, "Take a load off, Eye."

I do not have a load to take off. They do not mean what They say, but I know what They mean. I sit down in my chair at the end of the table closest to the opening of the hallway. I look down at my plate of egg. I already had breakfast and I do not want any more egg today. If I unfold the newspaper over my plate, maybe They will not notice I am not eating.

When I am done placing the newspaper, I look up. The yellow-topped One makes a too-big smile at me across the table. "So, Eye, did you read about Dr. Fred H. Schuman? It sounds like the Presence he's earning from his reality TV show might be artificial." The yellow-topped One seems to wait to hear my answer, which I know is hard for Them. Even to seem.

I look down at the newspaper that They make me read so I can talk to Them about the news before I interview Them about Their Presence. I think it is supposed to make Them comfortable, but I did not read the newspaper today so I am not comfortable. I read the first three sentences as fast as I can. The newspaper says that Their president has already been in charge of the West Coast League of States for ten months. In only two more months, a new president will be appointed. They think one of Them who calls Themselves Dr. Fred H. Schuman will be the new president because of how much Presence They earn from Their reality TV show, Emergency Room Live.

"Yes," I say, "what do all of you think about Dr. Fred H. Schuman?"

The One with short hair looks up from Their Rectangle. "Dr. Schuman, like, has more Presence than anyone in the West Coast League of States. I watch Emergency Room Live and post about it literally every day and so does basically everyone I know. I bet he earns more Presence in a week than I do in a year. He's gonna be president for sure. Who cares if the show is scripted, it's still, like, the best thing on Pangaea."

The long, black hair next to the short hair leans forward in Their chair and looks down at me. "You haven't said what you think yet, Eye. You're the professional here. Is it possible someone at the Office of Governance could determine Dr. Schuman's Presence is artificial before the next president is appointed?"

My head fills with static again. They say They are worried Their next president might have artificial Presence because the events on Their show are lies that would not happen unless They made them happen. They are not really worried. Disputes about Presence could all be resolved by using The Machine, but They will not use The Machine. They have not used it for years, even though They made it. The Machine can look into Them and tell how much of Their Presence is natural and how much is artificial. Once The Machine is finished, it deletes all Their artificial Presence.

I make sure to look at Them when I respond. "They could find out today if They made Them use The Machine."

They all stop scrolling. The One at the head of the table to my right with long, black hair around a long head squishes Their chin into Their neck. The One who let me in shuts Their eyelids very hard and puts Their hands on the table. They are big and I watch the extra skin around Their mouth shake when Their head shakes. The short hair next to the long, black hair has Their face open and I can see into Them more than I want to, so I go back to the big One. But now They open Their face too. Their teeth are yellow.

"Eye, we would appreciate it. We would appreciate it if you would not mention The M-Word."

They do not like it when I mention The Machine. If They mention it, They do not seem to mind. Maybe They think I have the power to make Them use it. I will not tell Them They are wrong.

"I am sorry. I will not talk about it again." I am not sorry.

Their chin moves back away from Their neck and around the table the chewing noises begin again.

I take out my official notebook and ask the question I am supposed to ask. "How have Your profiles been going over the last week?" I do not direct it at any one of Them because They have a pattern that I cannot control.

The first One goes first and is the youngest. They read off Their Rectangle. "Well, I uploaded thirty-six posts, looked at four thousand eighty-three pictures and watched six hundred and seventeen videos." They take Their time describing the Presence They have earned.

I cannot tell if Their Presence is natural or artificial. Maybe They set up Their Rectangle to automatically watch videos even when They were not looking at it. Maybe the video They took of Their friend dancing with a stranger was planned beforehand. It is hard to care when They do not care.

They take Their turns around the table. They describe Their posts and how much Presence each post earned. I write down some of what They say in my notebook and nod and wonder how many Presence the hole in my house would be worth.

When I close my notebook, the One with long, black hair looks at me and clears Their throat to let me know They have something to say.

I do not understand why They think it is better to make me ask Them to talk. "Do You have a question?"

"Well, Eye, and I hope this isn't a rude thing to ask, but I've always wondered how someone like you passes the time without a profile. I mean, I've heard Eyes can't post or earn Presence or even go on Pangaea."

They all stare at me. Even the One with short hair stops scrolling through Pangaea to see what I will say. I know They want to record me even though They are not allowed to. I close my eyes and, in my head, I am in my house. I reach out and put a hand on Mirror. I could move Mirror and stare at the hole until it grows big enough to eat all of the West Coast League of States and swallow all of Them.

"I have to go now." I have finished writing in my notebook and I do not like Them now so I will leave. Maybe when I go to interview a different house-full of Them about Their Presence tomorrow, I will like Them. Liking and not liking and other contradictions.

-∽A∽-

I walk by The Store on the way back to my house. I do not slow down to look through the big windows that let Them see into The Store. Inside, They use the Presence They do not use for posting on Pangaea to buy food and clothes and new Rectangles. I used to like to look at Them when They were shopping because They looked so happy, but now it makes me think about the hole.

I reach my street and start to walk down it. I still cannot see my house. I cannot see it until I am very close to it and I worry that I will look and it will only be the hole.

The alarm on the watch They gave me goes off again. This time, it lets me know that The Game starts in one hour.

When I walk by the house that is five houses until I get to mine, two of Them are talking loudly at each other.

One of Them has Their Rectangle out and is pointing it at Their neighbor, who is sitting in a long flat chair on Their front lawn. "If you say so," They say to the One in the chair. They shake Their head and do not look or sound like They think Their neighbor should say so. Their neighbor is my neighbor and that makes my stomach pinched.

"I do say so, asshole! I was sitting here for at least fifteen minutes before you came outside. At least. So will you just take the video, upload it to Pangaea, and get us both some goddamned Presence! I haven't been able to get into The Stadium for The Game in over a month!" They are leaning out toward Them and off the long flatness.

"Tell it to The Machine." They do not stop recording, but They will have to edit Their conversation. At the same time, maybe it will get Them more Presence if They include Their argument. Maybe They planned the argument because They know it will get Them more Presence. I am bad at telling if Their Presence is natural or artificial even though it is my job to tell, and They will not tell it to The Machine. I smile at the grass underneath Them.

The One in the chair says, "What's the Eye smiling at?" Their face tightens and Their voice shakes. They could ask me, but this could be Their way of asking me, and I should not judge. I should not judge. That is a good one. I try not to let my smile get bigger and that is easy because I remember that there might be a hole where my house should be.

I am close enough to see my house, but I do not look up to see if it is a hole. If I respect the hole, I like to think it will not swallow my house. I do not know how to respect it, but if I was the hole, I would not like it if someone checked to see if I ate their house. The hole is not me and maybe I am only respecting myself.

I walk up the dirt path that goes to my front door. There is a brown, paper bag with my lunch in it. I pick it up and reach out my other hand and when I touch the door, I let myself look. My house is still there.

I go into my house and turn in a circle to make sure everything is where I left it. It is. Bed and Sink and Mirror have not moved. Dresser is still next to Mirror and Toilet is still in its corner. I put my lunch down on Dresser and look at Mirror to see if my teeth are yellow. They are a little yellow. I try not to think about how the hole is behind Mirror. I am looking at the hole, but I cannot see it. Looking and not seeing and other contradictions.

-∞A∞-

I take a towel out of Dresser and go outside to use the hose to take a shower. When I am clean, I go inside and take out the uniform They make me wear for The Game. The uniform is blue and tight and all one piece. I sent Them three letters telling Them the uniform has gotten too tight and that it leaves red lines around my wrists and ankles and neck. They ignored my letters. I stretch out the uniform as much as I can before I put it on. This helps a little, but now when I wear it I do not feel important anymore. It is hard to feel important when They ignore my letters, just like They ignore my reports.

I check the inside of my house before I leave. Everything in it is in the right place. I stop at Mirror. Everything on me is in the right place, but I do not feel right. I do not know how to check my insides to see what is in the wrong place.

When I go outside in the uniform, They make The Sign at me. They put Their left hand out with the palm facing in at eye level and place the first and middle fingers of Their right hand on Their left palm like it is a Rectangle. I walk down Main Street and They make The Sign at me even though They are not going to be at The Stadium. All of Them that will be at The Stadium already are. Only the fifty thousand of Them with the most Presence from the previous week get to go The Game. They all want to go The Game because The Game is not broadcast on TV. Instead, it is only available on the Pangaea profiles of the Ones at The Game, who will all have Their Rectangles out and be recording it. This means the Ones at The Game will get a lot of Presence because everyone else will have to watch Their profiles to see The Game.

There is a long tunnel that goes from an alley in Main Street next to The Store all the way to inside The Stadium. I walk down the alley and into the opening of the tunnel past three of Them that have the job of only letting me walk past Them into the tunnel. There is nothing to do now but look at my watch and make sure I get to the end of the tunnel in time.

At the end of the tunnel there is a circle of metal on the floor. I check my watch again and step onto the circle of metal with eleven seconds left. I look up and can see a circle of blue sky. The piece of metal I am on starts to go up like an elevator. It lifts me toward The Stage that is at the center of The Stadium. When I stop moving, I am standing in the middle of The Stage. Many thousands of Them are seated around me in The Stadium. They all make The Sign toward me, but it feels like They are only making it at the uniform I am wearing. Thousands of lefts hands go up and thousands of right hands point at them. They are quiet because the countdown has started, but the quiet ends.

"And now, ladies and gentleman, it's the moment you've all been waiting for. The Eye has arrived and the countdown clock reads all zeroes. The Players have been chosen and, you guessed it, not a one of them has requested The Machine. There's not a cloud in the sky…except for the one we put there. You know what time it is. It's game time!"

I mouth along to Their announcement that changes every week until it goes back to being the same. Changing and staying the same and other contradictions.

The twelve Players run out of the tunnels at the four corners of The Stadium and stand around me on The Stage. They carry Their Items in little, black, regulation backpacks. The Players are taller than me and none of Them look down to see me.

The Players are introduced by the Announcer, and then all but the Player who is first go back through the tunnels and into Their separate waiting rooms until it is Their turn. They are monitored to make sure They do not communicate with the Audience or the other Players so that They do not know what the Players before Them have done. All They are allowed to know before The Game starts is who the other Players are and the order They will go in.

-A-

The first Player's intestines hang from a slit just below Their belly button. I do not know why They chose something that has been done so many times before for Their first Act. I get very close to make sure it is not a hologram. It is not because Their intestines smell like sour rubber and They do not know how to make holograms have smells.

"Henrietta Collinsworth is really showing some guts here, ladies and gentlemen. But are they her guts?" the Announcer asks.

The Audience's laughter is joined by the laughter They pipe in through the speakers placed around The Stadium.

I put the first two fingers of my right hand on the center of my chest and my uniform goes green. They roar Their approval, but the scoreboard only registers a 32% because of how common self-disembowelments are.

"A real gamble there by Henrietta," continues the Announcer, "but she knew our second Player might be just the man to make that gamble pay off. You all know him from his starring role on the hit reality show, Emergency Room Live. Let's hope Henrietta brought him the right tools in her backpack. It's everyone's favorite emergency surgeon and presidential hopeful, Dr. Fred…H… Schuman!"

The second Player reaches the center of The Stage. They have ten seconds to decide whether They think They will score higher by helping the first Player, ignoring Them, or hurting Them.

The Announcer talks during the ten seconds. "Alright, Dr. Schuman, now's your chance to show us you have what it takes to be the next president of the West Coast League of States."

The second Player takes out a sleeve of medical tools from the first Player's backpack, and the first Player starts begging Them for help. The Players do not have microphones because They are not allowed to talk to the Audience, but I am close enough to hear.

"Please, Dr. Schuman, they want to see you help. Think of the score you'll get. I know—"

I put my hands on my hips and the Audience's shouts drown out the first Player's words when my uniform goes orange. They stop begging and look at my uniform angrily, but They should not blame me. I do not make the rules, I am only an Eye.

"Oh, and would you look at that," says The Announcer. "Henrietta's just talked that already pedestrian 32% down to an embarrassing 27%. But who can blame her, friends? She's dying for a better score. I do apologize for that joke, it's almost as overdone as Henrietta's first, and maybe last, Act."

The second Player holds a scalpel up to the Audience and walks in a slow circle around where the first Player lies squirming on the polished wood of The Stage.

The first Player is trying to put Their intestines back in, but Their hands are shaking and the slit in Their stomach gets bigger. The hole in Their stomach reminds me of the hole in my wall. I want to scratch at my uniform where it is digging into my neck, but I am not allowed to scratch during The Game. I try to pay attention to the second Player.

The second Player stops walking and stands at the first Player's feet and looks down at Them, waiting for Them to stop struggling and make eye contact. When They do, the second Player takes the scalpel and cuts a slit just below Their own bellybutton.

The Audience erupts with sound and movement. When I go green, right up next to the blood coming out of the second Player's cut, the Audience gives the loudest yell yet. But when the second Player takes needle and thread from the first Player's sleeve of equipment and starts fixing Their own cut, while again looking down at the first Player, the noise is deafening.

The Announcer shows Their skill and does not try to speak until the Audience begins to go silent. "Wow! I mean, wow! What a move by Dr. Schuman! And look at that score, 94%, and I think I can safely say that is very well deserved. Henrietta, if you can still hear me, don't worry, you didn't die for nothing. I mean, 27% is pretty close to nothing, but hey, it's better than 0, right? And now, my Rectangle is telling me it's time to reveal the name of the Audience member who's earned the most Presence after our first two contestants. This update is brought to you by Alonso S. Juarez, who reminds you that a subscription to his profile has been shown to increase your Presence by an average of 8 percent. And I can tell you, ladies and gentleman, that he really is the best because I use him myself. Now, here's someone who doesn't need any help from Mr. Juarez. It's the top Presence earner from The Game so far…Lisa R. Phelps!"

A small section of the Audience stands and yells around one of Them that calls Themselves Lisa R. Phelps. They are sitting in the best seats in The Stadium, right at the center of the tiered seating in the row closest to The Stage.

Two hours later, the bodies of the first, fifth, sixth, eighth and twelfth Players are incinerated during the end of The Game ceremony. After this, the winner stands alone on The Stage to make a short speech and ends it by saying, "And remember, if you enjoyed watching me today during The Game, you'll love watching me on my show, Emergency Room Live. Follow me on Pangaea for unlimited access to every breathtaking episode. Good night and god bless!"

-∾A∾-

On the way back to my house from the alley near The Store, none of Them make The Sign at me. They do not like to notice me after The Game. This did not bother me before, but now it does, even though what They are doing has not changed. How can what I think change when the thing I am thinking about does not? Changing and staying the same and other contradictions.

I am almost back to my house. They are not sitting in the long flat chair on Their lawn anymore. I am glad I do not have to see Them.

As soon as I am three houses away from mine and I can check to see if the hole has eaten it, I do. My house is still there.

Inside, Sink, Bed, Toilet, Dresser, and Mirror are happy to see me. They cannot tell me they are, but that is what makes them valuable. I do not know what makes things valuable, so I make things valuable.

I go into the middle of my room and turn in a circle to make sure everything is where I left it. It is, except there is a piece of paper on the floor, just in front of my front door. I pick it up. One of Them has written on it. It says, "You watched my mom die and you did nothing. How can you live with yourself?"

They like to leave notes for me after The Game. Sometimes there are many notes, sometimes there are none. Sometimes, on days like today, there is only one. If I could go on Pangaea, I know I would find that They posted a picture of the note before sliding it under my door. Maybe They are sad about Their mother, but They are happy to get Presence.

I take off the uniform and rub the red lines it left on my skin. I look at the closed door of my house. I am on the inside and They are not and that is good. I am on the inside. I look at mirror. Am I inside the hole? I do not know if I would be able to tell. I cannot see the hole because mirror is in front of it. If I move mirror and the hole is not there, does that mean I am in the hole or that the hole is gone? It cannot hurt to check. I will only look for a moment. If the hole is there, it will only get a little bigger, and then I will know that I am not in the hole.

I still have Their note in my hand. I read it again. Something smells like sour rubber. My official notebook is on Dresser, waiting for me to take it to the

Office of Governance, so that They can ignore the report inside it. My wrists and ankles and neck hurt from where the uniform was pressing into them. I think about the faded sign pointing toward The Machine.

Maybe I will look for more than a moment.

Mirror is as tall as me so I can see all of me in it. I look like Them.

I move Mirror. It is heavier than I remember.

The hole is a spinning, flat circle of black and it gets bigger when I look at it. It becomes the size of one of my fists. There is no thickness to it and I see that I was wrong. It is not in the wall. It is in place of the wall. It makes a kind of music in time to how fast it is spinning that gets louder the longer I look at it. It sounds like a song made of an endless, wordless question. I stare at it. When it is almost as wide as my stomach, it starts to feel like someone is pulling me toward it. I close my eyes. I listen to the noise coming from it and it sounds like it is reaching for me.

If I go into the hole, I will not be able to look at it anymore and it will not get any bigger. It will not grow large enough to swallow all of Them. It will only swallow me.

I keep my eyes closed and move Mirror back in front of the hole. When I look, I cannot see the hole anymore. The reaching sound does not go away, but it does not bother me. It lets me know the hole is still there.

The Dry Flood

Kev Harrison

Detective Rodrigo Lopez sat back in his worn leather chair and reached out for the box on his desk with no small amount of trepidation. He lifted the paper top off the box, revealing a single, plump churro. Lopez had only been allowed one churro a week since the heart attack. Even that was the subject of great debate as far as Sofia, his wife, was concerned. He glanced back from his desk to the frosted glass of his door and, seeing that no-one was planning to disturb his moment of bliss, he shoved the sleeves of his pressed white shirt up to his elbows, took hold of the sweet in both hands and took a bite. He chewed the warm batter, feeling the creamy chocolate ooze out and closed his eyes to savour the moment. Then the phone rang.

"Lopez," he said in to the receiver, the 'L' distorted by the tacky material that had glued itself to his teeth. He listened to the stunted words on the other end of the line, wiping the cinnamon and sugar from his lips and his bushy black moustache.

"So the girl drowned? Is that confirmed? OK, yes. And how old? University? Right. Can you pinpoint the location for me?"

Lopez froze.

"Say that again. The Turia? You're absolutely sure? OK, but I want to see the whole report."

He slammed the phone back down and dropped the remaining half of his chocolate churro into the bin, pushing himself back from the desk on his chair. He wiped his hands on a napkin and ran them through his thinning hair, letting out a deep sigh. As he did so, his office door swung open and his junior detective, Moreno, burst in.

"Chief, what's the matter?"

"A twenty-two year old girl drowned last night, Moreno."

"Jesus, I'm sorry. Still, new university year, this shit always happens. Probably drunk."

"She drowned in the Turia, boy."

Silence swept across the two men like a wave, Moreno's eyes telling the story of the horror he felt at this revelation. Lopez's told a different story: the resigned worry of a man who had been waiting for this moment for a long time.

-ஃ-

Growing up in the seventies in Valencia, one of his favourite tales told by his grandfather—himself a Rodrigo—was that of the great flood. It had everything a kid could want. Acts of god, furious action, daring rescues and, ultimately, a happy ending—for his family at least. Of course the river had been diverted before he had even been born. But one look at the dry bed that wove its way through the city spoke loudly of what a Turia flood may have looked like.

Sitting as he did now, on one of the wooden benches beside the orange trees, the autumn sun beating down, he felt a world away from that drama. And yet drama was precisely why he was here. Though the body was already being refrigerated in the lockers of the coroner's office, the tent was still propped up behind the police line, hugging the looming sandstone wall of what was now the Turia garden. Two young officers were helping the coroner's photographer to take images of the place where the body had been found and combing the thin grass to find any of the victim's possessions missed the first time around. Lopez popped a nicotine gum into his mouth and chewed, feeling his heart rate pick up. Then he stood, ducked under the tape and into the tent.

"Good morning, chief."

"Morning gentlemen. I've got a few questions for my investigation, before I take a look at the body, if you don't mind."

"Anything we can do to help," the second officer piped up, taking his cap off and mopping his brow.

"Is there any evidence that she was moved here from somewhere else, after death?"

The two younger men looked at each other and then at the photographer, before glancing back to Lopez.

"Nothing, chief. And there was not a mark on the body. No fingerprints, no bruising, the clothes are all intact – waterlogged but intact – as far as we can tell she died here."

"Drowned here." It wasn't a question, but Lopez left the words hanging in the air anyway, to see how the boys reacted.

The first officer audibly swallowed and nodded.

"Ok, thank you gentlemen. Proceed with the rest of your work."

He took his cap off and nodded to the group as he lifted the flap of the tent. As he was leaving he turned back to the first officer.

"Be sure that copies of all reports into this death are forwarded to me, understand?"

The two officers nodded again and Lopez stepped out into the bright sunlight.

-A-

It was nearly two hours later that Lopez entered the coroner's pathology lab. The coroner slid the body out of the chilled cabinet and pulled back the sheet on the shelf, revealing pale, puffy skin and cold blue lips, slightly parted. The girl's auburn hair was still matted together and held no small amount of slimy plant material.

"You're quite sure it was drowning, Samuel?" Lopez said as he stared down at her.

The pathologist looked down his glasses at the detective, wiping his hands on his scrubs. He walked to the filing cabinet and slid one of the draws open with a series of clicks.

"The young woman—as yet unidentified—was found with one hundred and twenty millilitres of water in the lungs, a further three hundred in the stomach, anoxia of the brain. Do I need to go on?"

"OK, OK, stop. But in the Turia garden, Samuel? How does a girl drown in the Turia?"

"I'm the coroner, Rodrigo, you're the detective."

The pathologist pulled the sheet back up over the body and eased her back into the chiller until the locking mechanism engaged with a crunch. Lopez took the folder from him and flicked through the papers. He closed the folder, handed it back. He rubbed his temples with his fingertips.

"Samuel," Lopez paced over to the desk where his old friend now sat, filling out the police clearance forms for the body. "You know what I'm thinking about, don't you?"

The pathologist put the pen down and took off his glasses, polishing the lenses with a tissue from the box on his desk.

"Rodrigo, this is not going to be 1997 again. It's weird, of course it is. But that was…that was something different. We won't see the like of that again."

"I wish I had your confidence. When you know more about the girl, you'll call?"

"You'll know everything. Almost before I do. Now sign here, Inspector Lopez." He thrust the pen into his friend's hand and offered him a sympathetic smile.

Lopez signed, shook the pathologist's hand and left.

-∞A∞-

Lopez, out on his sun terrace, didn't hear the door of his apartment close when Sofia got home from the school. But he did hear her yelling his name.

"Rodrigo, if that is cigar smoke I smell, I swear I will kill you!"

The inspector didn't flinch. He rubbed his little dog behind the ears. It wagged its tail as it watched the pigeons flapping across the square below.

"I think we're in trouble, Esteban."

Sofia was still mid-tirade as she pushed open the old wood-framed doors and stepped out on to the terrace.

"After everything we went through with your heart attack! All the promises you made and now I find you smoking and…brandy! Is this some kind of joke?! I mean seriously, what do you—"

"—stop woman. Just stop. And listen."

He had not interrupted his wife in full flow for perhaps twenty years. She stood, incredulous, her mouth somehow frozen in forming the next word. Then she saw them. On the small wooden table in front of him, between the ashtray and the brandy glass, was his collection of newspaper cuttings from what had been Rodrigo's third ever case. And the only one he had never got to the bottom of. The Turia drownings of 1997.

"Rodri, why? Why now?"

"Camila Ramos is why, my love. She drowned last night."

"Not in the Turia? It's not possible." Sofia planted herself in the chair opposite him and took a long swig from his brandy glass. Her husband's eyes locked on to hers and he nodded.

"It's the same, my dear. Just the same." He picked up the first news cutting, the grainy black and white photo showing the same corner of the orange grove in the Turia garden where he'd spoken with the officers and the woman from the coroner's office earlier that day. His heavy fingertips traced the spot where the body had been found as he closed his eyes. He felt the comforting touch of his wife on his shoulder, and placed his own hands on hers.

-A-

The next morning consisted of three painstaking hours of analysing the footage from the sixteen CCTV cameras trained on the Turia that night. He watched as she walked past the old city gate and the football pitches, down the old steps and into the garden. He saw as she disappeared under two bridges, then skipped and jumped onto the low walls of the beginnings of the water garden. Then she vanished out of the shot. Lopez paused the feed. Looked back at the report. Still between fifteen and thirty minutes before Samuel's estimated time of death. He restarted the recording and watched intently. Not a single sign of her. He wound the dial up to double time and then he saw it.

On the street level camera that peered down into the old riverbed, a head rose above the murky darkness and into the amber glow of the street lights. Only her head and shoulders were visible. Then one arm rising up after the other, thrashing in the air.

In the air.

Then she slipped back down. Out of sight. Into the dark. Lopez wound it back and replayed on one quarter speed. Focussed on the look of despair, visible on her face even at this definition. Even from so far away. As she began to fall, he noticed another figure in the shadows. In a dark shawl, leaning over the wall and calling out, an old, claw-like hand gesturing to the girl, imploring her. As the body sank out of view, the figure turned and vanished into the blackness of the old city walls.

He gripped his walkie-talkie instinctively with his right hand, unable to take his eyes from the screen.

"Moreno."

There was a pause of a few seconds. Static.

"Chief. What's up?"

"Is that gypsy group still sleeping rough by the walls above the Turia, between Serrans gate and the Fusta bridge?"

"A few tents, chief. Most of them were cleared and moved into temporary housing in the spring."

"Meet me at the gate, Moreno. Twenty-five minutes."

"Chief? What's going on?"

"Be there. Out."

-A-

Lopez felt his stomach rumble as he stood at the wall, overlooking the old riverbed and smelling the fragrance of chorizo bread wafting from the van next to the gate. He looked anxiously at his watch. Where was Moreno?

At five minutes before one, he finally saw his weary-looking deputy striding across the bridge towards him.

"I'm sorry chief, I was at the other side of town. I was meeting the girl's relatives today, remember?"

"Ah, boy, I completely forgot. Did they have anything we can use?"

"Nothing. No depression, no bad influences. She often used the park as a short cut. Nothing out of the ordinary at all."

Lopez spat his nicotine gum into a tissue and crumpled it with his large fist, stuffing it into his pocket. He shook his head.

"Why are we here, chief? The officer's report said there was nothing of interest at the scene."

"Quite right. I was here myself, after all. But it's not something, we're looking for. It's someone."

Lopez lifted up his small bag and unfastened the clasp, pulling out a folder. He opened it to a grainy screen grab of the shawled figure, leaning over the wall into the park. Only a hand was visible from what was to become the body of Camila Ramos at the other side of the image, the rest of her veiled in darkness.

"She looks ancient, Lopez. Is she a suspect?"

Lopez snorted gruffly.

"Until we figure this out, everyone in Valencia is a suspect. But I doubt she's responsible. To me it looks like she's trying to help the girl. Calling to her. Now, show me where those tents you were talking about are."

The two men walked away from the towering gate in silence, Moreno just in front. They approached the wall of an old governmental building, its sandstone façade blending seamlessly in with the hulking medieval walls. In front of a corner section, an irregular patch of grass jutted away from the walls, housing a clump of three flimsy tents. Inside the closest of the three sat a boy of perhaps fifteen. He was smoking a rolled cigarette and mending an unidentifiable item of clothing.

Lopez cleared his throat and waved awkwardly toward the boy.

"Good day. We're looking for an older lady who might be staying here. Is she around at the moment?"

The boy didn't respond. He placed the needlework on his lap and raised his right hand to his cigarette. He inhaled deeply, eyeing the two men standing above him. He took the cigarette from his mouth, flicking the ash on to the grass beside him without blinking.

"If you're law, you're in the wrong place. We've done nothing and we've got nowhere else to go."

Lopez took a deep breath and raised his hands in a disarming gesture.

"We're not here to make any kind of trouble. It's about the girl. In the Turia. We think an old woman from here might have seen something."

"About time the police got something right." The voice was hoarse and came from behind the boy. The tent on the right of the cluster trembled until the woman from the video stepped forward, still wearing the black shawl, in spite of the balmy autumn weather. She leaned heavily on a dark wood stick as she approached the two men.

"Señora, we'd like to ask you a few questions, if we may?"

Moreno gave her his best pleading look as he asked the question. He stepped forward, opening his jacket and taking his ID to confirm that he was on official business.

"I don't need to see a badge. The pair of you stank of police before I even laid eyes on you. If you want me to answer your questions, you can take me to a café so I can make myself comfortable. And a glass of wine couldn't hurt to stir my memory."

Lopez was nodding even before Moreno turned to see if it would be ok to comply with the woman's request. Moreno offered the woman his arm, which she refused, and they ambled slowly around the side of the building to one of the narrow streets and into a café bar. Lopez sat opposite her while Moreno went off to fetch the wine.

"Bring the bottle," she called after him as she leaned her stick against the wall, Lopez giving a thumbs-up to his deputy.

"Thank you for talking with us, Señora. It's about a very serious matter. A girl died in the Turia two nights ago. When we were inspecting the CCTV footage for clues, we spotted someone that matched your description. The thing we can't understand is that the girl—"

"Drowned. And it's not 'Señora,' my name is Elisa. I told the girl to swim for her life, but she didn't understand. And then she went under, and…"

Moreno deposited a glass noisily in front of the old woman, sloshing a generous measure of wine into it. He looked up, noticing his boss' expression.

"Everything ok, chief?"

Lopez nodded, rubbing his eyes.

"Please, Elisa, explain how you knew she was drowning," said Lopez.

"I've seen it before, detective. Many times, since the flood came and took my parents in fifty-seven. But you might not remember the others. The last time was back in the late nineties, I think. The phantom water."

The colour drained from Lopez's round cheeks.

"Get me a glass, Moreno."

Lopez filled the glass to the top, his usually strong hands trembling feebly. He reached forward and took a long swallow, then wiped his moustache with the back of his left hand.

"Tell me everything you know."

The old woman paused, glancing sideways at Moreno who hovered at the side of the table.

"Take a seat Moreno, Jesus."

Moreno pulled up a stool, sat, and called to the barman for a bottle of water.

"How old were you when the floods came in fifty-seven, Detective?"

Lopez shuffled in his seat.

"I was still six months from this world, being carried by my mother, God rest her soul."

Elisa smiled, revealing a gaping hole where pre-molars once were.

"I was eight years old. We were living downriver then. The city had grown, but it wasn't like today. The place where our caravans were lined up was more or less a flood plain, two months of the year—the early Spring. But the flood came in October. No-one had expected that."

She stared off into the distance, her eyes glassy, her voice trailing off to a whisper.

"Elisa?"

Lopez drained the last of the rioja bottle into her half-empty glass.

"Sorry. I was coming back from a walk with a cousin of mine. We knew the water had been rising, but we'd been gone all afternoon. The weather was… calm. The rain had stopped hours before. But as we came down the hill on to our patch we saw the water. It was so high. So high. There were objects floating in the water. Bobbing up and down in the flood water. We got closer and we could see. Not objects. People. My mother among them. She was face down, but I knew it was her from two hundred metres. I ran and…"

The old woman wept, her body shaking. She gulped thirstily from her glass. Lopez raised a hand to her arm. She took a napkin from the dispenser on the table and blew her nose. She looked up at the two policemen, their expressions imploring her to finish the story.

"He was never the same—my father. He'd been out selling something—contraband, probably—outside the city. Perhaps an hour away, on his horse carriage. But after that day, he always wore black. Usually it's the widow in black. But he never forgave himself. Ten years, and he never spoke about her. We tried, my brother and me, but he wouldn't allow it. Taboo. Then, it was the same day. The same day. 1967. I can see it now, like it was this morning."

"He told us he was going to the Turia, to pay his respects. My brother asked if he could go too. He was older than me. But my father told him not to. Of course we followed. She was ours too, wasn't it our right to grieve? It was a quiet night, a bit chilly. No-one was on the street, so we followed at a distance. Then he came to the wall, overlooking the dry riverbed. It was just dead ground then, not the park that's there today. A wasteland, no more, no less. He looked over that wall and he was talking. We stood back and we watched him. But then he climbed up on to the wall. Felipe reacted before me—my brother, Felipe—he ran towards him, he called out: 'Papa.' Our father turned, saw us and he just yelled to us. He yelled, 'the water is calling to me.' And then he jumped."

The woman put both hands around her wine glass and guzzled everything that was left. She looked into Lopez's eyes with her own, burning rings of red gathered around them.

"The fall, Elisa? He didn't survive it."

Lopez didn't want to push her any further, but he had to know.

"He drowned, detective. In water that was not there. I watched him, with Felipe. We couldn't understand it. Couldn't grasp it enough to act. And that has haunted me every day since. It's why, these three days in mid-October, I am here, every tenth year, trying to warn people to stay away."

Moreno stood from the table.

"I need to get some air, chief."

He scurried from the café into the faltering afternoon sunlight, the silence magnifying his every step on the tiled floor. Lopez stood, calling to the barman for three cortados, then slipped back into his seat. He knitted his big hands together and sighed.

"How much longer before this…curse, whatever it is, is gone for another decade?"

The old woman looked up to the calendar that hung on the wall of the café, then back to the detective.

"Today is the fifteenth, detective. The final night."

-~A~-

Moreno swung the door to Lopez's office open and burst in. The detective looked up from his desk, where he was poring over the case files from ninety-seven all over again.

"Give me some good news."

"Staffing told me to politely shove my request up my ass. I told you chief, we need a better reason for an extra six duty officers to patrol the walls tonight."

"Better than to save people's lives? Please, do enlighten me."

"Chief, I was there. I know what the woman said. I might even believe her, just a little bit. But as far as the beat police are concerned this is a hunch. No more."

Lopez leapt from his seat and swept the papers on his desk to the ground, his face purple. He sat back down and huffed.

"Not again, Moreno. This will not happen again. It simply cannot."

The deputy bent down and picked up the case file, gathering the scattered documents and photos. He held up the file photo of the victim from twenty years before.

"Margarita Dias. You told me about her on my first day after my promotion. The only case you never explained."

"Ha! And now it's explained, it makes less sense than ever."

"We'll prevent it, chief. If we have to stay out there all night, we're going to put a stop to this."

Lopez climbed out of his chair and began to collect up the remaining papers and stationary which he'd cast to the floor.

"Have you eaten, Moreno?"

The deputy shook his head.

"Let's go grab a bite. We can't be heroes on an empty stomach."

Lopez strapped his gun holster over his shirt and slipped on his jacket, turning off the lights and locking the door as they left. Outside, they climbed into Lopez's car, covered in police livery, and began to cruise in to the centre to find a restaurant. Less than a minute from police headquarters, Lopez's phone rang in his pocket. He handed it over to Moreno.

"Take a message, will you. If it's Sofia, tell her I'll call her back in ten minutes."

"Chief, it's a landline. Not in your phonebook."

"Answer it, man!"

"Detective Moreno speaking."

He listened intently for a moment, nodding, then covered the phone with his hand.

"Chief, it's the old woman from earlier. It's started."

Lopez swore, thumping his palm into the steering wheel and down shifted to overtake the car in front. He flicked the switch to turn on the siren and accelerated hard.

"Five minutes. We'll be there," Moreno said, and hung up the phone.

-A-

She was waiting for them at the wall of the Turia, on the corner of the Trinidad bridge. Lopez swung the car over on to the pavement and cut the siren. The two of them leapt from the car and came straight to the woman.

"What's happening? Are we too late?" Moreno's eyes were wild as he asked the question.

The old lady shook her head and gestured down towards the park. They leant over the wall and looked down. Two children, preteens, a boy and a girl, were kicking a football around no more than five meters from where the Ramos girl had been found two days before.

Lopez stood straight and shot the woman an accusatory look.

"They're fine. Why the hell did you say it had started?"

"Shut your mouth and listen, detective."

Moreno could already hear it. It was that familiar sound, like when you place a shell over your ear. Water, rushing. The kids were fine, for now. But it was coming.

Lopez leant over the wall and began waving his arms high above his head.

"Hey! Kids! You have to get out of there! Come out of the park!"

The young boy looked up, his face a picture of mischief. He waved back at the detective, before chipping another neat pass across to his sister. The sound of the rushing water was growing louder. Lopez looked upstream and saw orange trees being jostled back and forth by invisible currents. It was almost too late.

"Kids, I'm not messing around. This is the police. Get the hell out of there, right now!"

Lopez held his badge aloft, the golden shield catching the amber light of the street lights. The girl looked up from the park, her eyes fixed on the badge. He had their attention. She walked across to her brother, picking up the ball, and began to talk to him. Inaudible from that distance. The boy nodded and they turned to the bridge and began walking towards the exit steps. Lopez gesticulated wildly for them to hurry. They quickened their pace, noticing the alarm on the detective's face. Then the girl suddenly stopped.

She turned her head back and her face contorted into an expression of concentration. She lifted a hand to her ear. In an instant, she and the boy were bowled over by the onrushing water. The invisibility of it only made it more stomach churning. The three of them watched with unobscured clarity as the currents pushed and pulled at the children, throwing them up towards street level and then pulling them under. The boy, a little older, was the first to come to the surface, still clutching his sister's hand as he pushed his head up towards the fading sunset.

"Help! What's happening?! Heeeelp!" He screamed, his voice a frayed shriek of fear. Elisa put her hands on the barrier wall and called out to him to swim. He was dragged down again, sinking almost out of sight before coming back up, dragging his sister with him. She was choking, instinctively holding her face upward to take in air. The boy looked at the woman, incredulous.

"Swim? How? What's happening? Señora, Señora, help us!"

Again, he was dragged below. His sister tugged down with him as a new invisible torrent drove them under the bridge. Moreno took off his jacket and stepped out of his shoes. He handed his phone and wallet to Lopez and climbed onto the wall.

"Be careful, boy," said the old detective, and squeezed his deputy's shoulder.

Moreno dove into the open space and immediately felt the invisible waves buffeting him from more directions than he could comprehend, driving him on to where he could see the bodies of the children tumbling through thick air. He gathered his bearings and kicked with his legs, guiding himself against the currents with outstretched arms. A second passed. Another. And he was with them. He swept the girl up in one arm and gripped the neck of the boy's t-shirt, then kicked as hard as he could below himself, pushing the three of them awkwardly upward until they breached the surface. He could hear and feel the spray around them even if he couldn't see it, splashing him and rocking the children in his grasp.

"Chief!" he cried out before being sucked under once more. He pushed up with his arms, elevating the kids above the choppy surf and into the air. "Chief! I can't keep this up for long. We need to get them out of—"

He was dragged back under.

Lopez looked around for something to throw to his deputy. A rope, something wooden. He saw nothing. He turned to the old woman, now sat against the wall, weeping.

"Think woman. My partner is going to die with those kids if we don't get them all out of this, now!"

"They are going to die. Again. I was too late. I'm always too late."

She brought her hands up to cover her face, her body jerking with the sobbing. Tears were now streaming down her leathery, tanned cheeks. Lopez stood and radioed for back-up as he ran along the wall to where his partner had resurfaced. Still he held the girl closely to his side, dragging the boy out of the water by his clothing.

"Hang in there Moreno. Help is on the way. Five minutes."

"She's taken on a lot—" a phantom wave struck his face. He turned back and spat water out over his chin. "A lot of water, chief. I don't know if she's going to…"

Once more he was pulled down.

Lopez felt the valves in his heart straining to pump the blood that his brain and his lungs now frantically demanded. He held his right hand to his chest, his breath racing. He looked to his left, saw the woman approaching him. He strode forward, still holding his chest. When he reached her, he placed a hand on each of her shoulders.

"Look into my eyes."

The woman's eyes lolled in her head, her despair overcoming her. Lopez shook her, bringing her back into focus.

"What did you say, just a moment ago?"

There was no reply.

"What did you say?"

She looked directly into Lopez's eyes and took a moment to form the words.

"Too. Late. I was too late, again."

"Are you talking about the other night? I saw you. On the tape. You were here. You tried to help the girl. None of this is—"

"For my father, Detective. I was too late for my father."

Behind the wall, he heard the water break once more as Moreno managed to drag the boy and the girl up for more air. Lopez looked over to them and felt his despair grow at the sight of the seemingly unconscious girl—at the weariness of his partner, thrashing erratically and trying in vain to fight the swirling water as it dragged him down over and over again.

"Chief! I can't fight this any longer. Where is back up?"

"Stay with me, boy. They're almost here! Stay with me!"

He turned back to the woman, his hands still gripping her arms tightly. He shook her again to bring her from her daze.

"Your father's death here was his own choice. He told you. The water called to him. There was nothing you or your brother could have done."

"We should have stopped him. We should have been closer. We were too late."

She howled the words, animal like, against the deafening cacophony of the thrashing water. Lopez caught sight of the thrashing arm of his deputy flinging the girl up above the surface of the invisible maelstrom once more and then slowly sink down into the darkness.

"Señora, did you ever stop to think that the water came back the first time because of the guilt that your father carried?!"

Lopez was bellowing now. As the words left his lips, the woman opened her eyes. They lost their glassy appearance and her breathing slowed. She lifted her hand to her lips. The wall of sound was receding. Lopez rose up to his full height and looked down into the darkness. Everything was still. He waited.

The young boy's head rose above the gloom first, his hair plastered against his skin. He spluttered, bringing up water, but he was just able to steady himself and approach the side of the bridge. Still there was no sign of Moreno. Lopez detected the sirens of the back-up team approaching in the distance, but the deputy was still beneath the ethereal deep. So was the girl. He looked back to the woman.

"You have to believe it."

The woman shook her head. She was lucid now, but she still didn't see.

"This is not your fault. Just as your mother's death was not your father's."

She nodded, sniffling.

"When you became calm, the water became calm. But you have to believe this is over. You have to reject this blame you have taken on yourself, or my partner and that little girl are coming out of the Turia in bags, just like all the others."

Tears started streaming from her face again and Lopez followed suit. He held her head in his hands. Looked straight into her eyes.

"Not my partner, Elisa, please. Not another little girl. You have to believe."

The woman reached her frail arms around the detective's shoulders and held herself against him tightly. He felt her shudder as the violence of those fifty and more years of sorrow flooded from her. At the same time, he heard the deafening roar of rushing water. After a brief moment, he eased the old woman away from him and staggered to the wall. He looked down, shining the torch from his mobile phone. He could just make out the two figures, still connected, of Moreno and the girl. They were some fifty metres away, lifeless, on the ground. He got on the radio to headquarters to hurry with the ambulance and dashed for the steps.

His feet squelched through the boggy, waterlogged soil as he approached his partner, lying face down on the ground. He rolled him onto his side. Felt for a pulse.

Feint, but it was still there.

Moreno began to choke, Lopez shifting him into recovery position and then making for the girl. She wasn't breathing. He pressed his fingers to her carotid artery. No blood flowed. He checked her airway and started to apply CPR. Moreno was on his knees now, a ruin of the man who had dived into the water a lifetime of ten minutes earlier. He could only look on as the detective tried and tried again, tears streaming down his face.

Finally the emergency team rushed across the park, planting the stretcher next to the girl. They had her out of the park and into the ambulance within a minute. Some of the response officers had brought coffee for the two detectives and the old woman, who had traded her black shawl in for a heavy blanket from the paramedics. While the hot drink brought warmth to his body, nothing could detract from the cold dread Lopez felt about the girl. He put an arm around Moreno's shoulder and told him he was a hero, regardless of this latest tragedy.

Then the commotion started behind them.

"Detectives, we have a pulse."

They rushed to the ambulance and looked inside in time to see her being rolled and vomiting up what seemed like litres of brackish, dark water into a metal bucket. She was weak, pale, very sick. But she would survive.

Lopez walked over to the wall of the Turia and lit up the cigar he had demanded from one of the back-up officers. He blew smoke into the air over the riverbed park as he observed the quiet beauty of the place.

"Thank you, Detective."

Lopez spun around to look at the old woman, almost instinctively hiding the cigar behind his back.

"It's me that should be thanking you, Señora."

"For helping you save your only unsolved case?"

The old man nodded as he exhaled.

"That, and for finally bringing all this to an end."

Swallow Your Third Eye

Evelyn Deshane

"You see it?"

"No. Nothing. Wait..." Peter Spinelli knocked the base of his hand against the flashlight. The light flickered before turning off for good. He'd felt his way through the abandon building's narrow hallway and down into the next room using the light of his partner, Aaron Carlisle's flashlight, until the darkness had become too much. The call for the dead body in the abandoned warehouse hadn't specified where it was, so Peter didn't exactly want to walk through a crime scene itself—though by the smell, he knew they were getting close.

"I see it," Aaron said. His voice was heavy. He gasped and seemed to cover his mouth. Peter walked towards his partner's voice, hitting his flashlights a few more times.

Nothing. But by the time he'd turned the corner, Aaron's light shone into the room. Gold spilled from one fixed point, creating a halo around the body. And the bones.

Body and bones? As in, separate people? Peter paused next to Aaron and gagged as he took a deep breath. The light cascaded off a gold filing inside an open mouth of a body that was missing the top half of its head. Blood spilled around him like a crown. Save for the injury on his head, he was intact in a blue janitor uniform. A push broom was in his right hand, a macabre sceptre. He was surrounded by piles and piles of bones.

"Oh, God. Those bones. They're too small. They're..." Aaron turned away and with it, his light was gone. Peter should have jolted into action, turning away from darkness towards the light, or grasping his partner, his radio, something—but he stayed in front of the body.

"What do you think happened?" Peter asked a moment later. "This guy was sweeping and then found the makeshift graveyard? The killer deposited a new body and then took him out?"

"Why would anyone sweep an abandoned building? And would the supposed killer come by to deposit more bones? Bones of kids. Jesus. I mean, who would even want to call this in?" Aaron trailed off as he grasped his radio. "There is too much here that is unanswered and honestly, this is far, far above my pay grade."

Aaron walked out of the room and towards the front door, talking into the radio. It dawned on Peter that they hadn't even cleared the rest of the building. A prickling fear ran through his body which he pushed down and pushed away. There was no way there was life in this building, not anymore. And if there was danger here, then Aaron was right. This was above their pay grade and they simply needed back-up. Peter turned around, ready to leave, when his flashlight came on full power.

The bones seemed to sparkler and glint like diamonds. The blood was black and slippery around the head wound, as if it was fresh. The gold tooth refracted the flashlight beam again and drew Peter's gaze to the man's hand not holding the broom. On the centre of his palm was the crude drawing of an eye.

-ᘛΛᘚ-

All Peter could see for the next three days was the black outline of the eye on the palm of the dead man's hand. While everyone focused on the bones from dead children—aged twelve to fourteen, according to the femurs and the reporters who extracted information from the coroner—Peter was fascinated by the man they had been called to find. The dead man had no ID, no fingerprints on file, and no system match on the DNA. The distinct gold tooth that had light up the room was going to be the only way to find him—so that was where the detectives had gone.

At least, that was what Peter had gotten out of Marty over drinks at the bar. As some of the few gay men on the force, he and Peter had always already been friendly. Marty was a bit too much on the bear-side for Peter's tastes, especially as Marty packed on weight in his newly garnered detective role, but he was still cute and easy to talk to.

And Peter was still haunted by the eye.

"Why do you want to know so much about the Janitor?" Marty asked over the second round Peter bought for him. "Most everyone wants to know about the kids. All milk carton material. All talk show worthy."

"I'm not a reporter here to write a true crime tale and weep. I have no profit motivations."

"What are your motivations?"

Peter didn't answer. "Was the man actually the janitor of the building? Was he the one that called in the body in the warehouse?"

Marty gave him a look. The "you know I can't divulge too much" look. But Peter pressed a hand into Marty's thigh under the table. Each touch, each caress and drink, would get him the answers he needed.

The phone call reporting a body had been a dead end; a burner cell and no way to clearly recognize the male voice on the other end without something to compare it to. It was highly unlikely that it was the dead man on the floor, though, calling in his own demise. The timelines didn't quite match up—but they were still working on it.

"And the eye?" Peter asked.

A dozen ideas had already gone through his head. The Illuminanti, Cyclops, the Pale Man from Pan's Labyrinth, and another obscure occult reference he couldn't understand at first glimpse. Was it a cult, a conspiracy, or just a coincidence?

"The eye is fucking weird." Marty shook his head, his words slurring together slightly. "It's the one thing we can trace. It's come up in a couple other murders."

"Child murders?"

Marty shook his head. Peter added a couple more guesses, all with negative responses before he finally asked skeptically, “Janitor murders?”

“Yeah. Except they’re not janitors. Just wearing the clothing. But you didn’t hear that from me.”

Peter mimed closing his mouth and throwing away the key. He wanted to ask more, but the alcohol seemed to hit him in that moment directly. He didn’t want to talk anymore, and neither did Marty.

As they pressed together in the back of Marty’s dark car, a trill of electricity went through Peter’s body. In his mind, he saw the desire between their body stretched out like a red elastic pulled tighter and tighter.

As soon as he blinked, though, it was gone.

-A-

The janitor’s name was Elias Whitney. His gold tooth ushered in his dental chart, and they all matched. He’d been reported missing a week before his body was found.

“I know him,” Peter said. He and Marty were at the bar again, drinks and electricity between them. “I went to the same church as him.”

“You? A church-going man?” Marty let out a low laugh.

“When we were kids. Communion. I...” Peter closed his eyes as a wave of pain ripped through him. His memory felt like the beginning of a migraine, the ordered scenes of his life suddenly jagged and painful as they slipped together. Elias was a short, squat thirteen year old while Peter was skinny, blond, and far too arrogant for his thirteen years. But they had been casual friends as they went to St. Anthony church and prepared for communion. After the ceremony, he’d come into the back room of the church for his jacket and saw Father Donovan with his arms around Elias. Struggling. Breathing heavily. All clothing had been on—but it was clear to Peter even then that he was interrupting something shameful, something he shouldn’t see.

Peter conveyed the story in shorter sentences to Marty. He seemed to sober up in the two minutes it took for Peter to tell. He withdrew his notepad from his pocket and started writing, underlining the ages the two boys had been and the priest’s name.

“What happened after?” Marty asked. “You tell anyone?”

"No. Never did. But Donovan was moved around to a different parish, and a year later, Elias was gone too. He didn't say anything to me about that night, and well, I didn't say anything to him. We were kids, still, you know?"

"And the shame," Marty added. "Probably was upset with himself and just wanted to get away. But fucking preists, man. I swear to God they ruin everything."

Peter nodded, swallowing hard. He hadn't thought about that spring in such a long time, but deep down, it was the origin of everything he was now. The moment Father Donovan left, along with Elias, the final thread of his faith had snapped and allowed him to let go of God altogether. When he had been young, the spiritual life had appealed to him and he told his mother he'd wanted to be a priest. Since he was the fourth boy out of five in total, she approved. There would be no need to worry about supporting him for school or work if he devoted his life to a higher purpose—and since she already had Michael, James, Daniel, and Timothy, she would still get her grandchildren.

But as Peter aged, the pride in spirituality had been replaced by a heavy guilt from being gay. He listened to the sermons that criticized lying down with men with a burning hot sensation of guilt. At first, he thought that maybe he could stifle his desire down; swallow it back and repress it in order to be closer to God. But to see the red face and feel the heat of anger and fury in that back room between Elias and Father Donovan was enough to crush every last hope within himself—but also build something in its place. If he couldn't stop what had gone on in the back room at thirteen, then he was going to spend his adult like putting away the bad men that lurked in the holiest of places and made sexuality into something twisted.

"You okay?" Marty asked. He put a hand on Peter's shoulder sympathetically. As a professional, not a date, this time. "You want to talk about anything?"

"No." Peter shook his head, but caught the far-away sadness in Marty's gaze. "No, Marty. Nothing happened to me."

"It's not your fault if it did."

"I know. But nothing honestly happened to me. No bad touch priests.

Not even Donovan."

"Well, you know, I had a boyfriend back in the day who had to deal with it. The memories came back later. Bad dreams, repressed shit, and headaches." Marty paused and assessed Peter. "Headaches kinda like your migraines."

"No. My migraines are different. It's all…" He closed his eyes, seeing the light behind them and feeling the jagged edges of memories. He opened his eyes again and took a drink. "I'm fine, Marty. Sorry about your ex-boyfriend, but that's not my story."

Marty's gaze was hard and penetrating, but he finally let it go. They talked about the identification of some of the bones in the pit, something that made Peter feel more like they were working instead of wallowing. Marty soon started to openly speculate if these bones had been child victims from another priest cover-up. It was the closest thing they had to a lead, and even if it sounded far too conspiratorial to be true, there was at least evidence of wide spread prest corruption.

"You know, at one point, the Catholic Church considered buying an island to keep all the priests who couldn't interact with boys? Rather than kicking them out, they wanted to repopulate another place with filth." Marty shook his head and took a drink.

"It's easier to move your location than to fundamentally change your foundation."

"Oh? You seem like you did quite well."

Peter gave a hard-edged smile. "And I lost my faith in the process."

"You're better for it. We both are. I do sometimes wonder, though, whatever happened to Dale…"

Marty continued to speculate, if not about his ex then about more child abuse and the potential cover ups. Peter nodded along and listened, but he was only half into the ideas. If he hadn't seen what he saw in the back room first hand, he would have had a hard time believing even the tidbit about the island. Now the sex abuse scandals were as obvious as light itself.

But Peter wasn't sure if the violence depicted in documentaries was the same type of violence and evil he'd witnessed at thirteen. Father Donovan never seemed like the type of priest with the bad touch like all the others. Peter thought of his first Ash Wednesday ceremony, where Donovan's thumb had given him the mark that they'd keep until noon when his mother would make pancakes in the church directory for everyone. The feeling in the centre of his head had been white-hot, as if the flame had been real when he was touched. But maybe it was Donovan, lingering too long and leering too heavily. Peter wasn't sure. He tried to remember Elias during that ceremony, if Donovan had touched his head in the same way, and if that meant it lead to something else.

But he was never sure. His memories began to feel jagged again, and Marty was no longer droning on and on about the case. Instead, he was silent, looking at his phone.

"Oh shit."

"What?" Peter asked. His voice was thin, reedy.

"We got a couple IDs on those kids. And they all link back to Elias's school."

"What do you mean?"

"He was never a janitor, but a principal. We'd been working on the assumption that he'd been abducted and lured to the building, given the janitor uniform, like all the earlier victims. The other murders we'd connected were all school officials too, you know? We thought they were all collateral for whatever pervert is leaving the bones behind and knocking off these kids. Be it a priest or a monster or whatever."

"But...?"

"But Elias was linked to several of the victims he was surrounded by. Reports of abuse. The other kids he knew before they disappeared. Doesn't take a rocket scientist to figure this out. Elias is just as much a murderer as he is a murder victim." Marty's face twisted. He listed off a few more details, before he sighed. "You don't know this."

"Of course. So is he the only one?"

"I don't know. But there's a lot of speculation now that Elias was taken out and the first target. Maybe by a former student who survived his abuse. Damnit." Marty huffed. "Now I've wasted a week on a perv."

Peter touched Marty's shoulder in support. "You haven't wasted a week. The dead still deserve answers."

"Yeah, yeah. I just... wanted a better story. Good guys, you know?"

Peter thought of Father Donovan in the back room, flushed and red. And then Elias, pale and writhing. Elias, who would grow up to be a child abuser. Was it the cycle of abuse in action? Was it fate?

"What about the other victims?" Peter asked. "The ones dressed and janitors with the eyes on their hands?"

"I don't fucking know," Marty said. "I just don't know."

-ꕥ-

When Marty was asleep, Peter grabbed the ID from his jacket and snuck out of his apartment. Back at the station, he fed in Marty's clearance code in order to access the case files, along with the ones from other jurisdictions about the eyes on the hands. Each one was crudely rendered in black ink or Sharpie markers. The first case had been done with henna and was written off as nothing out of the ordinary. It was only when eyes piled upon eyes and the glare magnified that the police thought there may be a connection.

So far, though, it had been an odd quirk. The victims did not know one another in their personal or professional lives. Nothing was shared between any of them aside from the fact that each one who bore the mark of the eye had been dressed as a janitor and had a sketchy relationship to children. Either there had been accusations that had been hushed up like Elias, or they were legitimate sex offenders with statutory or other forcible rapes on their records. None had been found with a pile of bones and Peter could recognize none of the other names on file. When he started to type them into computers to see their other records, he came back with a startling revelation.

Each one had been in his hometown at some point in their life. And each one's parents were still part of the Catholic Church in some form. Not always the same church, but Catholic parents were consistent. The connection was so common—or tenuous—that no one had seen it yet. Peter swallowed hard. He knew that if he were to search Father Donovan, he would find a record of Donovan in each place as well. Instead, he typed out Father Donovan's full name and wrote down the address of his current residence. It was only two hours away by car.

Peter returned to his apartment to give back Marty's credentials. He kissed a sleeping Marty on the forehead, his lips white-hot as he did.

-∾A∾-

By the time he arrived at the farmhouse, it was dawn. The golden light spread out like another halo around the barn. Screams, muffled yet distinct, were present in the distance along with chamber music. Peter had a gun under his jacket, but he didn't draw it out. If he knew Donovan like he was sure he did—if his jagged memory were to actually slip and slide into place the way he wanted it to—he knew he'd find an unarmed man on the other side of the barn door.

He stepped inside without a knock.

On a table were bones. Some were criss-crossed like a half-cocked pirate flag, while others were scattered like they had been in the abandoned building. A man was on the centre of the table, the top of his head bearing a bloody wound. The man's eyes darted back and forth under the closed lids, as if he was in some advanced stage of REM sleep. He was bleeding out. He was still alive, but Peter knew there was nothing he could do to help him, especially since the man on the table was the one who had probably put the bones there in the first place.

When Father Donovan stepped out from another door at the back of the barn, he seemed so much older than Peter remembered. It had been over twenty years since their last meeting in the back of the church—but as Peter had gotten stronger, he supposed Donovan would have as well. Instead a frail man in a blue -black jumper, like that of a janitor, stood hunched over as he held a long hunting knife, fresh with blood. His hair was white, his cheeks and eyes sunken. When he saw Peter, he didn't startle. He stood up taller.

"Father Donovan," Peter said. "It's Peter Spinelli."

He smiled. His teeth were as white as his hair. He looked Peter up and down, from his shoes to his shirt. "I remember you. You're a police officer now."

"Did you know that when you made the call about the body?"

Father Donovan didn't answer. Peter had all the information he needed. Donovan, the father who had become an abusive devil who ruined Peter's faith in God, had actually restored it. Father Donovan, who was going to harm one of Peter's friends, was actually trying to protect a whole generation of children. Father Donovan who, when he touched Peter's third eye, came away with visions of someone's character and their life choices—or blinding headaches if he did not heed the visions.

At least, this was what Peter believed. That was what he hoped. Every last piece of memory, of blood lust, of his own desire for God and for his sense of self, faded away and then came into stark focus. He and Father Donovan were the same type of being, but it was never a bad man. It was a destroyer of bad men.

"What did he do?" Peter asked, gesturing to the body on the table. The man gasped, blood oozing from his head. Though he was not restrained in any way, he didn't seem to be able to move.

"He made children into bones." Father Donovan spoke to the body on the table. "So he is now held down by the weight of his sins. He will be crushed by the weight of his sins."

"And you're the one who gets to decide?"

"Don't look at me like that, Peter," Father Donovan said. "You came across this once before."

"In the back room."

"No. In your own life." A pause stretched between them, heavy and menacing. "You don't kiss people on their foreheads, right? Not unless you really love them."

Peter didn't say anything. His lips burned.

"You can sense what I can sense. I felt it in your eye the moment we met."

"And Elias? You knew that he would..."

"Elias, like you and me, senses as well. But he uses a different, baser purpose." A pause. The man on the table wailed and quieted. Donovan seemed pleased. "Him as well. We all see and feel and think things we shouldn't."

"But we don't always act."

"You're right. We don't always act. But we should." Donovan walked towards the man, his knife poised. He placed the blade along the already-made wound across the man's third eye. "It takes one to know one. You and I, this man and Elias all saw things that make us further and farther away from God. But we both went in different directions. Bobby, here, went towards depravity, the worst type of torment and torture, like Elias."

"And me?"

"And me," Father Donovan. "We are very similar. Detective work is looking for symbols, in hopes of finding the truth. I look for signs in hopes of finding God."

"And God?" Peter bent to his knees. The pain in the centre of his eyes was overwhelming, was blinding. Gold light, followed by blue and red surrounded him. He flashed back to the moment when he was fifteen and an eight year old crossed his path, looking for a way home. Peter had just gotten his first pen-knife. He'd felt a gross, base instinct inside of him. His head had ached, but he took the boy's hand and led him home instead of leading him into a ravine where no one would hear them.

How many more times had the incident repeated itself? During his first beat cop walk, the hustler who was strung out and wouldn't remember. Or the prostitute with one eye who didn't know how to get home. Over and over again, he put himself into danger. And over and over, he had come out by swallowing down the strange desires that came over him. In spite of feeling and seeing and thinking things he couldn't understand but still felt so alluring.

He'd always wanted to swallow his third eye, but he never, ever could. Neither could Elias. Neither could Bobby, who had also done horrible things though Peter was no witness to them. But where they'd followed their eyes towards depravity, Peter saw now that he could turn towards the light. He had always thought he was fighting off the impulse to kill—and he was—but it was to kill for the sake of the future. If he embraced this now, he could become something else.

Just like Donovan. With whomever else was here; a cult—a conspiracy.

An entire island full of people who had populated a new terrain with morals inside of immorality.

When Peter regained his composure, Father Donovan was in front of him. He looked down at Peter and extended the knife.

“You know the right answer.”

Peter rose. He stabbed Father Donovan in the side, twisted the knife, and watched as he bled onto the dirt floor of the barn. He then traced the blade across his head in an attempt to quiet the jagged pieces of his memory.

He finished by drawing two eyes on both Bobby and Father Donovan’s hand.

Then he drove home, slid next to Marty, and tried to forget again.

Tens of Thousands Isn't Proper English

Ransom Wall

When the vision hit Jeffrey, he was halfway to the couch, where he would have sat until the coffee had finished brewing. Instead, he froze in his tracks, standing completely still in his striped pajamas.

The vision seemed to be an actual sight; an appendage to what he was seeing in the room he was standing in. It was as if he had suddenly obtained a second pair of eyes, mind-eyes, that were transmitting what they were seeing in addition to what he was seeing with his physical eyes. His physical eyes just saw his living room, but his mind eyes saw a long stretch of highway lined by long grass as far as the eye could see. On the side of the road, an undead man with rotting flesh and maggots in his right eye socket kneeled. Beside him, an unconscious woman lay face-down with her shirt torn open, the bare flesh of her back exposed. The maggoty-eyed man was using a boxcutter to carve into her back, cutting deep into the soft flesh. Half of the blade of the boxcutter was missing, as if broken off, though it had snapped off cleanly, leaving the blade still usable, as boxcutters do.

The dead man was not just slicing in the woman's flesh madly though, he was writing a message, in bloody, jagged letters: SO FLIES THE MOCKINGBIRD.

The image did not move, but Jeffrey could feel it wanting to move, almost vibrating.

And then it was gone.

Jeffrey was sitting on the couch in his living room, but the memory of the vision still lingered. His mind went back to the message.

"So flies the mockingbird. What the fuck does that mean?" thought Jeffrey aloud.

Why don't you go outside and see for yourself?

He walked over to the door, his legs moving seemingly of their own accord.

Or someone else's.

Jeffrey placed his hand on the doorknob, it felt warm to the touch, almost like flesh.

He closed his eyes and took a deep breath.

See for yourself.

He swung the door open and stumbled outside. He walked out into his yard and stopped. He wiggled his toes between the grass.

The grass felt like flesh too.

Well, you know what they say Jeffrey; all flesh is grass, so maybe all grass is flesh.

"Be quiet."

He looked out over the fence and scanned the field behind it. There was nothing there. He let out a sigh of relief, and turned back to his house.

He froze.

There were mockingbirds on his roof. Hundreds.

No, thousands. Thousands of mockingbirds were packed onto the roof of his house, swaying back and forth as one, a field of living feathers.

Those were just the ones on the roof. There were thousands on the roof, but there were tens of thousands in the air.

Tens of thousands isn't proper English, Jeffrey.

"Shut up."

They were all circling the house.

Are they circling the house, or are they circling you, Jeffrey?

"Shut up!"

Tens of thousands of—

Not proper English.

"Shut UP!"

—mockingbirds circling the house. They were all silent; not a single chirp or squawk could be heard from the tens of thousands of—

I told you, Jeffrey, tens of thousands is not proper fucking English. The correct term is dozens of thousands.

"Shut UP!"

—birds swirling about in the air. They made no sound.

Or they not making any sound or have you just gone deaf?

"SHUT UP!"

The tens of *(dozens)* thousands of mockingbirds on the roof were startled at Jeffrey's outburst and took flight, joining the tens *(dozens)* of thousands in the air.

They still made no sound.

Jeffrey sank to his knees in the *(flesh)* grass and looked up in awe.

The awe was interrupted by an odd thought of his, spoken out loud:

"I'm getting my pajamas dirty."

It seemed like such a ridiculous worry considering he was looking, but it was what took priority in his mind; that he was going to get grass stains on his pajamas.

Grass stains, or flesh stains?

"SHUT YOUR FUCKING MOUTH!"

I DON'T HAVE A MOUTH TO SHUT, ASSHOLE!

"FUCK YOU!"

The mockingbirds became even more agitated, but they still made no sound. They broke out of their eerie but somewhat peaceful-looking circle, and began to twist into a giant mass of feathers and beaks that formed a lunatic spiral, tens of thousands—

Dozens of thousands.

"TENS OF THOUSANDS!"

Thousands of tens.

"THOUSANDS OF DOZENS!"

Dozens of tens.

"TENS OF DOZENS!"

Dozens of dozens.

"TENS OF TENS!"

Dozens of dozens!

"TENS OF TENS!"

Dozens of DOZENS!

"TENS OF TENS!"

DOZENS OF DOZENS!

"DOZENS OF TENS!"

TENS OF DOZENS!

"DOZENS OF DOZENS!"

DOZENS OF TENS!

"TENS OF TENS!"

BEN TEN!

"TEN BEN!"

BEN BEN!

"TEN TEN!"

DOZEN DOZEN!

"DOZEN TEN!"

TEN DOZEN!

"TENS OF DOZENS!"

DOZENS OF TENS!

"FUCK YOU!"

—thousands of birds strong, spinning and turning, the amount of mockingbirds so thick in some places it blotted out parts of the sun.

The tens—

DOZENS!

"FUCK YOU, ASSHOLE, YOUR MOTHER SUCKS COCKS IN HELL!"

—of thousands of birds moved as one being, the mass of feathers twisting and turning in such organized perfection that it looked like a single organism, like a demonic, feathered worm of gargantuan proportions, a worm that held an infinite presence of mystery.

"The worm," said Jeffrey—but again; it wasn't really him saying it. "The Mysteries of the Worm. *De Vermis Mysteris.*"

He looked up in awe at the worm of birds again, and he began to sweat blood, the red liquid coming out of his pores and soaking his pajamas, adding blood stains to the grass (flesh) stains.

For a brief moment, the mass of birds twisted so tightly, the sun blotted out entirely. A second later it was back, at least partly.

It all looked so apocalyptic; the feathery shrieking mass twisting and turning in a DNA shape, the sun's rays leaking out through the spaces of the spiral.

It looked like the end of the world.

In fact, it was the end of the world.

The end of his world.

The twisting mass of birds spiraled down to the earth like a rocket, its shrieks filling the air, moving with organization that seemed impossible coming from anything but a single organism.

Organization.

Organism.

Orgasm.

The mockingbirds surrounded Jeffrey, forming a whirlwind of tens of dozens of thousands of beaks and claws that spun at thirty-miles-per-hour, creating a lethal tornado of deadly instruments that sliced through Jeffrey's flesh like razors. Beaks became blades, and claws became scythes.

Before death, Jeffrey had one final thought:

I'm getting my pajamas dirty.

Luther's Foreskin

Thomas Vaughn

Luther deeply resented the loss of his foreskin. Every day its absence ate at him like a persistent parasite. He knew with unflinching certainty that men without foreskins were unnatural. Despite his efforts to mimic the atavistic practices of Paleolithic humans in both diet and lifestyle, this void between his legs thwarted him at every turn and he felt like an imposter in his own body. It filled him with anger every time he thought about the millions of victims wheeled into sterile surgical chambers and subjected to a humiliating trauma that would haunt them for the rest of their lives. The machinery of modern culture had desecrated the human soul. Fortunately, for him, he had found Dr. Crites.

"So, I understand that you are interested in my foreskin restoration surgery?" Dr. Crites had a small office on the third floor of a dilapidated office building in downtown Van Nuys. Most of the other rooms were vacant and the structure permeated with the sweet smell of decaying wood. The sign on the door stipulated that he specialized in non-traditional cosmetic surgeries and voluntary limb amputations. The first thing that one noticed about him was the sweating.

"That's right," replied Luther. "Every time I look at myself in the mirror that's all I see. I feel like a piece of me was stolen before I even had a chance to know it."

"Yes, of course," affirmed the doctor. "Many men feel this way. They just don't talk about it. Now, let me tell you a little about my procedure. Most people resort to attaching tension cords or weights to the skin around the glans to stretch it and thus stimulating mitosis, but this can take months or even years. It is also, shall we say, unpleasant." Here the doctor paused, studying some distant object on the ceiling. After this momentary sojourn, he seemed to return to his body and wiped the beaded sweat from his forehead with a yellowed towel. "But I approach things a little differently. I prefer to use donated tissue. It is much quicker and yields better results."

"You mean like an organ donor?"

"That's exactly right."

Luther nodded. "I didn't know they could do that. I mean, I knew people donated body parts, but not that one."

The doctor smiled. "It just so happens that one is available. Shall I pencil you in for tomorrow?"

"You mean someone with an intact foreskin just died?"

"Some poor soul had an unfortunate accident. But that should not prevent us from extracting a small victory from his tragedy."

Luther hadn't expected things to move this fast, but then he thought about the years of suffering he had already endured. Why wait another day? "I will never really know who I am until this is done. This world is killing my spirit with all of its artificial technology. Let's make it happen."

-∞A∞-

The next day Luther's girlfriend, a local tattoo artist named Mayra, drove him to the appointment. "You're sure you are ready to do this?" she asked. He studied the Asian dragon that coiled around her arm, deriving comfort from the image's power. The rings in her ears and nostrils clinked like insect chatter.

"If I don't take my stand now, then I will never know what it means to be whole. I can't wait forever."

"I mean, aren't they worried about donor compatibility? And why aren't they doing this in a hospital?"

"I am pretty sure I can trust Dr. Crites. He radiates positive energy and the guy has some of the healthiest pores I have ever seen. You know how sick and twisted mainstream medicine is with all of its toxic pills and coercive procedures. They are the ones who put me in this position to begin with. You think I am going to trust them? No way."

As he entered the doctor's consulting room he saw the gurney. Dr. Crites' bored looking assistant, a Colombian woman named Artesia, instructed him to remove his clothes and put on the surgical smock. He had never gone through a surgery and therefore did not think to question why there was no attending anesthesiologist. As he situated himself on the table Artesia clamped a wet rag over his mouth and nose, infusing his lungs with an acrid smelling vapor. He fought for a moment against her relentless grip, but within seconds his arms dropped. As his eyes closed he saw Dr. Crites enter the room, rolling up his sleeves. His head glistened under the florescent lights.

When he awoke his head throbbed and his mouth was dry. Dr. Crites was gone so it was left to Artesia to instruct him not to remove the bandages for two weeks. She gave no indication that there was anything abnormal about the violence by which she had expertly chloroformed him. Once he could stand, she delivered him into the hands of his anxious companion.

Over the next two weeks Luther fretted, wondering if he had made the right decision. Dr. Crites had assured him the dissolving stitches would leave no trace. The days limped by and Luther grappled with the nebulous anxiety growing in his chest. When the day for the unveiling came Mayra gently unwrapped the bandages while Luther hid his eyes.

"Wow," said Mayra after the last bandage came off.

"What is it? What's wrong?"

"Nothing. It looks great."

Luther allowed himself a glance. She was right. It blended perfectly. There wasn't a trace of a scar. He ran to the full length mirror and stared at himself. It was truly beautiful.

"This is the best day of my life," he said with a tear forming in one eye.

"Say," said Mayra. "It has been a while. What do you say we try that bad-boy out?"

That was when Luther had a strange feeling. Normally this request would have been accepted enthusiastically, but for some reason he didn't feel like it. In fact, the idea disgusted him. To buy himself some time he lied to her, explaining that the doctor had specified no sex for at least two weeks after the bandages came off.

"All right," she pouted. "But I'll be waiting."

After this Luther was elated. There was a spring in his step that he had never felt before. Whenever the opportunity presented itself, he walked around the apartment naked, looking at himself in every mirror. He felt closer to his primal ancestors than ever before. The only nagging anxiety was the fact that he was no longer attracted to Mayra. At first, he told himself it was just a phase. He began to manufacture reasons in his head for why she no longer deserved his love. But, these rationalizations crumbled when he realized that every woman he saw did nothing for him. They were just inert pieces of matter.

Eventually his two weeks were up and he began making excuses. He told her he was having some pain or that he was still in shock from the restoration of his masculinity. At first she was patient, but it was clear that she was getting increasingly confused and frustrated with his evasions.

As time went by, Luther realized that his new foreskin had changed him in some fundamental way. He no longer liked to jog in the forested park. Instead, he found himself drawn to industrial areas. He liked the smell of car exhaust and the shadows of vapor trails in the sky. One day he came across a burned-out lamp pole. The maintenance plate was missing and the circuits were hanging out. Kneeling he placed his hand inside the opening so the he could caress the wires.

Not long after this he wandered by a fast food restaurant with outdoor seating. It was located in one of those East Hollywood slums that was transitioning into a hip commercial center. The smell of the burning meat hung in the air like a toxic haze. Usually the thought of eating meat, much less non-organic meat, nauseated him. The idea of fast food, with its artificial hormones and antibiotics, was unthinkable. Following some irresistible compulsion, he found himself staring at the restaurant's menu. He was almost frantic as he ordered the largest burger he could find. With anticipation overcoming his shame, he sat at one of the outdoor tables and unwrapped it. The bun was covered in a greasy sheen and ketchup was smeared on the wrapping. He had forgotten something as atrocious as ketchup even existed. Here before him was everything that he hated about the artificial culture of endless reproduction and yet he wanted it. Before he knew what had happened he crammed the burger into his mouth and began to chew. The meat was a little tough and he could actually taste an entire day's ration of sodium, but it was glorious.

As he plowed through the burger, he did not notice Mayra standing next to him with a look of horror on her face.

"Luther? My God. What are you doing?"

He looked up at her with his mouth full of genetically modified organisms, ketchup smeared on his face. "I was hungry."

She slowly sat down across from him, the shock evident on her face. Luther kept chewing.

"Luther, I need to talk to you. You are going to sit there and listen. Do you understand? Just listen. I don't know what happened. You act like you don't want me around. I know you've probably found someone else. Ever since you had your foreskin restored, you have acted like a different man. I don't even know who you are any more. Here I am just walking down the street and I find you in here—doing this..." Her voice trailed into condemnation.

Luther finished his burger and tried to ignore her. That was when the train went by. The tracks crossed the street about fifty yards from where they sat. It was the line that ran scrap metal to Long Beach. When Luther heard the whistle the hairs stood up on his arm. Then the train came into sight and his mouth hung open. He watched as the rail cars clattered by the restaurant. His heart accelerated and he could not take his eyes off of those wheels as they pounded out their terrible rhythm against the street. Soon he realized that his passion was aroused in way he never dreamed possible. He had to grip the table to keep from going into a state of erotic paroxysm. It was a long time after the train had passed before he regained his composure. When he looked up Mayra was gone.

Over the next couple of days he couldn't stay away from the trains. He had always hated machines and was proud of the fact he usually took public transit to reduce carbon dioxide emissions. Why had he failed to notice their indescribable beauty with their powerful engines and that steady, pounding rhythm? Sure, he had some residual self about the change. But, how can something be wrong if it feels so right? Sometimes he would stand dangerously close to the train so he could feel the kinetic vibration in his body—only to be left with that terrible, hungry mourning when it had passed. It was all he could do to stop himself from reaching out to touch it as it rumbled by.

In an effort to explain this change in his personality, he returned to Dr. Crites' office only to find it empty. The entire building had been cleared and there was a demolition notice on the door. Breaking the warning tape Luther entered the office and looked around. It was almost barren. He sat on a lone plastic chair and pondered his next move. That was when he noticed the folder on top of the dilapidated filing cabinet. He walked over and picked it up. To his surprise, it was his. He flipped through it until he found was he was looking for.

Donor Name: Benoit, Roger M.

"Roger Benoit," he mouthed to himself. A quick search on his phone revealed a very unhelpful obituary. There was no cause of death or next of kin listed. All that it said was that a sample of his art would be displayed at a gallery in Santa Monica for a limited time. An hour later he was stepping out of an Uber in front of the gallery. It had a low-rent vibe, blending perfectly into a neighborhood where a burned out shack could sell for a million dollars. He stepped inside and looked around at the paintings and blown glass. The framed pictures were mainly stills or photographs taken at awkward angles. Nothing really appealed to Luther.

"Can I help you?" The owner's voice was dripping with that sleek ennui that made his customers feel as if they were participating in some cosmic joke. Here was a man that would greet the apocalypse with nothing more than a casual flick of his cigarette.

"You still have any of Benoit's work? I was told I could see some down here."

The owner's expression changed. "You want to see a Benoit? You're the first person that has asked about him. I had his work up for two weeks. I couldn't give it away."

"You still have it?"

"Oh yeah. No one else wants it, at least no one around here. You see, this is a nice neighborhood full of well-medicated clientele. I have it in the back."

Luther licked his lips. "You mind if I have a look?"

The owner lit another cigarette. "You don't look like the type of guy who would be into Benoit."

"What do you mean?"

"Well… you're too healthy. You know, kind of granola. It's not like he was painting earth goddesses or candy skulls. You know that right?"

"No," said Luther shaking his head. "I don't know anything about him. I just need to see the work."

The owner waved lazily and said "All right. It's not like I will see anyone else this afternoon other than the homeless guy who keeps trying to get high in the restroom. Follow me."

As they walked to the back of the store the owner told him about Benoit's brief career. "He came out here from New Orleans. Cute guy, but he didn't take care of himself. Terribly unhappy and a tad obsessive. He really would have been better off back in the nineties during the whole industrial, techno craze. He's a little too gritty for the steampunk crowd. I promoted him for a while because I liked his energy—the way he rattles the cage."

Once they were in the backroom, Luther did not need to be told which works belonged to Benoit. There was an ensemble of crudely cut pieces of sheet metal soldered to a steel surface depicting gears, springs, and the insides of turbines. After studying the geometry of the metal parts for about a minute, Luther could see the phallic and vaginal imagery, one bleeding into the other. It was almost as if the gears were churning with their own frenetic energy as each formed a part of a whole, snapping into shape in Luther's mind like one cosmic orgasm.

"You see it…Don't you?" said the owner studying Luther.

"Yeah… I see it," said Luther in a faraway voice.

"Not very many people do. I believe the psychiatric term is mechanophilia, only in this case it's more than just a concept. It really hits you on an existential level. I believe it was Fromm who said it was a type of necrophilia—because the machine is dead. You see Benoit's work and you know that psychobabble is total bullshit. I have never seen anything so alive."

All Luther could do was nod as he felt his pulse quickening.

"But that's not the only thing I have. To my knowledge, he only did one painting. It was his last piece."

With that, the owner removed a bedsheet from a massive canvas in the corner. Luther gasped. It depicted a powerful locomotive churning through a lonely desert at night. The moon highlighted the rivets and the machine seemed to surge from the canvas. But, it was more than just an object. The locomotive looked back at you like a sentient being.

"How did he die?" asked Luther.

"You don't know?"

"No. Tell me." Luther's voice dropped to a low rasp.

The owner looked at him with some concern. "He said he had to merge with his subject. He was really quite insistent about it. He said it was the only way to find peace. I didn't know what he meant by that when he said it. As it turns out he was talking about getting knocked into the hereafter by the Frisco-Pacific Express. Hey, where are you going?"

As Luther fled, he waved the owner away. Once he was in the street, he gripped a lamp pole and began to weep. He shook his head, trying to steady himself against the approaching storm of realization. That was when he saw the girl cruising up the opposite sidewalk on a pair of roller skates. Steadied by the comforting hum of the wheels he managed to return her smile. That night one of those fogs that carries sound over long distances slipped through the streets. While everyone else in the city clung to one another for comfort, Luther stood naked astride the trestles, panting like an animal and listening to his oncoming lover braying in the distance.

Puke

Paul J. Lashway

Thad Johnson goes into Benjamin Franklin Middle school every morning by the same manner. He counts each step by lightly tapping the middle and ring fingers of his right hand on the black lacquered metal railing in between the bus circle and the main school building. Usually Thad counts between thirty-five and thirty-eight steps from the building doors to his locker. Thirty-six was good, Thad liked thirty-six. Thirty-six meant the day would be a good day. Anything but thirty-six steps made Thad feel out of sorts and a bit off.

Most days Thad wore a short-sleeve button-down shirt with no more than six buttons. These shirts always caused problems for the lefty, but his mother insisted he wear them anyway.

"Oh, they make you look so handsome," she often said. "And besides, I need you to start learning how to do things for yourself. I won't be around forever, ya know?"

The buttons were meant to be fastened from right to left, denoting it was in fact a male shirt. Thad found this to be an oddity considering his mother's blouses were the exact opposite. He first noticed the discrepancy last summer when his mother was running late for her job at the diner. She burst out of her room flushed and panicky and left the house still buttoning up her smock. Puzzled by his observation, Thad made a trip to the library the next day where an afternoon of research help from the librarian showed him this fashion style actually stemmed from Victorian culture; during the period, men dressed themselves while women were dressed by others, probably handmaids.

The memory struck Thad, causing him to stop dead in his tracks and interrupt his step count. He didn't know why. He did his best to refocus, like he'd been working so hard on, and entered the building. Thad's Bus drop-off times were staggered so he usually arrived at school ten minutes before the rest of the students. This was to give Thad and his fellow riders extra time to put away their effects and find their classrooms before first bell. His bus was short and cramped and the only one of its kind in his rural school district. He wanted to ride the other buses whenever he overheard his classmates talk about how much fun it was to bounce while sitting in the back seats whenever going over a large bump in the road. Instead, Thad rode the different bus and could only chalk it up to his living so close to school.

The scarcely populated corridors made finding his locker and classroom easy for Thad. Once in front of his dull green locker, he began his fastidious morning routine. To him, locker organization was essential. "Everything has its place," his mother would say. These words reverberated inside him like gospel, causing Thad to mumble the phrase over and over until everything was perfectly organized to his eye. His jacket, no matter the season, had to be placed on the inside left hook before taking his lunch bag out of his backpack and placing it in the upper cubby compartment, then came the books. Each textbook and corresponding notebook with folder would be meticulously placed in the bottom shelf in order of class period. Thad would then do a double, triple check, count to five by tapping his middle and ring fingers together with his thumbs and finally go into his classroom.

There were days, usually when he counted anything outside thirty-five to thirty-eight steps, when Thad could not break away from his locker routine. This almost always ended badly. Whenever Thad fell into this black hole, groups of kids from different grade levels, would gather to stare and usually mock him. The commotion would then draw the attention of the hall monitor, who would then proceed to break up the scene by stepping in and forcibly shoving Thad's effects haphazardly into the locker before turning his strength on Thad. Some harsh words usually accompanied the ordeal along with the expected bruises where the hall monitor grabbed his arm before dragging him into his classroom.

The empty classrooms all looked the same, for the most part. The room was large but would soon shrink down once Thad's fellow classmates entered, gyrating and eager, ready for the day. Thad took his seat when the urge struck and resisted the temptation to reach into his pocket and take out his BIC Round Stic medium pen. This persistent urge caused a slight tic in his face and cheek to develop. As annoying as it was to Thad, his tic actually represented progress in his focus training. He had come a long way from not having any control over himself to now only having a facial tic. Long excruciating summer hours were spent seated at the kitchen table desperately trying not to grab his BIC pen and make those countless, endless circles. His mother did her best to teach him different ways he could redirect his concentration whenever his disorder would suddenly get the better of him. Thad knew how hard she worked to help him and he knew removal of the pen from his pocket now would mean failure.

The hallway behind him suddenly roared to life with incoming students who quickly spilled their energy into the classroom. Thad smiled in an attempt to greet his fellow students as they settled into their assigned seating around him.

"Pssh, where's your cornfield, scarecrow?" one girl jeered.

"And look at those teeth," another boy laughed, "didn't know we had a class jack-ass o'lantern."

Thad didn't think much about his appearance. Were he to look in a mirror, Thad would have seen two sunken in eyes under a mop of curly straw hair looking back at him with a mouth full of stunted, spaced teeth and crusted-over skin flakes under the crook of his right nostril. The final and warmest welcome he received was simple "ewwah-hh, no," from the girl who sat next to him. Thad slowly turned, disheartened, when his teacher burst in the room with a mug of freshly microwaved coffee in her left hand and a manila folder of papers under her right armpit.

Puke

"Class, Class! Good morning class."

"Go-od Mor-ning, Mis-sus O'Tur-ley," the class droned in unison.

"Now I want everyone to get out last night's assignments and pass them forward while I take roll," said Mrs. O'Turley as she straightened up her desk.

Sudden panic swept across Thad's brow. He wracked his brain. *Assignment? What assignment?* he thought. Frozen, like a deer caught in headlights, the sound of the other's papers rustled like orchestral strings tuning before curtain went up. Brassy bellows of binders began clipping open and shut with all the grace and dulcet of "CA-CHUNK, Ki... CUNK." The en masse crescendo began swirling around Thad's head and filled his ears while his internal percussionists, the churning cymbalist of his stomach and the slave-driving timpanist of his heartbeat, limbered up for (what one snooty critic might lazily describe as) the Big Finish.

The orchestra's opus suddenly gave way as the new sounds of paper passing descended upon Thad from the back of the room. The race began without a starting gun. He contorted his back with each rustle of papers creeping up towards him as if they were individual chills up his spine. Papers collapsed and stamped into uniform piles by each new handler jockeying their three page masterpiece into the top position. Thad began to taste traces of blood; he did not realize his jaw was clenched down on his lower lip.

Seemingly in unison, students shuffled, tapped, and passed each pulpy baton forward like a step in the process of some manufacture assembly line: Snatch, Shuffle, Tap-Tap, Pass, repeat. Snatch, Shuffle, Tap-Tap, Pass, repeat. Snatch, ShuFFLE, TAP-TAP, PASS, repeat. SNATCH, SHUFFLE, TAP-TAP, PASS....

-ॐA ॐ-

Thad didn't know what happened when he came to, until he looked down. A pile of his classmate's papers sat disheveled in front of him. Numerous scribbled circles covered each exposed page with wet black ink as if tattooed by some tribal shaman. Then he noticed the shadow encroaching over him—he felt especially small.

"What do you think *YOU* are doing," a voice shrieked from above, "Do you think this is *FUNNY*…or *CLEVER*?"

Thad felt the moisture accumulate in his hand. Clenched within his fist was his BIC Round Stic medium pen. It was the smoking gun—the bloody hook—Col. Mustard in the library with the candlestick. All at once his body jerked back into reality with one uncontrollable motion. Thad began furiously rocking back and forth as the realization sunk in that he was the culprit who drew all of the circles. He was the shaman; he was Col. Mustard.

"What's he doing, now?" one girl said.

"Hey, I worked hard on that, ya Retard!" said another boy.

"ENOUGH!" said the voice from above.

Thad didn't know what to expect next. He was a rat trapped in a corner with no escape. Thad sat as still as he could manage. Then just as he braced for impact, "Hopeless," the voice above disgustedly sighed before forcibly snapping the papers off the desk and marching back to the front of the room. The snickering voices of each classmate rang in his ears as the clunky black shoes of his teacher reverberated off the tile flooring. Her strut made her seem more like a schoolmarm disciplinarian than the doe-eyed nurturing educator Thad first met at open house last year.

The rest of the morning passed in a quiet haze and soon the lunch bell invitingly rang. Thad came into the cafeteria equipped with a standard issue brown paper bag, properly weighted and in sequential order of eating: turkey sandwich without crusts, mixed berry juice box, gummy snack and granny-smith apple.

An *Amazing Spiderman* comic was his usual companion at lunch. He wasn't particularly fond of spiders. In fact, they gave him the heebie-jeebies. Mostly, he identified with Peter Parker because whenever things got rough, Peter would simply put on his mask and become the hero; become somebody else. Thad always wanted to be somebody else. The school district recently made a push for healthier lunch options, all within budget of course. Thad's laundry list of food allergies precluded even the slightest inclination of him ever actually buying lunch. So, given that most of the children purchased their victuals, anyone brown-bagging it naturally stood out like a big sore toe—Thad was that toe.

Puke

Thad found his usual spot in the lunchroom at the last empty, out-of-date, fold--up table. He didn't mind that the built-in stools sagged too low to the floor making sitting an impossibly uncomfortable task. He instinctively rectified the situation by curling one leg underneath him. This effectively propped Thad up to the perfect height for both eating and looming over his comic. Most days he found balance between devouring his food and reading. Today was not one of those days. The newest issue had Spiderman pitted against the evil Doc Ock who, in the last issue, kidnapped Mary Jane and left her dangling off the Brooklyn Bridge for ransom. Thad couldn't wait, he poured himself into the story. One minute he was swinging from building to building with Peter, the next he was right alongside his hero being taunted by Doc Ock's henchman. Thad left his lunch bag on the table corner untouched.

"Mr. Johnson, aren't you gonna—Thad, THAD!" a woman's voice cried, startling Thad out of deep concentration, "Mr. Johnson, aren't you gonna eat your lunch? You only have fifteen more minutes before…"

"S-sorry Ms. Nealon," Thad stammered, "But Sp-Spiderman just got cap-captured trying to save Mary Jane and I kn-knew it was a trap this whole time, and you have a st-stain just above your left pocket on your pants. Did you know you have a st-stain on your pants? Right there, see it, M-Ms. Nealon? Ms. Nealon?"

"…Mr. Johnson! I don't care about SpEH-SpEH-SpEH-Spider-whoever!" the Lunch Monitor said tauntingly, "Eat your lunch. Go to recess, got it?"

Thad looked down in confusion as if trying to figure out the New York Times Sunday Crossword.

"Look at me!" She said louder, letting her anger show, "*Got it?*"

Thad awkwardly shook his head in approval causing a little bit of spittle to drop from his upper lip. Ms. Nealon rolled her eyes and walked away, shaking her head in disapproval.

He dug through his bag. Thad first pulled out the turkey sandwich his mother made only a few hours earlier. After close inspection he took a bite. Next came his juice box. Thad delicately removed the accompanying straw from its cellophane casement and punctured the flimsy foil orifice located on the top right corner. This caused a few purple droplets to scurry upwards and dribble out on the table as the outside air reached equilibrium within the cardboard container. Not a moment later, Thad felt something awful attack his left bicep causing him to drop his sandwich on the lunchroom floor. The initial shock made Thad jerk away and look down at his arm thinking a wasp stung him. The pain quickly escalated into a widespread throbbing sensation and before he knew it another shot came in harder than the first.

"Hey Retard!" a boy's voice rang, "hurts donut? Wanna'nother? Today only, free of charge!"

Before Thad could blink, the boy landed another punch, harder still.

"Owwah, wh-whadd'ya d-do that for, J-Jimmie?" Thad said, gripping his now dangling left arm with his right hand.

The lunchroom went quiet with curious onlookers; all eyes set on the two boys and Ms. Nealon was nowhere to be found.

"It's simple, Tard-o, you ruined my paper, so I'm gonna ruin you!" Jimmie said.

All at once the room spun as Thad was thrown to the ground. The next thing he knew, he was being pummeled by the contents of his lunch. In the background, Thad heard the chants, "Jim-mie, Jim-mie!" Thad was caught in the hysteria of the moment. He didn't even realize another boy joined in the drubbing until the cafeteria erupted in shouting and laughter of utter pandemonium. Every type of school lunch food item was thrown across the room and most of it aimed at Thad Johnson. The big toe suddenly became the carnival dunk-tank clown, the sideshow, the freak. By far, the worst thing to hit poor Thad was the shiny granny-smith apple he and his mother picked the weekend before. Jimmie specifically saved it for last.

"You're the apple of my eye, Fag-mo!" Jimmie mocked, before landing the projectile square on Thad's forehead. There seemed to be no end in sight to the beating when, "MR. LUBINOWSKI!" cried a voice. The raucous lunchroom dropped to stunned silence.

"I'm going to pretend I'm not actually seeing what I think I'm seeing and give you to the count of three to take your seat!"

It was Ms. Nealon. Everyone stood in place, stupefied, as if they could not remember authority ever having existed before this point.

"One…" Ms. Nealon said, sternly.

The cafeteria tensed then quivered as harsh screeches and squeals came from each of the lunch tables being manipulated back to order. Most of the student onlookers sheepishly tried to act as if they weren't involved. Their efforts were sorely in vain. Jimmie remained frozen, he was caught red-handed.

"Two…"

Upon hearing the digit, his paralysis subsided, giving way to a sudden burst of adrenaline-infused movement. His dirty blond hair swished in front of his eyes as he darted past the formidable Ms. Nealon and back into his seat proper located on the other side of the room. He just made it.

"Three…OK!" she said furiously, "Now who is responsible for this mess? They are gonna PAY!"

The lunchroom was hastily put back together. Thad Johnson was the only thing still out of place. He laid supine on the ground still in utter shock of the moment. There were bits of Cheetos' dust in his hair, congealed relish running down his right arm, miscellaneous tomato seeds mixed with whipped mayonnaise across his left thigh, and a welt beginning to raise near his right temple.

"MR. JOHNSON!" Ms. Nealon said, her anger began reaching fever pitch, "Why are you still on the floor?"

Thad could only mouth senseless words, but nothing came out.

"Everyone go to RECESS! Except you, Mr. Lubinowski," she said, "You are going to Asst. Principal Traegar's office."

As Thad lay there he thought the students' footsteps sounded like militaristic mice marching about as they scurried towards safety. Ms. Nealon stared coldly in Thad's eyes making him extremely nervous and uncomfortable. Not another word was uttered until everyone left. Ms. Nealon approached Thad and slowly squatted down next to him, never breaking eye contact.

"Now, Mr. Johnson, you have been nothing but a pestering little insect for me all day," she said, her sickly sour breath wreaked of stale cigarette smoke. "And…it appears you've dropped your lunch."

Thad didn't understand. He lifted himself up onto his elbows to look around. He sat confused for a moment but finally understood once he looked towards his feet. Underneath his left shoe laid the remnants of his turkey sandwich. The bread had imprints of shoe tread smashed onto one side. The other side held moist pieces of old spit wads embedded into the side of the crust. Miscellaneous crumbs and glops of pocket lint were scattered across the top, entangled with dandruff encrusted tufts of long knotty brunette hair. Thad thought he even saw what could only be described as greenish-white globs of gooey boogers smeared directly across the center of the sandwich.

"Go ahead…Eat It," she said with a snort.

Thad balked at the command. He had no idea what was going on but his innermost instinct told him not to move.

"I said, EAT IT!"

Thad started to rock slightly. He didn't know what to do. Even on his best days he was not mentally equipped to handle such a heinous situation. Tears of frustration and terror began forming in the corners of his eyes. Thad could not figure a way out and became helpless to resist.

"If I have to tell you one more time, there WILL be HELL..!"

Then in one swift movement the sandwich went from floor to hand to mouth. Thad tried his best to block out what was happening. He did well to get past the initial unknown crunchiness, but he gagged twice thinking about the hair and boogers mixing together in his mouth, then down his throat, and into his stomach. Seeing the reflex prompted Ms. Nealon to grab the crumpled up juice box lying next to Thad, the same one his mother lovingly packed for him that morning, and shove it into his mouth. "Here, drink this, Retard!" she said, squeezing the last remaining drops down his throat. He began to choke. Thad wanted to cough in the worst way but didn't dare for fear of what Ms. Nealon might do to him. He could only hold it in and wait. Then, as if coming out of a trance, Ms. Nealon carefully stood up. She appeared to be exhausted from the ordeal. Her left arm rested akimbo while the other swung haphazardly motioning towards the door. Thad was confused. She told him to get up and go to recess. After a couple poorly hidden convulsions, Thad finally let out a proper cough and did as she commanded. He felt disgusted in who he was and what he had done.

-ᴥ A ᴥ-

Outside Thad could barely move. No one would talk to him, everyone just stared. He found his way to where the shaggy grass met the white playground stone. The school board approved a budget which allowed for renovations to the recess facilities two years prior. Many updates were made aside from replacing the rusty old equipment. One such improvement was the addition of wooden railings marking the boundaries between the playground and the grass field. Thad went to this boundary. Normally, he would not have chosen this spot because to be so close to the pebbles meant he would have to constantly fight the urge to count them all and that was too risky. Thad found a compromise in himself and sat down with his back towards the play stones and faced out towards the field. It was easier for him to fight the urge to count the blades of grass since their color blended so well, masking their individuality, creating one great whole rather than many parts. It really didn't matter, though, he only stared at the plank of wood he was sitting on. Signs of wear already began to show against the finish on the woodgrain.

Thad could only stare downwards in shame. His right arm cradled his legs to his chest and Thad eventually found his balance. He began picking at the wood with his left hand until the weather-stained chips reminded him of those uncertain pieces of debris he ingested only fifteen minutes previous. His stomach let out a vicious growl causing Thad to break pose and helplessly clutch at his innards, a scowl took to his face. He knew something was seriously wrong, but before he had any time to reflect, the bell knelled twice, signaling it was time for the students to pack it in for the last part of the day.

-ᴥ A ᴥ-

An atmosphere of tense caution settled throughout the afternoon classroom as the students waited for Mrs. O'Turley to begin her lesson. Each student sat stone-faced and attentive, taking care to only make eye contact with the back of the head of the pupil sitting in front of them. Only Thad sat different, with his head hung low wishing he could disappear. Mrs. O'Turley sat writing at her desk with a downcast visage of disdainful indifference. As she finished, she let out three little "hmfphs" in concert with the last pen strokes marking down the roll from recess. Standing up, she snatched a heap of papers from the right upper corner of her desk. In the process, the backs of her knees pushed out her worn metal chair against the tile floor causing an awful screeching noise to fill the room. The entire class flinched in a collective wave as the piercing sound gratingly hit each individual eardrum. Normally, Thad would suffer worst of all from such a shrill sound, but not today.

"I'm handing out next week's spelling words," she said unimpressively.

Each student took a page before meekly turning to pass along the remaining papers to their rearward neighbor. All except Thad. When it was his turn to receive, the girl in front of him did her best to make the transaction as short and meaningless as possible. It didn't matter, though, because he never broke pose. He didn't even see her turn around, much less her attempt to hand him the dwindled pile. With a sigh of annoyance, she placed the papers on the top left edge of his desk where they sat miserably until finally the girl sitting next to Thad helped move the process along. She moved quickly so as to not disturb his semi-catatonic state. The only thing moving was Thad's anxious left thumb around the cap of his BIC Round Stic medium pen.

"All ready Class?" Mrs. O'Turley said. "Now the first word is…"

That's when it hit Thad. Something deep inside him let out a most awful gurgle, shaking him back into reality. Thad panicked, a cold sweat began to slightly break across his brow. The uninvited guest began announcing his arrival by way of clammy dewiness framing Thad's visage. He made a dry cough in hopes of covering up the rumbling noise, but he knew what was creeping along his innards.

"That's right, Victoria, and does anyone know what part of speech..."

Thinking about it only seemed to make it worse. Then another gurgle came spring-loaded from the opposite side of Thad's torso, causing him to shift sharply in his seat. The wagons were being circled, he could almost feel the prick of the enemy's arrows slinging inside him. Not knowing what to do, he began rocking faster. This only made matters worse.

"Not quite, Scott, anyone else? It's an adverb, remember adver—"

Pressure began collecting in his center. Thad did his best to reflexively keep in whatever was trying to come out. Each hand gripped the opposite side of his body in futile attempts to just hang on. That's when it all stopped. He stopped rocking and sat up straight. He didn't know what to make of it. In a matter of seconds, the nightmare seemed to be in the distant past. Forgetting his place, Thad stood up and surveyed the class around him. Mrs. O'Turley's back was turned as she wrote out the next definition on the classroom dry-erase board. No one seemed to notice him. Most of the students' eyes were half-glazed over due to the incessant drone of their teacher's voice pouring over some twenty monotonous vocabulary words. Thad was relieved his gastral distress timed out but was still unsure what to make of everything; he was in limbo. He wanted to say something, just to make sense of it all. So, without thinking, he opened his mouth.

A torrential flash flood of undigested bile shot out like a gush from an active fire hydrant. The festering solution began fountaining out everywhere. Thad froze in horror as he watched the scene unfold before him. He felt as if he was unleashing a new plague upon the world. His throat seemed an endless geyser of filth. The kids in the first two rows were instantly covered with the foulest smelling puke anyone has ever known. The retch slid down their fronts and backs before finally plopping onto the floor. The sludge quickly accumulated into ankle-deep pools of sour smelling sewage.

Thad could hardly believe his eyes. He broke trance and ran. He was a holy terror running up and down aisles, spraying everybody with his puke, especially Mrs. O'Turley. His head became a sprinkler system with enough pressure to rival that of every fire hose in the county. No one was safe. He wanted to scream except he couldn't, he would have choked first. It just kept coming and before long the vile juice seeped out from under the door of the classroom and out into the hallway. The hallway was transformed into a roaring river of barf. It spread to every classroom and poured into every office; after sloshing its way up the walls and seeping into lockers, the puke extended its slunky arm into the cafeteria where it met Ms. Nealon coming out of the back room office.

Leaving for the day, Ms. Nealon was absent-mindedly rifling through her purse in a desperate search for the last of her Newport menthols, when she first noticed the puke touching her foot. The combination of surprise, disgust, and momentum flung her body across ten feet or more of the greasy brown tile floor. She had all the grace and poise of a rhinoceros on roller skates and the shrieks of helplessness to match. What little innate balance she did have finally gave way and before she knew it, her protuberant body flew up, up into the air and careened backward towards the ground. With a mighty thud in the puddle of puke, she laid supine as a dazed limp bulbous mass. The puke rose higher and higher, until it covered every inch of the old bird. Though we may never know Ms. Nealon's last words, three little bubbles managed to find their way to the surface of the puke pool. They lingered and played but a minute, swirling on its surface, before collapsing and giving release to the contents of her final gasps, one by one.

It was finally over and the puke began receding. Everything touched the puke and the puke touched everything. Puke dripped from the ceiling and was splattered across the walls. The hair, teeth, ears, eyes, nostrils, arms and legs of every person in Benjamin Franklin Middle was covered in thick rancid puke. Everyone, except Thad Johnson who, once it was over, quietly and gingerly found his way back to his seat. He naturally feared the worst; he feared for his life. He waited for something to happen, except nothing happened. Mrs. O'Turley simply wiped her brow and with another barely noticeable "hmph" carried on with her lesson plan. Not another word was spoken on the matter. The afternoon continued on the same way as any other day. Then the final bell rang.

Thad went to his locker, but instead of gathering his things he stood, silently waiting. The idea was not lost on him that this is where his demise would ultimately occur. He waited, watching others pass him by, bracing for what he knew was to come. Except nothing ever did come. Much like the rest of the afternoon, the routine of dismissal unfolded as usual. The only real difference, Thad noticed, was the slimy brown footstep remnants left by his classmates throughout the hallway.

Thad smiled for the first time in quite a while. Turning towards the main doors, he made for his bus home. As he walked, he counted his steps by lightly tapping the middle and ring fingers of his right hand against his right thumb. Today, he counted thirty-six.

Sinistral

Meggie Nelson

They lived in colonies. Sometimes hundreds of them, and though they were scattered throughout the city's high-rise apartments, they still shared between the concrete walls and the open air above the alleys a sense of comradery.

Sometimes, the sense of constant peripheral companionship was comforting. More often than not, however, Snen found it crushingly lonely.

He was among the minority. This could be, perhaps, because in the haze that floated around him constantly, the ever-present distant echo of thoughts comingling, he never once found someone that resonated with him. None of the others seemed to have the same predicament. They had been designed for compatibility: biomechanical forms capable of prospering and producing their kind without the concerns of sexual incompatibilities, minds designed to link with ease.

Despite these facts, wired into his brain and skin, flesh and self, he had never been able to find someone in the constant haze that quite *fit.*

"Consider snails, then," Merriette said to him, rolling onto her side. She had scaled up the wall of his apartment and crept in through the window, like she usually did, always careful to avoid the glaring beam of the watchtower, which would certainly disapprove even if it didn't instantly register her as a trespasser. They had been neighbors in a past life, and though now Merriette lived half the city district away with her compatriot, she still came by to visit. An increasingly uncomfortable relationship with her housemate meant she was over more often than not, even though mingling between the districts was discouraged. Once a life was restarted, the reborn were strongly encouraged to sever ties with their past, but Snen was reluctant and Merrie was persistent.

"This again?" He asked, sighing. "You sure consider them an awful lot."

"And are we not supposed to? They helped inspire what we are. Don't you think you owe them at least a place in your thoughts?"

"Not as big of a place as you give them. Snails are small creatures. They don't need much space to thrive." And it wasn't like snails were the only inspiration for their forms. They were modeled as bipedal, humanoid even, their soft robotics mirroring softer creatures. Their Maker's reference to invertebrates almost seemed like an afterthought, like some cosmic joke about the spineless nature of life breathed into mechanical vessels. They were shells with shells. Snen shook his head, coming back to the conversation. "They don't need much space at all. Especially not snails of the mind. Most would say, give one maybe a corner. That should be enough. You, though, you give them free range."

"Yet, if you look around, there are snails even on the most remote of islands. They sure travel across large spaces for things so small," she said, nodding as if she had proved a point, and as if the ocean was real.

"And how do they do that? Get across the big blue?" He asked, not bothering to start the old argument about whether there really was anything beyond the city.

"Well, they can hitch rides. Latch on to something else and get carried to their destinations. They can stick to the leg of a bird, or the like."

"That doesn't seem safe."

She ignored him. "Some snails are so small, it's said they are light enough the wind itself could pick them up and carry them away without a second thought. "*Whoosh," she zoomed her hand above her head. "whoosh, whoosh. Some big adventure in the sky, going somewhere that no other snail has been before them." She was grinning at the ceiling, hand slowly meandering in lazy circles.*

"Whoosh indeed," Snen muttered with a small smile.

Merrie flinched out of her trance, and looked back at him, "Right. That wasn't where I was going. All snails can find love. They're some of the only true hermaphrodites out there and all. You'd think the pickings would be the tops for all snails, right?"

"Uh-huh."

"Well, see, a snail's shell curves to the right, right? And when it wants to get with another snail, any of the other right-curved-shelled snails, they fit together perfectly. The roles are irrelevant, since they work together either way."

With a sinking feeling, Snen knew where the conversation was going. "I don't know how this is supposed to make me feel better, Merrie. I'm happy for them and all, but I don't see why I have to think about a snail's sex life."

"No, you don't get it. Look," she said, sighing. "Sinistral. That's what they call snails with shells that curve leftwards. These snails, they can't click with the others. The biology is there, nothing is wrong with them, and everything about them is still right and good and in order, it's just that one little part isn't quite compatible."

"While I appreciate the attempts at reassurance, I'm fine," Snen said, turning away. "I don't need comforting, Merrie. It's fine. Let those snails have some peace in that mind of yours. They are allowed some privacy."

"But…"

"I'm *fine.*"

Snen merely muttered half-hearted responses to the stream of chatter after that, mind elsewhere. After a half hour or so of curt responses, Merrie left, climbing out the window reluctantly but without saying much else. The silence left in her wake was refreshing after the stream of daydream chatter, but also horrible, since she was the only thing drowning out the constant whispers that were always just out of his reach.

Snen stared at his ceiling, but found no answers in the cheap walls of the apartment complex, so he went up to the roof to stare up at the dark sky. Every now and again, he could see faint promises of stars from behind the city's smog. It was the only thing that seemed to whisper, "there's something else out there.

There is. There is."

Tonight, however, the haze was thick, and the haze of thoughts was just as oppressing. The only relief was a faint breeze, winding up through the alley.

Snen had thought that he was broken when he first filed for reassembly. The Deep-Resetting staff in the central Corrections facility didn't hesitate to dismantle him, give him a new form and a new identity with only echoes of his memories to give him vague reminders of how things were better for him now.

But, it didn't feel any different. His vague memories of being cripplingly lonely were only comforting in that they were less sharp than the overwhelming, suffocating lonely of the right now.

No matter how many times he put himself through Corrections, it never seemed to actually fix anything. Some of the people in the Deep Resetting wing had started to recognize him, but the alarm in their eyes was far from understanding. It was rare to willingly go through Corrections. It was more rare to do it again… and again, and again.

It never worked.

He stretched up his arms, as high as he could.

"Take me away," he whispered into the empty air that stretched between the apartments and up, above the city and above the wastes, above the distant ocean dream and above the stars, up into the sky and above. He whispered into the empty space where the echoes of comingling lingered just out of hearing, and he knew no one would ever hear him through the din.

"Take me away from here." He whispered. "Let me be somewhere new. Bring me over the ocean. Please." He teetered on the edge of the tiles, arms stretched out. He felt the stirring of a breeze drifting against the silky membranes ribbing his skin, and for a moment it was like the universe, some great voice, something had heard him and was whispering, another whisper just out of his reach, one he could almost touch somewhere in the empty space above the alley. He stretched out a foot hesitantly, and a small gust encouraged him to trust in what he could not touch.

But he was not a snail, and the wind hesitated.

When he woke up in the quick-repair wing of the nearest Corrections center, Merriette was glaring down at him with watery eyes. As soon as his eyelids peeled open, she began, "Were you just waiting for me to leave so you could try to off yourself?"

He tried to choke out words, throat too dry to manage, finally mustering, "I didn't, that's not what…"

"I knew something felt off, so I doubled back, but I didn't expect to find you cracked on the pavement right after I was gone. Seriously, Snen! Do you have *any idea what…"*

His voice was raspy when he cut her off, urgent. "Do you really believe in the ocean?"

"What?" She took in an angry breath, but stopped abruptly when she saw the desperate tears in his eyes.

"Do you really think that there's an ocean? And that there are things beyond it? And that we could get there somehow?"

"You dummy. Of course I don't believe in the ocean."

"Oh," he said.

It felt silly to feel so crestfallen, but she had always said it with such conviction he always could almost suspend his skepticism. He believed in her, and by extension, could almost believe what she believed.

It had never crossed his mind that her dreams were meant to comfort herself.

"But, you know, maybe that isn't a bad thing."

He turned to her, eyes glistening, and her face was soft.

"It means that there's nothing between you and the islands. No water you have to cross, no reason to latch onto anything, no reason to rely on the winds. You just have to start walking, and you'll get there one day, even all on your own."

"Aren't snails incredibly slow?"

"Well, duh. But so are you, dummy. It hasn't stopped you yet." She sat down on the bed beside him, and gently rubbed his shoulder. "I bet you can get there someday."

Together, they looked out the window, and through the city smog Snen thought he saw the glimmer of a single star. Though it could have just been a light in the watchtower, for just a moment his thoughts seemed to mesh with the babbling murmur in the background, and for just a moment with shocking clarity, the voice of an entire city echoed with his quiet whisper.

I wish...

TWILIGHT IN HEROLAND

Joe Baumann

When their powers started to flicker out, the superheroes gathered together and moved into an abandoned nursing home, long bankrupt and left to rot. They used their last bursts of superstrength and superspeed and the like to resurrect the building. Holed up inside, groceries were delivered to the front entrance along with piles of fan mail that went unanswered. When too many gawkers started poking around, they paid to have a high wrought-iron fence installed around the perimeter. When people started climbing over it, they strung electrified barbed wire around the top so the place looked like a prison.

Many a plucky wannabe journalist tried to wheedle their way into the sanctum of the superheroes, and the only reason I was admitted on my attempt was luck: Brainiac, who answered via the intercom affixed to the gate, recognized my name from the crossword puzzles I wrote for a few years over a decade ago. He called them the only thing in the world that gave him an intellectual challenge, and he buzzed me in. I'd stopped writing them after Clai died. He left me the money he had inherited following the passing of his parents, with the stipulation that I quit my job at the small newspaper that had printed my puzzles and instead devote myself to writing the novel I'd always dreamed of finding time for. It sold well, and I haven't spent a day in an office since.

Brainiac greeted me at the door, enveloping me in a hug. He smelled of camembert cheese and amaretto, and his cheeks were flush and tight. It was strange, not only seeing him in person, but seeing him in athletic shorts and a tank top instead of his signature lab coat and cartoonish safety goggles. Apparently the superheroes had invested in gym equipment so that those who had enjoyed massive musculature could at least keep up some sense of tone, and those like Brainiac who had never had such beach bods could work toward them.

"It's so great to meet you," he said as he led me inside. His voice was a gonging baritone. "Your one puzzle, 'Scrambled Eggs,' where every answer that was a kind of egg preparation had two letters switched in the middle? Genius. Pure and utter genius."

"Thanks," I said.

The superheroes had gutted the interior of the nursing home. Its antiseptic smell had been replaced by something cherry and earthy. The walls were gleaming wood, like a shellacked cabin in the middle of a forest, and aspen flooring ran underfoot, swept clean and with not a single groaning floorboard. Somewhere soft piano music—something slow but jazzy—tinkled on invisible speakers.

Brainiac led me into a cozy gathering space filled with a dozen wing-backed chairs and side tables adorned with reading lamps. A fireplace roared even though the weather outside was in the eighties. About half a dozen retired superheroes—some of whom I recognized, some of whom I did not—sat reading or chatting. Two were playing chess, staring down at their pieces in hearty concentration. No one noticed my presence, or if they did, they didn't show any interest.

"Here," he said, leading me to a corner where a thick history book I didn't recognize and a half-full rocks glass, sloshing with ice and amber-colored liquor lay. He gestured for me to plop into one of the chairs and he took the other. When he swirled the glass, he peered up at me and asked if I would like something to drink. I begged off.

"Well, Leonard. Can I call you Leonard?"

"Of course."

"Mr. Anders-Cline sounds so formal, after all."

"And that was my married name. It's just Anders now."

"Oh. Terribly sorry. Divorce?"

"My husband died."

"Ah." He propped one ankle on the opposite thigh and brought his hands together in a point below his nose. His shorts slid up toward his waist, revealing lean but muscled thighs dotted with blond hair that matched that on his head, which was cut short and spiky, glistening in the low light with gel. Brainiac was young, probably in his late twenties, but he had dark circles under his eyes. I wondered what kept him up at night. He took a long glug from his drink.

"So," he said, "I can tell you just about anything you'd like to know about us, but there's a price."

"I have money."

"No, nothing like that. No fees. I want your secrets."

"My secrets?"

"One for one seems like a fair trade. You tell me something about you, and I tell you something about me."

"But I don't have any secrets."

"Oh come now." He scratched at an armpit. "That's all we are is secrets. Without our secrets, we're nothing."

"Really, though. There's nothing about me I wouldn't willingly share with you."

"Well, that doesn't mean they're not secrets."

"Isn't that what makes things secrets?"

He let out a short *pft* and took another deep, finishing slurp of his drink, then reached under his chair and fished out a bottle of Disaronno and unscrewed the cap, filling his glass so full I was sure it would spill onto his lap.

"Secrets are just the things that make us tick. Our versions of our own experiences. They don't have to be dark or dirty—though those, of course, are the ones that are the most fun. Tell me, for example, what you think of me."

I looked him over. Brainiac had settled himself in a chair pressed up against the wall, so I didn't have a view of anything but him and a corporate-fuzzy painting hung at a slight, annoying angle, of a cityscape whose sky was dazzled with bioluminescent laser beams.

"Well?" He leaned back, smiling, cupping the glass in his hands.

"You're either older or younger than you look, but it's hard to tell which. You're smart, but you've spent a lot of your time in retirement working out too. The combination makes you a bit ageless. The circles under your eyes mean you're either restless or, more likely, an alcoholic, the former of which would indicate youth, the latter, age."

He said nothing for a long, stretchy minute, and I thought I'd made the wrong move—offended him beyond repair. I saw my story escaping into the dark ether.

I should explain that my interest in the superheroes was purely literary. I had no interest in selling a story to a tabloid or writing a tell-all. The truth was, after my first and only novel, from which I was still miraculously receiving royalty checks thanks not only to a sale of the film rights (it was nominated for an Oscar but didn't win) but also two new editions, one translated into French, the other Mandarin Chinese, I had run out of ideas, in that I'd only ever come up with the one good one. I'd tried, of course, to write a second book. My computer was a graveyard full of at least a dozen half books, but the problem with books is you usually can't just sew two random halves together and end up with a singular whole. The entire mess would probably end up just like Frankenstein's monster, pissed off at the world and its master and leaving behind it a wake of bodies.

Finally, Brainiac moved. He'd become so still I thought he might have passed out from too much amaretto; his eyes were shut in that hard-but-soft way of someone who has not chosen to but has fallen asleep, conked out by external forces, like a blow to the head or a bloodstream thick with alcohol. But then he let out a short bray of laughter, almost a cough mixed with a screeched out, "Ha!"

"Quite good, Leonard," he said, voice so jovial I thought he would have slapped his own knee if it weren't for his precious glass of liquor. "Excellent observations, and quite a secret, too. Most brave of you to share so much so quickly."

Then he called out to the other half-dozen superheroes poised in the room, gesturing for them to come to our corner, abandoning their paperbacks and chess matches and, in the case of a woman whose hair coursed with crackling electricity, her crocheting. Quicker than I could process, I was surrounded.

-~A~-

The superheroes were much kinder than the outside world had painted them to be; I suppose isolation will do that. As soon as Brainiac introduced me, they let out a collective murmur of recognition: apparently the adoration for my crossword puzzles was not specific to just him. Rather, solving them was a fetish shared by those with powers beyond the human pale. I was thrown into a tour of the building, with each superhero taking a moment to walk me through his or her—or in the case of The Springy Chair, its—private quarters. The intimacy of individual spaces was taken quite seriously, so when we approached a particular hero's personal domain, the rest of the pack slowed their pace and eventually stopped, so that I was drawn through rooms with only the owner. Lordy Lordy sauntered through his room filled with marble and gilt, crosses on every wall, a baptismal font in the bathroom where a sink should be. The Mandrake's rooms were covered in vines and portraits of screaming, crying babies. Stepping into The Belle's quarters was like traveling to pre-industrial France. Brainiac's space, cavernous and sterile like a laboratory—it *was* a laboratory—came last, smelling like bromide and sulfur. He pointed to a beaker full of purplish liquid that was sending steam into the air.

"The fountain of youth right there," he said.

"So does that mean you're older or younger than you look?"

"All things in good time. Besides, you're racking up quite the debt. We've shown you so many secrets, you probably owe us your life story."

They had gutted what was once either a cafeteria or activity room where the least-senile residents might play bingo or bridge while the near-vegetables, wheeled into corners, drooled into their laps. The large room had been transformed into an elegant dining room in walnut hues, complete with a trio of crystal chandeliers that dangled down over a long table with eight high-backed, hand-carved chairs on either side and one at each end of the table. Brainiac gestured for me to sit at the head, and he lowered himself into the seat to my right while the rest of the superheroes gathered in what I assumed were their own usual spots. Fourteen heroes lived in the complex although they'd started with sixteen; as most of the world knew from sightings, Star Seeker and The Crumbler had left some months into their stay. When I tried to ask Brainiac why, he smiled like a coy, guilty child and held up his hands, one high, the other dipped low. I got the message.

"What do you want to know?" I said.

"We want to know about you," he said. "Tell us about your husband. The one who died."

"You want to know about Clai? Why?"

"Because you're a person who has experienced loss," said The Mandrake, his voice hissy as a slithering snake. His legs were the color of wet soil, and he left a tiny trail of dirt behind him everywhere he walked.

"So you want me to depress you?"

"Look around," The Mandrake said. "Could it get much worse?"

I thought: *Yes, of course it could*, but said nothing. I wondered when food of some kind would arrive. Who would serve it?

"Come on," Brainiac said. "Don't be shy."

"Okay. Well, let's see. He proposed to me twice. I said no both times."

The Belle, four seats down on my left, gasped and pressed her hands to her chest. "Why ever did you do that?"

"I wasn't ready," I said. "Isn't that good enough reason?"

"But you did end up married," Brainiac said.

"Yes. I eventually asked him. I thought he was either going to punch me or kiss me. Fortunately, he did the latter."

I had felt bad about my refusals, both of which, fortunately, happened in the privacy of the home Clai and I shared, which he'd owned before I was even in the picture. I had no real good reason to say no when he presented me with the onyx ring that I would eventually wear for more than ten years, only finally taking it off three months after his funeral when the ache I had been feeling over my entire body seemed to concentrate itself in my fingers. We had, by the time of his first proposal, been living together for half a year, an exclusive couple for eighteen months before that, a time which included a trip to Hawai'i that may as well have been a honeymoon for all the sex and glow it included. But we had agreed, back when I moved in with him that marriage wasn't for us—a shackling constriction that I, especially, found weighty and permanent in all the wrong ways. He must have thought that I'd changed my mind, but he'd been wrong. When I said I wasn't ready he didn't blurt out any rages or sorrows. He simply shrugged and closed the small velvet box he'd presented and stuffed it in his pocket. I don't know where he kept it until he tried again the following Christmas, his eyes aglow with the lights of our tree.

"And yet you said no a second time," Lordy Lordy interrupted. He was seated halfway down the right side of the table, his hands propped in exaggerated prayer, like a child on his way to his first communion, palms pressed perfectly together, fingers aligned. His cheeks were tattooed with elaborate, identical crosses, garish and curly. Whatever he worships does not believe the body is a temple to remain untrammeled, apparently.

"I didn't really have to say so. He could tell by the look in my eyes that I wasn't ready. He laughed, he smiled, and he put the ring away again."

"What changed?" Brainiac asked. He was leaning back in his chair, his tank top off kilter so one of his nipples was exposed.

"I'm not sure," I said, which was true. Nothing momentous happened in the eight months between Clai's second proposal and mine. No one was born, no one died. Clai's bitch of a sister who I always knew was uncomfortable with the fact that her brother hadn't settled down into marital dysfunction with a woman, one who would pop out a few kids and make him miserable for the rest of his life, hadn't gone to rehab, or killed herself. My parents were their same selves, living thousands of miles away in coastal Oregon, calling me once every three weeks and talking over one another on their split landline.

"Maybe I got older," I said.

Brainiac nodded. "We are, after all, more an accumulation of the small details of our lives than the singular big ones."

This drew a round of somber, synchronized nods. I wondered if, like me, they were in fact thinking of those singular large moments—for me, Clai's death, sudden and sharp and horrible—or if this head-bobbing was all a show. Or maybe, they really did believe what Brainiac was saying—I would never know.

"Well," said The Mandrake, positioned at the other end of the table, his elbows leaving dirty coin-sized spots where he propped them up, "You must be getting hungry. Let's eat."

-❧A❧-

Dinner was served collectively. At The Mandrake's pronouncement, the superheroes rose in a single synchronized motion and paraded through a door cut into the wall so seamlessly I hadn't noticed it. Minutes went by, and I heard nothing. Then they marched back in, each armed: Brainiac with plates, The Belle with cutlery, The Mandrake a gravy boat—everyone held something, Lordy Lordy last with a huge roasted turkey on a silver platter, and The Springy Chair managed to balance purple cloth napkins across its back, although I suspected someone placed them there; The Belle plucked them up with a dainty, gloved finger and distributed them as she set out the knives and forks.

We ate in silence, except for the periodic request that the green beans or mashed squash be passed, and the dish would make a clockwise promenade around the table, even if the request would be faster filled if the bowl in question moved the other way. Food steamed from its crockery. Everything was perfectly seasoned, perfectly done.

"Who cooks?" I asked finally, after the final bite of my slab of turkey melted down my throat.

The superheroes looked up from their plates as if startled.

"We all do," Brainiac said. "We take turns."

I frowned. "But when? How? You were all here."

"Some of us," said Lightning Strike, the woman whose hair was drizzled with glowing crackles, "happen to move fast."

"You have the ability to make the oven move that fast, too?" I said. Brainiac snorted. The Belle glowered at him.

Lightning Strike crossed her arms and frowned. She looked ready to fry me. I said nothing else. The silence resumed, broken only when, by some invisible signal, they stood again and completed their little dinner dance in reverse, each hero taking up that which he or she or it had brought in. When Brainiac tried to take my plate, smeared with gravy and leftover asparagus shoots, I offered to help. He looked at me as though I'd spoken an ancient language, one of the few he was not versed in.

"But it's my job."

"You wouldn't like a break?"

"A break?"

"Yes."

"But what would I do while everyone else is doing their job?"

I let it go, and the superheroes, led by Brainiac—they'd all been waiting, like a growling, agitated mob—departed again through the near-invisible door. I realized that what had goitered Brainiac was the possibility of interruption of duty, not because he felt some particular fealty to dirty dishes, but because the clearing of plates was his singular responsibility. Part of the problem the superheroes had faced in the weeks prior to their exodus from the outside world had to do with balance: there were no more supervillains. They were too good at what they did, the superheroes, taking down black-masked psychopaths intent on destruction. They tried to be helpful in other ways, knocking out drug cartels and helping NATO and the UN establish peace and stability in the Middle East, taking down a rising despot in a small country near Indonesia. But these things were small fry. Yes, there would always be bad guys of one flavor or another, but eventually all that was left was the riff-raff that even local Dudley Dorights could handle. It was akin to telling a professional football player that instead of keeping up with his frothy two-a-day workouts, he would have to satisfy his body with a single pushup every afternoon at two o'clock.

The superheroes filed back into the dining room and bid me adieu in a chorus line of handshakes and salutes. Most of them skittered away, but Brainiac invited me back into the lounge for a nightcap. None of the other superheroes were lodged in the wing-backed chairs, and most of the reading lamps had been extinguished. The fire had been reduced to a smattering of glowing, periodically

-popping embers. We sat in the same spot as before, and Brainiac armed himself with another glass of amaretto.

"Do you have what you need?" he said.

"I'm not really sure what I need."

He smiled and set his drink on the side table. "You haven't written a book since your first, correct?"

We hadn't discussed my writing much, and, as if he could see my hesitant surprise by the look on my face, added, "We do our homework around here."

"But we never met before today."

"That doesn't mean we didn't know you were coming. You think there's not someone here who can see the future?"

"I suppose that makes sense."

"I also know you've got at least one more question you want to ask."

"Did your fortune teller give you a list?"

"No," he said, picking up his glass again and taking a fluttering sip. "My intuition did. Go on."

"Okay. Why did you all come here? What made you leave the world? Besides the lack of the criminal element, that is."

Brainiac nodded. I'd picked the right question.

"It is hard," he said, "to be in the world when there is nothing left for you there." He raised his blond eyebrows in a pair of high arches. I said nothing. He took another drink. "We were defined so totally and completely by fighting crime. It was what kept us going, one and all. We relished justice."

"But you relished big-scale justice."

"Yes. Admittedly. We kept waiting for some new threat, some sparkly, monstrous end-of-times catastrophe."

"And instead you got purse-snatchers and cocaine."

He chuckled. "Something like that. You understand."

I said that I did.

"Of course you do. That's why we let you in. You're one of us, really."

I frowned. "I don't have any super powers."

"We both know that's not what I mean, Leonard."

Brainiac said my name with a swooping gait, as if he was swallowing air as he said it. Every time, the same hitch, the same drop in pitch and rise at the end, almost like he was surprised to be calling me by name. I'd caught it the first time, but thought that maybe he was uncertain as to whether he had it right. But no.

"I have a place in the world," I said.

"And what is it?"

I told him that I still gave periodic readings, went on book tours. My agent, who had stopped galling me for a second book years ago, was in the process of pinning down a Portuguese translation of my novel, which might eventually spin into a publicity tour of Argentina or Brazil.

"Home away from home?" Brainiac said.

"I'm not sure I'd call Rio home."

"What do you call home?"

I told him that I lived on the other side of St. Louis. "About a twenty-five minute drive."

"That's where you live. Is it home?"

"Where else would home be?"

Brainiac leaned back and shut his eyes. "Isn't that the ultimate question?"

I left soon after that. The front gate swung open for me, and as I walked out someone darted from behind the saffron-yellow forsythia bush blossoming along the fence line and squirted in, squeezing between the shutting grates just before they clamped shut like a powerful crocodile jaw. I watched for a minute as the shadowy body skirted up toward the front door, zigzagging as though a series of floating sentries watched the main walkway. My inclination, at first, was to press the buzzer and rat the interloper out to Brainiac, but I decided not to. If nothing else, catching and tossing out this quick-stepping intruder would give him and the other superheroes something to do. Maybe one or two of them would even doff their abandoned spandex, capes, and masks. No one would be hurt, I told myself, except maybe the fool cavorting through the calla lilies planted along the walls.

I turned away, leaving the superheroes to do their duty, and marched headlong into the deepening night.

A Jade Superfox Adventure

Claude Lalumière

Through the lens of his telescope, Keller watched the new girl coordinate the movers. He couldn't shake the notion that he'd seen her before. Or maybe this feeling of déjà vu was caused by the fact that she was killer cute, the kind of girl he fantasized about every night, every morning, and every moment that he thought about girls, which was basically all the time. The girl moving into the ritzy condo development across the street from their shabby apartment building was short, no more than five foot two, max, and that was with low-heeled sandals that showed off her lustrous green toenails. Her was hair tucked into a tight-brimmed army cap, her eyes obscured by designer sunglasses, and her lipstick bright green. Fiddling with her necklace, she exuded brash, sexy confidence as she directed the big, buff guys doing all the heavy lifting.

Keller momentarily lost himself in a daydream of being a swashbuckling swordsman, of shredding the girl's clothes with such mastery that the tip of his blade never touched skin. He hugged the near-naked girl in his arm while he ripped off the remaining rags with his other hand, revealing...

"So, you gonna stop bogarting the view? I wanna check out the new hottie, too." Laurel's palpable impatience interrupted Keller's flight of fancy.

"Okay, but it's my telescope; I'm giving you two minutes. Not a second more." He moved back from the window and tripod to give her access to the view.

"You're so greedy, Kell," Laurel said as she positioned herself.

"Greedy, nothing. It's all lust. Wait till you get a good look. She's scorching. Exactly our type." Keller and Laurel had always loved the same stuff. The same comics. The same TV shows. The same games. The same superheroes. The same porn. The same girls. Everything. They'd been friends from birth; they were practically brother and sister. Keller Christopher Tobin and Laurel Andrea Fort both arrived in the world at the Toronto General Hospital, on Thursday, 13 April 1995, at noon precisely. Their dads had met that day in the hospital and instantly bonded, linking their families from then on.

"Holy fuck, Kell! Why didn't you tell me it was her! Holy fucking fuck. I am so wet now."

"What? We know her? I thought she looked familiar..."

"You really didn't recognize her? Take another look." Laurel gave up the telescope, and Keller peered at the girl intently.

"I still can't place her...But the way she moves..."

Laurel prodded him. "Look at her necklace."

He zoomed in. Around the new girl's neck: a jade fox on a simple gold chain. "No way, Laurel. No way it's her." Those lips. That chin. That figure. It was her.

Jade Superfox.

-ꟷA-

Laurel said, "This has got to stop. You're getting creepy. I don't like you creepy."

"Oh, shut up," answered Keller, without taking his eyes away from the telescope. "How is this any different from watching episodes of *Jade Superfox Adventures*?" Every week, there was a new ten-minute short up at jadesuperfox.web. The adventures were kitsch and campy, with a bit of coy cheesecake to spice up the action.

"She expects people to watch her website. That's what it's for. She's an actor. This is her private life. I know it's fun to be a voyeur, but the voyee has to be in on it. Or else it's creepy. As I said: I don't like you creepy. You're better than that."

"Cut me some slack, L. It's Jade Superfox, for fuck's sake. Anyway. I want you to look at this. It's not pervy or anything."

"Kell, you've been spying on the girl for three weeks. Give it a rest. If you want to talk to her, go and do it."

"What am I gonna say, L? 'Hi. Me and my semi-sister roommate wank off to your superhero webisodes a gazillion times per week? Wanna come over for a board-game night?'"

"Leave me out of it, perv-boy. I'm perfectly content with my fantasies."

"Coward. Truth is, you're just as shy as I am. When's the last time you asked a real girl out?"

"Hey, I'm busy with grad school. I've got no time for that. You should remember that, too. You've got papers due, math genius. You can't afford to waste hours peeking at that girl, no matter how hot she is."

"Excuses. Whatever. Truce, okay? Here, I'll make a deal with you. You take a look at what's going on in Jade Superfox's condo. If you still think we should stop spying, I promise not to do it anymore. But, if you get as curious as I am, no more nagging."

"Ah! Deal. No-brainer, Kell. You lose."

"We'll see about that." Keller moved aside to let Laurel position herself at the telescope.

Laurel shouted, "Holy shit! Why didn't you tell me about this sooner? What the hell is that thing? We have to take pictures."

"Way ahead of you, L." Keller's telescope was connected to his computer, and he could snap pictures that were automatically saved onto his hard drive. "Who's the loser, now, L?"

"Oh, shut up. Don't be a sore winner."

Keller swivelled his monitor so Laurel could see it. He clicked a few times and ran a slideshow of the inside of Jade Superfox's condo.

Laurel said, "I've never seen anything like it. We have to get in there. I've got to get my hands on that thing. Whatever it is."

Her whole life, Laurel had loved taking things apart, figuring out how they worked, and putting them back together again. By the time she was eight, she often put them back together better that they'd been before she took them apart. She was almost finished her MA in Geomatics Engineering at York, but, truth was, she was already drafting her PhD in Transdimensional Quantum Engineering. She'd showed her work to Keller, because she needed help with some of the equations, but most of it was beyond him. He understood the theory—the math made sense—but he couldn't grasp the practical side of it, no matter how Laurel explained it. For him, math had always been an abstract game that lost its beauty once the equations were translated into concrete reality or applications.

He knew Laurel was anxious about school because, no matter how well she might ace her MA, she suspected no teacher would dare take on her PhD project. It sounded too loony, too much like science fiction.

The weird machine that Jade Superfox was building in her condo? That, too, looked like something out of science fiction, something from a mad scientist's lab or something.

"So, L—are you gonna go talk to her? What's the plan?"

"We can't just say we've been spying on her. Let me think, Kell. And wipe that smug smile off your face."

-A-

Laurel had lined the walls of her room with diagrams and printouts, all relating to the machine in Jade Superfox's condo.

"Wow, L. Obsessive much?" Keller said this with a grin and an appreciative bob of the head.

"Don't be patronizing. I have to figure out what that contraption of hers is exactly."

"I'm not being patronizing. I approve of irrational obsession. Aren't you having fun?"

"Yeah, I am."

"So it's all good."

Laurel scrutinized Keller's grinning face. "There's something you're not telling me. I know that look of yours. Don't try to lie to me."

"Come in the living room. I have something for you."

On the table, there was an open cardboard box.

Keller said, "I know I shouldn't have opened it, but...Whatever. You should take a look at what's inside. You really, really should."

"Fine. I'll bite, but you know I hate surprises."

"Whatever, L. You'll like this one."

Laurel read the shipping label: it was addressed to Jade Superfox Adventures.

Keller said, "Her apartment number is the same as ours. But someone mistyped the street address, 1963 instead of 1962. It was delivered here by mistake."

"This is so wrong, Kell." As she spoke, though, she nevertheless removed the contents from inside the box. It was a piece of machinery. "Kell, I don't even know what this could be." She held it delicately, inspecting it from every angle. "I'm completely stumped."

"Look in the bottom of the box."

Laurel carefully set down on the table the strange object and pulled out some papers from the box, which Keller had already inspected before: blueprints and an instruction manual. "Ohmygod."

She put everything back in the box very carefully. She stood up and picked up the box. "I'll be in my room."

"How wet are you, L?"

Laurel stuck her tongue out at him but mouthed a silent *thank you* before sequestering herself.

-∞A∞-

Keller knocked on Laurel's door. The door was postered with blueprints of rockets, space stations, submarines, and other things Keller thought big, ponderous, and unbeautiful. Math had been responsible for the creation of all these things, and whenever Keller was reminded of that connection it complicated his relationship with the pure beauty of abstract mathematics. He didn't want math to have any applications in the real world. For him, math was an untarnished, perfect plane of existence. Letting it seep into reality that way—it sullied it.

"Come in," Laurel answered.

Laurel was sitting on her bed, staring at the object. "I think this is the most beautiful thing I've ever seen."

It didn't look beautiful to Keller: an asymmetrical metal contraption bulging with a mess of wires and plastic parts. "Have you figured out what it is yet?"

"I think so. The paperwork calls it a 'magnetomic dimensional threshold compensator'; I didn't know anyone else was working on this stuff. I'm so awed I've barely touched it. I'm afraid to take it apart. I always take new gizmos apart. It's what I do. But...this...what I think this is...it's, like, a religious icon for me. This whole discovery is a transcendent experience."

"Dimensional threshold...? Holy shit, does that mean what I think it does?"

"Yeah, I think so. Screw grad school. I should just send my draft PhD paper to these people to convince them I should work there. How have I never heard of them before? 'Superdimensional Labs: A Division of the Dent-Robeson Corporation'—does any of that ring a bell to you?"

"No, but now that you know all that—there's no reason to not return this dimensional threshold contraption to Jade Superfox. You can contact them yourself. Get one of your own. You've been staring at that thing nonstop for three days now. I was gonna propose that we return it anyway."

"I dunno, Kell. What if I never get so close to technology like this again? These people may not want to hire me. I can't even begin to imagine how much this compensator costs. Or how they figured out how to build it."

"All the more reason to return it. It's the right thing to do. It's hers. Not ours."

As if Keller hadn't said anything, Laurel continued: "This is way ahead of any science I know. I read all the journals. This goes beyond what I was working on, and already people think I'm a crackpot."

"Listen to me, Laurel. We go over there and bring it back. We apologize. And hope that she's as nice as her online superhero character is."

"You're the one who took it in the first place. You gave it to me. I don't want to give it up."

"Don't be bratty, L. We're not thieves. I should never have opened that box. I was wrong, and now you're being stupid. And you're too smart to be so stupid."

Laurel held up her hands in surrender. "Okay, okay. Just give me one more day with it. One more—"

The doorbell rang.

Keller said, "I don't think we should wait another minute. Stay here while I get that. We're not done talking."

He opened the door to find a freakingly tall middle-aged dude he'd never seen before. The guy was wearing a grey domino mask, a studded metal cap sizzling with miniature lightning, and some kind of weird black leather fetish gear. "Who the hell are you?"

"I am Madman Mastermind! Give me the device!" The electrical sizzle of his helmet intensified.

Keller had no idea what was going on, except for the fact that there was no doubt this dude was exactly what he said he was: a madman. Keller tried to close the door, but a bolt of energy sprang from the helmet and knocked him clear across the apartment. Madman Mastermind walked inside. "Tell me where it is, you insignificant idiot!"

Scanning the apartment, Madman Mastermind spotted Laurel's door, with its engineering posters. "Mmm...there perhaps?" He glanced at Keller again, who was terrified but nevertheless trying not to betray anything. "Your mind is so weak. I have my answer. If you stay down and don't make any noise I might let you live." Before Madman Mastermind could turn back toward Laurel's room, something flew in the air toward his head. It froze in the air a few centimetres from his helmet; it was a wrench, now crackling with the same energy emitted by the intruder. Laurel's door slammed shut. "So there's another bothersome gnat to deal with." With a flick of Madman Mastermind's head, the wrench shot toward the door, which shattered on impact.

"Don't try anything else, you cowardly simpleton," Madman Mastermind threatened as he advanced toward Laurel's room. "Surrender the compensator!"

That's when something smashed through the outside wall and into the apartment.

Not something, but someone.

Keller gasped in awe.

Madman Mastermind shouted, "Jade Superfox!"

She wore the costume Keller recognized from *The Adventures of Jade Superfox*: purple facemask and leotard; green boots, belt, and cape; on her chest, a stylized green S. Around her neck, the green fox amulet glowed. Behind her, there was huge hole in the wall, revealing the sky beyond. At her feet were shattered brick, wood, plaster, and metal. "I'm gonna kick your sleazy ass, Madman Mastermind!"

"Yes, I do believe you would," said Madman Mastermind with a sneer. "I'll confront you when the time is right. Then, that'll be the end of you, Jade Superfox." With a crackle of energy, he vanished.

The supergirl walked toward Keller. She extended a hand to help him up. "Are you alright?"

He nodded as Laurel emerged from her room.

The supergirl said, "Sorry about the wall. Emergency and all that. Now, you two have a lot of explaining to do." Addressing Laurel, she continued: "You must be Laurel. Thanks for contacting me."

Laurel said: "We have a lot of explaining to do? What about you? You have superpowers! For real! And who was that evil creep? How is any of this possible?"

Jade Superfox giggled, just like she did in her webisodes after defeating the menace of the week. "You may have a point. Give me the magnetomic dimensional threshold compensator, and we'll head over to my place before the police get here. We'll talk there."

Keller was dizzy. He didn't know if it was from dealing with the impossibility of having been slapped around by a supervillain and then saved by a superhero, from the mesmerizing sound of that supersexy giggle, or from the realization that he'd just been invited to Jade Superfox's home by the supergirl herself. Probably all of the above, he decided.

-~A~-

The supergirl's apartment was supercool. On the walls were framed prints of the title cards to various episodes of *The Adventures of Jade Superfox*. Everything was decorated in muted colours that matched her uniform, all in a sleek, minimalist Art Deco style. The superhero herself, sitting on the couch opposite Keller and Laurel, kept fiddling with her jade fox pendant.

Laurel quickly explained about the parcel, and Jade Superfox was totally forgiving. Keller tried very hard to pay attention, but everything about the supergirl distracted him. The slightest motion of her head, hands, or hips sent him daydreaming to a hazy, blissful nirvana that smelled of everything girl.

Jade Superfox was saying, "...so at the end of our last fight, Madman Mastermind somehow sent me whirling into this mundane universe—your world. I've been trying to get back home ever since. I've been obtaining parts from various labs and manufacturers. I've been sourcing from different places already working on technology close to what I need, ordering custom-made pieces. But I have to be careful because I don't want to tamper with your native scientific development. Plus, superscience isn't really my thing—I'm just a dabbler back home. Still, I did pick up a few things from my dad, Doc Wonder, he's a supergenius. I know just enough to figure out how to assemble a quantum probability engine, and the magnetomic dimensional threshold compensator should be the last piece. Once I fit it in, I should be able to get back home. I think. I hope."

It was Laurel who asked, "But why only pretend to be a superhero online instead of, well, you know, being the real superhero that you are?"

"There are no supercriminals or giant monsters or anything like that in your universe. Being a superhero here...who knows what the consequences would be? Plus, I needed money—lots of money—to get the parts for the machine, and all I know is superheroics; so I created *The Adventures of Jade Superfox*."

Laurel said, "You made enough money for all this..."she made a swooping gesture, "—this luxury apartment, this lifestyle, this state-of-the-art tech—from internet ad revenue and merch sales?"

Jade Superfox giggled. "Fuck, no. The real money came from johns – and even janes—with an appetite for superpowered sex."

"Superpowered sex?" Laurel and Keller said in unison.

It rankled Keller that a multitude of strangers had touched Jade Superfox. But she giggled again, and he so melted with lust that the jealousy was pushed out of his mind.

"You guys look like you haven't had a good fuck in long, long time. Don't you ever have fun with each other?"

Laurel said. "No. We're like siblings, even though we're not really related. Plus, I'm into girls."

"This world with its endless taboos and sexual categories! Why can't you just be into people, and not worry about it? You need to relax. I know just the thing." Jade Superfox wriggled out of her uniform.

-∞A∞-

Jade Superfox put her uniform back on. Keller and Laurel were lying on the floor in a post-orgasmic stupor.

"By the way, since your place is wrecked, you guys are welcome to stay here after I return to my universe. The condo is all paid up. Now, it's time for me to activate the quantum probability engine and go back home." She took the magnetomic dimensional threshold compensator and fitted it in the machine.

Laurel said, "How are you powering that thing? You'd need a lot more energy than you can get from plugging it into the wall..."

"That's the easy part." Jade Superfox's pendant glowed, and an aura of green energy enveloped the supergirl. She inserted her hand into a slot in the quantum probability engine, and the machine started to hum. "Goodbye."

Keller and Laurel, still lying naked on the floor, watched with fascination as the air next to the machine shimmered. Jade Superfox removed her hand from the quantum probability engine, but glowing with green energy it continued to function. The air in the room ripped apart and a gateway opened into...

"No!" shouted Jade Superfox.

...Into...Keller could not tell into what exactly. All he saw through the hole in the air was a vaguely menacing blur; the sounds that seeped through the portal made his skin crawl. There was a flash of darkness, and the portal blinked out.

The hum of the quantum probability engine died, as did its aura of green energy. Jade Superfox murmured, "What did I do wrong? What? What?" She again inserted her hand into the slot, but this time the machine remained inert. "No! Work! You have to work, you stupid machine!"

Laurel shot up from the floor and hugged Jade Superfox. The supergirl leaned into her and collapsed into a sobbing mess. Laurel motioned at Keller with her head. He joined the two girls in the group embrace.

Laurel said, "Don't worry, Jade. We can help you."

Keller said, "We can?" After a beat, "You're right! We can!" He hugged the girls tighter.

-∾A∾-

Jade Superfox slammed the door to her bedroom, shattering it to pieces. Laurel said, "Now, there's a girl not used to rejection."

The biggest challenge for Laurel and Keller wasn't the superscience—no, that came easily to them; no, the real challenge was keeping up with Jade Superfox's superlibido. For the first few days, the previously undersexed pair had revelled in the supergirl's constant desire for three-way sexual interaction, but after three weeks they agreed that they both felt raw and overdosed. And most of all: emotionally awkward. But it was so hard not to give in to her desires. Whenever she directed her lustful gaze at him, Keller's resolve to end things with Jade washed away, forgotten. Sex with Jade Superfox was never boring. She always brought to it superhuman levels of enthusiasm, lust, and imagination. But Keller and Laurel were only human. And finally, this morning, the two had turned her down in unison. Keller and Laurel loved each other but they weren't into each other, not at all. That was a source of growing unease between the two. Keller and Laurel shared a profound bond, but lust wasn't part of it, would never be part of it, and would only risk sabotaging their relationship. The current situation was already dangerously close to doing that.

"I'm worried about Jade," said Keller.

Grabbing his hand, Laurel said, "She's just homesick, Kell. She'll be fine. We're almost done, right?"

Keller had been working on transdimensional quantum equations, using the data collected from Laurel's multidimensional vibration metric analyser, which she'd built with parts salvaged from the old, fried quantum probability engine. Using it on Jade Superfox, Laurel had determined the correct frequency to which to tune the new, improved quantum probability engine she'd built for the supergirl. The project had taken this long partly because they'd needed to order more parts, but also partly because both Keller and Laurel were meticulous about triplechecking every aspect of the insanely complex formulae; this was weird science, even for them. Even though Jade Superfox had put both the webisodes and the supersex-for-hire on hold since Keller and Laurel had moved in with her, funds, fortunately, were not a problem.

Keller said, "The math checks out. Here's how you need to calibrate the quantum probability engine." He pushed his papers toward Laurel.

"I can do that." Laurel walked up to the remains of Jade Superfox's bedroom door and knocked on the frame. "Fox—we're ready. We can get you home."

The supergirl emerged flying from her room, "Really?" In excitement, she pirouetted in the air; her feelings of rejection had obviously dissipated. "I knew you guys loved me!" She giggled. That giggle... "We should celebrate...one last time..."

Loss and sadness hit Keller like a punch in the heart; he would never again touch Jade. But before he could respond Laurel was already answering: "Jade!...No. We talked about this. Let's all be happy that you'll finally get to go back home."

Jade floated between them, and gave Laurel, then Keller, a chaste kiss on the cheek. "You're right. Thank you! I am so happy!"

Keller thought, *Right. Happy. Is this what happiness feels like?* It was as if his insides were being shredded by a horde of tiny Madmen Masterminds with sharp, sharp claws.

-∞A∞-

Jade Superfox was in full uniform, her hand next to the slot on the new, improved quantum probability engine. Laurel was busy checking that the machine was calibrated just right. Keller, whose contribution had been the math, sat back and admired the two girls he loved each doing what made her special.

Holy shit, he thought. *Love! I do. I do love Jade Superfox and all her crazy superlibido and supergiggling and super-everything*. He would always love Laurel. She was family. More than family. But he was undeniably in love with Jade Superfox.

Laurel said, "Are you ready, Fox? This is it."

"I love you guys! I'll miss you! But I have to get back home."

Laurel said, "Power up the quantum probability engine."

Jade Superfox touched her pendant, activating her superenergy; she inserted her hand into the slot. The machine hummed and glowed. The air shimmered, and a portal appeared. Beyond, Keller could see a futuristic city filled with flying people and biomechanical architecture. Jade Superfox's world of the impossible. Where the craziest math became the wildest superreality.

Laurel whispered to Keller, "See? It can be amazing that math has practical applications."

"Home!" shouted Jade Superfox. "You guys are superscience geniuses!" She looked at Laurel and Keller. "Thank you! Thank you so much. For everything."

Laurel said, "Goodbye, Fox! It was incredible to know you."

But Keller couldn't say anything. His throat felt all tight and tangled, and his eyes moistened with the hint of tears. *Control yourself. Don't spoil this for her. You should be happy.*

Jade Superfox's gaze lingered on Keller's face. He tried but failed not to let his emotions show. The supergirl whispered, "Oh, Keller...I didn't know." Biting her lower lip, half-turning toward the portal, she hesitated.

Laurel said, "Fox! Go! The machine won't be stable much longer. It'll start breaking apart soon. Plus...the longer it stays open, the more both universes risk becoming unstable. You have to go now!"

Jade Superfox said, "You guys are wasted here. This world has no use for superscience. But there would be a place for you both in Doc Wonder's Challengers of the Impossible."

Keller's heart filled with elation. He whispered, "Yes..."

Laurel said, worry creeping into her voice, "You can't be serious."

"L, no teacher on this world will ever understand or approve your doctoral thesis. You're smarter than any of them."

Laurel frowned. "This is crazy—"

Jade Superfox giggled. "There's no time to discuss it. The machine is breaking up." She flew toward Laurel and Keller, grabbed one in each arm, and sped the three of them through the portal, to her world of superscience.

Keller reached out to take Laurel's hand. He saw her face shift from irritation to wonder as she took in the sprawling supertechnology of this impossible universe.

Never before had the applied aspect of math interested Keller, but if supermath could produce all this—there was too much novelty to take in to even begin to understand everything he was seeing—he might broaden his horizons. He looked up into Jade Superfox's eyes and mouthed the words *I love you.*

Jade Superfox winked at him.

Bibliography

Images

Licensed

Cover:

Luadthong, Tithi, "Dark Fantasy Concept Showing the Boy with a Torch Facing Smoke Monsters with Demon's Horns, Digital Art Style, Illustration Painting - Illustration." *Shutterstock*, ID: 695511787, https:/www.shutterstock.com/image-illustration/dark-fantasy-concept-showing-boy-torch-695511787?src=gU_R9THfTY9Jlh1oIa6r4g-1-6&studio=1. Accessed 19 July, 2019.

-A-

The following images have been used with the permission of Amazing Stories *magazine.*

Film Scripts Section:

Paul, Frank R. "The Giant Mogul of Jupiter." *Amazing Stories*, Vol. 2 No. 7, p. 626, Oct. 1927. *Internet Archive*, Identifier: AmaingStoriesV02N07192710, _sas_, 19 Oct, 2017, https://archive.org/details/AmazingStoriesV02N07192710/page/n7. Accessed 29 Jan. 2019.

Novelettes Section:

Paul R. Frank. "The Chemical Magnet." *Amazing Stories*, Aug. 1927 p. 486. *Internet Archive*, Identifier: ams_1927_08, aeakett, 6 Apr., 2014, https://archive.org/details/ams_1927_08/page/n71. Accessed 29 Jan. 2019

-A-

Every attempt has been made in good faith to locate copyrights on images by researching the publications through online, libraries, archives, and the Library of Congress's Catalog of Copyright Entries database: http://www.archive.org/details/copyrightrecords/.

No copyright source and/or contact could be found. It assumed that the following images are free for use, having been posted online and freely available through the Internet Archive organization. If person know of copyright owners, please contact the publisher, Forty-Two Books, to correct future citations.

Book Chapter Section:

Flagg, Francis. "His Clutch Hands Closed on Something Small and Hard." Vol 9, No. 1, Jan. 1932, pg 81. *Internet Archive*, Identifier: Astounding_Stories_of_Super_Science_1932, https://archive.org/details/Astounding_Stories_of_Super_Science_1932. Accessed 29 Jan. 2019.

Flash Fiction Section:

"The Marble Virgin." *Startling Stories*, Vol. 8 No. 1, July 1942, p. 87. *Internet Archive*, Identifier: StartlingStoriesV08N01194207,_sas_, 22 Nov., 2017, https://archive.org/details/StartlingStoriesV08N01194207/page/n85. Accessed 29 Jan. 2019.

Novellas Section:

"The Master." *Strange Stories*, Vol, 2 No. 2, Oct. 1939, p. 55, Better Publications. *Internet Archive*, Identifier: StrangeStoriesV02N02193910, _sas_, 22 Feb. 2018, https://archive.org/details/StrangeStoriesV02N02193910/page/n53. Accessed 29 Jan. 2019.

Play Section:

Novick, Irv. "The Power and the People." *Future Fiction*, Vol. 1 No. 4, Nov. 1940, p. 61. *Internet Archive*, Identifier: FutureV01N04194011, _sas_, 3 Apr. 2018, https://archive.org/details/FutureV01N04194011/page/n59. Accessed 29 Jan. 2019.

Short Fiction Section:

"The Spacer Lurched from the Recoil!" *Future Fiction*, Vol. 1 No. 4, Nov. 1940, p. 9. *Internet Archive*, Identifier: FutureV01N04194011, _sas_, 3 Apr. 2018, https://archive.org/details/FutureV01N04194011/page/n7. Accessed 29 Jan. 2019.

Works Cited

Introduction

Ashley, Mike. "Strange Stories." In Clute, John and Grant, John (eds.). *The*

Encyclopedia of Fantasy. St. Martin's Press, 1997.

Flanders, Judith. "Penny Dreadfuls." *Discovering Literature: Romantics and Victorians*, 15 May 2014. *British Library*, https://www.bl.uk/romantics-and-victorians/articles/penny-dreadfuls. Accessed 1 Aug 2019.

Paulnack, Karl. "We Need Music to Survive." *The Christian Science Monitor*, 4 June, 2009, https://www.csmonitor.com/CommentaryOpinion/2009/0604/p09s02-coop.html. Accessed 24 Jan., 2019.

About the Editors

Daniel Cureton is a writer, editor, publisher, and avant-garde poet. He holds an MA in English from Weber State University. He currently lives in Salt Lake City, UT with his cat Oliver, a cross eyed Siamese.

Kylie Williamson has been a guest editor for *Strange Stories* and participated in putting together *Metaphor* at Weber State University, where she currently teaches while pursuing her MA in English.

Amy Pittman is a writer, teacher, and editor in Salt Lake City. She graduated

NOTES

www.ingramcontent.com/pod-product-compliance
Lightning Source LLC
Chambersburg PA
CBHW081353090726
47908CB00011B/2650

* 9 7 8 1 7 3 4 0 0 6 7 0 4 *